Praise for
Jill Shalvis
and Her Novels

"Shalvis writes with humor, heart, and sizzling heat!"
—Carly Phillips, *New York Times*
bestselling author

"Jill Shalvis is a total original! It doesn't get any better."
—Suzanne Forster, *New York Times*
bestselling author

"Count on Jill Shalvis for a witty, steamy, unputdownable
love story."

—Robyn Carr, *New York Times*
bestselling author of *Harvest Moon*

"A Jill Shalvis hero is the stuff naughty dreams are
made of."

—Vicki Lewis Thompson, *New York Times*
bestselling author of *Chick with a Charm*

The Lucky Harbor Series
The Sweetest Thing

"A wonderful romance of reunited lovers in a small town. A lot of hot sex, some delightful humor, and plenty of heartwarming emotion make this a book readers will love." —*RT Book Reviews*

"A Perfect 10! Once again Jill Shalvis provides readers with a sexy, funny, hot tale...The ending is as sweet as it is funny. Tara and Ford have some seriously hot chemistry going on and they make the most of it in *The Sweetest Thing*. Trust me: You'll need an ice-cold drink nearby." —RomRevToday.com

"Witty, fun, and the characters are fabulous." —FreshFiction.com

"It is fabulous revisiting Lucky Harbor! I have been on tenterhooks waiting for Tara and Ford's story and yet again, Jill Shalvis does not disappoint..." —RomanceJunkiesReviews.com

"A fun-filled, sexy, entertaining story...[satisfies] one's romantic sweet tooth." —TheRomanceReader.com

Simply Irresistible

"Heartwarming and sexy…an abundance of chemistry, smoldering romance, and hilarious sisterly antics."
—*Publishers Weekly*

"The title says it all! Fans of Shalvis will recognize her trademark humor and sensuality."
—TheRomanceStudio.com

"Five stars!…A talented writer. *Simply Irresistible* is fun, full of humor, and simply delightful in every way."
—HuntressReviews.com

"This series is going to be one to watch as Jill Shalvis combines her quirky writing with a small-town America setting, while adding in some sizzling heat to make *Simply Irresistible*…simply irresistible!"
—RomRevToday.com

"A beautiful start to this new series. The characters are as charming as the town itself. A pleasure to read."
—FreshFiction.com

"The very talented Jill Shalvis delivers up a delicious romance…hilarious…sparkling…one of her best books so far."
—TheRomanceReadersConnection.com

"Jill Shalvis seems to have a golden touch with her books. Each one is better than the previous story."
—RomanceJunkiesReviews.com

Also by Jill Shalvis

Christmas in Lucky Harbor

Jill Shalvis

GC

GRAND CENTRAL
PUBLISHING

NEW YORK BOSTON

First omnibus edition copyright © 2013 by Jill Shalvis
Simply Irresistible copyright © 2010 by Jill Shalvis
The Sweetest Thing copyright © 2011 by Jill Shalvis
"Kissing Santa Claus" copyright © 2011 by Jill Shalvis
"Under the Mistletoe" copyright © 2012 by Jill Shalvis
Excerpt from *Always on My Mind* copyright © 2013 by Jill Shalvis

Grand Central Publishing
Hachette Book Group
237 Park Avenue
New York, NY 10017
www.HachetteBookGroup.com

Grand Central Publishing is a division of Hachette Book Group, Inc.
The Grand Central Publishing name and logo is a trademark of Hachette Book Group, Inc.

The Hachette Speakers Bureau provides a wide range of authors for speaking events. To find out more, go to www.hachettespeakersbureau.com or call (866) 376-6591.

The publisher is not responsible for websites (or their content) that are not owned by the publisher.

Printed in the United States of America

First omnibus mass market edition: September 2013

10 9 8 7 6 5 4 3 2 1

OPM

Contents

♥

Simply
Irresistible

To another middle child, the middle sister,
the middle everything. To Megan, the peacemaker,
the warrior princess, the fierce, loyal protector
of our hearts.

Chapter 1

♥

*"I chose the path less traveled,
but only because I was lost. Carry a map."*
PHOEBE TRAEGER

Maddie drove the narrow, curvy highway with her past *still* nipping at her heels after fourteen hundred miles. Not even her dependable Honda had been able to outrun her demons.

Or her own failings.

Good thing, then, that she was done with failing. *Please be done with failing,* she thought.

"Come on, listeners," the disc jockey said jovially on the radio. "Call in with your Christmas hopes and dreams. We'll be picking a random winner and making a wish come true."

"You're kidding me." Maddie briefly took her eyes off the mountainous road and flicked a glance at the dash. "It's *one* day after Thanksgiving. It's not time for Christmas."

"Any wish," the DJ said. "Name it, and it could be yours."

As if. But she let out a breath and tried for whimsy. Once upon a time, she'd been good at such things. *Maddie Moore, you were raised on movie sets—fake the damn whimsy.* "Fine. I'll wish for…" What? That she could've had a do-over with her mother before Phoebe Traeger had gone to the ultimate Grateful Dead concert in the sky? That Maddie had dumped her ex far sooner than she had? That her boss—may he choke on his leftover turkey—had waited until *after* year-end bonuses to fire her?

"The lines are lit up," the DJ announced. "Best of luck to all of you out there waiting."

Hey, maybe *that's* what she'd wish for—luck. She'd wish for better luck than she'd had: with family, with a job, with men—

Well, maybe not men. Men she was giving up entirely. Pausing from that thought, she squinted through the fog to read the first road sign she'd seen in a while.

WELCOME TO LUCKY HARBOR!
Home to 2,100 lucky people
And 10,100 shellfish

About time. Exercising muscles she hadn't utilized in too long, she smiled, and in celebration of arriving at her designated destination, she dug into the bag of salt and vinegar potato chips at her side. Chips cured just about everything, from the I-lost-my-job blues, to the my-boyfriend-was-a-jerk regrets, to the tentatively hopeful celebration of a new beginning.

"A new beginning done right," she said out loud, because everyone knew that saying it out loud made it true. "You hear that, karma?" She glanced upward through her slightly leaky sunroof into a dark sky, where storm clouds tumbled together like a dryer full of gray wool blankets. "This time, I'm going to be strong." Like Katharine Hepburn. Like Ingrid Bergman. "So go torture someone else and leave me alone."

A bolt of lightning blinded her, followed by a boom of thunder that nearly had her jerking out of her skin. "Okay, so I meant *pretty please* leave me alone."

The highway in front of her wound its way alongside a cliff on her right, which probably hid more wildlife than this affirmed city girl wanted to think about. Far below the road on her left, the Pacific Ocean pitched and rolled, fog lingering in long, silvery fingers on the frothy water.

Gorgeous, all of it, but what registered more than anything was the silence. No horns blaring while jockeying for position in the clogged fast lane, no tension-filled offices where producers and directors shouted at each other. No ex-boyfriends who yelled to release steam. Or worse.

No anger at all, in fact.

Just the sound of the radio and her own breathing. Delicious, *glorious* silence.

As unbelievable as it seemed, she'd never driven through the mountains before. She was here now only because, shockingly, her mother's will had listed property in Washington State. More shockingly, Maddie had been left one-third of that property, a place called Lucky Harbor Resort.

Raised by her set-designer dad in Los Angeles, Maddie hadn't seen her mother more than a handful of times since he'd taken custody of her at age five, so the will had been a huge surprise. Her dad had been just as shocked

as she, and so had her two half-sisters, Tara and Chloe.
Since there hadn't been a memorial service—Phoebe had
specifically not wanted one—the three sisters had agreed
to meet at the resort.

It would be the first time they'd seen each other in
five years.

Defying probability, the road narrowed yet again.
Maddie steered into the sharp left curve and then immediately whipped the wheel the other way for the unexpected
right. A sign warned her to keep a lookout for river otters,
osprey—what the heck were *osprey?*—and bald eagles.
Autumn had come extremely late this year for the entire
West Coast, and the fallen leaves were strewn across the
roads like gold coins. It was beautiful, and taking it all
in might have caused her to slide a little bit into the next
hairpin, where she—oh, crap—

Barely missed a guy on a motorcycle.

"Oh, my God." Heart in her throat, she craned her
neck, watching as the bike ran off the road and skidded
to a stop. With a horrified grimace, she started to drive
past, then hesitated.

But hurrying past a cringe-worthy moment, hoping to
avoid a scene, was the old Maddie. The new Maddie
stopped the car, though she did allow herself a beat to
draw a quick, shuddery breath. What was she supposed
to say—*Sorry I almost killed you, here's my license,
insurance, and last twenty-seven dollars?* No, that was
too pathetic. *Motorcycles are death machines, you idiot,
you nearly got yourself killed!* Hmm, probably a tad too
defensive. Which meant that a simple, heartfelt apology
would have to do.

Bolstering her courage, she got out of the car clutching

her BlackBerry, ready to call 911 if it got ugly. Shivering in the unexpectedly damp ocean air, she moved toward him, her arms wrapped around herself as she faced the music.

Please don't be a raging asshole...

He was still straddling the motorcycle, one long leg stretched out, balancing on a battered work boot, and if he was pissed, she couldn't tell yet past his reflective sunglasses. He was leanly muscled and broad shouldered, and his jeans and leather jacket were made for a hard body just like his. It was a safe bet that *he* hadn't just inhaled an entire bag of salt-and-vinegar chips. "Are you okay?" she asked, annoyed that she sounded breathless and nervous.

Pulling off his helmet, he revealed wavy, dark brown hair and a day's worth of stubble on a strong jaw. "I'm good. You?" His voice was low and calm, his hair whipping around in the wind.

Irritated, most definitely. But not pissed.

Relieved, she dragged in some air. "I'm fine, but I'm not the one who nearly got run off the road by the crazy LA driver. I'm sorry, I was driving too fast."

"You probably shouldn't admit that."

True. But she was thrown by his gravelly voice, by the fact that he was big and, for all she knew, bad, to boot, and that she was alone with him on a deserted, foggy highway.

It had all the makings of a horror flick.

"Are you lost?" he asked.

Was she? Probably she was a little lost mentally, and quite possibly emotionally, as well. Not that she'd admit either. "I'm heading to Lucky Harbor Resort."

He pushed his sunglasses to the top of his head, and

be still her heart, he had eyes the *exact* color of the caramel in the candy bar she'd consumed for lunch. "Lucky
Harbor Resort," he repeated.

"Yes." But before she could ask why he was baffled
about that, his gaze dipped down and he took in her favorite long-sleeved tee. Reaching out, he picked something
off her sleeve.

Half a chip.

He took another off her collarbone, and she broke out
in goose bumps—and not the scared kind.

"Plain?"

"Salt and vinegar," she said and shook off the crumbs.
She'd muster up some mortification—but she'd used up
her entire quota when she'd nearly flattened him like a
pancake. Not that she cared what he—or any man, for
that matter—thought. Because she'd given up men.

Even tall, built, really good-looking, tousled-haired
guys with gravelly voices and piercing eyes.

Especially them.

What she needed now was an exit plan. So she put her
phone to her ear, pretending it was vibrating. "Hello," she
said to no one. "Yes, I'll be right there." She smiled, like
look at me, so busy, I really have to go, and, turning away,
she lifted a hand in a wave, still talking into the phone to
avoid an awkward good-bye, except—

Her phone rang. And not the pretend kind. Risking a
peek at Hot Biker Guy over her shoulder, she found him
brows up, looking amused.

"I think you have a *real* call," he said, something new
in his voice. Possibly more humor, but most likely sheer
disbelief that he'd nearly been killed by a socially handi-
capped LA chick.

Face hot, Maddie answered her phone. And then wished she hadn't, since it was the HR department of the production office from which she'd been fired, asking where she'd like her final check mailed. "I have automatic deposit," she murmured, and listened to the end-of-employment spiel and questions, agreeing out loud that yes, she realized being terminated means no references. With a sigh, she hung up.

He was watching her. "Fired, huh?"

"I don't want to talk about it."

He accepted that but didn't move. He just remained still, straddling that bike, sheer testosterone coming off him in waves. She realized he was waiting for her to leave first. Either he was being a gentleman, or he didn't want to risk his life and limbs. "Again, sorry. And I'm really glad I didn't kill you—" She walked backward, right into her own car. Good going. Keeping her face averted, she leapt into the driver's seat. "Really glad I didn't kill you?" she repeated to herself. *Seriously?* Well, whatever, it was done. *Just don't look back. Don't—*

She looked.

He was watching her go, and though she couldn't be certain, she thought maybe he was looking a little bemused.

She got that a lot.

A minute later, she drove through Lucky Harbor. It was everything Google Earth had promised, a picturesque little Washington State beach town nestled in a rocky cove with a quirky, eclectic mix of the old and new. The main drag was lined with Victorian buildings painted in bright colors, housing the requisite grocery store, post office, gas station, and hardware store. Then a turnoff to the beach itself, where a long pier jutted out into the water, lined with more shops and outdoor cafés.

And a Ferris wheel.

The sight of it brought an odd yearning. She wanted to buy a ticket and ride it, if only to pretend for four minutes that she wasn't twenty-nine, broke every which way to Sunday, and homeless.

Oh, and scared of heights.

She kept driving. Two minutes later, she came to a fork in the road and had no idea which way to turn. Pulling over, she grabbed her map, watching as Hot Biker Guy rode past her in those faded jeans that fit perfectly across his equally perfect butt.

When the very nice view was gone, she went back to studying her map. Lucky Harbor Resort was supposedly on the water, which was still hard to believe, because as far as Maddie knew, the only thing her mother had ever owned was a 1971 wood-paneled station wagon and every single Deadhead album ever recorded.

According to the lawyer's papers, the resort was made up of a small marina, an inn, and an owner's cottage. Filled with anticipation, Maddie hit the gas and steered right…only to come to the end of the asphalt.

Huh.

She eyed the last building on the left. It was an art gallery. A woman stood in the doorway wearing a bright pink velour sweat suit with white piping, white athletic shoes, and a terry-cloth sweatband that held back her equally white hair. She could have been fifty or eighty, it was hard to tell, and in direct contrast to the athletic outfit, she had a cigarette dangling out the corner of her mouth and skin that looked as if she'd been standing in the sun for decades. "Hello, darling," she said in a craggy voice when Maddie got out of her car. "You're either lost, or you want to buy a painting."

"A little lost," Maddie admitted.

"That happens a lot out here. We have all these roads that lead nowhere."

Great. She was on the road to nowhere. Story of her life. "I'm looking for Lucky Harbor Resort."

The woman's white eyebrows jerked upright, vanishing into her hair. "Oh! Oh, finally!" Eyes crinkling when she smiled, she clapped her hands in delight. "Which one are you, honey? The Wild Child, the Steel Magnolia, or the Mouse?"

Maddie blinked. "Uh..."

"Oh, your momma *loved* to talk about her girls! Always said how she'd screwed you all up but good, but that someday she'd get you all back here to run the inn together as a real family, the three of you."

"You mean the four of us."

"Nope. Somehow she always knew it'd be just you three girls." She puffed on her cigarette, then nearly hacked up a lung. "She wanted to get the inn renovated first, but that didn't happen. The pneumonia caught her fast, and then she was gone." Her smile faded some. "Probably God couldn't resist Pheeb's company. Christ, she was such a kick." She cocked her head and studied Maddie's appearance.

Self-conscious, Maddie once again brushed at herself, hoping the crumbs were long gone and that maybe her hair wasn't as bad as it felt.

The woman smiled. "The Mouse."

Well, hell. Maddie blew out a breath, telling herself it was silly to be insulted at the truth. "Yes."

"That'd make you the smart one, then. The one who ran the big, fancy production company in Los Angeles."

"Oh." Maddie vehemently shook her head. "No, I was just an assistant." To an assistant. Who sometimes had to buy her boss's underwear and fetch his girlfriend's presents, as well as actually produce movies and TV shows.

"Your momma said you'd say that, but she knew better. Knew your worth ethic. She said you worked very hard."

Maddie *had* worked hard. And dammit, she had also pretty much run that company. May it rot in hell. "How do you know all this?"

"I'm Lucille." When this produced no recognition from Maddie, she cackled in laughter. "I actually work for you. You know, at the inn? Whenever there's guests, I come in and clean."

"By yourself?"

"Well, business hasn't exactly been hopping, has it? Oh! Wait here a second, I have something to show you—"

"Actually, I'm sort of in a hurry..." But Lucille was gone. "Okay, then."

Two minutes later, Lucile reappeared from the gallery carrying a small carved wooden box that said RECIPES, the kind that held 3x5 index cards. "This is for you girls."

Maddie didn't cook, but it seemed rude not to take it. "Did Phoebe cook?"

"Oh, hell, no," Lucille said with a cackle. "She could burn water like no other."

Maddie accepted the box with a baffled "Thanks."

"Now, you just continue down this road about a mile

to the clearing. You can't miss it. Call me if you need anything. Cleaning, organizing...spider relocation."

This caught Maddie's attention. "Spider relocation?"

"Your momma wasn't big on spiders."

Uh-huh, something they had in common. "Are there a lot of them?"

"Well, that depends on what you consider a lot."

Oh, God. Any more than one was an infestation. Maddie managed a smile that might have been more a baring of her teeth, gave a wave of thanks, and got back into her car, following the dirt road. "*The Mouse*," she said with a sigh.

That was going to change.

Chapter 2

♥

"Don't take life too seriously. After all, none of us are getting out alive anyway."
PHOEBE TRAEGER

Turned out Lucille was right, and in exactly one mile, the road opened up to a clearing. The Pacific Ocean was a deep, choppy sea of black, dusted with whitecaps that went out as far as Maddie could see. It connected with a metallic gray sky, framed by rocky bluffs, misty and breathtaking.

She had found the "resort," and Lucille had gotten something else right, too. The place wasn't exactly hopping.

Dead was more like it.

Clearly, the inn had seen better days. A woman sat on the front porch steps, a Vespa parked nearby. At the sight of Maddie, she stood. She wore cute little hip-hugging army cargoes, a snug, bright red Henley, and matching high-tops. Her glossy dark red hair cascaded down her back in an artful disarray that would have taken an entire beauty salon staff to accomplish on Maddie's uncontrollable curls.

Chloe, the twenty-four-year-old Wild Child.

Maddie attempted to pat down her own dark blond hair that had a mind of its own, but it was a waste of time on a good day, which this most definitely wasn't. Before she could say a word, a cab pulled up next to Maddie's car and a tall, lean, beautiful woman got out. Her short brunette hair was layered and effortlessly sexy. She wore an elegant business suit that emphasized her fit body and a cool smile.

Tara, the Steel Magnolia.

As the cabbie set Tara's various bags on the porch, the three of them just stared at one another, five years of estrangement floating awkwardly between them. The last time they'd all been in one place, Tara and Maddie had met in Montana to bail Chloe out of jail for illegally bungee jumping off a bridge. Chloe had thanked them, promised to pay them back, and they'd all gone their separate ways.

It was just the way it was. They had three different fathers and three very different personalities, and the only thing they had in common was a sweet, ditzy, wanderlusting hippie of a mother.

"So," Maddie said, forcing a smile through the uncomfortable silence. "How's things?"

"Ask me again after we sort out this latest mess," Tara murmured and eyed their baby sister.

Chloe tossed up her hands. "Hey, I had nothing to do with this one."

"Which would be a first." Tara spoke with the very slight southern accent that she denied having, the one she'd gotten from growing up on her paternal grand-parents' horse ranch in Texas.

Chloe rolled her eyes and pulled her always-present asthma inhaler from her pocket, looking around without much interest. "So this is it? The big reveal?"

"I guess so," Maddie said, also taking in the clearly deserted inn. "There don't appear to be any guests at the moment."

"Not good for resale value," Tara noted.

"Resale?" Maddie asked.

"Selling is the simplest way to get out of here as fast as possible."

Maddie's stomach clenched. She didn't want to get out of here. She wanted a place to stay—to breathe, to lick her wounds, to regroup. "What's the hurry?"

"Just being realistic. The place came with a huge mortgage and no liquid assets."

Chloe shook her head. "Sounds like Mom."

"There was a large trust fund from her parents," Maddie said. "The will separated it out from the estate, so I have no idea who it went to. I assumed it was one of you."

Chloe shook her head.

They both looked at Tara.

"Sugar, I don't know any more than y'all. What I *do* know is that we'd be smart to sell, pay off the loan on the property, and divide what's left three ways and get back to our lives. I'm thinking we can list the place and be out of here in a few days if we play our cards right."

This time Maddie's stomach plummeted. "So fast?"

"Do you really want to stay in Lucky Harbor a moment longer than necessary?" Tara asked. "Even Mom, bless her heart, didn't stick around."

Chloe shook her inhaler and took a second puff from it. "Selling works for me. I'm due at a friend's day spa in New Mexico next week."

"You have enough money to book yourself at a spa in New Mexico, but not enough to pay me back what you've borrowed?" Tara asked.

"I'm going there to work. I've been creating a natural skin care line, and I'm giving a class on it, hoping to sell the line to the spa." Chloe eyed the road. "Think there's a bar in town? I could use a drink."

"It's four in the afternoon," Tara said.

"But it's five o'clock somewhere."

Chloe's eyes narrowed. "What?" she said to Tara's sound of disappointment.

"I think you know."

"Why don't you tell me anyway."

And here we go, Maddie thought, anxiety tightening like a knot in her throat. "Um, maybe we could all just sit down and—"

"No, I want her to say what's on her mind," Chloe said.

The static electricity rose in the air until it crackled with violence from both impending storms—Mother Nature's *and* the sisters' fight.

"It's not important what I think," Tara said coolly.

"Oh, come on, Dixie," Chloe said. "Lay it on us. You know you want to."

Maddie stepped between them. She couldn't help it. It was the middle sister in her, the approval seeker, the office manager deep inside. "Look!" she said in desperation. "A puppy!"

Chloe swiveled her head to Maddie, amused. "Seriously?"

She shrugged. "Worth a shot."

"Next time say it with more conviction and less panic. You might get somewhere."

"Well, I don't give a hoot if there are puppies *and* rainbows," Tara said. "As unpleasant as this is, we have to settle it."

Maddie was watching Chloe shake her inhaler again, looking pale. "You okay?"

"Peachy."

She tried not to take the sarcasm personally. Chloe, a free spirit as Phoebe had been, suffered debilitating asthma and resented the hell out of the disability because it hampered her quest for adventure.

And for arguing.

Together all three sisters walked across the creaky porch and into the inn. Like most of the other buildings in Lucky Harbor, it was Victorian. The blue and white paint had long ago faded, and the window shutters were mostly gone or falling off, but Maddie could picture how it'd once looked: new and clean, radiating character and charm.

They'd each been mailed a set of keys. Tara used hers to unlock and open the front door, and she let out a long-suffering sigh.

The front room was a shrine to a country-style house circa 1980. Just about everything was blue and white, from the checkered window coverings to the duck-and-cow accent wallpaper peeling off the walls. The paint was chipped and the furniture not old enough to be antique and yet at least thirty years on the wrong side of new.

"Holy asphyxiation," Chloe said with her nose

wrinkled at the dust. "I won't be able to stay here. I'll suffocate."

Tara shook her head, half horrified, half amused. "It looks like Laura Ingalls Wilder threw up in here."

"You know, your accent gets thicker and thicker," Chloe said.

"I don't have an accent."

"Okay. Except you do."

"It's not that bad," Maddie said quickly when Tara opened her mouth.

"Oh, it's bad," Chloe said. "You sound like Susan Sarandon in *Bull Durham.*"

"The *inn,*" Maddie clarified. "I meant the *inn* isn't so bad."

"I've stayed in hostels in Bolivia that looked like the Ritz compared to this," Chloe said.

"Mom's mom and her third husband ran this place." Tara ran a finger along the banister, then eyed the dust on the pad of her finger. "Years and years ago."

"So Grandma ran through men, too?" Chloe asked. "Jeez, it's like we're destined to be man-eaters."

"Speak for yourself," Tara murmured, indeed sounding like Susan Sarandon.

Chloe grinned. "Admit it, our gene pool could use some chlorine."

"As I was saying," Tara said when Maddie laughed. "Grandma worked here, and when she died, Mom attempted to take over but got overwhelmed."

Maddie was mesmerized by this piece of her past. She'd never even heard of this place. As far as she knew, none of them had kept in regular contact with Phoebe. This was mostly because their mother had spent much of her life out of contact with anything other than her own whimsy.

Not that she'd been a bad person. By all accounts, she'd been a sweet, free-loving flower child. But she hadn't been the greatest at taking care of things like cars, bank accounts... her daughters. "I wasn't even aware that Mom had been close to her parents."

"They died a long time ago." Tara turned back, watching Chloe climb the stairs. "Don't go up there, sugar. It's far too dusty; you'll aggravate your asthma."

"I'm already aggravated, and not by my asthma." But Chloe pulled the neckline of her shirt over her mouth. She also kept going up the stairs, and Tara just shook her head.

"Why do I bother?" Tara moved into the kitchen and went still at the condition of it. "Formica countertops," she said as if she'd discovered asbestos.

Okay, true, the Formica countertops weren't pretty, but the country blue and white tile floor was cute in a retro sort of way. And yes, the appliances were old, but there was something innately homey and warm about the setup, including the rooster wallpaper trim. Maddie could see guests in here at the big wooden block table against the large picture window, which had a lovely view of... the dilapidated marina.

So fine, they could call it a blast from the past. Certainly there were people out there looking for an escape to a quaint, homey inn and willing to pay for it.

"We need elbow grease, and lots of it," Chloe said, walking into the kitchen, her shirt still over her nose and mouth.

Maddie wasn't afraid of hard work. It was all she

knew. And envisioning this place all fixed up with a roaring fire in the woodstove and a hot, delicious meal on the stovetop, with cuteness spilling from every nook and cranny, made her smile. Without thinking, she pulled out the BlackBerry she could no longer afford and started a list, her thumbs a blur of action. "New paint, new countertops, new appliances..." Hmm, what else? She hit the light switch for a better look, and nothing happened.

Tara sighed.

Maddie added that to the list. "Faulty wiring—"

"And leaky roof." Tara pointed upward.

"There's a bathroom above this," Chloe told them. "It's got a plumbing issue. Roof's probably leaking, too."

Tara came closer and peered over Maddie's shoulder at her list. "Are you a compulsive organizer?"

At the production studios, she'd had to be. There'd been five producers—and her. They'd gotten the glory, and she'd done the work.

All of it.

And until last week, she'd thrived on it. "Yes. Hi, my name is Maddie, and I am addicted to my BlackBerry, office supplies, and organization." She waited for a smartass comment.

But Tara merely shrugged. "You'll come in handy." She was halfway out of the room before Maddie found her voice.

"Did you know Mom didn't want to sell?" she asked Tara's back. "That she planned on us running the place as a family?"

Tara turned around. "She knew better than that."

"No, really. She wanted to use the inn to bring us together."

"I loved Mom," Chloe said. "But she didn't do '*together.*'"

"She didn't," Maddie agreed. "But we could. If we wanted."

Both sisters gaped at her.

"You've lost your ever-lovin' marbles," Tara finally said. "We're selling."

No longer a mouse, Maddie told herself. Going from mouse to tough girl, like…Rachel from *Friends.* Without the wishy-washyness. And without Ross. She didn't like Ross. "What if I don't want to sell?"

"I don't give a coon's ass whether you want to or not. It doesn't matter," Tara said. "We *have* to sell."

"A coon's ass?" Chloe repeated with a laugh. "Is that farm ghetto slang or something? And what does that even mean?"

Tara ignored her and ticked reasons off on her fingers. "There's no money. We have a payment due to the note holder in two weeks. Not to mention, I have a life to get back to in Dallas. I took a week off, that's it."

Maddie knew Tara had a sexy NASCAR husband named Logan and a high-profile managerial job. Maddie could understand wanting to get back to both.

"And maybe I have a date with an Arabian prince," Chloe said. "We *all* have lives to get back to, Tara."

Well, not all of us, Maddie thought.

In uneasy silence, they checked out the rest of the inn. There was a den and a small bed and bath off the kitchen, and four bedrooms and two community bathrooms upstairs, all shabby chic minus the chic.

Next, they walked out to the marina. The small metal building was half equipment storage and half office—and one giant mess. Kayaks and tools and oars and supplies vied for space. In the good-news department, four of the eight boat slips were filled. "Rent," Maddie said, thrilled, making more notes.

"Hmm," was all Tara said.

Chloe was eyeing the sole motorboat. "Hey, we should take that out for a joyride and—"

"No!" Maddie and Tara said in unison.

Chloe rolled her eyes. "Jeez, a girl gets arrested once and no one ever lets her forget it."

"Twice," Tara said. "And you still owe me the bail money for that San Diego jet ski debacle."

Maddie had no idea what had happened in San Diego. She wasn't sure she wanted to know. They moved outside again and faced the last section of the "resort," the small owner's cottage. And actually, *small* was too kind. *Postage-stamp*-sized was too kind. It had a blink-and-you'll-miss-it kitchen-and-living-room combo and a single bedroom and bath.

And lots of dust.

"It's really not that bad," Maddie said into the stunned silence. They stood there another beat, taking in the decor, which was—surprise, surprise—done in blue and white with lots of stenciled ducks and cows and roosters, oh, my. "Mostly cosmetic. I just think—"

"No," Tara said firmly. "Bless your heart, but please, *please* don't think."

Chloe choked out a laugh. "Love how you say 'bless your heart' just before you insult someone. Classy."

Tara ignored Chloe entirely and kept her voice soft and steely calm. "Majority rules here. And majority says we should sell ASAP, assuming that in this economy we don't have to actually *pay* someone to take this place off our hands."

Maddie looked at Chloe. "You really want to sell, too?"

Chloe hesitated.

"Be honest with her," Tara said.

"I can't." Chloe covered her face. "She has Bambi eyes. You know what?" She headed for the door. "I'm not in the mood to be the swing vote."

"Where are you going?" Tara demanded.

"For a ride."

"But we need your decision—"

The door shut, hard.

Tara tossed up her hands. "Selfish as ever." She looked around in disgust. "I'm going into town for supplies to see us through the next couple of days. We need food and cleaning supplies—and possibly a fire accelerant." She glanced at Maddie and caught her horror. "Kidding! Can I borrow your car?"

Maddie handed over her keys. "Get chips, lots of chips."

When she was alone, she sat on the steps and pulled Lucille's recipe box from her bag. With nothing else to do, she lifted the lid, prepared to be bored by countless recipes she'd never use.

The joke was on her. Literally. The 3x5 cards had been written on, but instead of recipes for food, she found recipes for...

Life.

They were all handwritten by Phoebe and labeled *Advice for My Girls*. The first one read:

Always be in love.

Maddie stared at it for a moment, then had to smile. Years ago, she'd gotten the birds-and-bees speech from her father. He'd rambled off the facts quickly, not meeting her eyes, trying to do his best by her. He was so damned uncomfortable, and all because a boy had called her.

Boys are like drugs, her father had said. *Just say no.*

Her mother and father had definitely not subscribed to the same philosophies. Not quite up to seeing what other advice Phoebe had deemed critical, Maddie slipped the box back into her bag. She zipped up her sweatshirt and headed out herself, needing a walk. The wind had picked up. The clouds were even darker now, hanging low above her head.

At the end of the clearing, she stopped and looked back at the desolate inn. It hadn't been what she'd hoped for. She had no memories here with her mother. The place wasn't home in any way. And yet... and yet she didn't want to turn her back on it. She wanted to stay.

And not just because she was homeless.

Okay, a little bit because she was homeless.

With a sigh, she started walking again. About a mile from the inn, she passed the art gallery, waving at Lucille when the older woman stuck her head out and smiled. Snowflakes hovered in the air. Not many, and they didn't seem to stick once they hit the ground. But the way they floated lazily around her as the day faded into dusk kept her entertained until she found herself in town.

She suddenly realized that she was standing in front of a bar. She stepped back to read the sign on the door, tripped off the curb, and stumbled backward into something big, toppling with it to the ground.

A motorcycle. "Crap," she whispered, sprawled over

the big, heavy bike. "Crap, *crap*." Heart in her throat, she leapt to her feet, rubbing her sore butt and ribs and mentally calculating the cost of damages against the low funds she had in her checking account.

It was too awful to contemplate, which meant that the motorcycle had to be okay. *Had* to be. Reaching out, she tried to right the huge thing, but it outweighed her. She was still struggling with it when the door to the bar suddenly burst open and two men appeared.

One was dressed in a tan business suit, tie flapping, mouth flapping, too. "Hey," he was saying. "She was asking for it..."

The second man wasn't speaking, but Maddie recognized him anyway. Hot Biker from earlier, which meant— Oh, God. It was *his* motorcycle she'd knocked over.

Karma was such a bitch.

At least he hadn't seen her yet. He was busy physically escorting Smarmy Suit Guy with his hand fisted in the back of the guy's jacket as he marched him out of the bar.

Smarmy Suit pulled free and whirled, fists raised.

Hot Biker just stood there, stance easy, looking laid-back but absolutely battle ready. "Go home, Parker."

"You can't kick me out."

"Can, and did. And you're not welcome back until you learn no is no."

"I'm telling you, she wanted me!"

Hot Biker shook his head.

Smarmy Suit put a little distance between them then yelled, "Fuck you, then!" before stalking off into the night.

Maddie just stared, her heart pounding. She wasn't sure if it was the volatile situation, ringing far too close to home, or if it was because any second now, he was going to notice her and what she'd done. With renewed panic, she struggled with his bike.

Then two big hands closed around her upper arms and pulled her back from it.

With an inward wince, she turned to face him. He was bigger than she'd realized, and she took a step backward, out of his reach.

His dark hair was finger-combed at best, a lock of it falling over his forehead. He had a strong jaw, and cheekbones to die for, and disbelief swimming in those melted caramel eyes. "Mind telling me why you have it in for my bike?"

"Okay, this looks bad," she admitted. "But I swear I have nothing against you or your motorcycle."

"Hmm. Prove it."

Her gut clenched. "I—"

"With a drink." He gestured with his head to the bar.

"With you?"

"Or by yourself, if you'd rather. But you look like you could use a little pick-me-up."

He had no idea.

He righted his bike with annoying ease and held out a hand.

She stared at it but didn't take it. "Look, nothing personal, but I've just seen how you deal with people who irritate you, so…"

He looked in the direction that Smarmy Suit had vanished. "Parker was hitting on a good friend of mine and making an ass of himself. Yeah, he irritated me. You haven't. Yet."

"Even though I've tried to kill your bike twice?"

"Even though." His mouth quirked slightly, as if she

were amusing him. Which was good, right? Amused at her klutziness was better than being pissed.

"And anyway, the bike's going to live," he said, directing her to the door, the one whose sign read THE LOVE SHACK.

"This is a bad idea."

He flashed her a smile, and holy mother of God, it was wickedly sexy. It might even have been contagious if she hadn't been so damn worried that any second now he was going to morph into an angry, uptight, aggressive LA attorney who didn't know how to control his temper.

No, wait. That'd been her ex, Alex. "Honestly," she said. "Bad idea."

"Honestly?"

"What, don't people tell the truth around here?"

"Oh, the locals tell the truth. It's just that they tell *all* the truth, even when they shouldn't. It's called gossip. Lucky Harbor natives specialize in it. You can keep a pile of money in the back seat of your unlocked car and it'd be safe, but you can't keep a secret."

"Good thing I don't have any."

He smiled. "We all have secrets. Come on, I know the bartender. It'll help you relax, trust me."

Yes, but she was in the red on trust. Way overdrawn. In fact, the Bank Of Trust had folded. "I don't know."

Except he'd nudged her inside already, and her feet were going willingly. The place snagged her interest immediately. It was like entering an old western saloon. The walls were a deep sinful bordello red and lined with old mining tools. The ceiling was all exposed beams. Lanterns hung over the scarred bench-style tables, and the bar itself was a series of old wood doors attached end to end. Someone had already decorated for Christmas and huge silvery balls hung from everything, as did endless streams of tinsel.

Hot Biker had her hand in his bigger, warmer one and was pulling her past the tables full with the dinner crowd. The air was filled with busy chattering, loud laughter, and music blaring out of the jukebox on the far wall. She didn't recognize the song because it was country, and country music wasn't on her radar, but some guy was singing about how Santa was doing his momma beneath the tree.

Shaking her head, Maddie let herself be led to the bar, where she noticed that nobody was here to drink their problems away.

Everyone seemed...happy.

Hoping it was contagious, she sat on the barstool that he patted for her, right next to a woman wearing sprayed-on jeans and a halter top that revealed she was either chilly or having a really, really good time. Her makeup was overdone, but somehow the look really worked for her. She was cheerfully flirting with a huge mountain of a guy on her other side, who was grinning from ear to ear and looking like maybe he'd just won the lottery.

Hot Biker greeted them both as if they were all close friends, then moved behind the bar, brushing that leanly muscled body alongside of Maddie's as he did.

She shivered.

"Cold?" he asked.

When she shook her head, he smiled again, and the sexiness of it went straight through her, causing another shiver.

Yeah, he really needed to stop doing that.

Immediately, several people at the bar tossed out orders to him, but he just shook his head, eyes locked on

Maddie. "I'm done helping out for the night, guys. I'm just getting the lady a drink."

The other bartender, another big, good-looking guy—wow, they sure grew them damn fine up here in Lucky Harbor—asked, "What kind of wing man just takes off without proper clearance? Never mind." He slapped an opened sudoku puzzle in front of Hot Biker. "Just do this puzzle in three minutes or less."

"Why?"

"There's a woman at the end of the bar, the one with the fuck-me heels—Jesus, don't look! What, are you an amateur? She said she'd do things to me that are illegal in thirteen states if I did the puzzle in less than five minutes. So for all that is holy, hurry the fuck up. Just don't let her see you doing it."

Hot Biker looked at Maddie and smiled. "Trying to impress a woman here, Ford."

Ford turned to Maddie speculatively. "I suppose you already know that this guy here has got some charm. But did he tell you that in our freshman year we nicknamed him Hugh because his stash of porn was legendary? Yeah, he had more back issues than eBay. And maybe he mentioned that he can't pee his name in the snow anymore because the last time he did, he gave himself a hernia trying to cross the X at the end of his name?" Ford turned back to Hot Biker and slapped him on the back. "There. Now you have no hope of impressing her, so get cranking on that puzzle—you owe me."

Hot Biker grimaced, and Maddie did something she hadn't in weeks.

She laughed.

Chapter 3

♥

*"A glass of wine is always the solution.
Even if you aren't sure of the problem."*
PHOEBE TRAEGER

So you collect porn."

Jax Cullen took in the genuine amusement on the woman's face and shook his head. Fucking Ford. "Past tense," he corrected. "I sold the collection to an incoming freshman when I left for college."

"Uh-huh. That's what they all say."

Liking the way the worry had faded from her eyes, which were now lit with good humor, he leaned over the bar and whispered near her ear, "Want to swap stories, Speed Racer?"

She composed herself enough to grimace. "I'm just glad you can laugh about me almost killing you."

"As opposed to?"

"I don't know. Yelling."

Jax studied her face before she turned away from him, purposely eyeing the bottles of alcohol lining the back of the bar, trying to conceal her discomfort. "Not much of a yeller," he murmured and reached out to play with one of her dark blond curls. He couldn't help himself—they were irresistible.

So was she.

"I've heard that LA women are pretty aggressive in their pickup tactics. But this just might be one for the record books. You should probably just save us both some trouble and ask me out directly."

"Hey, I didn't nearly run you over on purpose. And I tripped on the bike trying to read the sign."

"Ah, but you don't deny the attempting to pick-me-up part." He nodded. "You want me bad."

She laughed and then shook her head as if surprised at herself. "If you plan to keep stalking me like this, we should be on a first-name basis. I'm Jax." He held out his hand. "Jax Cullen."

She slid her smaller, chilled-to-the-bone hand in his. "Maddie Moore."

He knew the name, more than he wanted to. She was Phoebe's middle daughter. Giving himself a moment, he rubbed her hands between his, trying to warm them up. Earlier when she'd been using the highway—and nearly his body—for offensive-driving practice, he'd gotten the impression of a sweet, warm, and very stressed-out woman, and that hadn't changed. He loved the wild, curly hair which was barely contained in a ponytail, but her long side bangs brushed across one eye and the side of her jaw, nearly hiding her eyes and her pretty face.

She'd dressed to hide her body, as well. Watching her squirm on her barstool under his scrutiny, he wondered why. "What's your poison?"

"A beer, please."

Jax grabbed two Coronas, lifted the walk-through, and took the barstool next to her. Ford, who was a coowner of the place—and until about two minutes ago also one of his best friends—came back and jabbed a finger at the sudoku book. "You haven't even started it? Killing me, Clark."

Maddie frowned. "Thought your name was Jax."

"It is, but Leno-wannabe here thinks he's being funny when he calls me Clark. As in Superman," he clarified, making Ford snort.

"As in *Clark Kent,*" Ford corrected. "See him squint at the puzzle? Yeah, that's because he needs reading glasses and he won't wear them. He thinks he won't ever get laid again if he does. Because apparently squinting is sexier than admitting his vision sucks."

"Thanks, man," Jax said.

Ford clapped him on the shoulder. "Just keeping it real."

Maddie was looking at him. "Actually, you do sort of look like Clark Kent, if he were really fit. And tough. And edgy. What's your superpower?"

Ford grinned in approval at her and opened his mouth to answer, but Jax reached across the bar, put a hand on Ford's face, and shoved. "I try to keep the superpower on the down-low," he said. "Because the people here like to gossip."

Even with Jax's hand on his face, Ford managed another snort and tapped the sudoku book in front of Jax. "If he's a superhero, ask him why the puzzle's still blank. Tick-tock, bro. Tick-tock."

"Forget it. And maybe you could actually be the bartender and serve us." Jax looked at Maddie. "Food?"

She was too nervous to eat and shook her head.

"That's all right," Ford said. "This guy'll eat me out of

house and home all on his own." He leaned over the bar, smiling at her, pouring on the charm that got him laid so regularly.

"Hey," Jax said.

Ford grinned at Maddie. "He doesn't like to share. It's because I'm hotter than he is."

Maddie was smiling again. "You always make fun of your friends?"

"Hey, you can't make fun of your own brother, who can you make fun of?"

Maddie took a long pull on her beer, set it down, then once again turned to face Jax, eyeing him for a long beat. "You're brothers?"

Jax understood the question. Ford had lighter hair, lighter eyes, and more bulk to his muscle, like a football player. He mostly sailed these days and was, in fact, a world-class pro. When on the water, he moved with easy, natural grace, not that you could tell by looking at the big lug. "Not by blood."

"Yeah, by blood," Ford said. "We cut each other's palms and spit on them in the third grade, remember? Misfits unite."

Maddie was still dividing her gaze between them. "Neither of you look like misfits."

"Ah, but you didn't see us back then," Ford said. "Two scrawny, bony-ass kids. The best that could be said of us was we knew how to take a beating."

"And run fast," Jax reminded him.

Maddie looked horrified. "How awful."

"It wasn't so bad." Ford lifted a shoulder. "We had Sawyer."

"Sawyer?"

"Our secret weapon. He'd been wrestling with his older brothers since before he could walk. It's why we let him hang out with us."

Maddie finished her beer and set the empty down, looking infinitely more relaxed. "Another, please."

Ford obliged. "So is this a social second round or a get-shit-faced one?"

She pondered that with careful consideration. "Does it matter?"

"Only if I have to peel you off the floor and call you a ride."

She shook her head. "No floor peeling."

Ford nodded and smiled, then turned to Jax and pointed at the puzzle before moving off to serve his other customers.

Maddie sipped her second beer. "So you and Ford are close."

"Yeah."

"Do you two fight?"

"Occasionally."

"And how do you settle these arguments?"

"Depends. Fight night in town square usually works."

At that she gave him a long look, and he smiled, making her shake her head at herself. "You'd think LA would have beaten the gullible out of me," she murmured.

"Nah. I'm just good at pulling legs."

"So what do you and Ford argue about? Women?"

"We try to avoid that."

"Okay, not a woman. Something else. Would you solve it with, say, a diplomatic coin toss?"

"Probably not," he admitted. "Loudest usually wins. A well-placed punch is always a bonus."

When she narrowed her eyes in blatant disbelief, he smiled again. "See, you're catching on to me already."

"Actually," she murmured, "it's not a bad idea. But I'd lose a fight against my oldest sister. Tara's got some *serious* pent-up-aggression issues." She considered her beer for a minute, her fingers stroking up and down over the condensation, drawing Jax's full attention.

"Probably I could take Chloe on account of her asthma," she said. "But that'd be mean. Plus I'm out of shape, so..."

At that, he gave her a slow once-over, fully appreciating her real curves, and shook his head. "Not from where I'm sitting."

She blinked. Compliments obviously flustered her, which only stirred his curiosity all the more. "You could challenge your sisters to a street race in your Honda," he said. "My money's on you."

She choked out a little laugh, set down her beer, and pointed at the opened puzzle book. "Four."

"Excuse me?"

"Four goes there. And six goes there." Leaning in, she took his pencil and filled in the two spots while he found his mouth so close to her ear he could have taken a nibble. Instead, he inhaled her scent. Soft. Subtle. *Nice.*

She cocked her head sideways, concentrating, and he just breathed her in. Which was how she filled in the rest of the puzzle before he realized it. "Damn."

"Don't be impressed," she said. "I've got a little compulsive problem. I can't stand to leave anything unfinished." She hopped off the barstool. "Unfortunately, they don't have a twelve-step program for such things."

"Ford's going to owe you," he said, snagging her wrist to halt her getaway.

"You could have done it if you'd worn your glasses." She pulled free. "It was only a moderately hard one. Oh and FYI? Women think glasses are a sign of brains, and also, they're sexy."

Cocking his head, he took in the slight flush to her cheeks, the humor in her gaze, and felt something stir within him. She might be struggling with some demons, but she was sweet and sharp as hell and a breath of fresh air. "Are you flirting with me?"

"No. The porn thing was a dealbreaker."

That made him laugh, and even better, so did she, and something flickered between them.

Chemistry.

A shocking amount of it. Clearly she felt it, too, because suddenly she was a flurry of movement, pulling some cash from the depths of her pockets, setting it on the bar for Ford, and turning for the door like she had a fire on her ass.

"Maddie."

She turned back, looking a little frenzied again, a little panicked, much as she had when he'd first seen her across the expanse of highway. He wondered why.

"I have to go," she said.

"Puzzles to solve?"

"Something like that."

"It's not really a puzzle-solving night," he said, slipping her money back into her front jeans pocket, his knuckles grazing her midriff. She went stock-still while he pulled his own money out to cover the drinks. "It's more of a make-new-friends night," he said. "And Ford's putting out peanuts. We can throw them at him. He hates that."

She closed her eyes, and when she opened them again, emotion flickered there. "I'd really like that, but tonight I have to have that fight with my sisters."

She was clearly vulnerable as hell, and he needed to get away from her before he took advantage of that. But then her bright blue gaze dropped and homed in on his mouth, and all his good intentions flew out the window.

"I'm working on a new beginning here," she said.

"New beginnings are good."

"Yeah." Her tongue came out and dampened her lips, an unconscious gesture that said maybe she was thinking of his mouth on hers. Seemed fitting. He'd been thinking about her mouth on his since he'd seen her outside the bar.

It'd been a hell of a long time since he'd let himself feel something, far too long. That it was for this woman, here, now, was going to make things difficult, but he was good at difficult and wouldn't let that stop him.

Reaching for her hand, he pulled her in, lowering his head. His jaw brushed her hair, and a strand of it stuck to his stubble. He was close enough now to watch in fascination as her eyes dilated. Her lips parted, and—

"You two need a hotel room?"

Ford, the resident nosey-body.

Maddie jumped and pulled free. "I've really got to go. Thanks for the drinks." She whirled around and stumbled into a table. With a soft exclamation, she righted the spilled drinks, apologizing profusely. Then she hightailed it for the door, not looking back.

"You're an ass," Jax said to Ford, watching her.

"No doubt. So, you going to collect her, too?"

Jax slid him a look.

"Come on. Try to deny that out of guilt you collect the needy: the homeless dog, friends who need loans, the chick with the sweet eyes and even sweeter ass—"

"You know I'm not interested in a relationship." It wasn't that he didn't believe in the concept. In spite of his parents' failed marriage and Jax's own close call with his ex, he understood wanting someone, the right someone, in his life. But he wasn't sure he trusted himself. After all, his past was freely littered with the debris of his many, many mistakes.

"You don't have to have a relationship to get... *involved,*" Ford said. "Not the naked variety of involved, anyway. But she did run out of here pretty darn quick. Maybe she wasn't feeling it."

No, that hadn't been the problem. There'd been chemistry, so much that they could have lit all of Lucky Harbor's Christmas lights from the electricity. And that chemistry had scared her. She'd been hurt, that was plain as day. Knowing it, hating it, Jax headed for the door, because bad idea or not, he felt compelled to get to know more about her.

"Hey, what about my tip?" Ford called after him.

"You want a tip? Learn to keep your big trap shut." And Jax stepped out into the night.

"Rule number one of drinking without a wing man," Maddie chided herself as she walked away from the Love Shack. "Don't do anything stupid."

She walked faster and found herself at the beginning of the pier, pushed around by the wind. But she hardly felt it. Nope, she was still all warm and tingly thanks to a certain gorgeous guy with a mischievous, bad-boy smile and an even better body—

You gave up men!

She had no idea why she kept forgetting that. She wasn't ready to let one near her. Not after leaving Alex six months ago now. She hadn't looked back. Hadn't looked forward, either, to be honest.

And yet she'd let Jax near enough to touch her.

Since going into the bar, dark had fallen. The main street was lit up like a Christmas card, and the quaint historical architecture was a great distraction.

She passed a beauty shop. It was open, the front chair filled with a client, the hairdresser behind her, and the two of them talking and laughing together like old friends. On the corner, where the pier met the street, came the delicious, mouth-watering scent of burgers from a little restaurant.

The Eat Me Café.

Her stomach rumbled. With good reason, as all she'd given it in the last few hours were chips and beer. She thought about a loaded burger, fries, and maybe a pie…

Instead, she had to go back and face her sisters.

Past the lights of the town stood a set of craggy bluffs, nothing but a dark, shadowy outline in the night sky now, most likely teeming with coyotes and bears. With a shiver, she turned and took in the coast, lined with impressive ancient rock formations and granite outcrops.

She hoped those coyotes and bears stayed up there and kept away from the beach. The pier was lit up by twinkling white lights strung on the railings. Someone had added red bows and mistletoe at regular intervals.

It could have been a movie set. Well, except for the realistic icy wind. Waves slapped at the pylons beneath her, far more real than any sound effect. She shivered in just her sweatshirt, but she shoved her hands into her pockets and kept walking because she needed another moment.

Maybe two.

She stopped at the base of the Ferris wheel and looked up. And up. Just thinking about riding it, sitting on top of the world, had the bottom falling out of her stomach.

Stupid fear of heights.

One of these days she'd conquer that fear, but it would have to get in line behind all the others, the ones she was letting rule her life—like her fear of being a mouse forever.

She passed the arcade and came to an ice cream shop. Just what the doctor ordered, she decided, and in spite of the chilly night, she requested a chocolate shake.

"How about a chocolate–vanilla swirl?" the guy behind the counter asked. He was young, early twenties, and had a smile that said he knew how cute he was. "It's our bestseller."

"Okay." But as soon as he turned away to make it, she smacked her forehead. "Don't let people make decisions for you! Dig deep and be like...Thelma. *No, wait. Louise. I want to be Louise.*" Crap. Which one had Susan Sarandon played? And did it matter? If she couldn't be strong, she was going to have to fake it until it sank in. "I'm *Louise.*"

"Ah, a fantasy. I like fantasies."

Heart in her throat, she whirled around and came face to face with Jax, looking dark and delicious, and instead of fear, something else entirely quivered low in her belly.

"But probably we should wait until after our first date to role-play," he said.

Jax and *fantasy* in the same sentence made her shiver. Jax slipped out of his jacket and offered it to her, leaving him in just a long-sleeved black shirt. She opened her mouth to tell him she wasn't cold, but then he drew the ends closed around her and her nipples pebbled as if he'd touched them, and she promptly forgot what she was going to say.

The leather held his body heat, wrapping her in it like a cocoon, and she murmured her thanks. "When I first heard you walk up behind me, I had visions of a wild animal from the cliffs dragging me off to its den to eat me, so I'm glad it was you."

"What makes you think you're safer with me?"

A laugh escaped her. "Well, it is true that you aren't looking so Clark Kent–like right now, not out here in the dark." Nope, he seemed much more like a superhero, all tall and dark and focused on her. It made it difficult to breathe, in fact. "I need to walk."

He gave her a single nod.

Apparently that meant he was coming along, because he kept easy pace with her. The back half of the pier was empty except for the occasional bench. There were no stars visible through the clouds, and, other than the pounding surf and gusts of wind, no interruptions. She slurped on her shake, then offered some to Jax.

He searched her gaze a moment, his own quiet and reflective. Then, instead of taking the cup, his hand enveloped her own as he leaned in to draw on the straw. Her fingers itched to run over his stubble to see if it would feel rough or silky. And then there were those sinfully long, dark eyelashes, practically resting on his cheekbones, wasted on a man. But her gaze locked in on the way the muscles of his jaw bunched as he sucked the shake. When his tongue released the straw, she actually felt an answering tug deep in her womb. She must have made a noise, because he sent her a curious glance.

"It's nothing." Well, nothing except she was all alone with a complete stranger on the far end of the dark, nearly deserted pier. No one to save her from herself.

"It's a different pace out here, isn't it?" he said quietly.

"From LA? A different world entirely." Her daily drive to work had been like riding the bumper cars at the fair. Funny thing was, she'd never really minded because *everything* in her life had been like a ride at the fair—fast and just a little out of control. Her commute, her job, her boyfriend...

Especially her boyfriend.

Alex had been all charm and sophistication on the outside. On the inside, though, he'd been a simmering Crock-Pot of negative emotions.

She drew a deep breath recalling her secret shame, that it had taken her so long to realize that she couldn't change him, that instead she'd slowly changed herself into someone she didn't recognize.

Standing up for herself when he'd started hitting her had been empowering. Unfortunately, he hadn't taken it well, and a couple of weeks ago, after *months* of trying to talk her into reconciling, he'd cornered her in her office at work. She'd taken care of herself, but it turned out that the brass frowned on anyone tossing hot coffee into the lap of their high-powered, expensive entertainment attorney.

Needless to say, Maddie no longer had her crazy daily drive to make.

Her mother had died that same week.

Maddie was working on being okay with all of it, but she hadn't gotten there yet. Maybe she'd schedule it into her BlackBerry.

Jax was watching her, as if something didn't quite add up. She could have told him not to bother trying to figure her out. No one had managed yet, not even herself.

"You okay?"

"Working on it," she said and gave him a small smile.

He returned the smile and stepped a little closer to her, which is when she discovered several things. One, she still had to fight her automatic flight response and purposely hold her ground, not taking a step back. *Not all guys are capable of smiling, stepping close, and then hitting,* she reminded herself. But while her brain knew this, her heart still wasn't ready to buy it.

Two, and even more unsettling, he smelled good— sexy and alluring. Closing her eyes, she felt her body actually tingle, brought to a hyper-awareness that felt almost foreign as something zinged through her.

Desire. Bone-melting desire.

When she opened her eyes again, he was even closer. His eyes weren't the solid warm caramel she'd thought but had flecks of gold dancing in them, as well. She could have drowned in all that deliciousness.

Not a bad way to go, she figured—death by lust.

Taking the shake out of her hands, he put it on the railing. "Maddie," he said. Just that, just her name in a deep voice that promised things she no longer believed in. And suddenly the part of her brain that had dictated the whole giving-up-men thing went on a vacay somewhere on the other side of reality, probably sharing a suite with the same gray matter that thought she could make a go of the inn. So instead of taking a step back, she took one forward and met him halfway on wobbly legs.

And what happened next was the oddest thing of all.

Odd and scary and amazing.

A heavenly sigh drifted past her lips as his arms came around her, and then his mouth touched hers, warm and tasting like the chocolate shake and forgotten hopes and dreams, and then...

And then there were no more thoughts.

Chapter 4

♥

*"Never sweat the small stuff.
And remember, it's all small stuff."*
Phoebe Traeger

Maddie's eyes had slayed Jax from the very start, but her mouth...Christ, her mouth. The kiss started out gentle, and he'd meant for it to stay that way, but then she pulled back just enough to stare up at him, all flushed and wide-eyed.

Lowering his head, he pressed his mouth to the hollow of her throat. Beneath his lips, he could feel her pulse racing, and he touched his tongue to the spot. At her gasp of pleasure, he made his slow way along her jaw, over warm, soft skin to her ear. When he finally lifted his face to hers, her eyes were huge, a sea of dazed heat as she clearly wondered exactly what he was up to.

No good. That's what he was up to.

Proving it, he kissed her again, her little whimper for more going straight through him. He heard her purse hit the pier at their feet, and then her arms wound around his neck and she was kissing him, an all-consuming, earthy, raw kiss, and he was a goner. He groaned into her mouth at the pleasure of her touch, at the rush of heat, at the anticipation that swam through him instead of good sense.

Again she tore free of his mouth and stared up at him, eyes feral, mouth wet, breathing wildly. He had no idea what she was looking for, but apparently she found it because she tugged him back down, her fingers digging into his biceps as if she couldn't get enough.

That made two of them.

He kissed his way down her throat, and she gave a low, sexy gasp when he got to the spot where her neck met her shoulder. Her eyes slid closed, and she shuddered with the intensity. "You taste good," he murmured.

"Like chocolate–vanilla swirl?"

He lifted his head as she opened her eyes, opaque with hunger and desire. "Like woman." Her hair was wild, a few curls clinging to her face and dancing in the wind, calling to him. Needing to touch her, he raised a hand to stroke her hair back, and she flinched, hard.

Shock had him going still, fingers hovering near her forehead, but she went even more still. Slowly he lowered his hand. "Maddie—"

With a quick, single shake of her head, she took a giant step back, her eyes shuttered from him. "I have to go."

"Okay." His brain raced, trying to figure out what had just happened. She'd acted as if he'd meant to hit her, which was crazy—he wouldn't.

Ever.

But someone had.

That was clear. So was the heat that rushed to her

face, knowing her involuntary gesture had just given her away.

Feeling sick for whatever she'd been through, sicker still for reminding her of it if only for a second, he stepped back. "Maddie—"

Tightening her lips, she bent for her purse, then turned away, walking back toward the street. "I *really* need to go."

Letting out a long, careful breath, he gave her a head start. He was quite certain that she'd like him to vanish entirely, but he couldn't do that. There was nowhere to go but back up the pier. So he followed, doing his best to give her the space he figured she needed.

Maddie walked fast down the pier, not slowing until she came to the Ferris wheel. Too bad her life couldn't be as simple as going round and round...

"You okay?"

Turning, she faced Jax, who stayed about five feet from her, hands in his pockets. "I'm fine." A little white lie that didn't count because she *wanted* to be okay. "About that kiss. I shouldn't have—We can't—" She blew out a breath and went with honesty. "Obviously I'm not in a place to start anything up."

"I'm getting that. It's okay, Maddie. I've been there."

She doubted he'd ever let anyone take advantage of him or hurt him, but she didn't want to talk about it. He was giving her an out, which she was going to take. Turning, she started walking. Not surprisingly, he kept pace. "I'm going back to the inn," she said. "Alone." She glanced over at him, not knowing what to expect, but it wasn't the quiet intensity she found. And it certainly wasn't feeling her own heart skip a beat.

They passed the ice cream shop, and the guy who'd served her waved at Jax. "Hey, man. Hot chocolate tonight?"

"Sure. A large to go, Lance. Thanks." He paid, then exchanged the warm cup for Maddie's shake. "For your hands," he said and guided her off the pier and onto the main street in front of the Love Shack.

A cute blonde burst out of the bar, teetering a little on her heels, laughing with a pretty brunette. "... and he wanted to drive me home!" she exclaimed.

"Well, you said you wanted to get laid," the brunette said.

"Yes, but look at me! I'm a nine tonight, maybe even a ten. And nothing less than an eight takes *this* body home—" Catching sight of Jax, she threw her arms around him. "Hey, sexy! Haven't seen you around all week. You working hard, or hardly working?"

"A little of both," Jax said, steadying her.

"Join us for a nightcap," Blondie said, slipping her arms around his neck.

Maddie looked down at herself. Yeah, okay, so she was dressed as a four, tops, but she wasn't invisible.

A cab pulled into the lot, and Blondie smiled. "There's our ride. Jax?" she murmured throatily, tugging his hand. "You coming?"

He shook his head, and Blondie and Brunette sighed in joint disappointment, then slid into the cab and vanished into the night.

"You could have gone," Maddie said after a minute. "Wouldn't want to hold you back."

"From . . . ?"

"A threesome."

He arched a brow. "Is that what you think I want?"

"Well, it does seem to be the top male fantasy."

"Maybe I'm content with my current company."

She felt herself soften in spite of herself and decided it was all the emotion of the day. The wind was kicking hard now, but Jax's jacket was protecting her, and she was content to just stand there. "Are you cold?" she asked, really hoping he wasn't.

"I'm good. Let me drive you to the inn." He gestured toward a red Jeep.

"What about your bike?"

"Both mine. But the Jeep'll keep you warm."

"I don't know."

He met her gaze evenly, his eyes dark and warm, quietly assessing. "It's a long walk."

"Yes," she agreed. "But taking a ride from a stranger would be even more stupid than kissing one."

"I can provide references if you'd like."

"From Blondie and Nine-Maybe-Ten?" she asked.

He burst out laughing, and the sound sent heat slashing through her. Sliding his hand to the small of her back, he walked her to the Jeep. "I think I can provide better than that for you." He opened the passenger door and waited while she hesitated. Gallant superhero, she wondered, or smooth bad boy who'd just managed to talk her into his lair?

Hard to tell.

She buckled herself in. The interior of the vehicle

was dark, and he wasn't giving any hints as to his thoughts while he put the Jeep into gear and headed out of the lot.

She stared out the windshield, thinking that so far, superhero and smooth bad boy seemed to be running neck and neck. Not that it mattered, not when deep down, she secretly wanted both.

Chapter 5

♥

*"Just when you think you've hit rock bottom,
someone will hand you a shovel."*
PHOEBE TRAEGER

Jax pulled up to the resort, and they both eyed the dark buildings. "Problem with the electricity?" he asked, idling the Jeep.

She hoped not. "I don't know."

"Your sisters are here?"

"I don't know that, either."

Jax thrust the Jeep into gear again and drove around to the back of the inn. Maddie held on to the dash and gulped. "This isn't the part where the big bad wolf eats me, is it?"

He sent her a mischievous glance. "What is it with you and things eating you?"

A nervous laugh burst from her, and he let loose a smile that was just wicked enough to boost her pulse and scare her at the same time. "Tell you what," he said silk-ily. "If *I* ever get the chance to eat you, I promise you'll like it."

Her stomach quivered. Her body had other reactions, too, but she kept them to herself as he pulled up to the cottage, where the windows were lit.

"How did you know to come back here?"

"I spent time out here as a kid. Once, with Ford and Sawyer, I TP'd the entire place."

It didn't surprise her that he'd had a wild youth. She suspected he'd had a wild everything. "You did?"

"Yeah, and Sawyer's father beat the shit out of us when he found out, and then turned us over to your grandpa. Instead of handing out our second ass-kicking of the night, he made us clean up our handiwork and paint the entire inn. He was a good guy." He flicked his gaze to the cottage, and she followed his line of sight to where both Chloe and Tara stood inside, staring out the window.

"They don't look very happy," he noted.

"Yes, I tend to have that effect on people."

His callused hand slowly slid up her back. When she started because she was looking out the Jeep window and not expecting the touch, he very gently touched the back of her neck. Warmth engulfed her.

"I don't know," he murmured very quietly. "You did a decent number on me tonight." His thumb swept over her nape, urging her to look at him.

One of them leaned in, she wasn't sure who, but suddenly her hands were on his chest and his hands were sliding up her arms, pulling her in as close as she could get with the console between them. "My sisters—"

"Can't see inside the Jeep." He kissed her once, and then again—small, brushing kisses that weren't enough, not even close, but when she heard a soft moan and realized it was hers, she pulled back.

"Yeah," Jax said, studying her intently. "I like this look on you a lot better."

"What look?"

"Heat. Desire. Not fear."

It took her a second for the words to register. When they did, she turned to open the door to get out, but he gently pulled her back and kissed her again, deep and hot. Her eyes drifted shut as she gave herself over to it, to him, and what he made her feel. He was such a good kisser, and his taste, his touch, his scent, the heat off his body—it all combined together so that she couldn't talk herself out of having this moment. She *needed* this moment. She deserved this moment, and, giving herself permission to enjoy it, she slid her hands over every part of him that she could reach, absorbing the groan of approval that rumbled from his throat.

"Haven't made out in a car in a damn long time," he said when they broke apart, his voice low and gravelly.

"Me either." In fact, she wasn't sure she'd *ever* made out in a car. She looked around. "We steamed up the windows."

He slid a hand over her shoulder, up her throat, his thumb skimming her pulse point. "We steamed up a lot of things."

Yes. Her body was humming with it. She ran her gaze down his body, past his broad chest, the flat abs she wanted to lick, and the button fly of his Levi's, which were strained over an intriguingly large bulge. Her gaze flew to his, which was both scorching hot and just a tad bit amused.

"I have to go in." But she didn't move. Well, actually, she did. She moved to give his mouth better access to her throat, which he took full advantage of, his lips rubbing

slowly back and forth over her skin. "B-before they...
Oh, God," she whispered. "Before they come out here to
investigate."

He had a hand at her waist, beneath his jacket and her
sweatshirt, his fingers gliding over the bare skin of her
belly, and she let out a shaking breath. "You're going to
have to take your hands off me, or..."

He met her gaze, his eyes dark and heated. "Or?"

Or she was going to crawl over the console and straddle him. "You don't play fair."

"I don't. You should remember that."

Telling her body to behave, she extricated herself from
both his hands and the Jeep. "Thanks for the ride."

And the kiss...

He opened his door. "I'll walk you in—"

"No, don't." She didn't want to explain this. She
dashed out of the Jeep and made her way up the rickety
porch, but the door opened before she'd reached it.

Chloe stood there, a small smile on her lips as she
peered past Maddie at the Jeep. "Who's that?"

Maddie watched the brake lights of the Jeep as it vanished into the night. "Jax Cullen. And that's all I know,"
she said before Chloe could ask anything else.

Well, except that he had a voice that went down like
smooth whiskey, a way of looking at her that tended to
get her to say more than she should, and oh, yeah, he
kissed like heaven on earth.

"I want a Jax," Chloe said.

"You didn't even see him."

"No, but I can see the look he put on your face plain
enough. Nice jacket."

"I forgot to give it back." *Maddie, Maddie, Maddie,*

she told herself. *That's a big fat lie. You didn't forget. You wanted the excuse to see him again.*

"I drove through town three times," Chloe said. "I never found a Jax."

Maddie slid her a look. Perfect dark red shiny hair. Cute, sexy clothes. Tight, toned body. An arresting face with piercing green eyes that said Trouble with a capital T, and that she was worth it. "There's no way you have a hard time attracting men."

"It's not the attracting that's the problem. You ever try to have sex with a third wheel in the bed?"

"Um, no," Maddie admitted. "I've never—"

"I meant my asthma," Chloe said dryly. "But good to know how your mind works. My *asthma* is the third person in my bed. And it usually kicks ass."

"You mean you can't—"

"Not in mixed company, or I end up needing an ambulance for the ensuing asthma attack." She sighed. "I really miss co-partnered orgasms."

"Oh, my God, will you get over the no-orgasm thing?" Tara said, coming up behind them. "Some of us *never* get them."

"Never? But you're married."

"Okay, so never might be an exaggeration. The point is, there are more important things than sex."

"Name one," Chloe said.

Tara lifted a bottle of wine.

"A close second," Chloe admitted. They moved through the living room as the wind rattled at the living room windows. The shag carpet had once been some sort of blue but had faded to a dingy gray, looking like a dead lawn that hadn't been watered in two decades.

"The place needs Christmas decorations," Chloe decided. "And a tree."

Maddie plopped down on the faded blue quilted couch and a huge cloud of dust arose. Chloe joined her, immediately drawing the neck of her shirt over her mouth and nose to protect herself. "And possibly a fumigation."

Tara shook her head and pulled Chloe off the couch. "Kitchen. The dust in here will kill you, sugar."

Maddie followed her two sisters, musing on the odd dynamic between them. Tara clearly cared while pretending not to. Chloe soaked up that caring like a love-starved child, while also pretending not to. As for Maddie, she had no idea where she fit in, or even if she could.

A loose shutter slapped against the side of the house and made her jump. The lights flickered off and then, after a long hesitation, back on again.

The three of them grabbed each other's hands and eyed the kitchen. It looked like the one in the inn, minus the table and *many* square feet. They sat hip to hip on the Formica counter. Tara poured the wine, handing a glass to Maddie, then poured one for herself.

"Hello," Chloe said, holding out her hand for a glass. "What am I, chopped liver?"

"Too young," Tara said.

"I'm past legal by three years!"

"Do you need a bra to keep your boobs from falling?" Tara asked. "Do you need a pair of Spanx to keep the tire hidden?"

"Tire?"

"Yes, the tire, the spare tire around the middle that doesn't go away in spite of a rigorous workout regime."

Tara gestured to her stomach, which in Maddie's opinion looked damn fine. She'd like to have a "tire" like that.

And probably she could, if she gave up chips.

"Do you get hot flashes that keep you up at night? Then you're not old enough to drink."

Chloe rolled her eyes and snatched a glass for herself anyway. "You know, you have some serious anger issues. And resentment issues. And holier-than-thou issues."

Maddie braced for the yelling. "Listen—"

"*Excuse me?*" Tara tossed back her wine and poured another, topping off Maddie while she was at it as she whirled on Chloe. "Holier than thou?"

"If the shoe fits," Chloe said. "*Sugar.*"

"Never mind, Miss Perky Boobs. I'll talk to you when you're sober."

"And I'll talk to you when you're not a bitch."

"Yeah, well, that might be a while," Tara said.

Chloe shook her head. "And for the record, you're thirty-four, Tara, not seventy-two."

Maddie snatched the wine bottle, because it was going to be that kind of a night.

"And another thing," Chloe said, taking the bottle from Maddie. "Maddie's boobs are just as perky as mine."

Everyone looked at Maddie's breasts. They were full C's, and the only reason they were anywhere even close to *perky* was thanks to her clearance sale push-up bra. She blew out a breath and looked at her empty wineglass. "I should stop now. Beer and wine don't mix well."

Tara looked at her empty glass, then over at the garbage can, confused. "How did I miss the beer?"

"She drank with Hot Guy," Chloe said.

"Hey." Maddie tried to find the indignation but had

some trouble working around the alcohol. "He has a name."

"What is it?" Tara wanted to know.

"It's a really, really, really good name."

"Can you even remember it?" Tara asked wryly. "Or did he suck your memory out along with your tongue?"

No, but he'd sure had a nice tongue. "His name's Jax. Jax Cullen."

Tara choked on her wine.

"Know him?" Maddie asked.

Tara set her glass aside and tipped the bottle to her mouth, taking a long time to answer. "How would I know him?" She dabbed delicately at the corners of her mouth. "And what do you see in this guy anyway?"

Chloe held up her hands about ten inches apart.

At that, it was Maddie's turn to choke. "I didn't sleep with him! I gave up men," she added much more weakly. "And anyway, penises that size don't really exist."

"Then why did you come in grinning?"

Maddie sighed. "Has anyone ever told you that you're a tattletale?"

"Always has been," Tara said. "Once when I was fifteen and sneaking out the back door, Chloe told Mom on me. I was grounded for the rest of the summer."

Chloe grinned. "Good times."

Maddie had lived with Phoebe only until she'd gotten pregnant with Chloe. After that, Maddie's father had taken custody. Maddie had visited during vacations or whenever her father couldn't have her with him at work, but it hadn't been often. As a result, she had only sparse memories of her sisters. But Tara had spent most summers with Phoebe and Chloe.

"Where were we that summer?" Chloe asked Tara. "Northern California somewhere, right? In that trailer Mom rented on some river with friends?"

Tara nodded. "Sounds about right."

"You wouldn't take me with you wherever you were sneaking off to. That's why I told on you."

"You were a baby!"

"I was five. And I wanted to be fifteen like you."

And Maddie wanted memories with them.

Tara sighed and leaned back. "I completely wasted fifteen. Youth is wasted on the young."

Chloe snorted.

"I'm not kidding!" Tara said. "If I was fifteen again, I'd definitely know what to do with it now."

"Really," Chloe said with disbelief heavy in her voice.

"*Really.*"

Outside, the wind battered the windows, the storm in full swing. They all paused and glanced uneasily out into the dark night. "I hated being fifteen," Maddie said quietly, feeling the wine. "The doubts, the lack of confidence, the despair." And damn if much had changed. She sighed and held out her glass for more wine. Tara obligingly topped her off again.

"If you're having what-ifs," Chloe said, "you're *still* wasting life."

"Not me." Maddie shook her head. "I'm not wasting anything, not ever again. I'm on a new life's lease. I'm starting over." She emphasized this with a wild swing of her glass. Wine splashed out over her hand, and she licked it off. "No more letting anyone speak for me, roll over me, step on me, slap me..."

The shattering silence that followed this statement sobered her up a little. "See, this," she said. "This is why I shouldn't drink." Ignoring the startled look exchanged between her sisters, she held out her glass. She definitely needed a refill.

But Tara gently took it away. "Somebody hit you?" she asked softly.

"Slapped." Big difference. A slap was humiliating and hurtful, but it wasn't like he'd punched her. Or caused her real harm. Well, except for that last time, when the corner of a cabinet had broken her fall, requiring stitches just outside of her eye. But hey, she was single now. All was good. Or as good as it could be.

"Maddie—"

"It's over and done." She dropped her head and studied her shoes. Sneakers, scuffed and battered. That had to be symbolic somehow, she thought unhappily.

Chloe was wearing cute ankle boots, not a scratch on them.

Tara was wearing stylish heels, so shiny they could have been used as a mirror.

"I need new shoes," she said out loud.

Chloe reached out and squeezed her hand. "New shoes rock," she whispered, sounding like her throat was too tight.

Maddie squeezed her fingers back while her wine-soaked thoughts rambled in her head, not quite readily available for download. "Oh! I forgot to show you guys something." She pulled the recipe box from her bag and told them about Lucille. She flipped through for a random card. "Bad decisions make good stories," she read.

"Lord," Tara said.

"Not 'bless her heart'?" Chloe asked, grinning until a gust of wind hit so hard that the entire house shuddered.

This was followed by a thundering *BOOM*. The ground shook, the lights flickered, and all three of them jumped.

"Holy shit." Chloe scooted over on the counter until she was right up against Tara, nearly in her lap.

Maddie hopped down and opened the back door, flicking on a flashlight that didn't do much for cutting into the utter blackness of the night.

"Where did that flashlight come from?" Chloe asked.

"My purse."

Chloe looked at Tara. "She carries a flashlight in her purse."

"For emergencies," Maddie said, trying to see into the yard.

"You have any chocolate?" Chloe asked hopefully. "For emergencies?"

"Of course. Side pocket, next to the fork."

"You're good," Tara murmured, holding out her hand for some.

"Are you of age?" Chloe asked snidely.

Tara growled, and Chloe hastily handed her a piece.

"You are a lifesaver," Tara said to Maddie, who smiled. She'd learned at work to be prepared for anything and everything. She'd never given it a second thought, but sensing her sisters' relief, and maybe just a little bit of admiration, as well, felt good.

Even if they were chomping on her secret chocolate stash.

But she'd always wanted a true family, wanted to be counted on. Oh, she loved her dad, and he loved her, but she had always yearned for more.

That her family could be here after all this time, right here in front of her, gave her a warm fuzzy in spite of the frigid, windy night, slapping her in the face as she started outside. Sweeping her flashlight from right to left, Maddie stopped when she came to the newly fallen tree bisecting the yard. "We lost a tree," she called back to her sisters. "A big one."

"Come back before one of them falls on your head," Tara called out.

Maddie kept going until she stood where the very top of the fallen pine tree had landed, trapping a scrawny baby pine tree beneath it. And damn if the sight didn't break her heart. It took her a moment to free it, and then she hoisted the tree into her arms, turning back to the porch, where both her sisters still stood.

"Found us a Christmas tree," she said.

Chapter 6

♥

*"Obeying the rules might be smart,
but it's not nearly as much fun."*
PHOEBE TRAEGER

They decorated the tree with what they had on hand, which turned out to be some kitchen items and a string of chili pepper lights left over from what Chloe claimed to remember as a wild block party in the nineties.

Tara found a stack of twenty-year-old *National Enquirers*. "Phoebe's gospel," she said with a fond smile, holding up one with Mel Gibson on the cover. She cut out the picture and hung it on a branch. "What?" she said when Chloe and Maddie just stared at her. "I'd do him."

"You do realize he no longer looks like that, right?" Chloe asked.

"Hey, *my* fantasy."

They spent the next half hour drinking another bottle of wine and cutting out pictures of all the guys they'd "do." Turned out there were quite a few. Maddie claimed Luke Perry and Jason Priestley—pre all their horrible movie-of-the-week specials. Chloe went for the boy bands. All of them.

"It can't be just a hottie tree," Tara decided.

Chloe nodded and hung a serving spoon, then cocked her head to study it critically, moving it over an inch like she was creating the *Mona Lisa*. "I once dated a guy who had a face like this serving spoon. He was ugly as hell, but man, *oh, man,* could he kiss. He gave me a nightly asthma attack for the entire week we dated." She sighed dreamily. "Ugly men make good lovers."

"Logan's gorgeous *and* good in bed," Tara said. "What does that mean?"

"Um, that you're lucky to be married to him?" Chloe asked.

"No." Tara shook her head with careful exaggeration. "Gorgeous men are flawed. Seriously flawed."

"Not all of them," Chloe said.

"*All of them.*"

Maddie found a doily. "My ex is good-looking. And good in bed. And..." The shame of it reached up and choked her as she carefully folded the doily so it looked like a star. "And, as it turns out, violent." She nodded to herself and set the "star" on top of the tree. Yep. Perfect. Especially if she scrunched up her eyes. "Which I guess makes him pretty damn flawed."

There was a long beat of loaded silence. When she managed to turn to her sisters, both were looking at her with shock and rage and regret in their eyes.

"Is that who hit you?" Tara finally asked quietly. "Your ex?"

Maddie nodded, and Chloe let out a breath. "You hit him back, right?"

"And then called the police," Tara said. "You called the police on him, didn't you, sugar? Put him behind bars so he could be some big bubba's bitch?"

No, she hadn't. And it was hard to explain, even to herself. But it'd happened slow, the gradual teardown of her self-esteem until she'd no longer felt like Maddie Moore. She'd felt awkward and stupid and ugly.

Alex had done that.

No, scratch that. She'd let Alex do that to her, one careful, devastatingly cruel comment at a time before she'd walked out on him.

Without her confidence, without her savings, without anything.

It sounded so pathetic now, which she hated. "I dumped his coffee on his family jewels," she said. "Ruined his new Hugo Boss suit, which was pretty satisfying, since he looked like he'd peed his pants." Too bad her bosses hadn't appreciated her show of feminism and she'd gotten fired.

Details. But for the first time, she shared them over a third bottle of wine, while they cleaned and decorated the cottage into the night.

And much later, lying under the tree together, the three of them stared up at the chili pepper lights and grinned like idiots.

Or that might have just been Maddie.

She couldn't help it. The top of her head was bumping up against the scrawny trunk of the tree, and she was breathing in the scent of pine. Above her, she could see a set of barbecue tongs dangling off the branches next to a picture of Jon Bon Jovi, a whisk, a Tupperware lid, and a near-naked shot of a very young Johnny Depp.

"I've never had a more beautiful tree," she whispered reverently.

"That's because you're drunk, sugar. Drunk as a skunk."

Chloe sighed dreamily. "I haven't had a tree in years. Not since I left Mom's when I was sixteen."

Maddie sighed, too. They were as much strangers to each other as she was with Jax, really, and yet since arriving in Lucky Harbor, she'd never felt less alone. "I know you guys are out of here as soon as possible, but—"

"Maddie, darlin'," Tara said softly. "No buts."

"Just hear me out, okay? What if we refinanced? We could hire someone to renovate, and we could run the inn the way it should be run. And we have a part-time employee already in Lucille! Sure, she's ancient, but Mom trusted her."

"Mom trusted everyone."

"My point is, we could probably even make decent money if we tried."

"Do you have any idea what it takes to refinance these days?" Tara asked, ever the voice of reason. "We'd need a miracle."

"Then we try to find out who Phoebe left all her money to in that trust. Obviously, it's someone she cared about, which means this person cares about her in return. Maybe they'd be interested in investing in the inn. We could—"

"No," Tara said harshly, and when both Maddie and Chloe stared at her, she closed her eyes. "Think about this logically, okay? Running an inn is a lot of work." She waved her arms and nearly knocked the tree over. "And the marina, good Lord. Do either of you even know the first thing about boats or the ocean or—" She stopped because a spoon had fallen from a branch and hit her in the nose. "*Ouch.*"

"Mom wanted this." Maddie reached up and removed a fork from the branches before it fell, too, and maybe poked out an eye. "She wanted this for us."

Tara and Chloe lay there, silent. Silent and contemplative. Or so Maddie hoped. Exhausted, she let her eyes close, her thoughts drifting. She wanted this to work. She wanted it bad. So maybe her mother hadn't tried to get close to her. Maybe her sisters hadn't, either, and maybe, possibly, she'd even *allowed* her mother to rebuff her because it'd been easier. But now, right now when she'd needed an escape, one had appeared. "It's meant to be," she whispered, believing it.

For a long beat, no one said anything.

"My life is crazy," Chloe said quietly. "And I like crazy. It doesn't lend itself to responsibilities, and I'm sorry, Maddie, so very sorry, but this is a pretty big responsibility."

"And my life is in Dallas," Tara said. "I'm not a small-town girl, never have been."

"I get that," Maddie said. "But maybe we can put it all into motion, and I'll run the place. Maybe I'll send you both big fat checks every month. Maybe by this time next year, we'll be celebrating."

"That's a lot of maybe-ing."

"It could happen," Maddie insisted. "With a little faith."

"And a lot of credit card debt."

Sitting up again, brushing pine needles out of her hair, Maddie went to the kitchen and came back with a

Lucky Harbor phonebook. "I saw a bank right next to the Love Shack in town. I'll go there tomorrow and see about refinancing."

"What do they sell at this love shack?" Chloe wanted to know. "Is it a sex shop?"

"It's a bar."

"Even better," Chloe said.

"I'm leaving here by the end of the week," Tara warned. "Sooner, if I can manage it, with or without refinancing."

"You really get hives in a place like this, huh?" Chloe asked.

"Sugar, you have *no* idea."

Maddie had put her finger on a list of general contractors. "Two of them say they specialize in renovations." She pulled out her BlackBerry.

"Maddie," Tara said.

"Just calling, that's all." She dialed the first.

"Isn't it the middle of the night?" Chloe asked, looking out the window.

"Oh, yeah…" Still buzzed, Maddie grinned. "I'll leave a message." Except the number she'd dialed had been disconnected or was out of service. She punched in the numbers for the second listing, a JC Builders. "Hey," she said to her sisters. "I got an answering machine, and it says they have a master carpenter on staff. A *master!*"

"She's drunk dialing contractors," Chloe said to Tara. "Someone should stop her."

"Shh." Maddie closed her eyes as she listened to a deep, masculine voice instructing her to leave a message. "Hi," she said at the beep. "Potential new client here, looking for a master—er, renovation expert. We're at

Lucky Harbor Resort, at the end of Lucky Harbor Road, you can't miss us. Oh, and we're in desperate need of mastering. You're probably busy, seeing as you're the only master in town, but we're short on time. Like *really* short on time. In fact, we're sort of desperate—" She broke off and covered the mouthpiece because Tara was in her face, waving wildly. "*What?*"

"You said *desperate* twice. You can't tell him that—he'll raise his price! And what the hell is your fixation on being mastered?"

Maddie rolled her eyes—which made her dizzy—and uncovered the mouthpiece. "Okay, forget the desperate thing. We're not desperate. Hell, we could do the work ourselves, if we wanted. So come or don't come, no worries." She paused, turned her back on her sisters, and lowered her voice to speak extra softly. "*But please come first thing in the morning!*" And then she quickly ended the conversation and smiled innocently at Tara.

"Stealth," Chloe said with a thumbs-up. "Real stealth."

As always, Jax got up with the sun. Apparently, some habits were hard to break. Once upon a time, he'd have hit the gym and downed a Starbucks while racing his Porsche on the highway to take his turn on the hamster wheel with the rest of the city. As a very expensive defense attorney for a huge, cutthroat law firm in Seattle, where winning cases at all costs had been the bottom line, he'd gone by his given name, Jackson Cullen III.

It'd been comfortable enough, given that he'd been raised by a man with the same philosophy as his firm. Jax had spent his days doing his thing in court, schmoozing with the other partners in the law firm, and in general sucking the very soul from himself and others. And then repeating the entire thing all over again the next day.

He no longer owned the snooty condo, fancy Porsche, or even a single suit, for that matter, and he was five long years out of the practice of schmoozing anyone.

But he was still working on recovering his soul.

Just being back in Lucky Harbor helped. It was a slower, simpler lifestyle, one he'd chosen purposely. He'd gone back to his first love, rebuilding and restoration, while trying to help people instead of acquit them.

Until yesterday anyway, when for the first time in far too long, he'd actually felt something real. He'd felt it with shocking depth for a curly-haired, endearingly adorable klutz, a woman with unconscious warmth and an innate sexiness, and a set of sweet, haunted eyes.

Devastating combo.

He pulled on his running gear and nudged Izzy, his two-year-old mutt. She was part brown Lab, part possum, and proved her heritage by cracking open a single eye with a look that said *Dude, chill.*

"You're coming," he said.

She closed her eye.

"Come on, you're getting a pudge."

She farted.

He shook his head, then dumped her out of her dog bed, no easy feat since she weighed seventy-five pounds.

They ran their usual three miles along the beach. Well, Jax ran. Izzy sauntered a hundred yards or so, then slowed, dragging her feet in the sand until she found a pelican to pester. Then, apparently exhausted from that effort, she plopped down and refused to go another step until Jax roused her on his return.

He entered his house through the back door and stepped into his office. Surprised to see a blinking light on his machine at seven in the morning, he hit play, then realized it was a call from last night. He stood still in shocked surprise at Maddie's soft voice.

"Hi," she said. "Potential new client here, looking for a master."

The loud knocking startled Maddie out of a dead sleep. Discombobulated, she blinked, and then blinked again, but all she could see was a sea of green and a flashing red that had her groaning and lifting her hands to hold her pounding head.

Taking stock, she realized that she was flat on her back beneath the tree, staring up at a string of obnoxious chili pepper lights.

Or maybe that was the hangover that was so obnoxious.

With another groan, she managed to sit up and nearly took out an eye with one of the low, straggly tree branches. Slapping a hand over it, she looked down at herself. Huh. She was completely tangled in red yarn. And she was pretty sure she had sap in her hair.

Even more odd, the cottage was spotless. Maddie had vague recollections of a tipsy Tara moving through the place with a broom in one hand and a rag in the other, bossing Maddie to assist as she went.

Which didn't explain the yarn. But she also remembered going through the cottage's bedroom, where they'd found some of their mother's things. There'd been a basket full of loose pictures, an empty scrapbook that Phoebe had clearly meant to use but never had, and another book, as well—*Knitting for Dummies*. Maddie had stared at the book and at the half-knitted scarf beneath it and felt her heart clench at the long-ago memory—she and her mom, sitting together, trying to learn to knit.

Trying being the operative word.

Phoebe had laughed at their pathetic efforts, saying how the fun wasn't in the final product, but in the journey. At the time, it'd frustrated Maddie.

Not last night. Last night, it'd been a precious memory, one of far too few, and she'd laid claim to the book, the knitting needles, and the half-finished scarf from all those years ago. While Chloe had sorted through the pictures and Tara had cleaned, Maddie had re-taught herself how to knit.

Loosely speaking.

Her sisters were still prone under the tree, out cold. Chloe was snoring. Tara was...*smiling?* Not a sight Maddie had seen often. Hell, none of them were exactly free with their smiles, she'd noticed. She shook her head, then groaned at the movement.

Note to self—*never drink again.*

At some point, they'd clearly decided pj's were a good thing. Maddie was wearing her favorite flannel Sponge-Bob drawstring pants and a Hanes beefy tee with the words BITE ME across the chest. Chloe's pj's had come from Victoria's Secret, but with her body, she could have worn a potato sack and looked good. Across her teddy the words JINGLE MY BELLS were delicately embroidered. Tara was wearing men's boxers, a cami, a silk bathrobe, and a pair of knee-high socks.

Maddie nudged Chloe's foot.

"No more, Juan," Chloe whispered. "My inhaler's too low."

The knock on the front door came again, and in unison Chloe and Tara sat straight up, conked their heads together, and moaned.

Maddie staggered toward the door, taking a second to stare in shock at their tree. Last night, it had been the most gorgeous tree she'd ever seen. This morning, it stood barely three feet tall and looked like... "A Charlie Brown Christmas tree," she whispered. She stepped over her sisters' legs, caught sight of herself in the small mirror over the little table in the foyer, and just about screamed.

Her hair had rioted. The little mascara she'd had on her lashes was now outlining her eyes, and she had a crease down one cheek from whatever she'd used as a pillow, which she suspected had been the yarn she was still wrapped in. "Never again," she told her pathetic reflection and then pointed at it for emphasis.

Her reflection stuck her tongue out.

With a sigh, she opened the front door, then stood there in a stupor. Standing on the porch, wearing faded Levi's, a black sweater over a black T-shirt, mirrored sunglasses, and a crooked smile was Jax Cullen.

Chapter 7

♥

"Experience is something you get…
after you need it."
PHOEBE TRAEGER

Maddie stared up at Jax, who was not hung over and didn't have a crease on his face. He looked big, and bad, and so sexy it should be a crime, and she reacted without thinking.

She shut the door in his face.

Tara gasped.

Chloe laughed.

And Maddie covered her face. "Quick, somebody shoot me."

"Honey." Tara's hand settled on her shoulder. "Maybe you don't know this being from LA and all, but shutting the door on someone's nose is considered rude in almost all fifty states."

"You don't understand. It's him. *Jax.*" And maybe it was the fact that her brain was on low battery, but just looking at him made her hot and bothered. Her! The woman who'd decreed that the entire male race was scum. "What do I do?"

"Well, for starters," Chloe said, "You stop slamming doors on guys who look like *that*."

"He has superpowers," Maddie said, nibbling on her thumbnail.

"Yeah?" Clearly fascinated, Chloe took another peek. "Like being hot as hell?"

Tara lightly smacked Maddie's hand from her mouth. "What does he want?"

"I'm going to guess SpongeBob Pants here," Chloe murmured, still looking at him.

Maddie pushed her away from the window so she could take her own look. "Oh, my God," she whispered.

On the porch, Jax turned his head and gave her a slow, mischievous wink, making her jump back as if he'd bitten her. "*Oh, my God.*"

"She's starting to repeat herself," Chloe said to Tara, who took her turn at the window.

"Oh, sugar." Tara took her time looking him over. "You're not ready for the likes of him."

"I hate to agree with her on anything," Chloe said to Maddie. "But she might be right on this one."

Drawing in a sharp breath, Maddie put her hand on the door handle. With a sister crowding her on either side—she wasn't sure whether it was for moral support or to make sure she didn't jump his bones—she opened the door.

She had to give Jax credit. Certainly, the three of them looked like wild, grossly unpredictable creatures from Planet Estrogen. But much as he had at the bar in the face of that pissed-off Smarmy Suit, he stood his ground. He even smiled.

"Hey," Maddie said, taking a step forward to give them some privacy, but she tripped over the yarn. It took her a few seconds and most of her dignity before she fought her legs free.

He pulled off his sunglasses to watch her, revealing those melted caramel eyes, which seemed to be both amused and heated. Amused, no doubt, because of the little yarn incident, not to mention the bedhead and SpongeBob pj's. As for why his eyes were also heated, she could guess—he was thinking of last night.

Which made two of them, because the kisses—oh, good Lord, the kisses—were suddenly all her brain would upload. The memory of those delicious, hot, deep, amazing kisses had kept her up most of the night. And then there'd been how his hands had felt all over her. Just remembering had something tingling behind her belly button and heading south.

"You okay?" he asked.

Sure. She was peachy. Or she would be soon as she cleared a few things up. Because as much as just looking at him put a big, goofy smile on her face, she had to be honest with him. Or at least as honest as she could. "About last night. I'm sorry if I gave you the wrong impression, but I'm really not in a good place for this right now."

He didn't say anything to this, and the silence was worse than the hangover.

"It's nothing personal, of course. But I can't, I just can't go there." Why wasn't he saying anything? "I'm... not interested." Okay, so that was liar, liar, pants on fire, but his silence was unnerving. "I mean, I realize that I probably didn't *seem* uninterested last night, but that was extenuating circumstances." Those being that he was far too good-looking and he'd tasted like chocolate—lethal combination.

Fighting a smile, he reached out and started unwinding some of the yarn still around her shoulder. His fingers brushed her collarbone and sent yippee-kayee messages to her nipples.

She snatched the yarn from him. "And as for the pier and then needing a ride, well, I'm not usually so helpless. In fact, you should probably know..." She drew a deep breath. "I've given up men."

At that, he arched a brow.

Be strong. Be confident. Be...Neytiri from Avatar. *Okay, so Neytiri was a mythical creature, not to mention animated, but still. She was strong and confident, and that's all that matters at the moment.* "It's true. At first, I was just going to give up attorneys, but that seemed immature—and far too exclusive, so I'm playing it safe and giving up all the penis-carrying humans." Because that was so much *more* mature.

Tara peeked out from behind the door with an apologetic wince in Jax's direction. "It's possible she's still tipsy," she explained.

"I'm not still tipsy!" She didn't think so, anyway. "So I'm sorry if you drove all the way out here looking for a repeat of last night, but it's not going to happen. I'm not interested." She held her breath in case karma was listening, ready to flatten her with a bolt of lightning for lying.

Nothing. Well, nothing but more silence, and this time she bit her tongue rather than try to fill it with more embarrassing chatter.

"Okay," Jax finally said with a single nod. "That's all... very interesting. But I'm not here for a 'repeat.'"

A very bad feeling began to bounce around in her gut. "You're not?"

"No. You called and asked me to come here."

Maddie took a second, deeper look at him and his attire: the black sweater that upon closer inspection was really a North Face hoodie and had JC Builders embroidered on his pec. His jeans were baggy but still emphasized his long, hard body in a way that suggested they were old friends. He wore work boots, and, given the battered, beloved look to them, they were not for show. But most telling was the measuring tape sticking out of a pocket and the clipboard he held resting against his thigh.

In the yard behind him was his Jeep with a big, brown dog riding shotgun.

"You're the contractor," she said weakly.

"Uh-huh." He was definitely amused now. "Unless you're no longer interested in my... *mastery*."

Oh, God.

"After all," he said. "I am a penis-carrying human."

Chloe laughed.

Tara grimaced and shut the door on his face, but she did hold up a finger first and say, "Just a moment, sugar." Once a steel magnolia, always a steel magnolia.

"Jeez," Chloe said in disgust. "How is it the so-called baby of this family is the only one who knows *not* to shut the door on the unspeakable hottie? I mean that's just sacrilegious."

Maddie groaned. "I called him. Omigod. *I* called *him*. I'm such an idiot."

"Aw, honey." Chloe stroked a hand down Maddie's out-of-control hair, her fingers getting caught in the tangles and tree sap. "You're not an idiot. Not exactly."

"It's the kissing! It's the stupid kissing! It's like he kissed all the vital brain cells right out of my head!"

"A good kiss is a signature," Chloe said, and when both sisters looked at her, she shrugged. "Hey, don't blame me, it was on one of Mom's cards."

Maddie shook her head. "What do I do?"

"You stick with your resolve. You're giving up men," Tara reminded her. "Next problem. We're selling this property. We need to tell him so before we waste any more of his time."

Maddie held her breath—and her head. Damn, she really needed Advil. "Last night, we said we'd give this place a shot."

"That was three bottles of wine talking," Tara said.

Suddenly Maddie's heart pounded in tune with her head. "Give me a month. Until Christmas," she said. Begged. "We fix the place up a little, and if you still don't want to make it work, we'll sell. And with the improvements, we'll get a better price. You'll have lost nothing."

Chloe looked at Tara.

Tara sighed.

"You know I'm right," Maddie said, sensing their capitulation. This was it. She had to convince them. She wanted, *needed,* this month. "We'll be better off for it, I promise."

"But what will we use for money for the renovations?" Chloe asked. "All I have is a Visa card, and there's not much left on it after last month's trip to Belize."

"I have an unused MasterCard," Tara said slowly.

"Me, too." It was Maddie's entire emergency contingency plan, since Alex had so unsuccessfully "invested" her small nest egg. "It's a start, and it shouldn't take us more than a few weeks to refinance. And I'm still determined to find out about that trust and talk to—"

"Let the trust go," Tara said firmly. "Mom went to great lengths and expense to separate it and protect it, and it's none of our business. Besides, that's not our real problem."

"What's the real problem?" Maddie asked.

"That I don't want to be here," Tara replied.

"You don't have to be," Maddie said. "We put this into motion, and I'll stay. You two can go, and I'll handle it."

"Until Christmas," Tara said. "And then we'll sell."

Not a mouse...Fake the strength. "If that's how the majority votes," Maddie said carefully, forcing herself not to back off.

"And you're okay doing this by yourself," Chloe clarified. "Really?"

"Yes." Maddie looked at the closed door and drew a deep breath. "Well, maybe not *all* by myself."

"A partner will definitely help," Chloe said, nodding. "And I have a feeling that man knows how to *partner*."

Maddie remembered how it'd felt to be in his arms and got a hot flash. No question, he knew how to *partner*. She'd be willing to bet her life on it. Not that it mattered.

"Sugar, how do you plan to get his help when you just rudely told him you weren't interested?"

Oh, yeah. That. "I'm going to wing it." With a steady breath, she pulled open the door while simultaneously attempting to tame her hair—a losing battle.

Jax had moved along on the porch and was hunkered

down, arms braced on his thighs, studying the dry-rot on a post. When she stepped out, he straightened to his full height and looked her over. "Everything okay?"

"Sure. We were just, um, discussing what we're going to have for breakfast."

"Really."

"Yeah. You know, pancakes or Cap'n Crunch."

"Cap'n Crunch. Always Cap'n Crunch. And you're going to have to work on your lying." Leaning in, he tweaked a curl. "Thin door."

And here she'd been worried that she wasn't going to make enough of a fool of herself in front of him today. She glanced over her shoulder for assistance, but her sisters had vanished. *Traitors.* "Okay, listen. I'm sorry."

"For?"

"The drunken phone call. Shutting the door in your face twice this morning alone. The whole spiel you just heard—pick one."

Jax looked out into the bright, sunny, icy-cold morning, and then back into her eyes. "And about the kiss. Are you sorry about that, too?"

She'd thought that she would be. After all, she'd been so easily drawn into Alex's ready charm, and look at what a nightmare that had turned out to be.

They both knew the truth. If she'd felt any more "interested," she would have spontaneously combusted.

At her silence, he stepped in a little closer. Close enough that her body tensed with the need to step back, but then his scent came to her, his soap or deodorant or whatever that delicious male scent was, and her nostrils twitched for more. "I don't want to talk about it," she whispered.

"You have a lot of things you don't want to talk about."

Last night, he'd been kind enough not to ask questions. She hoped that was still the case. "I know." She braced for the inquisition, but he didn't go there. He kept it light.

And sexy. God, so sexy.

"I understand," he said, nodding. "All that kissing was...awkward. Messy. Completely off."

It'd been deep and erotic and sensual, and even now, just thinking about how his mouth had felt on hers sent butterflies spiraling low in her belly.

No.

No, she wasn't sorry about the kiss.

Clearly reading her mind, his mouth slowly curved. "So no interest, and certainly no chemistry," he murmured, dipping his head to take in the fact that her misbehaving nipples were pressing up against the words BITE ME on her T-shirt.

"R-right," she managed. "No chemistry whatsoever." But then she took a step into him instead of away, and look at that, suddenly his mouth was right there, and her hands were fisting in his fleece hoodie.

How had that happened?

His eyes were heavy lidded now and locked on her mouth. Beneath her hands, he was warm and hard with strength, and she tightened her grip. To keep him at arm's length, she told herself. "You don't want chemistry with me," she said. "I have...faults."

"Like you can't hold your liquor?"

"Ha. And no. I mean..." She searched for something suitably off-putting. "I'm twenty-nine, and I keep a flashlight on me, just in case I need to hold the closet monsters at bay. I can't let foods touch on my plate, everything has to be in its own quadrant. And my go-to movie is *The Sound of Music*. I can sing every song." There. Didn't get more embarrassing than that. But just in case, she added one more. "I can also burp the alphabet. I won an award for it in college, and sometimes when I'm alone, I practice in the mirror."

"The whole alphabet?"

"Yeah, so it's for the best that we don't . . . you know."

"You're right. That *Sound of Music* thing is totally a dealbreaker. Thankfully, we have no chemistry at all." He was teasing her, but when she met his gaze, he wasn't smiling. Nope. His eyes were lit with something else entirely, and it wasn't humor.

And she knew something else, too. She hadn't scared him off. Not even a little.

Chapter 8

♥

*"The easy road is always under construction,
so have an alternate route planned."*
PHOEBE TRAEGER

Maddie rushed through a shower with water that wouldn't go past lukewarm, and worse, it looked suspiciously rusty. She'd be worried except she'd gotten a tetanus shot just last year when she'd stepped on a nail at a movie set in Burbank. And anyway, it was hard to find room for worry when her body was humming and pulsing.

And he hadn't even kissed her again.

Dammit, how dare he bring her body parts back to life with nothing more than his presence after she'd decided to go off men entirely?

It was rude, it was thoughtless, it was...

Not his fault.

Getting out of the shower, she stood in the bathroom and rummaged through her duffel bag. She'd packed only the essentials, leaving the rest in storage with her dad in Los Angeles.

She pulled on a pair of Levi's and struggled with the top button. Damn chips. She pulled on a tank top, then added a big bulky sweater, not letting herself hear a certain ex's voice whispering in her ear that she should hit the gym. Instead, she didn't look at herself too closely in the mirror. Ignorance was bliss, right? Maybe she ought to put *that* on a 3x5 card and add it to the box.

As always, her hair had a mind of its own. Battling with the blow-dryer helped only marginally. She took a couple of swipes with the mascara wand and declared herself good to go.

Jax had offered to wait for her to take a quick shower and dress so that she could walk him around the property. She found him in the small kitchen, which was made even smaller by his sheer size. He was drinking something out of a mug and talking to Tara, but when she walked into the room they both fell into a silence of the shhh-here-she-comes variety. "What?" she said, looking down at herself. Nope, she hadn't forgotten her clothes.

"It's nothing, sugar." Tara handed her a steaming mug. "It's only instant from the store, and trust me, it's no Starbucks." She shot Jax a look like this was his fault. "I picked it up last night when I bought the cleaning supplies."

"It's good enough for me," Jax said. "Thanks."

Maddie told herself not to stare at him, that it was like staring directly into the sun, but she'd never been good at following advice. Plus she found she couldn't stop looking at his mouth. It was a good mouth and made her think about things she had no business thinking about. "So about why we called you."

A faint smile hinted around the corners of his mouth. "You needed a master."

"Well, your ad did say you are an expert." Look at that, she sounded cool, even smartass-like. She'd always wanted to be a smartass. *Nicely done, keep it up. Do not let him see you sweat.*

And whatever you do, don't look at his mouth.

Or at the way his jeans fit, all faded and lovingly cupping his...cuppable parts. "Does your expertise include dusty hundred-year-old inns decorated in early rooster and duck?"

"Ducks and roosters are no problem. The cows are new to me. And I specialize in fixing things up and restoring them to their former glory."

She wondered if that talent extended to humans, maybe even humans who never really had a former glory. "So how much can we get done between now and Christmas?"

"And think cheap," Tara cut in to say. "Aesthetic value only, for resale purposes."

"The inn didn't come with an operating account, unfortunately," Maddie explained. "Just a big fat mortgage payment, so money's a problem."

Jax's eyes flicked to Tara, then back to Maddie, and once again she wondered what she was missing.

"So you're going to sell?" he asked.

"Hopefully," Tara said.

"Hopefully not," Maddie said.

Jax nodded as if this made perfect sense. "I'll walk the property and work up a bid."

"And I'm off to shower." Tara turned back at the door. "Sugar, tell me you left me some hot water so I'm not forced to head to Alpine and bathe outside like a cretin."

"Alpine?" Maddie asked. "What's that?"

"There's a natural hot springs about three miles up the road," Jax said. "The locals think of it as their own personal hot tub."

Maddie looked at Tara. "How do you know about the hot springs?"

"Doesn't everyone?"

"No," she said, but Tara was gone. Alone with Jax, she pointed to his clipboard. "Better put a new water heater in that bid."

"All right."

The kitchen seemed even smaller now that it was just the two of them. She moved to the slightly larger living room and was extremely aware that he followed. "I don't think we'll waste any money in here," she said. "Just the inn." She reached up to shove her too-long bangs out of her face and realized what she'd done when she caught him staring at her right eye, at the scar on the outside of it that she knew was still looking fresh. Before she could turn away, he was there, right there, and gently—God, so gently it nearly broke something inside of her—brushed the hair from her face and stared at the mark.

For the longest heartbeat in history, he didn't say anything, but the muscles in his jaw bunched. From his fingers, so carefully light on her, she felt the tension grip his entire body. "What happened?"

"Nothing. I don't want to talk about it."

Another agonizing beat pulsed around them before he let go of her, allowing her bangs to fall over her forehead again.

He let out a long breath and eyed their Charlie Brown Christmas tree. When he spoke, his voice was low but normal. "You have an eyelash curler on your tree."

Grateful, so damn grateful that he wasn't going to push, she let out a breath, too. "We improvised."

He took in the pictures of their teen crushes and shook his head, not smiling but letting go of some of the tension racking him.

"You don't like?"

"Actually, I do like," he said, and when she glanced over at him, she found him looking directly at her.

"I meant the tree."

He just picked up his leather jacket from its perch by the front door, the one he'd given her to wear last night. Once again he held it open for her, then nudged her outside ahead of him.

The morning was clear and crisp, and the trees and ground glittered with frost. The sun was so bright it hurt her eyes and head, and also her teeth, which made no sense.

"Hangovers are a bitch," Jax said and dropped his sunglasses onto her nose.

He walked away before she could thank him, so she closed her mouth and pushed up the glasses a little, grateful for the dark lenses. She tried to remember the last time anyone had done such a thing for her without anything expected in return—and couldn't.

"Also going on the list," he said when she'd run to catch up with his long-legged stride. "Making sure no more trees are in danger of killing you in the next windstorm. We'll chop that up for firewood."

She stared at the massive tree bisecting the yard. "Where I come from, firewood comes in a small bundle at the grocery store, and you set it in your fireplace to give off ambience."

"Trust me, ambience is the last thing you'll want this tree to give you. It's going to keep your fingers and feet warm."

She hugged his jacket to her and not because it smelled heavenly. Okay, because it smelled heavenly. And did he never get cold? She looked at him in that slightly oversized hoodie and sexy jeans and boots, carrying that clipboard. She wished she had a clipboard. Instead, she pulled out her BlackBerry to make notes, too. "Do I need to call a tree guy?"

"I can do it. Those two trees there..." He pointed across the yard to the left of the marina building. "They're going to need to be seriously cut back. I'm sure there's others."

They walked the rest of the property and outlined all the obvious problems. There were many. After discussing them in detail over the next half hour, they were back in the center of the yard, next to the fallen tree.

"So," he said. "Your sisters want out."

"Yesterday," she agreed.

"I think your mom hoped you three would stick around and take care of this place the way she always intended to. You know how she was."

"Actually, I don't," she said. "I didn't know her very well. I was raised by my father in Los Angeles. She sent postcards from wherever the Grateful Dead were playing, and we had the occasional whirlwind visit. But she never mentioned this place, not once." She realized how detached that sounded and just how much she'd revealed about their lack of a relationship, and it both embarrassed and saddened her. Having bared herself enough for one day, she turned away.

"Some kids might resent their parent in this situation," he said quietly.

"There's some of that."

She felt a big, warm hand settle at her back, and he led her to his Jeep. The huge brown dog in the passenger seat sat up and gave a single, joyous *woof!*

Jax opened the door and the Lab mix leapt out, all long, gawky limbs and happy tongue. Two huge front paws hit Maddie in the chest, making her stagger back.

Jax's hands settled on her arms from behind, steadying her. Leaning over her shoulder, he gave the dog a friendly push. "Down, you big lug. You okay?" He turned Maddie around to face him, eyeing the two dusty paw prints on her chest.

She backed away and brushed herself off before he got any notions about helping. "She's very pretty."

"Pretty *something,* anyway." He sent the dog a look of affection. "I just haven't decided on what. Izzy, sit," he directed, and the dog promptly sat on his foot, looking up at him in clear hero worship.

Maddie bent for a stick and threw it. Izzy craned her neck, took in the stick's flight through the air, and yawned.

"She's not much for chasing sticks," Jax said dryly. "She'll chase her tail, though, all day long. She's a rescue. She didn't get the Labrador handbook."

Izzy nudged her head to Jax's thigh, and Jax crouched to give her a hug and a full-body rub, and Maddie felt a moment of jealousy as Izzy slid bonelessly to the ground in clear ecstasy, groaning loudly.

"She likes that," Maddie managed.

"I have a way with my hands."

She bit her lower lip to keep the words "show me" inside.

He laughed again, soft and sexy, as he straightened and apparently read her mind. "We don't have chemistry, remember?"

She closed her eyes. "Okay, here's the thing. We have *some* chemistry," she allowed.

"Some? Or supernova?"

"Supernova. *But,*" she said to his knowing grin. Good Lord, he needed to stop doing that. "I really did give up men."

"Forever?"

"My gut says yes, but that might be PMS talking. Let's just say I'm giving up men for a very long time."

"You going to try out women?"

He was teasing her. She pushed him back a step, knowing damn well he only went because it suited him. No one pushed him around unless he wanted to go—something she wished she could say about herself. "I'm trying to say I'm not cut out for this, for the casual-sex thing."

"But you've given up men," he pointed out, still teasing her. "Sounds like there's going to be no sex, period."

"None."

He merely arched a brow. "Aren't you going to miss it?"

"No."

"Not at all?"

"Not even a little."

He shot her a look of blatant disbelief. "How is that even possible, not missing sex? That's like saying you wouldn't miss having a cold beer on a hot summer night or the sound of the ocean pounding the surf while you run, or...air in your lungs."

She had to laugh at his adamancy. "Maybe sex isn't all that important to me."

"Then you've been doing it wrong."

His voice dripped with innuendo, and her body tightened involuntarily while the meaning behind his words thrummed through her veins. It was a foregone conclusion that the man knew how to use his muscular body and talented hands to make a living. She figured it wasn't a stretch to imagine he could also use those things to make a woman very happy.

"Still with me?" he murmured.

A warm flush spread through her body, and she lost her ability to speak.

His mouth was serious, but his eyes were laughing. With a quick playful tug on a lock of her wild hair, he walked off, heading toward the inn in that long-limbed, confident stride of his.

She stared after him, a little flummoxed by the funny something still happening very low in her belly, something she was pretty sure meant her body was *not* on board with the giving-up-men thing.

Not even close.

Chapter 9

♥

*"If you're going through hell…
keep moving."*
PHOEBE TRAEGER

By the time Maddie gathered her wits enough to follow Jax to the inn, he'd opened the front door. "Did your mom have a set of blueprints for this place?" he asked.

"I don't know. It looks like she kept all paperwork in the office in the marina. We could check there."

"You'll need it for the escrow contract, because anyone who buys this place is going to need to make sure the entire property passes inspection and is up to code. It's probably got more violations than you can count, and that'll all have to be dealt with at the building department. But I think Phoebe dated Ed for a while, and he works there. He'll help you through it."

She paused, a little dizzy at his knowledge and the educated, professional way he spoke. Her first impression of him had been Hot Biker. Her second impression had been Hot Biker Who Could Kiss.

Now she was seeing yet another side. She asked the question she'd been dying to ask. "You liked her. My mom."

"Yes. You resemble her, you know." He took his time letting his gaze run over her, leaving her breathless. "It's in the eyes," he said. "She could see right through a person, right to their soul, and know."

"Know what?"

"What they were made of."

She'd had a knot in her chest since Phoebe's death, a thick ball of grief and regret, and it tightened now. "I don't have that ability. I'm actually a terrible judge of character."

He didn't say anything for a long moment. "Your mom was fun and a little flighty, but she had substance where it counted. She had heart."

"Yeah, well, the flightiness was self-induced."

A little smile crossed his face. "No doubt."

Given the fondness in his tone, she figured he'd known Phoebe well. Certainly better than she had, and the ball tightened a little more. "So what about you?"

"What about me?"

"I know next to nothing about you. Tell me something."

He shrugged. "Not much to tell. I was born and raised here. My mom died of a stroke a few years back. No siblings."

"Except for Ford and Sawyer," she said.

"Except for them."

"What about your dad?"

"He's in Seattle."

There was something there, something in his voice

that had her taking a closer look at him, but his face was calm. "You've always been a carpenter?" she asked.

"No. I went away to college, then stayed away for several years after that. I've been back five years now. Boring story."

She doubted that, but he took himself and his clipboard inside the inn, and she and Izzy followed. The dog sniffed at every corner as Jax and Maddie went through room by room. He showed her what could be done to update and modernize, sometimes stopping to sketch things out for her as he talked, his love of a challenge shining through.

Maddie had enjoyed her job, sometimes, and it'd fulfilled her. But she'd never loved it. It was fascinating to watch him. *He* was fascinating.

They finished the main floor and headed up the stairs, while Izzy slept in the sole sun spot on the kitchen floor, snoring like a buzz saw. Jax made suggestions for the bedrooms and bathrooms. At some point, he'd gone out for his tool belt. There was something disturbingly sexy about the way it sat low on his hips, framing everything. She did her best not to notice, but he sure had a very nice...everything.

Together they crawled through the attic space, looking for the source of a roof leak they'd discovered in the last bathroom. Jax was out in front, braving the spiderwebs. Maddie was behind him, working really hard at not looking at his butt.

And failing spectacularly.

So when he unexpectedly twisted around, holding out his hand for the clipboard she was now holding, he caught her staring at him.

"I, um—You have a streak of dirt," she said.

"A streak of dirt."

Yes." She pointed to his left perfectly muscled butt cheek. "There."

He was quiet for a single, stunned beat. She couldn't blame him, given that they were both covered in dirt from the filthy attic. "Thanks," he finally said. "It's important to know where the dirt streaks are."

"It is," she agreed, nodding like a bobble head. "Probably you should stain-stick it right away. I have some in my purse."

"Are you offering to rub it on my ass?" She felt the heat flood her face, and he grinned. "You're a paradox, Maddie Moore. I like that about you."

"Is that because I said nothing was happening between us, and then I..."

"...Wanted to touch my ass." He finished for her. "You can, by the way. Anytime."

She squeaked in embarrassment and covered her cheeks.

"See? Paradox."

"You know, you don't sound like a contractor. You sound like..."

"Like?"

"Well, before the ass comment, I was going to say professional. Educated."

"Maybe I am those things, as well."

She followed some more, crawling along behind him, her eyes automatically locking in on the way his jeans stretched taut when he moved. Which meant it wasn't even really her fault. It was his. His and his tight—

"I'm pretty sure," he murmured without turning

around, "that it'd be a lot easier for you to give up sex if you stop thinking about it."

"How do you know I'm thinking about it?"

He didn't dignify that with an answer.

"Because I'm not. I'm thinking about..." What? "About how hard it'll be to get your jeans clean."

He laughed softly. "Hold that thought. I found the leak. It's fixable."

"Good."

"But you're going to need a new roof next year."

Not good. "What else?"

"Besides the fact that I like to look at your ass, too?"

With a moan that was only half embarrassment, she shook her head. "Stop it."

"Stop the looking, or the telling of the looking?"

Oh, God. "You're not helping me with this giving-up-men thing."

"I don't intend to."

There in the dark, dusty attic she stared at him. "You have a stake in this, too. You said you weren't interested, either."

"No, I said I've been there. *There* being fresh out of a bad relationship and so sure I never wanted to be in another again."

She sucked in a breath and considered denying that, but in the end, her curiosity won. "What happened?"

"I got over myself. Sort of. And for the record, I am interested. Very."

Oh, boy. "Let's go back to talking about the inn," she said shakily.

"Safer?"

"Much."

His eyes smiled. "The windows are single pane. If you replace them with energy efficient and insulated, you'd make the place far easier to heat, plus get an updated look at the same time. Parts of the porch have to be repaired. It's not up to code, it'd never pass inspection. There's the leaking roof. You need interior and exterior paint, and the carpet is trashed. I'd suggest ripping it out and restoring the hardwood that's beneath it. You want to replace the water heaters. You could easily update the bathrooms by putting in new vanities and cabinets when you fix the leaking pipes."

"Sounds like a lot."

"No, a lot would also be renovating the kitchen and replacing the entire roof."

True.

Back outside, they headed to the marina with Izzy trotting along after them. The sun wasn't assisting much in warming the air, and their breath crystallized in front of their faces. A long, shrill whistle came from the water. "What's that?" she asked.

"A seine boat searching deep waters for crab."

As always, she walked quickly, almost running. Jax's stride was long-legged and sure but as unrushed as everything else about him. He liked to take his time, she was learning. He took his time measuring, he took his time talking, he took his time drinking the water bottle he offered her from the back of his Jeep, and he took his time giving Izzy a hug when she roused a very pissed-off squirrel and got scared.

Maddie couldn't help but wonder if he took his time in bed, too, and just the thought caused a rush of heat to places that had no business getting all heated up.

He slid her a look, and his mouth twitched. "Again?"

"So your superpower is reading my mind?"

"Anyone can read your mind, Maddie. You wear it—along with your heart—on your sleeve."

She blew out a breath. "That's going to have to stop. Soon as I figure out how."

"You could start by letting go of some of the stuff you're holding in."

"I'm not holding anything in."

"Do we need to go over the long list of things you don't want to talk about? Like your thing against educated and professional and...lawyerly?"

She put her hands on her hips. "What's your thing with my thing against lawyers?"

He did the brow arch. "Nice deflection. You're getting better at it, actually."

"Consider it step one in learning how to *not* wear my thoughts on my sleeve."

He laughed softly and tugged on a curl. "If you're not going to tell me any deep, dark secrets, let's do the rest of this."

Inside the marina, they decided there was nothing critical to be done here on Jax's part. But taking a look at all the gear—kayaks, canoes, paddles, and more—her thumbs itched to get busy itemizing and cataloguing on her BlackBerry. She had a month to prove to her sisters that this could be a viable business for them, and she didn't intend to fail.

"You seem pretty comfortable out here," she said to Jax. "Even for someone who once painted the inn."

"See that fourteen-foot sailboat in slip three? And the thirty-two-foot one in four? They're both Ford's. He leases year-round and sometimes drags me out on the water with him. But even before that, we used to come out here late at night."

"To TP."

"Just the once. Trust me, we learned our lesson on that one. Look out past the slips, to the woods beyond the marina. There are trails leading up to the bluffs. It's rough going, and the bush is really overgrown. It's a deterrent for everyone except the occasional teenager who wants a quiet place to go make out. Gives a whole new meaning to the name Lucky Harbor."

The thought of a teenage Jax hiking out there with nefarious intentions should have made her laugh. Instead, she wished she'd grown up here in Lucky Harbor, and that maybe she could have been one of those girls. "Even in the winter?"

"All the better. There isn't any poison oak in the winter. It's hard to convince a girl you're sexy when you can't stop scratching your ass because of the rash."

She laughed. She'd done that a few times now, when up until yesterday, being amused at anything had seemed so far out of reach. How it was possible that just one day and one tall, dark, and enigmatic man had changed things, she had no idea.

The marina office was small and held an ancient couch, a huge, beat-up, old desk piled with papers, and a filing cabinet. Drawers were open, and files were in complete disarray.

Jax shook his head. "You've got your work cut out for you."

Maddie shrugged. "I've organized worse." And what was the alternative, going back to LA with her tail between her legs? Hell, no. The thought brought her up a little. She'd been faking strength for so long now that it was starting to stick. About time.

Jax pointed out the window beyond the marina to the thick, overgrown woods. "Shortcut to the bluffs is right past that isolated, small rocky beach. Another good makeout spot, FYI. Especially when you're sixteen and grounded from a car."

She smiled. "Were you grounded a lot?"

"Pretty much 24/7 until I left for college."

"And did you miss small-town living when you were gone?"

"Not even a little. I didn't just walk out of Lucky Harbor; I ran like hell."

There was that same something in his eyes that had been there when he'd mentioned his father. She wasn't the only one keeping her own counsel. "And yet you came back."

His gaze met hers, clear now. Relaxed. "And yet I came back."

"Why?"

"Funny what a couple of years' perspective can do."

Growing up on movie sets as she had, just about everything in her life had been an illusion. The illusion of friends, the illusion of home. The question was—was Lucky Harbor just another set, or would it turn out to be the real thing?

Back at Jax's Jeep, he opened the driver's door, set his clipboard on the dash, then gestured for Izzy to jump in.

The dog leapt up, limbs akimbo, and sat. "Scoot over," Jax told her.

Izzy grinned.

Jax shook his head, leaned back against the Jeep, and looked at Maddie. "I'll work up a bid and email it to you."

"Thanks."

He looked behind her to the inn. "Phoebe left you the property because it meant something to her. If you really don't want to sell it, stand your ground." He flashed her a smile. "Be Louise."

The smile was devastating and contagious, damn him. "I'm trying. But there are problems."

"Yeah. It's called life."

"The mortgage is in arrears. I think the property is actually upside down on its loan. Which is a mystery to me, because like you said, I believe this place meant something to Phoebe, sentimentally anyway. But if she wanted us to keep it, why did she leave every last penny in a trust for someone else?"

He paused, as if carefully picking his words. "There are things you can do. Talk to your original lender, for one. Get an appraisal and refinance. And have you actually verified that there are no funds other than the trust? You've talked to the probate attorney and have a list of Phoebe's assets and accounts? Because that might lead you to...other avenues."

"There you go," she murmured, a little surprised to find that even more attractive than his butt were his brains. "Sounding like more than a pretty tool belt again. Maybe even like a...lawyer."

"And that's bad?"

She didn't answer, didn't know how. It wasn't exactly a rational fear she was carrying around.

"Let me guess," he said. "It's one of those things you don't want to talk about."

"Definitely."

Their gazes collided.

Held.

Time seemed to stand still, which was not only odd, but silly. Time never stood still, not even for sexy super-heroes. When he pushed off the Jeep and stepped close, her pulse immediately kicked into high gear. "Thanks for coming," she whispered. "I—"

Slowly, purposefully, eyes still locked on hers, he invaded her personal space bubble.

She sucked in a breath as heat spiraled within her.

"You..." he said, trying to help her along.

"I can't remember a single thought in my head."

Gentle but firm hands settled on her hips, and he backed her into the Jeep.

"What are you doing?" she asked breathlessly.

"Giving you a new thought." Leaning in, he covered her mouth with his and kissed her, his tongue teasing lightly, keeping it soft until she moaned. Then he deep-ened the kiss into a hot, intense connection that had her head spinning and her blood pumping as their bodies molded together. Unlike last night's tender kisses, this was a little demanding, and a whole lot wild, and when he slid a thigh between hers, she lost her ability to think.

Last night, he'd been seeking permission. Not this time. This time, he buried his fingers into her hair and claimed her mouth, pulling her in even closer, a hand caressing down her back as if to soothe as well as incite, claiming another little piece of her heart in the process.

Sneaky bastard.

She'd tell him so, but her tongue was a little busy. So were her fingers, first enjoying the play of the muscles on his back, then holding on tight just in case he had any ideas about trying to get away. Because she wasn't done, not even when Izzy gave a little whine of unhappiness at sharing her man.

Maddie slid her hands over Jax's shoulders, reminding herself that enough was enough, but she tugged a thrillingly rough groan from deep in his chest so she tightened her grip instead. By the time they broke apart, she was completely out of breath. If it wasn't for the Jeep at her back and the thigh he still had wedged between hers, she'd have dropped to the ground in a puddle of lust.

"Maddie."

His voice was low and gravely and sexy as hell. "Yes?"

"I'm going to touch your face now."

Remembering last night and her mortifying reaction, she should have been grateful for the heads-up, but she was still dizzy from the kiss. "Oh. Well, I—"

He ran his hand up her arm, to her shoulder, over her throat, going slowly, achingly slowly, so that by the time he cupped her jaw, she was quivering, all right, but not from fear. Lifting his other hand, he slid a curl from her temple, tucking it behind her ear. With her pulse somewhere at stroke level, she closed her eyes to better absorb his touch. His fingers were warm and callused. Strong, though not using that strength against her, but in a protective way. And in spite of her admittedly irrational fear of men, her body and heart wanted him.

Bad.

"Maddie."

"Huh?"

There was amusement in his voice. "Are you still giving up men?"

He was pressed against her, deliciously warm and hard. *Everywhere.* She wanted to give him a chance, but she'd meant it when she said she wasn't ready. She needed a clear head first, and her life straightened out. A relationship of any kind at this point would be ludicrous. "Yes," she said, but it came out as more of a croak. She cleared her throat and said it again. "Yes, I'm still giving up men."

He studied her face, then gave her a very small smile before backing away, pulling his keys from his pocket. "I'll be in touch."

"Just the minimum," she reminded him. "That's all I need."

With a nod, he got into the Jeep, nudging Izzy to the back seat. He rolled the window down for the dog, and Maddie reached in to stroke her soft, silky coat.

"Just the minimum," she repeated softly, taking a step back as two warm doggy eyes laughed into hers, silently calling her out as a big liar.

Chapter 10

♥

*"Smile... it makes people wonder
what you're up to."*
PHOEBE TRAEGER

Two days later, Jax was in his home office plowing
through paperwork. He'd put together the bid for Lucky
Harbor Resort and emailed it off to Maddie. He'd handled all his city council duties, but being Lucky Harbor's
mayor for his second term now was a relatively easy position to manage and didn't take much of his time. He was
signing accounts-payable checks that his part-time office
worker Jeanne handed to him one at a time.

"Electric bill," she said, standing over him like a
mother hen, even though they were the same age. Her
headband had reindeer antlers with bells on them that
jangled with every bossy statement she uttered. "Gas
bill," she said, bells jingling. "Visa bill. And here's my
paycheck. Thanks for the raise."

He slid her a look, and she laughed. "Kidding. You
already pay me too much. Oh, and here's the bill for those

supplies you sent over to the Patterson family. Nice of you to do that, since they lost everything in the fire. So... who's the woman?"

Jax pushed all the checks back at her. "What woman?"

"The one you were kissing on the pier the other night."

He arched a brow, and she grinned. "Oh, come on. You can't be surprised that I know."

"Call me naive, but I'm surprised."

She shook her head, like *You poor, stupid man.* She gave him that look a lot. He put up with it because she ran his office with a calm efficiency that was a relief to him. He hated office work.

Jeanne was flipping through the checks, putting them in some mysterious order that worked for her. "Jake told his sister, who told Carrie at the grocery store, and I happened to run into my sister today when I was loading up your refrigerator. And by the way, you were down to an apple and a piece of leftover pizza. I also found what looked to be a science experiment growing in a Tupperware container. I made an executive decision and tossed it. How do you live like that?"

"It's called takeout. What did you put in my refrigerator?"

"Fruit, cheese, beer, and a loaded pizza."

"I love you."

She laughed. "If that was true, you'd tell me about the woman."

He smiled but kept silent. Mostly because it would drive her crazy, but also because he didn't feel like sharing. Truth was, he'd been thinking about Maddie for two days now, and not as a future client. He thought about strangling whoever'd hurt her. He thought about how in spite of that hurt, she'd seemed so honest and artless—not like the women in his past. She was obviously afraid but doing her damnedest to move forward. He admired that.

He'd also given a lot of thought—*a lot*—to how she'd looked after he'd kissed her: ruffled and baffled and turned on. It was a good look for her. So was how she'd looked when she'd opened the door to him, sleepy and hung over, no bra, just a very thin T-shirt, the one that invited the general public to bite her.

Christ, he'd wanted to do just that.

"Rumor has it," Jeanne said, shoving another check under his nose. "She's Phoebe's middle daughter. She was at the hardware store today, and Anderson rang her up. He said she was pretty and sweet, and even though she knocked over his entire display of five-gallon paint cans, she got a big thumbs-up. Oh, and because she has a nice rack, he asked her out."

Jax's pen went still. "What?"

"Hey, I didn't see the rack myself, I'm just passing on the information." Her smile went sly. "Betcha you want to know if she said yes."

He said nothing, and she grinned. "You want to know."

"I don't gossip. I'm a guy."

"You *so* want to know."

"No, I don't."

"Yes, you do."

"No, I—" *Fuck.* He pinched the bridge of his nose because yeah, he did. He wanted to know. "You used to be so sweet and meek."

"That was back in the days when your badass scowl used to do it for me." Delighted at whatever she saw in his face, she waggled a brow. "Okay, I'll tell you, but first you have to tell me how you met her, and how it is that you were kissing her on her first night in town, and if you plan to fight Anderson for the rights to her rack."

"Jeanne," he said in warning.

"Use that tough-guy voice all you want. I'm not married to you. I don't have to cave so that you'll keep my feet—and other parts—warm at night." With that, she scooped up all the signed checks and sashayed out of his office, humming "We Wish You a Merry Christmas."

"You know where I'll be," she called back. "Sitting at my desk working my fingers to the bone. Oh, and I'm decorating your place for Christmas, so be afraid. Very afraid. Anytime you want to come up with some answers for me, I'll be happy to do the same."

Shit. Shaking his head, he turned to something new, drawing up plans for a new client in Portland who wanted a handmade front door with cherry overlay and stained glass. It would take weeks to construct and was the perfect job for when the weather went bad, which it always did for about a month after Christmas. He needed work for when the weather went bad—not for his bank account, which was plenty flush—but so that he wouldn't be stuck with nothing to do but think.

Though all he could think at the moment was that Anderson had asked Maddie out.

He could hear Jeanne in the front room, talking to her computer. He'd gone to high school with her and had even briefly dated her—if one could really call it dating when all you did was climb the bluffs and make out. When he'd gone off to USC, she'd married Lucky Harbor's high school quarterback and given him three kids. She was still happily married but bored beyond tears. So when Jax had come back to town five years ago, she'd shown up on his doorstep one day and announced that she was his new, perfect, part-time office assistant. Perfect because she had no interest in his money or his bed.

Which was a lie. She'd been harping on his heart and soul, trying to save him, ever since she'd demanded the assistant position. Not that he had much of a heart and soul left after he'd detonated both in his last job practicing law. He'd talked himself into embracing the lifestyle: the big salary, the corner office, the penthouse condo, the trophy fiancée. And he'd reaped the benefits, plenty of them.

The firm he'd worked for had been the best of the best at getting people acquitted of their white-collar crimes. It was a multibillion-dollar industry, and Jax had been good at it. Good at twisting the facts, good at misdirecting, good at getting their clients off with their crime of choice, even when it meant that innocent people paid the price.

Jax's discontent over that had started small and slowly grown. And then came to a head when the wife of one of their clients had paid the ultimate price.

With her life.

Her husband had been guilty as hell, and Jax had known it. Hell, everyone had known it. Yet Jax had gotten the man acquitted of embezzling from his wife's family, a family with known mob connections, so there'd been little sympathy for either side.

Except for the wife. She'd grown up as a pawn, and she'd been married off as a pawn. She'd never known life as anything else. An increasingly disenchanted Jax had known her enough to understand that when this went down, in all likelihood her assets would be confiscated and she'd be left penniless and alone. Unable to live with that, he'd broken attorney–client privilege to warn her, but instead of heeding his advice and taking off for parts unknown, she killed herself.

Forced to face his own part in her self-destruction, not to mention just how ethically indecent he'd become, Jax had quit. His fiancée left him shortly after. Game over. He'd left Seattle without looking back. Alone, unsettled, even angry, he'd somehow ended up back in Lucky Harbor.

The last place he'd been happy.

That had been five years ago. Sawyer had come back to town, as well, and after a wild, misspent youth had become a Lucky Harbor sheriff, of all things. Ford was around, in between sailing ventures that'd included the world-class circuit. The three of them had gravitated together as if they'd never been apart.

His first year back, Jax had lived on Ford's second sailboat in the marina. He'd practiced a little law here and there, for friends only, and he'd hated it. So he'd gone back to basics, which for him had been building things with his own hands. As he'd worked on getting over himself, he'd designed and built the house he'd always wanted. He did what he could to give back to the community that had welcomed him without question, including somehow, surprisingly, being elected mayor two terms running.

He was jarred out of his musings when his father strode into his office and immediately set Jax on edge with nothing more than his stick-up-his-ass gait and ridiculously expensive suit. They hadn't spent much time together, mostly because his father was still good and furious over what he saw as Jax's failure in Seattle.

"Got a case for you." His father tossed down the file.

This wasn't surprising. His father often felt the need to manipulate his son's emotions. Which was ironic, since Jax had been trained by the man himself that emotions and business never mix. Hell, in their little family of two, emotions didn't even *exist*. "You haven't spoken to me since I refused to represent that charming Fortune 500 sex offender you brought me last time. That was three months ago. Now you walk in here like you own the place and toss me yet another case I don't want. I'm too busy for this, Dad. Jeanne and I have billings to go over—"

"He said I should go home," Jeanne said softly from the doorway. "I'm done for the day anyway," she said in silent apology, jerking her head toward his father, indicating that they should try to talk.

Fat chance.

Jax didn't often feel his temper stir. It took a lot, especially these days, but his father could boil his blood like no other. "Still minding your own business, I see," he said when Jeanne had left.

"Get over yourself, son. This is a simple, open-and-shut case."

Everything in Jackson Cullen's world was open-and-shut—as long as he got his way. "If it's so simple, you take it."

"No, they want someone young, an up-and-comer."

"I've up and come. And gone," Jax reminded him. "Now if you could do the same..." He gestured to the door.

"Jesus Christ, Jax. It's been five years since you let your job go. You let your fiancée go, too. Time to stop feeling sorry for yourself and get back on the horse."

Jax shoved the file back across his desk and stood up. "Get out."

"You're not listening. Elizabeth Weston is thirty, loaded, beautiful, and her daddy's going to be the next state governor."

"Which matters why?"

"She's looking to settle down. You'll do."

He choked out a laugh. "Now you're whoring me out? Not that this surprises me."

"What, you're not seeing anyone, are you?"

Was he? He'd like to say hell, yes, but the facts were simple. He was guessing Maddie's ex had been an attorney, and a real asshole, to boot. When she learned about Jax's past, she'd run for the hills. Even if he somehow managed to show her that he'd changed, he doubted she'd understand his morally and emotionally bankrupt history. He wouldn't expect her to.

Hell, just being a man was a strike against him. She wasn't in a place to trust any person with a Y chromosome.

"A wife like Elizabeth will be an asset when you take over my practice," his father said.

"I've told you, I'm not taking over your practice."

"You're a Cullen. You're my only son. You have to take over the practice. I spent the past thirty-five years building it for you."

"You built it for you," Jax corrected. "Come on, Dad, doesn't this ever get old? You bullying me, me refusing to be bullied. Hire an associate and be done with it."

"This is asinine." Jaw tight, his father scooped up the file and moved stiffly to the door. "No one can disappoint me quite the way you can."

Ditto. "Dismiss Jeanne or interfere with my work again, and you won't be welcome back."

When the front door slammed, Jax picked up a paperweight on his desk and flung it against the wall, where it shattered. There. Marginally better. And it seemed that he and his father had something in common, after all—sometimes Jax disappointed himself, too.

He was still struggling with his own temper when Ford strode into the office and kicked Jax's feet off his desk. "Get up. Water's calm. Wind's kicking. We're going sailing."

"Not in the mood."

"I'm looking for a first mate, not a sex partner. Besides, you need some tranquility."

Jax slid him a look. "Tranquility? A big word for you, isn't it?"

"What? The bar's been slow. I've been reading."

"You didn't get that word out of *Penthouse Forum*."

"Hey, I read other stuff." He paused. "Sometimes. Now get up. Jeanne's got the afternoon off, and so do you."

He looked at the one person who knew his entire sordid story and didn't seem to blame Jax for being an asshole. "How do you know Jeanne's got the afternoon off?"

Ford didn't answer.

"Shit," Jax said. "She called you."

"A little bit," Ford admitted. "She wanted me to give you a hug."

"Fuck off."

"Figured you'd say that. Also figured you'd be needing to get out."

Which is how Jax ended up on the water on Ford's thirty-two-foot Beneteau. It was late in the year for a leisurely sail. Far too late. Most sailing enthusiasts had long ago winterized their boats, but Ford being Ford, he never let a little thing like winter slow him down. He always thrived on pushing the envelope, and not just in sailing.

They were rewarded by an unexpected cold, hard wind that took their breath and every ounce of questionable talent they owned. The swells rose to nearly eight feet, ensuring that their planned easygoing few hours turned into an all-out work-their-asses-off-fest just to stay alive, much less afloat.

"Christ," Ford breathed when they'd made it back to the slip. He slumped against the hull, head back. "I sailed the West Indies and nearly died three times. That was nothing compared to this. What were you thinking, letting me take us out there?"

Jax didn't have the energy to kick Ford's ass, so he slid down the hull next to him and mirrored his pose, his every muscle quivering with exhaustion and overuse, even his brain. "Forgot what a drama queen you are."

Ford choked out a laugh. "If I could move, I'd make you eat that statement."

"You and what army?"

"Fuck you," Ford said companionably. "And when were you going to tell me about Maddie? I have to hear about some supposedly hot kiss on the pier from Jeanne, who heard it from—"

"I know this story, thanks." And in tune to Ford's soft laugh, Jax thunked his head back against the hull and closed his eyes. He wondered what she was doing right now, if she was working at the inn. He knew everyone, himself included, had found Phoebe fun and free-spirited, but having met her daughters now, Jax found himself angered at how Phoebe had neglected them.

Maddie deserved better. They all did.

"Did you know that Anderson asked Maddie out?" Ford asked.

"Yes!"

"Hell, man, sailing's supposed to relax you."

Jax *was* relaxed. He was easygoing and laid-back. It'd taken him five long years to get there. He no longer let things stack up on his shoulders until he was ready to crumple. He no longer kept secrets for a living, his clients' or his own, secrets that had the ability to burn holes in the lining of his stomach.

So why hadn't he told Maddie that he'd been a lawyer?

Because he was a dumbass.

And a chicken, to boot.

And because you know she'd stop looking at you like you're a superhero...

Oh, yeah, *that*.

Maddie and her sisters spent their days going through the inn and marina, each for different reasons. Chloe was bored. Tara didn't want to miss anything of resale value. But for Maddie, it was about sentiment and about learning how the inn could run. She'd hoped to have everything computerized by now, but she'd spent most of her time digging her way through just to see what she had to work with.

On the second day, she headed into town with a list of errands. When she saw Lucille out in front of the art gallery, she pulled over. Lucille was thrilled for the company and after hugging Maddie hello said, "I hear you've been kissing our Jax on the pier."

"Oh. Well, I—"

"You've picked the cream of the crop with that one, honey. Did you know he lent me the money to help my granddaughter stay in college? Don't let the motorcycle, tattoos, and aloofness fool you; he's a sweet, caring young man."

Maddie hadn't found him aloof. Big and bad and intimidating, maybe. Sexy as hell, certainly. And—Wait. Tattoos? He had tattoos? Just thinking of ink on that body of his had heat slashing through hers.

"Come in, come in," Lucille said. "I just put up my Christmas decorations. And I have tea. And brandy."

She wasn't sure what it said about her that she was tempted. "I'm on a mission for Tara, running some errands, but thank you."

"Going back to the hardware store?" Lucille cocked her head. "Heard Anderson asked you out."

Maddie had gone yesterday to get some organizational supplies. The guy behind the counter had been wearing a Santa hat, and was extremely cute and extremely funny, but she'd left with only her supplies, gently turning down the date.

She'd given up men.

Or she was trying. "Does everyone know everything around here?"

"Well, we don't know which guy you're going to date, Anderson or Jax. But if you could tell me, I'll be real popular tonight at bingo," she said hopefully.

Maddie's next stop was the pier for another shake, which she needed bad.

She smiled at the familiar guy behind the counter. "Lance, right? Straight chocolate this time."

He smiled and nodded. He was in his early twenties, small boned, and had a voice like he was speaking through gravel.

He told her that he had cystic fibrosis. He had family in Portland, but he lived here in Lucky Harbor with his brother, priding himself on his independence in spite of a disease that was slowly ravaging his young body.

Listening to him, Maddie decided she had nothing, absolutely nothing, to complain about in her life. And on the way back to her car, she stared up at the looming Ferris wheel.

Had her mother ever ridden it? From all that she'd read on Phoebe's "recipe" cards, Maddie had to believe her mom had lived her life fast, and just a little bit recklessly.

Chloe was a chip off the old block.

Tara hid her wild side, but she had traveled far and wide, as well, and she had a lot of life experiences under her belt.

Maddie...not so much. Sure, she'd lived in Los Angeles, but that was because her father had brought her there. Those adventures she'd had on movie sets were because of him, not because she'd had some deep yearning for the profession.

She'd fallen into it. She'd fallen or been dragged into just about everything she'd ever done.

Including the inn.

No, she decided. This was going to be different. She was going to make this adventure her own. Nodding, she walked along, listening to the rough surf slap at the pier. The slats of wood beneath her feet had spaces between them, and in the light of day that gave her vertigo and a fear of falling through.

"The trick is not to look at your feet when you walk."

Maddie turned toward the voice and found a woman busy nailing a sign to a post. Appearing to be about Maddie's age, she was petite and pretty, with dark waves of hair falling down her back. She wore hip-hugging pinstriped trousers and a business jacket fit for her toned figure, looking cool and composed and far too professional to be standing on a pier with a hammer and nails in her manicured hands.

"If you look straight out to the horizon," she told Maddie, "you won't feel like you're going to fall." Looking quite comfortable with the hammer in spite of her outfit, she pounded a last nail into the sign, which read:

**Lucky Harbor's Annual Shrimp Feed
this Saturday at 6:00
The Biggest and Bestest in the State:
Dinner, Dancing, and
Kissing The Mayor—Don't Miss it!**

"You're new." Smiling, the woman thrust out a hand. "I'm Sandy. Town clerk and manager. I also run the library." She smiled. "You know, you look like your momma."

"You knew her?"

"Everyone knew her. Be sure to bring your sisters to the feed. Here." Reaching into the bag at her feet, she pulled out a round of what looked like raffle tickets. She tore off a long strip of them and handed it over. "On the house. A welcome-to-town present."

"What are these for?"

"The guessing tank. You write how many shrimp you think'll get dragged in on the shrimp boat parade that night. Winner gets to kiss Jax when he comes in off the Jet Ski leading the boat parade."

Maddie blinked. "Jax? Jax Cullen?"

"The one and only."

"Why does the winner get to kiss Jax?"

"Besides the fact that he is one *fine* man?" Sandy grinned. "Because someone always gets to kiss the mayor. We like to torture our own here. Especially someone as popular as Jax. Before Jax, it was me, actually. I was mayor for three terms. I got lucky one year—a board member won the raffle and he was a cutie pie. Couldn't kiss for beans, though. The other years I had to kiss frogs."

"But mayor?" Maddie shook her head. "Jax is a contractor. He restores things."

"He's a man of many talents." Sandy said this with a secret little smile, and Maddie knew a moment of horror.

Oh, God. "He's your boyfriend." She'd kissed another woman's boyfriend.

"No," Sandy said with a sigh. "Much to my utter dismay—and not for lack of trying—Jax and I are just friends." She dropped her hammer into her bag and smiled. "See you at the feed. Oh, and are you going to hand out coupons for the inn? Phoebe did that last year, and it was a big success."

"It was?" How was that even possible? The place was a complete wreck.

Seeing Maddie's expression, Sandy smiled. "Yeah, probably she didn't charge them, but the point is, she could have. She was a wonderful lady, your momma, but not much for business. Maybe she didn't mention that."

No, Phoebe hadn't mentioned that. Phoebe hadn't mentioned much of anything. "I'll talk to my sisters about it, but the inn won't be reopened until..." Well, maybe never, but since she was done with negativity, she said, "Hopefully right after the new year."

Sandy nodded. "Can't wait to see what you do in the way of updating and modernizing. The whole town is buzzing about it."

"How does anyone even know we're doing anything?"

"Well, you've asked Jax for a bid. Jeanne had lunch with Tracy, her best friend, who told Carla, my sister-in-law, who's the local newspaper reporter. Lucky Harbor prides itself on keeping up with the news, and you three are big news."

Maddie tried to wrap her mind around the thought that she was news. Maddie Moore, assistant to the assistant, was news. "We're not really that interesting."

"Are you kidding? Three new women in town, running the inn? It's the biggest news this month. Well, maybe not quite as big as the upcoming shrimp feed, or watching Jax freeze his most excellent butt off leading the parade, but big enough." She smiled. "Okay, I'm off to hang more signs. See you!"

"See you," Maddie said softly and sipped her shake. She wanted to think about all Sandy had mentioned. She needed to wrap her head around the Lucky Harbor grapevine, the possibility that people were excited to have her in town, and the inn, but her brain kept stuttering on one thing.

Jax—the mayor!—and his most excellent butt.

Chapter 11

> *"A sister is a forever friend."*
> PHOEBE TRAEGER

That's not a quote about men or sex," Chloe said, scooping up another piece of pizza. She was wearing a snug black hoodie, zipped to just between her breasts. There was a single bright white word emblazed across the front—NAUGHTY.

They were on the counter at the cottage having dinner, where they'd taken to pulling out a random Phoebe quote from the recipe box because otherwise they argued. They argued about the inn, about the sole bed in the cottage, about the cottage kitchen—mostly because only Tara could cook, but she refused, saying she was on vacation. They argued about Phoebe's wishes, clothes...there was no sacred ground.

Tara and Chloe were going back to their lives in a matter of days. Maddie was staying.

So the cards were just about the only safe subject.

Most of the cards were outrageous. Some were downright absurd.

But once in a while there was a treasure, something so real, it caught Maddie like a one–two punch. *A sister is a forever friend* was one of them. "I like that one," she said quietly. "I like it a lot."

Tara tapped her perfectly manicured nails a moment, clearly uncomfortable with Maddie's obvious emotion. Finally, she blew out a breath and spoke with more emotion than Maddie had ever heard from her. "I agree, it's a keeper."

"Aw, look at you." Chloe nudged shoulders with her. "Going all Ya-Ya Sisterhood on us."

When Maddie and Tara both gave her the stink eye, she rolled her eyes. "Jeez, just lightening up the moment so we're not reenacting a Lifetime movie."

Maddie sighed, then carefully put the card back in the box, hoping the quote proved to be true.

The next evening, Jax stood behind the bar drying glasses, waiting for Ford to finish his shift so that they could go grab a late dinner. Jax had spent the day finishing up a mahogany dining room set for a client, and though he'd showered, he still smelled like wood shavings. He had two splinters in his right hand that he hadn't been able to remove himself, and a pounding headache that he suspected was directly due to the scathing email his father had sent him earlier regarding his last visit.

He was starting to wish he'd snagged himself a shot of 151 instead of a beer.

Ford was down at the other end of the bar. He turned and looked at Jax, brows up.

Jax shook his head. He was fine.

Fine.

A breeze hit him as the door opened, accompanied by a sizzle of awareness that zinged straight through him.

Maddie walked in and slid onto a barstool. He took in her jeans and soft, fuzzy, oversized sweater the exact blue of her eyes and was powerless against the smile that crossed his lips. "Hey."

"Hey Mr. Mayor."

He grimaced and served her a beer. "Discovered that, did you?"

"I can't believe you didn't tell me."

"It never came up."

"It could have," she said. "Maybe between the 'so glad I didn't kill you' and, oh, I don't know, when we played tonsil hockey."

"Which time?"

She rolled her eyes. "You know what I'm saying. You've encouraged me to blab all about myself, but you seem to have managed to remain quiet about you."

Yeah, and he was good at it. He came around the end of the bar and sat next to her. "In a town this size, being mayor is more of a dubious distinction than anything else."

"A pretty *fancy* dubious title." She sipped her beer and studied him.

He studied her right back. It'd been two days since he'd emailed her the bid. Three days since the aforementioned tonsil hockey. He'd thought of her, a lot more than he'd meant to.

He wondered if she'd done the same.

"So what's the protocol here?" she wanted to know. "Do I curtsy when I see you? Kiss your ring?"

He felt a smile curve his mouth. "A curtsy would be nice, but you don't look like that kind of girl. And I don't wear a ring, but I have something else you can kiss." He tapped a finger to his lips.

She laughed, and he decided that was the best sound he'd heard all day.

She handed him a file folder.

He opened it and found she'd printed his bid. He looked at what she'd circled and signed and then into her face.

"I got my sisters to agree."

There was a world of emotion in her voice, though she was trying to hide it. She'd gone up against her sisters and stood her ground. "Proud of you, Maddie."

"Thanks. And you're hired," she said quietly. "Assuming you still want the job."

The job, the woman . . .

"I circled what we can afford to do right now. Some of the other stuff, like the interior painting and the hauling of any demo debris, I'm going to do myself."

"Yourself?"

"My sisters aren't staying, just me. When can you start?"

The days of working 24/7 and cultivating as many clients as he could handle, maybe even more than he could handle, were long gone. Happily gone. These days, he took only the jobs he wanted. At the moment, all he had waiting on him was a wood-trim job in town, but his materials hadn't come yet. He also had to finish a front door design and the final touches on the dining room set. "I can start the day after tomorrow."

"Fair enough."

There was something in her voice, something she'd held back until now, and he realized she'd been avoiding direct eye contact. Removing the beer from her fingers, he set it down, then put his hands on her hips. Gently he turned her on the stool to fully face him, waiting until she tilted her head up and met his gaze.

Yeah, there it was. *Damn.* Unhappiness. "You wanted this," he murmured quietly. "The renovation on the inn."

"Very much."

"Then what's wrong?"

She looked away. "That whole superpower mind-reading thing is getting old."

He let his fingers do the walking, up her arm, over her throat, giving her plenty of advance warning before he cupped her jaw. Just as slowly, he brushed her long side bangs away from her right eye.

Her breath hitched, but she didn't pull away. The scar there was fading, and he let his thumb brush over it lightly, hating what it represented. He wanted to know the story, wanted to know how badly she'd been hurt, and whether she'd managed to give as good as she'd gotten.

He realized that he'd tensed, and that Maddie had stopped breathing entirely. When he purposely relaxed, she responded in kind, her eyes drifting closed, and she surprised the hell out of him by tilting her head slightly so that his hand could touch more of her. His heart squeezed up good at that, and his fingers slid into her hair, and then around to cup the nape of her neck.

Obeying the slight pressure he applied, she slid off the stool and then, of her own accord, stepped between his legs, dropping a hand to his thigh. When her chest bumped his, she let out a soft sigh. "You touch me a lot."

"I like to touch you. That's not what's making you unhappy."

She shook her head. "This is still a bad idea." She looked at him then. "Just so we're clear. We are, right? Clear?"

He didn't take his eyes off hers. "Crystal."

She nodded, then backed away from him. "Then I'll see you the day after tomorrow."

"Yes, you will." He snagged her wrist. "Maddie—"

"Listen, I'm not trying to be coy, or play a game, I promise. It's me. I'm just…" She shook her head. "It's me," she repeated softly. "I'm just trying hard to be who I want to be, that's all. I'm okay, though. Really."

"Good." He slid his hand to hers and stroked his thumb over her palm. "One more thing."

"What?"

He covered her mouth with his. He kissed her until his headache vanished and so did his bad mood. He kissed her until he felt her melt into him, until she was gripping his sweatshirt like a lifeline and kissing him back with enough passion that he forgot what the hell he thought he was doing.

Lifting his head, he ran his thumb over her slightly swollen, wet lower lip and struggled to put his brain into gear. "Saying that this isn't going anywhere doesn't change the chemistry problem we have. Just wanted to make that clear, as well."

Eyes huge on his, she licked her lips and made him want to groan. "Crystal," she whispered breathlessly and pulled free. This time she didn't stumble into a table—instead she plowed over some poor sap at the door. Apologizing profusely, she vanished into the night.

"Always in a hurry," Ford said conversationally, leaning on the bar.

"Always," Jax murmured.

"Ah, so you do still have a tongue. For a minute there, I thought maybe she sucked it out."

"Fuck you, Ford."

"You keep saying that, but you're not my type. And do you realize you're still looking at the door?"

"Just reminding myself to keep my distance," Jax said. "Distance is good."

"Yeah, that was some nice distance you had going there a minute ago."

Jax opened his mouth, but Ford held up a hand. "I know, fuck me, right? So tell me this, is keeping your 'distance' why you bid the inn renovation? Or why you stopped by the hardware store earlier to what, *chat* with Anderson? Because I heard you set him up on a date with Jeanne's cousin. Smooth, by the way. Real smooth."

"Okay, so the distance thing has gone out the window," Jax admitted. "I don't know when or why, but it has."

Ford laughed, easily vaulted over the bar, and clapped a hand on Jax's shoulder. "Maybe because she's hot and sweet? Or because you two have enough chemistry to light up this entire town? Because karma's a bitch?"

Jax shoved him off. "This isn't funny."

"Yeah, it is. Come on, I'm starving. You can brood over a burger."

Five minutes later, they walked into Eat Me Café to grab burgers. Maddie was at a semicircular booth with her sisters, the three of them bent over a stack of paperwork. Jax looked at her frown and figured they were going over the inn's outstanding bills and the refinancing forms.

Jax stopped, fighting the urge to yet again hint that she should approach her current note holder, but she hadn't asked his opinion and probably wouldn't.

Tara sat on Maddie's left, facing Jax and Ford. Her eyes locked on Ford, then widened right before they darkened. If looks could kill, Ford would be six feet under. Then, smooth as silk, she cleared her face until it was blank, got up from the table, and headed in the opposite direction, slipping into the restroom.

Jax looked over at Ford, who was watching Tara go with a tight look to his mouth, eyes shuttered.

What the hell?

He was unable to ask Ford about it, because they were now even with Maddie's table. Jax greeted her and then introduced Ford to Chloe.

While Maddie and Chloe made casual pleasantries with Ford, Jax took in the paperwork on their table.

Yeah, bills. And by the looks of things, lots of them.

The waitress came by to seat Jax and Ford, and they ended up on the other side of the café. Tara came out of the restroom, and Ford followed her with his eyes.

"What's going on?" Jax asked him.

"What? Nothing."

"You're staring at Maddie's sister."

"Maybe Tara's staring at *me*."

Jax leaned back and studied his oldest friend. "I never said which sister, and I sure as hell didn't say her name, either. *And* I was under the impression you didn't know any of them."

"I'm a bartender. I know everyone."

"You're an athlete who happens to own half a bar. Cut the shit, Ford. What's going on?"

Ford just shook his head, silent. Since Jax had given up destroying souls for a living, he'd admittedly become more easygoing and laid-back, but even so, Ford was just about catatonic in comparison. He was so chill that sometimes Jax felt like checking him for a pulse.

But nothing about Ford looked chill now. His mouth was grim, his eyes inscrutable, and he seemed shaken.

Except nothing shook Ford. *Nothing.* "What the hell's up with you? You bleeding from where her eyes stabbed daggers into your sorry ass?"

Instead of smiling, Ford shook his head. Thing was, if Ford didn't want to talk about something, then Jax would have better luck getting answers out of a rock. He looked at the table where the three sisters sat, Tara on one side of Maddie, looking tense enough to shatter, Chloe on the other, slouched back, a little distant, a little bored, and clearly frustrated.

Between them, Maddie was talking, probably trying to make everyone happy. Ever the peacemaker. Even as he watched, Maddie looked at Tara, then over at Ford.

She'd noticed the tension, too.

Ford slumped in the booth a little, face turned to the window.

"Ford."

"Let it go, Jax."

"I will if you will."

Ford was silent a long moment. "You ever make a stupid mistake, one you think you can run from, only no matter how fast and far you run, it's still right there in front of you?"

"You know I have."

Ford let out a long, shuddery breath. "Well, chalk

it up to that. One I don't want to talk about now, maybe not ever." The door to the café opened, and a uniformed sheriff strode in. He was built almost deceptively lean. Deceptive because Jax knew that the guy could take down just about anything that got in his path. He'd seen him do it. Actually, he'd seen him do it to Ford.

And okay, also himself. The guy was a one-man wrecking crew when he wanted to be, and the three of them had gone a few rounds with each other over the years.

Sawyer, the third musketeer.

He made his way directly to their table and sprawled out in the chair Ford kicked his way. "Shit, what a day." He turned down the radio at his hip and looked around. "I'm starving."

The guy had been born starving. He ate like he had a tapeworm, and he eyed the burgers lined up on the kitchen bar, waiting to be served. Both Jax and Ford gave him space. You didn't want to get any key body parts, like, say, a hand, in between Sawyer and grub when he was hungry.

Jax waved over their waitress, and between the three of them, they ordered enough for a small army. Sawyer didn't speak again until he'd put away two double doubles. Finally, content, he sighed and leaned back. "So. Why are we staring at the sisters?"

Not much got by Sawyer.

"What do you know about them?" Ford asked him.

"Other than Jax going at it with the middle one on the pier the other night? Which, by the way—nice, man."

Jax let out a long breath and felt a muscle bunch in his jaw. "People need to mind their own business."

Sawyer flashed a rare grin and helped himself to Jax's fries. "Not going to happen in this town. As for the other sisters, I know the oldest has a sweet ass to go with her sweet-ass accent when she's pissed, and she was pissed earlier at the post office when she found out that we don't have guaranteed overnight from here. And the youngest, she might be hot, but she's also crazy. I clocked her at seventy-six on a fucking Vespa 250. When I pulled her over and wrote her up a ticket, she said I was committing highway robbery because there was no way she'd been going a single mile per hour over sixty-five. She chewed out me, my radar gun, and my mama, and I gotta tell you, that girl has a mouth on her. Oh, and apparently I need some sort of guava shit facial because my skin is dry in my 'P' zone. Like I care about my P zone. She's going to be trouble, big trouble."

"I think it's a 'T' zone," Ford said, pointing to his own.

Sawyer sent him a look of banality. "Is there something you want to tell us?"

"Yeah, I'm fucking gay." Ford shook his head, confident in his sexuality. "And *all* women are trouble, man. Every last one."

At this, Sawyer raised a brow. Ford loved women. Always. *Period.* Sawyer looked at Jax for answers.

Jax shrugged. "It's a sucky day in Mayberry," he said and took another look at the table of sisters.

Tara was saying something through tight lips to her sisters. Chloe downed her drink and raised her hand for another.

Maddie shoved the stack of papers aside and reached into her purse, pulling out two knitting needles and a bright red skein of yarn. Jax wondered if it was the same one he'd seen wrapped around her the other morning.

Biting her lower lip between her teeth, she slowly and awkwardly worked the knitting needles, murmuring to herself as she did, clearly talking her way through each stitch with heartbreaking meticulousness. It got him right in the gut.

She got him right in the gut.

"Earth to pussy-whipped Jax."

Jax slid Ford a long look. "Pussy-whipped?"

"I thought you gave up that shit when you ran away from Seattle."

He hadn't run away from Seattle. He'd walked. Fast.

Sawyer was looking like he'd found a bright spot to his day. "So exactly how many women do you figure have thrown themselves at you since you've been back in Lucky Harbor?"

"I don't know."

"All of them," Sawyer said. "But this is the only one to hold your interest, and don't even try to tell me I'm full of shit." He hitched his chin to indicate Maddie. "So basically, it's Murphy's Law now. Sheer odds say you're about to make an ass of yourself." He said this as if it was Christmas morning and Santa Claus had delivered.

"And this makes you happy?" Jax asked in disbelief.

"Oh, fuck, yeah."

Jax took another look at the sisters. The three of them were talking, but Tara was looking at her watch. Chloe was now making eyes at the busboy's ass. Maddie still had her brow furrowed in fierce concentration as she carefully talked herself through another stitch.

"Christ, you have it bad," Ford said in disgust.

It was entirely possible that for once, he was right.

Chapter 12

♥

*"You're as happy as you make up
your mind to be."*
PHOEBE TRAEGER

For the third morning in a row, Chloe whipped the blanket off Tara. Maddie knew this because Tara's distinct screech echoed in the small bedroom they'd been sharing in the cottage.

Where there was only one bed.

At least it was a queen-sized, and it'd been cold enough that they hadn't minded being packed in like a litter of kittens. Well, they minded Chloe talking in her sleep, because it was usually things like "harder, Zach, harder," which both Tara and Maddie could do without hearing.

Tara was still complaining about being woken up, her drawl thick and sweet as molasses. This was in direct opposition to the words she was saying, something about Chloe's questionable heritage and the turnip truck she rode in on.

Cocooned in between the wall and a pillow, Maddie snickered and burrowed deeper into her own warmth. And then the blanket was rudely ripped off her, as well. "*Goddammit!*"

Looking disgustingly cheerful and put together in black, hip-hugging yoga pants and an eye-popping pink sports bra, Chloe smacked Maddie's ass. "Get up."

"Touch *my* ass," Tara said, sitting up and pointing at her, "and die."

Chloe grinned. "Two minutes."

When she'd left the room, Tara gritted her teeth and rolled out of bed, wearing only a cami and boxers, looking annoyingly fabulous with her hair only slightly mussed. "I intensely dislike her."

"You seem to intensely dislike a lot of people. Like Ford, for instance—who I didn't realize you knew."

Tara stiffened. "I don't."

"Your accent definitely thickens when you lie. You might want to work on that."

Tara let out a long, shaky breath. "What do *you* think of him?"

"Ford?" She thought of him standing behind his bar, tall and sexy, that easy grin charming anyone in its path. "I like him. What's going on, Tara?"

"Nothing."

Maddie understood that sentiment. She had a lot of stuff that she didn't want to talk about, either. She sat up in bed and patted her hair, knowing it resembled something from the wild animal kingdom. She sighed and staggered off the bed. By day, they'd been doing their own thing. She'd been going through the "office" in the marina, trying to make sense of the wacky accounting system—which seemed to be one step above a shoebox. Tara had been cleaning. Chloe couldn't do either. She'd decided she was going to create a line of skin care products with the inn's name and give away baskets to their customers when the time came. And when they sold the inn, she hoped the new owners would want the line.

It was a great idea, unique and perfectly suited for a small, cozy beachside inn—assuming they got customers.

When Chloe wasn't working on that, she spent her time looking for trouble—and, given the two speeding tickets she'd already racked up, she'd found it.

At night, they ate as a family, which meant they fought. Maddie had discovered that it didn't matter what subject they tackled. Tara and Chloe could argue about the sky being blue.

Mostly they fought over the inn. Tara wanted a commitment from her sisters to sell. Maddie wanted a commitment to give the place a fair shot. Chloe wanted... well, no one really knew. But one thing was certain, she still didn't want to take sides.

So the tension mounted and manifested itself in stupid little disagreements. Like over yoga.

"Sixty seconds!" Chloe yelled from the living room.

Maddie tied back her hair. "Coming!"

"Liar!"

For being such a tiny thing, Chloe was a purebred pit bull. Maddie staggered to the living room, where Tara was already sitting obediently, legs crossed.

As they'd learned the hard way for three mornings running, Chloe took her yoga seriously. For the next forty-five minutes she chided, bossed, demanded, and bullied myriad poses out of them until Maddie was dripping sweat and barely standing on muscles that were quivering. "I need food," Maddie gasped.

"*Eat me?*" Chloe asked.

"If I have to eat one more greased up, heart-attack-on-a-plate meal from that place," Tara said from flat on her back, "I'm going to kill myself. *I'm* cooking."

"*Finally,*" Chloe said with relief. "What took so long?"

"I don't do it for people I don't like."

"But *sugar,* you don't like *anyone.*"

Maddie shook her head at Chloe, then looked at Tara.

"It's more that I've decided I don't *not* like you," Tara said.

Even flat on her back and sweaty, Tara exuded confidence. Maddie flopped down and sighed. She'd been working on her own confidence, but even faking it, it was still hard to go toe-to-toe with her sisters.

Half an hour later, Tara had food spread in front of her sisters that blew Maddie's mind. Blueberry wheat pancakes, egg-white omelets, turkey bacon, and fresh orange juice.

"Not a river of grease in sight," Tara said. "Chloe, stop wrinkling your brow or your face will stick like that."

"I don't like wheat pancakes—they taste like dirt." But she took a bite, chewed, then shrugged. "Okay, never mind. These don't taste like dirt."

"I don't give a flip," Tara said, mixing up more batter.

"Well, flip this," Chloe said and gave her oldest sister a middle finger.

"No, that's what I call them—'I Don't Give a Flip'

Pancakes. I could make peace on earth with those pancakes."

"You should really work on that self-esteem issue you have," Chloe said dryly, gathering ingredients of her own into a bowl—almonds, jojoba oil. "Making a cracked-heel treatment today. Because Maddie's feet need help."

"Hey," Maddie said.

"You keep rubbing those babies against my legs at night, and it hurts. And," Chloe said, looking at Maddie's plate and the way she'd carefully arranged her food, nothing touching, "you're a freak."

Maddie looked at her large plate of food and tried not to get defensive and failed. "I'm hungry. I just burned a million calories doing yoga."

"The way you do it? Not quite. And I was talking about how you're trying to keep your syrup off your eggs, not about how much food you have on your plate."

"I don't like my foods touching."

"Like I said...freak."

"Hey, I don't mock you."

"What's to mock? I'm normal." Chloe began whisking up the ingredients in her bowl for her balm, or whatever it was. "Oh, and I know I told you I was leaving tomorrow, but good news. I'm not leaving for two days, because my thing got pushed back."

"Yay for us," Tara said dryly.

Chloe ignored her. "First up is New Mexico, and then I'm thinking about going to meet a friend in Houston, who's interested in buying some of my recipes." With a sly look in Maddie's direction, Chloe set down her whisk to turn to her plate, where she purposely mixed her eggs with her pancakes, smeared it all in syrup, then dipped a huge bite…into her orange juice. Watching Maddie squirm, she sucked it into her mouth, making "mmm-mmm" noises.

Maddie couldn't even watch. "You're disgusting."

Chloe just moaned in pleasure. "This is damn good food. Boggling really."

"Why is it *boggling* that I cook well?" Tara asked in a tone that had the air around them going frosty.

"First off, you don't cook 'well,' you cook *amazing,* and it's boggling because I thought I was the only one who got Mom's artistic streak. Not to mention that people who can cook are usually more outgoing and friendly than you are, and—"

"And," Maddie said, quickly jumping in because she'd learned that was the best way to keep things from escalating, "you just don't seem like the cooking type."

Ignoring Maddie, Tara narrowed her eyes at Chloe. "Finish your sentence."

"Are these blueberries fresh?" Maddie asked desperately. "Cuz they taste fresh."

"You seriously think that you're the only one who got anything from Mom?" Tara asked Chloe.

"I know I'm the only one who liked her."

"You didn't even know her, not really!"

"And the orange juice," Maddie interjected into the very tense room. Her first instinct was to find a hole to crawl into. Her second was to grab her knitting, which she'd discovered was not only a sentimental escape, but was also a great relaxation technique. Better than chips. Problem was, she couldn't look away from the impending train wreck. "The orange juice is amazing, Tara. How did you get out all the pulp?"

"I knew her better than you," Chloe said to Tara. "At least I called her."

"I called." Tara's voice was pure South, dripping with fury. "She screened me!"

"Well, maybe there was a reason."

"Like what?"

"Like maybe because you're controlling and anal and a b—"

Tara slammed her hands down on the counter.

Maddie nearly leapt out of her skin, and her elbow hit Chloe's bowl of . . . whatever concoction she'd been making. The contents flew out, splattering across Tara's face.

After a horrendous, thundering beat of silence, Tara scraped herself clean and glared at Chloe. "This is because I asked you to leave my house when you visited me for Easter last year."

"Hey, it's Maddie's elbow that got you all covered in liquid, not me."

"I didn't mean to," Maddie said, gaping at the goop dripping off Tara's nose. Maddie had some of Chloe's foot balm on her, as well, but she didn't look at it because she had a burning question. "And how come I never got an Easter invite?"

"You were somewhere on a movie set, I think," Tara said. "This year I'll ask you instead of her, believe me."

"And you didn't ask me to leave," Chloe said. "You *kicked me out*. Because your husband's friend kissed me!"

Tara was holding a ladle full of pancake batter, and she pointed it violently in Chloe's direction. "He was *my* friend, too. And *you* kissed *him!*"

Chloe jumped to her feet. "I knew you didn't believe me!"

Tara tossed her plate into the sink with enough violence to splash soapy dishwater all over Maddie.

"Great!" Maddie said, pulling her shirt away from her skin with a suction sound.

"I'm done talking," Tara informed them loftily, which was hard to pull off with some balm on her face, but she managed.

"Good tactic," Chloe said. "Ignore all your problems—because that seems to be working out so well for you."

Maddie stood up. *Quiet strength,* she told herself. *Just project quiet strength, like...Julia Roberts in* Erin Brockovich. Okay, so Erin wasn't always quiet in her strength, and you know what? She didn't have to be, either. So with a deep breath, Maddie said, "Shut up."

Both sisters stared at her.

"We all know what we're really tense about."

The inn. How the final vote between the three of them would go. What would happen...With a sigh, she picked up her knitting instead of inhaling any more food and continued from where she'd left off last night. "In, wrap around," she said to herself. "Pull out."

"You know," Chloe said, licking some batter off her thumb. "The way you knit always sounds a little dirty. I bet if you knitted in earshot of a guy, you'd get laid for sure."

Tara was tossing breakfast dishes into the running sink, each harder than the last, if that was possible.

Chloe responded by cranking up her music via her iPod Touch parked in the dock on the counter. Hip-hop thumped out of the speakers. Tara hated hip-hop, and her head whipped around like the possessed victim in a horror flick.

"In, wrap around," Maddie said, trying to find the calm. "Pull out—"

The back door opened, and all three of them swiveled to look as Jax filled the doorway. He looked like sin on a stick in faded Levi's, a long-sleeved graphic Henley, and—there went her pulse—that damn tool belt slung low on his hips.

Izzy was at his side, alert and panting happily until she caught the tension in the room. With a soft whine, she sat on Jax's foot. Jax set a hand on her head as his gaze went straight to Maddie. "Problem?" he asked over the booming bass.

Yep, Maddie thought, more reading his lips than actually hearing him. A big problem, actually. Because whenever she so much as looked at him, no matter what was going on around her, her body got all quivery. Some parts more than others.

"No problem, sugar," Tara drawled, a polite smile on her face as she slapped the power button on the iPod dock, forcing a sudden quiet over all of them. "Blueberry pancakes?"

With a sound of disgust, Chloe pushed her way to the door. "They're both nuts," she warned Jax as she passed him. "Freaking nuts. I'm going for a ride."

Giving up the pretense, Tara wiped her hands on a towel, her dignity somewhat ruined by the sole blueberry left in her hair. "Me, too. I need to get out."

Maddie handed over her car keys.

"Thanks, sugar." And then Tara was gone, too.

Still covered in a sticky, wet combo of batter and soapy water, Maddie remained seated, carefully holding her knitting so it didn't get dirty. To her left, the water was still running in the sink, bubbles rising high. Jax came toward her in that easy, steady stride of his. The singular intent in his gaze had her faltering on the next knitting stitch, partly because she couldn't look at him and knit at the same time. Much like how she couldn't look at him and breathe, either.

Two big, warm hands pulled the large plastic needles and yarn out of her fingers and set them on the counter in the sole clean spot left in the whole kitchen. "Want to talk about it?"

Which—that her sisters were crazy, and she might be, too? Or that she'd been dreaming about him, nightly fantasies involving a lot of nakedness with all his good parts getting intimately acquainted with all her good parts?

"I . . . it's . . . No," she finally managed. "Not really." She looked down at herself. "I need to take another shower."

Grabbing a chair, he spun it around and straddled it directly in front of her. He gazed at the batter and water splattered on her, taking his time about it, too. "Ford and Sawyer are never going to forgive me for missing the girl-on-girl fight. Can I at least lie and say I saw a little of it? And that you guys were all wearing tiny tank tops and panties?"

A reluctant smile tore from her lips, and, given the warmth that filled his eyes at the sight of it, that's what he'd meant to happen. "Guys are perverts," she said.

"Mmm-hmm." He was busy watching a glob of batter make its way down the curve of her right breast, disappearing down the front of her shirt.

Maddie swiped at it with a finger, but before she could wipe it on a napkin, Jax took her hand and, still holding eye contact, sucked it off her finger.

At the strong pull of his warm, wet tongue, she shivered.

"You taste good enough to eat," he said, eyes darkening as he watched her nipples pebble against her T-shirt.

"Shower," she said out loud, reminding herself. "I need to shower."

His fingers sank into her hair, his thumb gliding softly along her jaw. "I'm good in the shower, Maddie."

She shivered again, heat swamping her. "Do you always say everything that comes to your mind, no holding back?"

"Usually, but I'm holding back right now."

"You are?"

He nodded with eyes so hot they scorched her skin. "If I told you what I was thinking," he said, voice low and seductive, "you'd probably run for the hills."

She shuddered again. Strength... "Tell me anyway."

"Maddie—"

"*Tell me.*"

Leaning on the back of his chair, he was so close now that when he spoke, his lips lightly brushed hers with every word. "I want to put my hands all over you. I want to..."

Her breath caught, and she felt herself go damp. "What?"

"Touch. Kiss. Lick. Nibble. And then—"

At that moment, the sink—still running—finally overfilled, and water splashed to the floor. Jumping up, she cracked her head on Jax's chin. Staggering back, she held her head. "Ouch!"

Jax shut off the faucet. His boots squeaked in the water on the floor as he turned back to her, a red spot already blooming on his chin.

Staring at the spot in horror, she took a step backward out of sheer instinct. "I'm sorry, I'm so sorry—are you okay?"

"Your head isn't that hard." Calmly, he crossed the room to her, not allowing space between them. "You have two choices." His tone was light and easy, his hands going to her hips to gently squeeze. "You can kiss it better, or you can go take your shower."

It was as if her body took over the decision-making process from her brain, because she went up on tiptoes and pressed her lips to the spot she'd hit. He had a little stubble going, just enough to feel deliciously male beneath her lips, and she slowly inhaled against him, breathing him in.

A low groan rumbled from his chest, and his hands tightened on her, just as Tara walked back in.

She took a moment to glare at Jax, who held her gaze with an even look of his own.

"Sugar," she finally said to Maddie, grabbing the jacket she'd forgotten off the hook by the back door. "You can either fuck him or hire him, but you shouldn't do both. That's the advanced class, and you're not ready." She walked back out, and a minute later they heard the car start up.

Maddie let out a long, shaky breath. Tara was usually the voice of reason, but this decision was not majority rules. This decision was hers alone.

Jax was still in her space, quiet, watchful.

Sexy as hell.

Patient.

He wanted her. His body was tight with the wanting, but it was her decision.

Alex had made all the decisions. Maybe not in the beginning, but somewhere along the way with him she'd lost herself. She'd let it happen. That was another thing that was going to change. If she wanted something, she was going to get it. If she wanted someone, she was going to take him.

She wanted Jax. She wanted the oblivion, she wanted to feel good, she wanted...

To be wanted. And a little bit of ravishing and cherishing would be good. Love would be better, but as Tara had noted, she wasn't ready for that. She was, however, ready for this, this one time. And even if she wasn't, it didn't matter. She wanted him.

Grabbing his hand, she pulled him with her out of the kitchen. Allowing it, he brushed his big, hard body up against her back.

In the small bathroom, she dug through Chloe's bathroom bag on the counter and came up with a condom, which she handed to Jax, who hit the lock on the door.

She started the shower, then reached for the hem of her shirt. He took over, slowly pulling it off, tossing it to the floor. Then he repeated the gesture with his own shirt.

She found the tattoos, which made her weak in the knees. A tribal band around a bicep, another down one side from the top of his ribs to his oblique muscle.

She wanted to lick them.

"Maddie."

She couldn't stop staring at him, all hard and warm and delineated with strength. "I don't want to talk," she said.

Amusement crowded for space with the hunger in his gaze. "What do you want?"

"You. Now. Fast. Maybe hard, too."

"You got me. But not fast, not hard." He ran a long finger over the front hook of her bra. "Not our first time."

"Our *only* time," she corrected.

"Hmm," he murmured noncommittally, and with a flick of his wrist, her bra fell to the floor. He covered her mouth with his and unbuttoned her jeans, slowly sliding them to the floor.

"Christ, Maddie. Look at you. You take my breath away." His dark gaze took her in and got darker as he kicked off his boots and shucked his clothes, revealing the rest of his mouthwatering body in its entirety, including the part of him she wanted inside her, *yesterday*.

Leaning past her, he checked the temperature of the water while she checked out his perfect ass. As usual, he caught her at it and sent her a heated smile that dissolved her bones as he tugged her into the shower with him. In contrast to the hot water, his hands were still a little chilly from being outside, giving her a zing when he slid them up to cup her breasts.

Her eyes drifted shut and her other senses took over. His body was unyielding, strong, rippling with power against hers. He was hard, and huge.

It should have made her nervous. Instead, it turned her on, and she pressed closer, wrenching an appreciative male growl from him.

"Be sure, Maddie."

She opened her eyes. The steam from the shower was fogging the tiny bathroom, making it hot and humid. "If you even think about stopping now, I'm going to have to hurt you."

He stared down at her for a beat, then murmured her

name before kissing her, slow and deep. She'd never felt more aroused, more wanted, and it made her tremble.

Jax pulled back, his hands threading into her hair, holding her gaze. She had no idea what he was looking for, but something in her expression must have reassured him, because he brought his mouth back to hers, his tongue flicking out over her bottom lip. His hands slid down her body, cupping her bottom, lifting her to grind his hips to hers. He was hard and thick against her, straining between them. Pushing her back farther into the shower, he kissed his way over her, starting with her throat and working his way down. He had a nipple in his mouth, sucking it hard between his tongue and the roof of his mouth when she reached down and wrapped her hand around his hard, pulsing length. When she stroked him, he groaned and covered her hand with his, moving with her, showing her what he liked, until suddenly he stopped her.

"You don't like that?" she asked.

"I love that." His voice was hoarse, unsteady. "But it's been too long." With the water washing over their bodies, he nibbled at her neck, cupping a breast, rasping his thumb over her nipple, none of which deterred his free hand from slipping between her thighs. When he felt how ready she was, he dropped his forehead to hers and said her name in a jagged whisper.

She clutched at him. "Now, Jax. Please, now."

His finger was tracing over her, stroking, teasing. "I love how wet you are," he murmured against her ear, sucking the lobe into his mouth as he slid a finger inside her.

With a strangled cry, she rocked to him. "It means I'm ready."

He brushed his lips against hers. "Just making sure."

"I'm *sure!*"

He added another finger, gliding deep while brushing his thumb over her in just the right rhythm until she came with a rush. While she was still shuddering, he rolled on the condom and slid inside of her with a single, sure push of his hips.

She gasped, arching helplessly as it extended her orgasm. When she could open her eyes, she blinked him into focus. His eyes were solid black and locked on hers, intense and fierce. As he began to move within her, she felt the tile at her back, warm from both her own body heat and the hot water pulsing down over them. His strokes were strong and steady and sent her spiraling. He came with her, the both of them rocking together, gasping for breath. Unable to stand, they slid to the shower floor, still entwined.

Completely spent, Maddie dropped her head to his chest, managing a smile when he drew her in against him with a wordless protective murmur, pressing his face in her hair. At the tender touch, something came over her, something new. It was both warm and wonderful.

And terrifying. Because he'd given her just what she wanted.

Only she already wanted more.

Chapter 13

♥

"My momma always said that two rattlesnakes living in the same hole will get along better than two sisters. So I had three daughters to improve the odds."
PHOEBE TRAEGER

The next day Jax spent most of his time at the inn, stripping old windowpanes and carpeting.

And watching Maddie.

She'd pretty much kicked him to the curb after yesterday's shower. It was a first for him, not being the one to need space, and he hadn't known what kind of reception to expect this morning.

She'd greeted him with a sweet, warm smile, and because she wasn't one to fake anything, that had told him that they were okay. "How about dinner tonight?" he asked her midday.

Maddie glanced at him, then back to her task of hauling out the debris. She was looking hot and just a little bit breathless. Her hair was wild, her shirt untucked, and the seat of her jeans was dirty.

He couldn't take his eyes off her.

"Can't," she said.

He tossed the load in his arms into the back of the Dumpster they'd had delivered and brushed his hands off on his jeans, catching her arm before she could turn away. "Can't? Or won't?"

She closed her eyes but then surprised him by dropping her head to his chest. "I'm all dirty and sweaty, Jax."

"I like dirty and sweaty," he said, drawing her into his arms. "And it's just dinner, not a ring or a white picket fence."

Choking out a laugh, she pressed in even closer, sighing when he kissed her temple. But then after a moment, and far before he was ready, she backed away from his touch and met his gaze. "But no condom on this dinner date, right? Because..."

"...Because you're not ready for this."

"I just need...I really need to take a step backward from anything serious."

And sex for her was serious. He understood. Hell, what they'd experienced in the shower was so serious, he still hadn't recovered. "Take the step back if you need it. Hell, take two. Just don't go running away."

That brought a small smile. "I no longer run."

"Good," he said and went back to work, for the first time in five years wanting something he couldn't have.

Maddie divided her time between the marina office and painting the inn's bedrooms. Tara helped with the painting. Chloe couldn't do much because of her asthma. Maddie got that, but the way she held herself separate from them, working on her skin care line instead of the inn, was more worrisome than annoying. At some point, Chloe was going to have to exercise the swing vote, and Maddie had no idea which way she'd go. With a sigh, Maddie watched Tara walk across the yard, gingerly carrying paint supplies. Tara had at least deigned to get her hands dirty, risking her manicure. Not because she believed in the cause.

Nope, what Tara believed in was saving money.

Over the past few days, Maddie had finished the paperwork for refinancing their loan and filed it at the bank. Her fingers were crossed. Tara and Chloe were both leaving tomorrow, and Maddie would be on her own. But that was a worry for later, she told herself. For the moment, she was covered from head to toe in paint.

"I'm changing my penny-pinching stance," Tara huffed at her side, with hardly any paint on her. "We should have hired someone to do this part."

Maddie had no idea how her sister had managed to stay clean, but it was really annoying. Perhaps it was the invisible bubble of righteous perfection that clearly surrounded her. "We should have hired someone? You did not just say that."

Tara sighed. "I hate being peasant stock." She swiped her brow, but Maddie didn't see a drop of sweat on her. Maybe she had a sweat-gland disorder or something. That thought made her smile a little. Only Tara could have a medical condition that aided her perfect southern belle image.

"You okay?" Tara asked.

"Yes, why?"

"Because for the past few days, you've been . . . different somehow."

Yes. Multiple orgasms tended to do a body good.

"You went out with Jax last night."

"Just for dinner." And a few hot-as-hell kisses. Turned out, she didn't really want to take *too* many steps backward, only a little one. A real little one.

"So you're okay?"

"Yep."

Tara nodded and looked at her hands. "You know, I'm not normally one to gripe." She narrowed her eyes when Maddie snorted. "But I would like to make an official complaint that *I* didn't get the asthma in the family."

Maddie had to give her that one. Chloe was sitting a hundred yards away on the dock, free of the chemicals that would have sent her into asthma hell, surrounded by bowls and containers filled with ingredients like eggs and honey and almonds. "What is she making today?"

"Some facial to clean out our pores when we're done," Tara said. "And she's brewing some sort of soothing homemade sun tea that reduces stress." Her tone said this was as likely as them making a go of the inn. "She said it'd be better than a spa day."

"I've never had a spa day," Maddie said on a sigh.

"And you have the pores to prove it."

"What? I do not." Maddie moved to the hallway and stared at herself in the full-length mirror leaning against the wall, the one they'd pulled off one of the interior guest room doors. Oh, boy. Her hair looked like she'd stuck her finger in a live electrical socket, and her skin was shiny with perspiration, but she didn't see any pores. Probably because she was layered in a fine dusting of paint. She paused, searching for a natural transition to the question she wanted to ask and found none. So she jumped right in. "Why are you mad that Chloe kissed Logan's best friend?"

"Because *she* wanted Scott for herself," Chloe said from behind them, having come inside without either of them noticing. She was wearing leggings, a miniskirt, and a sweater that said DEAR SANTA, LET ME EXPLAIN. Eyes inscrutable, she handed them each a small vial. "Try this. Let me know if you notice a difference in the next twenty-four hours."

"But you're both leaving in the morning," Maddie said.

Chloe shrugged.

Tara didn't say anything. Done painting, she pulled on her sweater and wrapped a red scarf around her neck. Maddie had finished the scarf the night before, when she couldn't sleep because she'd been too busy reliving Jax's hands on her body.

The scarf was crooked, but just looking at it gave Maddie a little tug of pride. Her next project, started this morning, was with the green skein of yarn she'd commandeered from her mother's stash, which made it feel just as special as the red one. It wasn't quite as crooked—yet—but give her some time.

"You can text me," Chloe told them, voice flat.

Tara sighed. "I didn't want Scott for myself."

Chloe just gave her a long, level look.

"I didn't. I was just jealous because... well, because you make it so damn easy. You make friends in the blink of an eye, and I don't. This may come as a surprise to both of you, but some people find me... unapproachable."

Chloe was quiet for a long moment, and it wasn't clear if she was trying to fight a grimace or a smile.

"You shouldn't be here," Tara told her. "You'll get an asthma attack."

"I know but the bank just called. You and I each missed signing one of the loan docs. I'll take you on the Vespa."

"Are you going to promise not to kill me?"

"Only if you promise not to irritate me."

They left, and Maddie figured the odds were fifty–fifty that they'd both survive the short trip. She stared at herself in the mirror. She was wearing a long-sleeved knit tee and jeans, and she realized that for the first time in recent history, the button on the jeans wasn't cutting into her belly. Huh. She lifted the hem of the shirt and stared at her middle. It might have been wishful thinking on her part, but it seemed flatter. "Maybe I should forget to eat potato chips more often."

Two big, warm hands slid beneath hers, callused palms flat on her stomach. Her gaze collided with Jax's warm, amused one in the mirror.

For two days, he'd found a way to have his hands and/ or his lips on her every chance he got. Yesterday morning, he'd been wielding a huge power saw like a sexy lumberjack, cutting the fallen tree in the yard. When he'd caught her watching him, he'd pressed her up against the stack of cut wood, slid his hands beneath her shirt, and kissed her senseless.

Yesterday afternoon, he'd backed her into the upstairs linen closet and she'd spent the best five minutes of her life making out like they were teenagers.

Except she was fairly certain that a teenage boy couldn't have brought her to orgasm with nothing more than a touch of his fingers.

"Mmm," Jax murmured now, those magic fingers stroking lightly across her stomach. "Soft and warm."

"But not hard and ripped like you." She tried to say this critically, but it was difficult not to sound breathless with his hands on her bare skin, his chest plastered to her back, and his hips snuggled to hers.

"I've definitely got the hard taken care of." Still holding her gaze in the mirror, he rubbed his jaw to hers as he slowly rocked into her.

He was right. He had the hard taken care of. She thrust her bottom into him, moaning when he thrust back. At the sound, he whipped her around to face him, slowly pressing her back into the wall.

"You've had a rough morning," he murmured, his mouth descending to her neck.

"Yes. I'm dirty, Jax."

"Don't tease me."

That got a low laugh out of her, and she shifted closer. She felt him smile against her skin as she obviously acquiesced, not caring as long as he didn't stop.

He didn't. His lips brushed just beneath her ear, and his hands headed north.

"You're tense."

"A little," she admitted. Her fingers were in his hair. He had better hair than she did, the bastard, all soft and silky.

"A lot," he murmured against her, spreading hot, open-mouthed kisses along her jaw and down her throat, which he then gently bit.

A gasp escaped her, and she clutched at him, moaning when he licked the spot to soothe the slight sting. His hands slid up her ribs and very lightly grazed the undersides of her breasts. "I'm excellent at relieving stress," he said, and his thumbs glided over her nipples, wrenching a shocked, aroused cry from her that he swallowed with his mouth, kissing her until they had to tear apart to breathe.

"Still need space?" he asked.

"Maybe later."

His smile was sheer sex. "Are we alone?"

"Yes, but—" She looked around the hallway. "Here? You want to do it here?"

"Yes or no, Maddie."

"*Yes.*"

He kissed her again, slipping a hand between her thighs, his fingers pressing on just the right spot to drive her even more wild. It'd taken him four and a half minutes to get her to the toe-curling point yesterday. Right now she was pretty sure he could have her there in half the time, which was more than a little embarrassing.

"Jax—"

His fingers began to move, but a low growl conveyed his frustration with her jeans. A second later, he'd unbuttoned them and slid a hand inside. "Jesus," he murmured reverently.

Lost, she ground her hips against him and heard him swear roughly into the side of her neck. All this while his fingers continued to give her exactly what she needed. Like yesterday, it took shockingly little to topple her over the edge. She burst with a shudder and a soft cry and would have fallen to the ground if he hadn't supported all her weight.

When she stopped panting and her vision cleared, she realized she had a death grip on him. "Sorry," she managed a little hoarsely.

"Christ, are you kidding? I'll be thinking about that all day." Tucking a damp curl behind her ear, he buttoned and zipped her back up, and then studied her face. "Better. You look a lot less tense now."

"And you look more tense."

"I'll live."

"Or I could..." She pulled him toward her and placed her lips on his jaw. "Repay the favor."

He groaned and pulled her in tight, but they both went still as a car pulled up in the yard.

Jax looked out and groaned, dropping his head to Maddie's shoulder. "Material delivery."

When he was gone, Maddie sat down right there on the floor. He had a way of filling her with mind-blowing pleasure. She wanted to lose herself in it, but she wouldn't. She'd made that mistake before and still wasn't ready to trust herself.

Fifteen minutes later, Tara walked back inside the inn and executed a double take at Maddie sitting on the floor in the dirty foyer. "What are you doing?"

Waiting for her bones to reappear. "Nothing."

"So why do you look like you either just ate a bag of chips or got lucky?"

"What?" Maddie dragged herself upright and looked in the mirror. Flushed. Damp. Glowing.

Well, hell.

"Don't let Chloe know you're still eating chips," Tara said on a sigh. "She'll triple our yoga regimen."

Maddie nodded. "Okie-dokie, I won't tell Chloe about the chips..."

Or the orgasms...

Chapter 14

♥

"Life is short. Eat cake."
PHOEBE TRAEGER

Their last night together, Maddie and her sisters ended up at Eat Me Café. Silver and blue tinsel hung everywhere, and cutouts of Santa's reindeer were hanging from the rafters. Tara was, as usual, overdressed in designer jeans and a blazer. Maddie had gone with her decidedly not-designer jeans and her thickest sweater in deference to the chilly weather. Chloe was wearing denim leggings, kickass boots, and a long-sleeved shirt that read I MELTED FROSTY.

"Now we're going to get along," Maddie told them, walking through the decorated café. "Or I'm going to let my pores get big and go back to eating potato chips three meals a day."

"I don't believe you," Tara said, cool as a cucumber. "You're going to hit the Love Shack, get trashed, and do something extremely inappropriate with our master renovation expert."

Chloe raised her hand. "Can I vote for that? I think getting mastered by our sexy carpenter is a good idea."

Maddie's good parts all stood up and voted for that, too.

Tara shook her head. "Bad idea, sugar. Still not ready."

"Are you saying he's out of her league?" Chloe asked.

"I'm saying he's so far out of her league that she can't even *see* his league." Tara looked at Maddie. "No offense. I don't mean he's too good for you. I mean he's too..."

"Hot," Chloe supplied.

"Yes," Tara said. "Hot. You have to work your way up to a man like that. Maybe start out with a basic model." Her eyes roamed the bar and landed on a good-looking man who was pulling a bag of tea leaves from his plaid coat pocket and signaling the waitress for a cup of hot water. "Someone like him," she said. "A training-bra version of Jax."

Maddie sighed. "Subject change, please." She lifted her water glass. "How about a toast to Mom, for bringing us together."

Chloe and Tara lifted their glasses. "To Mom," they said in unison.

"Aw." Maddie smiled. "You two are so cute when you're in accord." Empowered, she lifted her glass again. "To our new venture, the three of us."

Silence.

"To our new venture," Maddie repeated, giving them the evil eye.

"To our new venture," they murmured.

"*The three of us,*" she said firmly.

"The three of us," they muttered.

"But we're still selling," Tara said.

"Maybe selling," Maddie said, looking at Chloe. "You going to pick a side anytime soon?"

"Soon," she said noncommittally.

"Admit it," Tara said. "You like being the swing vote."

"Well, I do live to annoy you."

Thirty long, awkward minutes later, they still hadn't been served. The tension was rising. Tara and Chloe had a limit on the amount of time they could spend in close quarters, and they'd met it. "So about that weather, huh?" Maddie asked.

Both sisters just stared at her.

Cripes. She searched her brain for a joke and came up empty. Desperate, she flagged down the only waitress in the place.

"Sorry," the waitress huffed out, not stopping. "Our chef quit, and we're going nuts."

"*Chef*," Tara said under her breath. "That guy wasn't a chef. He was a short-order cook trained at Taco Bell, bless his heart."

"Hey, I like Taco Bell," Maddie said.

"You would, darlin'."

Chloe snorted. "You are *such* a food snob."

"I beg your pardon." The South dripped from each word. *Delta Burke save us.* "I'd work here."

"Right," Chloe said. "*You'd* work *here*."

"Absolutely."

"Admit it, you'd *never* lower yourself to work in a place like this, with real people and real food," Chloe said.

Tara's jaw began to spasm, and Maddie's belly matched it. Instead of pulling out the Tums, Maddie grabbed the half of a green scarf and knitting needles. True to form, this scarf was already crooked.

"Food. Snob," Chloe repeated softly to Tara, who abruptly stood, tugged on the hem of her perfect little blazer, and strode purposely toward the kitchen, heels clicking on the chipped linoleum.

"Holy shit," Chloe said, watching her go. "She's going to do it." She grinned and leaned back, like she'd just completed a job well done. "God, she's so easy."

"Why?" Maddie asked, baffled. "Why do you mess with her?"

"Because it's fun?"

Tara talked to the owner and vanished into the kitchen. In twenty minutes, the bell started ringing, accompanied by Tara's voice demanding that the waitress hustle because she didn't want the food served cold.

In another hour, the owner of Eat Me Café was begging Tara to sign on until they could get a permanent replacement. Maddie and Chloe had left their table and were in the kitchen now, staring in shock at how fast the chaos had been organized.

"I suppose I could stay a little longer," Tara said. "If they get me *real* garlic, no more of this dried crap."

"So you're *not* leaving in the morning?" Maddie asked.

"No." Tara was chopping onions at the speed of light. "I'm not leaving."

"But your husband. Your great job. Your perfect life."

Tara never even looked up as her hands continued to move so fast they were a blur. "Truth?"

"Please," Maddie said, confused.

"I don't have a great job. I do inventory for a chain of hotels' cafés and restaurants, and I hate it."

Maddie blinked. "And Logan?"

Pain and wistful regret came and went in Tara's gaze. "He's driving NASCAR, he's on the road 24/7. I gave up traveling with him two years ago. I was jealous of his career and bitter about being relegated to third place in his life behind his car and crew. I divorced him. I'm alone and have been for a year and a half."

"There's been no one else?"

"Well, for a little while I thought maybe I could start a thing with a close friend, but *someone* else got in the way."

"Me," Chloe said softly. "I got in the way."

Tara sighed. "I don't blame you for it. I was still missing Logan. It wouldn't have been right."

"Excuse me, girls."

The three of them turned to face Lucille. She wore her eye-popping pink track suit, minus the white headband. Today it was a rainbow-colored knit cap. Maddie introduced her to her sisters.

Lucille smiled at Chloe. "The wild one."

Chloe saluted smartass-like, but with a genuine smile. "At your service."

"And you," Lucille said, pointing to Tara. "You're the Steel Magnolia who sometimes forgets to breathe. Just wanted to say that was the best turkey club I've ever had, thank you. You're gifted. Oh, and I hear the inn's coming along. Looking forward to working for you girls."

Tara blinked as the older woman smiled and walked away. "I don't forget to breathe."

"Sometimes you do," Chloe said. "Can we rewind a minute? Back to the you-don't-blame-me thing? Cuz I gotta tell you, it feels a little like you do."

Tara took a deep breath, her fingers still chopping, chopping, chopping. "I might have a few anger issues."

"*No,*" Chloe said in mock disbelief.

"And maybe some misplaced resentment."

"How long is it going to be misplaced?"

Tara grimaced and stopped chopping. "I'll let you know. But I am sorry for being a bitch, if that helps. And I'm sorry for any future bitchery."

Chloe cupped a hand behind her ear. "I'm sorry, what was that?"

"*I'm sorry! Okay? I'm very, very sorry!*" she yelled.

Chloe grinned. "I heard you. I just like hearing you say sorry."

Tara narrowed her gaze and tightened her grip on her knife, but Maddie stepped between them. "We'll just get out of your hair now," she said quickly, grabbing Chloe by the back of her shirt. She turned and bumped into Jax.

Ford was with him, and they were both eyeing the mountain of food with interest. "Heard there was a new chef," Ford said and met Tara's shocked gaze.

An awkward silence filled the kitchen. Maddie decided it wasn't the mouse who needed to fill it, but the new, improved, strong Maddie. So even though Tara and Ford obviously had some connection, she went with the benefit of the doubt. "Tara" she said. "Have you met—"

"Ford," Tara said calmly, her eyes anything but.

"Tara," Ford said just as calmly.

"So you two *do* know each other," Chloe said.

"No," Tara said.

"Yes," Ford said.

Maddie could have cut the tension with the knife in Tara's hand, the one that was currently looking a little white-knuckled for her taste. She reached out to try to take it, but Tara began slicing a tomato.

Actually, *slicing* was too gentle a word for what Tara was doing with deadly and lethal precision. More like making ketchup.

"Everyone who wants to keep all their body parts needs to get the hell out," Tara drawled coolly.

"Tara," Ford said quietly.

"No." She pointed the knife at him, not threateningly, necessarily, but not exactly gently, either. "No talking in my kitchen."

Ford's jaw bunched as he turned to Jax. There was some silent communication thing, and Jax opened the kitchen door, nudging Maddie and Chloe out ahead of him.

Ford shut the door.

On the other side of it, Maddie looked at Jax, who shook his head. "I don't know," he told her. "I don't know any more than you."

"Yeah, well, I hope you weren't that fond of him," Chloe said.

But Ford came out three minutes later, unscathed. At least physically.

"You going to explain that?" Maddie asked him.

Looking uncharacteristically tense, Ford shook his head. "No."

No. Of course not.

The next morning, Jax was on the second story of the inn sanding the wood floors into submission when he heard the rumble of Chloe's Vespa start up.

Setting down the sander, he walked past a snoozing

Izzy to the window. In the yard below, Chloe sat on her bike. Tara was on one side, hands shoved in the pockets of her long coat. Not Maddie. Nope, she stood directly in front of the Vespa, hands on hips.

Chloe said something.

Maddie said something.

Tara didn't.

Then Maddie removed the god-awful green scarf she wore, the one she'd been making for the past few days, and wrapped it around Chloe's neck.

Chloe looked down at it and grinned. Whatever she said had Maddie throwing herself at Chloe and hugging her tight. After a single beat of hesitation, Chloe returned the hug, awkwardly patting Maddie on the back.

Maddie craned her neck and sent Tara a *get-your-ass-over-here* gesture.

Jax watched Tara fight with herself, then capitulate to the "Mouse," who'd never really been much of a mouse at all. Tara stepped forward and nudged Chloe in the shoulder. Chloe nudged back, and then Maddie yanked them both closer and into a hug.

Afterward, Chloe drove off, and Maddie swiped at her eyes like a mother seeing her baby off on the first day of kindergarten.

Tara went into the cottage, but Maddie stayed there on the driveway, watching until the Vespa vanished from view.

Without taking the time to drop his tool belt, Jax headed for the stairs with a sleepy Izzy at his heels. He half expected Maddie to have vanished by the time he got outside, but she still stood in the same spot. Her eyes were wet but no longer leaking, for which he was infinitely grateful, though his heart clenched hard at the sight of her misery. "You okay?"

At the sound of his voice, she angrily swiped her nose on her sleeve. "No, and don't be nice." Her voice cracked, and she turned away. "Not yet, not until I . . . get this thing out of my eye."

"Aw, Maddie. Come here."

With a soft sniff, she whirled and threw herself at him, making the tools on his belt jangle as his arms came around her hard.

"I'm going to miss her," she whispered, her hands fisted in his shirt and her face plastered to his neck. "Which is ridiculous. We hardly know each other—"

"It's not ridiculous." Sliding a hand into her hair, he tugged her head up so he could see her eyes. "You love her."

"Every pissy, sarcastic, bitchy inch." She dropped her forehead to his chest and sniffed again.

He squeezed her tight and gave her a few minutes. Finally she relaxed and lifted her head.

"She'll be back," he said.

"Yes," she agreed, sounding better, much to his relief. "She'll be back." She shifted against him, then sucked in a breath when his hammer jabbed into her hip.

"Sorry," he said. "Let me drop the belt—"

"No." She held on when he would have pulled away. "Don't. I like it."

Again, he lifted her face, and he smiled. "The tool belt turns you on."

"No." She closed her eyes and thunked her forehead to his chest. "Little bit."

Delighted and also immediately aroused, he laughed,

and she groaned. "Don't judge me. Apparently *everything* turns me on here in Washington. I think it's the ocean air." She rubbed her forehead back and forth over his chest. "Or..."

"Or..." He tightened his grip on her hair when the tip of her nose brushed over his nipple.

"Or learning to stand up for myself." Going up on tiptoe, she pressed her face into his throat and inhaled, her hips bumping his.

His eyes drifted shut as he held her to him. "Try again," he murmured against her mouth.

She stared into his eyes. "It's you."

"*Us,*" he corrected and kissed her, hot and insistent. She responded with a satisfying, soft whimper of need that went straight through him. He still held her ponytail, controlling the angle of her head, but he didn't have anything to do with the way she melted against him, trying to climb into his skin to get closer. Their tongues slid together in a rhythm that made him groan, as did her hands, which were all over him, slipping beneath his shirt, gliding over his back as if she couldn't get enough.

He sure as hell couldn't, but he wasn't going to get what he wanted out here in the yard, even when her hands came around to his front, playing with his abs, then with the waistband on his jeans, which were loose enough to allow the tips of her fingers to slip inside. He held his breath and wished she'd go south another half an inch—

"Oh, for the love of God."

Tara was hands on hips when they broke apart. She glared at Jax. "So was that tongue lashing you just gave her included in the bid?"

Chapter 15

♥

"Men are like parking spots. All the good ones are taken, and those that aren't are inaccessible."
PHOEBE TRAEGER

Maddie rounded on Tara. "You'll have to excuse me," she said. "Since I didn't get the memo about you having the right to butt in on my business."

"How about I just remind you that you gave up men for a damn good reason. You need to slow down and think before acting."

"I spent my life doing that. It hasn't worked out so well. I'm trying something new."

"At our expense," Tara said.

"Well, excuse me for lacking the *perfect* gene from the Traeger pool."

Tara nearly choked at that. "Sugar, if you think my life is perfect, you need to take off the rose-colored glasses."

"Hey, until last night, you wanted *all* of us to believe it."

Tara stared at her, myriad emotions dancing across her face, with hurt leading the pack. "Well," she finally said a little stiffly. "Nobody's perfect." And with a final glare in Jax's direction—one that he didn't need translated—she stalked off.

Maddie blew out a breath, then looked at Jax. "Tell me why I feel like I just kicked a kitten."

He gave a slow shake of his head. "A wild tiger, maybe. Not a kitten."

She smiled grimly and backed away. "I need something to do. Work, maybe."

"You could help me sand the floors."

"Tempting, but I need something more physical. I need to tear something up. You got anything like that?"

You could tear me up. In bed. For a minute his head actually spun with that image, but he shook it off and grabbed her hand. "I've got just the thing."

"Is it X-rated?"

He nearly smiled at the slightly hopeful tone in her voice. "Maybe later."

In less than five minutes, he had her suitably protected and holding an ax. He pointed to the pile of huge wood rounds he'd created from the fallen tree earlier in the week. "Have at it."

With a tight, thankful smile, she gripped the handle but then hesitated.

"Problem?"

She gave him an apologetic glance. "Feels weird with you watching."

"I like to watch."

She rolled her eyes and shoved a few curls out of her

face. "I know it's silly, but this feels like a...solo thing." She paused. "I'm used to doing things on my own."

"Solo isn't all it's cracked up to be. Maybe it's time for a new tactic."

No doubt. She gestured for him to step back a little.

"Go for it," he said.

Trinity in *The Matrix*, she decided. That's whose strength she was going for. She wriggled her hips a little, getting into position, and then swung the ax. It barely budged, much less flying through the air in slow-mo like in *The Matrix*. Damn, the thing was heavy.

"Put your weight into it."

She narrowed her eyes and looked at Jax. "Maybe you should go first and show me how it's done."

"Sure." He came close, moving with his usual innate and easy grace even in the tool belt. He was wearing Levi's again. This pair had a hole in one thigh and on the opposite knee. He had on an opened flannel over a caramel brown Henley that brought out his eyes.

Their fingers collided as he took the ax from her, and then he set his open hand low on her stomach, the hot, callused palm gently pushing her out of harm's way. As always at his touch, heat slashed through her, and for a minute, she closed her eyes and wavered.

She should have chosen sex. Note to self: *always* choose sex over physical labor!

"It's not too late," he said very softly.

Afraid to speak and give herself away, she pointed to the wood. With a knowing smile, he lifted the ax and swung it. Muscles bunched and worked with an effortless ease that left her mouth dry and other parts of her not quite so dry. He swung for five straight minutes without faltering in his rhythm, then stopped. He shrugged out of the flannel, leaving him in just the Henley, the sleeves of which he shoved up to his elbows. "You ready to try?" he asked.

Hell, no. Not when she had a view like this. She shook her head. "Watching you do it is helping a lot. Keep going."

He gave her an amused look but turned back to the wood.

"Um, Jax?"

He glanced over his shoulder.

"You look..." *Hot.* "Overheated. Probably you should take off your other shirt, too."

"You think?"

Oh, yeah. Not trusting her voice, she merely nodded.

His lips quirked, but he said nothing as he reached up and behind him, tugging the shirt over his head in one smooth, very male motion.

And then he stood before her in those low-slung jeans, tool belt, and nothing else but a gleam of sweat.

"Better," she tried to say, staring at his tatts, but it came out more as a squeak. She was lucky not to be a puddle on the ground. Honest to God, the man shouldn't be allowed to look like that. It just wasn't fair to all the other men on the planet.

Turning back to his task, he went at the wood for a while. Maddie backed up to a large wood round and plopped down. After a few minutes, Tara came out with a peace-offering tray of iced tea and glasses. "Oh, sweet merciful Jesus," she whispered, eyes locked on Jax as she sank to the log next to Maddie.

The two of them sat there in companionable, lust-filled silence watching Jax like he was must-see TV until finally he stopped and gave them a long glance, swiping his brow on his forearm. "Your turn, ladies."

Tara jumped to her feet. "Oh, not me, honey. I have a thing in the thing…" She waved vaguely behind her. "Enjoy the rest of the tea. There's plenty." And then she was gone.

Maddie poured him a glass, which he downed in a few gulps while she watched a drop of sweat slide down his chest. "I don't think I can pull that off," she murmured, nodding to the wood.

"That's okay. I have something better for you."

Oh, boy. "Is *this* X-rated?"

He flashed that badass grin, grabbed his shirts, and took her to the second floor of the inn, in one of the bedrooms that had been used as a storage room, gesturing to the stack of wooden crates that someone had piled there. The plan had been to tear them up and use the wood for kindling. Jax handed her a much smaller ax than the one he'd used outside and nodded for her to have a go.

So she gave it a shot and found that she could do this. She swung and chopped until she was shaking and sweaty and feeling much better. "Whew," she said, dropping the ax. "How long was that?"

"Two minutes." He laughed at the look on her face and stepped up right behind her, dipping his head so that his mouth brushed her ear. "You look overheated. Probably you should take off your shirt."

He was playing with her and thought she wouldn't dare. Something came over her at that—the exhilaration that came from discovering a man found her sexy, maybe.

In any case, she took a deep breath and stripped out of her sweatshirt, leaving her in just a cute little baby blue tank that she'd borrowed—okay, stolen—from Chloe.

He went still, his eyes eating her up.

With a small smile, she put a hand to the middle of his chest and pushed him back, once again grabbing the ax.

She lasted a whole minute before dropping the heavy tool and gasping for breath.

"Feeling better?" His eyes were lit with heat, amusement, and something even better. Pride.

"Getting there," she murmured.

Stepping forward, eyes locked on hers, he swiped at a smudge on her jaw. "What would make it even better?"

She closed her eyes for a beat, swaying toward him. *You,* she thought. *In me.* That's what would make it alllll better.

From somewhere below, Izzy barked. She was looking for her human. "You going down?" Maddie asked him.

His eyes flamed. "Any time."

And just like that, her nipples did their Jax Happy Dance. Much as she hated to admit it, Tara had been right. He was out of her league. She grabbed her sweatshirt and turned to go downstairs to open the door for the dog herself, but he reeled her in until she was up against him, her back to his front. "Remember this place," he said, voice low. "Remember where we are. Right here, this very spot."

"You mean here in this room, all hot and sweaty?"

His teeth nipped her ear, and she shivered.

"You keep taking those steps back," he said. "Not enough forward." Turning her in his arms, he lightly brushed his lips over hers before pulling back to meet her gaze. "Save our place," he said quietly, all signs of teasing gone, and turned to go.

He cared about her, he liked her, just as is. Her hands caught him, brought him back, pulling him down to her. "I won't forget." And then she kissed him, loving the ragged groan she wrenched from his chest. She loved the way he kissed, too. He tasted warm and tangy sweet from the iced tea, and it was intoxicating. So was the solid feel of his body pressing into hers, making her want to forget about her to-do list, about Tara just next door in the cottage, the dog wanting in, everything. "We have to go," she said.

"Uh-huh." Dropping her sweatshirt back down to the floor, she accepted that she was making the slippery descent into oblivion and slid her arms around his waist, losing herself in their connection.

In him.

With a rough sound, he took control, backing her to a beam. He palmed her breast, thumbing her already erect and straining nipple over her thin tank top.

"God, you're soft," he said. "Soft and warm and perfect. I have to feel you again, Maddie." His hands slid beneath the tank. Pushing the material up, his mouth took itself on a tour along her collarbone and down, his tongue gliding over the lace of her bra, right over her nipple as he ground his pelvis into hers.

He was big, which no longer scared her, and extremely aroused, which excited her beyond belief. "Jax."

"I know. I can't get enough of you." Tugging the cups of her bra down, he licked her again, over her bared flesh this time so that she clutched at his biceps and arched up into him. "Not even close," he said. He gripped her bottom, squeezed, then brought his hands around and was heading for the button on her jeans when the dog barked again.

Their eyes met, and Jax let out a breath of male frustration. "She's got timing, I'll give her that." They were still both breathing erratically when he stepped back, his eyes blazing with heat.

He wanted her. Again. *Still.* It was a powerful feeling.

"Save our place," he repeated in a soft but direct command and was gone.

For two mornings running, Maddie and Tara did yoga. Chloe's legacy, they decided. Plus it burned calories.

They did it in silence. Well, Tara was silent. Maddie had been asking questions like "Why did you agree to the job at Eat Me when you wanted to leave?" and "Are we celebrating Christmas together?" and "How do you know Ford?"

None of which Tara answered.

Finally one morning Maddie sat on her yoga mat and refused to do a single pose. "Not until you answer at least one question."

Tara sighed. "Fine. Regarding Christmas, I don't think we should exchange gifts that cost any money, not when we're spending every spare penny we have on this place."

"Fair enough," Maddie agreed. "But expect another scarf, probably crooked. And that wasn't the question I most wanted answered and you know it."

Tara sat and faced her, stretching her long, perfectly toned body. "If I answer another, you have to do the same."

"Deal. Why didn't you tell us about Logan?"

Tara's cool expression crumpled. "I don't know, probably because I didn't want to look like a loser."

"We're sisters. Sisters are supposed to tell."

"Yes, but I'm the oldest." She went into some complicated upside-down yoga pose. "Oldest sisters are supposed to be perfect."

"Says who?"

"Older sisters." Tara sighed and changed positions with ease. "And I realize it's no secret that when we first got here, all I wanted was to get back out again. I really can't explain why I agreed to stay. I don't know. Temporary insanity."

"Or... we're growing on you."

"Or I'm enjoying the weather."

Maddie sighed. "So about Ford."

"Oh, no. I just answered *two* questions. Now you. What are you doing with Jax?"

"Huh," Maddie said. "Suddenly I'm seeing why it's more fun to be the one asking the questions. Would you believe me if I say I have no idea? I mean you saw me when I first got here. I didn't want to even think about men." She hesitated. "Problem is, he's hard *not* to think about."

"If I looked like him," Tara said. "I'd want to have sex with myself. All the time."

Maddie laughed. "Now you sound like Chloe."

"No need for insults."

"She should have stayed with us."

"Aw, you missed me."

They turned in shock to face *Chloe.* "Hi, honey," she said with a wave. "I'm home."

"Already?" Tara asked. "What about New Mexico?"

"Didn't quite get there." Chloe rolled out her yoga mat.

"Texas?" Maddie asked, mimicking Tara's pose so it looked like she'd been working hard all morning.

"Didn't get there, either. Decided you two were going to have too much fun without me. Besides, I love the natural sea salt here. I came up with an idea for a body lotion. Maddie, focus. Hold your pose."

What, was she kidding?

"You're moving too fast, as usual. You're always in a hurry. Got to take a moment to smell the roses." Chloe began to stretch, bending in one fluid movement to lay her palms flat on the floor, legs straight.

"I'm working on other things," Maddie said.

"Like?"

"Like changing my moniker from 'the Mouse.'"

"To?" Tara asked.

"Actually, I'd like to be more like you. You know, the strong, take-no-shit Steel Magnolia."

Chloe chortled, then zipped it when Tara sent her a narrowed gaze before turning to Maddie with clear surprise. "Sugar, you don't want to be like me. I'm as messed up as they come."

"Yes, but you pretend not to be. And you, too," Maddie said to Chloe. "I like that. And I'm starting to see it's all in the pretending. And the attitude. You know, act tough, be tough."

"You going to be bitchy, too?" Chloe asked. "And say 'bless your heart' and do the holier-than-thou shit?"

"Or maybe she could just get whiny," Tara said smoothly. "Or better yet, take off on her Vespa when the going gets a little rough."

The tension ratcheted up a notch. "Maybe I'll do a combination," Maddie said. "Bitchy *and* whiny, with only a dash of anxiety. We'll call it 'the Blend' and make a recipe card about it for our kids."

Both sisters stared at her for a shocked beat, then looked at each other. That was the only warning Maddie got before they both tackled her down to the yoga mat for a wedgie.

Yeah, Maddie thought, lying there with her underwear twisted in places it shouldn't be as Tara and Chloe got up and bumped fists. They were really starting to gel together as a family.

Chapter 16

♥

"Never leave a paper trail."
PHOEBE TRAEGER

Maddie sat at the desk in the marina office. It was beginning to become clear why the inn hadn't been successful. Phoebe hadn't charged enough for any of the services, and sometimes, when she'd known her customers, she hadn't charged at all.

That would have to change—assuming they got their financing, that is. And assuming that by fixing the place up, they got customers. And that both of those things helped Maddie convince her sisters to keep the inn instead of selling. She dropped her head to the desk and hit it lightly a few times as a man let himself into the marina building.

He was six foot four, at least two hundred and fifty pounds, and looked like Sulley from *Monsters, Inc.*, minus the smile and blue fur.

"Need to rent a boat." His voice thundered like he'd spoken through a microphone. "Fully equipped."

She jumped in automatic response. "Have you rented here before?"

"Yes."

Good. So one of them knew what they were doing.

"Name's Peter Jenkins." He pounded his finger on her desk. "And I get a deal. Phoebe always gave me a deal."

Since Maddie had just yesterday organized the accounts receivables, she was proud to be able to go right to the file cabinet and locate a stack of boat rentals, where she pulled out one with his name on it. *Please have notes, please have notes . . .*

"Make sure it's gassed up," he boomed. "And I'm in a hurry here."

Yes, she was getting that. And she was getting something else—nervous as hell. He yelled when he talked. It was making her fingers refuse to work and her brain uncooperative. Plus, she hadn't yet studied any of their rental agreements or learned the procedure.

"What the hell's taking you so long?"

"I'm sorry." She reached for the file of blank rental agreements, looking for one for the fishing boat. "I'm new at this, so—"

"Oh, for fuck's sake." He slapped some cash onto the desk, making everything on the surface bounce. Maddie nearly jumped out of her skin. She took a careful breath, working really hard to find her nerve. She located it about the same time she put her fingers on the right form. "Got it—"

But he'd taken the keys off the hook on the wall and was already out the door and on the dock, stalking toward the boat.

"Hey," she called out, grabbing the cash and stuffing

it into her pocket to add to the cash box later. It wouldn't be difficult. The cash box was currently empty. "Excuse me!"

He'd boarded the boat by the time she caught up to him. "Mr. Jenkins, I need you to sign—"

Ignoring her, he untied the rope and pissed her off. She hopped on board before he could pull away, but as she jumped down, the boat pitched violently.

"Stern!" he bellowed. "Stern!"

Gripping the side of the boat, Maddie crouched low and looked at the very cold water, trying not to panic as they rocked hard. Logically she knew *stern* had to mean right or left, or maybe front or back. For all she knew, it meant go to hell, but with no idea which direction to move, and with the boat still pitching side to side and threatening to capsize, Maddie dropped to her butt.

"Get *off* the goddamned boat!"

Oh, hell no. "Not until you sign!"

Mr. Jenkins sent her a hard, long look, but she didn't cower.

Much.

Instead she whipped a pen out of her pocket and offered it up. He snatched the paper from her, signed it, then tossed it in her lap. Gee, guess he was in a hurry to get rid of her. She very carefully climbed out of the boat and stood on the dock as he headed out of the marina, muttering something about suing her for stupidity.

Rude. She stalked back to the office, talking to herself.

"Did you skip the caffeine again?" Jax asked.

She took in the unexpected sight of him standing in the doorway, palms up on the wooden frame above him.

Just looking at him made her feel better.

A lot better. He was watching her with a little smile on his face, wearing his usual uniform of a pair of jeans and battered boots, today with a merino wool hoodie sweatshirt.

And his tool belt.

Let's not forget the tool belt. "I've had caffeine," she told him. "And a blast of Mr. Jenkins. He called me an idiot."

Jax's lazy smile vanished. "What?"

"Yeah, I didn't know stem from stern. Hell, I barely know what horses have to do with engines." She smiled, but he didn't.

Instead, he pushed off from the door frame and came close. "He's an ass."

"Agreed. But he's a paying ass. Why would my mom have given that man a deal?"

"I think she dated him briefly, but even her sunny nature gave up trying to cure his chronic grumpiness. Tell me you kicked him out of here when he mouthed off at you."

"I was tempted. But truthfully, it was my own fault."

Jax stilled, his expression going very quiet, very serious. "Maddie."

She stared at him, her stomach pinging hollowly. "Dammit," she whispered. "It *wasn't* my fault. I did it again." She closed her eyes. Whirling, hands fisted, she flew to the marina door with some half-baked idea about climbing back onto that boat and—

"Maddie."

"No, I have to go. I have to give him a piece of my mind and maybe a foot shoved up his—"

Two warm arms surrounded her, pulling her back against a solid chest. "I'm all for that," he said in her ear. "In fact, I'll hold him down for you if you'd like. But unless you want to go for a swim to retrieve him, you're going to have to wait a few hours."

She turned to face him. He was still dangerously quiet, and there was an anger in his eyes she'd not seen since he kicked that patron out of the Love Shack that first night. It gave her yet another heart lurch, even though she knew he wasn't mad at *her*. "Being the strong female lead star of my own life is harder than I thought."

"You're doing good. You're doing real good."

She let out the breath that she hadn't realized she was holding and tipped her face up to his. "Yeah?"

His eyes warmed. "Yeah."

She managed a little smile. "Would you really hold him down for me?"

"In a heartbeat."

For some reason, that gave her a warm fuzzy, and her smile spread. "It's not exactly...politically correct."

The look he gave her said he didn't give a shit about being politically correct, he only cared about what was right.

And God, even from here, he smelled delicious. How was it that he always smelled so good? But rather than grabbing his sweatshirt and pulling him in, she stepped around him to her desk. "I've got to finish getting all this straightened out. I don't want to lose money because I don't know what I'm doing. And Mr. Jenkins threatened to sue me for stupidity, which would really suck."

"Tell him you're going to countersue for emotional damages."

She smiled at the thought. "Can someone really do that?"

"If you could prove you were negligently injured."

"You sound like a lawyer." She grinned. "Good thing you're not, because then I'd probably not like you as much."

"Come here," he said softly and pulled her in for a hug. "Kiss me, Maddie. Show me you remember our place."

She went up on her tiptoes and kissed him until she couldn't remember her own name, then pressed her face to his throat, feeling an odd tug in her chest at how much this meant. At how much he meant.

"Maddie—"

"I love how open you are," she said. "How honest. Do all the women you date appreciate that?"

"I'm not dating anyone else right now. Tell me that you know that we wouldn't have had sex if I was seeing someone else."

"Well, you'd think I'd know that, but I've made some bad choices," she said. "I no longer trust my judgment. It's easier for me to hear it straight from you, because I can believe what you say."

That odd something crossed his face, coming and going so fast she couldn't identify it. For a long moment, he watched his thumb glide along her jaw. "How about what I don't say?"

"What?"

"I haven't been in a relationship for five years," he said. "Since before I moved back here. Opening up isn't exactly second nature for me, Maddie."

"Five years is a long time to go without sex."

His eyes cut to hers. "I didn't say I'd gone without sex."

"Oh." *Oh.*

"But before you, it'd been a while for that, too."

"There's plenty of women in town."

"Yes, and most of them take their dating far more seriously than I do. Maddie, you need to know something about me."

God. "You're married. You're a felon. You're—"

"A lawyer. Before I moved back to Lucky Harbor, I was in Seattle. I was practicing law."

Jax spent a few days building new bathroom vanities at his own home wood shop on the other side of town. Maddie hadn't said much about his revelation, but then again, she'd made herself scarce.

There was nothing Jax could do about his past, it was written in ink. And he'd done the right thing by telling her. Especially since he'd held back other things—secrets that weren't his to share.

He only hoped Maddie saw it the same way. He kept telling himself that she would, that what they were beginning to feel for each other would be stronger than extenuating circumstances.

As he made his way through his house to leave for the shrimp feed, he shook his head at all the decorations Jeanne had put up, complete with mistletoe hanging from his doorways. It was clear that she was optimistic for his shot at having a woman in the house. Probably he'd blown that.

He drove to the pier. In a few hours, just about everyone in town would arrive for the annual event. The money raised tonight would supplement the funds for the police and fire departments, which was important but definitely not the first thing on people's minds as they paid to get in.

Nope, that would be the events. First up was the parade of shrimp boats, always led by the mayor on a decorated Jet Ski. Then the person who came closest to guessing the amount of shrimp brought in would get to kiss the mayor.

Man, woman, or child.

With Jax's luck, it'd be Ford or Sawyer. Last year it'd been his mail carrier—much to everyone's utter delight. Hopefully this year, plenty of the other two thousand people in town had bought tickets.

Afterward, they'd eat until their guts hurt and then dance to the Nitty Gritty, the local pop-rock band. People would probably still be dancing as the first pink tinges of dawn came up on the horizon.

Sawyer arrived right after Jax. He was in uniform, there on official crowd-control duty. And to make fun of Jax, of course. Ford showed up, too, setting up a booth for the Love Shack from which beer, wine, and eggnog would be floating aplenty.

Jax eyed the Jet Ski waiting for him. It was a loan from Lance and his brother—when they weren't manning their ice cream shop, they were big Jet Skiers. In the summertime, like normal people.

Not many were crazy enough to go Jet Skiing in the dead of winter, but tradition was tradition.

Lance was grinning when he handed over the key. The kid was facing a virtual death sentence with his cystic fibrosis, but he knew how to enjoy life. He'd lavishly decorated the Jet Ski with Christmas lights. Sawyer had helped him, and both had promised that everything was battery operated and waterproof so Jax *probably* wouldn't get electrocuted.

Good to know his friends had his back.

Out on the water about two hundred yards, three shrimp boats waited, also lavishly—aka garishly—decorated, ready for him to escort them in parade-like fashion. "Good times," Lance said and grinned.

Jax turned his face upward. Lots of clouds, but no snow or rain. That was good. But it was forty-eight degrees, so "good" was relative. He pulled on the thick, waterproof fisherman gear the shrimpers wore so at least he wouldn't freeze off any vital parts.

The crowd woo-hoo'd as if he was stripping instead of putting on gear, and he rolled his eyes. Looking out into the faces, he locked gazes with Maddie.

She shook her head. Obviously, she wasn't over the whole lawyer thing—not that he blamed her—and just as obviously, she thought he was crazy.

He'd have to agree there. He smiled at her. She didn't return it. Ouch. He'd have to work on fixing that, but onc problem at a time. Stepping into the water, he straddled the Jet Ski and took another look at the shore.

Ford and Sawyer were grinning. So was Chloe.

Bloodthirsty friends.

Maddie had her hand over her mouth, so he wasn't exactly sure what her expression was now. He hoped it was sympathy, and he also hoped that he could get that to work in his favor in a little bit when he needed warming up.

As he'd imagined, the next ten minutes passed in a frozen blur as he rode the Jet Ski and led the shrimp parade. Then he was back on shore, being warmly greeted and wrapped in blankets. Sandy shoved a mic into his hand and a piece of paper. The crowd hushed with expectant hope.

"Eight hundred and fifty-six shrimp," Jax called out.

No one had guessed that exact amount, but one person had come close at 850. He accepted another piece of paper from Sandy with the winner's name. He read it silently and looked at Maddie, who stared back, thoughts closed but a little pissiness definitely showing.

Trying to convey both apology and self-deprication, he smiled at her. "Maddie Moore," he said to wild cheers.

Maddie's mouth fell open.

Chloe helpfully shoved her forward.

"But I didn't put any tickets in," Maddie said as Jax grabbed her hand in his and pulled her up onto the makeshift stage.

Ford and Sawyer were cracking up. So was Chloe, and Maddie narrowed her eyes at her. "How many tickets in my name did you enter?"

"Fifty."

"Me, too," Ford called out.

Sawyer grinned. "A hundred from me. Good cause and all."

Okay, Jax thought, so maybe sometimes his bloodthirsty friends came in handy.

"I entered my name one hundred times," Lucille called out, disappointment clear across her face. "Damn. Maybe next year..."

"*Kiss, kiss, kiss,*" chanted the crowd.

Jax had stopped shivering, but he still had some serious warming up to do. Both his own body, and Maddie, because her eyes were on him, cool and distant.

Yep, definitely needed some warming up. Kissing sounded like a great way to do that. Holding Maddie's very resistant gaze in his, he tugged her close, looking forward to this for the first time all day.

"You're freezing," Maddie whispered.

"Yes."

She sighed and slipped her arms around his waist, tipping her face up to his. "I'm still mad at you."

"I know." He stared down into her beautiful eyes and felt his heart catch with all the possibilities he felt, not to mention hope—an extremely new emotion for him. "I plan on changing your mind about me."

"Jax—"

"I'm sorry, Maddie. I'm sorry I didn't tell you sooner, but you have to know, I'm not a lawyer now. That was my past."

"I know."

"Kiss!" yelled the crowd.

Maddie fidgeted in his arms, clearly not thrilled with having an audience for this. He ran a slow hand up her throat before cupping her jaw, leaving his other hand low on her back in what he hoped was a soothing gesture. "You okay with this, Maddie?"

Surprising the hell out of him, she answered by cupping his icy face in her hands and going up on her tiptoes to reach him. He met her halfway, bending low to cover her mouth with his. He heard her suck in a breath and knew his lips were icy. Apologizing with a soft murmur, he changed the angle to get a better taste of her.

Then she surprised him again.

Her mouth opened for his, and the sweet kiss turned into something else, something sensuous and intense.

Heat exploded within him, melting all the iciness from the inside out.

Around them, the crowd whooped and hollered, and Maddie began to pull back, but he held her tight.

"Need a minute?" she whispered, a hint of humor behind the heat in her eyes as she brushed up against his erection.

"Maybe two—" He broke off with a jagged groan when she put her mouth to his ear. "Maddie, that's not helping."

But then she whispered something that did help.

"Just think," she whispered. "It could have been Lucille."

Ford was bartending, serving beer on tap to a line of customers. Jax, warmed up now, was behind the bar getting cups and restocking the alcohol. The booth was good for Ford because it made the Love Shack even more popular, which in turn was good for Jax because he owned the other half of the bar.

In fact, Jax coowned several businesses in town. It was what he'd done with his money when he'd come back to Lucky Harbor. He'd bought up properties in a sagging market to help the people who'd known and loved him all his life.

They were thankful, but he was the one who felt the gratitude. They'd welcomed him back, given him a sense of belonging when he'd so desperately needed it.

"Wake up," Tara said with a little wave in his face. She'd come to his end of the bar, away from the line and the crowds, and was looking at him expectantly. "Yeah, hi. I'm looking for a drink."

"The line's over there. I'm not serving, I'm just—"

She tapped the bar. "Listen, sugar. Lucille just asked me about the stick up my ass, okay? I need a drink pronto. Make it a double."

He grimaced. "Beer, wine, or eggnog?"

"Well, hell. Wine."

Jax poured her a very full glass and handed it over, watching as she tossed it back like a shot of Jack. "Tara."

"Yeah?"

"You have to tell her."

Tara stared at him, then sat and dropped her head to the bar. "I'm going to need more alcohol for this. And something far stronger than wine."

Jax reached beneath the bar for a shot glass and a bottle of Jack that Ford had squirreled down there for... hell, he had no idea.

"Bless your heart," Tara said fervently as he poured her two fingers.

"You can't keep this from Maddie any longer."

"Watch me."

Jax shook his head. "When Phoebe asked me to draw up the blind trust five years ago, she also asked me for a promise. That you be protected at all costs."

"Not me." Tara shut her eyes. "My secret. She wanted my *secret* protected." Her eyes flew open. "Which means you *can't* tell." She sounded relieved. "You can't, you promised—"

"But *you* didn't," he said.

"Jax."

Who'd have thought that a promise to a dead woman would result in betraying a person he'd come to care

for so deeply? "I don't break my promises, Tara. Ever."
Not to mention professional confidentiality. "But when
Phoebe put all her liquid assets into that blind trust—"

"It left her in a precarious position when she needed
cash. And then you gave her the loan against the inn."
Tara's eyes filled with misery. "I never meant for either
of you to have to be in that position—"

"I know," he said quietly. "But now I'm sitting on *two*
secrets from a dead woman. Secrets that aren't fair to
either of your sisters."

"You care about Maddie."

"Yes, I do."

"A lot." She leaned in and looked deep into his eyes.
"She's not just a quick lay to you."

Hadn't been for a while now, the knowledge of which
had pretty much sneaked up on him. "You have to find
a way to tell her," he repeated softly. "Or I'll find a way
for you."

Tara stared at him, then thrust out her glass.

He obligingly refilled it, and she drank it down with a
shudder. "I haven't told anyone," she whispered. "Ever."

"This isn't just anyone. It's Maddie. She deserves
to know what you're holding back and why. And she
deserves to know the domino effect of it all, the inn, the
loan, the trust, all of it."

Tara closed her eyes and let out a long, slow breath.
"I'm just so...ashamed."

Understanding that all too well, he covered her hand
with his. "You were just a kid, Tara. You got in over your
head and paid dearly. There's no shame in that. You're
giving it more power by keeping it a secret."

"I know." She pulled her scarf closer around her neck.

It was green and sparkly, and very, very crooked. "She's making you one now," she said, seeing where his gaze had gone. "It's multicolored. And ugly as sin, bless her heart. I need another shot, sugar."

He poured, then watched her toss that back, as well. "You okay?"

"Fan-fucking-tastic."

"Liar."

Tara blew out a breath. "She made me this scarf with love, and lots of it, even though I'm the one who stresses her out when I fight with Chloe."

"So stop fighting with Chloe."

"She wants us all to be together." She closed her eyes and pushed the empty shot glass his way. "Here in this town where I made my biggest mistake."

"Maybe it's time to stop looking at it as a mistake. There's got to be *something* you like about being here, or you'd have left when you had the chance."

She stared down at the scarf, fingering the yarn. "I've been cooking."

"And damn well. I'm partial to those bacon bleu cheese burgers, myself."

"I am good," she said, looking both proud and a little surprised. "And somehow I agreed to work at the café and stay for the rest of the month, which is crazy, given how badly I want to be anywhere other than here. I'm working at Eat Me Café, for God's sake." Lifting her head, she leveled her baffled gaze on his. "Let me repeat that. *I work at a café called Eat Me.* What kind of idiot does that make me?"

"The good-sister kind," he said. "Tell her, Tara."

She closed her eyes, then opened them. They were

shiny now, and he feared that she was going to cry. But he should have known better.

"I can't, Jax," she said. "Not yet. I'm not ready."

He let out a long breath. Not what he'd wanted to hear. He ached for Maddie, ached for what he was beginning to feel for her, knowing that they'd all held so much back from her. Taking Tara's shot glass away, he poured another glass with water.

"She wants things we can't give her, Jax. She wants us to be a family. I don't know anything about family."

"You're wearing the scarf she made for you," he pointed out. "That seems like a sisterly thing to do."

"She's been so alone. Her father's a good man, but he's a set designer. She spent most of her childhood on location, in the makeup and hair trailer or the production office. Her friends are all transient by the very nature of her job, changing from one project to the next. None of them have called her that I can tell. Her closest friend was her boss, and he dropped her like a bad habit when she got laid off due to the...situation." She put her hand over his, making him realize he was squeezing the bottle of Jack with white knuckles. "He wasn't the one who hurt her physically," she said softly.

"Someone did," he said flatly. "Someone hurt her plenty."

Tara nodded and sipped her water. "Past tense, though. She's getting stronger. You should have seen her giving poor old Mr. Jenkins what-for when he tried to rent another boat this morning." She smiled fondly. "She got all up in his grill, made him sign the form at her desk and say please and everything."

He would have enjoyed seeing that. "She was down

a quart in self-esteem and confidence when she first got here."

"And that's changing, in good part thanks to you." She stared into her glass. "She wants to make a go of this place. Only a complete bitch would turn her down."

"Then don't turn her down."

Chapter 17

♥

"Learn from others' mistakes. You don't have enough time to make them all yourself."
PHOEBE TRAEGER

A few days later, Maddie headed into the tiny laundry room of the inn carrying a load of rags and towels. As an afterthought, she added in her filthy sneakers.

"That's a pretty flimsy excuse to get some dryer therapy," Tara said, folding her clean clothes into perfect piles.

"Dryer therapy?"

"Sugar, everyone knows the shoes-in-the-dryer trick. But the dryer's got nothin' on the spin cycle." She gave a wicked smile and left.

Maddie shook her head, then added detergent. While the load ran, she padded to the linen closet to continue cataloguing sheets and towels on the computer for inventory purposes. She'd downloaded several new programs designed specifically for running a small inn and was having more fun than she'd thought possible organizing and modernizing the place. Both Tara and Chloe were amazed and thrilled at her skills but baffled as to the happiness it gave her to organize.

That was okay. She didn't understand enjoying cooking or practicing yoga or making spa treatments, either. Hell, she barely enjoyed *using* the spa treatments.

She glanced at her watch. For two days running, Ford had been giving her boating lessons. He was teaching her about all the marina's equipment, how to use and care for it, but her favorite part had been learning what *stern* and *stem* meant.

Take that, Mr. Jenkins.

Jax was still building their new vanities at his shop, so he'd not been around during the day. She realized he was giving her the space he thought she wanted. But she'd come here to Lucky Harbor not wanting her past to count against her—which meant she had no right to count Jax's against him.

That was logic.

Her heart wasn't feeling so logical. She knew that Alex's law degree wasn't what made him an abusive asshole, and a lying one at that.

Jax hadn't lied, but he had held back. She'd be the liar if she said that it didn't bother her.

But then there was the biggest problem: was she ready to trust herself again with a man? Blowing out a breath, she went back to the laundry room to check on the loud clunking sound coming from the washer. Her tennis shoes. Tara's words floated in her head—*the dryer's got nothing on the spin cycle.*

Suddenly it hit her what Tara had meant. Surely she couldn't—could she? She glanced out the small window. No cars in the yard. She was alone.

As usual.

She stared at the shuddering washer and bit her lip. Then she hopped up on it. Just to disprove the theory, of course.

Wow.

Gripping the sides of the machine tightly as the ride began, she had to admit that Tara had been on to something.

The thing had great rhythm.

Eighteen minutes later, she shuddered in brief ecstasy then slumped back against the wall. Eyes closed, she stayed there catching her breath. Not nearly as good as Jax's fingers—or other parts—but it had definitely taken the edge off—

The washer suddenly stopped.

In the jarring silence, she opened her eyes. Jax stood in front of her as if she'd conjured him up, his finger on the off button.

Oh, God. Arousal and embarrassment warred for space inside her, but she managed both with equal aplomb—she was nothing if not an excellent multitasker. "How long have you been there?"

He stroked a damp curl off her forehead and pressed a single soft kiss to the pulse racing at the base of her throat. "Just got there. You okay?"

Lord, the things he could do to her with those lips. "Y—yes."

"Sure?"

"Uh-huh." She tried to look innocent. Like maybe she always just sat around. On a washer. While it was running. "Why?"

"Because you're all breathless and a little sweaty." His

eyes were darkening, his voice lowering in timbre. "And you're sitting on a washer."

"Well, look at that, I am. There's a perfectly good reason, actually."

"Yeah?" he asked huskily.

"Yeah." She bit her lower lip. "Except I don't want to say."

He looked at her for a long moment, his eyes hot enough to fry her brain. Bracketing her hips with a fist on either side of her, he ran his tongue along the outer shell of her ear, his voice soft and thick. "Was this one of those solo expeditions, Maddie?"

"No." She closed her eyes and shivered when he lightly bit her earlobe. *Oh, God.* "Maybe."

He groaned, and she drew in a shuddery breath. "And other than you, it's my most successful expedition in a long time."

He let out a soft bark of laughter and ran his thumb along her lower lip until her mouth trembled open, then leaned in for a kiss. "There's nothing wrong with solo," he murmured against her mouth. "But *not* solo is preferable."

"Oh," she breathed, trembling as he ran his hands down her body, his fingers grazing the sides of her breasts, then her hips and thighs.

"Are you still thinking, Maddie? About us? Still taking a step back?"

She stared up at him, wanting him more than her next breath, but... but. He'd held back, and she couldn't help the feeling that there was more.

"Ball's in your court," he said, and before she could finish catching her breath, he hit the power button. The clunking started up again, and she let out an involuntary gasp, gripping the sides of the washer for all she was worth.

Flashing her a slow, heated smile, he left her alone.

Two weeks. Maddie had been in Lucky Harbor for two weeks, and they'd been the best fourteen days of her life. Now she had two weeks left until Christmas to do what she had to do.

All along, she'd hoped that she'd be able to convince Tara and Chloe to give the inn a real shot.

She'd believed she could.

But that belief had just died with one shake of her loan officer's head.

Denied.

With a rough sigh, she left the bank, got into her car, and dropped her head to the steering wheel. She had the start of a headache pounding behind her right eye, her stomach was in knots, and the interior of her car felt like it was closing in on her as the loan officer's words echoed in her brain.

I'm sorry, Ms. Traeger, but you've been turned down for the refinancing. In today's economy, we have to work up against tougher regulations and qualifications, and you and your sisters didn't qualify.

Didn't qualify...

You're a loser...

Okay, so she hadn't said that last part, but Maddie had felt like a loser. Dammit, they'd needed that loan, both for the renovations and to get the inn up and running.

Not to mention paying off the credit card debt the three of them were racking up.

A shuddery sigh escaped her, but she refused to cry. *Couldn't* cry. She hadn't told her sisters that she'd had the bank meeting this morning. They thought they wouldn't be hearing until the end of the week.

Now she was glad she hadn't told them. Mostly because she wasn't quite sure they'd be as devastated that it was over.

She pulled out her cell and called her dad. She had no idea why, other than she needed to hear the voice of someone who loved her.

"Hey, sweetie," he yelled into the phone, sirens and screaming in the background. "How are you?"

"Dad?" Her heart stopped. "What's going on, are you okay?"

"I'm terrific. I'm on a set in New Orleans, filming a horror flick."

"Oh." Like a dope she nodded, even though he couldn't see her. His voice helped though, a lot. "Miss you."

"Well, then come on out here. We could always use another hand."

The thought was oddly tempting. "I might do that." Since she'd be homeless soon enough.

They spoke for a few more minutes, and then she hung up without telling him about the mess she'd made of her life.

And her heart...

God, she needed some chips. An entire bag. With a sigh, she drove to the inn, but neither sister was there, and Chloe's Vespa was gone. Turning around, Maddie headed to the café and found Tara working the lunch shift.

"Go away," Tara said from the chef's window. "I'm snowed under."

Okay, so that took care of telling Tara now. "I need something warm and fattening." *To ease the hot ball of anxiety choking the air out of me.* "And if you remind me that my jeans are finally fitting, I'm going to knit you another scarf."

To her credit, Tara merely nodded. "I've got just the thing—Life Sucks Golf Balls casserole. Eggs, bacon, cheese, and veggies for a healthy touch."

"But it's a *casserole.*" Maddie shuddered. "The ingredients will all be touching."

"Don't be a child."

"*Touching,* Tara."

"Yes, the ingredients are all touching, good Lord, but I'll put the bread waaaaay on the other side of the plate, okay? Maybe even on its *own* plate if you stop your bellyachin'. Now sit down and shut up, and I'll bring it out to you."

"Fine. But I also need hot chocolate and extra whipped cream. *Extra* extra." Because whipped cream was a solve-all. It would ease the dull throb of bitter discontent and swirling anxiety in her gut. She was counting on it.

In a few minutes, she was inhaling the amazing casserole and simultaneously spraying more whipped cream into her hot chocolate when she felt a shiver of awareness race down her spine.

Jax.

Already horrifyingly close to losing it, she didn't dare look up when his boots and denim-clad legs came into her line of vision. "How?" she asked, nose deep into her hot chocolate. "How do you always know?"

"That you're OD-ing by whipped cream? I didn't. I have a business meeting with a potential client." He nudged her over and slid into the booth next to her. She felt his long, searching look, then his warm palm sliding along the back of her neck at the same time as he pressed a hard thigh to hers, making her want to crawl into his lap and inside his opened jacket.

Instead, she squirted whipped cream directly into her mouth. She swallowed the mass and licked her lips, then happened a glance at Jax.

Whose eyes were locked on her mouth.

It was interesting, watching him watch her. Her life was in the toilet. Circling the drain, in fact, and he still wanted her. She hadn't thought that could matter, or that it could help, but somehow it did. "Thought you had a meeting."

"He can wait a minute. Talk to me, Maddie."

"About what?" She shook the nearly empty can of whipped cream. "How I just ran out of my drug of choice, or that I failed at yet something else?"

Her only defense at letting that last part slip was sugar overload. She read the label on the whipped cream, but nowhere did it say that mainlining this substance might cause low self-esteem and diarrhea of the mouth.

He took the can from her fingers. "What do you think you failed at?"

Life. She closed her burning eyes and swallowed past a thick throat. The beginning of a headache had turned into an entire percussion band sitting on her right lobe. "I need some chips," she whispered. "Layered in greasy, salty goodness. It soothes being rejected." Downing her hot chocolate, she went to stand, but Jax grabbed her wrist.

"Rejected?"

Rejected. Stomped on. Decimated… "You have a meeting."

"I do," he said, but didn't let go. She tried to tug free, but he reeled her in, then lightly kissed the corner of her mouth.

"Whipped cream," he explained.

She drew a shaky breath. She wanted him, bad, but even that wouldn't soothe the ache from knowing her dream was in its death throes. "I think your client is waving at you," she whispered.

He turned and eyed the man two booths over trying to get his attention. Jax nodded his head and held up a finger, and then turned back to Maddie. "Talk to me," he repeated firmly.

"The bank turned us down for the refinancing." Just saying it out loud made her want to be sick, but that might have been all the junk food she'd consumed. She shot a guilty look in the direction of the kitchen. "And I still have to tell Tara and Chloe, but we should cancel the new interior doors we ordered. Obviously, we need to put in the new windows when they come and fix the roof to sell, and I'll finish the painting, but little else. And your client's about to fall out of his chair trying to overhear us. You have to go."

"Maddie."

Oh, God, that low, husky voice filled with all that empathy was going to break her into a million little pieces. *Not here,* she told herself sternly. *You will not fall apart in a public place again.* Besides, this time there was no one to dump coffee on.

"Gotta go," she choked out. She'd used up all the fake strength in her arsenal. She needed to reboot, that was all. Pulling free, she got up and walked out.

•   •   •

Back at the inn, Chloe's Vespa was still gone, so Maddie headed directly into the marina office. If the ship was going down, the books were going to be balanced when it did.

Less than a minute later, she heard the marina building door open and shut, and then the slide of the lock, and she looked up into Jax's caramel eyes. Her heart skipped a beat. "What happened to your meeting?" she asked.

"Suddenly canceled."

By him. God. She was costing him work left and right. "Jax—"

He came around the desk and leaned back against it, facing her, with his long legs stretched out in front of him. "You can try to get a revolving line of credit as a second mortgage. Or try another bank. Or your current lender, who's far more likely to—"

"If we go to the current lender, they'll know we're in trouble."

"Maddie, in this market, *everyone's* in trouble, not just you. This doesn't have to be over." His voice was low and serious. "I can help—"

"No." She swallowed hard and shook her head. "Thank you. It's incredibly kind of you to even think it, but—"

"Jesus, would you stop trying to figure this out all on your own? You're not on your own, not anymore, not unless you want to be."

Suddenly uncomfortably aware that he'd never gotten frustrated with her before, she stared at him.

He stared right back, unwaveringly. "Maddie, remember when you listed all your faults for me?"

"Jax—"

"*Do you?*"

"Yes," she said tightly, hating that her stomach had knotted at the first sign of his frustration. He wouldn't hurt her, she told herself. He'd never hurt her.

"I'm going to guess you're still using a night-light for the closet monsters. And I know you still don't like your food touching." He cocked his head. "What else was there?"

"*The Sound of Music,*" she said, then rolled her eyes. "And the burping the alphabet."

"You forgot one."

She'd forgotten many. On purpose. But hey, if he wanted to think she had only one more fault, she wasn't about to dispel that notion.

"You forgot that you're the most mule-headed, stubborn-assed woman on the planet." Crouching at her side, he put his hands on the arms of her chair and turned her to face him. She saw that his frustration was with the situation, not her, that he was indeed looking at her with warmth and affection.

"I can help," he said. "By extending a second loan, or helping you apply to another bank."

His offer tightened her throat so that she could barely breathe. "I don't want to think about that right now."

"What do you want to think about?"

"Maybe about inhaling some chips."

He nodded, letting her lighten the mood. "Except that might clash with all the whipped cream."

"True," she said. "I could work on another crooked scarf."

Holding tight to her chair, the very sexy, gorgeous man shook his head, and she worried that he was going to force this conversation that she didn't want to have.

But she shouldn't have. "I have something better," he said very quietly, his eyes heated.

Everything within her quivered at that. He was close enough to block out the sharp fluorescent light with his shoulders, shoulders that were broad enough to weather whatever burdens came his way.

And hers.

And he could make everything go away for a while, help her let go of all that was wrong, and embrace the one thing that was right.

Him. *He* was right, she thought, staring at his hard chest. It would be warm to the touch and strong enough to offer comfort and safety while making her feel desire.

He slid his hands up her legs and settled them on her waist, just beneath her sweater. His hands were big and callused and felt so damn good on her bare skin.

"You're tense again."

"Yes." She bit her lower lip, but the words escaped anyway. "You fixed me last time. You're good at fixing things."

"Yes. Anything you need, Maddie."

That. That right there was another thing that made him different from the men in her past. He was willing to put her first. They'd known each other two and a half weeks, and he'd do anything for her, and at the knowledge, a powerful emotion surged through her. Desperately afraid to trust it, she shoved it aside, forgetting it entirely when he slid his hands up, taking her sweater up, too, up and over her head.

This left her in just a plain white bra, but when she'd dressed this morning, she hadn't exactly planned on being seduced.

Jax's eyes dipped downward, darkening as he took in the soft curve of her breasts, not appearing at all bothered by the plainness of the bra. This was good. She sucked in her stomach, but he didn't take his gaze any farther south.

In fact, he lifted his head and looked straight into her eyes. "You're so beautiful, Maddie." And then he kissed her.

Yes. Oh, yes, this was definitely going to go a long way toward making her feel better, and when he deepened the kiss, stroking her tongue with his, she slid her hands beneath his shirt to touch his warm skin. "Here?" she whispered.

"No." He lifted her from the chair and set her on the desk. "Here." Eyes hot, he spread her legs with a big hand on the inside of each of her thighs, then pressed close. When he slowly ground his erection against her, she nearly lost it. She tore at the button on his jeans and was going for his zipper when he captured her hands. His mouth skimmed her jaw, heading toward her ear, his hands dropping to her hips to hold her still so that she couldn't climb him like a tree. "Slow this time," he murmured against her skin, letting go of her hands to stroke her body, his fingers teasing her nipples. "We have as long as we want—"

Yes, but she didn't want to think. She needed the oblivion. *Now*. Maybe she wouldn't have thought of getting it in quite this way, but he'd started it, and she was on board. So completely on board. Again she reached out, this time getting his jeans opened and…oh, yes, her hands inside to wrap around him, so big and hot and hard—

"Maddie."

She tipped up her head to say he'd better not be thinking of stopping just as he raised his hand toward her face.

In a completely involuntary motion, she flinched back.

He went still. For a single, horrified beat, she did the same. Then she closed her eyes and thunked her head back to the desk, swamped by embarrassment, unease, and frustration. "I'm sorry, I have no idea where that came from. None."

Calm, silent, he leaned over her and slid a hand to the nape of her neck, cupping the back of her aching head, probably checking to make sure she hadn't cracked it.

She could have told him the only thing that was cracked was her damn, worthless heart. Horrified, she kept her eyes closed. She trusted him, maybe more than any man she'd ever been with, so she really couldn't explain why she'd—

"Maddie, look at me."

When she talked herself into opening her eyes, he shook his head. "Don't be sorry. Don't ever be sorry."

How could she not be? Because a minute ago she'd been half an inch from getting her hands on him, and now...now he was moving away from her, easing out from between her legs.

"We're not doing this." His voice was quiet. Terrifyingly gentle. "Not like this, not again."

"Jax—I know you wouldn't hurt me."

"No, you don't. Not yet. But you're getting there. That's not why we're not—"

"*Then why?*"

A muscle in his jaw bunched, as if it was costing him to back off. It sure as hell was costing her; her entire body was humming, throbbing.

"Because I just realized I don't want to be your escape. I want more. Yeah," he said when she gaped at him. "I don't know when or how exactly that happened, but there it is." He looked at her for a long beat, clearly waiting for her to say something, like maybe she felt the same, but she couldn't say a word with her gut lodged in her throat. He nodded and handed over her sweater before zipping up his jeans and turning to the door, where he paused.

She held her breath. Surely he wasn't really going to walk away. He was going to come back to her, and they'd laugh this off and agree they were just playing...

Any second now...

"Take care of yourself, Maddie."

She blinked at the sound of the door shutting. It sounded pretty damn final.

Apparently, they were not playing. Not even close.

And how had he done that so calmly, when everything within her still trembled and quivered? Whipping around, she grabbed the first thing she could—a file—and chucked it at the door where he'd vanished. It made it only about two feet before it opened and fluttered uselessly to the floor. Dammit. And damn him.

"Fine," she said out loud. But it wasn't fine, and she had the shakes to prove it, not to mention the churning in her stomach. She took in the desk, the organized mess she'd been working so hard on. She needed something to do *now*. Something big. Something new.

Her gaze fell on the key hooks lining the wall behind the desk. Specifically onto the fishing-boat keys. Snatching them in her fingers, she flew out of the building and headed down the dock. It was time for a solo expedition of a different kind.

With Ford's patient, calm voice in her mind, she sailed out of the marina. The wind was low, and the swells even lower. Because the skies were overcast, and also because she wasn't stupid, she stayed very close to the shore. It was a smooth ride, and it felt incredible to do it by herself, for herself.

When she got cold, she turned back to the marina. She did have a bad moment trying to dock. But she managed, and if she accidentally hit the side of the boat hard enough to jar her teeth, that was okay. That's what rental boats were for.

She tied up the boat, hung up the keys, and nodded. She'd done it. She'd actually done it. And if she could do that, she could do anything. Maybe even have a relationship without self-destructing it.

Chapter 18

♥

*"Always get the facts first.
You can distort them later."*
PHOEBE TRAEGER

Today would have been Mom's birthday."

Both Tara and Maddie stopped eating when Chloe said this casually over blueberry pancakes. "It's true. She'd have been fifty-five today. She was looking forward to this one because it meant she could get a senior discount in some places. She always wanted to be able to get that damn discount."

Tara looked at Maddie. "Did you know?"

Maddie shook her head. She hadn't been able to think of anything but how Jax had looked walking away from her. "Whenever I asked her how old she was, she said she was ageless. She celebrated Jerry Garcia's birthday as her own."

Tara let out a reluctant smile. "That's what she always told me, too."

"Grandma showed me Mom's birth certificate," Chloe said. "That's how I know."

Maddie dropped her jaw. "You have her birth certificate? Where was she born?"

"Here." Chloe smiled. "Well, in Seattle, which is close enough, right? She grew up in Lucky Harbor, from what I heard."

Thinking about Phoebe going to school here and having a home made Maddie wistful. She was working hard on not resenting how little she'd known about her mother, or how her father hadn't encouraged her to breach that emotional and physical distance. Instead she was trying to concentrate on the here and now that Phoebe had given her.

She'd told her sisters about yesterday's bank rejection. Surprisingly enough, they'd been disappointed. Or at least they'd been kind enough to pretend. They'd agreed to find another lending institution, though Maddie was fairly certain neither Tara nor Chloe expected that to happen. In the meantime, they were going to stick out the month, finish up the bare-essential renovations, and then put the place on the market. Maddie hoped to open the inn and run it until it sold. Hell, who knew, maybe it'd do so well they would miraculously turn it around.

Worst-case scenario, she'd go back to LA and try to get a job through her dad's connections, but she hoped it didn't come to that. She was doing her damnedest not to think about it, not yet anyway. A picture of Jax flashed in her mind—the other thing she was trying not to think about—and her heart pinged, but she hoisted her glass of orange juice into the air. "To you, Mom."

Tara and Chloe looked at her like she was nuts, but she gestured to their glasses, and they obediently picked them up. "I'd love to celebrate who you were," Maddie said to the ceiling. "But I didn't know you well enough. So instead, I think I'll celebrate who we are because of you."

"I like that," Tara said. "Here's to letting go of regrets and even resentments. Here's to what might have been, and to what we will be."

"Happy birthday, Mom," Chloe said quietly, for once her eyes devoid of the mocking sarcasm.

"Happy birthday," Tara and Maddie echoed.

"Oh, and happy birthday to Jerry, too," Chloe added, and they all laughed. It was a rare moment of peace and solidarity as they clicked their glasses together.

Chloe knocked her orange juice back and set the glass on the table. "So, Tara, Maddie wants to tell you something—you snore."

"Excuse me?" Tara's eyes narrowed. "I do not."

"Yes, you do. Like a buzz saw. Or a grizzly bear with sleep apnea. Tell her, Maddie."

Maddie winced. "Okay, well—"

"You did *not* just compare my breathing to a grizzly bear," Tara said to Chloe.

"And/or a buzz saw."

Maddie sighed and reached for her knitting. Solidarity was officially over.

At dawn, Jax gave up on the pretense of sleep and got out of bed. It was ironic that he'd come back to Lucky Harbor to lead the lazy, kick-back life he'd always wanted, and yet it wasn't in him to be lazy.

Unlike Izzy, who was sleeping like…well, a dog. "Time to get up."

Izzy squeezed her eyes tight.

"We're going for a run."

Jax could have sworn that she shook her head. With a sigh, he got up and ran alone. When he got back, Izzy was waiting for him on the porch. "Did you cook breakfast?" he asked her.

She looked at him balefully, like *Dude, no opposable thumbs, or I totally would have.*

Jax showered and dressed, then headed into his office, where Jeanne handed him coffee and left him to himself. Three hours later, she reappeared.

"I'm all caught up. I'm going shopping for some lingerie."

Jax winced. "And I want to know this why?"

"Because maybe you'd like me to pick up a present for somebody."

"Like who?"

"Like the cute curly-haired Traeger sister. The one you're in a fight with."

"What?" He shook his head and stared at her. "How could you possibly know that?"

She smiled. "I didn't, but you're all broody and mopey-looking. What did ya do? Don't tell me, it was something stupidly male, right? Should I get black and lacy, or white and sheer?"

Jesus. "You should mind your own damn business."

"Well, that's no fun." She came close, gave him a sympathetic look, and kissed his cheek. "You could solve it the way Steve solves all of our fights."

He sighed. "How does he do that?"

"Easy. Just admit you were wrong. His always being wrong really works for us." She gently patted his arm and left him alone.

But it didn't feel wrong to want Maddie to see him as more than an escape. It felt…weak and vulnerable, which he really hated.

But not wrong.

Stop thinking, you idiot. He moved through the office and out the back door. The morning was frosty, the cold biting into his skin, reminding him that winter had arrived. Instead of going into his wood shop, he loaded himself and Izzy into his Jeep and went for a drive.

And found himself at the inn.

It looked deserted. He let himself in, noting that it was colder inside than outside. The heater hadn't been turned on today. He walked the ground floor, the sanded but not-yet-finished floors creaking beneath his boots as he took in the walls that still had to be painted, and the bathrooms waiting for their new vanities. He felt a surge of frustration.

It didn't have to be like this.

When something thudded above him, he took the stairs two at a time but found the second floor empty. He hit pay dirt in the attic. The room ran the entire length of the inn. At the moment, it held most of the furniture from the other floors that had been moved to finish the floors. There were tarps everywhere and also stacks of boxes filled with God knew what, dating back to Maddie's grandparents' era.

It was the approximate temperature of the Arctic Circle up here, thanks to the icy air and the equally icy glance Maddie sent his way. She was sitting on the floor, holding her BlackBerry as she went through the box in front of her.

"Hey," he said, risking frostbite by moving farther into the room.

She didn't answer.

"What are you doing?"

"Trying to figure out what pieces of furniture are worth selling to cover this month's bills."

Ah, hell. "Maddie—"

"This is a no-talking zone."

When he didn't leave, she sighed, her expelled air coming out in a puffy mist, testament to just how cold it was. "Fine." She jerked her head toward an unidentifiable pile in the far corner. "Can you peek under that tarp and tell me if you see an antique walnut hall bench? I know we had one. Someone's selling a match to it on eBay for three hundred fifty dollars. If I could get half that, I'd be happy."

He moved toward the pile. "You shouldn't be working up here. It's too cold."

"Turns out financial anxiety is a great way to keep warm."

He hated that she was so stressed about money. "Where are your sisters?"

"Drove into Seattle to check out two antique consignment shops to see if they'd be interested in working with us."

"If you sell all the furniture, what will you use if you reopen?"

She shot him a look that said she was worried about his IQ and went back to working on her BlackBerry. There were two spots of color high on her cheeks. Her eyes were shiny, too shiny. And her lush, warm, giving mouth was tight and grim.

That's when it hit him. She wasn't mad at him.

She was hurt. "Maddie."

"Go away. I hate everyone right now, and I'm pretty sure that includes you."

"No, you don't."

"Yes, I do. I really do."

"I could change your mind about me."

"I have no doubt, but try it and you'll be walking funny tomorrow."

He couldn't help it, he laughed, and she swiveled her head toward him. "This isn't funny! I wanted you, and you walked away!"

"I wanted you to want *me,* not just the—"

"You're not just an escape, not to me. I'm just a little slower at this than you are."

He looked into her eyes and saw the truth. Remembering Jeanne's words, he shook his head. "I was wrong to push."

"Wow. A man who can say the W word. What else do you have up your sleeve?"

"I don't know. You'll have to look yourself."

She arched a brow. "Strip."

Not much surprised Jax anymore, but this did, and he laughed again as he willingly pulled off his shirt.

She stared at his chest, then his tattoos. Her eyes went a little glazed, but she lifted a shoulder, feigning indifference.

Indifference his ass.

"I've seen you without your shirt before," she pointed out coolly, then murmured so quietly he would have missed it if he hadn't leaned in, "And maybe I'd rather see you without your pants."

"You've seen me without those, too."

"You'd argue with a woman on the very edge?"

He nearly laughed again but recovered quickly, especially since she was still giving him that eat-shit-and-die look. But at least she *was* looking. And the rosiness of her cheeks was no longer about hurt or embarrassment. Mission half accomplished.

Holding her gaze in his, he tore open the buttons on his Levi's, held his breath to brace for the cold, then shoved them down to his thighs.

Her eyes locked in on his forest green knit boxers. Slowly, she set down her BlackBerry and then, just as slowly, rose to her feet. "I'm trying to hate you."

"But you can't."

"I could. With some more time."

"Then I'll change your mind," he said.

"But I'm stubborn, remember?"

"Yes, but I'm *very* persuasive."

She nibbled on her lower lip and stared at him, definitely not hating him if her hardened nipples were any indication.

"You're..." She gestured to his erection. "Um."

"Yeah." He was just as shocked as she. It was fucking freezing in here.

"I thought it was supposed to shrink in the cold," she said, eyes on "it."

He opened his mouth, then shut it again. She was the only person on earth who could render him speechless. While he stood there, shirt off, pants at his thighs, she stood up and tore off her own sweatshirt.

She wore a pale blue satin bra that barely contained her full breasts. As he soaked in that mouthwatering sight, she unbuttoned and unzipped her jeans and shoved them down. "Crap," she said and glanced up at him.

"Okay, keep in mind I didn't plan on a striptease today. I've got to learn to plan ahead."

If she was talking about the fact that her underwear was a purple lace thong instead of a match to her bra, he could care less. Combined they were going to give him a brain aneurysm.

She tried to kick her pants off, but they got caught on her boot. "And some practice wouldn't hurt, either."

He laughed, and she grumbled, turning away from him to bend over to untie her bootlaces.

And abruptly his amusement was gone, replaced by a wave of sheer, unadulterated lust. It was her cute little thong's fault, the one bisecting her sweet heart-shaped ass and shooting the temperature in the room straight into the stratosphere. "Maddie—" His voice was gruff and hoarse. Probably from blood loss.

She was still fighting with her shoelaces. "Yeah?"

Before he could answer, her cell rang from the floor about five feet in front of her. Shifting gears, she crawled forward.

Yeah. He was going to have an aneurysm. He could feel it coming on.

"Can't," she said into her cell, still on her hand and knees. "I..." She shot him a look over his shoulder, her gaze again dipping down to the front of his tented boxers. "Gotta go." She disconnected with a tap of her thumb. Still staring at him, she paused. "We're in this freezing attic showing our...parts to each other."

"Yes."

"We need to grow up."

"Maybe. But not today."

She drew a breath, still staring at his erection. "Yesterday you said you wouldn't be my escape."

"That was a stupid statement by a very stupid man who wasn't thinking clearly."

"And you're thinking clearly now?"

"Yes. This isn't just sex between us. So if you want escape, and you want to use my body to do it, then I'm your willing victim."

"Magnanimous of you."

Done playing, he crooked his finger at her in the universal "come here" gesture.

She rose to her feet, took a step, and hit the floor with a heavy thud.

"Jesus." He surged toward her and dropped to his knees, pulling her up to face him. "You okay?"

She grimaced. "Tell me you have a clumsy dork fetish."

"Oh, I have a fetish." Her nipples appeared to be a fraction of an inch from breaking free of her bra. He slid his hands up her ribs, his thumbs rubbing over them. "For you. For everything about you."

She sucked in a breath.

"We have some more clothes to lose." He bent to work on untying her shoes, and then his. They kicked them off and then finally lost their pants.

"Maybe we should lose the underwear, too," she whispered and ran a finger over the front of his boxers, right down the length of him, making him groan and reach for her, just as the doorbell rang downstairs.

"I'm going to shoot somebody," Maddie said.

"Sawyer hates when people do that. It's a whole bunch of paperwork."

The doorbell rang again, and Maddie crawled to the window.

Jax stared at her ass and crawled forward, too, planning on tearing those cute little panties off with his teeth. Then he'd grip her hips and bury himself deep in one thrust. Yeah, and then—

"It's Lucille," she hissed. "I can't shoot Lucille."

"She'll go away." Bending, he put his mouth to her hip, then let his tongue snake beneath the string.

"But she's—" she whispered, slapping a hand to the window when he nipped at her with his teeth. "Oh, God."

"Give me a minute and you'll be saying 'Oh, Jax.'" He slid a hand up the inside of her leg, not stopping until he hit lace. "Spread your legs, Maddie," he said, kissing the back of her thigh.

She did just that, and then her other hand hit the glass, and then suddenly she stiffened, but not in a good way. "She sees me," she hissed. "She thinks I'm waving to her." She dropped to her knees and stared at him. "She knows you're here. Your Jeep's here. And I'm in the window without a shirt."

"She's a hundred and ten. There's no way she could see you clearly." He kissed her neck. "She'll go away."

"No, she won't." She batted at his hands as he went for the hook on her bra. "The last time you and I were seen together, our kiss on the pier was the talk of the town. This can't be the talk of the town. This," she said, giving him a poke with her elbow, "is just for you and me."

He blew out a breath and sat back on his heels as she pulled her jeans back on, covering up that sweet ass, jumping up and down a little to work them over her hips. Her breasts jiggled, and he watched as first one and then the other nipple struggled and then managed breakaway status. *Damn.*

She grabbed her sweatshirt and yanked it on, inside out, covering the best view he'd had all week. "*Crap.*" Yanking the shirt back off, she fumbled to right it, then noticed he was just standing there. "Get dressed!"

"Can you be this bossy when we get to a bed? Cuz it's turning me on."

She threw his shirt at him. "Hurry up! You're coming with me!"

"Yeah, now, see, I'd kind of hoped you'd be the one coming by now."

She groaned. "Stop teasing me!"

Lucille talked for eight minutes. Maddie lost track of what the conversation was about, struggling to nod and act as if she was following along—for *eight* long minutes. And for each and every single one of them, she was overwhelmingly aware of the big, tall, silent man standing behind the door, just out of view from Lucille, radiating heat and a sexual frustration that undoubtedly matched hers.

The old Maddie had gone with the flow. Had allowed others' needs to come before her own. "Lucille," she said suddenly. "I'm sorry. I'm really sorry, but I have to go."

Lucille looked puzzled, but she nodded. "Okay, dear. Just come by when you get a chance, and we can finish talking about the project."

"Sure thing. I will, I promise. The, uh, project sounds really worthwhile. A great project, as far as projects go."

She shut the door and closed her eyes. She felt Jax come up behind her, exuding testosterone and pheromones, the only project she was interested in.

A hand brushed aside her hair, and then she felt his mouth on her neck. Her head dropped back to his shoulder as his arm came around her, his hand running up her belly to cup her breast.

"I'm taking you home," he said in a thrillingly rough voice, his thumb brushing over her nipple before he took her hand firmly in his. "To my place."

She opened her mouth to say "Hell, yes," but he pushed her out the door ahead of him, barely giving her time to grab her purse, his big body giving her the bum's rush.

"Jax—"

"This," he said in a repeat of her own words, "is a no-talking zone."

"Lucille at twelve o'clock!" she hissed, jerking her head toward the yard, where Lucille was making her way to her car. Slowly.

"Shit." Jax yanked Maddie back inside as they watched Lucille *finally* get into her car.

"She's killing me," Jax muttered.

It took Lucille even longer to turn her car around and pull out. And then Jax was tugging Maddie down the steps, his long legs eating up the space, forcing her to run to keep up. Izzy loped alongside, ears perked up at the hope that something fun was about to happen. A laugh escaped Maddie, half nerves, half anticipation, and one hundred percent hunger.

At the Jeep, Jax pressed her up against the door and leaned in to kiss her, possessive and deep, as if he had to convince her that she wanted this as badly as he did.

Wrapping her arms around his neck, she plastered herself even closer. "Drive fast," she said and licked the rim of his ear.

He shuddered, then practically shoved her into the Jeep. They drove in silence across town, the only sound being her own heartbeat drumming in her ears. She was so worked up she nearly hit the roof when he touched her thigh. "That was anticipation," she said. "Not... you know."

"Good." He entwined their fingers and didn't speak again.

That worked for her. She couldn't have kept up her end of a conversation to save her life. Not as revved up as she was. Nope, the only thing going to fix this was a man-made orgasm.

A *Jax*-made orgasm.

Driving faster than the speed limit, he turned into a quiet neighborhood on the bluffs three hundred feet above the ocean. His house was the last on the street and the closest to the cliff.

Jumping out, she glanced at his view and stopped in shock. Deep blue ocean as far as she could see, sparkling from the sun's glow. "It's breathtaking," she whispered, taking a step toward it.

"Later. Much later," he said and dragged her inside, giving her nothing but a quick peekaboo hint of wide-open rooms, high wood-beamed ceilings, and gorgeous wood trim and floors before he had her in his bedroom. "I'm going to toss you onto the bed now and have my merry way with you," he said against her lips.

"*Oh*," she whispered, trembling in anticipation, already wet for him.

"Yes or no, Maddie."

"Yes. God, *yes*."

Before she'd even gotten the words out, he'd done just

as he'd promised. He'd picked her up and tossed her to the bed. Before she bounced, he was on her, the fire he'd ignited in the attic flaming back to life. Mouth on hers, he slid his hands beneath her shirt, his fingers teasing her nipples. She gasped, and he pulled back only long enough to peel her shirt over her head, and then his own.

She couldn't take her eyes off him.

He bent and kissed the curve of her breast that spilled out of her bra, and then suddenly even that barrier was gone. "Love your skin," he whispered against her nipple, flicking the pebbled peak with his hot tongue before sucking it hard into his mouth until she was writhing beneath him. "You're so soft."

"It's Chloe's lotions," she said inanely, and he huffed out a rough laugh against her.

"I'm pretty sure it's all you."

His voice couldn't get any lower or any sexier, and she felt like she could come from the sound of him alone. Then he upped the tension by sliding the tips of his fingers into her hip-hugging jeans. "Oh, my God," she whispered.

"I know."

She laughed breathlessly. "No, you don't understand—" She pushed at his chest until he lifted his head. "You got your hand in my pants!"

"Uh-huh." His expression was a mix of lust and amusement. "I was hoping to get even more than that."

Giddy, she grinned. "No, you did it without unbuttoning them. I think it's all that hauling of debris and chopping wood. I'm toning up!"

His eyes were dark and very, very hot. "And that turns you on?"

"Yes." She cupped his face and smiled. "But you turn me on more."

"Good. You turn me on, too." Taking her hand, he placed it over his erection to show her just how much. "We're done talking now. I have other plans for our mouths." To prove it, he tugged her jeans off and then rose off the bed to do the same with his.

Her breath caught at the sight of him in silhouette. Gorgeous. That went without saying. The air shuddered out of her when he bent and kissed her, low on her stomach as he hooked his thumbs in her panties and slowly tugged them down. "You're beautiful, Maddie."

While she melted, he made himself at home between her thighs, taking so long to look at the view in front of him, she squirmed. "Jax."

"If you could see from my point of view..." His broad shoulders nudging her legs wide, he bent and kissed an inner thigh, and she had one thought; *Please be as good at this as you are at everything else.*

Then he gently stroked her with his thumb and she had no more thoughts. With a groan, he ran his tongue over her wet, throbbing skin. She bit her lip and fisted her hands in his sheets, unable to stop from writhing beneath him.

Newsflash— he was indeed as good at this as he was at everything else.

"I love how you taste," he murmured, and when her hips rocked against him, he slid both hands beneath her bottom, holding her still for his ministrations. Quicker than she could have believed possible, she was quivering, on the very edge of an explosive orgasm, and—

And he paused.

"*What?*" she gasped.

Lifting his head, he met her gaze, his own glittering. "The last two times we even got to this spot, we were interrupted. I'm just waiting for it."

She gaped at him in disbelief, panting for breath as she sat up. "You *want* to be interrupted? Because I have to tell you, if we are, I'm going to scream at someone."

He flashed her a devastatingly wicked grin. "Better idea. *I'm* going to make you scream." With that outrageously confident statement, he leaned over her, using the fact that she'd sat up to his advantage. "Soon as I find all your sweet spots." He laved his tongue over a nipple, pressing her back down to the bed. "What you like..." He dipped his tongue into her belly button, then nipped at her hip, taking his cues from her reactions, which she couldn't seem to help.

"How about this?" he murmured, licking the spot where her leg met her body, lingering, taking his time while she shifted restlessly beneath him, trying to get him where she wanted him to go. "Maddie?"

"Y—yes, I like that."

"Good." He kissed her there, then brushed his lips over her mound. "This?" When she didn't answer, he lifted his head.

"*Yes!*"

Doing it again, he slid first one finger into her, and then another, stroking slowly.

She gasped his name.

"Good?"

"*Ohmigod,*" was all she could manage.

"Good," he decided and gently closed his teeth on her center.

She just about lifted off the bed, would have if he wasn't anchoring her with his body. "Jax. Jax, please..."

"Anything," he promised and sucked her into his mouth.

"Don't stop."

He didn't, not when her hands came up to tangle in his hair, not when she cried out and came, shuddering endlessly beneath him. When she was limp, he kissed his way up her still-quivering body.

She tightened her grip on him and kissed him back, feeling him hard and throbbing at her hip. "I need you inside me."

Reaching over her, he took a condom from his night-stand, groaning when she helped him roll it down his length. Then he entwined their fingers and brought their joined hands up to rest on either side of her face. Already cradled by her open thighs, he slid into her. She gasped, rocked to her very core by how good he felt filling her, and he went still. "No, don't stop," she whispered, barely recognizing her soft and throaty voice.

He dropped his forehead to hers, his eyes closing, clearly trying to give her a minute to adjust to him. Wrapping her legs around his waist, she arched up and felt herself soften for him.

"God, look at you," he whispered hoarsely. Squeezing their entwined fingers, he touched his lips to hers. "I love your smile."

She hadn't even been aware that she was smiling. But when she was with him like this, she felt sexy and wanted and beautiful, and on top of her world. And then he was moving with her, setting a pace that stole her breath and captured her heart. Freeing her hands from his, she threaded her fingers into his hair, holding his gaze, knowing her own was filled with shock and wonder.

This. *This* was what it felt like when it was right.

Jax banded his arms around her, sliding them beneath her, up her back to grip her shoulders. The movement pulled them closer, allowing him even deeper inside her, and she cried out, shuddering in pleasure. Her eyes started to drift closed, but he tangled a hand in her hair, tugging gently until she opened them again, allowing him to see everything, allowing her the same as she quivered and trembled against him.

He seemed to lose himself in her eyes. God knew she'd lost herself in his, and as she came, she took him with her for the free fall.

But in his arms, the landing was safe. She had a feeling that with him she'd always be safe.

Chapter 19

♥

*"Since it's the early worm that gets
eaten by the bird, sleep late."*
Phoebe Traeger

The sun was slanting much lower in the sky out Jax's bedroom window when Maddie opened her eyes and blinked into focus a well-defined, muscular chest. Tipping her head back, she met a pair of warm golden eyes that were looking pretty damn alert for a man who should have nothing left in the tank.

"I fell asleep," she said in surprise.

"Just for a little while." He was playing with a strand of her hair, wrapping the curl around and around his finger. "You okay?"

She knew why he asked. He'd seen her face that exact moment he'd pushed inside of her, the single sole heartbeat when her world had slammed to a halt on its axis.

Fear.

Not that he'd hurt her, never that. No, this fear hadn't been physical. Instead, she was afraid of the emotions he had awakened in her. Of what she could feel for him if she let herself.

Jax was on his side, holding her snugged up against him, one hand propping up his head, the other stroking her under the blanket he must have pulled up over them.

"I'm more than okay," she said.

"Then what was the look?"

Trust him to ask bluntly, to put it all out there. She dropped her gaze from his and stared at his throat. "It was good, so very, very good."

"And this surprises you?"

"No. It scares me." She met his gaze. "You've made sure to touch me, to try to put me at ease, as often as possible, and yet you've never asked me about it. About my past. My relationships."

"I figured you'd tell me when you were ready."

And she finally was. "I dated a guy that...well, he wasn't good for me."

Something flickered in his eyes. Something hard. But when he spoke, his voice was as calm and gentle as his hand still whispering over her. "Figured that."

"Until I met you, I'd talked myself into believing all guys were assholes." She chewed on her lower lip, closing her eyes when he lifted his hand to stroke the hair from her forehead, brushing his fingers across her scar.

"Maddie, look at me."

She opened her eyes and found his eyes warm and waiting. "We can all be assholes. I want five minutes alone with your ex to prove it, and I want that badly, but I'd never hurt you. Never."

"Only five minutes?" she asked, trying to lighten the mood.

He wasn't feeling playful. "Violence should never happen in a relationship."

She listened to the vehemence in his voice and took strength from it. "Alex was quiet. Controlled. And when he got pissed, he got *more* quiet and *more* controlled, until he wasn't either of those things." She drew a deep, shuddery breath, remembering how awful it'd been. "The first time he hit me, he seemed so horrified. I can't even explain to myself how I forgave him. He was so sorry and promised it'd never happen again. Then it did. It was..." She swallowed hard, knowing this all played into her fears, how she had no idea what people were really capable of, and how frightening that was. "It escalated, and I left. But I still hate that it happened more than once." She shut her eyes and admitted her secret shame. "It's humiliating that I didn't see him for what he was. That I'd be with a guy like that—"

"You got out," he said quietly, firmly. "You managed a difficult situation, and you got out. That's all that matters now. You have nothing to be ashamed of." He waited until she met his gaze again and softly repeated it. "*Nothing.*"

She nodded, and he kissed her softly. "You're one of the bravest women I know."

That made her laugh.

"You are."

Looking deep into his eyes, her amusement faded, replaced by awe. He meant it. And suddenly, she didn't have to fake the strength. The bravado. It was real. "Did you build this house?"

"Yes. And time for a subject change, I take it."

She smiled at him. "You're a smart man. And I think the house is beautiful."

"You haven't seen much of it."

"That's because you practically shoved me straight to your bed." She looked around at his large bedroom, sparsely filled with big pieces of dark oak furniture that were both masculine and inviting. His sheets were earth tones and luxurious. There were a couple of towels tossed onto a chair in a corner and running shoes lying beneath it. A forgotten pair of jeans was discarded on the floor.

Izzy was snoozing on top of them.

The room was clean but not necessarily neat. Good to know he wasn't a perfect superhero. "I like your furniture."

"I built that, too."

"So you're multitalented."

He smiled wickedly, making her laugh.

"And full of secrets," she added.

His smile faded some. "Yes."

She felt her heart catch at the way he looked at her as he ran the pad of a finger over her lower lip. "You going to share them?" she asked.

He just rolled her over the top of him and ran his hands down her body. "Yes. Secret number one. I'm not finished with you."

"You're right," she said, feeling him hard beneath her. "One of us definitely isn't finished."

With a grin, he pulled her thigh over his hips so that she straddled him, opening her to his touch. "Only one of us?" he murmured and stroked her with his thumb.

It came away drenched.

"Okay, as it turns out, I might not be finished with you, either."

"Feel free to take your time."

She set her hands on his pecs and stared down at him, feeling shockingly at ease given how naked she was. His hands were everywhere on her body, rough and strong and gentle all at the same time. Then he produced another condom and guided her down on him.

It was a deliciously tight fit, and her hands clung to his biceps as she rocked. This wrenched a hungry groan from him, but he gripped her hips. "Slow this time," he demanded, lazily stroking her where they were joined, making her crazy. "Real slow, Maddie."

And he meant it. For torturously long minutes, he languidly stroked, teased, and drew her nearly out of her mind, until she was panting out his name like a mantra, desperate for release. When he finally moved, it was in fluid, rhythmic motions that had her crying out, arching into him, clinging to him as if he was her own personal life support. He was everything.

Simple and terrifying as that.

Eventually they staggered into the kitchen for provisions. Jax made grilled cheese and soup, and then they somehow ended up naked on his big leather couch in the living room. Maddie was currently lying there, gasping for breath, thinking that at this rate, they'd kill each other by Christmas. Damp with perspiration, she shifted, and the friction of her moist skin on the soft leather made a sound that had her going utterly still in horror. Then she became a flurry of motion trying to re-create the sound so Jax would know it was the couch and that she hadn't—

They both clapped their hands to their noses at the same time as the odor hit them, hard and merciless.

"Christ," Jax said, sitting straight up.

"It wasn't me, it wasn't!" Maddie shook her head wildly. "It was my skin against the leather, and—" She broke off because Jax was doubled over, gasping for breath. God. He was dying, he was—

Laughing his butt off, she realized. "It wasn't me," she repeated, beginning to feel insulted.

Jax managed to regain control of himself and then turned to the dog lying at their feet. "Iz, we've been over this—*not* in front of guests. You have to go out?"

The dog leapt to her feet and barked joyously, and—

Let out an audible fart.

Grinning, Jax got up to open the door for her.

"You knew it wasn't me," Maddie accused when he came back, crossing her arms over her chest.

Still grinning, he sank back down and hauled her into his lap. Pressing his face into her hair, he kissed her behind her ear.

Her sweet spot, and he knew it. "Let me make it up to you," he said with a low, masculine laugh.

She lifted her chin softly. "I can't think of anything good enough."

"I can." His eyes were lit with the challenge. "And it's going to be good, Maddie. *Very* good."

Not going to cave, she told herself, holding her body rigid. *Not going to—*

Taking her earlobe gently between his teeth, he tugged lightly. An answering tug occurred between her legs. Cause and effect...

She caved like a cheap suitcase.

Chapter 20

♥

*"If you're going to walk on thin ice,
you might as well dance."*
PHOEBE TRAEGER

Much later, Maddie put a hand to her heart to keep it in her chest. She was trying to think of something to say, but the only thing that came to her mind was *"WOW."* So she murmured it softly and then again, because frankly, it bore repeating.

Next to her, Jax let out a very male sound of agreement and reached for her hand. Entwining their fingers, he brought her palm up to his mouth and brushed his lips across it. "It's dark out," he noted. "When did that happen?"

She had no idea.

"Thirsty? Hungry?"

In response, her stomach rumbled loud enough to echo off the walls, and she closed her eyes in answer to his laugh. The couch dipped as he rolled over her and placed his forearms on either side of her face, his body lowering to hers. "My plan was to keep you naked until one of us begged for mercy. We'll circle back to that."

They showered, dressed, and made it to the Jeep just as a sleek Mercedes pulled up the driveway. Beside her, Jax stiffened. Glancing into his face, she was surprised to see that his look of satisfaction had vanished. "What is it?"

Before he answered, a man stepped out of the car wearing a well-cut suit and a flash of sophistication. His eyes went straight to Maddie.

Resisting the urge to pat down her crazy hair and squirm, she jumped a little when Jax took her hand in his and ran his thumb over her fingers. Other than that small, comforting gesture, he didn't move a single muscle.

"So I see why you haven't returned my phone calls," the man said to Jax.

Jax didn't respond. Maddie wasn't even sure he was breathing. The other man was as tall as Jax and incredibly fit, and could have been anywhere from late forties to sixty. "As I told you in the emails you didn't answer," he said to Jax. "We need to talk about Elizabeth."

"And as I told you, don't show up here without an appointment." Jax's eyes were colder and harder than Maddie had ever seen them.

"Christ," the man said. "You're worse than a damn woman. Fine. Can I…*please*…" He paused for sarcasm's sake. "Have an appointment?"

A tight smile curved Jax's mouth, but it wasn't a pleasant one. "Busy."

The man let out a snort, his gaze flicking back to Maddie, who hadn't been born in a barn, so she held out her hand. "Maddie Moore."

"Jackson Cullen. Are you a client, or a friend?"

"None of your business," Jax said and put a hand on Maddie's lower back, nudging her to the Jeep. "Let's go," he said. "Now."

Only a little while ago, she'd been kissing her way down his amazing body, licking and nibbling, coaxing the sexiest sounds from him, including lots of that "now," in a different context of course.

She loved knowing she had the power to make him lose control. She loved his warm body, his scent, the texture of his skin, the taste of him on her tongue, and the strength of his hands, and how she trusted that strength. She loved his generosity of spirit, loved the way he could be gentle and endlessly patient, and yet still vibrate with testosterone. She loved how much he cared about his friends, his dog, everyone in the town. She loved his mischievous smile. The way he looked at her. How he teased her, laughing with her, not at her.

And she was desperately afraid she *loved* him.

Jax opened the Jeep's passenger door for her, and she started to get in. "He'll never love you, you know," Jackson said directly to Maddie.

When she looked up at him, he nodded. "He's cold. It's what made him so successful. Ask his old bosses. Ask Elizabeth. His fiancée." He cocked his head and studied her face. "Did he tell you about her?"

"Dad," Jax said tightly. "Back off."

Jackson sent his son a long look. "Oh, he talks a mean game," he said, still speaking to Maddie. "And he can spin wheels of logic in your head until you think you're getting what you want from him, but it is a game. It's *all* a game." His smile was dark and grim. "You seem like a nice girl, Maddie, but you're out of your league here. I'd get out while you can."

"Maddie, get in," Jax said and stood there as if guarding her until she did. Then he turned to his father. "Get off my property and don't come back."

Violence shimmered in the air, and Maddie stared at them through the windshield, her pulse kicking hard. Jax looked at her. With a flash of something that might have been regret, he moved around to the driver's side.

"You're fucking up your life," his father said, grabbing Jax's arm as he turned away.

Jax spun back, and at whatever Jackson saw in his son's face, he dropped his hands from him.

"You can't push me around anymore, Dad," Jax said. "You can't get to me."

"It's not too late to get your life back on track."

Again, Jax locked eyes with Maddie through the windshield. "I'm on track." With that, he slid into the driver's side and thrust the engine into gear.

Jax was silent as he pulled out.

She was silent, too, though she eyed him very carefully as he drove. Had he inherited his father's temper? It was possible. She of all people knew anything was possible, that people could hide parts of themselves and keep those parts under wraps until they decided to reveal them.

He finally spoke. "You okay?"

"I was thinking of asking you the same. You're... mad."

He shifted his inscrutable gaze to hers, then turned back to the road. "And that worries you."

She squirmed in her seat over that one, and he blew out a low breath. "I was hoping we were past this, Maddie."

Her, too, but unbidden came the images of Alex, how he'd lashed out when he appeared so calm and in control. It pissed her off that her brain could do this to her, betray her now, make her feel so irrational. But that was the thing about fear. She could ignore it all she wanted, but it didn't go away. Nope, it merely hung out, biding its sneaky time.

Jax let out a long breath and didn't speak again. As they got on the highway, with the mountains on their left and the ocean churning on the right, the silence grew.

And grew.

And thickened into something ugly.

"You believed him," he finally said, voice low.

"No. I—"

"You did."

"I'm sorry. I'm..." What? *Overwhelmed by seesaw emotions?* Check. *Unnerved because even not wanting to, I let your father scare me?* Check and check. Both were ridiculous and childish and stupid, and she knew this. "I'm sorry," she repeated lamely.

"Don't," he said, voice tight. "You don't mean it. So don't apologize."

He was right. She hadn't meant to apologize. She'd meant to ask him how he planned on releasing his anger, because he clearly *was* angry. She could read the tension still in his body—she'd become somewhat of an expert on the subject. "For what it's worth, I really do know you wouldn't hurt me. Logically, anyway."

He slid her a searching look but said nothing.

She let out a breath. "So what's your father's problem with what you do for a living?"

He was quiet so long she'd decided he wasn't going

to answer. Then he suddenly spoke. "He sees working with one's hands as beneath him." He turned off onto the asphalt road at the end of town. Lucille was on her front porch and waved.

Maddie automatically waved back.

They drove down the dirt road, and then they were at the inn. Jax parked, and they both sat there.

"What does he do?" Maddie eventually asked.

"He's a lawyer. We used to be one and the same."

She tried to picture Jax in an expensive suit and an uptight expression and couldn't. "No. I don't believe you were ever like him."

"Believe it. Hell, I even thrived on it."

She searched his face for the easygoing, sexy, playful lover she'd been with all afternoon but couldn't find him. This did not help her nerves. "Why did you quit?"

"Lots of reasons, but mostly I hated who I'd become."

"Elizabeth?"

He shrugged. "She was part of the lifestyle."

"You don't talk about her."

"I try not to think about that time in my life."

She stared at him for a full minute, waiting for more. When it didn't come, she felt her own temper stir. "I've learned the hard way that when people aren't forthcoming, there's a good reason."

"I'm not like him, Maddie. Not even close. Don't compare us."

She felt like he'd slapped her. *Not a mouse,* she reminded herself. Hold your ground. "So you didn't keep parts of yourself purposely hidden from me? You're not still keeping parts hidden?"

A muscle ticked in Jax's jaw. "You're going to let him

win." His words were short and clipped. He was pissed. "You're going to let him drive that wedge he wanted between us."

"This isn't a court case to win or lose, Jax. It's my life." She stared at him while he stared straight out the windshield. "Is there anything else about your past I should know?"

He was quiet for a beat too long, and she let out a breath. "Jax. Is there?"

"There's always something."

"That's no answer, and we both know it."

But given his silence, it was the only answer she was going to get. Honestly, she couldn't quite believe it, that they'd found themselves here, in this place. She'd had little hints from him that he hadn't been the open book she'd thought, but she'd ignored them.

Logically she knew that, given how hard it'd been for *her* to open up about her past, she needed to cut him some slack for not being completely forthcoming himself. But she couldn't find it in her at the moment. "I have work to do."

He shoved his fingers through his hair. "Maddie—"

"Lots of work." She hopped out and shut the door hard. Her exit wasn't exactly graceful, since she had to yank it open again to pull out the hem of her shirt, which had gotten caught.

Without looking at him, she walked into the inn and shut that door hard, too, then put her forehead to the wood. When she couldn't stand the suspense and peeked out the window, he was gone.

Chapter 21

♥

"Men are like roses.
You have to watch out for the pricks."
PHOEBE TRAEGER

The three sisters sat in the back booth at Eat Me Café having a late night dinner. Tara had just gotten off shift, and at this hour, there were more Christmas decorations than customers.

Chloe was eating the night's chicken special. Tara was carefully stirring her hot tea and adding honey with the precision of a drill sergeant moving troops.

Maddie was knitting, and *not* with the precision of a drill sergeant. She was also thinking too hard: about Jax's father, about Jax's ex-fiancée, about Jax. About their fight. At the moment, she wasn't sure where they stood, or even where she wanted them to stand, but with a few hours of distance, she could definitely admit one thing.

She'd overreacted.

Fear did that to a person, made them completely... *stupid*. She hated that. She thought about going over to his house to talk to him. Or better yet, *not* talking. She could let her fingers do the talking for her.

Chloe glanced at her and rolled her eyes. "You and your orgasmic glow need to shut it."

"Don't mind Chloe," Tara said. "She's just jealous, bless her heart."

"I'm going to bless your dead body," Chloe said. "And are you saying you're *not* jealous? The Mouse is clearly getting some, and we're getting the big fat zip."

"Sugar, you can't miss what you can't even remember."

Maddie sighed. "There's really nothing to be jealous of."

"Uh-oh." Chloe cocked her head. "Trouble in paradise? What happened? Don't even try to tell me he didn't fill out a condom. I've seen how he fills out his jeans."

Tara choked on her tea.

"Oh, like you haven't noticed." Chloe turned back to Maddie. "Before we get to why you're pouting, can we at least hear the juicy details? Does he talk dirty in bed? He's good with his tongue, right? Please tell me he is."

So good, Maddie thought and wriggled as she felt her body respond at just the memory.

"This isn't fair." Chloe slouched in her chair, pouting. "I'm good with my tongue, and I can't even do it without getting an asthma attack."

"I know I'm going to regret asking," Tara said. "But how do you know you're good?"

"I practiced with zucchinis. What?" she asked when both sisters laughed. "You asked."

Tara rubbed her temples as if trying to remove the image burned into her brain. "So what happened?" she asked Maddie, clearly desperate to move on. "What happened with you and Jax?"

"I happened," she said miserably. "I let my past dictate my present and possibly ruin the future."

"Huh?" Chloe asked.

"I met his father. Who's not a nice guy, by the way. And I found out that Jax gets really quiet when he's mad. Like the calm-before-the-storm quiet."

"Ah, sugar." Tara pushed aside Maddie's knitting to squeeze her hand. "That doesn't mean he's going to blow up."

"I know that." Sort of.

"And we all have pasts," Chloe pointed out, surprisingly void of sarcasm. "*And* exes."

"I know that, too. I just realized that, for as open and laid-back as he is, there's more to him, a lot more than he's shown me. I'm tired of playing the game when I don't get a copy of the rules. He can go play with himself." She paused. "Okay, that came out wrong."

"But it sure is a great visual," Chloe said.

"I say back off," Tara said. "You've had your fun with him, and that's all you need for now."

"But—"

"Trust me," Tara said. "Backing off *before* you fall is the safest." She got up and came back with an apple pie and a quart of vanilla ice cream. "This is my Can't Get It Together apple pie. It's got a million calories, but it cures everything. Broken budget, broken heart, you name it."

They each took a huge piece and added ice cream.

"Uh-oh," Chloe said to Maddie. "Your foods are touching."

"Shut up." The warm, buttery crust melted in Maddie's

mouth and made her moan. Not as good as being naked with Jax, but a close second.

"So one week left until Christmas," Chloe said, mouth full.

Maddie set down her fork, her stomach clenching.

"Honey." Tara shook her head, looking surprisingly upset. "It all comes down to money. Our cards are maxed out now. We have no buffer. We're finishing up the bare necessities and getting it on the market. It's for the best."

"Plus you two want out of here," Maddie said softly.

"And that," Tara said honestly.

Chloe took Maddie's hand. "Come on. Let's go back to the cottage, turn on our Charlie Brown Christmas tree lights, and sing bad Christmas songs. I have a brand-spanking-new facial mask to try out on you guys that takes away fine wrinkles."

"I don't have wrinkles."

Chloe patted her hand. "And remind me to remind you to get your eyes checked."

The next morning, Maddie opened her eyes and had to laugh. Once again she'd fallen asleep knitting and was wrapped in her yarn. And also once again, she was entangled with her sisters beneath their tree like a pack of kittens. She crawled over a snoring Tara and pulled herself free from her latest knitting project. She'd finished it last night, and beautiful as she thought it was, she had to admit—it was her most crooked scarf yet. "Okay, one of these days, I'm going to get the hang of this."

Chloe sat up, and Maddie gaped at her. And then at Tara. "Why is your hair green?"

"What?" Chloe touched her hair. "*What?*"

"And your face is white."

"Omigod. So's yours! And yours!" Chloe said, pointing at Tara, too.

It was like a bad game of blind man's bluff. They all ran to the tiny bathroom and fought for space in front of the mirror.

Each of them had green-tipped hair and a face mask that had hardened like clay, cracking across their skin.

"Oh, God," Tara groaned, then whirled on Chloe. "This is your fault."

Chloe tossed up her hands. "Why is it always the baby who has to take the blame?"

"Because you are to blame? You said the mask would soak in overnight."

She'd talked them into some new conditioner she'd made out of seaweed and avocado. "It must have stained. Okay, no one panic."

"Why, because I'm sporting a hair dye that makes me look like I should be starring in a Dr. Seuss book?" Tara yelled.

Maddie bent to the sink and scrubbed off the face mask and brushed her teeth. Chloe and Tara followed suit, then they all stared at themselves until the doorbell rang.

Maddie went to the door.

Jax stood on the porch holding a container of four steaming hot coffees. Something tumbled inside her at the sight of him, but the warm fuzzy was immediately chased by a cold dose of reality. She had no idea where they stood.

He was wearing his usual sexy-as-hell work

uniform—jeans, boots, and a big, warm-looking hoodie sweatshirt. Minus his usual easy smile. He handed her a coffee. "About my father and my ex," he said, characteristically going right to the meat. "I don't talk about them because neither are involved in my day-to-day life anymore. I spend long chunks of time not thinking about them at all. We don't keep in touch; we don't have fond memories. Both of those relationships ended badly, so believe me, there isn't anything you'd want to hear."

Fair enough. She and her father had a very decent relationship, but her time with Alex certainly wasn't anything anyone would want to hear, either. "I'm sorry. I overreacted." She offered a small smile. "I guess I'm still working on those trust issues. But you can't deny that I really don't know very much about you."

His warm caramel eyes met hers. "We could work on that."

Out of everything he'd given her—his time, a sense of renewed confidence, his friendship and more—this was perhaps the most meaningful of all. "That'd be nice," she said. "Getting to know each other even better."

"Maybe we could start with why you have green hair."

"Basically, it's because Chloe's evil. Notice my scarf matches."

"There's a lot of green going on," he agreed.

She pulled off the scarf and wrapped it around his neck, holding the ends. Playfully, she went up on tiptoe and brushed his lips with hers. "It's a little crooked, but I prefer to think of it as unique. And it's warm."

"Reminds me of you," he said softly, hands going to her hips to hold her against him. "Unique and warm."

She kissed him again. "Thanks for the coffee, and especially thanks for being so patient with me."

He tightened his grip when she moved to pull away. "Have we negotiated a truce, then?"

"I think so. We're..." What? What were they? She realized she had no idea what he wanted from her.

He looked at her for a long moment. "I'd like to keep going with us, Maddie. Adding in more talking, minus a few misunderstandings. You?"

She stared at him, feeling her emotions swing like a pendulum. Not only had he said what he'd wanted without a sign of panic or fear, he'd asked her what she wanted. "I'm on board with that. Though I'd add in more of what we did yesterday at your house before your dad showed up."

With his first real smile and a soft laugh, he pulled her in and pressed his mouth to her temple. He ran a hand down her hair, tugging very lightly on the green tips, the small smile still curving his mouth, the one that tended to melt her bones with alarming alacrity.

Her sisters appeared on either side of her, green hair and all. Jax offered them coffees, which were gratefully received.

"You need a clone," Chloe told him and sipped. "To share with the rest of the female population. What are we doing today?"

Maddie knew what she wanted to do. *Jax.*

But clearly his superhero powers of ESP were broken. "Painting," he said to Chloe. "An entire day of painting."

Damn.

They painted.

And painted.

Well, Tara and Maddie painted. Chloe worked on her skin care line.

Jax worked outside and away from them on the wood trim. By the time Tara and Maddie quit at sunset, Maddie's arms felt like overcooked noodles.

Chloe, restless as usual, rode off into the sunset on her Vespa.

"Stay out of trouble," Tara called after her. Shaking her head, she sighed. "She's not going to stay out of trouble." She turned to Maddie. "I'm going in for my dinner shift. Come over when you're hungry, and I'll feed you."

"Will do." Maddie stood in the middle of the living room of the inn and took stock as if she were looking at the place for the first time. The floors were looking good, and without the rooster and cow wallpaper, the rooms looked bigger and more airy. Even so, there was still something almost antiquated about the place, which was okay, because it fit like an old glove. It had character. And charm. It felt like a place that she could get comfortable in and stay awhile.

Too bad that wasn't going to be the case. For her entire life, "home" had been transient, a place to hang her coat, to rest her head, but not a place to stop for any length of time. Now she'd finally found a true home, one that embraced her, comforted her, and gave her peace.

But just like everything else in her life, it hadn't worked out. She'd been trying to keep that thought at bay, but the Denial Train was leaving the station.

And soon, all too soon, Maddie was going to have to leave, too.

Chapter 22

♥

*"Catch and release when you're fishing,
and catch and release when you're dating."*
PHOEBE TRAEGER

Jax spent the next few days installing the bathroom vanities and finishing the floors. The painting was done, as well. Tara had wielded a paintbrush with predictable meticulousness. Maddie had painted as she did everything else in her life. She'd started out tentative but had ended up giving her entire heart over to the process.

She made him smile.

And ache. He had no idea what would happen—if and when she'd be leaving, if she'd ever let herself fully trust him—but he knew what he wanted to happen.

He wanted her to stay.

As darkness fell on Christmas Eve, he stood outside the inn in the blustery, frigid air, cleaning up his tools, watching as first Tara sped off in Maddie's car, and then Chloe on her Vespa.

He turned to take in the single light shining into the

dull, foggy dusk from the marina building. Setting down his tool belt, he headed that way and found Maddie at her desk. She was lit by the soft glow of the lamp, the rest of the marina in shadow. She had her back to him in her chair, feet braced up on the wall, computer in her lap, fingers clicking away.

Helpless against the pull of her, he stepped in a little closer. She'd showered and changed from the day's work and wore a pair of bright red sweats, snug enough to show her curves, yet covering her from head to toe. The hood was edged in white and had two white tassels hanging down, dangling to her breasts like two arrows. Along one leg were white letters spelling out "Mrs. Claus."

Her hair was piled messily on top of her head, held there with her knitting needles, and she was frowning, looking tousled and annoyed and beautiful. "Hey," he said.

She didn't budge, and he realized she wore earphones, the cord trailing to her pocket, a tinny sound giving away her iPod. Smiling, he pulled out his phone and IM'd her.

(JCBuilder):   Busy?

(ILoveKnitting): Trying to relax.

(JCBuilder):   I could help with that.

(ILoveKnitting): Yes, you could. By telling me something about you. Your favorite childhood memory, your most embarrassing moment, what makes you tick—*something*.

(JCBuilder):   Eating ice cream on the Ferris wheel, plowing my first truck into Lucille's mailbox, and living for the here and now. Now you.

(ILoveKnitting):   Making s'mores on a movie camp-
fire set with my dad, every single second of that
first time we met, and knowing that there's always
tomorrow to get it right.

(JCBuilder):   It?

(ILoveKnitting):   Life. You got a recipe for life that I
can follow?

(JCBuilder):   Feeling brave?

She laughed when she read that one, and Jax felt a
weight fall off his shoulders.

Tugging out her earphones, she leaned back even
deeper in her chair. "If you only knew..." she murmured.

"What?" he asked her, stepping closer. "If I only knew
what?"

She gasped and whipped her head around, losing her
balance in the process and crashing to the floor.

"Christ." He came around the desk and crouched
down at her side. "You okay?"

"I've *got* to stop doing that." Still in her chair, she
was flat on her back on the ground, clutching her laptop,
appearing annoyed until she got a good look at him and
the crooked green scarf around his neck. "*Aw.* You're
wearing it."

"Yeah." He'd been taking shit about it from Ford and
Sawyer, too. He took her computer and set it on the desk,
then reached for her, holding her down when she tried to
scramble to her feet. "Wait. Just lie there a minute. What
hurts?"

"Besides my stupid pride? My butt."

Still on his knees, he lifted her out of the chair and pulled her over to him so that she was straddling his thighs in those Mrs. Santa sweats. "Cute," he said, sliding his hands to said butt. "Better?"

"Mmm. The sweats are Chloe's. It's laundry day. All my clothes are in the washer."

"Don't tease me with the washer, Maddie."

She bit her lower lip between her teeth, and he laughed softly. "You know, I've never been jealous of a spin cycle before."

She grimaced in embarrassment. "Stop."

"You have no idea what the thought of you on that thing does to me." He was hard already. And since his hands were on her ass, cupping her, he realized something else.

She wasn't wearing any underwear.

With a groan, he slid his hands up to her breasts. No bra, either.

Oh, Christ, he was a goner. "Maddie, where's your underwear?"

She lowered her voice to a whisper, as if imparting a state secret. "In the washer."

"You realize that puts you on the naughty list." He slid a finger into her drawstring resting just below her belly button and very slowly began to tug.

"What are you doing?"

Unwrapping you . . . "Checking for injuries."

"Jax—"

"That's Dr. Jax to you."

Her eyes lit with humor, but she put her hands over his, stopping their progress. "I feel different with you. Good different. I just wanted you to know." She removed her hands from his. "You can carry on now. Doctor."

He kissed her, then pulled back to look into her eyes. "I feel different, too."

"You do?" she breathed, her entire body softening for him. "What else are you feeling?"

Hot. Hungry. Devastatingly seduced by the look in her eyes, the one that said she was falling for him. "Like I want you. All of you. Wrapped around me. Lost in me." Having untied her bottoms, he reached for the zipper of her sweatshirt.

She held her breath as he slid it down, revealing a strip of her creamy skin from chin to belly button, and more than a hint of the curves of her breasts.

"I'm going to be cold," she whispered.

"I'll keep you warm." Leaning forward, he pressed his mouth between her warm, full breasts. Gently scraping his lips over one plumped curve, he worked his way to her nipple, which had already tightened for him.

"I don't think I got hurt there." But her fingers slid into his hair to hold him in place.

"You can never be too sure." Slowly, he drew her nipple into his mouth and sucked.

Her head fell back, and she let out an aroused murmur that went straight through him. "But I fell on my butt."

"You're right. You need some serious TLC." He slid his hands into her loosened sweatpants, tracing his fingers down the center of her sweet bare ass. Lingering... "Here?"

She gasped and shifted away. "No!"

With a smile, he slid his fingers lower. Wet. God, so wet.

Her arms clenched around his neck, and her breath was nothing more than little pants of hot air against his skin as he stroked her. "How about here?" he asked, slowly rubbing the pad of his callused finger over her, groaning when she spread her legs a little farther apart for him, giving him room to work. "Are you injured here?"

"N—no." She clutched at him, panting for breath in his ear. "Jax—Jax, please—"

He loved the sweet begging, but it wasn't necessary. Because he was going to "please." He was going to please the both of them.

She rocked into him, her hands running over his chest, his abs, trying to get inside his clothes, trying to get inside him. He felt the same. He couldn't get close enough. She was warm and curvy and whispering his name, and that worked for him, big-time. He reached down to tug off her shoes so he could get her out of the Santa sweats when red and blue lights flashed from outside, slashing into the office window.

Chapter 23

♥

"Sisters are the true friends who ask how you are, and then wait to hear the answer."
PHOEBE TRAEGER

Maddie straightened and stared at Jax, before zipping herself back up. She got to the window just as Sawyer opened the back door of his sheriff's car.

Chloe huffed out and stormed toward the cottage.

"Oh, boy," Maddie said, feeling Jax at her back.

"Sawyer's pissed," he said.

"How can you tell? He's wearing a blank expression."

"*That's* how you tell. He gives nothing away when he's in that kind of mood."

Maddie's gut tightened. "What do you think she did this time?"

"This time?"

Maddie hurried outside. "Chloe?" she called out.

Both Sawyer and Chloe turned around.

"It wasn't my fault," Chloe said.

Sawyer snorted.

Chloe tossed up her hands, whirled, and started walking again.

"You're welcome for the ride," Sawyer said to her back.

Chloe flipped him the bird and slammed the cottage door.

"What happened?" Maddie asked Sawyer.

"She talked Lance into taking her hang gliding by moonlight. The two of them climbed Horn Crest and flung themselves off the cliff, landing on Beaut Point with about six inches to spare before they would have plunged to their deaths."

At 6,700 feet, Horn Crest was the highest peak in the area. Beaut Point was the plateau overlooking Lucky Harbor, and it was about the size of a football field, sitting three hundred feet above where the Pacific Ocean smashed into a valley of rocks below. Picturing what Chloe had done, Maddie felt sick. "Is she all right?"

"Are you kidding me? She's like a cat with nine lives. I don't know how many she has left, though." Sawyer shook his head in disgust. "Lance was under the influence. I'm hauling his ass in until he sobers up. Chloe wasn't drinking, so technically, I can't hold her. And they didn't actually break any law since it's actually not illegal to be stupid, but they were trespassing, and I should have ticketed her." He blew out a breath. "At this point, it's a waste of paper."

He rubbed his hands over his face and turned to Maddie. "She was lucky tonight, damn lucky. I'd ask you to try to talk some sense into her, but I'm not sure that's even possible."

• • •

A few minutes later, after having said good night to Jax and Sawyer, Maddie walked through the cottage to the small bedroom, where she found Chloe sprawled facedown and spread-eagle across the bed, already out cold.

The Wild One...

Maddie had always secretly yearned to be the Wild One. Anything would have been better than the Mouse. Except that no longer really applied, did it? A mouse wouldn't have given this place a shot. A mouse wouldn't be having spectacular sex with a man who had a singular ability to obliterate her heart. A mouse wouldn't be fighting to get to know her sisters, and herself.

Maybe what was happening with the inn was inevitable, and maybe she couldn't save it. And maybe what she had with Jax was truly just a little snapshot in time and couldn't be saved either.

But she *could* save her relationship with her sisters. And she could save herself from going back to the way she'd been before.

She could be whoever she wanted. Knowing it, she felt herself smiling and pulled out her phone. "Still close by?" she asked when Jax picked up.

Jax watched Maddie peer out the Jeep's windshield at the unlit, unmoving Ferris wheel. "It's closed," she said with disappointment.

"It's Christmas Eve." He had the Jeep running, the heater on full blast. The interior of the vehicle was dark except for the glowing light from the instrument panel, but he had no trouble seeing the life in her eyes or the smile on her face.

He knew if asked, she'd say he put that smile there. She'd been coming to life a little more every day, but the truth was that he'd had nothing to do with it. She'd taken on her world, and it was sexy as hell to watch.

"I guess I'll have to find another adventure tonight," she said and turned to him. Her hair fell around her face in soft curls, just past her shoulders. He knew what it smelled like, knew how it felt brushing over his bare skin. He knew how she tasted and how to make her moan his name. He knew she was slow to open her heart, but that once she did, she was fiercely loyal to those she cared about. He knew what foods she craved, that she had a low tolerance for alcohol and a penchant for drinking it anyway. He knew that she pretended to be annoyed by Tara's steely resolve but really admired it, just as he knew she also admired Chloe's spirit. He knew that after a life in Los Angeles, she thought Lucky Harbor would be heaven. He knew she was looking for more...

And that she hoped she'd found it.

She knew things about him, too, more than he'd revealed to a woman in a long time. Unable to help himself, he ran a finger along her temple, tucking a strand of hair behind her ear. "Name it," he said. "Tell me what you want."

"But we don't have a condom."

He couldn't help it, he laughed.

She grinned. "I'm sorry. I think it's the fresh air here. And the pounding surf. And maybe also, it's you."

"No," he told her quietly. "It's all you. Come on." He turned off the Jeep, pulled two heavy coats from the back seat, and handed her one. When she was bundled up, they walked the pier.

They passed Eat Me, and Maddie's stomach growled. "I could use some of Tara's Badass Brownies right about now."

"Badass?" he asked.

"As in they're so badass that you turn badass just by smelling them."

He laughed and pulled her in close for the sheer pleasure of touching her. "Do you want to go in? I'll buy you a Badass Brownie."

"No, Tara's in there. She'll be annoying."

They hadn't gotten five steps past the café when they heard a loud voice.

"Maddie Moore, I see you."

Maddie jerked around. "What—"

Jax pointed to the loudspeaker on the corner of the building, just above the large picture window on the café, where several faces were pressed up against the glass, watching them.

"Step away from the good-looking man," came the disembodied voice.

Tara.

Maddie groaned but surprised him by tightening her grip on his hand instead of dropping it. "What does she think she's doing?"

"Amusing her customers." Jax's gaze locked in on their audience in the window, some shoving for better position, a few others waving.

"Madeline Annie Traeger, this is your conscience speaking," the loudspeaker said. "We're watching you. And—Hey, are those my Gucci boots?"

Maddie tipped her face up to the stars as if looking for divine intervention. "Some people have normal families," she said. "They get together once a month or so and have dinner. My family? We have pancake batter food fights, steal each other's footwear, dye our hair green, and yell at each other over loudspeakers in public."

"Keep it moving, sugar. No loitering on the pier."

"Everyone loiters on the pier!" Maddie yelled at the speaker.

"And especially no standing beneath the mistletoe for any reason at all."

Both Maddie and Jax looked up at the mistletoe someone had hung on the building's eaves. "What does it say about me that now I want to stand beneath it?" Maddie asked him.

"That we think alike?" Jax stepped closer, bent his head, and—

"Hold it!" the voice of Maddie's "conscience" called out.

Maddie sighed. "Jax?"

"Yeah?"

"I need a chocolate shake."

He didn't point out the fact that it was thirty degrees or that her breath was crystallizing in front of her face. They headed toward the ice cream shop.

It wasn't Lance serving tonight, mostly because he was still sitting in the single holding cell at the sheriff's station. Instead, it was Tucker, Lance's twin brother.

"Sawyer's keeping an eye on him," Jax said to Tucker's unasked question. "He'll be out in time to celebrate Christmas. He's okay."

"He's an idiot. We'll have the rent to you next week. We're a little behind."

"It's okay," Jax said. "It's a slow time for everybody."

Tucker nodded his thanks, handed over a chocolate shake, and Jax and Maddie walked on.

"You're their landlord?" Maddie asked.

"Yes."

She thought about that a minute. "Do you own the whole pier?"

"No. But I own some of the businesses on it."

She walked to the end of the pier. Leaning over the railing, she stared at the churning sea beneath her, clearly thinking and thinking hard.

She needed answers, deserved answers, but the truth was he wasn't sure where to start. For a man who'd made a living spinning words his way, it was pretty fucking pathetic. He came up beside her. "I own some businesses in town, too."

"Interesting that you've never mentioned this, Mr. Mayor."

He winced. "You really do know a lot about me." *Lame.*

"Hmm," she said, distinctly unimpressed.

He drew a deep breath. "You once told me some of your faults."

"I told you *all* my faults."

He smiled and played with one of her curls. "Want to hear mine?"

"I know yours. You don't like to share yourself. You think dog farts are funny."

"Everyone thinks dog farts are funny."

"You make me talk during sex."

He grinned. "You like that."

She blushed. "That's not the point."

When she didn't come up with anything else, he

raised a brow. "Is that it? Because I have more faults, Maddie. Plenty of them. Like...I ate only cereal until I was five."

"I like cereal."

"I jumped off Mooner Cliff into the water when I was ten. I thought I could fly, but I broke both legs."

"So you were all boy. Big deal."

"I got laid in the USC law school library when I was nineteen and nearly got arrested for indecent exposure. I failed the bar exam the first time because I had a hangover." He paused and let the big pink elephant free. "Then I took a case where an innocent woman got trapped between both sides. I tried to warn her, breaking my oath as a lawyer to do so, and instead of using the info to get herself out of a bad situation, she took her own life."

He paused when she inhaled sharply. He couldn't read the sound and had no idea if it was horror or disgust. But he'd gone this far—he had to finish. "I stopped practicing law after that. It'd sucked the soul right out of me." He paused. "I haven't gotten it back yet."

She stared at him then, and he held the eye contact. He figured she was going to walk away from him in three, two, one—

She moved, but not away. Instead she came close, her hand on his chest, gently stroking right over his heart. "You have a soul," she whispered, her voice shaking with emotion. "And a huge heart. Don't ever doubt it. You have a *superhero* heart," she said fiercely.

He shook his head. "I'm not a superhero, Maddie, not even close. I'm just a guy, with flaws. Lots of them. I do the restoration and the furniture making because I love it, but neither is all that profitable."

"But you have that big, beautiful house. How could you..." She paused. "Your father," she breathed.

"No. *No*," he said firmly. "Not my father. I'm good with investments."

She searched his face. "This bothers you," she said.

He shook his head, unable to put it into words. He'd tried to give back some of what he felt he'd taken by his years at the firm, but instead he'd profited.

"You know, you're standing right here," she said softly. "And yet I feel like you're far away. You hold back so much. Do you do it on purpose?"

"Yes. I've done it on purpose for so long I'm not sure how to do it any differently. You know me, Maddie. You know what I do, where I like to go—"

"I know that about a lot of people, Jax. I know that about Lucille, about Lance. Hell, I know that much about Anderson." She poked him in the chest. "I want to know more about *you*. I want—" She was toe to toe with him, getting mad, standing up to him.

She wasn't afraid of him. She was in his face, holding her ground, and he'd never been more proud of her. "You know more," he said quietly. "You know my friends, and that I have a screwed-up relationship with my father. You know I drive a beat-up old Jeep so that my big lazy dog can ride with me wherever I go. You know that I don't pick up my clothes and that I like to run on the beach."

She made a soft noise, and he stepped closer and brushed his hand over her throat, where, to his chagrin, she had whisker burn. "You know how much I like to touch you."

Her eyes drifted shut. "And I like all those things about you," she admitted. "Especially the last..." A soft sigh escaped her, and she met his gaze. "But you're still hiding—I can feel it. What are you hiding, Jax?"

With a long breath, he took her hand. "Telling you would involve breaking a promise. I can't do that."

"Because of what happened to you when you were a lawyer?"

"Nothing happened to *me*," he corrected, voice rough with the memory.

She slid a hand up his stomach to his chest, holding it over his heart. "You were trying to help her, Jax. You didn't know what she'd do. You couldn't have known."

"I failed her." He closed his eyes, then opened them again. "And now here I am, back between the rock and a hard place."

"I don't understand."

"I know you don't." He looked into her face, so focused on him, so intent, and drew a deep breath. "Your loan on the inn. I know who holds the note. I know that if you'd make contact, your refinancing would be approved."

Her brow furrowed. "You can't know that for a fact."

"I do. I know it *for a fact*. I've tried to get you to look into it, but—"

"Oh, my God." Her mouth dropped open, and she stepped back from him. "It's you. *You* hold the note."

He reached for her, but she slapped his hands away. "No. No," she repeated, her chest rising and falling quickly. "Is it you?"

"Yes."

She stared at him. "Why didn't you tell me? All those times we talked about it—"

"And every single time, I tried to steer you—"

"You *tried* to steer me. You tried to *steer* me." Her eyes were filled with disbelief. "I'm not a sheep, Jax. I was lost and stressed and overwhelmed and freaked out, and you . . . you had the answer all along."

"I was trying to protect the here and now, and also you. I wanted you to refinance. With me. But your stubborn-ass pride would have reached up and choked you if you thought you were accepting anything from me that you didn't earn. I knew that unless it was your idea, you'd go running hard and fast."

She shook her head. "So you kept it from me to be noble?"

He grimaced, swiping a hand down his face. "Yes, but in hindsight, it sounded a lot better in my head."

Rolling her eyes, she turned away from him, then whipped back. "And the trust outlined in Phoebe's will. You know all about the trust, too?"

He wished she would just kill him dead and be done with it. "Yes."

"Is it you? Did she leave the trust to you?"

"No."

"Then—"

"I can't tell you."

"You mean you won't."

"That, too."

She jerked at his answer as if he'd slapped her, and she pretty much sliced open his heart at the same time.

"I remember distinctly asking you if there was anything else I should know about you," she said very quietly.

"This isn't about me. It wasn't my place. It still isn't my place—"

"You're my friend. You're my—" She broke off,

staring at him from eyes gone glossy with unspeakable emotion. "Well," she finally said quietly with a painful pause. "I've never been exactly sure what we are, but I'd hoped it was more."

"It was. It is. God, Maddie. I *couldn't* tell you. I made a promise—"

"Yes. I'm getting that. And since you certainly never made me any promises, I have no right to be mad." She ran a shaky hand over her eyes. "I'm tired. I want to go back to the inn."

"Not until we finish this."

"Finish this?" She let out a mirthless laugh and started walking to the Jeep, her steps measured and even, her fury and hurt echoing in each one. "I think we just did."

Maddie tiptoed into the dark cottage. The only lights came from their Charlie Brown Christmas tree. Pressing a hand to her aching heart, she went straight to the kitchen, to the cupboard where Tara kept the wine.

It was empty. "Dammit."

"Looking for this?"

She whirled at Tara's voice, squinting through the dark to find her sister sitting on the kitchen counter in a pristine, sexy white nightie, holding a half-empty bottle of wine in her hand.

"I'm going to need the rest of that," Maddie said.

"No. The sister getting regular orgasms doesn't get to have any pity parties."

"Yeah, I'm pretty sure the orgasms are a thing of the past."

"What? Why?"

"Because he hid things from me. From us." Moving

into the kitchen, Maddie hopped up on the counter next to Tara. "You're probably too drunk to retain any of this, but it's Jax. *He's* the note holder."

Tara had gone very still. "Did he...tell you that?"

"Yes, because suddenly he's a veritable pot of information. He knows about the trust, but he remained mum on that, the rat bastard."

Tara stared at her for a long moment. "He probably had his reasons. Good reasons. Maybe even *very* good reasons."

Maddie sighed and thunked her head back on the cabinet. "Why are you drinking alone?"

"I do everything alone."

"Tara..." Was there no end to the heartaches tonight? "It doesn't have to be that way."

"Oh, sugar." Tara tipped the bottle to her mouth. "Are you always so sweet and kind and...sweet and kind?"

"I'm not either of those things right now."

Tara closed her eyes. "I look at you, and I feel such guilt. I'm so full of goddamn guilt, I'm going to explode."

"Guilt? Why?"

"You maxed out your card for me. You were willing to stay here, even alone if you had to, to take care of things. And all I wanted was to leave. You have so much to give, Maddie. You're a giver, and I'm a..." She scrunched up her face to think. "Sucker. I'm a life sucker. I suck at life."

"Okay, no more wine for you." Maddie took the bottle. "And we *all* maxed out our cards. Well, except Chloe, cuz she turned out not to have any credit, but you and I both—"

"For different reasons," Tara whispered and put a finger over her own lips. "Shh," she said. "Don't tell."

"Okay, you need to go to bed," Maddie decided.

"See that." Tara pointed at her and nearly took out an eye. "You love me."

"Every single, snooty, bitchy, all-knowing inch," Maddie agreed. "Come on." She managed to get Tara down the hall and into the bedroom, where Chloe was still sleeping. Tara plopped down next to her and was out before her head hit the pillow.

Kicking off her shoes, Maddie changed into pj's and crawled over one sister and snuggled up with another, both making unhappy noises as she let her icy feet rest on theirs beneath the covers.

"Maddie?" It was Tara, whispering loud enough for the people in China to hear. "I'm sorry."

"For drinking all the wine?"

"No. For making Jax hurt you."

"What?"

Tara didn't answer.

"Tara, what do you mean?"

Her only answer was a soft snore.

Maddie bolted awake sometime later, fighting for breath. Gasping, she sat straight up as horror and smoke filled her lungs. "Oh, my God!" she cried, fear clenching hard in her gut. Fingers of smoke clouding her vision, she shook her sisters. "Get up, there's a fire!"

"Wha—" Tara rolled and fell off the bed.

Chloe lay on her back, eyes wide, wheezing, hands around her throat, desperately trying to drag air into her already taxed lungs.

Maddie leapt off the bed and dragged a suffocating Chloe with her. God, oh, God. "Who's got their phone?"

"Mine's in the kitchen," Tara rasped through an already smoke-damaged voice.

So was Maddie's.

Nearly paralyzed with terror, they turned to the door and staggered to a halt. There were flames flicking in the doorway, eating up the doorjamb, beginning to devour their way into the room.

No one was getting to the kitchen.

Tara ran to the window and shoved at it. "It's jammed!"

Chloe dropped to her knees, so white she looked see-through, and her lips were blue. Maddie grabbed a T-shirt off the floor, dumped water from the glass by the bed onto the material, which she then held over Chloe's mouth. "Inhaler. Where's your inhaler?"

Chloe shook her head. It was clenched in her fist and clearly hadn't given her any relief. By the way she was fighting for air, she was deep in the throes of the worst attack Maddie had ever seen.

"Maddie, help me get this open!" Tara cried, straining at the window.

Maddie already knew that window was a bitch. The sill and window frame had been heavily painted over several times, the last being a decade ago at least. They hadn't worried about that before because it'd been too cold to open it.

"Air," Chloe mouthed, no sound coming out of her, just the wheezing, her eyes wide with panic.

Her panic became Maddie's. The window wouldn't budge, and they didn't have time to fight it. Chloe was going to pass out. Hell, Maddie was going to pass out. The smoke had thickened in the past sixty seconds, the heat pulsing around them and the fire crackling at their backs.

Maddie grabbed the small chair in the corner, dumped the clothes off of it, and swung it at the window. She used the chair legs to smash out the last of the sharp shards and grabbed the blanket from the bed, tossing it on the ledge so they wouldn't get cut on the way out.

They shoved Chloe out first, and she fell to the ground, gasping for fresh air. Tara went next, holding on to Maddie's hand to make sure she was right behind her.

Maddie hit hard and took a minute to lie there gasping like a fish on land. From flat on her back in the dirt, time seemed to slow down. She could see the stars sparkling like diamonds far above, streaked with lines of clouds.

And the smoke closed in on the view, clogging it and blocking out the night.

Sounds echoed around her, the whipping wind, the crackle of flames, and, oh, thank God, sirens in the distance.

"Good," she said to no one and closed her eyes.

Chapter 24

♥

*"If you're always saving for a rainy day,
you're never going to get out of the house."*
PHOEBE TRAEGER

At two o'clock in the morning, Jax was lying in bed attempting to find sleep when his cell rang. Hoping it was Maddie saying that she'd changed her mind, that she wasn't dumping his sorry ass, he grabbing the phone.

It was Sawyer, and Jax took a long breath of disappointment. "Been a while since you've called me in the middle of the night. Ford need to be bailed out again? Or are you just that excited for Santa?"

"You need to get out to the inn, now. There's been a nine-one-one fire call."

Jax rolled out of bed, grabbed his jeans off the floor and a shirt from the dresser. He jammed his feet into boots, snatched up his keys, and was out the door before Sawyer got his next sentence out.

"—Fire and rescue units have been dispatched. Do you have Maddie?"

"No." Christ. He sped down the highway, heart in his throat. "I dropped her off an hour and a half ago."

"I'll be there in five," Sawyer said.

"I'll be right behind you."

It took him an agonizing seven minutes to get into town, and when he passed an ambulance racing in the direction of the hospital, his heart nearly stopped.

He flew down the dirt road, his heart taking another hard hit at the sight of the inn with flames pouring out of the windows and leaping high into the night.

The lot was a mess of vehicles and smoke and equipment, making it nearly impossible to see. He peeled into the area, pulled over, and barely came to a stop before he tore out of his Jeep. His pulse was pounding, and his legendary calm was nowhere to be found.

The cottage was gone. Completely gone. The second floor of the inn was on fire. It was a living nightmare. The lights from the rescue rigs slashed through the night as he passed police and fire crew and leapt over lines of hoses and equipment to come to a halt before the blackened shell of the cottage.

No Maddie.

A hand settled on his shoulder. Sawyer. Through the thick, choking smoke, his friend's face was tight and drawn, but he pointed to the low stone wall between the inn and the marina.

Huddled there, wrapped in a blanket, face dark with soot, sat Maddie.

He took his first breath since Sawyer had called. An EMT was talking to her. Her head was tilted up, facing the still-blazing inn, devastation etched across her face.

Jax crouched in front of her, his hands on her legs. She was shaking like a leaf. Or maybe that was him. "Maddie, Jesus. Are you okay?"

She met his gaze, her own glassy. "It's gone. The cottage is gone. And the inn—"

"I know, sweetheart." Just looking at the charred remains made him feel like throwing up. Very carefully, he pulled her against him, absorbing the soft, sorrowful sound she made as she burrowed against him. She wrapped her arms around his neck so tight he couldn't breathe, but he didn't need air. He needed her. "I saw the ambulance, and then the remains of the cottage, and I thought—" He closed his eyes and held her in that crushing hug, pressing his face into her neck. "How did you get out?"

"Through a window. The flames were blocking the door, and the window was painted shut. I broke out the glass with a chair."

He was probably holding her too tight, but he couldn't let go. She smelled like smoke and ash, was filthy from head to toe, and she'd never looked better to him. "Chloe and Tara?"

"Chloe had an asthma attack. That's who is in the ambulance. Tara rode with her."

Weak with relief, Jax sat on the rock wall and held her in his lap, opening the blanket she had around her so he could get a good look at her. She wore only a T-shirt and panties. Her arms and legs were streaked with dirt and soot. Her knees were scraped and bleeding. Gently he took her hands in his and turned them over. She had a few cuts on her palms.

The thought of that stuck window had his blood

running cold. A couple more minutes and it would have been too late. With as much care as he could, he wrapped her back up in the blanket and looked at the EMT. Jax had gone to school with Ty Roberts, and they sometimes played flag football together on the Rec league.

"She's refusing to be taken in," Ty said.

"It's just a few cuts," Maddie murmured. "That's all." She was back to watching the inn. The firefighters had a good handle on it now. The flames were nearly gone.

Ty looked meaningfully at Jax and then to the ambulance. He wanted to take Maddie in.

"Maddie." Jax made her look at him. "Let me take you to the hospital. We can check on your sisters and get you cleaned up."

"Not until it's over."

So they sat there and watched the blaze. When the flames were completely out, Sawyer spoke to the fire chief, then came over. "When the cottage caught fire, the wind carried sparks to the inn's roof. That's how the second floor ignited. They were able to contain it there." He squatted beside Maddie and ducked his head until he could see into her eyes. "They're not going to let you go in there until tomorrow. It's okay to leave. I want you to get into the second ambulance and go get checked out."

"No, I'm fine, I—"

"You're going," Jax said, willing to out-stubborn her. "I'll take you."

Maddie opened her eyes when the Jeep came to a stop. It wasn't quite dawn, and the sky was still inky black.

Christmas morning.

For a minute she sat still, remembering the panic of

waking up choking on smoke, the flames licking at the bedroom door, and watching Chloe fight for air...

God. Chloe was okay, or she would be. At the hospital, they'd learned she was being held overnight for smoke inhalation. Tara was staying with her, and Maddie could have, as well, but Jax had stepped in. "She's coming with me."

Four simple words that had filled Maddie's head while the nurse had cleaned and dressed her wounds—no stitches required, thankfully—and then given her a pair of scrubs to wear.

She'd been too numb and tired to argue with Jax.

No, that wasn't true. She was tired, to-the-bone exhausted, but she could have still argued. After all, she had no reason to go home with him.

Except she didn't want to be alone in a hospital chair.

She wanted to be held.

She wanted to feel safe.

The Jeep's heater had been on her full blast as they left the hospital, but she was still shivering. She felt like her teeth were going to rattle right out of her head. Jax had driven with his left hand, keeping his right hand on her, rubbing up and down her thigh, squeezing her icy fingers with his warm ones.

The passenger door opened, and she jerked.

"Just me," Jax murmured, having exited the Jeep and come around for her. Crouching at her side, he unhooked her seat belt and held her for a moment, fiercely, before lifting her into his arms.

"I can walk," she said, even though she made no attempt to do just that.

"Pretend you still believe I'm that superhero."

With a sigh, she looped her arms around his neck and pressed her face to his throat, breathing him in. The scent of him filled her, and her burning throat tightened.

She already missed him. Letting out a shuddery breath, she kept her eyes closed as she heard him open his front door and make a low comment to a sleepy Izzy. A few moments later, he let her feet slide to the floor.

Because she was still barefoot, she could tell she was on tile. But this tile was deliciously warm thanks to his heated floors.

Keeping one arm around her, he leaned away for a beat, and she heard the shower go on. "You're shaking," he said.

"I think that's you."

"Maybe."

She opened her eyes and found his, dark and shadowed with concern.

"Do you know how fast that fire moved?" he asked. "How much of a miracle it is you all got out?" He ran a hand over his eyes. "Christ, Maddie. If you hadn't woken up when you did..."

Her heart caught at his raw voice. "But I did," she whispered, reaching for him. "I'm okay, Jax. Look at me. I'm indestructible, apparently."

"*Resilient,*" he said and tilted her face up, looking at her from fathomless eyes. "Strong and giving and resilient."

She thought about the things that meant so much to her and could count them with the fingers on one hand. Her sisters. The inn.

Jax.

And all of it was in jeopardy. "I'm still mad at you," she whispered.

"I know."

She pressed a hand to her heart, which ached more than her cuts and bruises, and then to his. "I don't want to be alone tonight. Today. Whatever it is." Words failed her past that. She wanted comfort, and she wanted to feel alive, and she knew he could provide both.

"You need to get in the shower and warm up."

"With you."

Pressing his forehead to hers, he let out a slow breath. His hands, when he lifted them to her, were careful on her body as he stripped her out of the scrub top, taking in each and every one of her cuts and bruises. Then he slid the bottoms down her legs and paused at the sight of her Supergirl bikini panties. "Did I ever tell you," he murmured, dropping to his knees to press a kiss to her bruised hip, "that I'm pretty convinced you have your own superpowers?"

Bending her head to take in the top of his, she gave him a shaky smile that she knew didn't make it to her eyes. "What are they?"

"The power to get past all my walls..."

"Jax." She closed her eyes as he hooked his thumbs in the sides of the undies to slowly drag them down. She gasped when her world tilted as he picked her up and deposited her into the shower. He stepped in behind her and, without a word, washed her hair and then her body, quickly and efficiently.

She could feel him behind her, hard and aroused, but his touch remained gentle and soothing. It was just as well. With exhaustion sneaking up on her again, she could do little more than lean against him.

The next thing she knew, the water was shut off, and he wrapped her in a big, soft towel. He redressed her cuts, drew one of his own big, soft T-shirts over her head, and placed her on his bed.

She heard him move to the door. "Jax—"

"Sleep."

"'Kay." She listened to him moving around the house for a while. His phone rang, and she heard him quietly telling someone he had her.

He had her.

It was true, she realized. He had her heart and soul...

No. That wasn't right. He'd held back from her. Was still holding back...

Or was that her?

God, she was so confused, and tired...

"Sleep," he said again, back in the room now, running a hand down her arm.

She caught his fingers in hers. "Stay," she said, tightening her fingers on his.

"Always." The mattress dipped beneath his weight, and then she was carefully scooped up against his big, warm body. Their legs were entangled like it was the most natural thing in the world, as if they'd been sleeping together for years. His touch slid over her like a soothing balm, making her ache from deep inside, making her shiver for more. "Just for tonight," she whispered, snuggling in, feeling the steady beat of his heart beneath her ear.

Just for tonight.

Another lie, of course. She'd fallen for him, just as she'd fallen for her sisters, for the inn. And she was losing them all, one by one. She felt the sting of tears against her closed eyelids and, to hide them, buried her face into his throat.

His hands slowly stroked over her body, tender but sure. She knew he was offering comfort, but she took more, pressing in closer, anticipation humming through her. They were on their sides facing each other, and she drew a leg over his. Rocking her hips, she let the very tip of him, velvet over steel, slide into her.

He groaned roughly and tightened his grip on her, holding her still. "Maddie. You're hurt—"

She impaled herself, and, with another groan, he rolled her beneath him, filling her so entirely she saw stars. Bending low, his lips rested on the strong pulse in her throat, and she both felt and heard her name on a whispered breath.

Restless, she ran her hands down his back, digging her fingers into him, urging him on. Lifting his head, he held her gaze prisoner as he began to move within her, long, slow, delicious thrusts, a mind-blowing grinding of his hips. On the edge, her eyes began to drift shut in sheer, numbing pleasure.

"No, look at me. Feel me. Feel *us*."

Opening her eyes, she looked right at him. She saw her life, her heart echoed in his eyes, and she burst in a kaleidoscope of colors and emotion, unlike anything she'd ever felt.

When she could breathe again, he was waiting for her, still hard inside her. His forearms were alongside her face, his hands cupping her head. "I love you," he said, honest and sure, more a vow than a confession as he thrust into her and came, sending her spiraling again.

It was the last thing she remembered before sleep claimed her.

Twice she woke them both up with nightmares, hyperventilating and caught up in the sense of being trapped. In between the dreams, she tossed and turned.

Jax would have fought her demons for her if he could, she knew that by the way he spent the hours holding her close. It was close to noon before she woke up fully, and she opened her eyes to find Jax watching her.

"It's gone," she said, voice still a little hoarse. She knew her eyes were puffy and red, and that her hair had to be as wild as ever. "It's Christmas, and it's all gone."

Propping his head up on his hand, he used his other to tug her in close. "Yes."

Closing her eyes, she swallowed hard and pressed her face into his chest, her scratched-up arm gliding up to hook around his neck. She felt her tears wet both of their skin, and he made a low sound of regret. "You'll rebuild," he said.

She shook her head.

"There's fire insurance on the property."

It wasn't the words that set her off. It was the reality that he'd always known more about all of this than she did, even though it was her life. Not his fault, not her fault, she got that. It was no one's fault, but it didn't make it any easier.

Worse, even if they rebuilt, they'd still sell, because that's what her sisters wanted. Majority rules.

It devastated her.

As did knowing that walking away meant walking from Jax, too. She rolled out of the bed and began jerking on clothes. *His* clothes.

"Let me guess," he said. "You just remembered you're mad at me."

Mad? More like confused as hell. She turned to the door, wearing his sweatpants, a Henley, and her heart in tatters on the sleeve.

"Maddie." He snagged her hand in his, halting her progress.

"I'm going to call a cab to go to the hospital."

A muscle in his jaw ticked. "I'll take you."

He drove her in silence, not saying a word until she went to get out of the Jeep. Taking her hand in his, he brought it up to his mouth and kissed her bandaged palm. "You used to be afraid of me, and I understood that. But now it feels like you're afraid of what you feel for me. Of what I feel for you. And that I *don't* understand. Not one bit, Maddie."

Her eyes misted, and she shook her head in denial, causing him to pull her over the console and into his lap, nose to nose. Though he was careful not to hurt her, he wasn't gentle. "You think you're losing everything," he said, running his hands up her arms. "But it's not true. You have the power to stop this, Maddie. To not give up. Make a stand. Make a stand and take what you want."

Chapter 25

♥

"Remember, it's always better to be the smartass rather than the dumbass."
PHOEBE TRAEGER

Maddie sat on the dock at the marina, each exhalation a little white cloud in front of her face as she watched the sun make its route across a quiet sky. Behind her was the burned-out shell of her dream. In front of her, the Pacific Ocean was rough and churning this morning, matching the pitch in her stomach.

She dropped her head to her bent knees and squeezed her eyes shut. She'd just left the hospital. She was supposedly grabbing breakfast for her sisters and then going back to pick them up. But she needed a moment to herself, so she'd come here first. She felt empty and exhausted and defeated.

And sad.

So damn sad. It wasn't the loss of the cottage or her things. She'd survived far worse.

Jax loved her. Her. He wanted her to make a stand. Take what she wanted.

But it wasn't that easy, not for her.

It could be, said a little voice. Angrily, she swiped at a tear, then went still when she heard footsteps. Someone steady on their feet, but not trying to sneak up on her.

Jax.

She felt the weight of his jacket as he wrapped it around her, surrounding her with warm leather and his scent.

Lethal combination.

He crouched at her side, eyes dark and full of so many things she couldn't put her finger on a single one of them. His familiar easy smile was nowhere in sight. The lines etched around his eyes and mouth spoke of exhaustion and worry.

"What are you doing here?" she whispered.

"There are some things that need to be said."

"Jax—"

"Not by me." He looked over his shoulder at someone and nodded.

More footsteps sounded. Tara. She walked past Jax, and the two of them exchanged a long look. Jax's was warm and encouraging, but Tara's was guarded and tense, and dread filled Maddie. "What's going on?"

Tara sat next to Maddie. She was wearing scrubs and smelled like some odd combination of hospital disinfectant and smoke, but other than that, she appeared no worse for wear from the fire. "We need chairs out here, sugar. This is beyond undignified."

Maddie looked at Jax, who gave her a tight smile that didn't come close to reaching his eyes. Then he turned and walked away. She opened her mouth, but Tara reached for her hand. "He brought me here. Said it was time. He's been telling me that for weeks now, but I think he's about done with subtleties." She sighed. "So am I."

"Oh, God." Maddie stared at her, afraid to breathe. "This isn't the part where you tell me you're sleeping with him, right?"

"Oh, Lord love a duck. No, I'm not sleeping with him—not that he isn't one fine man. One really fine *hot* man, but honey, he's yours. He's been yours from day one."

Maddie started to shake her head, but Tara squeezed her hand. "I know you're upset with him. He was holding back information you feel he should have shared, and you're right. You're one hundred percent right to believe that when you're in love with a man, he should definitely tell you he's holding the note on the property that you consider your home, except—"

"Wait a minute." Maddie could have used some oxygen from that cute EMT about now. "No one said anything about love."

Tara rolled her eyes. "…Exceeeeept," she said. "It wasn't his place to tell you. He'd made a promise."

"But—"

"I know. In a relationship, you share things, but as it turns out, he was protecting someone." She paused, and when she spoke again, her voice was very quiet and halting. "He was protecting someone you know."

"Who?"

"Phoebe. And…" Tara shook her head and slumped as if the weight of the world was heavy on her back. She covered her face with her hands. "Me. I lied to you, Maddie. From the very beginning, I lied right to your face, and then I pulled a double punch by going to Jax and begging him to keep his promise, to keep this from you and Chloe." Shame laced every word that tumbled from her mouth.

Maddie stared at her, floored. "But...why?"

"Because I couldn't handle the truth coming out, not if I had to be here again. God, it hurt to be here again, still does."

"You couldn't handle *what* coming out? And what do you mean 'again'? You told me you've never been here before."

"No. You assumed that." Tara rubbed at her chest absently, as though to soothe an unrelenting ache, and cleared her throat. "I should start at the beginning."

"Okay." Maddie nodded, heart pounding. "That's a good idea."

Tara stared out at the water. The air was heavy with sea salt and the acrid scent of burnt wood. It was chilly, but Maddie wasn't feeling a thing past the icy ball of hurt in her chest.

"A few years back," Tara said. "Someone near and dear to Phoebe needed money. Phoebe didn't have any, but she wanted to help. She mortgaged the resort property." Her voice seemed distant, as though she was trying to remove herself somehow from the words she was saying.

"To Jax," Maddie said. "He lent her the money."

"Yes. He'd grown up here and had always been kind to her, and he'd recently come back to town and had been known for helping out financially when anyone needed it. She needed it."

"Why?"

Tara drew a deep breath. "I spent a summer here in Lucky Harbor when I was seventeen. My grandparents were going on a world cruise, and my daddy was working all the time. I was a lot like Chloe back then. Wild, spoiled, unrepentant." She shook her head. "No one could tell me what to do, but no one was listening to me, either. I was shipped here without ceremony. I arrived with a chip on my shoulder and a bad attitude, neither of which endeared me to any of the girls my age that were around. There was only one person who'd talk to me, and he..." She closed her eyes. "I got pregnant that summer."

"Oh, Tara," Maddie whispered. "I had no idea."

"No one did. No one knew but me and him, and Phoebe. God, it was awful. I felt...well, there's no way to explain how I felt, really. There's not many missteps you can take in life that can change you the way that can." She looked off onto the water as if there was something only she could see, and whatever it was made her ache. "And it did change me. It never left me," she whispered. She shook her head as if disgusted with herself for going down that road. "We were young and stupid and immature, and not in any position to be parents. I knew that even then." Her eyes were haunted. Hollow.

"I went to Seattle for the pregnancy, then gave the baby up for adoption—" Her voice broke, and she shook her head again, unable to go on.

Heart squeezing, Maddie hugged her even though they mostly showed their affection in other ways—like dying their hair green together. "I'm so sorry. You must have been so scared."

"Yes." Tara sniffed and searched her pockets for a tissue, which of course, she found. "I was terrified. But I knew enough to understand that I was just a kid. I...I did the right thing."

"Well, of course you did."

"I left Lucky Harbor and never looked back. I planned to never come back."

"What about the father?"

"We never spoke again. I went on with my life," Tara said. "Spending the next years *purposely* not thinking about it. But then..." She paused, her eyes solemn. "The baby grew up and got sick. Her heart had a faulty valve and required surgery. There were lots of medical bills, and Phoebe—" A shaky smile crossed her lips. "While I'd been doing my best *not* to think of what had happened, Phoebe had never *stopped* thinking about it. She found out that money was needed for medical care."

"So she mortgaged the place to help." Maddie shook her head. "I'd never have guessed that one. I never thought much of her mothering skills, but no one can deny she was a genuinely good person."

"Yeah." Tara dabbed at her eyes. "She made the donation to the baby's adopted family anonymously. She didn't want the child or her family to feel indebted."

Maddie squeezed Tara's hand again and smiled. "You had a girl."

Tara's smile was weak but proud. "A beautiful girl, and healthy now, thank God. By all accounts, she's happy and settled, and..." Her smile faded. "And I'm not a part of her life."

"Are you okay with that?"

"I have to be. I chose it," she said simply. "I chose it a long time ago, and I live with it. But Mom never really accepted it. I think maybe she felt her own guilt, you know, because maybe she didn't give her daughters up, but she sure didn't raise us. Anyway, she arranged a trust." She held Maddie's gaze. "She left the resort to us, but everything liquid went to her only grandchild. She hid the details from everyone but me in order to protect all parties, but mostly to protect me." Tara's eyes filled again. "I'm sorry, Maddie. I've been holding this in for so long, and truthfully, I would have held it forever, except..."

"Except?"

"You," she whispered. "You came here ready to accept what Mom wanted from us, what she hoped for. You came ready to accept us as a family. You maxed out your credit card to improve the inn that had been mortgaged to save my daughter." She shook her head in marvel. "You gave this place your all, when the only thing I could think about was running like hell." She swallowed hard and repeated, "I'm so sorry, Maddie. I'm so very sorry."

"No." She wrapped her arms around Tara. "You did what you had to. I'm proud of you, Tara. So proud."

Tara dropped her head to Maddie's shoulder, her body shuddering as she tried to keep her pain inside. Maddie held Tara tight and stroked her sister's hair as she lost more than a few tears of her own.

Tara finally pulled back, carefully swiping the mascara out from beneath her eyes as she let out a shuddery breath. "Well. That's never pretty."

"Feel better?"

"No, but I will. It's Christmas, sugar. We have to get Chloe sprung from the hospital, and you have a man to forgive."

"There's nothing to forgive," Maddie said, realizing it was true. It wasn't about what Jax hadn't told her. It wasn't that simple. "There's nothing to forgive, but—"

"Nothing good ever comes out of a *but.* Listen, I realize I did my part in keeping you from falling for him, but I was wrong. I was acting out of my own fears and past."

"Yes. And now I'm acting out of mine," Maddie admitted.

"You're afraid of him?"

"No." She hesitated. "Maybe. Yes. But not how you think. Dammit," she muttered, rubbing her temples.

Opening herself up and making herself vulnerable to a man didn't always end well, but even she knew that Jax was unlike any man she'd ever known. He was worth it. He was worth the potential heartache, because without him she was pretty sure her heart would cease to work anyway. "I'm not afraid of him. I'm afraid of what I feel for him—which means he was right. God, I really hate that. I mean, how do you deal with a guy who's always right?"

Tara laughed ruefully. "Sugar, if I knew that, I'd still be married."

The three sisters sat at Eat Me Café, which was open for a big brunch special for Christmas. Tara was mainlining caffeine in the form of a lethally strong coffee, and Chloe and Maddie were stuffing their faces.

Tara had made Bottom-of-the-Barrel Waffles, made with pumpkin and cinnamon and topped with lots of whipped cream. Heaven on earth. Maddie was shoveling them in, momentarily letting her mind go blank. It might have been the sugar high. She was keeping an eye on Chloe, as was Tara, but Chloe's color was good and she wasn't wheezing at all. Maddie knew Tara planned to tell Chloe about her past. She also knew that she wasn't eager to do so.

"We look like hell," Chloe said, eyeing herself in the reflection of her spoon, turning her head left and right.

"At least we're breathing," Tara said.

And breathing was good, Maddie thought, looking at her sisters, the two women who'd been like strangers to her only a month ago. "Last night in the terror and chaos, something became crystal clear to me," Maddie said softly. "I love it here. And I love you guys, too."

Chloe slid her a long look. "I'm not sharing my waffles."

Tara rolled her eyes and sent a small but warm smile to Maddie. "I love you, too, sugar. Both of you."

She and Maddie both turned to Chloe, who sighed. "Well, way to make me feel like a bitch." She kept eating, until she realized they were still staring at her. "What, I feel it. I just can't say it."

"Ever?" Maddie asked.

Chloe shrugged. "Maybe I'll work on it."

Everyone in the café came by their table. Hell, it felt like everyone in Lucky Harbor came by, wanting to commiserate and express their sympathies and condolences. Word spread quickly, because people were bringing them stuff—clothes, bathroom essentials—things to get them through the next few days since everything they had was destroyed.

Afterward, Tara cleared her throat and told Chloe everything, every painful detail. It was no easier for Maddie to hear the second time, but there were cleansing tears and a group hug.

"Wow," Chloe kept saying. "Wow."

"Okay, we're going to need a new adjective," Tara said. "That one's getting old."

"Well something finally makes sense to me," Chloe said. "Mom asking me when I was going to give her *more* grandkids. I never understood that."

"You were in regular touch with Mom?" Maddie asked.

"Well, yeah. I was her soft spot, I think. You know, because I'm so sweet and adorable." Her mouth quirked, but she looked a little shy about it. "I called her. I did it every week or so, just to check in from wherever I was. It seemed to mean something to her."

"And it meant something to you," Tara said softly.

"It did." Chloe nudged Tara. "And from what she told me, you were a lot like me before you grew up and got old and snooty—you were reckless and wild."

"Hey, I'm only ten years older than you. *Not* old." She sighed. "But yeah, I was. Your point?"

"Well, that there's hope for me, of course." Chloe shrugged. "It tells me that someday I can get myself together as well as you have."

"You think I have it together?" Tara asked in disbelief. "I had a baby when I was little more than a baby myself and gave her up. I have a failed marriage and a job I hate, and I'm in debt up to my eyeballs."

Chloe laughed. "Well, when you put it like that..." She turned to Maddie. "Maybe I should covet your life instead."

"You might want to wait until I get it together first."

"Oh, jeez, you still holding back on the sexiest mayor in Whoville?"

"You don't understand."

"Let's see...He only saved the resort when Phoebe needed a loan, then as much as promised us a refinance even though at least one of the three of us is incredibly financially unstable. He did the morally right thing and protected Tara's secret and proved himself trustworthy over and over again. What a self-serving bastard. Do you think we can drag him to the middle of the town square and stone him?"

Maddie sighed, then went still as a shiver of awareness shot up her spine. When she looked up, Jax was coming toward them in his usual long-legged, easy stride.

"Now's probably not a good time," Chloe said to him when he got within hearing distance. "I haven't quite finished talking you up."

Maddie shot Chloe a dirty look and, in doing so, realized the entire café had gone silent.

Everyone was listening.

"I was just listing all of your positive attributes," Chloe told him. "Leaving out the parts where you didn't tell her shit and kept yourself from her, of course. That was your bad."

Jax never took his eyes off Maddie. "Okay, first, I never kept myself from you. Maybe I didn't tell you enough about who I used to be, but Christ, Maddie, I hated that guy. And I guess I was hoping the man I am now would be enough for you."

"*Aw.*" Chloe's head whipped back to Maddie. "Did you hear that?"

Maddie's heart swelled painfully, pressing against her ribs. "I'm right here, Chloe."

"Sounds like a reasonable request to me," a guy from two tables over said. Maddie recognized him because he worked at the gas station. "And I can vouch for Jax being a good person. He gave my sister a loan when the bank wouldn't. She'd have lost her business and her house otherwise."

"And he did our house addition," a woman called out. "And when my husband lost his job, Jax accepted small, irregular payments. He didn't have to do that."

"Jesus," Jax muttered, hands on hips, eyes closed.

"And he donated new flak vests for the entire PD," Sawyer said, having just come inside.

"That was supposed to be an anonymous donation, you jackass."

"It looked to me like you were sinking fast. Thought I'd toss that in."

Shaking his head, Jax grabbed Maddie's hand and pulled her out of the booth and toward the door, moving so fast she had to run to keep up.

"Where are we going?"

"To talk without the entire fucking town throwing in their two cents."

He opened the café door, and they ran smack into a man wearing a rain slicker and carrying a clipboard with the name of a national insurance company on the front. "Excuse me," he said. "I'm looking for the owners of the Lucky Harbor Resort."

"That's me," Maddie said, very aware of Jax at her back, protective. Steady. "Give me a minute?" she asked the insurance guy, and at his nod, she pulled Jax aside. "I'm sorry," she whispered. "We have to have this meeting before any of us can leave town."

"Leave?"

"Yeah." She met his gaze, her chest so tight she could

scarcely get the words out. "I'm pretty sure that's what Tara and Chloe are planning on doing now. We have no place to live, and they've been wanting to get back to their lives for weeks now."

"And you?"

"It's majority rules."

"Bullshit." He shook his head and said it again. "You came here a fighter, Maddie. Maybe you'd lost a round or two, but you were on your feet. You want to stay in Lucky Harbor? Fight for it. You want a relationship with your sisters? Fight for it."

"What about you? What about a relationship with you?"

He pulled back to look into her face as if memorizing her features. His voice, when he spoke, was low and gravelly with emotion. "I'm already yours. Always have been. All you have to do is step into the ring."

Chapter 26

♥

"My motto was always: never chase after person, place, or thing, because something better will come along. Turns out I was wrong."
Phoebe Traeger

The insurance adjuster slipped out of his rain slicker and introduced himself as Benny Ramos. He was tall and lanky lean, wearing cowboy boots, a matching hat, and Wranglers that threatened to slide right off his skinny hips. It was impossible to tell if he was barely twenty-one or just really good with a razor.

Jax had led both Maddie and Benny back to their table. Jax gave Maddie a quiet, assessing look that she had no idea how to read and then left.

Her head was spinning. He'd given everything he had, and he wanted the same from her. He wanted her to fight for what she wanted.

Made sense. Made a lot of sense. It's what any good, strong leading lady would do.

"So," Benny said. "The cottage is a total loss."

"No duh," Chloe said. "Now tell us something we don't know."

"The fire department believes the fire originated with a set of old faulty Christmas lights that were strung..." He consulted his clipboard. "On a dead plant of some sort in the living room."

Tara snorted.

Maddie closed her eyes. *Poor Charlie Brown Christmas tree, may you rest in peace...*

"Anyway," the adjuster went on. "The inn isn't as bad as it looks. The bedrooms upstairs need a complete renovation, new carpeting, walls and bathroom replacement. New roof. But the downstairs is all cosmetic and can be cleaned. You're in decent shape there."

They were in decent shape. Good to know.

Step into the ring.

Jax thought she was a fighter. That hadn't always been anywhere close to true. She'd let life happen to her. She'd gone with the flow.

She hated the flow. The flow was working like a dog at a go-nowhere job, trying to please too many people who didn't care. She was done with going with the flow. She wanted to be a fighter. "Excuse me," she said to Benny. "But the downstairs *is* water damaged, so we're not in 'decent' shape there. We expect proper compensation."

Tara raised a brow, like *Go, kitten. Show him those claws.*

Chloe out-and-out grinned and gave her a thumbs-up. "You heard my sister," she said to Benny. "We expect proper compensation. You go back and tell your people that."

"Actually, we're on the same side," Benny said and

made some more notes on his computerized clipboard. Maddie was dizzy. She was heartsick. She was out of control, but she was having some serious clipboard envy. She needed a clipboard like that. She also needed to fight for her new life. "We'll need rental compensation, as well."

"Of course," Benny said.

She blinked. Was it really that easy? Say what you want, get what you want? Jax had suggested it was, and it'd always seemed to work for Tara.

Benny looked over his clipboard. "I figure we can get all the paperwork taken care of by next week and get you a check to get started."

"And I figure today or tomorrow would be better," Maddie said smoothly. "Bless your heart."

Tara grinned. *Grinned.* Maddie took in the rare sight and returned it.

Benny went back to his clipboard, his ears red. "Tomorrow. How's tomorrow?"

"Fan-fucking-tastic," Chloe said. "Thank you." She beamed at him.

Benny looked a little stunned. "Uh... You're welcome."

Chloe walked him to his truck, then came back with a piece of paper in her hand.

"Are you kidding me—you got his phone number?" Tara asked. "He's barely twelve. I bet they haven't even dropped yet."

"Hey," Chloe said. "Don't talk about my future boyfriend's balls. He was cute, and Maddie scared the hell out of him."

"I thought you thought Lance was cute," Tara said. "And his brother."

"Uh-huh. And your point?"

"And Officer Hottie. Sawyer, right? You were looking at him the other night like you wanted to eat him up alive."

"If I was looking at him at all, I was planning his slow, painful death. Did you hear what we were just told? We're getting a big fat check tomorrow." Chloe looked at each of them. "Our plan?"

"Big fat checks divide into three nicely," Tara noted.

"True." Chloe nodded. "I guess that means by this time tomorrow, we're cut loose." She smiled. "You guys will miss me. Say it."

Maddie tried to sit there calm and in control, but suddenly it was all too much. The fire. The terrifying escape. Tara's revelation, making her realize that she'd misdirected her emotions. Her sisters all gung ho to take the check and run. Jax saying those three little words that she'd never heard before, three words that meant so much more than she'd imagined they could. Her heart clenched hard. "I'm the middle sister," she said softly, then repeated it more strongly.

"Very good," Chloe said. "Can you say the alphabet, too?"

"As the middle, I'm the logical choice for mediator. We have decisions to make, and they get made right now. Majority rules." She looked at each of them. "We walk away or rebuild. We're voting, now. Youngest first."

Chloe pulled out an iTouch, which Lance had lent her in the hospital, and brought up a Magic 8-Ball application. "Magic 8-Ball," she intoned with great ceremony. "Should I stay here in Lucky Harbor?"

Maddie was boggled. "What? You can't leave your vote up to a Magic 8-Ball!"

"I can't?"

"No!" But Maddie bit her lip, trying to see the iTouch screen. "What did it say?"

Chloe looked down and sighed. "*Outlook not so good. Just as well. I'm ready to blow this popsicle stand anyway.*"

Disappointment practically choking her, Maddie turned to Tara.

Tara held her hand out for Chloe's iTouch. "Let me see that thing."

"You aren't serious." Maddie's throat felt like she'd swallowed shards of glass. "Please say you're not serious."

"Okay. I'm not serious." Tara reached for Maddie's hand, her smile a little watery. "I vote we stay here."

"Me, too," Chloe said. "I was only kidding before. We can't leave now. Things are just getting good."

"Two yeses," Tara said. "Maddie?"

She was dizzy, overwhelmed, and confused as hell.

"Aw, look at her," Tara murmured. "Like a long-tailed cat in a room full of rocking chairs."

"She's got fear written all over her," Chloe agreed. "Definitely a high flight risk. Makes me wonder if she wanted us to vote the other way."

"Huh," Tara said, nodding. "Interesting. You mean she wanted us to make the decision for her so she didn't have to be accountable?"

"Exactly."

"I'm right here," Maddie said. "I can hear you."

"You know what you need?" Chloe asked. "You need to get over yourself."

"Hey," Maddie said. "When you first showed up here with your bad 'tude, did I tell you to get over it?"

"Yes, actually. Several times."

Okay, true. Maddie turned on a smug Tara and narrowed her eyes. "And you."

"Me? What did I do?"

"I gave you sympathy. *I* want sympathy!"

"Are you kidding me? You have the sexiest man on the planet wanting you. You're getting laid regularly. No sympathy for you!"

Maddie stood up. "I need some fresh air."

"Last time you said that, you went to the bar, got toasted, and kissed a hottie."

Halfway to the door, Maddie came back and snatched Chloe's iTouch out of her hands. "And I need this."

Just outside, she closed her eyes and whispered, "Am I going to get it right this time?"

The iTouch clouded and then cleared with her answer:

Ask again later

Dammit! She shoved the thing in her pocket and got into her car. She drove along the beach, which was dense with fog. The water was gray and choppy today, an endless cycle of unrestrained violence.

Sort of how her gut felt.

Somehow she ended up at the pier, ticket in hand, staring up at the Ferris wheel. *Do it,* the brave little voice in her head said.

Live.

Which is how she found herself in the swinging seat, clinging to the bar in front of her, her legs like jelly as she rose in the air.

And—oh, shit—rose some more.

And more...

And then, when she was as high as she could go—and not breathing—the Ferris wheel stuttered to a stop.

Her heart did the same.

Around her, the few others on the wheel with her gasped and woo-hoo'd their delight.

She wasn't feeling delight. She was feeling stark terror. Whose idea had this been? What the hell had she been thinking? Life was just as good on the ground!

She tried to look at that ground, but her forward motion had the bucket tilting forward, and she felt her head spin. "Oh, God, oh, God—" She had a death grip on the bar now. She couldn't feel her legs at all. And her stomach was sitting in her throat, blocking all air from coming through.

Stop looking down. Forcing her head up, she stared out at the view. It was incredible. If she discounted the vertigo, that is. From this high, she had a three-hundred-sixty-degree vista of the sparkling Pacific Ocean and the rocky shores for as far as she could see.

And the town. She could see all of Lucky Harbor from here, and it was as pretty as a postcard. It was a perspective she never would have appreciated had she not faced her fear and come up here.

Okay, so she hadn't quite overcome the fear, and she was a minute from hyperventilating, but she'd get there.

Thing was, she had a lot of fears to overcome. She had a lot of "roads not taken," or "rides not taken." There'd been things she'd convinced herself she couldn't do.

For instance, she'd convinced herself her mother hadn't been interested in more of a relationship. It was too late for what-ifs on that one, but what about her sisters? It didn't seem too late for them, even though she'd told herself that they hadn't wanted her in their lives. The truth was, she hadn't reached out, either, and she could have. She should have.

She'd done the same to Jax. He might not have been forthright, not completely, but he'd shown her from the beginning how he felt, without words. He'd pushed her to want more—more of the truth from him, more of everything. Why hadn't she wanted to hear it?

Fear. She'd let it rule her.

That had to change. If she lived through this stupid ride.

Just as she thought it, the Ferris wheel jerked and her bucket swung as the ride started moving again. And ten minutes later, after she'd gone around three times and finally had her feet firmly back on the ground, she grinned.

She'd made it. She got back into her car feeling better and more determined and drove without a destination in mind.

No, that was a lie. She knew *exactly* where she was going. She pulled into Jax's driveway and parked. It was forty-five degrees out, and she was sweating.

You know what to do, he'd said.

And he'd been right. She wanted to stay in Lucky Harbor, and she wanted to be a family with her sisters.

Both of those things were within her reach.

She also wanted Jax.

Hopefully he was still within her reach, as well. She knocked on his door, and when he didn't answer, she twisted around and eyed his Jeep. He was home...

Then she heard it, the steady, rhythmic banging,

and she followed the sound around to the back of the house. He was there in battered boots, a gray Henley, and beloved old Levi's faded to threads in spots. He was chopping wood, the ax rising and falling with easy grace. His shirt was soaked through with sweat and clinging to his every hard inch.

He had a lot of hard inches. Just watching him gave her a hot flash.

He had to have seen her come around the side of the house. He had instincts like a cat, and she was making no move to be secretive, but he kept chopping.

Saying nothing.

Finally, she risked life and limb and stepped close enough that he was forced to stop or put her in danger from the flying shards of wood.

Lowering the ax, he leaned on it, his breath coming steady but hard.

Still saying nothing.

"Hey," she said softly.

"Hey. What are you doing here?"

Fair enough question, since she'd asked him the same only this morning. It figured that he'd get right to the point. He was good at that.

She wasn't. "I was...confused. And I guess a little mad at everyone, and then I went for a drive and my car came here."

His mouth quirked very slightly. "Did your car forget that you're mad at me, as well?"

"Well," she said, "out of all the people I'm mad at, I think I'm the least mad at you."

"Why's that?"

Maddie fought the urge to pull out Chloe's iTouch and

ask the Magic 8-Ball how she was doing with Jax, but she had a feeling she knew.

"Why, Maddie?"

Dammit, he wasn't going to let her off the hook. She went with flippant. After all, it was her number-one defense mechanism. "You did recently put a damn good smile on my face. Maybe you get partial immunity. I don't know."

He eyed her for a long moment, clearly seeing right through her. "I gave you more than a smile," he said, setting down his ax and walking into the house.

Jax headed into his kitchen and straight for the refrigerator, pulling out a bottle of water for his suddenly parched throat.

Do-or-die moment. Either she'd come to say thanks for the memories and vanish off into the sunset, or she was here to... Hell, he was afraid to hope.

When he'd been a lawyer, he'd walked into court every day knowing he was going to win. Always.

It'd be nice to know the verdict on this.

Distance. He needed some. He downed the water, tossed the bottle aside, and moved through the house. Not a total ass, he'd left the slider open in case she wanted to come in and destroy him some more, but without looking back, he went into his bathroom. Stripping out of his sweaty clothes, he cranked the shower up to scalding and stepped in. Bowing his head beneath the spray, he let the water bead down his back and tried to clear his mind.

Not happening.

Instead, images came to him: Maddie standing beneath the hot water with him, glistening and soapy, her eyes soft and warm on his; him gliding his hands over that body until those eyes glazed with passion, listening to her pant his name over and over as she came—

When the door opened behind him, he didn't move, didn't lift his head, didn't open his eyes. Her arms came around him, and he felt her naked body press up against his.

And here was the thing. All his good intentions went out the window as those hands drifted down his chest and over his abs, because it was hard to remain distant with the hard-on of his life.

"Why are you here?" he asked again.

Maddie swallowed hard and tried to channel... which actress? Damn, she couldn't think of an actress to save her life! She was on her own. "Well, you seemed pretty sweaty," she said in her best come-hither voice. "Thought maybe I could help wash your back." She leaned in and licked a droplet of water off his neck.

She felt him draw a deep breath. "Maddie."

Okay, so he wasn't in the mood for flippant. She could understand that. She paused, her eyes on the smooth muscles of his back. "You bared yourself to me."

He turned to face her. "Yes, as it happens, I'm as bare-ass naked as it gets."

They both looked down. Yeah, he was naked. Gloriously so. "I meant more than your body," she whispered. "You bared yourself to me, and... and it took me longer than it should have to notice."

God, he was perfect. Hard and ripped and heart-stoppingly perfect. She ran her finger over the drops of water on one pec, and, whoops, grazed his nipple.

"Maddie?"

"Yeah?"

"Up here."

She tore her gaze off him and met his eyes. They were slightly warmer, and maybe, possibly, amused. Relief hit her so hard she nearly slid to the tile floor. "Oh, Jax. I'm sorry that it took me so long to get with the program. That I doubted you, that I pushed you away. I wasn't looking for this. And I know you weren't, either, even less than me, but you...you handled it better."

His hand slid over her stomach and settled on her hip, which made it all but impossible to think, but she struggled to try. "I know I said some things...about where we're at."

"Actually, you made yourself pretty clear about where we *weren't* at." Reaching for the soap, he turned away and began to scrub up.

"About that. I was wrong." She was a little breathless just from watching his hands run over his body, leaving soapy trails in their midst, and lost her train of thought.

He didn't say anything, just finished what he was doing. Finally he put the soap back, rinsed off, and then moved unexpectedly, pulling her in close, wrapping his arms around her and just holding on. Tight. She didn't mind. She could have stayed like that forever, feeling safe and warm and stupidly happy. But she had more to say. "Jax, I—"

"Whatever you want," he said, his voice low and raw. "Except for letting go. I'm not going to let go."

"I hope you mean that. Because you were right about something else, too. I *was* scared, scared to the bone." She grimaced. "I might have panicked even."

"You did do a lot of knitting," he said with an utterly straight face and then moved his lips down her neck.

Shivering at the feel of his mouth brushing over her wet skin, she clutched at him. When he lifted his head, he was smiling. The sight threatened to short out her brain. Or maybe that was his touch. She wasn't sure, except she was breathing hard and was dangerously close to leaping into his arms and impaling herself on him. "You said to fight for what I want. You said to get into the ring." She looked down. "Um, not to change the subject, but you want me."

"Hard to hide it."

"I want you back," she whispered, which isn't what she'd meant to say. Exactly.

"For how long?"

"As long as you'll have me."

He drew a shuddery breath. "So this is you, fighting for what you want?"

"Yes." It was hard to concentrate. His hand was on her hip, slowly making its way north until it cupped her breast. His thumb glided over her already pebbled nipple, his expression a mixture of heat, affection, need, and so much more that it took her breath. She slid her arms around his waist and laid her head on his chest, shivering when he cupped the back of her neck. "I came to Lucky Harbor out of obligation, but really, I was looking for something."

"Did you find it?"

She loved the way his voice rumbled through his chest, his body radiating into hers. "Yeah, I found it. I'm staying in Lucky Harbor, Jax. We're going to rebuild. For the first time in my life, I fit. I have my sisters, a place that's mine—well, it's only one-third mine, and we still owe you a ton of money, not to mention it's half charred—but you know what I mean."

His lips twitched.

"And!" She drew a breath, because this was the big one. "I let myself love and, in return, be loved."

He went utterly still, his eyes twin dark pools. His fingers brushed up her spine, sinking into her hair. "Did you?"

"Yes." Her heart clenched that he'd doubted it, even for a minute. "I love you, Jax. And you love me back."

"I do," he said, warm emotion thickening his voice, and all her worries began to fade completely away. He pressed his mouth to the beat of the pulse at the base of her neck. When he lifted his head and met her gaze, his eyes were shining fiercely. "I love you more than you'll ever know."

Looking at him, she saw her future and felt all the ragged tears in her heart heal themselves. "I fit," she whispered in marvel, stepping into him. "I fit with you."

He nodded and wrapped his arms around her. "Perfectly."

Maddie's Boyfriend Scarf

Materials:
One skein super-bulky yarn, at least 100 yards
1 pair size 13 needles (straight)
1 size G (4 mm) crochet hook

Instructions:
1. Cast on 15 stitches (or enough stitches to make the scarf 6 to 8 inches wide).
2. Knit every row—this is called a garter stitch—until your scarf is 60˝ long. (If you have more yarn left and a very tall boyfriend, you may choose to make the scarf a bit longer.)
3. Bind off.
4. Use your crochet hook to weave in the ends at the top and bottom. See how easy that was!

Personalize your gift:
1. Feel free to use a different weight of yarn but check on the label to see what size needles are recommended and use them instead.
2. Knit with two different strands held together throughout. This creates a unique yarn only your beloved will have.
3. Create stripes by buying several colors of yarn, starting a new color at the end of a row, and leaving a tail for each color (which will be woven in with the crochet hook during step #4 above).
4. Add fringe: Cut 64 lengths of yarn approximately 10˝ each. Take four lengths of yarn and fold them in half. Insert the crochet hook into one of the corners of the scarf. Pull the loop through the scarf with the crochet hook. Then bring the ends of the yarn through the loop and tighten. On the narrow edges of the scarf, make 8 tassels spaced evenly.

The Sweetest
Thing

*To another oldest sister, Kelsey, who always knows
what to do and how to make us feel better.
Love you forever.*

Chapter 1

♥

"There is no snooze button on life."
TARA DANIELS

Muffin?" Tara asked as she walked along the long line of people waiting on the pier to enter Lucky Harbor's summer festival. "Have a free Life's-a-Peach Muffin?"

The large basket was heavier than she'd anticipated, and the late afternoon June sun beat down on her head in tune to the Pacific's thrashing waves beating the shore. Perspiration beaded on her skin, which really chapped her hide. It was the steel magnolia in her. Perspiring wasn't just undignified, it contradicted her *never let 'em see you sweat* motto.

Telling herself that she was merely glistening, and hopefully looking luminous while she was at it, Tara amped up her smile and kept going. At least her sundress was lightweight, the material gauzy and playful against her skin. She'd bought it to look sophisticated and elegant. And to boost her confidence.

This was a tall order for a dress.

"Muffin?" she asked the next woman in line.

Mrs. Taylor, the owner of the local craft and supply shop, looked the basket over carefully. "Are they low-fat?"

Before coming to Washington State, Tara had spent most of her life just outside of Houston on her grandparents' ranch, where holding back the use of butter and lard was considered sacrilegious. Low-fat? Not exactly. She gave a brief thought to lying, but she didn't want to be struck dead by lightning—it would ruin her good hair day. "Definitely not, sorry."

"Do you know the calorie count?"

Tara looked down at her beautiful muffins, fat and soft and gently browned, each perfectly baked and undoubtedly overflowing with calories. "A gazillion," she said. "Per bite."

"I'm surprised at you," Mrs. Taylor said disappointedly, "promoting cholesterol consumption like this."

Tara had read somewhere that it took less effort to be nice than bitchy. And since she was all for energy conservation, she let her mouth curve into a smile. "Actually, what I'm promoting is the renovation of the inn my sisters and I are opening in two weeks—" She broke off when Mrs. Taylor held up a polite finger and pulled out her vibrating phone.

Tara had a finger of her own to hold up, but since it wasn't a polite one, she refrained. She moved on, assuring herself that the continuous swallowing of her pride since coming to Lucky Harbor only *felt* like it was going to kill her, but surely it wouldn't.

Probably.

"Muffin?" Tara asked a new section of the line, handing them out as people expressed interest. "Y'all want a free Life's-a-Peach muffin?"

Each had been painstakingly wrapped in cellophane with a folded flyer for the Lucky Harbor Beach Inn tucked into a ribbon. It was part of Tara's mission, and that mission was different than it'd been last year. Last year, she'd wanted peace on earth and a manicure that lasted a full two weeks. This year, things were more basic. She wanted to be able to pay her bills at the end of the month without robbing Peter to pay Paul, and maybe to feel like she was in control of her own life.

That was all.

Just a single month in which her ends met her means. Thirty days during which she wasn't constantly in angst over the arrival of a paycheck.

Or lack thereof.

The sun continued to beat down on Tara as she walked the length of the pier. Behind her, the sharp, craggy cliffs were cast in shadow. Out in front, the surf continued to pound the beach, shuddering the pier beneath her feet. She passed the beauty shop, the Eat Me Diner where she worked four nights a week, and then the arcade, ice cream parlor, and the five-story-high Ferris wheel.

The crowd grew around her, seeming to surge in closer. It was as if the entire state of Washington had showed up for the Summer Arts and Musical Fest, but that wasn't a surprise to Tara. The only thing the people of Lucky Harbor liked more than their gossip was a social gathering, and there would be plenty of both to be had tonight. A warm night, good music, dancing, drinking... a recipe for a good time, no doubt.

"I'll most definitely take a muffin," Chloe said, appearing at Tara's side.

At twenty-four, Tara's sister was the baby of the family, and as such had inherited all the free-spiritedness—aka wildness—of their mother, Phoebe Traeger. Chloe wore snug hip-hugging cargo shorts and a sunshine yellow tank top that required sunglasses to look at. Her glossy dark red hair was streaked with twin hot-pink highlights, one down each temple, the rest cascading down her back in a perfect disarray of waves to give her a just-out-of-bed look.

She could have been a cover model.

Well, except for the fact that she was five foot three in her high-tops and had absolutely no discipline nor inclination to follow instructions. Chloe was freshly back from a two-month trip traveling through Miami Beach's high-end hotel spas, where she'd put her aesthetician license to good use while fine-tuning her own natural skincare line. And probably also finding trouble, as was Chloe's habit.

Tara was just glad to have her back in Lucky Harbor. She'd worried the entire time Chloe had been gone. It was a lifelong thing for Tara, worrying about her troubled baby sister.

Chloe, looking tan and happy and sporting a new Chinese symbol tat on the inside of her wrist that she'd refused to translate, bit into a muffin and let out a heart-felt moan. "Damn, Tara, these rock. Can you tell me something?"

"If you're going to ask me if the muffins are low fat," Tara said, "you should know I'm running out of places to hide all the dead bodies."

Chloe laughed. "No, I can feel my arteries clogging even as I swallow, and I'm good with that." She licked the crumbs off her fingers. "Just wanted to know if you noticed Ford making his way toward you."

Tara turned to follow Chloe's gaze and felt her breath catch. Ford Walker was indeed headed her way, moving sure and easy, his long-legged stride in no hurry. Which was a good thing, as he was stopped by nearly everyone that he passed. He didn't appear to mind, which made it damn hard to dislike him—although Tara still gave it her all.

"You ever going to tell me what's the deal with you two?" Chloe was digging into a second muffin as if she hadn't eaten in a week. And maybe she hadn't. The perpetually broke Chloe never seemed to worry about her next meal.

"There's no deal with me and Ford."

Chloe's low laugh rang in Tara's ears, calling her out for the liar she was. "You know what you need?"

Tara slid her a look. "A trip to some South Pacific island with no sisters named Chloe?"

"Hmm. Maybe for Christmas. For now, you need to relax. More yoga, less stress."

"I'm plenty relaxed." Or she had been until she'd looked at Ford. He'd gotten stopped again and was talking to someone in the line behind her, but as if he felt her appraisal, he turned his head and met her gaze. An odd tension hummed through her veins. Her pulse kicked up as well, not quite into heart-attack territory, but close enough. "Totally, completely relaxed," she murmured.

"Uh-huh," Chloe said, sounding amused. "Is that why you're hugging the basket so tight you're squishing the muffins? Or why you compulsively cleaned the cottage from top to bottom last night?"

"Hey," Tara said in her own defense. "There was a lot of dust, which would have aggravated your asthma. *And*, if you remember, it's only been two weeks since you've landed in the hospital unable to breathe thanks to nothing more than a pollen storm. So you're welcome."

Chloe rolled her eyes and turned to the woman behind her in line. Lucille owned an art gallery in town and was somewhere between seventy and two hundred years old. She wore white-on-white Nikes and her favorite track suit in hot, Day-Glo pink. She took a muffin, bit into it, and sighed in pleasure. "Tara, darling, you're as amazing as you are uptight."

"I'm not—" *Oh, forget it.*

Lucille looked her over from eyes lined thickly with blue eye shadow. "Pretty dress. You always dress so nice. Ross? Wal-Mart?"

Actually, Nordstrom's, Tara thought, back from her old life when she'd had a viable credit card. "It's several years old, so—"

"We have a question," Chloe said to Lucille, interrupting. "Tell me, does my sister look relaxed to you?"

"Relaxed?" Taking the question very seriously, Lucille studied Tara closely. "Actually, she looks a little constipated." She turned to the person who came up behind her, but Tara didn't have to look to see who it was because her nipples got hard.

At six-feet-three inches, Ford was pure testosterone and sinew. His build suggested one of those lean extreme fighters but Ford was too laid-back to ever bother being a fighter of any kind.

He wore low-slung, button-fly Levi's and a white button-down shoved up to his elbows, yet somehow he managed to look as dressed up as Tara. His brown hair was sun-kissed, his green eyes sharp, his smile ready. Everything about him said *ready*, from his tough build to the air of confidence he wore like other men wore cologne. Half the people in Lucky Harbor were in love with him.

The other half were men and didn't count.

Tara was the odd person out, of course. Not only was she *not* in love with him, he tended to step on her last nerve.

There was a very good reason for that.

Several, in fact. But she'd long ago given herself permission to pretend that the thing that had happened between them *hadn't* happened.

"We're trying to figure out what's wrong with Tara, dear," Lucille told him, having to tilt her blue-haired head way up to meet his eyes. "I'm thinking constipation."

Chloe laughed.

Ford looked as if he wanted to laugh.

Tara ground her teeth. "I'm not—"

"It's okay," Lucille said. "It happens to the best of us. All you need are some plums and a blender, and you—"

"*I'm not constipated!*" Great. Now everyone within a thirty-foot radius was privy to the knowledge.

"Well, good," Lucille said. "Because tonight's Bingo Night at the Rec Center."

Extremely aware of Ford standing *way* too close, Tara shifted on her wedged sandals. "Bingo's not really my thing."

"Well, mine either, honey," Lucille said. "But there are men there and lots of 'em. A man could unwind you real nice. Isn't that right, Ford?"

"Yes, ma'am," Ford said with an utterly straight face. "Real nice."

"See?" Lucille said to Tara. "Sure, you're a little young for our crowd, but you could probably snag a real live wire, maybe two."

Tara had seen the Bingo Crowd. The "live wires" were the mobile ones, and using a walker qualified as mobile. "I don't really need a live wire." Much less two.

"Oh my dear," Lucille said. "*Every* woman needs a man. Why even your momma—God rest her soul—used to say it was a shame you couldn't buy sex on eBay."

Beside her, Ford laughed softly. Tara very carefully didn't look at him, the man she'd once needed with her whole being. These days she didn't do "need."

Chloe wisely and gently slipped her arm in Lucille's. "I have friends in high places and can get around this line," she told the older woman. "Come tell me all about all these live wires." She shot Tara a you-owe-me smile over her shoulder as she led Lucille away.

Not that Tara could think about that because now she was alone with Ford. Or as alone as one could be while surrounded by hundreds of people. This was not how she'd envisioned the day going when she got up this morning and made that bargain with God, the one where she promised to be a better person if he gave her a whole day where she didn't have to face anything from her past. But God had just reneged on the deal. Which meant she didn't have to be a better person...

Ford was looking at her. She could feel the weight of his gaze. She kept hers resolutely out on the water. Maybe she should take up knitting like her other sister, Maddie. Knitting was supposedly very cathartic, and Tara could use cathartic. The late afternoon sun sank lower on the ocean as if it was just dipping its toes in to cool off. She stared at it until long fingers brushed hers.

"Tara."

That was it, just her name from Ford's lips, and just like that she...softened. She had no other word for what happened inside her body whenever he spoke to her. She softened, and her entire being went on full alert for him.

Just like old times.

Ford stood there, patient and steady, all day-old scruff and straight white teeth and sparkling gorgeous eyes, bringing out feelings she wasn't prepared for.

"Aren't you going to offer me a muffin?" he asked.

Since a part of her wanted to offer far more, she held her tongue and silently offered the basket. Ford perused his choices as if he was contemplating his life's path.

"They're all the same," Tara finally said.

At that he flashed a grin, and her knees wobbled. Sweet baby Jesus, that smile should come with a label: WARNING: *Prolonged exposure will cause yearning, lust, and stupidity.* "Don't you have a bar to run?" she asked.

"Jax is there, handling things for now."

Ford was a world-class sailing expert. When he wasn't on the water competing, or listed in *Cosmo* as one of the year's "Fun Fearless Males," of all things, he lived here in Lucky Harbor. Here, with his best friend, Jax, he co-owned and ran The Love Shack, the town's most popular watering hole. He did so mostly because, near as Tara could tell, he'd majored in shooting the breeze— which he did plenty of when he was behind the bar mixing drinks and enjoying life.

She enjoyed life, too. Or enjoyed the *idea* of life.

Okay, so she was *working* on the enjoying part. The problem was that her enjoyment kept getting held up by her reality. "Are you going to take a muffin or what?"

Ford cocked his head and ran his gaze over her like a caress. "I'll take whatever crumb you're offering."

That brought a genuine smile from her. "Like you'd settle for a crumb."

"I did once." He was still smiling, but his eyes were serious now, and something pinged low in her belly.

Memories. Unwelcome ones. "Ford—"

"Ah," he said very softly. "So you *do* remember my name. That's a start."

She gave a push to his solid chest. Not that she could move him if she tried, the big, sexy lout.

And she'd forgotten nothing about him—*nothing*. "What do you want?"

"I thought after all this time," he said lightly, "we could be friends."

"Friends," she repeated.

"Yes. Make polite conversation, occasionally see each other socially. Maybe even go out on a date."

She stared at him. "That would make us more than friends."

"You always were smart as hell."

Her stomach tightened again. He wanted to sleep with her. Or not sleep, as the case might be. Her body reacted hopefully to the mere thought. "We don't—" She closed her eyes to hide the lie. "We don't like each other like that anymore."

"No?" In the next beat, she felt the air shift as he moved closer. She opened her eyes just as he lifted his hand and tucked a strand of her hair behind her ear, making her shiver.

He noticed—of course he did; he noticed *everything*—and his mouth curved. But his eyes remained serious, so very serious as he leaned in.

To anyone watching, it would look as if he was whispering something in her ear.

But he wasn't.

No, he was up to something far more devastatingly sneaky. His lips brushed against her throat, and then her jaw, and while she fought with a moan and lost, he whispered, "I like you just fine."

Her body quivered, assuring herself she returned the favor whether she liked it or not.

"Think about it, Tara."

And then he was gone, leaving her unable to do anything *but* think of it.

Of him.

Chapter 2

♥

*"Good judgment comes from bad experience.
Unfortunately, most of that comes
from bad judgment."*
TARA DANIELS

A week later, the heat had amped up to nearly one hundred degrees. The beach shimmered, the ocean stilled, and Ford came back into Lucky Harbor after a sailing event he'd competed in down in Baja.

He wasn't on the world circuit anymore, but sometimes he couldn't help himself. He liked the thrill of the race.

The sense of being alive.

He'd like to say that he'd worked his ass off most of his life to be the best of the best, but he hadn't. Sailing had come relatively easily, as if he'd been born with the knack to read the waters and handle the controls of a boat, outguessing and outmaneuvering the wind as he pleased. He'd lived and breathed racing for as long as it'd been fun, in the process leaving blood and sweat and little pieces of his soul in every ocean on the planet.

These past few days had been no different. And as it had been just last month in Perth, his time had been well spent, paying off big. Ford had placed in the top ten, pocketing a very lucrative purse for the honor.

Once upon a time, it'd been all about the money. Back when he'd been so poor he couldn't even pay attention.

Now it was about something else. Something... elusive.

The win should have left him feeling flush and happy, and yeah, for a brief moment, the adrenaline and thrill had coursed through his body, fooling him with the elusive, fleeting sense of having it all.

But it'd faded quickly, leaving... nothing.

He felt nothing at all.

And damn if he wasn't getting tired of that. He'd gotten back late last night, docking at the Lucky Harbor marina. He'd spent the morning cleaning up his Finn, the strict, simple design solo boat he raced in. Then he'd done a maintenance check on his thirty-two-foot 10R Beneteau, which he'd slept on last night rather than drive up the hill to his house on the bluffs.

Moving on from his boats, he worked on the Cape Dory Cruiser docked next to his Beneteau as a favor to Maddie Moore.

The favor had been a no-brainer. Maddie was one of Tara's two sisters, and together with Chloe, they ran and operated the marina and inn. And when a pretty lady like Maddie asked Ford for help getting her boat to run, he did his best to solve her problem. Even if said pretty lady was sleeping with his best friend Jax.

The problem with the Cape Dory had been a relatively

easy fix. It hadn't been properly winterized, and condensation had formed on the inside of the fuel tanks.

The repair, along with some other things, had taken several hours in the unbearable heat, but Ford hadn't cared. It'd occupied his brain and kept him from thinking too much—always a good thing.

As a bonus, getting his hands dirty had done more for his mental health than the racing had. He loved wrenching. It was something else that came easy to him and gave him great pleasure.

When he'd finished, he pulled off his trashed shirt and washed up the best he could in the marina building. Then he headed across the property to the inn, looking for a big, tall glass of ice water.

Sure, he could have just gone home, but Tara's car was out front, and he...hell. She tended to look right through him, and in return, he liked to drive her crazy. Home was a short drive on the best of days, and a vast improvement from being ignored by her. He toyed with coming right out and asking what her problem was, but he realized that if she said, "You, Ford, *you're* my problem," he'd still have to see her daily for the duration of her stay here in Lucky Harbor. And that would suck.

This was at least the hundredth day he'd come to this "realization," and he was no closer to figuring out what to do than when she'd first come back to town six months ago. So mostly, he'd steered clear. It'd seemed the easiest route, and he was all about the easy.

But today he had a gift to deliver. Lucille had cornered him when he'd stopped by his bar last night to check in after his trip, handing him a wooden box with the word RECIPES written across it.

"Can you give this to Tara for me?" she'd asked. "Don't peek."

So, of course, he'd peeked. There'd been nothing inside but plain—and blank—3×5 index cards. "For her recipes?"

Lucille snapped the box shut, narrowly missing his fingers. "No."

Ford recognized the spark of trouble in Lucille's rheumy eyes. There was no bigger gossip or meddler in town, and since Lucky Harbor was chock-full of gossips and meddlers, this was saying a lot. Lucille and her cronies had recently started a Facebook page for Lucky Harbor residents, bringing the gossip mill to even new heights.

"Okay, spill," Ford said, pinning her with a hard look that wouldn't slow her down—she was unstoppable *and* unflappable. "What are you up to?"

She'd cackled and patted him again. "No good. I'm up to no good. Just see that Tara gets the box."

So that's what he was doing.

Delivering the box to Tara.

She wouldn't be happy to see him, that was for damn sure. Her eyes would chill and so would her voice. She'd pretend they were virtually strangers.

And in a way, they were. It'd been a damn long time since they'd known each other, and the past was the past. He wasn't a guy to spend much time looking back. Nope, he liked to live with both feet firmly in the present, thank you very much. He didn't do regrets, or any other useless emotions for that matter. If he made a mistake, he learned from it and moved on. If he wanted something, he went about getting it. Or learned to live without it.

Period.

Of course, as it pertained to Tara, he'd made plenty of mistakes, and he wasn't all that sure he'd learned much except maybe how to bury the pain.

He'd gotten damn good at that.

But lately, whenever he caught a glimpse of Tara in those look-but-don't-touch clothes and that hoity-toity 'tude she wore like Gucci, he had the most insane urge to ruffle her up. Get her dirty. Make her squirm.

Preferably while naked and beneath him.

Ford swiped the sweat off his forehead with his arm and strode up the steps to the inn. A two-story Victorian, it'd been freshly rebuilt and renovated after a bad fire six months ago. There was still a lot to do before the grand opening: painting and landscaping, as well as interior touches, and the kitchen appliances hadn't yet been delivered. Still, character dripped from the place. All it needed were guests to come and fill it up, and Tara, Maddie, and Chloe could make a success of it.

As a family.

To the best of Ford's knowledge, the whole family thing was new to the sisters. Very new. And also to the best of his knowledge, they weren't very good at it. He just hoped they managed without bloodshed. Probably they should put that into their business plan and get everyone to sign it: *Murder Not Allowed*. Especially Tara.

Bloodthirsty wench, he thought fondly, and walked across the wraparound porch. There were seedlings laid out to be planted along the new railings. Someone had a green thumb. Not Chloe, he'd bet. The youngest sister didn't have the patience.

Not Maddie either, since she was currently spending every spare second in Jax's bed, the lucky bastard.

Tara then?

Ford tried to picture her pretty hands in the dirt...and then his mind went to other places, like her being dirty with him.

Shaking his head at himself, he stepped inside. Before the devastating fire, the interior decorating had been *Little House on the Prairie* meets the Roseanne Conner household. Things had changed once Tara had gotten hold of the place. Gone were the chicken, rooster, and cow motifs; replaced by a softer, warmer beachy look of soothing earth tones mixed with pale blues and greens.

Not a cow in sight.

As Ford walked inside on the brand-new wood floors, he could hear female laughter coming from the deck off the living room. Heading down the hall, he opened the slider door and found the party.

Seated around a table were four women of varying ages, shapes, and sizes. At the head of the table stood Tara. She had eyes the color of perfectly aged whiskey, outlined by long black lashes. Her mouth could be soft and warm—when she was feeling soft and warm, that is. Today it was glossed and giving off one of her professional smiles. She'd let her short, brunette layers grow out a little these past months so that the silky strands just brushed her shoulders, framing the face that haunted his dreams. As always, she was dressed as if she was speeding down the road to success. Today she wore an elegant fitted dress with a row of buttons running down her deliciously long, willowy body.

Ford fantasized about undoing those buttons—one at a time.

With his teeth.

She held a tray, and on that tray—be still his heart—was a huge pitcher of iced tea, complete with a bucket of ice and lemon wedges, and condensation on the pitcher itself, assuring him it would quench his thirst. He must have made a sound because all eyes swiveled in his direction. Including Tara's. In fact, hers dropped down over his body, and then jerked back up to his eyes. Her gaze was gratifyingly wide.

There were a couple of gasps from the others, and several "*oh my's*" mixed in with a single, heartfelt "*good Lord*," prompting him to look down at himself.

Nope, he wasn't having the naked-in-public dream again. He was awake and wearing his favorite basketball shorts—admittedly slung a little low on the hips but covering the essentials—and running shoes, no socks.

No shirt, either. He'd forgotten to replace the one he'd stripped off. "Hey," he said in greeting.

"What are you doing?" Tara asked, her voice soft and Southern and dialed to Not Happy to See Him.

And yet interestingly enough, she was looking at him like maybe he was a twelve-course meal and she hadn't eaten in a week.

He'd take that, Ford decided, and he'd especially take the way her breathing had quickened. "I have a gift for you from Lucille."

At the sight of the small wood box, Tara went still, then came around the table to take it.

"It looks just like the one we lost," she murmured, opening it. When she looked inside, a flash of disappointment came and went in her eyes, so fast Ford nearly missed it.

"What?" he asked, ignoring everyone else on the deck as he took a step toward her. "What's wrong?"

"Nothing." Tara clutched the box to her chest and shook her head. "It's just that we lost the original in the fire. It was filled with Phoebe-isms."

"Phoebe-isms?"

"My mom. She'd written these little...tidbits of advice, I guess you'd call them, for me and my sisters over the years. Things like 'A glass of wine is always the solution, even if you aren't sure of the problem.'"

The four women at the table, each of whom had known and loved Phoebe, laughed softly, fondly.

Ford had a soft spot for Phoebe as well. She'd been in Lucille's "gang" and one of Ford's best customers at the bar. As he smiled at the memory, Tara did that pretend-not-to-look-at-his-bare-chest thing again, then quickly turned away.

Interesting reaction for someone who'd exerted a lot of energy and time over the past months *not* noticing him.

"Get him a chair, honey," one of the women said— Rani, the town librarian.

Tara turned to Ford, panic growing in her eyes at the thought of him hanging around.

Yet another interesting reaction. "Ford can't stay," she said, eyes locked on his. "He's...busy. Very busy. I'm sure he doesn't have time to bother with our little meeting."

"I'm not that busy," Ford said, looking around the table. Each woman had an assortment of plates in front of her, filled with what looked like delicious desserts that Tara must have baked at the diner since the inn's kitchen wasn't yet functioning.

They looked good, real good.

There was also wine, mostly gone now, and everyone

but Tara was looking pretty darn relaxed for a *meeting*. "Besides," he said, "this looks more like a party."

"It's the Garden Society." Tara was still blocking his way from moving farther onto the deck. "The ladies here were gracious enough to come and sample some snacks that I hope to have available for our inn guests upon request."

His belly stirred, reminding him he'd skipped lunch. "I'm an excellent taster," he said with his most charming smile.

"But you're *so* busy," Tara said, with *her* most charming smile, although her eyes were saying *Don't You Dare*.

"Aw, but I'm never too busy for you." Ford had no idea why he was baiting her. Maybe because she'd spent so much time pretending he didn't exist, and this was much more fun. Plus there was the added benefit that he knew her Southern manners wouldn't allow her to say what she *really* wanted to, not in front of company, anyway. *Heaven forbid we be rude in front of guests*.

Tara was now giving him the look that assured him that she was indeed imagining wrapping her fingers around his neck. He smiled wider. He couldn't help it. For the first time in too damn long, he was feeling alive. Very alive.

Admitting defeat with her usual good grace, Tara never let her smile falter as she shifted to the railing, where she had supplies stacked up. She grabbed a spare plate and loaded it with her goodies before wrapping it in foil.

Ford was getting the to-go version.

"He looks thirsty, too, Tara," Rani said.

Ford loved Rani.

"Yes, dear," another of the women said. "Pour the

poor, overworked man a glass of tea. You don't let a man of this caliber drink from a garden hose."

"Thank you, Ethel," Ford murmured, and since he was watching Tara's arresting face, he saw the flicker of surprise cross her features. Yes, he knew Ethel, too. She ran the Rec Center. She'd been there when, twenty years ago now, he'd hit a baseball through her office window, nearly decapitating her. Good times.

"Please stay," Ethel said to Ford, and patted an empty chair right next to hers.

"But he's not dressed for this," Tara said, once again eyeing Ford's bare chest. Her pupils dilated. "There are health codes, and—"

"We won't tell." This from Sandy, the town clerk and city manager of Lucky Harbor. "Besides, we're outside. He's dressed just *perfect*."

Sandy had gone to school with Ford. She'd been class president, head cheerleader, and a lot of fun. Ford smiled at her.

She returned it with a saucy wink. "My sister's husband is looking into buying a boat," she told him. "A fixer-upper. I told her that I'd ask your opinion."

"It's a good time," Ford told her. "The market's down so you could get a deal. If he wants my help working on it, have him call me."

"A man who can wield a set of tools *and* read the market," Rani said on a dreamy sigh.

"Yes," Tara said, grinding her back teeth together as she looked at Ford. "Bless your heart."

She didn't mean it, of course, which only made him smile again. Sure, her voice was all gentle and soft, but her real feelings were visible if you knew her.

And whether she wanted to believe it or not, Ford knew her. He knew she wanted to knock him into next week.

"A moment?" Tara requested sweetly.

"Sure," he said just as sweetly as he leaned back against the railing and got comfy.

"*Alone.*"

And then, without waiting for an answer, she dropped his foiled to-go goodies into a pretty bag, poured one of the glasses full of iced tea, and walked right past him, hips swinging with attitude, inside the inn.

Clearly assuming he'd follow.

He watched her go, enjoying the view, but he didn't move. He wasn't much into being bossed around, even by an incredibly beautiful woman who was anal retentive and a bit of a control freak.

Well, unless they were in bed. He didn't mind then, not as long as he got to return the favor.

But there was something about Tara that drew him in spite of himself, that snagged him by the throat and held tight. Maybe it was the tough-girl exterior, which he knew barely covered a bruised and tender heart. He'd seen that heart once, and truth be told he wasn't all that interested in going back there. But he wouldn't mind seeing her other parts.

He couldn't help it. She had really great parts.

And he wanted that cold iced tea, bad. Almost as much as he wanted...

Her, he realized grimly. Against all caution and sanity, he wanted her. So he followed her inside the inn.

Chapter 3

♥

"Change is good but dollars are better."
TARA DANIELS

Tara waited in the freshly painted hallway off the inn's large, open living room with what she felt was admirable calm until *finally*, a half-naked Ford slowly strode inside.

Not hurrying.

Of course not. Ford never hurried when he could saunter. He never rushed a damn thing in his life. The big, sexy lug moved when and where he wanted.

She knew she was just damn lucky he'd decided to move at all. He was unpredictable.

Spontaneous.

Not to be confused with uncontrolled. Because Ford, for all his sense of humor and smart-ass-ness, was one of the most controlled people Tara had ever met. It was one of the few things they had in common. She did her best to keep her eyes on his, but she couldn't seem to help herself. She'd seen him without a shirt before, of course. But it'd been a while.

Watching her watch him, he reached out and played with the lace on her collarbone. "Why are you always dressed like you're going to a business meeting?"

"I *am* at a business meeting. Sort of." She paused and admitted the truth. "But mostly I wear dresses or skirts because I don't have a good butt in jeans."

With a laugh, Ford stepped close, so close that she could smell the ocean on him. He was salty and tangy, and so indelibly male that Tara almost closed the last inch between them simply so that she could lick him like a lollipop. Just one lick, she told herself, from sternum to the very low waistband of the basketball shorts...

His eyes lit with wickedness, as if he knew her secret longings, but he said nothing as he leaned over her shoulder to view her backside.

Ford Walker, Resident Butt Inspector.

"Looks fine from here," he assured her in a low, husky voice that scraped at every single erogenous zone she owned. "Damned fine." He paused. "Maybe I should give it a hand test to be sure." Before she could say a word, he slid a hand down her spine, heading south with wicked and nefarious intent.

With a shocked laugh, she shoved him away. "I'll take your word for it."

"So," he said, recovering far faster than she. "Still constipated?"

Tara choked. "What?"

Ford lifted a broad shoulder and unsuccessfully bit back a smile. "After the other day, it got around town that you were having troubles."

" 'Got around town,' " she repeated faintly and closed her eyes to count to ten. For peace and Zen.

Neither made an appearance.

"I think Lucille tweeted it, and it ended up on Facebook," he said, amusement heavy in his voice. "She took the opportunity to put up a recipe to fix the problem. You take a few plums, pit them, get a blender and—"

"I'm not—" Tara broke off, glancing through the inn to the sliding glass door before purposely lowering her voice. "*Constipated!*"

"You sure?"

"Very!"

He grinned, and she felt conflicting reactions—her brain melting, and steam coming out her ears.

How could this be? How could he drive her so insane and make her want him with equal intensity? She didn't understand, she really didn't. "Here," she said and thrust the glass of iced tea and the bag of desserts at him. "And you should know, regarding your *friend* request the other day at the music fest, I've thought about it. Us." Fact was, she'd done nothing *but* think about it. But they'd failed once. More like crashed and burned, spectacularly, and she shook her head. "I can't go there again, Ford." The last time had nearly destroyed her. Only he seemed to have the power to do that, and she wouldn't, *couldn't*, let it happen again.

"I didn't ask you to go there again," he said.

She met his gaze, his giving nothing away, and she flushed because he was right. He hadn't asked her to fall in young, crazy love; he'd only suggested they have sex. *Very* different. "That's an equally bad idea. You know it, and I know it. Now please go."

"You're big on that word," he noted. " 'Go.' "

His was a not-so-subtle rebuke, and an unpleasant reminder of their past. And she resented like hell that he was throwing it in her face. By leaving as she had, she'd done him the biggest favor of his life. And not for one minute did she believe he hadn't been thrilled to see the last of her, given how she'd turned his life upside down. He certainly hadn't chased after her. He'd just let her go. The painful memories reared up and bit her, making her voice tight. "We are not doing this now, Ford."

"Fine. Later then."

"Never."

"Never is a long time," he said evenly, calmly, and since she couldn't find her *even* or *calm* to save her life, it pissed her off. That he could be so relaxed through this conversation made her fingers itch to pour the tea right over his damn sexy head. Two things stopped her. One, he'd be half-naked *and* wet, and watching the iced tea drip down that bronzed chest, with its barely there spattering of sun-kissed hair and six-pack abs, might just be too much for her to take. And that was just his upper half. Lord almighty, if his basketball shorts got wet, they'd cling to all his glory.

And there was a lot of glory.

The second problem, the *real* problem, was that dumping the tea over his head would show her hand to him, because she could make no mistake with Ford. He might look and act like a frat boy with no concerns beyond the next good time, but she knew better. Behind that lazy smile was a mind as sharp as a tack. She thrust the goodie bag and the glass at him.

Ford accepted both. Their hands brushed together, his

tanned and big against her much smaller one. "Thanks," he said. "I'm sure it's perfect, as well as the desserts."

"Are you buttering me up?"

"Trying." He smiled. "Is it working?"

"No." *Yes*. Dammit.

Through the sliding glass door, she could still hear the ladies chattering amongst themselves, and she kept her voice as low as possible. "Just drink up. You looked parched, and I don't want you passing out."

"Aw. You care."

Yes. But caring wasn't the problem, for either of them. Longevity was. His. She was no longer seventeen and looking for a good time. She wanted more. Certainly more than Ford was looking to give. She knew him, or at least she was pretty sure she did. She'd read about him over the years and followed his career. For the six months she'd been in Lucky Harbor, she'd paid attention to his current life as well.

He'd grown up, there was no doubt. Once upon a time, he'd been headed for trouble but he'd gotten it together. He was a good man who was doing exactly as he wanted for a living and making it work for himself. But he was still content to live his life *c'est la vie*, to let the cards fall where they might, not all that interested in keeping anything, or anyone, long term.

And then there was her real stumbling block. They'd already had their chance and had missed it. End of story. "I don't want to make Lucky Harbor's Facebook page again," she said. "We don't need that kind of publicity."

"You care," he repeated softly.

She paused, but there was no reason not to admit it when he'd always been able to read both her heart and her soul like a book. Once, he'd seen everything she was, and he'd made her feel like the most beautiful, love-worthy woman on the planet—at least as much as a seventeen-year-old could feel. "Yes," she said softly. "I care."

He looked at her for a long moment, clearly surprised at the admission. Then he broke eye contact and downed the iced tea she'd given him in approximately two huge swallows. Letting out a heartfelt sigh of appreciation, he smiled down at her from his towering height as he handed back the glass.

Which was another thing. She wasn't petite. She was five-seven in her bare feet, but today she was wearing three inch heels, and she *still* felt small next to Ford.

Small and... feminine. "Okay, then." Tara set the glass aside and turned him toward the front door, ignoring the way her hands tingled at the feel of his biceps beneath her fingers, hard and warm. "This has been fun," she said. "But buh-bye now."

"What's your hurry? Afraid you'll be unable to keep from having your merry way with me?"

Since that was far too close to the truth for comfort, she nudged him again, a little harder now. "*Shh!* If the women hear you talk like that, I'm going to blame you."

"Not my fault. You're the one who can't keep her hands off me."

She looked down and realized her fingers were indeed still on him, practically stroking him. *Crap*. She snatched her hands back and searched for her dignity, but there was little to be found. "I didn't say it would be your fault. I said I'd blame you."

He laughed. "Since when do you care what anyone thinks of you?"

"Since I want to impress these women—all of whom have connections and will hopefully send their family and friends here to the inn. So please. *Please*, Ford, you have to go. You can mess with my head another time, I swear."

From outside on the deck, the women were still talking and their voices drifted in. "Lord alive," someone said, possibly Ethel. "I'm *still* having a hot flash. If this inn comes with that man walking around like that, I'll shout recommendations for this place from the rooftops."

Ford's gaze met Tara's, and he slowly raised a brow.

"Oh, for God's sake." She gave up trying to push him out. "It's your damn body, that's all!"

"I have charm, too," he cajoled. "Let me back out there, Tara. It'll help, you'll see."

And here was the thing she knew about Ford. He never made pie-crust promises. His word was as good as money in the bank. If he said he'd help, he would.

She could trust him.

Problem was, she couldn't trust herself.

Not even a little bit. Leaning back against the wall, she covered her eyes, thinking that *not* looking at him might help clear her thoughts.

Except that he planted a hand on the wall next to her head and leaned in.

"Stop that," she said weakly when he leaned close. "You're all..." *Delicious.* "Sweaty."

He sidled up even closer, so that their bodies were brushing against each other. "You used to love it when I got all sweaty."

Oh yeah. Yeah, she had. She'd loved the way their bodies had heated and clung together. She'd loved how they'd moved together, she'd loved… "That was a damn long time ago," she said, ruthlessly reminding herself how it'd ended.

Badly.

Eyes holding hers prisoner, Ford remained against her for an interminable beat before finally taking a slow step back, still far too close for comfort.

She busied herself by grabbing the empty glass and striding back out onto the deck to refill it. She smiled at her guests and said, "I'll just be one more moment."

"Take your time, honey," someone replied. "I certainly would."

Doing her best not to grimace, Tara once again entered the cool interior of the inn.

Ford was almost at the front door, but he turned when she said his name. She watched the surprise cross his face when he took in the refilled tea. He moved back toward her and never took his gaze off her face as he accepted the glass.

"Why?" he asked.

"Because you looked like you're still thirsty."

His mouth quirked. "Thanks. But that's not what I meant."

Tara exhaled in an attempt to hold it together. No, she knew that. "You make me forget my manners. I hate that."

"Can't have you without your manners." He ran his fingers over her jaw, his eyes at half-mast as he took in her expression. "You ever remember it, Tara? Us?"

She'd done little but remember. Her emotions had long ago been shoved deep down, but being back in Lucky Harbor had cracked her self-made brick walls, and all those messy, devastating emotions came tumbling down every single time she looked at him.

She'd first arrived in town, a pissed-off-at-the-world seventeen-year-old, banished here by her father and her paternal grandparents for the summer, and she'd resented everything about Lucky Harbor.

Until her second night.

She'd had a simple but particularly nasty fight with her mother. Tara hadn't known Phoebe well, which hadn't helped. The fight had sent Tara sulking off to the marina, where she'd run smack into another seventeen-year-old. A tall, laid-back, easygoing, sexy-as-hell Ford Walker.

He'd been sprawled out on one of his boats, hands behind his head, watching the stars as if he didn't have a care in the world. One slow, lazy smile and an offer of a soda had pretty much been all it'd taken for her to fall, and fall hard.

He hadn't been like the guys back home. He hadn't been a rancher's kid or a cowboy. Not an intellectual or the typical jock, either.

Ford had been the bad boy and the good-time guy all in one, and effortlessly sexy. He'd drawn her right in, making her laugh when she hadn't had much to laugh at. His eyes had sparkled with wicked wit and a great deal of promised trouble, and yet he'd also been shockingly kind. They'd gone out sailing by the light of the stars and swam beneath the moon's glow.

She'd escaped to his boat every night after that.

As unbelievable as it seemed, they'd truly been just friends. She'd come from a broken home and had all the emotional baggage that went with that, including anger and confusion and restlessness.

She'd felt...alone.

Ford had known what that was like. His parents had split up when he was young, too, and his father had taken off. His mom had remarried a few times, so he also knew how tenuous "family" was.

But he'd been far more optimistic than she, possessing a make-your-family-where-you-can mentality. And actually, she'd loved that about him. She'd loved a lot about him, including the fact that he'd been a bit of a troublemaker and had encouraged her to step outside her comfort zone.

It hadn't taken much encouragement. That's when they'd become more than friends.

They'd gone for a long sail, dropped anchor... and their clothes. They'd made love—her first time.

Not his.

Ford had showed her just how good it could be, how amazing it could feel, and for that one long, glorious month of July, Tara had found herself hopelessly and thoroughly addicted to his body.

He'd felt the same about her; she'd seen it, felt it. There'd been no spoken vows of love between them, but it'd been there. They'd been lovers in every sense of the word.

A very grown-up word, *lovers*. And given that Tara had ended up pregnant and giving the baby up for adoption before hightailing it back to Texas, she hadn't been ready for all that went with being grown up.

No matter what Ford thought, neither of them had been.

Tara hadn't come back to Lucky Harbor after she'd had the baby, not once in all these years. She'd moved on. She'd gone to college. Traveled. Sown some wild oats.

She'd even fallen in love. Logan Perrish had been charming, funny, and accepting, and a huge NASCAR star. Tara had married him, and, determined to get things right, she'd done everything in her power to fit into Logan's world of whirlwind travel, press, billboards, and cereal boxes.

She'd lived and breathed the part of a celebrity wife, always on the go, doing whatever it took to make Logan love her as much as he loved his racing world.

Even when it had all failed, she'd still stuck in there. She'd made a commitment, and she'd faked it.

Fake it until you make it; that had been her motto.

But somewhere along the way, she'd lost herself. It seemed she always lost herself. And what made it even worse was that Logan hadn't been a bad guy, just the Wrong Guy.

So she'd escaped back to Texas once again, to lick her wounds in private, struggling to remember who she was—a woman who'd lived through some bad things and still persevered.

A woman who wouldn't lose herself again.

The steel magnolia within her had finally served Logan divorce papers. Due to his celebrity status, they'd had a prenup, of course. Without kids to complicate things, she'd willingly walked away free and clear. Still Logan had insisted on giving her a very fair settlement, which she had used every last bit of when she and her sisters had needed money for the inn.

She was now a take-no-prisoners sort of woman, and maybe also a don't-get-too-close-to-me woman. It was necessary, in order to keep her heart protected and safe.

And to keep herself pain free.

Unfortunately, she'd just broken her own rule by

tangling with Ford. Problem was, when it came to him, her mind and body appeared to be at war.

Want him.

Hold him at arm's length.

Want him...

The ongoing battle was complicated by the fact that she now lived within a stone's throw of him. As she knew all too well, Ford was lethal up close, especially when he wanted something.

And he'd admitted to wanting her. Her body, anyway.

He was just watching her now, and when she said nothing, he slowly shook his head, a bittersweet smile twisting his lips. "Thanks again for the tea," he said, and when the door shut behind him Tara drew in a shaky breath and let it out slowly, struggling for her equilibrium. As always, she eventually found it, and once she had, she headed back outside to the deck.

"There you are," one of her guests said slyly. "Everything okay?"

Tara smiled. "Absolutely," she said, taking her own advice—*fake it until you make it*.

Chapter 4

♥

"A conclusion is the place you get to when you're tired of thinking."
TARA DANIELS

Two days later, Tara woke up when someone plopped down on her bed. "It's Wednesday," Maddie said, adding a bounce to make sure Tara was up.

"It's also the crack of dawn." Tara pulled her pillow back over her head and turned over. "Go away."

Maddie yanked off the pillow. "*Wednesday.*"

"Sugar, you'd best at least have coffee brewing."

Maddie reached over to the nightstand and handed her a cup.

Tara sat up and sipped, repressing the sigh that wouldn't help anyway. Maddie had decreed Wednesdays to be "Team Building Day." The three of them had to spend every Wednesday together from start to finish until they learned to get along.

It was no surprise that they didn't. They'd grown up separately, thanks to the fact that Phoebe had loved men.

A lot of them.

Tara's father was a government scientist who'd come into Phoebe's orbit and not known what hit him. After their divorce, Tara had lived with her father. Actually, her father's parents, since he'd traveled so much. Tara had spent only the occasional summer with Phoebe, before her mother had inherited the Lucky Harbor Inn, so those visits had consisted mostly of camping and/or following the Grateful Dead tour.

Maddie's father was a Hollywood set designer. He'd also taken Maddie with him when his relationship with Phoebe had gone kaput. Maddie hadn't come back for summers, so she and Tara had been virtual strangers when Phoebe had died.

Chloe had no idea who her father was and didn't seem to care. The only daughter raised by Phoebe, she had traveled around at Phoebe's desire. As a result of that wanderlust upbringing, Chloe tended not to worry about convention the way her sisters did. She didn't worry about much, actually. She lived on a whim.

Unlike Tara, who lived for convention, for order. For a plan.

When Phoebe died and left her daughters her parents' inn, not one of them had intended to stay. And yet here they sat over six months later: the steel magnolia, the mouse, and the wild child.

Having a Team-Building Wednesday.

This was their third month at it, and the days still tended to be filled with bickering, pouting, and even all-out warfare. Today, Tara guessed, would be more of the same, but for Maddie's sake she gamely rose and dressed.

First stop—the diner for brunch. Tara took grief from

Jan, the woman who owned the diner. Tara's boss was fifty-something, mean as a snake unless she was taking money from a customer, and liked Tara only when Tara was behind the stovetop.

Which she wasn't at the moment.

Tara managed to get them seated with only the barest of snarls. Chloe ordered a short stack and consulted with the Magic Eight app on her iPhone, asking it if she was going to have a date anytime in the near future. Maddie ordered bacon and eggs with home fries and talked to Jax on her cell about something that was making her blush. Tara ordered oatmeal and wheat toast, and was busy calculating the balance in her checkbook. If that didn't explain their major differences right there, nothing could.

Afterward, in the already blazing sun, they walked the pier for the purpose of buying ice cream cones. In Maddie's case, they also went for getting on the Ferris wheel she'd once been so terrified of. They did that first, holding Maddie's hand. They might not see eye to eye on much, but some things could be universally shared, and ice cream and Ferris wheel rides were two of them.

Lance served them the ice cream. In his early twenties, he was small-boned enough to pass for a teenager, and thanks to the cystic fibrosis slowly ravaging his body, had a voice like he was speaking through gravel. He and Chloe were good friends, or more accurately cohorts, trouble-seekers of the highest magnitude. Lance tried to serve them for free, but Chloe refused. "We've got this," she told him firmly, then turned to Tara expectantly.

Maddie snorted.

Tara rolled her eyes and pulled out her wallet.

"I'll pay you back," Chloe said.

"You always say that," Tara said.

"Yeah? How much do I owe you?"

"One million trillion dollars."

Chloe grinned. "I'll get right on that."

Tara looked at Maddie.

"You spoil her," Maddie said with a shrug.

"Shh, don't say that," Chloe said. "She's right here."

Tara knew she wasn't exactly known for the warm, loving emotions required to spoil someone, and that she could come off as distant, even cold. This actually surprised her because she didn't *feel* distant, although she'd like to try being so sometime.

It'd be nice not to worry about things like money, or the future, or her sisters. And Tara did worry continuously, about Maddie and Chloe more than anything else—like whether Maddie was getting over her abusive ex and if Chloe would ever get over her inability to show or trust love.

Because of these things, Tara stayed in Lucky Harbor longer than planned. Or so she told herself.

"So what's next?" Chloe asked as they walked back to the inn. "I wore my bathing suit in hopes of getting a tan."

"We're going sailing," said the Team Building Day's president.

"We went sailing last week and nearly killed each other," Chloe said.

"We went *canoeing* last week," Maddie corrected, "and Tara nearly killed you because you tipped her over, and she'd been having a good hair day. Keep your hands to yourself and you'll survive today's Team Building Adventure."

"Hmm," Chloe said, sending a long, steady look in

Tara's direction as they boarded the Cape Dory Cruiser, the sailboat that had come with the marina.

They'd also inherited kayaks, canoes, a fishing boat, and one dilapidated houseboat. Most of these equated to some modest rental income, and they were determined to wring every penny out of the place that they could.

They had to, seeing as they'd gone through money with alarming speed to get everything up and running. Maddie's savings was gone. Tara's, too. It was a small price to pay, she reminded herself, for a new lease on life. A life that was lived the way she wanted, and not for anyone else.

"Tara," Maddie said, pointing, "you're in the cockpit."

"Yes!" Chloe triumphantly pulled off her skimpy sundress, revealing an even more skimpy red bikini beneath. "Time to sun, ladies."

Tara motored them out of the marina and looked at Maddie for further instructions.

"Point the bow into the wind," Maddie said. She was the only one who knew what she was doing, having taken a few lessons from Ford.

Tara had taken lessons from Ford, too. But that had been seventeen years ago, and the lessons she'd taken had *nothing* to do with sailing.

"What?" Maddie asked, making Tara realize she was smiling at the memory.

"Nothing."

"That's more than a 'nothing' smile," Chloe noted.

Tara ignored her.

"Into the wind," Maddie repeated to Tara.

Tara looked around to figure out which way the wind was coming.

"Quickly," Maddie said. "Or you'll swamp us."

Tara didn't know exactly what that meant but it didn't sound good. The boat was lurching heavily to the right and then the left on the four-foot swells; the wind was whipping her hair from all directions so she had no idea exactly which way was "into the wind."

"West!" Maddie yelled. "To the west."

"Okay, okay," Tara said, having to laugh at the sharpness in the former mouse's voice. "To the west it is." Just as soon as she figured out which way was west exactly . . .

"*Left!*"

So Tara steered left.

"Pull the halyard!" Maddie called out.

Tara looked at her. "Say that again in English?"

"Hoist the sail!"

"You should add 'aye, mate' at the end of that," Chloe told Maddie, spritzing herself with suntan lotion.

Maddie stood there, feet planted wide, wind whipping at her clothes, indeed looking like a modern-day pirate. "Pull it," she commanded as Tara hustled to do her bidding. "Crank it around the winch."

Tara glanced at Chloe.

Chloe had her face tipped up to the sun, and she was smiling, the little witch. "Isn't it Chloe's turn?" Tara asked hopefully.

"Not yet," Chloe said. "I feel my asthma acting up." She gave a little *cough-cough*, then affected a wheeze. "See?"

Maddie laughed. "At least put some phlegm into it."

Chloe began to work at wheezing and ended up coughing for real.

Tara sighed and began to hoist the sail. *She* wanted to be the pirate, dictating orders, thank you very much.

"Harder," Maddie told her. "You have to do it harder."

"That sounds dirty," Chloe said.

"Unfurl the jib," Maddie said, ignoring Chloe. "Hurry." She actually made a very cute tyrant in her snug capris and a tank top, looking fit and quite in charge even as she nibbled on potato chips—

Wait a minute. Tara narrowed in on the chips. How unfair was that? "Hey, if you were a really good captain, you'd share those."

Maddie peered in the bag, probably to assess whether she had enough to share. Tara knew that Maddie believed that chips were God's gift, the second best thing on earth. They used to be Maddie's *numero uno*, but then she'd fallen in love with Jax, so sex had been moved to the top of the list.

Maddie had her priorities straight. And as she reluctantly offered Tara some chips, Tara knew it was time she got her priorities straight as well.

They sailed for an hour, with Chloe sprawled out for maximum sun coverage, her fast-acting asthma inhaler tucked into the string low at her hip. Her long red waves were corralled prettily in a ponytail sticking out the back of a baseball cap that read: DARE TO BE NAUTI, and she had huge movie-star sunglasses perched on her pert nose.

Tara looked down at herself. She hadn't dressed special for this adventure. She'd worn thin trousers and a fitted knit top that was probably better suited for a day at the office, but it was what had been clean that morning. Besides, everyone knew that it wasn't so much what you had in the bank, or even where you rested your head at night—it was what you wore and how you wore it. She turned to Maddie. "Tell me again why Chloe's just lying there looking pretty?"

"Aw, thanks, hon," Chloe said, not opening her eyes.

"Chloe's going to get up now and reverse the entire process," Maddie said. "And bring us back to the marina."

Chloe sighed but obeyed and rolled lithely to her feet.

Tara gave Chloe a very immature *ha!* smirk and took the sun-worshipping spot. It took another hour to get back, and she spent that time enjoying the feel of the boat rocking beneath her, the scent of the salty ocean air, and the warmth of the sun drying her damp clothes and skin. She listened while feeling smug and superior as Maddie turned her bossiness on Chloe for a change.

"Watch your starboard," Maddie called out when Chloe steered toward the marina as they came back in. "Starboard!"

"What the hell's *starboard*?" Chloe yelled back.

"The right side! Watch your right side! Cripes, don't you people retain *anything*?"

Chloe slid the usually easygoing Maddie a look. "Either you had too much caffeine this morning or you didn't get laid when you got up."

Maddie rolled her eyes.

"Didn't get laid," Chloe decided.

"For your information, I got up too early to get…" Maddie lowered her voice to a whisper, "*laid*. And I have no idea how that matters."

"It matters because you're much more relaxed after Jax—"

"Chloe," Tara said, not wanting her to tease Maddie, not about this. "Not *everything* revolves around sex."

"It does when you're not getting any," Chloe muttered.

"Internal editor," Tara said. "Get one."

"I don't want to hear from you. *You* could be getting plenty of the good stuff from Ford, you know that? I mean have you *seen* him look at you?"

Tara sighed. "You could start an argument in an empty house."

"Or on a boat," Chloe agreed, not insulted in the least. "And nice subject change. Why does talking about sex bother you?"

Tara shook her head. "You know that sometimes it's okay to not talk at all, right?"

Chloe smiled good-naturedly. "I do tend to miss most opportunities to shut up."

"Hey," Maddie said. "That would make a good quip for the recipe box, Tara. *Never miss an opportunity to shut up*—Chloe!" she yelped, pointing ahead. "Watch the swell—"

Too late. The five-foot swell rose up and over the nose of the boat, splashing them all.

"You're not paying attention at all," Maddie said with reproach after she'd swiped the ocean spray off her face.

"You know what?" Chloe asked, tossing up her hands. "Sailing is too stressful for me."

Maddie took over as Chloe pulled out her inhaler and took a puff.

"Who are you writing those recipe cards for anyway?" Chloe asked Tara.

"My daughter," Tara said without thinking.

"Aw." That made Maddie smile. "That's sweet. Think she'll get to read them?"

Tara shook her head. "The adoption was closed. I can't find her. She'd have to find me." She heard the wistfulness in her voice and purposely closed her mouth, not wanting to go there. She'd spent a lot of time not going there. It was her own private guilt and shame, that she'd had to give up a baby.

"While we're on the subject," Chloe said, "you ready to tell us who was the father yet?"

Tara gave her a long look. Her ex had called it her "Don't Make Me Kick Your Ass" look.

It didn't daunt Chloe. "Tell the truth," she said. "It's Anderson from the hardware store. Yeah? Because he totally has the hots for you."

"No," Tara said. "He has the hots for *Maddie*. Or he did, before she broke his heart and started dating Jax."

"Then it's Ford." Chloe nodded. "Ford's totally your Baby Daddy."

Tara froze, then carefully, purposely, forced herself to relax. "What?"

"Yeah," Chloe said, and grinned. "We've known forever, actually. I was just pulling your leg with the Anderson thing."

"Chloe," Maddie said quietly, "you're ambushing her. That wasn't in the plan."

"The plan?" Tara repeated. "There's a plan? What was it, to get me out on the water under the guise of Team Building, where you could grill me?"

"No one's grilling you," Maddie said gently. "We're your sisters. Your support system."

"And seriously," Chloe said. "You doing the whole

Ignore-Ford thing was a dead giveaway anyway. *No one* ignores a man that fine."

"We're not discussing this," Tara said firmly.

Chloe sighed. "I'm telling you, if we just talked instead of being repressed all the time, we'd be less grumpy. And by 'we,' let's be clear. I mean you."

"*Not* discussing," Tara repeated.

"Sure," Chloe said. "Fine. How about your blind date tomorrow night? Can we talk about that?"

Maddie was steering the boat back into the bay with more skill than Tara had shown earlier, but Tara didn't care about that as she stared at Chloe. "How did you know about the blind date?"

"Are you kidding? This is Lucky Harbor, remember? Ethel told Carol at the post office, who told Jeanine at Jax's office, who told Sandy, who told Lucille that Ethel set you up with her grandson—the one coming through town for a short visit. So then Lucille tweeted it to Facebook."

Tara just barely resisted groaning. After serving the ladies of the Garden Society the other day, Ethel had cornered Tara to ask if Ford was courting her. Tara had choked on one of her own lemon bars, both at the old-fashioned and quaint connotation of the word "courting" and at the question itself. First of all, nothing about Ford was old-fashioned *or* quaint. Not given what he really wanted from her. Tara had firmly told Ethel no, that there hadn't been any courting—she'd kept the mutual lusting to herself—and that's when Ethel had mentioned needing a favor.

Tara had reluctantly agreed, and Ethel had laughed. "Oh, no, dear," she'd said. "You don't understand. I'm doing *you* the favor. I'm setting you up with my grandson Boyd. He's a wonderful, sweet, kind man, with a great personality."

Chloe was grinning, and Tara refused to say that she was already regretting her decision to accept a blind date. "So I'm going out to dinner. So what?"

"So if you were as smart as I thought you are, you'd be having breakfast with Ford instead."

Tara's belly tightened at the thought. "I'm sure Boyd's very nice."

"You haven't dated in how many years? Two? Three? Ten?"

Tara didn't bother to answer. Mostly because she didn't actually know.

"*Nice* isn't what you need," Chloe said. "You need—"

Maddie "accidentally" hit Chloe upside the head with a buoy. Tara ignored the following scuffle but took over the cockpit so they didn't all drown. The sails were down now so she motored them back to the docks, maybe hitting the gas a little more energetically than necessary. She ignored Maddie's squeak and Chloe's whoop and concentrated. She concentrated right into a big swell, rocking the boat hard.

"Ohmigod," Maddie gasped, lifting her head, "*you have to steer into—*"

"My bad," Tara said.

"And the—"

"I *know*," Tara said.

"Do you also know that you're a know-it-all?" Chloe asked casually, straightening up and adjusting her bikini.

When Tara just gave her a long look, Chloe shrugged. "We were just wondering."

"*We?*" Tara glanced over at Maddie, who winced.

Wheezing audibly now, Chloe pulled out her inhaler again, shook it, and took another hit. She paused to hold her breath for ten seconds, then exhaled. "I'm not supposed to wrestle," she said reproachfully to Maddie, then turned back to Tara. "And yes, *we*."

Tara swallowed a ball of unexpected hurt. "You two were discussing me being a know-it-all."

"Actually," Chloe said, "we were discussing your anal-retentiveness, your obsessive need to be right, and your all-around general crankiness."

"I'm not cranky."

Chloe laughed. "But you *are* anal and always right?"

"I'm *careful*," Tara said, lifting her chin, feeling defensive. Dammit. "And as for always being right, someone has to be." Okay, so she knew she wasn't always right but they'd been talking about her. And yes, maybe she was a little hard on them sometimes, but she was hard on everyone she cared about. She didn't see the value in letting Chloe suffer through mistakes she'd made due to the wild abandon of youth. Chloe hadn't had any guiding hand growing up with Phoebe, but Tara had at least had her father.

Which hadn't saved me from a few pretty major lapses in good judgment...

Tara shrugged that off, focusing on navigating the boat into the slip. She wanted a good relationship with her sisters, and in spite of the bickering, she knew it was happening. They were getting closer.

But the real goal here was making a go of the inn. It had to be. Distracted, she miscalculated how much to crank to the left and hit the boat slip. "Sorry," she called out as they all nearly fell to the deck. "But some assistance would be helpful!"

"You're doing fine," Maddie murmured.

"For a know-it-all, right?"

"Tara," Maddie said softly, apology heavy in her voice. "I—"

"No, it's okay." Tara shook it off. "Really. It's okay that you two discussed my personal life without me around to defend myself—"

"Hey, we do it right in front of you, too," Chloe said.

Tara shook her head and moved to follow Chloe off the boat, but ended up plowing into the back of her when Chloe stopped suddenly. "What are you—"

Chloe was staring ahead, and Tara joined her at it, even letting out a soft "oh my."

Ford stood on the deck of his racing Finn. Every single inch of him was drenched, making his board shorts and T-shirt cling to that built body as he maneuvered into his slip, his arms outstretched as he reached out to tie up the boat.

Tara had always loved his arms. They were sinewy and strong, yet capable of incredible tenderness. He gave some damn fine grade-A comfort when he put his mind to it. And his hands...they could handle rough waters or stroke her into orgasmic bliss with equal aplomb.

"You okay?" Chloe asked Tara over her shoulder without tearing her gaze off Ford.

"Yes. Why?"

"Because you just moaned." She craned her neck and eyed Tara. "And probably you should check for drool."

Tara gave her a nudge that might have been more like

a push, then surreptitiously checked for drool. Then she went back to staring at Ford. Given the look of satisfaction on his face, he'd enjoyed his sail, and something pinged low in her gut because she'd seen that look on his face before: when he'd been stretched out above her, as intimately joined to her as a man could get.

She made another sound before she could stop herself, then bit her lip. Bending, she concentrated on tying up their boat, but her fingers wouldn't work. "Dammit."

Two hands appeared in her vision—big, work-roughened hands—not taking over the task, but guiding her into the correct knot. "Like this," Ford said.

"I was fixin' to do it myself."

"She can do everything by herself," Chloe told him, heavy on the irony. "Bless her heart."

Tara straightened and shot Chloe a look, and got an eye roll in return.

"Come on, Mad," Chloe said. "I think Tara needs a little time out." And then she took her itty bitty bikini-clad body toward the inn, Maddie in tow.

Once again leaving Tara with Ford.

Tara flashed a vague smile in his direction without looking directly into his eyes—the key to not melting, she'd discovered—and went to step onto the dock.

Ford slid his hand in hers to assist, not letting go of her, even after she tried to tug free. He merely tightened his grip and waited her out.

With a deep breath, she tipped her head back and met his gaze. And yep, right on cue, as she took in the two-day stubble on his square jaw, the fine laugh lines around his mesmerizing eyes and the effortlessly charming smile, she melted like a glob of butter on a stack of pancakes.

"What?" he asked.

She studied his big, wet, gorgeous self and slowly shook her head. "Why couldn't you have gone bald or gotten fat?" It really was a bee in her bonnet that he looked even better now at thirty-four than he had at seventeen. "The least you can do is burp or scratch an impolite body part, or something equally unattractive."

His brow shot up. "You want me to scratch my ass?"

"Yes," she said. "And maybe you could also pick your nose in public."

His smile came slow and sure.

"*What?*"

"You want to jump me."

God, yes. "Look, I have bigger problems than this, okay? Problems far more pressing than our being comfortable with each other now that we're living in the same town again."

Ford looked at her for a beat, then stepped into her space, crowding her up against the wall of the marina building. "I can give you something to take your mind off your other problems," he said in a silky promise.

There was no doubt in her mind.

Sensing capitulation, he pressed his mouth to the underside of her jaw. "Just say the word."

Word, she thought dizzily with a delicious shiver.

With a single stroke of his finger along her temple, he pulled back, eyes dark on hers as he waited.

Sex. Just sex. And it'd be great. But not enough. Not nearly enough. "No," she said with far more resolution than she felt.

If he was disappointed, he didn't let it show as he backed away, leaving her leaning against the wall for support, her clothes wet from his body, her body overheated to say the least.

Not a new state when it came to him.

When he was gone, Tara blew out a shaky breath and headed up to the inn. She entered the cool, fresh rooms and gave herself a minute.

"Ms. Daniels? You okay?"

Tara turned to Carlos Rodriguez, the local high school kid they'd hired for the summer to do odd jobs like moving furniture, painting, and cleaning. With his multiple visible piercings and homeboy pants that hung just a little south of civilized, they'd all been a little leery of just how good a worker he might turn out to be, but he'd done well. At seventeen, he was already six feet tall, with a lanky build that suggested he didn't get three squares a day.

Tara knew from his application and obtaining his work permit from school that he was smart but an under-achiever, and possibly a bit of a troublemaker. But that's what happened when a kid had no authority figure in his life and was forced to work odd jobs to support himself, his younger siblings, and his grandma.

"I'm fine," Tara assured him.

"I did the weeding and painted the laundry room."

"Perfect. Did you eat lunch?"

"Yes."

She bit back a sigh at the lie. "I left you a sandwich in the fridge."

"Thanks, but—"

"No buts. Eat it."

He turned away so she couldn't see his face. "I'll bring it home with me."

Where he'd undoubtedly give it to his sisters or grandma. "Eat it here. I'll make you more to bring home."

He turned back and looked at her for a long beat, clearly struggling between pride and hunger. The lure of food won out, and he went into the kitchen.

Chloe came into the room from the hallway, pulling her cute little sundress on over her bikini. "Hope you're pleased with yourself," she said to Tara. "You chased Maddie away again. Little Miss Hates-Confrontations just up and vanished for friendlier waters."

"There was no confrontation."

"Are you kidding me?" Chloe said. "You're a walking confrontation."

"What are you talking about? *You're* the one who starts everything. You never know when to just keep something to yourself."

Chloe stood hands on hips, irritated. "Because sweeping things under the carpet and keeping everything deep inside would make me what, *you*? Sorry, no can do, Sis. But since you're never going to see my side of this, maybe we should just agree to disagree."

"Fine," Tara said.

"Fine. And let's not speak for a while either, at least until you can admit you're actually wrong once in a blue moon."

"I'd be happy to admit I was wrong," Tara said. "If I was."

Chloe tossed up her hands, then turned to Carlos as he came back from the kitchen, eating the sandwich. "Hey, Cutie," she said with her usual easy charm, as if she hadn't just been snarling at Tara. "What's up?"

Carlos shot her a rare smile.

Chloe had that effect on men.

"Almost done for the day unless you have anything else."

"Yes," Chloe said. "I do have something else. Maybe you can tell my sister here that no one likes a sanctimonious know-it-all."

Carlos divided a glance between them.

"Don't put him in the middle," Tara said.

"You're just worried he'll side with me." Chloe turned back to Carlos. "I'll give you a raise if you'll also tell her she's getting wrinkles from holding all her shit in."

"There's a recipe on the Facebook page for that," Carlos said, stuffing in the last bite of his sandwich.

Oh for the love of God, Tara thought, grinding her back teeth together. "She means I'm—"

"Uptight," Chloe said helpfully, laughing. "And could you also tell her that it's annoying to have to look at her lingerie that she's got constantly hanging from the shower rod?"

"Actually," Carlos said, finally looking interested, "that wouldn't annoy me one bit. Uh, which bathroom was that exactly?"

Chapter 5

♥

"Never mess up an apology with an excuse."
CHLOE TRAEGER

A few days later, Ford was at The Love Shack, out back in the small yard hosing down the tables and chairs. He had his music on low, but no matter how low he kept it, his neighbor next door—Ted the used bookstore owner—would poke his head out and ask for it to be turned down. Ford tried to picture what the guy's house must look like and decided it was probably all Enya, cats, and houseplants.

Jax, who'd come to help, sat on top of one of the freshly cleaned tables, texting—obviously being hugely helpful.

"Working hard?" Ford asked, heavy on the sarcasm.

All hunched over so he could see his screen in the bright sun, Jax didn't answer.

"Earth to Jax."

"Hmm." Jax's dark head remained bent, his thumbs flying. "Working hard here, man."

Ford narrowed his eyes. Once upon a time, Jax had been a hotshot lawyer who wore designer suits and drove a Porsche, but these days he stuck with Levi's, tees, a beat-up old Jeep, and the laziest dog on the planet. He spent his days renovating and his nights doing Maddie, and he'd never seemed happier. Ford walked behind him to read what he was typing. "'That's very naughty, little girl; you know what happens to naughty girls,'" Ford read out loud. "Looks like work all right."

Unrepentant, Jax grinned and hit SEND. "Hey, a relationship *is* work."

"Yeah, I bet all the sex is killing you."

"You ought to try it sometime."

"Daily sex?" Ford asked.

"A relationship, you dumb ass. It's been a while since...what was her name? That hot snowboarder you dated last winter?"

"Brandy," Ford said and felt a fond smile cross his mouth.

"Yeah. Brandy." Jax smiled. "I liked her."

"That's because she always hugged you hello and she was stacked."

"Hey, she was also very nice," Jax said. "Why did you two break up again?"

"Because her mother kept instant messaging me, asking when I was going to marry her."

"Which sent you into flight mode," Jax said. "And what about Kara, the one you actually *did* almost marry?"

"That was a long time ago. She..." Got a little fame crazy. *His* fame crazy, back during his serious racing days. "Didn't work out. And you know all this already."

"Still haven't heard a compelling reason for you to be

alone," Jax said, "except that weird inability-to-commit thing you've got going."

"I do not have an inability to commit."

"Whatever, dude."

"I don't!"

"No? Then find someone to be with and let it work out for you."

"Yeah, I'll get right on that."

Jax slid his phone into his pocket and gave him a once-over. "You're in a good place, so why not?"

Ford knew damn well that his life, at least on the surface, *was* in a good place. He had everything he needed, and the ability to get things he didn't. Which was about as different from his childhood as he could get, having grown up wild and reckless and not giving a shit.

Good thing Jax and Sawyer had. Given a shit. The three adolescent best friends had stuck together like thieves, having each other's backs through thick and thin. And there'd been a lot of thin. They'd been each other's family, and still were.

But it wasn't as if Ford didn't believe in relationships. He did. In fact, he'd had his share of good ones. He just hadn't had one that had stuck.

His own fault, as Jax was not so subtly pointing out.

"How about Tara?" Jax asked.

"Huh?"

"Let me rephrase. You ever going to tell me about the thing with her?"

"What thing?"

Jax shook his head in disgust.

Fine. So they all knew there'd been a thing. A huge thing. That one long-ago summer Ford had never been able to forget. He'd been working his ass off, living on his boat so as not to put a bigger burden on his grandmother, and feeling pretty alone and shitty while he was at it. Jax had been sent off to some fancy camp by his father, and Sawyer, the third musketeer, had gone to juvie for some fairly spectacular and innovative "borrowing" of a classic Mustang that unfortunately had belonged to the chief of police at the time.

Ford had been left to his own devices, and even working his fingers to the bone at any and all odd jobs he could get hadn't kept his mind busy enough. There'd been long, hot nights alone on his boat until Tara had shown up.

With one glare of her angry, whiskey eyes, Ford had lost a piece of his heart.

He'd softened her up. She'd done things for him, too, but making him soft hadn't been one of them.

They'd burned hard and bright that summer. And when Tara had shown up on his boat in tears, pregnant, they'd had two very different knee-jerk reactions. His had been that they could make it work. They could make a family, a *real* one. He'd drop out of school and marry her.

But Tara had different ideas. She'd known that she needed to let the baby go, that she couldn't offer it any kind of life. Between the two of them, only she'd been grown-up enough to see past her own grief. She'd explained to Ford that they couldn't do this, that the baby deserved more than either of them could provide.

And she'd been right. They'd done the right thing. Ford knew that. He'd always known that, but losing the baby had been hard.

Losing Tara had been even harder.

When she'd shown up in Lucky Harbor again after seventeen years, the emotions he'd capped off had easily surfaced again, shockingly so, but he hadn't worried. He'd known she was only in town to inspect the inn Phoebe had left them. He figured she'd be in and out.

But here it was, six months later, and she was *still* poking at his old wounds just by being here. He scrubbed a hand over his face. It'd taken him a long time to be okay about all that had happened, but it still haunted him when he let it. He'd done the right thing by signing away his rights to his daughter, he had. He'd done the right thing for both the baby and Tara. But there was always the regret.

Since that time, he'd done his damnedest to live his life in such a way that there were no more regrets, so that *he* called the shots. And yeah, maybe he did so to the point of being too ready to just let things go.

And people.

He shrugged. It'd all worked out fine. Or it would have, but now Tara was back in his world, and in no apparent hurry to leave.

She'd lived her life very carefully, with purpose. She was a woman who knew what she wanted. And what she didn't. Ford knew he belonged firmly in the latter category.

Worked for him. He was an unhappy memory to her. And a risk, a bad one. He got that. But defying all logic, their attraction was still strong.

"You look like you just had a Hallmark movie moment with yourself," Jax said.

Ford ignored him and turned to the gate as someone came through.

Carlos. The kid often came by looking for extra work in spite of the fact that he already worked at the inn and also bussed at the diner, on top of going to school and being head of his grandmother's household.

A situation that Ford understood all too well. "Hey. Need some hours?"

"No, I'm good," Carlos said. "I'm on at the inn today. Maddie sent me into town to get some stuff. She asked me to come by and tell you that tonight's the night."

Ford nodded. "Tell her to consider it done."

"Consider what done?" Jax asked.

"The inn's appliances were delivered today," Ford told him. "Maddie asked me to stock their kitchen tonight, as a surprise for Tara."

Jax raised a brow. "Really?" he said, his tone suggesting that he found this little tidbit fascinating.

"Like you don't know that Maddie burns water," Ford said. "And Chloe would probably booby-trap the place just to irritate Tara. So Maddie asked me to do it. It's no big deal."

"I just find it interesting that you're helping the woman that you claim to not be interested in," Jax said in his annoying, lawyerly logical voice.

Ford had *never* claimed not to be interested, and Jax knew it. He'd simply refused to talk about it.

"Maddie said to remind you that it's a surprise," Carlos said. He grimaced and shuffled his weight, looking uncomfortable now. "She said I should mention that *twice*, since you don't always take direction well."

Jax grinned proudly at this. "That's my woman."

"And she said *you're* to stay out of it," Carlos said to Jax in apology. "She said... ah, hell." The kid pulled a piece of paper from his pocket. "'You're not to poke at Ford,'" he read. "'You're to leave him alone or else you can forget about tonight.'" Carlos carefully folded Maddie's note back up and didn't look at either man directly.

"That's your woman," Ford said to Jax dryly.

"Let me see that." Jax snatched the note from Carlos, unfolding it again to take a look. "Damn, she really did write that." He handed it back.

"So the inn will be empty?" Ford asked the kid.

Carlos nodded. "Maddie said she has plans with Jax— assuming he doesn't mess with you over this. Chloe's giving a yoga class at the Rec Center. And Tara will be out."

"Out," Ford said. "Out where?"

Carlos hesitated and went back to his notes, even turning the paper over, but apparently there was nothing there to help him.

Ford thought of all the things that "out" could mean. She could be out bossing people around at the diner. She could be out shopping for more of those fantasy-inducing, uppity clothes she favored. Hell, maybe she was out making a list on how to further stomp on his heart.

Nah, she'd already done that.

"She has a date," Carlos finally said.

"A date?" Jax looked surprised. "*Tara?*"

If things had been different, Ford might have laughed. As it was, suddenly he couldn't breathe very well. *Captain Walker to Air Traffic Control, we have a fucking problem.* "A date," he repeated.

Carlos was edging his way back to the gate. "Yeah, that's what Maddie said."

Huh. Ford should like the idea of her dragging some other guy's heart through the mud instead of his, but *Tara on a date*. Nope, he could roll it around in his head as much as he wanted, he still hated it.

• • •

Tara's blind date had made dinner reservations for them at a sushi joint in the next town over.

Probably for the best.

She'd asked Boyd to pick her up at the diner because one, she didn't want to have to go back to the inn to change after her shift, and two—and she really hated to admit this even to herself—she didn't want Ford to be at the marina and possibly see her getting picked up. She couldn't explain that one even to herself.

What she hadn't expected was for Boyd to be several inches shorter than her, fifty pounds heavier, and dressed in a suit. "Do you eat here for free?" Boyd asked. "Because we could stay here tonight if that's the case."

"Wow," Jan whispered as Tara walked by her perpetually grumpy boss. "He's a catch."

Tara ignored her.

"Do you have flats?" Boyd asked. "Because looking up at you makes my neck hurt. No offense."

Perfect. Because now they were going to have to go back to the inn after all, so she could change into flats.

It wasn't as if she was an Amazon, she thought to herself as they walked the pier to Boyd's car. Most men seemed to be okay with her height. Sure, once in a while she wished she was shorter so she could actually feel... petite. Protected.

Just right.

But the truth was that only one man had ever made her feel that way.

"I just really hate having a neck ache," Boyd said.

He hated a neck ache, and she hated a headache, which she could feel coming on. This did not bode well for the evening ahead. For a moment, she looked past the Ferris wheel, eyeing the way the pier jutted from the beach into the ocean almost as far as she could see, and wished she was...

Sailing.

Ridiculous. She got into Boyd's car. He kept his eyes on the road as he drove slowly toward the inn. Slowly, as in a-herd-of-turtles-stampeding-through-peanut-butter slowly. The guy didn't pass a single indent in the road that didn't require a nearly complete stop. When they finally pulled up before the inn, Tara checked for gray hair while Boyd took a good look at the place.

Tara looked, too. She was so damn proud of what she and her sisters had done here. It'd been a long haul but the beach inn looked warm and welcoming, and she couldn't wait to see it filled with guests.

"Are you going to paint it?" Boyd asked.

"Yes." In fact, the painters were due tomorrow. She'd been waiting for a week. If they didn't show, she was going to get out a paintbrush and do it herself.

"Because it really needs to be painted if you want to make any money."

"We're aware," Tara said as mildly as she could. "Thanks. I'll change my shoes and be right back."

"No, offense," he said, getting out of the car with her. "But in my experience, letting a date out of my sight never works out well for me."

Surprise. And if he said "no offense" one more time tonight, *living* wasn't going to work out well for him.

Boyd smiled grimly. "I don't think I make the best first impression."

"Maybe if you didn't require them to be shorter than you, that would help," Tara said.

He nodded. "That's good advice."

They walked up the steps to the inn. "Hey," Boyd said. "You could cook for us here; I wouldn't mind. Grandma said you were an amazing chef. What do you suppose you could whip up?"

A major attitude, that's what she could whip up. Bless his heart. And to make it worse, she was craving comfort food for some reason, hankering for hot fried chicken and cold potato salad like nobody's business. Which proved that while you could take the girl out of the South, you couldn't really take the South out of the girl. "I haven't stocked the kitchen yet," she said. Not to mention that she'd just spent the past eight hours on her feet cooking at the diner. "Our appliances were just delivered. I haven't even unpacked the dishes."

"Oh. That's too bad." He followed her inside, right on her heels, taking the whole not-letting-her-out-of-his-sight thing very seriously. As she moved through the bottom level on the brand-new wood floors, Tara drew in a deep, satisfied breath at the scent of fresh paint and polished wood. More pride filled her, as well as something more, that sense of...

Home.

She was still basking in the surprise of that sensation when she realized someone was rattling around in the kitchen.

The place was empty tonight, or was supposed to be, but there was a light beneath the double kitchen doors and from the other side she heard the low, unbearably familiar voice that she'd have recognized anywhere.

"Oh, fuck, yeah." Ford, speaking low and husky. "That's the way, baby. Just like that."

Boyd blinked at Tara. "Uh, that sounds a little like someone's... *you know*."

Yeah. She did know.

"That's right, nice and deep," came Ford's voice. "Right up the center."

Tara turned back to Boyd to tell him to wait and bumped right into him. "*Stay*," she said firmly, and pushed open the door to face her sexy-as-hell intruder doing God-knew-what in her kitchen.

Chapter 6

♥

"Never miss a good chance to shut up."
Tara Daniels

When Tara stepped into the kitchen, she found exactly what she'd expected. Ford: bartender, sailor, town cutup, and overall bane of her existence.

What she didn't expect was for him to be working.

He had his back to her and was gazing into the open cabinets, a canister of sugar in his hand as he considered where to place it.

"Ford," she said with what she felt was remarkable calm.

No reaction. He kept doing his thing, which appeared to be stocking her shelves. She waited until he set the canister next to the salt and pepper. Good decision, she thought approvingly, but what the hell? "Okay, listen," she said, hands on hips. "You're in *my* place and—"

"*Yes!*" he yelled suddenly, startling her. "That's the way, baby. Go-go-go, *take it all the way*!" He accompanied this with an innately male, testosterone-fueled fist pump, turning just enough that Tara could see a cocky grin cross his face.

Catching sight of her, he kept grinning as he pulled out an earphone. "Mariners," he said. "Top of the ninth. Bases loaded. *Sweet* game."

"Baseball." Not sex on her countertops.

Ford arched a brow. "Yeah, baseball. What did you think?"

"Nothing. I don't know."

He flashed another grin, and this one was pure badass. It went well with the perfectly fitted and professionally distressed jeans sitting low on his hips and snug across his very nice ass. He wore battered cross trainers and a black T-shirt that managed to emphasize the strength and build of his wide shoulders and broad chest. And a certain naughty look in his eyes.

"Anyone ever tell you that your pretty, Southern belle accent thickens when you lie?" he asked.

"No. What in Sam Hill are you doing here, Ford?"

He smiled. "And also when you're pissy."

"I'm not pissy!"

His eyes cut to the doors behind her as they cracked open to reveal Boyd peeking his head in.

Tara gritted her teeth and introduced them. The two men shook hands while Boyd sized up the much taller Ford. "It's the heels," Boyd said.

Ford cocked his head. "Excuse me?"

"The reason I'm so short is that she's in heels."

"Of course," Ford said after a full beat. "It's the heels." He looked at Tara, face bland.

She did her best not to squirm.

"Listen, Tina—" Boyd started. "We should really get going—"

"Tara," she said.

"Tara." He nodded. "Sorry. Anyway, we really need to get a move on if we're going to make the early bird special."

Right. Except she couldn't do it. She just couldn't. She wanted something fried, in her damn heels, with someone who knew her damn name. "I think it's best if we make it for another night." Like, say, never.

Boyd blinked, slow as an owl. "Is it because you have a headache? Because I have Advil in the car for when my dates get a headache."

"Yes, it's because of a headache," Tara said, very carefully not looking at Ford. "A massive headache. But it needs more than Advil. I'm sorry, Boyd."

He sighed. "It's okay. I got further with you than any of my other dates lately. So that's something, right?"

Ford raised a brow in Tara's direction. She sent him a glare and walked Boyd out. When she came back into the kitchen, Ford was waiting for her, clearly amused.

"You used me to dump your date," he said.

" 'Dumped' is . . . harsh," she said.

"And accurate."

"And accurate," she agreed and sighed. "He had bad breath."

"Well then."

He was laughing at her, the bastard. "This isn't funny, Ford. I really needed a date."

"That's not what I would have guessed."

"And what does that mean?"

"It means," he said, pulling a frying pan and some

oil out of her cabinets like he was right at home. "That I remember how you get when you're uptight and anxious. I also remember the only thing that relaxed you."

Tara had a flash to a certain long-ago night on the docks, after a fight with her mother that had left her shaky and alone. Ford had found her, and in shockingly little time, had her forgetting her troubles.

Naked therapy, Ford style.

It'd worked. Tara felt heat flood her face. "Yes, well, sex isn't on the table."

He gestured to the pan. "I was talking about fried chicken, but your idea has merits, too. Come here, Tara."

Said the spider to the fly. "I don't think so."

Ford smiled and pulled a package of chicken from the refrigerator. He located the seasonings and bread crumbs he wanted, heated the pan, and poured her a glass of wine.

Tara looked around, trying to put two and two together as to why the bane of her existence was trespassing on her territory. "I just don't understand why you're here."

"I'm surprising you." Ford poured another wine for himself, looking comfortable in his own skin as he got to work cooking for her, occasionally drinking from the glass in his big hand. He fried the chicken with the easy flicks of an experienced wrist, flashing her a look that did something funny to her stomach.

And south of her stomach.

She told herself to ignore the attraction that she didn't want, but her hormones had their own agenda. Forcing herself to tear her eyes off him, she took in the kitchen, and how it felt to use it for the first time. It felt good, she realized. Really good. And there was something else. With Ford in it, the room seemed cozy, intimate.

And damn if he wasn't taking up too much of it.

The air had begun to smell like heaven, and Tara could hear the sizzle and pop of the oil. Her mouth watered. "So about this surprising me thing."

"Hush," he said, and before she could hurt him for that, he nudged her wineglass to her lips. "Just stand there and give your brain a couple of minutes off. Five minutes, Tara. Better yet, sit." He gently pushed her onto a barstool. "Take a deep breath." He waited until she did. "Good," he said. "Now let it out, slowly. Repeat a few times."

She glared at him, but continued to breathe. Slow. In and out. She drank. Breathed some more. And damn if after five minutes she didn't feel a whole hell of a lot better about the evening. "It's the wine," she said.

He refilled her glass and handed her a plate loaded with fried chicken. "It's also the company."

Tara laughed at his cockiness and took a bite of his chicken. And then moaned. "Lord almighty."

He smiled. "Yeah?"

"Oh yeah. This is amazing." She pointed at him. "Which you already know and which doesn't get you off the hook. Okay, so one more time, slowly and precisely—why were *you* putting my spices away?"

"Because your sisters asked me to. They asked because you're a control freak who'll bitch the air blue if they get left on the counter."

"I am not a—" She broke off and drew in a deep, relaxing breath. She was. She really was a complete and utter control freak. Another deep breath. Another sip of wine.

His eyes were laughing at her, which she ignored

because he was back to unloading her spices. "You can't put the basil and cumin so close to the stove," she said. "They'll go bad."

"They need to be in easy reach, and if this place sees anything close to the kind of business I think it will, the spices won't last long enough to go bad."

She stood up and moved close to reach out and stop him, accidentally brushing against his big body. That was so supremely annoying—seriously, could he be any sexier?—that she forgot to apologize. In fact, she might have given him a little tiny shove to get out of her way.

He held his ground, refusing to budge.

"*Everything* goes bad," she murmured, trying to reach the basil. She couldn't have it next to the cumin—yuck.

"Not everything," he said, and shifted to come up right behind her, crowding her.

Of their own accord, her eyes drifted closed and her body quivered. Because no matter how much time had passed, every part of her remembered every part of him. Gripping the countertop in front of her, she bowed her head and choked out his name as his long arms came around her.

But instead of touching her, he grabbed the basil for her without even stretching, the tall, gorgeous bastard, and set it down in front of her.

"The poppy seeds will start to smell disgusting if they're not in the fridge," she said.

Lowering his head, he sniffed at her neck.

"Not me," she said with a low, helpless laugh. "The poppy seeds."

"You're right. Because you smell amazing. You always did."

Oh, God. Her knees actually wobbled at that. "I smell like fried chicken."

"Mh-mmm. Finger-lickin' good."

Her fingers turned white on the counter. "Why did my sisters pick you to do this?"

"Because I offered to. Jax offered, too, but he's kitchen-challenged, so they wouldn't let him."

"I didn't ask for help."

"No kidding." He turned Tara to face him, his expression amused. "You'd choke on your own tongue before you asked for help. This was to be a surprise for you, Tara. A fully stocked kitchen, ready to go."

That Maddie and Chloe had even wanted to do this for her touched Tara more than she could have imagined.

"Oh, and I brought you my crepe pan." Ford gestured toward the island counter. "Maddie said you'd wanted to make crepes but that you didn't have a good pan for it."

She glanced at it, then let out a low breath. A Le Creuset. She pushed past him to run a reverent finger over the beautiful pan and nearly moaned. "It's beautiful," she whispered.

He let her drool over it for a moment before speaking again. "As for why it's *me* specifically doing the stocking…" He shrugged. "I know what I'm doing."

Yes, this was true. Ford always knew exactly what he was doing.

"I was just startled to see you in here is all," she said. "Given that we…that I—"

"Hate me," he said mildly.

A knot formed in her throat and couldn't be swallowed away. "I don't hate you, Ford. I never hated you."

He was quiet a moment, just watching her. The earlier

spark in his eyes was gone. "They trusted me to do this for you," he said simply. "Just as, once upon a time, you trusted me, too." With that, he slid his earphones back in and dismissed her, going back to unpacking.

She stared at his broad shoulders, the stiff back, and realized she wasn't the only one with some residual resentment issues. Something sank low in her gut at that, possibly a big serving of humble pie. Dammit. She was a lot of things, but a complete bitch wasn't one of them. With a sigh, she came up behind him. "Ford."

Not answering, he opened another cabinet and studied the space.

Ducking beneath his outstretched arms, she stepped in between him and the counter and turned to face him.

He looked down at her, and she found herself holding her breath. Unintentional as it'd been, now she was standing within the circle of his arms, and more memories slammed into her.

Good, warm, fun, sexy memories...

Even with the wedged heels that Boyd had resented, she only came up to Ford's chin. When he'd been seventeen, he'd been this tall, but he'd been much rangier from not having enough to eat, and also from working two, sometimes three jobs in a day. That had been before he'd gotten onto the sailing circuit and made a decent living in endorsements. Though looking at him now, one would never know money was no longer an issue. The man might drive her crazy, but he didn't have a pretentious bone in his perfect body.

And the body...goodness. He'd filled it out, with solid muscle and a double dose of testosterone. There was also a level of confidence, an air that said he'd listen to whatever anyone had to say but that he wouldn't necessarily give two shits about it. She met his gaze and drew a shaky breath.

He didn't move. His eyes were dark and unfathomable, his body relaxed and at ease. He was waiting for her to speak, or maybe, better yet, to go away. "Thank you for doing this," she said.

"You're welcome." His voice was lower now, and slightly rough as well, leaving her with the oddest and most inexplicable urge to reach up and put her hand on his face to soothe him.

She'd done that for him, once upon a time. She'd been there to listen, to ease his aches, to touch him when he needed.

He'd done the same for her.

They'd healed each other.

And now there was a huge gaping hole between them, and she had no idea how to cross it.

Or if she even wanted to.

No, that was a lie. A part of her wanted to cross it. Badly. But before she could go there, he turned away, going back to stocking her cabinets. Which he was doing simply because her sisters had asked him.

They couldn't have found anyone better equipped for the job. Ford had always cooked. Hell, he ran a bar and grill for fun. He, better than anyone else she knew, understood what a kitchen needed and how it should be organized. She watched as he picked up a twenty-pound bag of flour as if it were nothing and set it on the counter to open it.

He had her pretty flour container next to it, ready to be filled, and she moved in. "Here, let me."

"I've got it."

"I'm here, Ford. You might as well make the best of it. I'm not going to just stand around and watch you do all the work."

When he didn't stop his movements, she gave him a little hip nudge and reached for the bag.

"Fine." Raising his hands in surrender, he backed up, just as she ripped the bag open with slightly too much force. Flour exploded out of the bag. After a few stunned beats, she blinked rapidly to clear her eyes, and looked at herself. *Covered* in flour. She lifted her head and eyed Ford, who was wisely fighting his smile. "You did this on purpose," she said.

"No, that was all you."

She attempted to shake herself off. "Better?"

He ran a hand over his mouth, probably to hide his smile. "Yes."

"You're lying," she said, eyes narrowed.

"Yes."

Okay, that was it. She stalked toward him.

Laughing out loud now, Ford straightened. "Whatever you're planning to do," he warned. "Don't."

"Oh, Sugar." Didn't he know better than to tell her what to do by now? "*Watch me.*" She backed him up against the counter and held him there—plastering herself to him from chest to belly to thigh...and everything in between—on a one-woman mission to cover him in flour, too. "Gotcha," she said triumphantly as she rubbed up against him. "Now you're just as big a mess as me."

His hands were at her hips. "Is that right?" His voice sounded different now. Lower. Rough as sandpaper.

And heat slashed right through her. "Uh-huh." She bit

her lip, realizing that her voice was different, too, and that she was staring at his mouth.

And then she realized something else. She wasn't breathing.

He wasn't, either.

Of their own accord, her hands slid up his chest, wrapped around his neck, and then...oh God, and then.

Ford said her name on a rough exhale. Holding her against the hard planes of his body, his eyes filled with a quiet intensity, he lowered his head. "Stop me if you're going to," he said in quiet demand, all humor gone.

Tara sucked in some air, but didn't stop him. Not when his lips came down on hers, and not when he kissed her until she couldn't remember her own name.

Chapter 7

♥

"Accept that some days you're the bug, and some days you're going to be the windshield."
TARA DANIELS

Dazed, Ford tightened his grip on Tara, hearing the groan that her kiss wrenched from deep in his throat. *She* was kissing *him*. He couldn't have been more surprised if she'd hauled off and decked him. But having her push him up against the counter and kiss him hard like she was...oh, yeah. *Way* better than anything that had happened all day.

All damn year.

Ah, hell. Clearly she'd finally done it, she'd driven him bat-shit crazy, but she felt so good against him. Warm and soft, willing. *Amazing*.

And aggressive.

Christ, there was nothing more irresistible than Tara on a mission. And that he was that mission made it even better.

She pulled back slightly and he smiled. "Was that supposed to be punishment?"

"Yes." Her fingers curled into his shirt. "So be quiet and take it like a man."

Ford was still smiling when she kissed him this time, but the amusement faded fast, replaced by a blinding, all-consuming need.

All too soon, she pulled back again, eyes dark, mouth wet from his. "Is there anyone in your bed?" she asked, her voice low and extremely Southern.

He loved the way her accent thickened when she felt something particularly deeply. "No," he said. "There's no one in my bed." Except for her, hopefully. Soon. Because this was waaay better than pushing each other's buttons.

"Just wanted to make sure." With each word, her lips just barely grazed his, making him all the hotter. Tightening his grip on her, he whipped them around, trapping her between him and the counter. The scent of her was as intoxicating as her kiss, and when she stared at his lips and licked hers, something inside him snapped. Hauling her up against him, flour and all, he let loose the pent-up yearning and temper and ache he'd been barely reining in.

She hesitated for less than a beat before tightening her grip on him and kissing him back with a passion that nearly knocked them both to their asses. "No one's here?" he asked against her mouth.

"No one."

He had her divested of her short, lightweight sweater and was working on the buttons of her dress, thinking this was the best idea he'd ever had. No more dancing around each other. From now on, all their dancing would be done naked. Naked was good. Naked was *great*.

Tara appeared to feel the same. Her hands were everywhere, his chest, his arms, his ass, stroking and tormenting. The only sound was their heavy breathing and the sexy little murmur she let out when he cupped her breasts.

He remembered that sound. He'd dreamed about that sound. She writhed under his touch, pressing closer, like she needed to climb up his body—which he was all for, by the way. Her fingers found their way beneath his shirt, running lightly over the skin low on his abs, just above his low-riding jeans.

Ford wanted more and took it, letting his hands do the walking and talking beneath her clothes. There was no question about what they were doing now, or why. No thinking. Just feeling, and God help him, he was feeling a whole hell of a lot. Soul-deep, wrenching hunger. And need.

Nothing new when it came to Tara.

His next staggering thought, more than the feel of her hands beneath his shirt gliding downward, caught him. The last time they'd done this, they'd nearly destroyed each other.

Or at least Tara had destroyed *him*. Ford still wasn't clear on what she'd felt. She'd been good at holding back. She didn't seem to be holding back now. Her touch felt so damn good his eyes nearly rolled back in his head, and that was before she went for the button on his Levi's, banishing his ability to think. *Yeah, baby. Go there.*

She played in the loose waistband of his jeans for a minute and he groaned. He had one hand threaded through her hair. The other was cupping a breast, his thumb teasing her nipple as he deepened their kiss until they were both panting.

"Ford," she sighed when he finally released her

mouth. Her lips traveled down his throat to the base of his neck, where she licked at his pulse. "Mmm," she said, then nipped him. When he jumped, he felt her smile against him.

"You think that's funny," he asked, dipping his head to return the favor, his hands sliding south, down her back to her sweet, sweet ass. He sucked at her neck and—

"Wow," Chloe said from the doorway. "Now *that's* a way to unpack a kitchen."

"I especially like the flour accents on your pretty dress, Tara," Maddie said from next to Chloe.

Ten more seconds and they wouldn't have seen the pretty dress at all. It would have been on the floor.

Tara jerked away from him, and given her pale face, she'd realized that same thing. Or maybe that was the flour. In any case, in an irresistible bout of multitasking, she was busy simultaneously brushing off her dress, checking her hair, and doing her best to look innocent.

"What happened to your date?" Chloe asked Tara.

"I got a headache."

Chloe's brows went up. She started to say something but Maddie covered her mouth. "Pay no attention to us," Maddie said, dragging Chloe to the door.

"If only that was possible," Tara muttered. "And what happened to going out with Jax? And the yoga class?"

Chloe shoved free from Maddie's hand. "Still happening." She looked at her watch. "We have some time yet. We just didn't realize you'd be having casting calls for Pimp My Chef...or was that *Ride* My Chef?"

"Internal editor," Maddie murmured to her, which meant nothing to Ford.

Chloe smiled.

"We were just having a little trouble with the flour," Tara said, still brushing at her dress.

"Yes, I can see that," Chloe said. "I especially like the handprints you left on Ford's butt. Nice job there."

Ford couldn't see the handprints himself but he'd sure enjoyed getting them.

"This is all your fault," Tara said. Ford assumed she was talking to him, but she was actually looking at Chloe. Good. He was off the hook.

Chloe tossed up her hands. "How is it always my fault?"

Tara turned to Ford for backup. So much for off the hook. Probably he'd have been safer in a gunfight. Chloe was looking at him, too. He shrugged vaguely and took over wiping down the countertops to avoid opening his mouth and making everything worse.

"You got Ford to unpack the kitchen?" Tara asked. "Without telling me?"

"Sort of the definition of 'surprise,'" Chloe said.

"Honey, you're looking at this all wrong," Maddie said. "This was about you. About how you're there for us, always. We wanted to be there for you for a change."

"Well, *I* voted to get you a stripper," Chloe said with a reproachful look at Maddie. "But I was vetoed."

Tara let out a short laugh. "Good call," she said to Maddie.

"We really were just trying to help."

"I know," Tara said with a sigh. "And thank you. It was sweet. I'm sorry if I overreacted."

Chloe pulled out her iPhone and hit a few keys.

"What are you doing?" Maddie asked her.

"Marking the event of Tara's apology on my calendar."

Maddie snatched the iPhone, then turned to Tara. "We're sorry, too. We should have thought that you'd want a hand in the unpacking."

"No, it was a lovely gesture and saved me from obsessing over it."

Ford did his best not to smile at that, because he knew that nothing short of the apocalypse could stop Tara from obsessing.

"And you made a good choice with Ford," Tara admitted.

Wow. But when all three women looked at him, he remained quiet, deciding that silence was the best course of action here. They were actually communicating and trying to get somewhere.

Sort of.

In any case, his purpose seemed to be as mediator of some sort, so he tried to look wise.

"Ford," Maddie said, "I have a large ficus in the back of my car. Would you mind unloading it to the deck?"

He recognized a ploy to get rid of him when he heard one, but he was game. "Sure." As he brushed past Tara, taking the time to shift closer than necessary, he pressed his mouth to her ear. "We're not finished."

When the back door shut behind him, Tara sagged against the counter, scrubbing her hands over her face. "Good Lord." She dropped her hands to her sides and found both sisters staring at her with twin expressions of amusement and avid curiosity.

Maddie cracked first with a grin.

Chloe followed.

"Fuck all y'alls," Tara said without much heat. She

did like to see their smiles; she just wished it wasn't at her expense.

"Hey, we're not judging," Chloe said. "If I had that fine a man sniffing after me, I'd grab his butt, too. In fact, I'd grab a lot more than that." She rustled through her purse and pulled out a string of condoms, which she slapped on the countertop with great ceremony. "Consider this an early birthday present."

Tara's jaw dropped. "I don't need those."

"You sure about that?"

"There's no sex happening here!"

"Really? So you were just what... playing doctor, checking his tonsils, that sort of thing?"

"We are *so* not talking about this," Tara said.

"Ah, don't be like that," Chloe said. "Join me in the shallow end of the pool, why don't you. The water's warm. Give us the details. Is he as good a kisser as he looks?"

Ignoring her, Tara shifted her gaze to the window to watch Ford unload the ficus plant from Maddie's car. He moved with economical grace and ease, lifting the heavy potted plant like it weighed nothing.

"He's ever so dreamy," Chloe said, coming up next to Tara and mimicking her Southern accent.

Tara slid her a look. "Thin ice, Chloe."

Chloe snorted. "Sorry. But I can't take you seriously with flour all over your face."

Dammit. Tara swiped at her cheeks.

"Are you going to tell her or what?" Chloe asked Maddie.

"Tell me what?" Tara asked.

"The reason for the ficus," Chloe said. "It was supposed to be a bouquet of balloons, but I'm trying to go green."

Tara looked at Maddie. "Translation?"

"We want you to quit the diner and make the inn a B&B," Maddie said, then smiled.

Tara stared at her. "What?"

"Yeah," Chloe said. "You cook like an angel but you make next to nothing at the diner, which is so unfair for how hard you work."

"That 'next to nothing' has kept us in food for six months," Tara said. "I can't just quit. We like to eat."

"Well maybe you can't quit *yet*," Maddie said. "But hopefully, once we open, you could. You hate working nights, so we figured you could work here instead, making big breakfasts for the guests. It would change everything. As a bed and breakfast, we'd attract more attention, and..."

"And you think that will make me want to stay," Tara said softly, "if I'm working for myself."

"Us," Chloe said. "You'd be working for *us*."

Tara raised a brow. "Says the girl who *always* has one foot out the door."

"Yes, but *my* foot comes back every time," Chloe pointed out. "And also, I'm not a girl. One of these days you're going to open your eyes and realize I've grown up."

"I'll believe that the day Sawyer stops bringing you home from whatever misadventure you've gotten into."

"One time!" Chloe huffed.

"Actually three times," Maddie corrected, then shrugged when Chloe gave her a hard stare before turning back to Tara. "But this is about you."

"Yeah," Chloe said. "Stop sidetracking, or I'll ask you about Ford and his amazing ass again. By the way, were you going to stir him up and fry him next?"

"Oh my God, please stop talking about flour, tonsils, and *especially* Ford's amazing ass!" Tara said—okay, yelled—just as Ford—naturally—walked back into the kitchen.

In the thundering silence, he met her gaze. She did her best to look cool. Not easy with flour all over her.

"Awkward silence alert," Chloe said. "Maybe you two should just go back to—" she waved her arms, "whatever it was you were doing."

Tara sent Chloe a long look.

"Right," Chloe said, smacking her own forehead. "Stop talking. You said *stop* talking."

"Okay," Maddie said brightly, grabbing Chloe. "We'd love to stay, but we can't."

"Yes, we have to go," Chloe agreed, nonchalantly nudging the string of condoms with one finger toward Tara before Maddie yanked her to the door.

And then, *finally*, they were gone.

Tara let out a breath and turned to the sink, filling a glass of water for herself. She needed a minute.

Or a hundred.

She drank and tried to unscramble her brain cells.

Not Ford. He was leaning on the same counter that he'd pressed her against, looking relaxed and calm and very sure of himself as he eyed the string of condoms lying incongruously on the counter in front of her.

She looked at them too, and suddenly the temperature in the room shot up.

So did her body's temperature. "Ignore those," she told him.

Ford slid her a look that ratcheted the tension up even more. "Can you?"

Lord knew, she was trying. Outside the night was gorgeous, and inside there was this man, also gorgeous. She shook her head and closed her eyes. "How is it that we still feel the pull?"

Ford stepped into her, letting her feel *exactly* how much he still felt it.

"I mean, it shouldn't still be here," Tara whispered against his throat as his arms came around her. "I shouldn't..."

Ache for you...

"Some things just are," he said softly against her hair. "Day turns to night. The ocean tide drifts in and out. And I want you, Tara. Damn you, but I do. I always have."

Chapter 8

♥

"Remember, a closed mouth can't attract a foot."
TARA DANIELS

Tara wanted Ford, too. More than she'd ever wanted anyone. The wanting was in the air around them. It was in his eyes and beating in time with her pounding heart. Maybe she couldn't have her happy ending with him, but surely she could have this.

Ford's mouth left hers to skim along her jaw to her ear. His hands were equally busy, molding her body through the thin, flowing cotton of her sundress. "Say it," he murmured, flicking her earlobe with his tongue.

Tara clutched at him. "I want you too." So much. *Too* much. "Should we—"

"Yes," he said.

She stared up at him. "You don't even know what I was going to say."

"Yes to anything."

"Are you crazy? You can't give me that kind of power. What if I wanted to tie you up and—"

"Still yes," he said and dipped his head to kiss his way down her throat.

She let out a low laugh and slid her hands up his arms, humming in pleasure at the feel of his biceps, hard beneath her fingers.

Nudging her dress off her shoulder, he continued to nibble on her. "You taste good, Tara. So damn good. You always did."

He was at her collarbone now, and her brain cells were shutting down one at a time, making it a struggle to think. "What if this makes things worse?"

His soft laugh huffed against her skin. "You've barely spoken to me the entire six months you've been in town. How can it get worse?"

Good point. "But—"

"Tara." His fingers were on the zipper low on her back. "Stop thinking."

Right. Good idea. "Stopping thinking right now." She paused. "So we're going to..."

"Yes." Ford had been very intent on her zipper but now he lifted his head, and his eyes looked both amused and aroused. "On one condition."

"Wait—" Tara shook her head, which was ineffective at clearing the haze of lust. "What? You don't get to have conditions."

"Just one."

She thought about pushing him away, but then she'd be left in this...this *state*. "What? What is it?"

"You can't go back to ignoring me."

"I don't—"

He put a finger on her lips to hold in the pretty lie. "Yes or no, Tara."

Dammit. "*Yes*."

"Yes what?"

She gaped at him. "You want me to repeat it like an oath?"

"Yes," he said very seriously.

Tara stared at him, into his stubborn green eyes. He stared right back. "*Fine*," she expelled, caving like a cheap suitcase. "I won't go back to ignoring you. Which was never about you, by the way."

Ford arched a brow and she rolled her eyes. "Okay, maybe a little. But it wasn't your fault, Ford. I want you to know that. Really. It was me, and my own...issues."

"You about over those issues?" he asked as he slid his hands down her back to cup her bottom, grinding her against a most impressive erection.

"I'm not sure," she said breathlessly, "but I'm working on them."

"Good."

"So we're done talking?"

"Christ, I hope so," he said fervently, eyes dark and hot when she grabbed the condoms from the counter. When she tucked them into the front pocket of his 501s, he went still, then sucked in a breath as her fingers brushed against the hard ridge of him through the denim.

She wanted more, much more. Taking his hand, she led him out of the inn and across the yard to the small owner's cottage where she lived with her sisters. This had been rebuilt as well. The rooms were no longer 1980s checkered blue and white, but now the same earth tones as the inn.

Home.

There was no sign of her sisters, but after earlier, Tara locked her bedroom door anyway. This room was a pretty pale green, and she'd put fluffy white bedding and a pile of pillows on the queen-sized bed. Her own little corner of heaven. She purposely left the light off, thinking that would be the wisest course of action. Much as she wanted to see Ford's glorious body, she was afraid to look too deeply into his fathomless eyes, knowing that if she did she might drown in them and never come up.

There was also the fact that the last time he'd seen her body, she'd been seventeen. She wasn't certain the years had been as kind to her as they obviously had been to him.

But Ford didn't get the memo about the light. He hit the switch, and a warm glow flooded the room.

Tara hit it again, and everything went blessedly dark.

"*On*," he said firmly, and once more the room lit up.

She opened her mouth to argue, but unceremoniously found herself pinned to the wall by a hard-muscled furnace with wandering hands.

"You still have flour everywhere," Ford whispered in her ear, right before he took the lobe between his lips and sucked. "We need the light to find it all."

Huh. This reasoning could be applied to him as well, and she could get on board with seeing his body up close and personal. To get started, she shoved his shirt up his abs. Happy to help, he tugged it over his head in one economical motion. Almost before it hit the floor, her dress did the same, pooling around her ankles. Before she could bend to pick it up, Ford slid his thigh between her legs and pressed in. He kissed her breast through the lace of her bra, and her brain went into total meltdown. She was kissing whatever part of his delicious body she could reach—his jaw, his throat, the corded muscles of his neck—when she couldn't resist taking a little bite of him.

He hissed in a breath, and she murmured an apology.

"No. Do it again."

Tara obliged, making him groan as she rocked helplessly against the thigh he had between hers, the sensation of him so hard against her making her dizzy. He tugged the straps of her bra to her elbows and trapped her arms at her sides, and then concentrated on driving her crazy. "Ford, my hands—"

"Mmm," rumbled from deep in his throat as his thumbs ran back and forth over her very interested nipples. "Missed this," he said, grinding his hips to hers. "Missed you." He kissed her, then he gave her a gentle but decided push onto the bed. Following her down, he trailed kisses across her jaw and down her neck—and slowly divested her of her bra and panties. When his tongue darted out and made direct contact with her nipple, she gasped, the sound turning into a moan as he sucked her into his mouth. Then he dragged hot, open-mouthed kisses along the undersides of her breasts, sending chills up her spine.

"What?" he whispered when she went still.

"You..." Tara had an image of him making love to her all those years ago, how he'd taken the time to learn how to pleasure her. She'd always loved having the undersides of her breasts kissed.

And he'd remembered. He remembered after all this time how she preferred to be touched.

"I what, Tara?"

"You remember me."

"Vividly."

Tara sat up and helped him shove his Levi's off. His skin was warm, and he engulfed her senses, making her sigh into his next kiss. She sighed again when he rolled her beneath him, kissing and nipping his way down her body until he was at the apex of her thighs. Holding them open with his big hands, he smiled. "My favorite part," he said, and then dipped his head and proved it.

He proved it until she was helplessly shuddering and panting for air. "In me," she whispered, pulling him up. "Right now."

She was rewarded with a full-wattage smile as he tore open a condom, rolled it on, and slowly slid inside her, their twin gasps of pleasure echoing around them.

"God, Tara." His voice was so low as to be nearly inaudible. "It's been so long." He pulled out slightly, then flexed his hips and thrust back in. "So good."

The sensation of being filled by him stole her breath. She tried to rock her hips against him but his body was like steel and he had his own pace—which was set to drive-her-out-of-her-mind slow. There was no rushing him. Ever. She knew this about him but still her hands roamed over his smooth, muscular body, urging, coaxing, demanding. When that didn't work, she tugged him down and bit his lower lip.

With a growl low in his throat, he finally set an agonizingly measured rhythm, his hips moving in a delicious circle, making her moan with every thrust. But he didn't speed up, even when her fingernails dug into his back and she whispered a desperate "please," arching up and bending her legs, angling him deeper within her.

"Oh, Christ." He dipped his head to kiss her. "Christ, that's good."

"Then go faster!"

"Not yet."

"Dammit—"

"Let go for me, Tara." He cupped her face. "Let someone else have the control for a little bit."

No, she wasn't good at that. "But—"

"No buts." Ford tangled his fingers in her hair and made sure she shut up by kissing her thoroughly, his tongue sliding against hers.

Probably if anyone else had tried this, they'd have ended up walking funny tomorrow, but when Ford kissed her, she always lost track of her senses, not to mention the time and place. Every. Single. Time. She lost track of *everything* as he moved within her, bringing it all to a slow build that started low in her body and spread.

It took all she had to keep her eyes open and on his. Normally, she needed to close her eyes to concentrate, but with Ford, concentration wasn't necessary. He took her where she needed to go with seemingly no effort at all, and she didn't want to miss a single second of it. Even when her eyes were beginning to flutter shut on their own, she forced them open, unwilling to tear her gaze off his face, not wanting to miss the pure pleasure etched on his features.

Pleasure she was giving him. It was seductive, erotic, and she was burning with need, her entire body throbbing with it.

"Tara," he said, voice rough and thick with desire. "Now."

With nothing more than the demand, he sent her skittering right over the edge. A low, keening cry tore from her throat that she couldn't have held back to save her own life.

She'd given him control after all, she thought dazedly. And as she burst, pulsing hard around him, he pressed himself deeper, then deeper still, coming with a raw, rough, very male sound of gratification as he followed her over.

Ford was still buried deep inside Tara's gorgeous body when they heard the front door of the cottage open and then shut.

"Tara?" a male voice called out, one that had Tara jerking beneath Ford.

"No," she whispered, then shoved Ford off of her and sat up, the sheet clutched to her chest, her eyes wide and horrified. "It can't be."

"Who is it?" Ford asked, frowning.

"Tara? You here?"

Galvanized into action, Tara leapt out of the bed and started yanking on her clothes. "Give me a minute!" she yelled. "I'm coming."

"Yeah, you did," Ford murmured. He had the nail marks on his ass to prove it. "Who's out there, Tara?"

She shoved her feet back into her heels, then did a double take as she realized Ford was still lying in bed. *Naked.* "Oh my God. *Get dressed!*"

She was attempting to work her hair back into submission as he rose and pulled her against him, stilling her frenetic movements. "Talk to me."

"It's Logan," she choked out and shoved at him.

He held on. "Logan," he said, searching his memory banks. "Logan, the ex?"

"Yes. Wait—" She stilled in the act of getting back into her dress. "You know him?"

"Only that he likes to be plastered all over the papers

and magazines. And once upon a time, you were plastered there with him." He caught her arm before she could run off. This had been supposedly just sex—but that didn't mean he was happy to find her ex-husband sniffing around. And actually, he was distinctly *un*happy about that. "Why is he here?"

"I don't know." Tara clapped her hands to her face. "And you're still naked."

"Yes, and less than three minutes ago you were enjoying that very fact," he said grimly. "You don't know what he wants?"

She dropped her head to his chest. "No idea."

Ford wrapped his hand around the bulk of her silky hair and gently tugged until she was looking at him. "You asked who was in my bed. Maybe I should have asked who's in yours."

"No one's been in mine! For two years!" She closed her eyes. "*Two years*, Ford."

He stroked a finger over her jaw. "You were overdue," he murmured. Okay, so she and Logan weren't still having sex. That was good. Not that he should care one way or the other. "Why so long?"

"Because I couldn't find anyone I wanted to be with," she said a little defensively. "And now there are *two* men, and one of them is naked and smells like me, and—"

He kissed her, long and deep. Crazy. Stupid. And Christ, so fucking good.

"—and *tastes* like me," she whispered with a moan when they broke apart. "Oh my God, Ford."

Since she looked so adorably miserable and confused, and sounded so panicked to boot—all a rarity for her—Ford let out a breath and stroked a hand down her hair. "I can fix the naked part. You're on your own for the rest, unless you want help encouraging him to get the hell out."

"What? *No.*"

Ouch. But a good reminder of what this was. And what it wasn't.

"Ford. I can't do this with you," she whispered.

"Do what?"

"*This.* It didn't work back then, and it won't work now."

Yes, he knew that. So he had no idea why he backed her to the wall and kissed her again, hard and ravishing, until she was clutching at him. It might have been a stupid, macho, asshole thing to do, but that she looked so dazed when he pulled back helped a lot. "I don't think we're done," he said with a calm he didn't come close to feeling.

"We have to be." She chewed on her lower lip. "I'm working."

"Everyone works, Tara."

"On myself," she blurted out, hurriedly, with a quick glance at the door, anxiety level clearly high. "When we were together last time, I was young, and I didn't know— I didn't know how to be in a relationship. I was bad at it, at giving myself."

"And with Logan? Were you bad at giving yourself then too?"

"No." She stared up at him, leveling him with those whiskey eyes. "With him, I did the opposite. I gave too much. I gave everything. Don't you see? I have to figure it all out so I don't just repeat my mistakes."

"So that's what you're working on?" he asked.

"Figuring out how to give yourself and not lose yourself at the same time?"

"Yes!"

Ah, hell. Out of all the things she could have said, this was the one that got to him, and he stroked a hand over her jaw. "How's that going?"

"Right now? Not so well, actually."

"Tara—"

But she backed up and shook her head sharply. She didn't want his help, or his sympathy. Fair enough. He didn't want to get tangled up in this again anyway.

At least not outside of the bedroom.

"*Tara?*" Logan called from down the hall.

Ford tensed.

Tara closed her eyes. "Just a minute, Logan!"

"Remember my condition," Ford said softly.

"Don't ignore you."

"That's right. And another."

"Ford—" She started to pull away but he grabbed her.

"Don't pull what you did last time," he said. "The running away thing."

"We were seventeen and stupid."

"I'll give you the stupid part."

Her mouth tightened. "I didn't exactly just run off."

"Bullshit." He risked her temper by pulling her in close. He couldn't help himself.

Her breath caught in panic. "Ford! I mean it, I can't do this with you. The first time nearly killed me. Let's just learn from our mistakes, and cut our losses now."

Yeah. Excellent plan. Cut their losses. It made perfect sense, especially given that the last time Tara was here in Lucky Harbor things didn't exactly work out for her—in no small part thanks to him. Chances were good that she'd get the hell out of Dodge sooner than later anyway. And that was okay. He knew she deserved a hell of a lot more than to be stuck in a place with nothing but bad memories.

Of which he was one. The biggest baddest memory she had, no doubt. He pulled on his clothes and without another word gave her what she wanted, what he told himself he wanted as well. He walked out the door and down the hallway, nodding as he came upon the man he recognized from the racing world.

Logan Perrish was just shy of six feet, dark-haired and dark-eyed. He was in more than decent shape and looked designer ready for a cover shoot. A good match for the elegant, sophisticated Tara, which made Ford want to shove the guy's ass out the door.

Logan looked at Ford, then purposely switched his gaze to where Ford had come from, obviously the bedroom. "Are you... a guest?" he asked. "I didn't think that the inn was open yet."

Ford opened his mouth to answer, but Tara, coming from the bedroom as well, beat him to it.

"It's actually going to be a B&B," she said. "But no, he's not a guest. And neither are you. You can't just show up. Did you even knock before you broke in?" She wore her now-wrinkled dress, no shoes. There was a definite glow about her, one Ford took some pride in since he'd put it there.

"Yes, I knocked," Logan said. "You didn't answer." He was staring at Ford. "I didn't realize you'd have company. I was going to wait for you to get home."

Ford stared back.

Tara let out a sound that was part disbelief and part irritation. Ford recognized the irritation since he tended to bring that out in her a lot.

"You didn't realize I'd have company," she repeated slowly. "Even though it's been...what, *months* since we last talked?"

"We always go that long." Logan looked confused. "Is something wrong?"

"No," Tara said. "I'm only having flashbacks to why our marriage failed."

Logan jerked his head in Ford's direction. "Who is he?"

The guy who just did your ex-wife, asshole, Ford thought. Maybe he didn't have a future with Tara, but it would appear he wasn't a big enough man to want her to have a future with Logan, either.

Tara looked at Ford and opened her mouth. Then closed it again. Clearly she had no idea how to explain him. "Ford Walker," she finally said. "Ford, Logan."

Logan held out his hand. "I'm Tara's husband."

"*Ex*-husband." Tara smacked Logan in the chest. "What's the matter with you? And why are you here again?"

"I missed you."

Tara shocked Ford by bursting out laughing. "Come on," she finally said, still smiling. "Truth."

Logan returned the smile with good grace and some chagrin. "I did miss you." He stepped close, but Tara put up a hand and took a step back from him.

"Logan, when I left you, it took you a month to even realize I was gone. A month, Logan. So what's this really about?"

Logan looked at Ford.

Then Tara looked at Ford, too. Clearly the public forum portion of the evening was over.

Fuck it. If she didn't want to kick her ex-husband to the curb, it was none of his business, and he headed to the door.

Chapter 9

♥

Tara heard the door shut behind Ford as he left and felt a quick stab of pain in her chest. What would it take for him to fight for her, she wondered. For him to take a stand and stick?

More than sex, apparently. But secretly she'd hoped for *exactly* that, for something, anything, to show her that this was more than just a good time in the sack, that...

That they *deserved* another shot.

"New boyfriend?" Logan asked.

She nearly snapped out a sarcastic answer, but as he'd asked quietly and utterly without judgment, she found herself being honest. "More like an old one," she told him. It felt so odd to see him, fit and rangy and beautiful as ever. She waited for the inevitable heart pang at just the sight of him, but all she felt was the ache for what had once been.

And what hadn't been.

"You once told you me that you'd only had one serious boyfriend before me," he said. "From when you were young."

"Yes."

Logan's eyes widened. "And that's him? That's the one you ... ?"

She grimaced. Logan knew about the baby. He'd been the only one she'd ever told, because she hadn't wanted that kind of secret between them after they'd married. "Yes."

"Are you together now?" Logan asked.

"No." But as soon as the word left her mouth, she wished it back—she and Ford *weren't* together, so why the little stab of regret and the uncomfortable feeling that somehow she'd just been disloyal? "I don't really know," she corrected.

"Okay," Logan said, nodding to himself. "Unexpected detour."

She shook her head, baffled by his presence here, so far from his world. "Why aren't you off somewhere racing for fortune and fame?"

"I'm taking a season off."

This made no sense. Racing was everything to Logan. Everything. Plus, it was difficult if not downright impossible to just "take a season off." There were contractual obligations to owners and sponsors to deal with, pit crews and garage staff to keep on the books. "How can you just..."

Logan shoved the sleeve of his shirt back, revealing his arm. And the brace on it. "That last crash caused some serious ligament damage. I'm facing a couple of surgeries, which means I'm a liability right now on the course. They've hired a replacement for me. Indefinitely."

"Oh, Logan," Tara breathed, knowing how much racing meant to him, and what *not* racing meant, too.

"It's okay," he said. "I don't mind the time off."

"Why?"

"Because the racing world cost me something I miss. You, Tara. It cost me you."

Tara stared at him. There'd been a time when she'd have given anything to hear him say that: her so-called career, her right arm, anything. But things were different now. *She* was different now. "Logan—"

He shook his head. "Don't say anything. Just think about it. Think about me, okay?"

She let out a low laugh and sank to the couch, stunned. "It took me two years to get over you. I can't just make all that happened between us vanish with a snap of my fingers."

"I know, and there's no rush," Logan assured her. "I'm going to be here all summer, so—"

"All summer? What do you mean, all summer?"

He grinned. "To win you back, of course." He knelt down in front of her and flashed the grin that had once been panty-melting. "No decisions now, okay? Like I said, we have all summer."

Oh, God. "You can't just hang around all summer."

"Why not?"

"Because..." She had no idea. "What will you do with yourself?"

He leaned in and kissed her cheek. "I'll figure it out," he said. She kept him from moving in closer with a hand to his chest. "And," he went on, looking amused at her boundaries, "it's a busy time for you with the opening of the inn. I can help."

The man had two personal assistants to do his every bidding. He didn't do his own laundry, cooking, housekeeping, accounting...anything. "How exactly can you help?"

"Hey, I'm new and improved." He shot her his most charming smile. "You don't know this about me yet, but you'll see."

"Logan—"

"No rush, Tara. I'm a patient guy."

And then, like Ford, he vanished into the night.

The next morning was damp and foggy. Tara got up at the crack of dawn to walk. Probably she should run, but she hated to run. Her carefully constructed life was going to hell in a handbasket, and she was already planning on inhaling crap food by the bundle. She needed to burn some calories as a preventative measure or she'd be forced to switch to loose sweats in no time.

Tara walked into town and down the length of the pier, waving at Lance, who was hosing down the area out front of his ice cream shop.

Turning around at the end of the pier, she walked back. She could have gone straight to the cottage and had a nice shower but she decided to walk through the marina to burn a few extra calories.

Or because Ford was out there on the dock.

She was drawn to him like a damn magnet. He was surrounded by sailing boat parts, with a tool in one hand, a part in the other, and a look of concentration on his face.

When he caught sight of her, the corners of that

amazing, fantasy-inducing mouth of his quirked. Only a few hours ago, he'd been buried deep inside her, their bodies slick with sweat, their breath mingling, moving in tandem. Just in the remembering, the air around them changed, and she was swamped with more memories.

And longing...

Their gazes caught and held, though neither of them spoke. Her nerves fluttered. So did a few other body parts.

"You okay?" he finally asked.

It wasn't a filler question. Last night had been emotional, and he had a look of genuine concern on his face. It conflicted with the picture she had in her head of him walking out the door without a backward glance. "I'm fine."

"Logan gone?" he asked.

"Not exactly."

His jaw tightened, and he took a moment to answer. "What then, exactly?"

"He's staying for the summer." When he locked gazes with her, she lifted her hands. "Not my idea."

He said nothing to this but his silence spoke volumes.

"So is this going to be uncomfortable now?" she asked.

He cocked his head. "Does it feel uncomfortable?"

"I'm not sure yet."

He sighed, muttered something to himself that sounded like "don't do it, man," then wrapped an arm around her waist. He snugged the lower half of his body to hers, rocking against her. "How about now?"

"No, uncomfortable is not the word I'd use," she managed. "Ford." Helpless against the pull of the attraction, not to mention his easy, sexy charm, she gripped his shirt in two fists and dropped her forehead to his chest.

He stroked his hand down her hair, a movement of affection and gentle possession, and she pressed even closer. *Not again*, her brain told her body. *You are not going to have him again.* But her brain wasn't in charge because she glanced over his shoulder at the sailboat, which had a bedroom below deck.

And a bed.

Ford followed her gaze and let out a low laugh. "Okay, but only if you ask nice."

"Not funny," she said and pushed away from him. "Besides, I'm all sweaty, and you're all dirty."

"Then we're already halfway to where I'd like to be."

"Stop it."

"Hey, you're the one who came out of your way to see me."

That was true, which didn't make it any less irritating that somehow he always knew what she was thinking. "I'm going to take a shower." A cold one.

"You want help with that?"

"No!"

"You want me bad," Ford called after her as she walked away.

Yes, she did. Quite badly, in fact. What woman could help wanting him in her bed? The problem was that Ford didn't tend to exert much energy on things that were difficult. And Tara was just about as difficult as they came. Which meant she needed to resist him and all his gorgeousness because she already knew the ending to their story.

A few nights later, Ford was at The Love Shack serving drinks. The place was busy, which usually gave him a surge of satisfaction. He loved being here, hearing the chatter and the laughter, knowing that he brought everyone together. He'd learned a long time ago to make a family and a home wherever he could. This was both.

The walls of The Love Shack were a deep, sinful bordello red, lined with antique mining tools that he and Jax had collected over the years on various adventures. Lanterns hung from the exposed-beam ceilings and lit up the scarred bench-style tables and the bar itself, which was made of a series of old wooden doors attached end to end.

If Ford wasn't on a boat with the wind hitting his face as he flew over the water at dizzying speeds, then he was at his happiest here.

It was a simple lifestyle, but when it came right down to it, he was a simple guy. Growing up poorer than dirt had ensured that. So had being loved and protected by his grandma to the best of her abilities as they'd worked their asses off. She'd always said that someday it would pay off and she'd get to retire to Palm Springs.

It gave Ford great satisfaction that he'd been able to give that to her, that right this minute she was probably on the deck of the Palm Springs home he'd bought her, sipping iced tea and watching the mountains. It was her favorite pastime after cooking for him on the rare occasions he made it down there to visit, that is. She'd marvel at his height and build every single time he walked in her door, as if she couldn't quite believe he'd grown up from that scrawny, undersized kid he'd once been.

Ford couldn't blame her. He'd managed to live through his teens, and then his twenties in spite of himself, and was now working on his thirties and being a grownup. On accepting his mistakes and living with no regrets, though his biggest regret was heavy on his mind lately.

Tara.

"Earth to Ford." Sawyer Thompson waved a hand in Ford's face. "You with us? Or do you need a moment alone?"

"Thought tonight was your night off." Sawyer was big and broad as a mountain, and could be as intimidating as hell—unless you'd grown up with him and knew that he wouldn't watch any Disney/Pixar flick because they made him cry like a chick. Ford poured him a Coke—Sawyer's standard order when he was on duty.

"Got called in." Sawyer's smile faded. "Unexpected trouble out at Horn Crest."

"Hang gliders again?" Last time, the hang gliders had turned out to be Chloe, Lance, and Tucker, and they'd been arrested for trespassing when they'd landed in Mrs. Azalea's prized field of rhododendrons. Lance was on a mission to accumulate as many crazy adventures as he could before his cystic fibrosis caught up with him, and Chloe and Lance's brother, Tucker, were dedicated to assisting him in his stupidity.

For some reason, this drove Sawyer insane.

Ford was just glad to see that it ran in the family, the unique ability of the three sisters to drive men right over the edge of sanity.

"Not hang gliders this time," Sawyer said, sounding relieved. Chloe was well-liked in town, and every time she ran into trouble and Sawyer had to deal with it, *he* got the backlash.

Ford knew that Sawyer liked order. *Calm* order. Which

meant that Sawyer and Chloe were oil and water. But like oil and water, they ended up together a lot. Karma was a bitch with a good sense of humor.

"It was a group of teenagers," Sawyer said. "Brought them home to their parents and caught hell from one of the mothers. She told me I'd be a better use of her tax money if I was out catching *real* bad guys." With a sigh, he sank to a stool and accepted the Coke. "And what are you doing here? I thought you were going to do that race in the Gulf this weekend."

Ford shrugged. "Maybe next time."

Sawyer lifted a brow. "You losing your edge?"

"What? No."

"What then? Over the hill already at thirty-four?"

"Shut up. You're the one who threw your back out playing foosball last month."

Sawyer scowled. "Hey, that was an amazing play. Genius even."

"So was your having to spend the rest of the weekend on the couch whining, and then desk duty for a full week."

"So?" Sawyer said. "It got me some great bedside treatment from the women."

Ford snorted. "What women?"

"Hey, I have women."

"Women on porn sites don't count."

"You're being an asshole," Sawyer said mildly. "Another sign of age. Should I tell Ciera to save you a spot in the retirement home? And get you a prescription for Viagra?"

Ciera was Ford's sister, a nurse who worked at a senior center in Seattle. "You're older than me," Ford reminded him.

"By two months, which is offset by the fact that I'm better looking. I'm also not picking a fight just to be an asshole."

Ford blew out a breath. "I'm not racing because I didn't feel like traveling."

"And?"

"And Jax is too nice to our regulars, and I needed to stick around to keep him in line."

"And?"

"And..." Shit. He had nothing.

"Admit it," Sawyer said. "You're not going anywhere because Tara's ex-husband has shown up, and you don't want to lose your place."

Ford shoved his fingers through his hair. "Yeah."

Lucille sidled up to the bar. She was in her pink sweats with her crazy white hair looking like a Q-tip. Her rheumy blue eyes landed on Ford. "A vodka on the rocks." She tapped the bar. "So how's it going with the Steel Magnolia?"

Ford handed her the drink. "What?"

"Don't play stupid, honey. It doesn't suit you."

"Actually, it does," Sawyer said helpfully.

Ford took away his soda.

"Hey."

"Tara," Lucille said to Ford. "I'm talking about Tara." She tossed back the vodka like someone who'd been doing it for a gazillion years. "Her ex is here. He's a real live celebrity, you know."

Ford sighed. He knew.

Lucille nudged him. "He's got the edge on you, boy."

Ford began to wish he didn't have a thing against drinking while serving. "We're not discussing this, Lucille."

"Well, maybe you're not, but everyone else is. You need to look sharp. *Sharp*." She reached over the bar and jabbed him in the gut with her bony finger. "Are you listening?"

"Yeah, I'm listening." Ford rubbed his belly. "And *ouch*."

"*Sharp*, I tell you!"

Like he didn't know that. Like that hadn't always been the problem, that he wasn't exactly up to Tara's standards. Something that had been slammed home to him anew now that he'd actually met Logan and seen the slick, polished ex up close. Not only that, he'd sensed a still-obvious chemistry between Logan and Tara.

Sawyer was taking all this in with his usual quiet calm. "What makes everyone think our boy here is interested in the girl?" he asked Lucille.

She cackled and slapped down her empty shot glass, indicating she wanted another. "Oh, he's interested."

Sawyer looked at Ford, studying him thoughtfully. After a beat, a slight smile curved his lips. "Yeah, I think you're right."

"Thanks, man," Ford said.

Lucille smacked Ford upside the head.

"Okay," he said. "Stop that!"

"You need to stop. Stop messing around. It's time to get serious now, Ford. For once in your life."

What made this all worse was that in a way she was right. Ford knew what people saw when they looked at him—a guy who'd never had a serious commitment in his life, except maybe to sailing. And other than Tara and that long-ago summer, he'd never really been with a woman with whom he'd truly been friends as well as lovers. In his mind, the two were separate things. His life went day to day. His sailing. The bar. Friends. Sure he was good to his grandma but she didn't require anything much from him. Money was easy to give once you had it.

The truth was for the past six months now, he'd been…restless. Unsettled. Unhappy.

Six months. Since the day Tara had come back to Lucky Harbor. Which was especially stupid because neither of them wanted to go down that road again.

And yet there was something undeniable between them, something far more than what had happened in her bed. Something that made him itchy to both run like hell and go after her at the same time.

The door of the bar opened and in strolled…*shit*.

Logan Perrish.

He was dressed more for a hot nightclub than a small-town bar, and looking pretty damn expensive while he was at it. Ford wanted to hate him on principle but the guy stopped to sign an autograph for anyone who wanted one. Hard to hate a guy like that. When Logan got to the bar, he was clearly surprised at the sight of Ford. "Hey. You're a bartender?"

"Yep. A drink?"

"Sure." Logan scanned the list of beers available on the blackboard behind Ford. "I've heard about something called a…Ginger Goddess?"

From the next barstool, Sawyer grimaced. "You've gotta be within fifty feet of a swimming pool in order to drink a fruity, girlie-ass drink like that. Otherwise, they revoke your guy card."

Logan smiled, unconcerned. He looked at Ford. "So you make them or what?"

"Yeah." Ford made them. For women. Sawyer was right; it was a complete pussy drink.

Logan laughed at his expression. "I know, I know. But if it has the name of a soda pop or any sort of female connotation, I'm hooked."

Ford went back to hating as he picked out a kiwi, a pear, and a cocktail shaker, and got to work. On a damn Ginger Goddess.

"Well, if it isn't the famous Logan Perrish," Lucille said in her craggy voice.

"Hello," Logan said with an easy smile. "You a racing fan, darlin'?"

She simpered. "Oh, yes." She pushed her napkin toward him. "Autograph?"

Ford shot her a level are-you-kidding-me look over his shoulder, but she just grinned at him before turning back to Logan. "And isn't it something to have you here in Lucky Harbor? Nice finish in Talladega. Sorry about the subsequent crash." She touched his brace. "I hope it's not too painful."

"I'm healing up just fine," Logan assured her, turning to include the two women who came up on his other side. They held out their napkins for him to sign as well, which he did with a flourish.

Ford added ginger, vodka, and ice to the shaker, catching Sawyer's eye.

Sawyer was back to smirking.

With a scowl, Ford strained Logan's drink into a flute, then topped it with sparkling wine.

By now Logan had half the bar circling him like he was the best thing since sliced bread, and he'd turned away from the bar, completely surrounded by fans.

"A real live celebrity," Sawyer noted to Ford. "People can't resist that."

Ford could. "I don't see what's so great about him," he muttered. "In his last eighteen starts, he's never so much as led a lap. And he dresses like he believes his own press."

"I think you missed your dose of Midol today."

"And what the fuck," Ford went on. "Driving isn't even a damn sport."

Sawyer was cracking up now. "Really?"

"Really what?"

"You're going to finally make a move for the woman you've been mooning over for what, six months now, because her ex-husband is in town? Lame, man."

"Who said I was making a move?"

"You're gearing up, I can tell," Sawyer said.

"You can not."

"I've been watching you make your moves since middle school. You haven't changed your technique much."

"Whatever." Ford slammed around a few shot glasses to look busy. "And technically, I made my move *before* Logan got here." He felt someone pat his hand and looked down at Lucille.

"Don't you worry, honey," she said in a stage whisper the people in Seattle could have heard. "We're going to help you get the girl."

"We?"

She gestured to four women that looked even older than she, all in an assortment of bright lipstick and blue hair. "We're going to tip the scales in your favor," she said. "But it'd really help if you'd ever been on TV for winning a race."

"I have!" Ford pinched the bridge of his nose. "Listen to me, Lucille. No meddling. Do you hear me?"

But Lucille had already turned to her posse. "It won't be easy, girls," she was saying to them. "But we can do it. For Ford, right?"

"For Ford," they all repeated.

Sawyer was grinning, the asshole.

"Okay, that's it," Ford said to Lucille, pointing at her. "I'm cutting you off."

"Hush, dear," she said with a dismissive wave. "We're working here. And while you're standing there looking pretty, we're going to need a pitcher of margaritas."

Jesus.

Ford was halfway through that task when Logan sauntered back up to the bar for another drink.

"Don't tell me," Ford said. "Another Ginger Goddess."

"Nah." Logan grinned. "I just wanted to see if you knew how to make a sissy drink. It was good though. Thanks."

Sawyer, still sprawled back in his chair, laughed.

Okay, that was it. Ford was cutting *everyone* off, the fuckers.

Lucille asked Logan for his autograph again.

"Didn't I already give you one, darlin'?" Logan asked.

"Yes, but that was for eBay." Lucille patted his arm and pointed to Ford. "Have you met our own local celebrity?"

Logan looked at Ford. "Yes, but I didn't know he was a celebrity."

Ford waited for someone to announce his two American Cup wins or maybe the ISAF Rolex World Sailor of the Year award. Or hey, how about either of his gold medals?

"Yes, sirree," Lucille said proudly. "Ford here makes the best margaritas on the West Coast."

Sawyer choked and indicated he needed water. Ford ignored him.

"And oh!" Lucille added. "He's real good on a boat, too."

Ford was sure that he could feel a blood vessel bursting behind his left eye. He took a deep, calming breath. It didn't help, but it wasn't worth the breath to point out that he'd also once been featured in *Sports Illustrated*.

Sawyer continued to cough, and Ford hoped he swallowed his tongue.

Lucille waved her glass around as she spoke. "Why, just the other day Ford was working on Lucky Harbor Inn's rentals for them. Such a good boy."

Logan grinned. "That's nice."

"Oh, our Ford is *quite* the catch," Lucille went on, and her blue-haired posse all nodded sagely. "Tara thinks so, too, seeing as she pulled him into her meeting the other day and made him take off his shirt for the ladies."

Now it was Ford's turn to choke. "Okay, that's *not* what happened. I—"

"Don't be shy, dear. You look good without your shirt." Lucille glanced at Logan. "Though I'm sure you look good without yours as well. In fact, maybe we could have a contest right here."

Jesus.

Lucille's posse all sat up straighter and nodded their blue-haired perms.

Logan laughed, but he looked Ford over for a long beat.

Ford looked right back. In Logan's eyes, he saw the light of challenge. No, they weren't going to have a shirt-off contest, but they *were* competing.

Game on.

Chapter 10

♥

*"Life isn't about finding yourself,
it's about creating yourself."*
TARA DANIELS

Tara spent the next few days organizing and then reorganizing the inn's kitchen.

They were going to open as a B&B.

Maddie had handled the paperwork for the license and inspection required, Chloe was working up ideas for special baskets for guests that could be ordered if they wanted meals on the go, and Tara was working on menu planning, recipes, and the additional supplies needed.

It could actually come together and work.

Tara could hardly believe it, both that she'd agreed and that the more time passed, the more she liked the idea. It was exhilarating to finally do something she'd always wanted—cooking for a living in her own kitchen.

It was terrifying as well, because the opportunity for an epic failure had never been greater. It wasn't as if she had a great track record succeeding at...well, anything.

But there was always a first time. This was what she told herself. It gave her hope. With the phones starting to ring and bookings coming in, and with Chloe still coming and going and Maddie feeling in over her head, they'd put out an ad for another part-time employee. They already had interviews set up with a few high school students hopefully willing to do grunt work relatively cheaply.

Plenty of the Lucky Harbor curious stopped by: Lucille toting recipes, Lance and Tucker proposing the possibility of delivering ice cream on the weekends from their shop, Sawyer to mooch coffee—the inn was on his way to work and he preferred Tara's coffee to the station's.

If nothing else, the distractions soaked up some of the terror over the upcoming opening, and took up all of Tara's available brain space, leaving none for her other problems.

Such as her man problems.

That she could even think that phrase—*man problems*—was as amazing as it was ridiculous. She never had man problems.

She never had men!

To her surprise, Logan had been serious about staying in town. He'd rented a small beach cottage a few miles up the road and had come by each day. Tara had no idea what to make of that. Her entire marriage had been about *her* chasing *him*. It felt odd, to say the least, that things were reversed.

As for Ford, he was around. He'd served her drinks the other night when she'd gone to The Love Shack with Chloe and Maddie. He'd been at the marina yesterday working on his boat.

But there'd been no one-on-one conversations between them. And given that she knew he was all too aware of Logan being in town, she got the unspoken message.

He wasn't going to press, push, or fight for her. Shock. Ford never pressed, pushed or fought. Things either came right to him, like moths to a flame, or they didn't.

Not being a moth, Tara was on her own to do as she pleased. She just wasn't exactly sure what would please her.

Okay, big fat lie. She knew what would please her, and that was one Ford Walker, served straight up. But hell if she'd go through that again....

A week after their not-so-awkward morning after, Tara headed out at the crack of dawn to return his crepe pan, which she'd used and loved. She needed to buy herself one the next time she had a couple hundred bucks lying around.

It took ten minutes to drive to his house, ten minutes she told herself she didn't have to spare. She should have given him the pan back at the marina. That would have been the logical and reasonable thing to do. Except as it applied to Ford, Tara didn't have a logical or reasonable bone in her body.

At least his house was easy enough to get to. He lived on the bluffs above the inn. As the sun rose over the mountains, casting a pink glow over the morning, she parked and headed up his walk. A small part of her secretly hoped she caught him in bed. But that really was a very small part.

The bigger part hoped he was in the shower.

She looked around and realized that she didn't see his car, which pretty much rained on the waking-him-up parade. Wondering where he was—or who he might be with so early—put a hitch in her step.

None of your business, she told herself. *None*. She blew out a breath, opened her cell phone, and called him.

"Hey," he said in his usual sex-on-a-stick voice. "Miss me?"

She ignored both that and the floaty feeling the sound of his voice put in her stomach. "I'm returning your pan," she said. "I'm on your porch." She paused, hoping he'd tell her where he was.

"Let yourself in," he said and gave her the code to unlock the door.

"Where should I leave it, in your kitchen?"

"Or on my bed," he said.

"You want the Le Creuset on your bed," she repeated, heavy on the disbelief.

"No, I want *you* on my bed. What are you wearing?"

She pulled the cell away from her ear and stared at it. "You did not just ask me that."

"Never mind," he said. "I'll just picture you how I want you."

"And how would that be?" The words popped out of her before she could stop them, fascinated in spite of herself.

"Hmm," he mused silkily. "Maybe a French maid outfit."

"That's..." She struggled a minute with why the thought turned her on. "Outdated and anti-feminist," she finally said, a little weakly. "Not to mention subservient."

"I like the subservient part," Ford mused. "A few 'yes sirs' would be nice."

"You are one seriously warped man."

"No doubt." His voice was low and sexy, and it made her forget herself, made her forget that all he wanted was her body. Especially since at the moment, she wanted his.

"I can be there in twenty minutes," he said, a smile in his voice.

"No. Don't even think about it." Tara ignored the flutter in her belly. She couldn't help it. Even when he was being a Neanderthal, he still turned her on. Sure, she'd just been fantasizing about catching him in the shower, but that had been just a fantasy. She needed to live firmly in reality. "We're done with that."

"Bet I can change your mind."

"I have no doubt," Tara said. God, she needed help. "But you're a nice guy, so you won't."

"I'm not that nice a guy."

Great. Just great. "You've been an absent guy."

He was quiet a moment. "Didn't see a need to complicate anything for you."

Like a reunion with Logan. Tara drew in a deep breath. "You ever think that sometimes complications are worth the trouble?"

"No."

Quick and easy and brutally honest. It was Ford's way. She'd have to think about that later. Right now, she punched in his front door code and listened to the lock click open. "Are you sure you don't want me to just leave the pan on the step?" she asked. "It'd be safe." In Lucky Harbor, just about everything was safe.

Except her heart, she was discovering.

"Are you afraid to step inside my lair?" Ford teased.

"Ha. And no. I'll leave it on your table."

"Ten-four." He paused. "Are you going to snoop around while you're in there?"

"No." Maybe. "What would I snoop around in?"

"I don't know. My underwear drawer?"

The last time she'd touched his underwear, he'd been wearing them. But just the thought of him in his BVDs brought a rush. "No," she said quickly.

Too quickly, because he laughed softly. "You can if you want to," he said, lowering his voice. "You can do whatever you want, Tara. Flip through my porn, eat the enchiladas I made last night from Carlos's abuelo's recipe..."

"Wait." She promptly forgot about underwear, porn, *and* jumping his bones. "Carlos gave you his abuelo's recipe? I've been asking him for it forever."

"Yes, but do you take him out on the water every week and teach him to sail? Or teach him how to pick up girls so as to achieve maximum basage?"

"Basage?"

"You know, first base, second base—"

"Ohmigod," she said. "You are such a *guy*!"

He was laughing now. "Guilty as charged."

Tara sighed. "So it's a boy's club; is that what you're saying?"

"Uh huh. And I'm glad to say that you do *not* have the right equipment to join."

"I want that recipe, Ford."

"Only men are allowed to have it. It's been handed down that way for generations."

"You're making that up."

He didn't say anything, but she could practically *hear* him smiling. "*Please?*" she asked.

"Oh, how I like the sound of that word coming from your mouth."

"*Ford.*"

"Right here, Tara." He was still using his bedroom voice. Which, as she had good reason to know, made her one hundred percent *stupid*.

"What would you do to get the recipe?" he wanted to know.

She shook her head. "I'm hanging up now."

"Okay, but if you change your mind and want to play with my underwear, text me and I'll be right there. You can play with the ones I'm wearing."

She felt herself go damp and hurriedly disconnected. She wouldn't be texting him. She wouldn't let herself go there. *Way* too big a risk when it came to him, because he wouldn't risk anything. Been there, done that.

She stepped into his big, masculine house, her heels clicking on his hardwood floor. He had a big couch and an even bigger flat screen. One wall was all windows looking out over the water. And, she realized, the marina.

Lucky Harbor Inn's marina.

She wondered if he ever stood right here and looked for her. Reminding herself that she was on a mission to drop the pan off and get out, she refused to let herself look at anything else as she headed toward his kitchen.

Except her eyes strayed to the mantel in the living room on the way and at the pictures there. There was one of Jax, Sawyer, and Ford on Ford's boat. Three hard-bodied gorgeous men, tanned and wet and mugging for the camera. She wondered who had taken the picture, and if the bikini top hanging from the mast behind them belonged to the photographer.

There was another picture of Ford with a group of guys all standing shoulder to shoulder, wearing USA track suits and holding their medals. The Olympic sailing team.

The last picture showed an older woman with two younger women, all of whom shared Ford's wide, open, mischievous smile and bright green eyes.

His grandmother and sisters.

Tara walked through an archway, past the laundry room, and into a kitchen that gave her some serious appliance envy. And Corian countertop envy. And, oh Lord, *look at his Japanese cutlery.* Just standing here was going to give her an orgasm. She set the pan on the table, forced herself to turn around, and headed back under the archway. There was a basket of clean clothes on the dryer. Drawn in by the fresh scent, she stood in the center of the laundry room and inhaled deeply.

She was pathetic.

On the top of the basket of clothes lay a T-shirt. It said LUCKY HARBOR SAILING CHAMP across the front. At one time, it'd been gray, but years of washing had softened it to nearly white. She knew this because he'd been given two of them. Ford had gotten them that long-ago summer during his first sailing race when he'd been nothing but the dock boy on a local team.

She had the other shirt. He'd given it to her all those years ago, and she'd worn it to sleep in. She'd kept it as one of her few true treasures. Unfortunately, she'd been wearing it the night of the inn fire six months ago, and it'd been destroyed. Unable to stop herself, she ran her fingers over the shirt and whoops, look at that, picked it up. Well, hey, he'd invited her to play with his underwear, and a T-shirt could be classified as underwear. She pressed her face to the soft, faded cotton and felt her knees go a little weak even though it smelled like detergent and not the man.

She wanted the shirt.

Don't do it . . .

But she did. She totally stole his shirt.

She drove back to the inn with it in her purse and walked straight to the marina, and then to the end of the dock.

She needed a minute.

She inhaled the wet, salty air. Sitting was a challenge in her pencil skirt and she had to kick off her heels, but once she managed, having the water lap at her feet and the sun on her face made it worth it. It meant unwanted freckles and almost dropping a Jimmy Choo knock-off into the water, but there was something about listening to the water slap up against the wood and watching the boats bob up and down on the swells that really did it for her.

It was better than dark chocolate for releasing endorphins and helping her relax.

Better than orgasms.

Okay, no. Nothing was better than orgasms, but this would have to be a close second.

She'd stolen his shirt. Good Lord, she was losing it.

Two battered cross trainers appeared in her peripheral vision. Long legs, dark blue board shorts, and a white T-shirt came next.

And then the heart-stopping smile.

"So you didn't climb into my bed," Ford said, sitting next to her.

"How do you know I didn't just get tired of waiting for you to show up?" she asked.

His brow shot up so far it vanished into the lock of hair falling over his forehead. "Are you telling me I missed my shot?"

"Sugar, you never even had a shot."

Ford grinned and slung an arm over her shoulder, pulling her into him. He smelled delicious. Like salty air and the ocean and something woodsy too.

And male.

Very male.

"Liar," he said affectionately.

This was true. "You're in my space," Tara noted.

"That's not what you said when we—*Oomph*," he let out when she elbowed him in the gut. Unperturbed, he grinned. "Aw, don't be embarrassed that you attacked me in your kitchen."

"*What?* That night was all your fault," she told him. "You were standing there putting away spices and making me fried chicken, looking all—" Sexy. Sexy as hell. "I mean you practically force-fed me the cuteness."

"Cuteness," he repeated, testing the word out like it was a bad seed. "I'm not cute."

"Okay, true. You're far too potent for *cute*."

He cocked his head. "And you really think that us having sex was all on me?"

Her cheeks were getting hot, along with other parts of her. "I'm saying you seduced me with all the—"

"Say '*cuteness*' again," Ford warned, "and I'm going to strip you naked right here and show you exactly how *not* cute I can be. I'm going to show it to you until you scream my name."

"Okay, wait. Does anyone really scream during orgasm? I mean, you read about it all the time in books, but—"

He laughed. "Okay, so you don't scream." He leaned in close. "But your breath gets all uneven and catchy— which I love, by the way—and then you let out this sexy little purr, and—"

She elbowed him again.

"Told you I wasn't cute," he said, rubbing his ribs.

She squelched the urge to say "cute" one more time just to see if he'd follow through on his threat. She took a look around them to see if they were alone, just in case—

He laughed again, then put his lips next to her ear. "Sticking with your story, Tara?"

She shivered. "That you seduced me? Yes."

"We're even, you know." He nipped her earlobe with his teeth, making her shiver. "Since you've been seducing me since I first met you." He kissed her just below her jaw then, and along her temple, while she worked on not melting.

"W—what are you doing?"

"Seeing how far you're going to let me go."

Get a grip, she ordered herself as he got to the very corner of her mouth, and she took a big grip herself. A two-fisted one. Of *him*. She was holding him so tight that he couldn't have pulled away even if he wanted to, and given the rough sound that escaped him, he didn't want to. "We're not doing this again," she said. "You know we're not."

He sucked her bottom lip between his teeth and gave it a light tug. "I do know. I just can't remember why."

She sank her fingers into his hair. It was thick and silky and wavy, and she loved it. "Because—"

He kissed her long and hard, his hand sliding low onto her back, pulling her in closer to him.

"Ford. Ford, wait."

He smiled against her lips. "Let me guess." His mouth ghosted over hers with each word. "You have something else to say."

"Yes! You're…" She couldn't think. "Trouble. You know that? You're bad-for-me *trouble*."

"Maybe. But I'm only trouble some of the time," he said in that husky, coaxing voice that made her want to give him whatever he asked for.

"And what are you when you're not trouble?" she managed. "A Boy Scout?"

"'Fraid not. But sometimes my intentions are honorable."

"Like now?"

"No." His deep-green eyes met hers. "Right now, my intentions are definitely *not* honorable." And then he kissed her again. He kissed her until she was gripping him like she was drowning and he was her lifeline.

"Oh! Um, excuse me…"

They both turned to the young woman standing on the dock in a cute short skirt and cotton top, shielding her eyes from the glare of the sun with her hands, her long, sun-streaked, brown hair flowing out behind her. "Hi, sorry. I'm Mia Hutchinson."

One of the Seattle high school students that had called about the ad and had an interview with Tara this morning. "Mia, hi!" Knees still knocking, Tara stood up. It was too much to hope that her little make-out session with Ford hadn't been seen, but her plan was to ignore it. *Denial, meet your queen*. "You're right on time."

Ford was on his feet as well. "I thought we set that up for this afternoon," he said to the girl.

Tara looked at him. "No, she's interviewing with me for a position at the inn."

"Actually," Ford said. "She called to interview me for an article she's writing on sailing."

"Um, yeah," Mia said with a little wince. "Actually, I contacted *both* of you. I brought my résumé." She pulled an envelope from her purse. "I didn't really have any previous work experience that applied, so I just used the résumé I made up in economics class last semester. And before you ask, no, I didn't really work for Facebook or Bill Gates. And I wasn't a personal assistant to the Mariners' manager either." She hesitated, looking younger than seventeen. "The references are real, though." She turned to Ford, apology in her gaze. "I need a job, but I made up the article thing."

"Why?" Ford asked.

"Because I wanted to meet you both in a setting where you wouldn't get all weirded out. Finding you both here was just luck, I guess."

Tara was very still, in direct opposition to the way her heart was threatening to burst right out of her chest. "You know us?"

Again, Mia dragged her teeth over her bottom lip, looking at them from mossy green eyes that exactly matched...

Ford's.

"I kinda know you," Mia said. "It's sort of a long story."

"The CliffsNotes version, then," Ford suggested mildly.

Good. Good, Tara thought. He was calm, cool, and collected. Normally that was her role, but she'd left calm a few minutes back and was quickly heading straight past cool and collected, directly to *Freaking Out*. Because looking at Mia was reminding her of a very young Ford.

If he'd been female.

With Tara's willowy build.

"I was actually really surprised to find you two . . . kissing," Mia said carefully. "I don't know what I expected, but it wasn't that."

"Why don't you enlighten us on what you did expect?" Ford said. "Or should I help you out with that?"

Mia cocked her head, her gaze as sharp as his. "You figured it out," she said, sounding relieved.

"Yes," he said.

Tara couldn't speak. Hell, she could hardly breathe. She reached out blindly for purchase and found Ford's hand.

"You're ours," Ford said quietly to the girl. "You're our baby."

Chapter 11

♥

*"Always tell the truth. It eliminates the
need to remember anything."*
TARA DANIELS

Up until that moment, Ford's plans for the day had
included talking Tara into going out for a sail. And then
burning off some excess energy.

With their naked bodies.

Yeah, that would have been right at the very top of
the to-do list.

But that all changed with Mia looking at him through
his own green gaze, her expression slightly challenging
and yet braced for...hurt and rejection, he realized as
something twisted hard in his chest.

How many years had he wondered about the baby that
he and Tara had given up at birth?

Seventeen.

And how many years had he wondered if that baby
would grow up happy and whole and smart and sharp and
then...someday show up on his doorstep.

Christ, he couldn't remember ever feeling nerves like this before. Not while facing forty-foot waves threatening to tear his boat apart. Not while standing on an Olympic podium accepting a medal in the name of his country. Not ever.

Tara hadn't taken her eyes off Mia, and she was looking nervous too, her eyes misty. "You're so beautiful," she whispered.

Mia's eyes cut to her, quiet and assessing. "I look like you."

"Not as much as you look like..."

They both turned to Ford.

Having the woman he'd once loved with painful desperation, along with the daughter he'd dreamed about, both looking at him with varying degrees of emotion, was a punch in the solar plexus. Ford found he could scarcely breathe.

"Can I hug you?" Tara asked their daughter.

Mia gave a halting nod, but it was too late; they'd all seen the hesitation. Awkwardness settled over them all as Mia moved into Tara for a quick embrace. Ford was next, and he was surprised that with him Mia didn't seem awkward at all. Anxious, even eager, but not reluctant, and as he wrapped his arms around this thin, beautiful teenager that was his—Christ, *his*—he closed his eyes and breathed her in. "How did you find us?"

Mia pulled back and shifted her weight nervously, although her voice never wavered. "I thought I'd tell you *after* I got hired."

Bold. Ballsy. Probably she'd gotten a double whammy of both of those things from the gene pool, Ford thought.

"I only have seven weeks," Mia said, and Tara's hand went to her chest as if to keep her heart from leaping out.

Ford understood the panic. Hell, he felt it as his own. When Mia had been young, she'd had heart problems. A leaky valve that had required surgery. The only reason either Ford or Tara knew about it was because Tara's mother had donated a very large chunk of money to the medical bills, taking a second mortgage on the inn to get it—something that had only been discovered after Phoebe had died.

"What's the matter?" Tara asked Mia, voice thick with worry. "Your heart again?"

"No. I'm doing my senior year of high school in Spain as an exchange student, and I'll be gone for nine months."

"Oh." At this, Tara sagged in visible relief.

"So you're healthy then?" Ford asked Mia. "Everything's good?"

"Yep. I haven't had so much as a cold in years."

"That's wonderful," Tara said. "And your parents are okay with you doing this? Coming here to meet us?"

Another slight hesitation. "Well, they wanted to come with me," Mia admitted. "To be sure I'd be welcome, but I wanted to do this alone." Something came into her eyes at that. More nerves. And a dash of defensiveness.

And there was something else, too, Ford noticed. Whenever Mia spoke, she did so directly to him, not Tara. Almost as if Mia somehow resented the mother who'd given her up, but not her birth father.

Worse, given the look on Tara's face, she knew it too, and was miserable about it. Up until now Ford had caught only glimpses of the guilt that haunted Tara, but seeing it etched so deeply on her face squeezed his heart.

"My parents know I'm applying for work," Mia told them. "They've agreed that I can drive back and forth from Seattle to Lucky Harbor. If, you know, I get the job."

Smooth, Ford thought. Also from the gene pool.

"I'll hire you," Tara said softly. "If that's what you want, to work for me."

"Really?" For a beat, the cool, tough-girl expression fell away from Mia, revealing a heartbreaking vulnerability.

"Of course," Tara said.

"But... you don't even know my real skills. Or me."

"You came all this way," Ford said quietly. "Don't lose your nerve now."

Mia turned to him, studying his face like she'd been hungry for the sight of it as he'd been for hers.

"You're hired," Tara said. "I can teach you what you need to know. And then maybe by the end of the summer, you'll be able to write a real résumé, with real experience."

"Thanks," Mia said, looking slightly softer. Younger. "And don't worry. I'm real organized and a big planner. My parents tell everyone I'm anal, and it's sorta true."

"One guess as to where you got that," Ford said.

Tara slid him a long look, making him smile.

"I think I'm more like you," Mia said, looking at Ford.

Tara looked away at the quick hurt of that, and Ford felt unaccustomedly helpless, not sure how to breach the gap between mother and daughter.

"Excuse me, Ms. Daniels?" Carlos called from the

marina office door. He was in baggy homeboy jeans and a T-shirt that advertised some surf shop in Cabo. His dark hair was in spikes today, his earrings and eyebrow piercing all black to match his untied, high-top Nikes. He'd been cleaning windows in the morning sun, and his arms and face gleamed with sweat. "You have a phone call."

Mia looked at him, and then kept looking.

"Thanks, Carlos," Tara said. "Can you take a message?"

The teen nodded, his gaze falling to Mia, meeting her outwardly curious gaze.

"Mia, this is Carlos," Tara said, introducing them. "He works for the inn part time as well."

Carlos smiled, and to Ford, the expression had *horny teenager* written all over it. A very new and entirely surprising emotion hit Ford squarely between the eyes.

Paternal protectiveness.

Which was ridiculous. Hell, when he'd been Carlos's age, he'd looked at Tara just like that. He'd also done a hell of a lot more than just look.

"I'm going to start planting those seedlings," Carlos said to Tara. "You said it was a two-person job, but everyone's busy so..."

"I could help," Mia piped up.

"No!" Tara and Ford said at the same time. Ford let out a breath. That settled it. He was going to have to kill Carlos. He glanced over at Tara and found her wearing what he imagined was a matching scowl to his.

Luckily, before either of them could do or say anything stupid, Mia's stomach growled into the silence.

"Oh, Sugar," Tara exclaimed. "You're hungry! Come on, come up to the inn. I'll get you some breakfast."

"But the planting," Mia said, still looking at Carlos.

"Maybe later," Tara said.

Much later, Ford thought. Like never.

Tara hustled them all into the kitchen. Well, except Carlos. Carlos she sent on a run into town on an errand. When he was gone, Tara sat Mia at the table and pulled ingredients out of the fridge until she had a mountain of food on the island. "What would you like? Omelets? Crepes? Pancakes? French toast? I have—"

"It doesn't matter," Mia said. She and Ford watched as Tara went to work, her hands a blur. "Anything's fine. So about you two. Are you...a two?"

"Veggie and cheese omelets?" Tara asked, looking a little desperate for a subject change. "With turkey bacon and fresh fruit?"

"Okay." Mia hesitated and then glanced at Ford. "Is she always like this?" she whispered.

Crazy? Yes. Often. "She loves to cook."

Mia nodded, glancing at the newspaper that had been left on the table. "Is this for real?"

Ford looked over her shoulder. "What?"

Mia pointed to an article on the front page and read: "It's neck and neck between two fine stallions in the race for Lucky Harbor's Beach Resort owner Tara Daniels's heart. Which sexy hunk will make it to the finish line? The NASCAR cutie Logan Perrish or our own sailing hottie, Ford Walker? This just could be a photo finish, folks. Be sure to vote in our new poll, up on Facebook now. We're looking for donations of a buck a vote. The pot goes to the pediatric cancer research center at General, so don't be shy. We all have a buck to give, right? Vote now." Mia lifted her gaze and stared at Ford and Tara. "Is this about you guys?"

Ford looked for the byline. *Lucille Oldenburg*. Nosy old bat.

Behind the stovetop, Tara had gone utterly still, her eyes horrified. "Are you kidding me?"

"Nope," Mia said. "It's all right here in black and white. Who's Logan Perrish? Cuz it also says he spent two hours of his time graciously signing autographs— and bikinis—on the beach yesterday."

Tara closed her eyes. "He's my ex-husband."

Mia turned to Ford. "You're in competition with her ex-husband? For real?"

"It's a joke." He wondered if Jax would find him a good criminal defender after he killed Lucille.

Mia glanced at the paper thoughtfully. "Do you think you're winning?" she asked Ford. "In the poll?"

"Pay no attention to that," Tara said, pointing with her spatula. "I'm not seeing either of them."

Mia looked at Ford.

Tara looked at him, too, sending him a silent plea to back her up. He refused to, on the grounds that . . . hell. He had no idea. But when he remained silent, Tara let out a noise that managed to perfectly convey what she thought of him. He was pretty sure he knew what that might be.

"So you're *not* dating each other?" Mia asked Ford.

"No," Tara said, answering for him.

"But if you're not seeing each other, why were you kissing on the dock?"

"Do you prefer Swiss, mozzarella, or American cheese in your omelet?" Tara asked a bit desperately, turning to the refrigerator again.

"I don't care." Mia was still looking at Ford. "So have

you two been...*not* seeing each other all this time? The past seventeen years?"

"No," Tara said. "Yes. Wait a minute." She pressed her fingertips to her eyes. "Can you rephrase the question?"

"Until about six months ago, Tara lived in Texas," Ford told Mia. "And I lived here."

"So you two were never together?" Mia asked. "Not even when...you know. When I was conceived?"

Ford drew in a deep breath. This part was going to suck. "We were seventeen," he said.

Mia nodded. "Like me."

Yes, and he wasn't proud to say that he'd been far too experienced for his age. He'd lost his virginity two years prior, after being seduced by a sexy waitress who'd promised to rock his world. She had. For one entire glorious spring break, she'd rocked everything he had.

But Tara hadn't been experienced. At all. He had no idea how, but she'd seen something in him that had inspired her trust. "We were too young for the kind of relationship that we found ourselves in," he said carefully. *Please read between the lines and never have sex. Ever.*

"Yeah," Mia said quietly. "I figured I was an accident. A really big one."

"No," Tara said fiercely.

"It's okay," Mia said. "The whole giving-me-up thing was a dead giveaway." She shrugged as she looked at a stricken Tara. "You needed to fix a mistake quick, so you gave me up. Easy enough."

Christ, those eyes, Ford thought. The both of them were killing him. "It wasn't easy," he said, hoping to God that Mia believed him. "And it wasn't about us giving you up to make things better for us. It was about making things right for *you*."

Tara had turned to blindly face the window, completely ignoring what she was cooking.

Ford imagined she was feeling sick over the same thing. Heartbreaking to hear that the child they'd given up was thinking that it had been an easy fix. More heartbreak that she'd felt unwanted, even for a minute.

"I think I forgot to do the dishes this morning in the cottage," Tara whispered. "I should go check."

Ford would bet his last penny that she'd done every dish in the place and he stood to go to her, but, eyes glittering, mouth grim, she shook her head.

They'd been kids when she'd gotten pregnant. Stupid kids. That was no longer the case, and yet the situation was bringing back all the emotions from that time—the fear, the stress, the anxiety.

The utter helplessness.

And that overwhelming, ever-present, life-sucking guilt. Looking at Tara, Ford saw it all. He knew that she felt that they'd done the right thing. She'd always felt that way. But any woman would still feel the pang of giving up her own flesh and blood. She'd carried Mia, had been the one to feel her wriggle and kick, to feel her every hiccup.

And then had been left with little choice but to sign her away.

"I smell something burning," Mia said, and pointed to the stovetop, which was now smoking.

Yep, something was burning all right. Ford stepped behind Tara, took the spatula out of her hand, and turned off the burner. He carried the pan, and the blackened omelet in it, to the sink, where it hissed and smoked some more when he added cold water to the mix.

"I burnt it," Tara murmured.

"Yeah," Mia said, eyeing the pan. "You killed it dead."

"I never burn anything."

"No biggie," Mia said quietly. "I wasn't that hungry anyway. Should I go?"

"No." Tara straightened, seeming to come into herself again. "Mia, my burning breakfast was an accident. Like forgetting to go to the dentist. Like running out of gas on the highway..." She paused and swallowed hard. "But having a baby, that would *never* be classified as an accident. Not by me. I want you to know that. I'm not good at this. At revisiting the past, or talking about things that— I'm not good at emotions and feelings. But I want—I *need* you to know that I never thought of you as an accident. And I want you to stay."

Mia didn't look away as a myriad of emotions crossed her face. After a long beat, she swallowed hard. "Okay. Thanks."

In the heavily weighted silence, Ford went to the refrigerator. Time for improvisation, and his eyes locked on a big, juicy-looking strawberry pie. Worked for him. He grabbed it, carrying the tin heaped with brilliant red strawberries and dripping with glaze to the table.

"That's my Kick-Ass Strawberry Pie," Tara said, surprised.

"Yes, and now it's Kick-Ass Breakfast." Ford pointed to the chairs. "Sit."

Tara shocked him by actually following his direction. Mia followed suit, and he cut the pie into three huge thirds.

Tara choked. "I can't feed our daughter strawberry pie for breakfast."

"Why not?"

"Yeah," Mia asked. "Why not?"

"Because…" Tara appeared to search for a reason. "It's not healthy."

"It's got fruit," Mia said.

Tara looked at her. The awkwardness was still there. The air was filled with it, as well as unspoken questions and answers. But finally she nodded. Kick-Ass Breakfast it would be.

Mia gazed down at her third of the pie, her pretty hair sweeping into her eyes—which might be Ford's own green but they were guarded like Tara's.

His daughter, he repeated to himself. *God*. His daughter. She was careful. Controlled. Smart. And when she reached up and impatiently shoved her hair out of the way, he couldn't hold back the smile.

"What?" she wanted to know.

"You remind me of Tara at your age," he said. "Ready to tell us how you found us?"

"My dad helped me."

Ford couldn't help it: he flinched at the word *dad*, something he'd certainly never been to her. Tara met his gaze, and the understanding and compassion in her eyes were far too much for him to take. Getting up from the table, he poured three glasses of cold milk.

"I'd tried to find you before," Mia said, "but I couldn't. Then when Phoebe Traeger died, she left me some money." She looked at Tara. "I'm sorry about your mom."

"Thank you," Tara said quietly. "You got the money around Thanksgiving."

"Yes, and with it came a letter from her. She said she wasn't supposed to make herself known to me. That she was breaking rules and promises all over the place, but that she was dead and if people didn't like it, they could suck it. *Her* words," Mia added with a small smile. "She included your contact information in case I ever wanted it. For both of you." She paused. "I've always wanted it, but it took me a little while to find the nerve to do anything with it." She looked at Tara. "It said you lived in Texas, so I was surprised when I saw that ad to find out you were here." She paused. "I have a good life only half an hour from here. Two parents who love me very much. It should be enough." She paused. "I wanted it to be enough."

"It's natural to be curious," Tara said quietly. "It's okay to be curious."

"Yeah, well, at first I told myself I didn't care, about either of you." Mia pushed a strawberry around on the plate. "You gave me up, right? So I didn't care. I wasn't going to be curious. I refused to be, natural or not."

Tara looked devastated. Ford reached for her hand and gave it a squeeze. "I'm glad you changed your mind," he said.

"Who says I did?"

"You're here," he pointed out. "That indicates a certain level of caring. Of curiosity."

She sagged a little. "Yeah. I always was too curious for my own good."

"And now that you're here?" he asked. "What do you want to happen?"

Mia very carefully cut a large strawberry in half with her fork. "I realize I really should know, since I came to you, but I don't. At least not exactly." She looked at

Ford's hand. He was still holding Tara's fingers in his, and had been stroking his thumb across her skin, soothing her without even realizing it.

"I know I've asked this already," Mia said wryly. "But it really does seem like you two are together."

Ford understood why she thought it. But he'd told himself it was about sex. Hell, Tara had told him as well. And he'd been absolutely sure that's all there could be. It was a self-protection thing. But when he met Tara's gaze, that protection urge turned to her, as she was revealing a heartbreaking vulnerability. She'd gotten hurt the last time they'd been together, much more than he. It'd left her gun-shy, no doubt. He couldn't blame her for that. She'd been the one to face the consequences of their relationship.

"It's hard to explain," Tara said.

To say the least. Ford braced for Mia's reaction, but she was as resilient as she was smart. She merely nodded and stood up. "Can I borrow a computer?"

Tara looked confused. "Computer?"

"I want to go to Facebook and vote." Mia turned to Ford. "I'm going to vote for you. It'd be nice to have my parents together."

Tara turned to Ford. "She wants to vote for you," she said faintly.

"That's possible, right?" Mia asked. "You two getting together? You're not going to give me a line of crap about how you care about each other but it's not in the cards or something, are you?" She drew a breath. "Or how you each want to live your own lives, you have to be true to yourselves, you won't be held back anymore—" She broke off and winced. "Sorry. Wrong kitchen."

"Your parents are splitting," Ford said.

Mia nodded.

Shit. Ford found himself wanting to reach for her, but she was vibrating with a very clear don't-touch vibe, so in the end he refilled her milk. It was all he could think of, but she clutched her refilled glass and smiled at him.

"Mia," Tara breathed. "I'm so sorry."

"Yeah. Thanks." Mia got to her feet. "So...a computer?"

"Mine's in the small office behind the laundry," Tara said after a beat. "Second door to the right."

"Thanks."

When she was gone, Tara moved to the sink to stare down at the blackened mess of an omelet pan. "I burned breakfast," she murmured. "Burned it black."

Ford came up behind her. Like mother, like daughter, she was also sporting a don't-touch vibe, but he walked right through it and slid his hands to her hips. "You okay?"

Surprising him, she turned and faced him. "She's... ours."

"Yes."

"I mean, did you get a good look at her? We did that. We made her," she marveled.

"We did good." He pulled her in close.

She swallowed hard, clearly fighting tears. "We did *really* good. God, it brings me back, you know?" She dropped her forehead to his chest. "Back to that time when it was all so messed up."

"I know." He felt the same. Tara had spent the last five months of her pregnancy in Seattle. When she'd gone into labor, she hadn't wanted him there. He'd gone to the hospital anyway, though as far as he knew she'd never known he was there. He'd sat in the waiting room by himself staring at the walls, agonizing over the hell she was going through for all those hours, terrified for her.

Afterward, he'd spent more long hours just staring at their daughter through the nursery glass until they'd eventually carried her away to deliver her to her new parents.

To her new life.

"When I had her," Tara said, voice muffled against him, "it was so much harder than I thought it'd be. The pain. The worry. I kept telling myself that it would be over soon, and then when it finally was, they asked if I wanted to hold her for a minute. I had told myself no, no way could I do it and give her up, but I did. I took her." She paused, lost in the memory. "It was only for a second, but she was awake. She opened her eyes and looked right at me and I knew," she whispered. "I knew she was going to be beautiful." She pressed her lips together. "And for a minute, I didn't think I could give her up."

"Tara." Ford pressed his forehead to hers and fought with the what-ifs.

"I'd made my decision, and I was okay with it," she said, nodding as if to help convince herself. "It was just that when she looked at me...God, those eyes. She still has your eyes, Ford. And her eyes—your eyes—they've haunted me for seventeen years."

"You're shaking," he murmured.

"No, that's you."

Well, hell. It was.

"You were so good with her today," she said and sniffed. "You knew just what to say, and I...I froze."

"You did fine. It was a shock." Ford slid his fingers in her hair and tugged lightly until she lifted her face to his.

Her eyes shimmered, and she gave him a small smile that reached across the years and all the emotions, and grabbed him by the throat. As if it was the most natural thing in the world, he cupped her face and lowered his mouth to hers, just as Mia came back into the room.

After an interminable beat of silence, she said, "I don't know whether to cheer or be grossed out."

"Did you find the computer?" Tara asked, clearly trying to change the subject.

"Yes." Mia turned to Ford. "You're up in the voting so far, but not by much. Maybe you should help a few ladies across the street today if you get the chance." She grabbed her plate of pie and paused, head cocked as she studied the both of them. "Were you two really just about to kiss again?"

Tara winced. "Only a little bit."

"But you're *not* together," Mia clarified.

Tara winced again. "No."

Mia studied them both. "I don't have any siblings, do I?"

Chapter 12

♥

*"For some unknown reason, success usually
occurs in private, while failure
occurs in full view."*
TARA DANIELS

Tara introduced Mia to her aunts, and both Maddie and Chloe fawned all over her, loving her up. They'd all gone to dinner, but not before Tara had called and checked in with Mia's parents, giving Tara some peace of mind that they were really okay with this.

With sharing their daughter.

Her daughter.

Mia had warmed up to Maddie and Chloe easily, telling them all sorts of things about herself, like how she planned on being a lawyer because she had a talent for arguing.

"You come by that honestly, honey," had been Maddie's response as she'd patted Tara's hand. They'd all laughed except Mia, who hadn't looked as amused as everyone else to hear she took after Tara.

Later, after Mia had gone home and it was just Maddie, Chloe, and Tara sharing some wine on one of the marina docks, Tara admitted her fear—that she and Mia wouldn't connect. Maddie assured Tara that Mia had only connected with Chloe and herself so quickly because they were aunts and not a birth mother, and therefore had the benefit of not carrying any emotional baggage into the relationship.

Tara was well aware of the emotional baggage. It was currently weighing her down so that she could barely breathe. So was the bone-deep, heart-wrenching yearning for more with Mia, instead of the awkwardness, unspoken questions, and tension.

It'll happen, Maddie promised. Tara wanted that to be true more than she'd ever wanted anything.

The next day, she tried to lose herself in routine. She made a trip to the grocery store, something that usually, oddly, gave her peace, except not this time. This time she ran into Logan, and there in the ice cream aisle he introduced her to the circle of fans around him as his ex-*and* future wife. Annoyed, she corrected him and pushed her cart onward, running into several acquaintances who couldn't wait to tell her which way they'd voted on Facebook. The poll seemed to be running about 60 percent in Ford's favor, but Logan was charming the pants off Lucky Harbor and steadily gaining ground.

It was official. Her life was out of control. She had a daughter looking for a first chance, an ex-husband looking for a second chance, and Ford looking for . . .

She had no idea.

Shaking her head, Tara made her way back to the inn. When she got out of the car to unload, she was surprised when Mia came out to help. "Thanks," Tara said with a heartfelt smile.

Mia returned it, though it didn't quite meet her eyes. It never seemed to when it came to Tara.

Something else to work on, Tara thought: getting her daughter to let go of seventeen years of resentment and trust her. "Mia," she said softly as they came face to face at the trunk of the car. "What can I do?"

Mia didn't pretend to misunderstand as she reached to grab bags of food. "I don't know. I just..." She shrugged. "I thought that this would be easier, that's all. That I'd instantly feel this bonded connection with you, that..." The girl sighed and shook her head. "I don't know."

"Tell me how to help," Tara said. "I *want* to help. I want the same thing you do."

Mia nodded. "I guess maybe I still have questions."

"Then ask. Anything," Tara said, and hoped that was true.

Mia hefted six bags in her thin arms. She was stronger than she looked. "Anything?"

"Yes." But Tara braced herself, hoping against hope that she'd start off light. Like maybe what was Tara's favorite color and astrological sign? They could work their way up from there.

"Was getting rid of me easy?" Mia asked.

Tara gulped. "Uh—"

"Did you think about me? Do you," Mia paused, "regret giving me up?"

So much for the light stuff first, Tara thought as her chest tightened. It hadn't been easy to give Mia up, and Tara had thought of her baby often. But as for regret... no. She hadn't regretted it, not at first.

That had come later.

But before she could find a way to articulate all this without hurting her daughter, Mia's face closed, and she took another step back. "You know what? Never mind." Turning away, she carried the grocery bags toward the inn's back door.

"Mia. Mia, wait."

Mia looked back, her face pinched. "My mom warned me this might happen."

Her other mom. Her *real* mom. "Warned you what might happen?"

"That you might not be thrilled to find your biggest mistake on your doorstep. That you might be upset because my adoption was supposed to be a closed, confidential case."

Tara stared at her, stunned. "Your mom said that? That you were my *mistake*?"

"She didn't have to."

"Mia, that's not how I feel at all. And I'm not upset. I—" Tara broke off, at a complete loss. She was just coming to terms with this all herself, and she didn't have a game plan to make Mia understand. This was so important, so very important, and Tara needed time and careful planning to make it all come out okay—

"I changed my mind, I don't want to know." Mia took a step toward the inn. "These bags are really heavy. I have to go in."

"*Mia*."

But she was gone.

Weeks ago, Maddie had arranged for a "trial run" for the inn. She'd set up a raffle at the last music fest and had drawn a winner. The lucky couple's prize—one free night at the inn.

They were due to arrive in the morning.

This left Maddie running through the place like a madwoman, checking on last-minute details and barking orders at Tara. In turn, Tara was going Post-it note crazy, leaving everyone little yellow stickies everywhere and on everything, outlining what Maddie needed done. Everyone was on hand, doing their bidding without complaint.

Okay, there was complaining, but Tara ignored it and continued writing notes. Eventually she realized that Maddie was no longer barking orders, that in fact she and Jax kept vanishing for long periods of time. "Where the hell do they keep going?" she asked Chloe, exasperated.

"The attic." Chloe snatched the yellow Post-it pad from Tara's fingers. "Give me those. You're grounded." Chloe was wearing low-riding, skinny-legged Army cargos with a red tank top and her bright red Nike trainers. She'd been a surprising help and had created a large gift basket filled with her spa treatments. But she'd clearly had enough of the bossing around because she snatched the sticky note pad.

"Why the attic?" Tara asked, fingers itching to grab the pad back.

Chloe wrote something on a Post-it and slapped it to Tara's chest. Tara pulled it off and read it out loud. "They like to do it up there." She stared at Chloe. "Are you shittin' me?"

"There you go losing your *g*'s again, Miss Daisy. But no, I'm not 'shitting' you. Remember back a few months ago when you sent them to the attic to get that antique end table? They took over an hour and told you they'd taken the time to polish it?"

Tara closed her eyes. "They weren't—"

"Yep. Totally doing it."

Lord. Maddie and Jax were like a couple of freaking newlyweds with a case of nearly expired condoms. "I'm surrounded by children."

"Not exactly children," Chloe said. "More like horn-dog teenagers. Come on, admit it. You'd totally do it up there if you could."

"No, I wouldn't."

"Oh, right. That's me. *I'd* do it up there if I could. Should I pull out my phone and ask Mr. Magic Eight app if that's anywhere in your near future?" Without waiting for an answer, she did just that, then smiled at the answer.

NOT LIKELY.

Chloe slid her phone away. She'd changed her hair streaks to midnight blue. They were twisted and pulled up, holding her hair in place like a headband. "So since Maddie and Jax are taking a break—and each other—and since you don't seem to have that kind of a break in your future, I think we deserve a break of a different kind."

"Can't." Tara handed over a bucket of bathroom cleaning supplies.

Chloe frowned down at them. "Cleaning is *your* thing."

"Not today it's not."

"What's wrong with our teenage slaves?"

"Carlos is cleaning the front yard, and I'm acclimating Mia to my kitchen."

Chloe blinked. "Huh?"

"Yeah," Tara said. "In a blatant attempt to bribe her

into liking me, I'm letting her bake the meet-and-greet cookies."

"Wait a minute." Chloe narrowed her eyes. "She gets to bake cookies, and I have to do toilets? I have seniority! Where's the justice in that?"

"You're completely missing the significance of my gesture. You know how important the meet-and-greet cookies are."

"How could I have forgotten?" Chloe said dryly. "What an honor you've bestowed upon her."

"Hey, she's my daughter." As the word left her mouth, Tara smiled. She couldn't help it, she liked the way it felt rolling off her tongue.

Chloe grinned unexpectedly. "You got a kick out of saying that."

"I'm just stating a fact."

"Admit it, Tara."

Tara nodded and let a small smile escape. "I like saying it." So very much.

"So she's baking cookies, huh?"

"Yes." Tara took in Chloe's smug smile. "What? What don't I know?"

"Nothing. Except that she's not baking. She's nose up against the living room window watching Carlos hose down the yard." Chloe smiled. "*Acclimating*."

Tara sighed.

"I saw her at the diner this morning with Ford," Chloe said. "They seemed to be having a good time."

Something inside Tara warmed a little at that. For a guy who'd grown up without much direction or authority, Ford had some amazing people skills. Caring for and about others came naturally to him. Mia *would* love him instantly. But along with the warm fuzzies the image of them together gave her, she also felt a twinge of regret that she hadn't yet gotten there with Mia.

"She has his smile," Chloe said. "And his laugh."

So Mia was laughing for him. Of course she was. Ford did things like take her out to breakfast, employing his effortless charm and likability, while Tara burned breakfast and froze up when answering the simplest of questions.

And now she was jealous. Perfect. Jealous, because Ford made it easy to love him, and Tara... well, she didn't make it easy for anyone to care about her; she knew that. "Get cranking on that bathroom. I'll be making beds."

"One," Chloe said. "You have to make *one* bed. For our two guests, who are married. Plus they're newlyweds. They probably wouldn't notice if you gave them no sheets at all. Now back to me for a minute—asthma makes me exempt from cleaning."

"I realize that your asthma is a free get-out-of-jail card for just about everything you don't want to do," Tara said. "But I bought chemical-free cleaning agents. Nothing in any of them should bother you."

"Fine. Just fine then. Call me Cinderella." Chloe blew out a breath and looked out the window, then let out a soft laugh.

"What?"

"Nothing."

Oh, it was something. Tara moved to the window. Indeed, Carlos was out there hosing down the yard.

With Mia now at his side.

Carlos was both tough and quiet, and for the most part, utterly unreadable. His clothes added to his bad-boy persona, but he showed up on time, and until today, had always worked his ass off.

At the moment, he wasn't so much working as . . . posturing. And although Tara had heard him utter maybe ten sentences total in the past three months, the two of them were talking nonstop.

Carlos smiled down at Mia and entirely missed the flower bed that he was supposedly watering.

Mia was standing as close to him as she could get without sharing his too big, unlaced Nikes. She was also doing something Tara had heard about but had not yet seen firsthand.

She was laughing, a warm, genuine laugh that transformed her face.

"It's sweet," Chloe said.

"No. Not sweet." Tara shook her head. "He's a seventeen-year-old boy, and there's only one thing seventeen-year-old boys want."

Chloe laughed. "Wow, you're *such* a hypocrite."

Tara sighed and rested her forehead on the glass. "She doesn't smile like that for me."

"Of course not. She's not hoping that you're going to kiss her later, either."

Tara sighed again, and Chloe slid an arm around her. Shocked, Tara turned her head and met her younger sister's gaze. They'd spent summers together as kids, and the past six months in each other's pockets, and yet Tara could count on one hand the number of times they'd touched each other in affection.

"It's going to be okay," Chloe assured her with a surprisingly gentle squeeze. "She's going to be okay. She's happy here."

At the unexpected comfort from the most unexpected source, Tara felt her breath leave her in a whoosh. "You sure?"

"Yes. And I get the feeling she hasn't been happy in a while. Breathe, Tara."

"I really hate it when people tell me to breathe."

"Then you should do more of it on your own."

Tara inhaled deeply, held it, then let it out. "I just wish she'd warm up to me."

"Hey, she's here, isn't she? It'll come." Chloe squeezed her again. "Let her be. For once in your life, don't direct. Just let it happen and enjoy the ride."

Tara paused and gave her the once-over. "Look at you, being all sweet."

"I know, right?" Chloe flashed a grin. "I think I'd be great at sweet, but the truth is, that's not what I'm doing."

Tara sighed. She knew that was too good to last. "Okay. What do you want?"

"To take off next week without you bitching about me leaving right before we open."

"Where're you going this time?"

"Cabo. Got a friend who works in a five-star hotel there, and they're interested in my skincare line."

"The last time you went to Cabo, you were gone for four days, dyed your hair platinum blond, and got a nipple pierced."

Chloe winced in recollected pain. "Yeah. I'll be working, so there'll be no alcohol involved this time."

"Good to know," Tara said. "You've got to be running out of parts to get pierced by now."

"Actually—"

"Don't." Tara held up a hand and grimaced. "I don't want to know." Oddly unwilling to break the rare sweet moment, she pressed her cheek to Chloe's. "Love you, you know."

Chloe hesitated a moment, then hugged her back, hard. She didn't repeat the vow of love, but then again, she never did. But perhaps in a gesture that meant even more than the words would have, Chloe took a long time to let go. Then she nodded and carefully steered Tara away from the window and the view of the teenagers. "Did you see the paper this morning? Logan and Ford are neck and neck in the townwide vote. Probably because of last night."

Tara went still. "Oh, God. What happened last night?"

"Logan was at The Love Shack again." Chloe smiled. "You had your current lover serving your ex-lover. Never thought you had it in you to catch two alpha men like that." She eyed Tara speculatively. "You must have some moves once you lose all the control issues you have going on. Or hell, maybe guys like that, I don't know. Do you boss them around in bed?"

Tara ignored that. "Logan was at the bar again?"

"Well, mostly it was Ford at the bar being accosted by Lucille and her friends. They're on a mission to see you settled with Ford. Not that they don't think Logan is hot, but you know how they all love and adore Ford."

This was true. The whole town loved and adored Ford. Everyone did. He had effortless charm and ease, no matter what he was doing.

Or who.

"They've decided to try to sway the vote in his favor," Chloe said. "There are signs up in town and everything.

The one outside the post office has Ford's high school yearbook picture. He was Class Flirt, did you know that?"

Tara stared at her. "There are *not* signs in town."

"Okay," Chloe said agreeably. "But there are."

Tara moaned. "Okay, new plan." She shoved the sheets at Chloe. "You're doing the bathrooms *and* the beds. I'm going to town to pull down the signs."

"How did your problems become my problems? And if you'd just pick one of the Hot Guys, the voting would be a moot point."

"It's not about picking one," Tara said. "Logan wants a woman who no longer exists, and Ford wants..."

But Chloe was gone. And Tara was talking to herself. Perfect. Turning, she walked directly into a brick wall that happened to be Ford's chest.

Chapter 13

♥

"It's impossible to be both smart and in love."
TARA DANIELS

Ford's hands went to Tara's hips to steady her. Dipping down a little, he met her eyes with his. "I want…what?" he asked.

Tara pushed past him and headed for the kitchen.

He followed her. Of course he followed. She was annoyed with herself for allowing it, but also a little discombobulated. Her usual state around him.

"Talk to me," he said. "I want what?"

"You tell me," she said, going for flirty because she wasn't at all sure whether or not she wanted to hear his real answer.

His eyes dilated. "I'd rather show you." He reached for her but she backed up, directly into the pantry.

He simply stepped in as well and shut the door behind them. His expression resembled that of a lion stalking its prey.

"Okay, here's the thing," Tara said, hand on his chest to hold him off. "I meant what I told you that night after we..."

He cocked a brow.

"Were together." She backed up a step and came up against the pantry door. "I told you I'm working on things. Things inside of me. And you—you distract me from those things." She poked him in the chest. "So I'm asking you to stop doing that. Stop distracting me. Yes, we slept together. Hell, we have *a lot* of chemistry, and I was out of control that night. But I have a lot going on, Ford. *We* have a lot going on, so we really need to try to ignore us. Okay? No more of this dance we have going on. We have to control ourselves."

His silence was deafening.

"Well," he finally said. "That's all *fascinating*, and informative as well. And we're going to circle back to parts of it, especially the part where you can't control yourself around me, but I was only trying to..." Slowly he reached out for her again and pulled a Post-it note from her back.

There were two words on it: Bite Me.

Tara groaned. "Chloe's idea of a joke. Can we focus here?"

"I'd rather bite you."

"Very funny. Look, I get how you might think that the natural progression would be for us to have sex again, but we can't. I can't."

"Because you're working on yourself."

So he *was* listening. "Yes. And because when I'm with you like that, I'm..." She searched for the right word.

"Multi-orgasmic?"

She closed her eyes. "You're not taking me seriously."

"On the contrary, I'm taking you very seriously."

Their gazes collided. Held. And something jumped in her stomach. His eyes were dark and solemn, belying his easy tone. He'd heard everything she'd said. He'd also heard everything she *hadn't* said. What she didn't know was if he agreed with her. "Someone's going to get their emotions in the wrong place, Ford." And by someone, she meant *her*. They had a track record. The last time she let her emotions get tangled up with his, it had been the most painful time of her life. People didn't recover from that kind of screw-up; they didn't get second chances.

"Ah," he said quietly. "*Now* we're getting somewhere." He ran a finger over her jaw. "You're afraid."

"Yes. Join me, won't you?" She gripped his shirt. "Mia—"

"Is amazing."

"Yes." Tara let out a breath. "She is. But that's what I mean. We're in danger of misplacing emotions—"

"I'm misplacing nothing." His eyes softened, and he touched her face. "Tara. It's not the same now."

Because it was just sex. She swallowed the hurt. "Look, all I need is for you to agree that we should just go back to how we were before."

"Before what?"

He knew before what. "Before we made love," she said uncomfortably, hating him for making her say it out loud.

"At least you know that that's what we did." He paused. "How much of this has to do with Logan?"

"None." She met his gaze head-on. "Okay, maybe a little, but not how you think."

"Well, that makes me feel all better."

"I tried to explain this to you before," Tara said with a sigh. "I've got some issues. And so do you."

"I thought this wasn't about me."

"It's a roundabout thing," she said.

Ford paused. "Okay, help me out here. Who exactly is working on whose issues?"

"I'm working on mine." She lifted her chin. "And you should be working on yours."

"And mine are?" he asked mildly.

"Well, for one, you don't stick."

"What does that mean?"

"It means that you're laid-back, easygoing, and you like your life the same way," Tara told him. "And let's face it, you're good at just about everything. So when something's hard, or difficult, or doesn't drop into your lap, you don't tend to work at it."

Only his eyes reflected his tension. "You think things drop in my lap? That I haven't had to work hard at life?"

"No," she said, shaking her head. "I know where you came from. I know how you busted your butt to get to where you are, but sailing...face it, Ford. Sailing came easy. And Logan hasn't been the only man in my life to find his face in the papers. You've been there, too. *Cosmo* had some really interesting things to say about your bachelor life and how you live it."

"So I haven't been a monk. Jesus, Tara, I was in my twenties with too much money and women throwing themselves at me. Yeah, I enjoyed it all *way* too much, but I also eventually grew up."

"Yes, you got engaged after your gold medal to

someone you met while training. You broke it off at the last minute."

Something flickered in his eyes at that. Annoyance at having to explain himself, probably. Typical male. "Because," he said, "she'd gotten caught up in the fame and fortune of the sponsorships and wanted to live in the public eye. She went nuts for the attention, and I—" He broke off and frowned. "I wanted my same old, simple life. The life I'd worked hard for."

"You took a huge contract for sponsorship and then dropped it."

He stared at her. "You *have* been reading the papers."

Truthfully, Tara had devoured every little scrap on him over the years. "Yes."

He was quiet a moment. "I wasn't feeling as competitive as I'd been, and I wanted to slow down. It didn't seem right to stick with that contract when I wasn't going to be giving them their money's worth. So yeah, maybe I haven't exactly done what was expected, but I've always done what I felt was right."

"And us?" Tara asked. "Seventeen years ago?"

His eyes hardened. "You're the one who walked away."

"Yes, but you let me."

"What? Are you kidding me?" He shoved his hands into his hair, and arms up, muscles taut, he turned in a full circle. When he faced her again, a very rare display of temper and frustration was showing on his face. "No one has ever had any luck stopping you when you have your mind set on something, Tara, and you damn well know it."

"But you never even tried." Her throat was tight with remembered pain. God, the pain. She didn't want to ever feel that scared and alone and anxious again. Yes, *she'd* been the one to walk, but she'd been so young and stupid. "You never even attempted to contact me."

She'd been okay with that in the end. Because the clean break had given her the time to get over the heartbreak without having to constantly relive it. But it was bothering her now, she realized. Deeply. She knew Ford felt very strongly about her, but she wasn't sure he felt strongly enough. Certainly not enough to want to stick for real, for the long haul. And with him, she was beginning to realize she could handle no less.

Sure, back then he'd been willing to make things work, but the promise and drive of a teenager didn't mean that it would have. And what did teenagers know about love anyway? If he'd really been right for her, wouldn't he have followed after her, or at least tried?

She knew he'd wanted to do the right thing by her, she believed that. And he was a good guy: reliable, warm, caring…but she could only go on what she knew. And she knew she hadn't been important enough to him.

She had no reason to think now would be any different.

"I remember things differently," he said quietly. "I remember that you gave up. *You* ran. I'd have gladly taken it to that happy-ever-after you were too guilt-ridden to allow yourself."

She swallowed hard against both the recrimination in his voice and the truth of that statement. "What's done is done," she said. "And it's not just us now. There's Mia. We can't play at this anymore, Ford, not when so much is at stake. She's fragile and working through her adopted parents' split. We can't mess her up. We can't."

She turned away, then changed her mind. He deserved the truth. "It's just that if by some miracle we made this work now, then..." She swallowed hard and whispered, "Then maybe we really might have been able to work it out back then, too. And that *kills* me, Ford. All that pain I caused...for nothing."

Looking stunned, he stared down at her. "Tara," he said softly, regret heavy in his voice. "You can't keep punishing yourself, sabotaging your life, your own happiness for your past."

She'd never really realized it but he was right. Deep down she felt she needed to be punished for giving up Mia.

Ford was watching her, eyes solemn. "I have all those thoughts too, you know," he said. "The guilt. You're not alone in this."

She let out a breath. "How do you always know what I'm thinking?"

Running his thumb along her jaw, he let out a small smile. "It's all over your face. You made a decision back then. It was the right decision for you. Don't let it eat away at you now. It's a new chapter. Turn the page."

He was still touching her face, his other hand low on her back, holding her against him, and she fought the urge to turn her face into his palm. "So if I turn the page, then what?"

"Your choice," he said. "It always was. But know this. You're not alone. There are two of us now. Actually, there are three."

She dropped her forehead to his chest. He was big and warm and strong. Strong enough to share her burdens, at least for this moment. She shifted closer without even realizing it, then closer still. His heart was beating calm and even. His eyes were warm as he looked at her.

Into her.

She thought about how he'd said that he felt all the same things that she did, and an old, familiar closeness and tenderness welled up within her. She lifted her head and leaned back against the closed pantry door. "Ford?"

"Yeah?" He was steady and even. A rock.

Her rock.

Tired of thinking, tired of trying to keep in mind a viable reason why they needed to steer clear of each other, she followed her gut and put her lips on his. Which was when the door of the pantry suddenly opened behind her, and she spilled out, right into Logan's waiting arms.

Chapter 14

♥

*"Generally speaking, if your mouth is moving,
you aren't learning much."*
TARA DANIELS

"What the hell?" Logan stared down at Tara in surprise,
then lifted his head and eyed Ford.

Before Tara could budge, Chloe came into the
kitchen. She took one look at Tara—in a Logan-and-Ford
sandwich—and tossed up her hands. "I swear to God, I
don't get it." With a shake of her head, she pivoted and
walked out.

Logan was still sizing up Ford.

Who was sizing up Logan right back.

Tara pushed free of both men. "This is awkward. I'm
going to go finish my work." She'd planned on going into
town, but she didn't want to go too far away. She grabbed
the vacuum cleaner and headed up the stairs. When in
doubt, vacuum. In fact, she was a vacuuming demon, well
into the second bedroom, when two arms reached around
her and turned the machine off.

Logan pulled her around to face him, a small smile on his face, his eyes serious. "Avoiding me?"

"Little bit." She blew out a breath. "Logan, why are you really here?"

"I already told you."

"You think you miss me."

"I *do* miss you," he said. "I miss you traveling with me, I miss the way you always made coffee in the mornings, and how you packed for me. I miss you taking care of me."

"Oh, Logan." She heaved out a sigh. "I'm not that woman anymore." Not even close. "And your world... it's big and shiny and exciting, and I'm...not. Lucky Harbor is not. So I don't understand."

"Don't you?" His eyes were soft as they skimmed over her features. "You're smart and funny, and you wanted to be with me for me, not for my stats or bank account. Everyone else yesses me."

"Is that what this is? You want someone who doesn't yes you?"

"See that?" he said, smiling at her raised voice. "No one ever gets mad at me. No one but you." He gave her the eyes—the Logan bedroom eyes—and in spite of herself, she sighed again.

"I really did miss you, Tara." He put his hands on her waist and his mouth to her ear. "Tell me you missed me, too."

He was familiar and comfortable, and a part of her wanted to sink into that.

Luckily, a bigger part of her wanted to smack him. "Logan, these past few years..." She'd ached for him. She'd *wanted* him to come after her. She'd dreamed about it, much the way she once upon a time had dreamed about Ford doing the same.

But he hadn't. No one ever had.

"I'm too busy to miss you," she finally said, unwilling to reveal something so pathetic. "I'm sorry."

Logan searched her gaze, his smile fading some. "No, I deserved that. I spent way too much time being too busy for you, didn't I?" Moving farther into her personal space, he gently tugged at a loose strand of her hair. His eyes were warm in that just-for-her way, the look that used to melt all her clothes off in a blink.

But that had been when she'd been Mrs. Logan Perrish, back when Tara Daniels had barely existed. She didn't want to go back to that.

"You're tired. You're overworked," he chided gently. "I called you yesterday, wanting to come help. And don't think the irony got by me. I realize it used to be *you* helping *me*. So really, it's *me* who's sorry, Tara. So damned sorry."

She pressed her fingers to her eye sockets. "I don't want you to be sorry. I got over it."

"And over me," Logan mused quietly. "I won the Sprint Cup last year."

"I know." She smiled at him. "One of your biggest dreams."

"My life's goal," he agreed. "Met by age of thirty-two. And then, when it was over, I looked around for someone to share it with, but you were gone. The best thing that had ever happened to me—gone." He cupped her face. "I want a family, Tara. With you. Maybe even a few kids—"

She choked. She hadn't yet told him about Mia showing up in Lucky Harbor. She hadn't told anyone but her sisters. She knew it would come out eventually, but she'd hoped to be in a better, stronger place with Mia first. "Logan—"

"I know. We never really talked about kids, but it's time, don't you think?"

Jesus. "No, you don't understand, I—"

"I'm going to win you back," he said softly but with steel laced beneath.

Tara sucked in a breath and tried to figure out how she felt. Flattered? Maybe. Vindicated? Definitely. A little bit heated? Well, yes, but hell, the man was gorgeous, and she wasn't dead.

But mostly she felt unease. "I'm not an upcoming race," she said. "I'm not available to be won."

"I don't see a ring on your finger."

"That's not what I meant."

"I'm not leaving town without you, Tara."

"Logan—"

He kissed her, then pressed up against her to deepen the connection, but she stepped back and put up her hand.

Eyes dark, breathing unsteadily, he let out a breath. "That got to you, right?"

It used to be he could rock her world, but she wasn't feeling rocked. Okay, maybe there'd been a mild tremor, but she hadn't been rocked. Her good parts weren't tingling. Not like when Ford kissed her. "Logan—"

"We have the entire summer," he said.

She knew exactly how big a gesture that was for him careerwise—had it not been a forced break due to his injury. "Because you're hurt," she reminded him.

"Yes, okay, so it was good timing," he said with a wry smile. "As far as these things go."

"Logan." She shook her head. "Please. I need you to be honest."

"Fine. I was forced to take the time off to heal. Even more honestly, I needed a break." He paused. "But mostly, Tara, I need us."

If that was true, it was only because he didn't have racing at the moment. That was all. Or maybe he was bored. "There's no *us*."

Logan shot her a smile that said he disagreed and was confident that he could prove her wrong. "I have to go," he said. "I promised Chloe that if she told me where you were, I'd clean a bathroom."

While Tara sputtered, trying to picture NASCAR star Logan Perrish wielding a toilet brush, he kissed her and was gone.

Tara stared down at the vacuum. Wasn't life supposed to get simpler the older you got? She'd been really looking forward to "simple." She turned on the vacuum, then squealed for a second time when two warm arms came around her a few minutes later. "Logan, dammit, I told you *no us*!"

But she instantly realized her mistake when the arms tightened and the scent of the man came to her.

"Just me," Ford said easily, turning her to face him. "Though I do like the 'no us' thing with Logan. Stick with that." He looked her over, and some of his amusement slipped. "You okay?"

"Me? Oh sure. I mean, sure, I'm back in a town I promised to never step in again, I'm having trouble connecting with my daughter—my fault—and my ex has shown up. And you..." She closed her mouth and shook her head. Not going there. "I'm great."

"You'll connect with Mia," he said. "Just give it some time. What did Logan want?"

"To know if his kiss got to me."

Ford tensed a little. "He kissed you?"

Well, look at that. The vacuum needed to be emptied. She bent, but Ford hauled her upright again. She tilted her head up to look at him. He certainly wasn't offering the comfort that Logan had, but there was something else. Something new, something edgy and dangerous.

To her heart, anyway.

And so damn tempting. She could admit that much to herself, but not to him. She moved to go around him, but Ford backed her to the wall and held her there with his big, warm body.

"What is it with you and the caveman thing?" she asked. *And why, oh why, do I like it so much?*

"So did Logan's kiss get to you, Tara?" He took her bottom lip between his teeth and tugged before freeing her. "Did it make your knees weak?"

No, but they were weak now.

Ford turned his attention to her upper lip, nipping that too. "Did his kiss make you tremble?" He kissed her full on then, a slow, hot kiss that branded her as his before finally pulling back only enough to let her breathe. "Did it, Tara? Did he get to you?"

By this time, she was so hot that she figured she was lucky she hadn't spontaneously combusted. Against her, Ford was humming with the same tension as she. His eyes raked down her body, sending sparks racing along every nerve ending she possessed. Then he leaned in, his mouth once again hovering over hers.

Her lips fell open as she waited breathlessly for the kiss, but instead he stepped back, and she nearly slid to the floor.

With a knowing look, he lifted her up and supported her weight with no effort at all. "Tara."

She closed her eyes, then opened them again. "No. Logan didn't get to me. You do. You always did."

His smile came slow and sinfully lethal, and she pushed at him, thinking it should be illegal to have a smile like that. "Which you already knew, damn you. It doesn't mean anything, Ford. Not without intent."

"I have plenty of intent."

No kidding. "Intent from *me*," she said. "And the only intent I have is to get to know Mia and make a wild success out of the inn this weekend. And then the next and so on, until we're making enough money that Maddie is stable here on her own."

Something came into his eyes at that. She wasn't sure what. "And then?" he said.

"And then I'll go."

Temper, she decided. *That's* what was in his eyes. A good amount of it, and frustration, too.

"You'll go where, back to Texas?" he asked. "Far away from all the strings on your heart because that's the easiest way?"

Ouch.

And true.

"Maybe," she admitted, and damn him for putting it so succinctly into words. "Which makes us one hell of a pair, doesn't it? The runner—that would be me—and the guy who..."

"Who what?" he asked, eyes narrowed.

"It's easy come, easy go for you, isn't it? Things either fall into your lap and work out, or they don't. And if they don't, you're never overly bothered much." Again she shoved clear of him.

And this time he let her go.

The next morning, Ford woke up in a rare, foul mood. Tara was right about him. He was easy come, easy go, and he didn't like what that said about him.

And then there was Tara. She was difficult and a pain in his ass, and he had no idea why he wanted her.

Except he did.

He wanted her because she saw the real him. She didn't take his shit. And she made him feel. Christ, did she make him feel. And what he felt at the moment was impatient and frustrated as hell.

Usually a sign for him to move on.

Hell if that urge didn't piss him off too, because it proved her point. Christ, he really hated that.

He didn't want to move on.

Another shock. He thought maybe he was falling for her all over again, maybe even harder than the first time. As for her, he had no idea what she was feeling. For all he knew, she was feeling everything he was—but for Logan. He hated that, too. Frustrated with her, with himself, with every fucking thing, he did his usual morning run and then walked to the post office to collect his mail. Logan happened to be at the counter and Ford shook his head. Fan-fucking-tastic, because they hadn't seen nearly enough of each other lately.

By the looks of things, the race car driver was attempting to reserve a mailbox for the summer and getting nowhere. "I was told it would be no problem," Logan was saying.

This was no mystery once Ford caught sight of the clerk. Paige Robinson had crushed on Ford all through middle school. And again in tenth grade. They'd gone to Homecoming together, after which Paige had pulled her father's pilfered vodka from her purse to share. Ford had hoped to get lucky that night, but unfortunately, Paige had tossed back too much and thrown up on his shoes instead.

Maybe she felt she owed him now, or maybe she was still harboring a secret crush, Ford didn't know; but for whatever reason, she was shaking her head at Logan, saying she was very sorry but there simply wasn't an empty post office box to be rented in Lucky Harbor.

Logan walked out of the post office looking annoyed but resigned, and Ford watched him go, torn. *Don't do it, man.*

Don't. Fuck. He gathered his mail and followed Logan outside. "There's a Mailboxes-R-Us on Fourth Street," Ford said. "You can probably get a box there."

Instead of thanking him, Logan gave him a suspicious look. "I don't suppose you know anything about why Jan at the diner told me they'd run out of coffee when I tried to get caffeine this morning. Or how it is that I was woken up at five, six, seven, *and* eight o'clock by someone playing doorbell ditch at the cottage? Or better yet, where my rental car went?"

"Why would I know anything about any of that?"

Logan laughed low in his throat. "Maybe because while the locals are impressed with my NASCAR status, they'd do just about anything for you. Hell, Facebook is proving that."

"Facebook? Is the poll still up then?"

Logan pulled out his BlackBerry and brought up the page. People's tweets were posted, and on top of that was the latest blog entry:

There's romance in the wind! Or at least on the docks, where Tara Daniels was seen kissing a certain sexy hometown sailor. Voting is still open but it appears Tara's running a poll of her own. And don't forget to weigh in on a side poll—should Ford ask Tara to marry him? Also, see tweets on how he should pop the question...

Ford stared at the screen. "What the fuck?"

Logan blew out a breath. "All I know is that she's not kissing *me* on the docks." He punched 9-1-1 on his cell. "Yes, dispatch? I need to report my rental car as stolen."

Ford waited with him, somehow feeling responsible. Plus, he had a feeling Sawyer would show up.

And sure enough, his best friend arrived in less than five minutes.

Sawyer got out of his squad car in his uniform and dark mirrored sunglasses, looking his usual badass self. At the sight of Logan and Ford standing together, he arched a brow. He was far too good to show much, but a slow smile crossed his face. "Either of you see Facebook today?"

"Yeah, yeah," Ford muttered. "Have a good laugh."

"Already did. I haven't voted on the new poll yet. I'm weighing some heavy questions. Like do guys still get down on one knee? And how much should the ring cost?"

Ford flipped him the bird.

"Verbal assault of an officer," Sawyer said. "I'd arrest you but I don't feel like doing the paperwork."

"There's a stolen rental car," Ford said. "How about you be a cop and get to that?"

"It's not stolen. It just showed up." Sawyer turned to Logan. "You parked in a no-parking zone and it got towed." He eyed Logan over the tops of his dark lenses. "The law applies even to celebrities here."

Logan sighed. "I'm going to need a ride."

Sawyer looked at Ford.

Oh, Christ. "No."

"I have to get back to work," Sawyer said.

"It's your job to take care of citizens in need," Ford pointed out.

"Unless I have a call. And I have a call."

"What, to get donuts?"

Sawyer pointed at him, miming shooting his gun. Then he got back into his squad car and drove off.

Logan looked at Ford.

"Shit." Ford shoved a hand into his pocket for his keys. "Come on."

They walked to the lot, where Logan looked at Ford's classic 1969 Camaro. "You ever race this baby?"

"I keep my racing to the water."

Logan gave him an evaluating look over the hood. "You any good?"

"Yes."

"Heard about the gold medals."

"Then you know I'm good."

Logan leaned over the roof. "How about letting me drive?"

"Maybe when hell freezes over. And get off the car, man. You lean on your car like that?"

Logan laughed. "I kill people for leaning on my car."

Ford pinched the bridge of his nose. "Where are you staying?"

"Well, I *was* at the Beachside Cottages. But when I went to the office to complain about the doorbell ditch this morning, I was unceremoniously kicked out. Something about last-minute renovations."

"They can't really do that."

"Can and did," Logan assured him. "I called Tara, and she agreed to put me up."

Oh, good. His greatest nightmare coming true. "Tara."

"Yeah," Logan said, laughter in his voice. "Guess my sabotagers didn't think that one all the way through. I'll be staying at the inn with Tara. Think she still loves to ... *cook*?"

Ford knew for a fact that she did, and thinking about it, he found himself driving a little faster, a little tighter than he normally would have.

"You're trying to impress me," Logan said. "It's okay. I get that a lot."

Shit. Ford slowed down but it was too late. Logan was grinning. "Do you also get that you're an ass?" Ford asked.

Logan shrugged, completely unconcerned.

Ford concentrated on not putting the pedal to the metal. "Why are you here again?"

"I let my wife get away from me. We were good together. She traveled with me, made my life bearable, and in return, I took care of her."

Ford thought about that for a moment. If Tara had

ever needed anyone, those days were long over. She'd grown up, and nothing about the new version was needy or dependent.

"And you?" Logan asked.

"Me what?" Ford slid him a look. "And be careful, because if you're about to ask about me and Tara, I'm going to kick your ass and enjoy it."

Logan snorted at the empty, hollow threat. Fan-fucking-tastic.

When Ford finally pulled up at the inn, Logan eyed him across the console. "If all you're looking for is a good time, she deserves better."

Ford was surprised he still had back teeth, what with all the grinding he'd been doing. "What I'm looking for is none of your business."

"Look, I was the guy that came along in Tara's life after you screwed her up. And she was damn tough to catch because of it. But my patience and perseverance paid off, and she married me. So man to man...." Logan gave him a tight smile. "You might *think* you have game with her now, but she isn't a game. Move onto someone else, Ford."

"Get out."

Logan did just that, then leaned in the window. "I've heard a lot about you, you know. Hard not to; you're the only thing anyone around here wants to talk about. You're the Good Time Guy, not the Keeper Guy. That's how I know I'm going to be the last one standing. And I think you know it, too."

Ford watched him walk away. It was true that all he and Tara had in common was a mutual desire, which they'd supposedly fulfilled. And Mia, of course.

502 Jill Shalvis

Except...

Christ, the *except*. He watched Logan vanish inside the inn, thinking about how much more than desire this was. How he wasn't feeling much like just a Good Time Guy.

He was feeling like the Confused Guy, one who wanted so much more than he ever had before.

Tara and Maddie were up at the crack of dawn, standing on the docks watching as, from the very far corner of the bay, Logan seemed to be struggling with the houseboat.

"Does he look like he's okay?" Tara asked, peering through the binoculars she'd found in the marina building.

"He has the two-way," Maddie said. "He'd call for help if he needed it, right?"

"No, he wouldn't. He's a guy. He'll call for help when he's dead."

The houseboat had come with the inn and marina as a part of their inheritance. Since this had happened in the dead of winter six months ago, they'd never had an earlier opportunity to use the boat.

But when Logan had called yesterday needing a place to stay, Tara had grabbed her sisters and cleaned the thing out, and placed Logan in it.

Better than having him underfoot at the inn.

Chloe came up behind them. "Hey, thought we were doing yoga this morning."

"I get enough exercise just pushing my luck," Tara said, still watching the houseboat through the binoculars. Logan was on the deck, messing with something in the open maintenance closet. She considered calling him, but probably it was his plan to look helpless so she'd go out there. He used to do that with all the kitchen appliances when they were married.

"Did anyone look through yesterday's mail yet?" Chloe asked. "I'm waiting for a few checks to come through for the classes I gave in Tucson last month."

"No checks, only bills," Maddie said.

Chloe sighed. "The bills always travel faster than the checks. Why is that?"

Neither Tara nor Maddie had an answer for that. Tara was still looking at the houseboat. Huh. Logan did seem to be genuinely concerned about something.

"Tell me again why he couldn't just rent one of our rooms?" Maddie asked, shielding her eyes from the early morning sun. "The rooms that we actually *want* to rent out? He's a paying customer."

"That would have put him too close."

Maddie glanced at her. "If you don't want him here, why don't you ask him to leave?"

"Because he said he wasn't leaving until he won me back."

"Is that even possible?"

The "no" was on the tip of her tongue, but she was having some trouble getting it out. She had no intention of starting anything up with Logan. None. But he'd been her only family for several years, during a time when she didn't have a lot of others in her life, and he'd stuck with her until she hadn't been able to make it work anymore. There were still emotional ties.

"And what about Ford?" Maddie asked.

"What about him?"

"Is he the reason Logan doesn't have a shot? And don't lie. I've seen the way you look at him. It's how I look at junk food."

"We are *way* too busy to discuss this," Tara said. "We have guests—"

"Who have been out sightseeing in the area and are no trouble at all." Maddie took in the heavy South in Tara's voice and smiled. "You do realize that you don't scare either me or Chloe anymore with that tone, right?"

"Like I ever scared you."

Maddie's smile turned into a grin. "You know what you should do with Ford?"

Tara gave her a droll look. "Drag him up to the attic like you do Jax?"

Maddie blushed. "Hey, we go up there to—"

"I'll pay you fifty bucks not to finish that sentence," Tara said fervently.

From behind them came the sound of a soda can being popped open, and they all whirled around.

Ford stood on the deck of his Beneteau, drink in one hand and a bag of chips in the other. Breakfast of champions. He wore a WeatherTech T-shirt, board shorts, and a backward baseball cap with his hair curling out from beneath. Looking better than anyone should this early, he toasted them with his soda, his eyes never leaving Tara's. "Morning."

Maddie gasped. Only she wasn't looking at Ford, but out at the water. "Do you think Logan's all right?"

"He's always all right," Tara said. "Why?"

"Because he's waving at us."

Ford looked out on the water, then swore as he set his

soda aside and leapt forward to start the engine on the Beneteau.

"What are you doing?" Tara asked.

"Saving the bastard." He paused and looked at her hopefully. "Unless it's okay with you if he dies?"

"*What?*"

"He's sinking."

Tara looked. Ford was right. Logan was definitely sinking.

"Oh my God," Maddie whispered, horrified. "I rented him that boat. Does that make me a murderer?"

Tara's heart clutched. "He's not dead yet."

"Hurry," Maddie called to Ford. "I can't be the one who killed Tara's ex! I look terrible in orange!"

Tara tried to remember if Logan was good in the water. He could drive like the best of the best, but she had no idea about swimming. She grabbed the two-way radio from Maddie's hip. "Logan, why aren't you wearing protection?"

The radio crackled, and then came Logan's voice. "I have 'protection' in my bag," he said. "But much as I don't want to say this, darlin', now's not the time to be asking if I'm carrying condoms. I have problems."

"A life vest, Logan! I'm asking where's your life vest!"

"Oh," he said. "I knew that."

Maddie was yelling at Ford. "Faster! I voted for you, and I want you to win, but not this way, not by killing the ex-husband!"

Tara shook her head in disbelief. "You voted for him? I told you and Chloe not to vote. None of us were going to vote!"

"Actually, this is pretty funny, if you think about it," Chloe said as Ford sped toward Logan.

Tara gaped at her. "What could possibly be funny about any of this?"

"How about the fact that your two men seem to be spending more time with each other than with you?"

Chapter 15

♥

"Experience is what you get when you didn't know what you wanted."
TARA DANIELS

By noon, the houseboat had been towed back to the marina, where it was determined that the bilge pump had failed. Logan was perfectly safe although slightly disgruntled, and settled back at his original beach cottage after a phone call to the owners from Tara.

The weekend guests were no trouble at all. Chloe had been right. They were in their mid-thirties, on their honeymoon, and hadn't noticed a thing about the inn. All they wanted was their bed.

Maddie was set to handle the afternoon and evening, with both Chloe and Mia for backup if needed. Tara had a shift at the diner, and she was running late. Keys in hand, she came running out of the cottage and nearly toppled over Mia, who sat on the top step.

Holding the recipe box.

"Hey, Sugar." Tara pulled up short. "Where did you get that?"

"From Chloe." Mia opened the box and pulled out the first card, on which Tara had written *For My Daughter*. "She thought I'd like to see it."

Tara was going to be late for work if she stopped but she knew it didn't matter. Talking to Mia was worth being bitched at by Jan—and Jan *would* bitch. Eyeing the wooden step, Tara bit back a sigh. Hiking up her pencil skirt to mid-thigh, she gingerly sat.

Mia pulled her lips in, trying to hide her smile, reminding Tara that in the girl's eyes, she was not only old but also probably embarrassing.

"The porch swing would have been more dignified," Tara told her.

"I like it right here. I can see the world sail by."

That was true. From here, there was a lovely view of the marina and any ships sailing past it. "Are you interested in sailing?" Tara asked her. "Because it just so happens, you're closely related to an expert."

Mia smiled. "I know. And yeah, I'm interested. Ford said he'd take me real soon." She pulled out a card and showed it to Tara. "'Never miss a good opportunity to shut up'?"

Tara sagged a little and let out a huff of laughter. "It fit at the moment."

"Chloe?"

Tara looked at Mia and found the girl still smiling, and felt the helpless curve of her own mouth. "Yes. She has a way, doesn't she?"

"Yeah." Mia looked down at the box and was quiet a minute. Normal for her, not normal for Tara. She had to bite her tongue to keep it from running away with her good sense, to keep from filling the silence. And damn, it was hard to do, but when Mia finally spoke, it was worth the torturous wait.

"You thought of me," she said.

Tara let out a low laugh. "A little."

Mia lifted her gaze from the box and met Tara's.

"A lot more than a little," Tara said very softly.

Her daughter's eyes warmed, those beautiful eyes that made Tara think of Ford every single time she looked into them. She wanted nothing more than to have Mia keep looking at her like that, but she had to tell her all of it. "I want you to know the truth, Mia. I need you to know the truth. I *don't* regret giving you up."

Mia went still. "Oh."

"I loved you," Tara said, and put her hand to her chest to absolve the ache she felt there at the memory of that sweet, sweet baby looking up at her. "Oh God, how I loved you, from the moment I first felt what I thought was a butterfly on my shirt and turned out to be you kicking. But I wasn't capable of the kind of love you needed." Tara paused, her throat tight. "Even in all my teenage selfishness, I knew you deserved more. You deserved everything I couldn't provide. So *that's* why I don't regret it, Mia. Because in giving you up, you had a childhood that I couldn't have given you."

Mia ran her fingers over the grooves in the wood of the recipe box, her silence killing Tara. "And something else I don't regret." Tara reached for Mia's hand. "Having you here this summer. I wouldn't have missed this for anything, getting to know you."

Mia's fingers slowly tightened on hers. "Even if it means facing your biggest mistake?"

"Oh, Mia." Tara risked all and slowly slid an arm around her beautiful, smart, reluctant daughter. "I meant what I said about that. You were never a mistake. You were meant to be, and I'm so very, *very* glad you're here."

"Really?"

"Really."

After a beat of thinking about that, Mia laid her head on Tara's shoulder, and Tara's heart swelled to bursting. They sat there quietly a few more minutes, Tara ignoring the occasional and insistent vibration of her phone. She knew it was Jan; she could *feel* the temper coming across the airwaves, but Tara didn't want to get up.

"I'm glad I'm here, too," Mia said.

Tara smiled. "It's been fun giving you the good jobs and making Chloe clean the bathrooms."

Mia's mouth quirked. Ford could do that, too, project an emotion with next to no movement. From within Tara's pocket, her cell went off yet again, but Mia was looking at her, something clearly on her mind, so Tara didn't move.

"I've just been trying to imagine it," Mia finally said. "Me, right now, having a baby at my age. It's...incomprehensible. The trauma. The utter responsibility of it all."

Tara laughed without much humor. "Don't forget the abject terror."

"Were your parents awful about it?"

"My dad, yes." Tara could still hear the bitter disappointment in his voice over the phone line. It'd taken him days to return her tearful message from wherever he'd been traveling for work. "But your grandma, she was surprisingly supportive."

"Why surprisingly?"

"We didn't see each other often. Just sometimes in the summers. But she didn't judge or yell. She didn't try to make me feel bad. She just found me a special high school to attend in Seattle, and she was there when I needed her. She came for your birth. And she was there for you later too, when—"

"When I got sick." Mia nodded. "My parents told me. She helped pay the medical bills."

"I didn't know it at the time," Tara admitted. "I never heard anything about it until she died. But I snooped through her papers and read about your condition. You had a problem with a heart valve."

"It was...*misbehaving*." Mia put finger quotes around the word. "That's what my parents called it. I had surgery, and now my heart's perfect. That's what my cardiologist said. *Perfect*."

"It must have been so scary for you."

She shrugged. "My parents kept buying me presents, and they took me to Disneyland afterward."

The resilience of youth...

"How about Ford? How did he handle the news of you getting pregnant?" Mia asked.

"Better than me. He was..." Strong. Steady. Calm. Looking back, Tara knew he must have been freaking out every bit as much as she was, but he'd never shown it. "Amazing."

"And you're not together why?" Mia asked, smiling when Tara sighed. "Sorry, couldn't resist asking again." She pulled out another index card. " 'The quickest way to double your money is to fold it in half and put it back in your pocket.' " Mia laughed again, and the knot in Tara's chest, the one that had been there since the girl had first shown up in Lucky Harbor, loosened. God. God, her baby was so beautiful. "This is nice," Tara said. "I like being with you like this."

Mia stared down at the box. "I'm sorry I said you were rigid and uncompromising and stubborn."

Tara blinked. "You never called me those things."

"Oh, right. Well, I thought them." Mia winced. "I'm sorry."

"It's okay. I *am* those things, and more."

"You're also smart, and pretty, and you care," Mia said quietly. "You're, like, all calm and collected, and you have this don't-mess-with-me vibe, but you also care about everyone in your orbit. Even people who drive you crazy."

Tara laughed a little, shocked. And touched. Unbearably touched that her daughter appeared to know her so well. "How do you know that?"

"Chloe told me. She said she drives you crazy and you're still there for her, no matter what. That's her favorite part about you, and mine too."

Tara's heart throbbed painfully. In a good way. "You know what my favorite part is?"

Mia shook her head.

"You."

Her daughter's eyes got misty as she smiled, and Tara had to fight for control as well. She reached for Mia, and then they were hugging just as Tara's cell phone vibrated yet again. Mia sniffed and pulled back. "Somebody really wants to get a hold of you."

"It's my boss." Tara swiped beneath her eyes. "Mascara?"

"Still okay," Mia assured her. "You need the waterproof kind, though. And a nicer boss, like I have."

Tara laughed and got to her feet, brushing off her butt and hoping she wasn't wrinkled. "Come to the diner after you finish here, and I'll make you dinner."

"Can I bring someone?"

Carlos, Tara thought, which was something else that had been keeping her up at night—the idea of the teens moving too fast. Already, they were inseparable. "Honey, about Carlos," she started slowly. "He's" —*A horny teen-age boy?*— "too old for you."

"He's my age."

"Well then, he's too . . ." Hell. He was too nothing. He was a great kid. But no boy was going to be good enough, she knew that already.

"Actually," Mia said. "I meant Ford. Do you have any objections to him? Because he likes to watch you cook. He told me."

Tara paused, struggling to change gears. "He did? What else did he tell you about me?"

"That he *loves* to see you and me together."

Aw. *Dammit*. There went her heart again, squeezing hard.

This question was accompanied by a certain look in her daughter's eyes, a speculative gaze that had Tara narrowing hers. "Sugar, you're not up to anything sneaky, are you?"

"Like?" Mia asked innocently.

Oh, Lord. "Like trying to get Ford and me together?"

"Hey, I didn't start the poll."

"Mia."

Mia was suddenly looking much younger than her seventeen years. "Would it be so awful?"

"I just don't want to disappoint you," Tara said. "Because Ford and I, we're not—"

"I know, I know. You've mentioned this a time or a hundred." Mia's attention was suddenly diverted by something behind Tara. "You'd better go. You don't want to be late to the diner."

Tara turned to look behind her at whatever had caught Mia's eyes and saw Carlos, walking across the yard toward the marina building.

"So have a good shift," Mia said, getting to her feet. "See you later."

"Mia—"

But Mia was already halfway to Carlos, and back to looking very much seventeen.

Much later that night, Tara awoke to someone trying to chainsaw their way into the cottage. She sat straight up and realized it was just her sister snoring.

From the next bedroom over.

Tara looked at the clock—midnight. *Great.* She slipped out of bed and down the hall to Chloe's room. "Turn over."

Chloe muttered something in her sleep that sounded like "a little to the left, Paco."

"Chloe!" Tara said, louder.

Chloe rolled over and blessed silence reigned.

With a sigh, Tara went back to bed and started to drift off. She got halfway to a dream that involved her naked and being worshipped by Ford's very talented tongue before Chloe began sawing logs again. Tara looked at the clock.

Midnight plus two minutes.

Hell. Sleep was out of the question, and anyway now she was hungry. She must have been channeling her sister Maddie because suddenly she wanted some chips. *Needed* some chips, quite desperately, as a matter of fact. Only problem, there were none in the cottage; she'd removed them for Maddie's sake. The only place she knew to get chips was in town.

Or...on Ford's boat.

Was it breaking and entering to board a man's boat and steal food? No doubt. But hell, she'd already stolen his shirt. In fact, she was wearing it right now, so what was one more act of pilfering?

Her stomach growled, and making her decision, she rolled out of bed once more. At the door, she realized she needed shoes, and slipped into the only ones she had out—her wedge sandals. She gave a brief thought to how she must look in Ford's shirt, panties, and the heeled wedges. Ready for a "Girls Gone Wild" video.

No one else will see you at this hour, she assured herself. The boat was only fifty yards across the driveway. She ran in the heels, skirting around the marina building and onto the dock, by some miracle not twisting an ankle or breaking her neck.

The night was noisy. No wind, but there was an owl hooting softly somewhere on the bluffs, and the answering cry of its mate. Crickets sang, and the water, stirred by the moon's pull, pulsed against the dock, slapping up hard against the wood.

In Houston, Tara had slept in a fourth-floor condo. City lights had slashed through her windows, blotting out the moon's glow, and there'd been no noise except for the drone of the air conditioning just about 24/7. Six months ago, when she'd first arrived in Lucky Harbor—bitchy, resentful, and unhappy—she'd hated the sound of nature at night. It'd kept her up, and she'd lay in bed for hours, mind racing. But somehow, over the months, she'd come to accept the noises. Even welcome them.

They soothed her now, as did the utter darkness of the night itself. There were no city lights here, nothing to mute the glorious stars. She would stay outside and enjoy the night but she wasn't exactly dressed for it. And those chips were calling her name. She did have a bad moment boarding the boat in the wedges, and pictured falling into the water between the boat and the dock and being found with Ford's T-shirt up around her ears.

Once she managed to board, she headed below deck, and as hoped found a bag of chips on the counter in the tiny galley. She downed her first mouthful, and her hand was loaded with her second when the light came on. Blinking in the sudden brightness, she turned and faced...

Ford.

He took in the fact that her mouth was full, her fingers loaded with more chips, and began to smile. By the time he eyed her undoubtably bedhead hair, bare legs, and heels, it was a full-blown grin. "Nice," he said.

"This isn't what it looks like."

"No?" He wore sweatpants low on his hips and nothing else. His hair was rumpled in that sexy way that guys' hair get when they've been sleeping. He leaned back against the opposite counter and slid his hands into his pockets. Relaxed. Watchful.

Amused.

Damn him.

"So what do you think it looks like?" he wanted to know.

Like she was a crazy chick so on the verge of losing it that she'd broken and entered and stolen his chips. "Uh…"

His eyes had locked in on her shirt. "You're either chilly or very happy to see me—is that my shirt?"

Crap. She looked down and crossed her arms over herself, which made the shirt rise up higher on her thighs, possibly exposing her pink lace panties.

This momentarily diverted his attention downward. His smile went naughty and the air around them heated to scorching.

Yeah, definitely she'd exposed her underwear.

"That *is*," he said. "That's my shirt."

She didn't really want to talk about the shirt. "I couldn't sleep. I got hungry and figured you had chips."

"So you committed felony B&E," he said, nodding. "Good plan. Except for the getting caught part. Were you going to sleep in my bed, too, Goldilocks?"

The way he said *bed* brought vivid memories of all the mind-blowing, amazing things he'd done to her in a bed. And *out* of a bed…"No," she said. "That would be rude."

He laughed softly. "Are you still working on your issues?"

"Yes," she said primly. "You?"

"I'm a work in progress, babe." He slid her a bad boy smile. "Still hungry?"

Oh boy. "Yes," she whispered.

He crooked a finger at her. "Come here, Goldilocks."

"That would be…a really bad idea."

"I can make it so bad it's good."

Gah. "You've *got* to stop that."

"Stop what?" he asked.

Looking hot, she thought. Talking naughty.

Breathing.

As she turned to face the counter and set down the bag of chips, she grabbed a bottle of water and washed down the crumbs. She knew by the tingling at the base of her neck that Ford was right behind her now. Then he was so close that she could feel his body heat seeping through the shirt to her skin. She could have moved away, but the truth was, she was exactly where she wanted to be.

"Okay," she said shakily. "Here's the thing. I'm... still attracted to you." Her breath shuddered out when he nudged her hair aside and brushed his lips along the nape of her neck. She locked her knees. Had to, in order to keep standing. "But I don't want to sleep with you again."

"And yet here you are," he murmured against her skin. "On my boat. In the middle of the night."

"Yeah. That looks bad," Tara admitted. "But really, it was all about the chips."

"And my shirt." He ran a finger down her spine, stopping far below the line of decency, making her breath catch in the sudden silence. "How is it that you have it?" he asked, his hand on her ass.

She fought against the urge to thrust her bottom into his palm.

Or better yet, his crotch.

"Tara."

She squeezed her eyes shut. "I stole it. The day I returned your crepe pan."

"Look at me."

No. No, thank you very much.

His hands settled on her hips and he turned her to face him. "Not that I don't like the sight of you in the shirt," he said. "Because I do. Very much. But you've been keeping your distance, and I've been trying to respect that. But you came to me tonight, so all bets are off. Tell me why you're in my shirt."

She nibbled on her lower lip. She didn't have an answer. At least, not one she wanted to give him. "You gave me one just like it when you first got them."

"I remember. I just didn't realize you did as well."

"Yes, well, I do. And I loved it," she told him. "And I lost it in the fire. I really missed it. So when I saw yours..." She closed her eyes. "Hell, Ford. I can't explain it. I lost my head and stole your damn shirt. There. You happy?"

"Hmm," he said noncommittally. "The fire was six months ago." He was still gripping her hips, his hands beneath the hem of the shirt now and his thumbs scraping lightly up and down on her bared belly, making her muscles quiver. "You had it all that time?"

"It was comfortable."

He smiled at that. "Comfortable. You kept a shirt for seventeen years because it was comfortable."

"Yes."

"Liar. Such a beautiful liar." Leaning in, he kissed her. Soft.

A warm-up round.

She knew just how potent the next round would be, so she put her hand to his chest, not quite sure if she was stopping him or making sure he couldn't stop.

In the silence, her stomach growled, and he grinned. "I stand corrected. You really *are* hungry." Turning to the small refrigerator, he pulled out tortillas, grated cheese, and salsa.

"What are you doing?"

"Making you a quesadilla. I'd grill it, but I can't do that in here."

She watched as he stroked a spoonful of salsa onto the tortilla, then layered grated cheese over it. There was something about the way his hands moved, his concentration, the obvious ease that he felt in his kitchen, that got to her.

And he did get to her, in a big way.

He waited until she'd eaten the entire quesadilla to take the plate from her and then lifted her up to the counter. Eyes on hers, he stepped in between her thighs.

"I didn't come here for this," she whispered as he slowly lifted his shirt from her and peeled it off over her head.

"Your nose is going to start growing, Pinocchio," he said, resting his hands on her waist.

"You didn't eat anything," she said inanely.

"Wasn't hungry for a quesadilla."

"What are you hungry for?"

His eyes were so heated that she felt her bones melt away. "Guess," he said, and slid his hands up her thighs. He hooked his thumb in her panties and inched them down. Then he dropped to his knees and proceeded to show her.

Over and over again.

Chapter 16

♥

Tara stood alone in the inn's kitchen in rare blessed silence. She was trying not to think about how many times Ford had taken her—and she him—last night before he'd walked her back to her bed at dawn.

Or how much he was coming to mean to her. Along with Mia. And her sisters. And Lucky Harbor...

It was all those strings that Ford had pointed out, tangling around her heart.

Damn strings. She didn't want them. She wanted to be able to protect her heart as needed, and that was getting damn hard to do. At least with Ford, she knew what she was getting. A good time. Okay, a *really* good time. She'd meant for it to be nothing more but it was...

Chloe came into the room just as Tara was staring blindly into the refrigerator. "Hungry?"

"No," Tara said. "Trying to decide between juice or the vodka."

Chloe laughed. "Always the vodka. It's fewer calories. But I've never actually considered vodka and OJ to be mutually exclusive. Go ahead, splurge, have both."

"Hmm," Tara said and pulled out the eggs.

"You're probably starving from burning all those calories having wild animal sex last night, right?"

Tara nearly dropped the eggs before turning to stare at Chloe. "What?"

"Well, you came in at dawn with crazy hair and a ridiculously wide smile for someone who hates early mornings." Chloe shrugged. "I figured it had to be sex. And given that it was Ford, I also figured it had to be a pretty fantastic night. It *was* Ford, right?"

"Oh my God," Tara said. "*Yes.*"

Chloe grinned at the confession.

"Stop that," Tara said. "We're not talking about this."

"Pretty please? It's so much better than what I have to talk to you about."

Tara opened her mouth to respond to that but Sawyer came in the back door with his usual long-legged stride. It faltered only slightly when he locked gazes with Chloe, whom he wasn't used to seeing in the kitchen when he made his early morning coffee run.

Tara pulled out a to-go mug from a stack that she kept just for him and filled it up.

Chloe watched the process, including Sawyer's quiet but grateful thank-you, although she didn't say a word until he was gone. "Why do you let him steal your coffee?"

"Because he's a good man with a crappy job, that you make all the more difficult for him, by the way. I feel like I owe him."

Chloe rolled her eyes. "Back to you, missy, and your just-got-laid expression. You should try to lose that. You know, for the children."

Tara attempted to catch sight of herself in the steel door of the refrigerator. Damn, Chloe was right. She was glowing.

"Oh, and I borrowed your laptop this morning," Chloe said casually, gathering strawberries, yogurt, and the blender.

"Don't tell me you were looking at porn again," Tara said. "You froze my computer last time you opened that *See Channing Tatum Naked* attachment."

"Hey, anyone would have clicked on that, and it was a total hoax. I never even got to see him naked. And no, I didn't do any of that today. I was just getting my mail. Oh, and I accidentally clicked on your Firefox history."

"So?"

"So I happen to know you went to Facebook, created an account, and voted for Ford."

Tara went still. "Did not."

"Okay. But you did."

Tara crossed her arms. "I'll have you know that there's not a single Tara Daniels on Facebook," she said with confidence.

Chloe looked amused. "And you know this how, *Tallulah Danielson*? Tallulah? Danielson? Seriously? Because Jesus, if you ever find yourself with the need to go deep undercover again, I'm begging you, ask for help. And never consider a job with the FBI."

Well, hell. This was embarrassing. Worse, she couldn't come up with an excuse. Not a single one.

Oh! Temporary insanity. That would work. Or avoidance, Tara decided, and turned away from a grinning Chloe, only to come face to face with the man himself.

Ford. Who was also grinning. "Bless your heart, Tallulah," he said.

Chloe laughed and walked across the room to hug him. "If you weren't so totally hung up on her," she told him, "I'd claim you for myself."

Ford hugged her back. "It's true. I'm totally hung up on her."

Aw. And *dammit*, he really had to stop doing that, Tara thought, watching them, her heart going all mushy. It was all those little things that added up, like making her a quesadilla in the middle of the night, or the way he looked at her, like maybe she was a better sight than say his first cup of coffee in the morning. Or, in the case of how he was looking at her right now, like she was greatly amusing him. "You might have told me he was standing there," Tara said to Chloe.

"I might have."

Tara shook her head and looked at Ford. "I meant to vote for Logan. I hit the wrong button."

Ford burst out laughing. He wore a T-shirt and Levi's that were faded into a buttery softness and doing some nice things for his bod. He had a day of scruff on him and looked so utterly delectable that she found herself just staring.

He looked right back, that small smile still hovering at the corners of his mouth.

Chloe cleared her throat. "Well. This is cute and

all…" She looked at Tara. "But I actually do really need to talk to you. Got a few?"

"Actually, not until later and neither do you. The guests are going to want breakfast."

"This is a quick thing," Chloe said, "but an important one."

Oh hell. It was something big, Tara could see it in Chloe's eyes. "Don't tell me you got arrested again, because I'm pretty sure Sawyer's going to throw away the key on you this time—"

"No. Jeez," Chloe said, tossing up her hands. "A girl gets arrested one time—"

"*Three* times."

Chloe sighed. "This is about *you*."

"What about me?"

Chloe glanced uneasily at Ford, who clearly wasn't budging, then sighed and pulled a white plastic stick from her pocket. "I was in the downstairs bathroom setting up a basket full of lotions and soaps, cleaning up, emptying the trash, that sort of thing."

"I emptied the trash just this morning," Tara said.

"I know," Chloe said. "I saw you. Which means you were the last one in there. So I figured you'd want me to give this to you so no one else could come to the wrong conclusion."

Tara looked down at the thing in Chloe's hands in shock. "That's a pregnancy test stick."

"A negative one," Chloe said. "Probably a relief for you guys, right?"

Tara nearly went into heart failure. "What are you talking about? It's not mine."

Ford's face was utterly blank as he stared at the stick.

After a beat, he lifted his head and met Tara's gaze, his eyes completely shuttered.

Because he knew what she did. They'd used a condom. Every time. It was an unspoken, very serious thing with them, and they both knew it. So undoubtedly his mind was now leaping to the next possibility, that she'd slept with…Logan?

"It's not mine," Tara said again and grabbed Chloe by the arm. "Excuse us a minute?" she said to Ford, then without waiting for an answer, yanked Chloe into the pantry and slammed the door.

"Yeah," Chloe said, looking around at the small but cozy space. "I can see why you pull Ford in here whenever you can. It screams 'do me.'" She tested a shelf. "Does this hold?"

"Chloe, *how could you*?" Tara demanded in a harsh whisper.

"I don't know. I guess I'd hop up right here, and then he'd stand between my legs and—"

"I meant how could you give this to me in front of Ford? My God, that was the most irresponsible, rude, grossly negligent sisterly thing you've ever done, and you've done a lot!"

Chloe paused a moment, clearly startled by Tara's fury, as if she sincerely, honestly hadn't given anyone else's feelings a thought. As always, though, she rebounded with an excuse for herself. "Hey, if you're close enough to need a pregnancy test with him, then he's close enough to go through the worry with you. For the second time."

"It's not mine!"

"Well, it's not mine," Chloe said emphatically. "I haven't had sex all damn year. Not since that hot Cuban guy in Miami, which landed me in the ER. A bit of a post-coital downer, I should add."

"Oh my God," Tara said. "It's Mia's."

"What?"

"The pregnancy test! It's Mia's."

Chloe contemplated this, then let out a slow breath. "Oh boy."

Tara gritted her teeth. "I'm going to kill Carlos—"

"It's not Mia's. It's mine."

Tara and Chloe looked at each other, and then at the door, which had spoken to them. Chloe pulled it open and there stood Maddie.

And Mia.

They stood side by side, Maddie looking sheepish. "I thought I wrapped it up so no one would see it," she said.

Tara stuck her head out into the kitchen and looked around for Ford.

"He left," Maddie told her.

Mia still hadn't said a word. She stood staring at Tara with barely veiled resentment. "You thought the stick was mine."

Tara opened her mouth but Mia shook her head and took a step back. "I have to go," she said and moved to the door.

"Mia, please." Tara rushed to her. "Wait—"

Mia whirled back, her eyes swimming. "You thought it was mine," she repeated. "You think I'm having sex and being stupid enough to do it without protection. You think I'd compound that stupidity by taking a pregnancy test here and then leave the stick where it could be found." She winced and shot Maddie a look. "No offense."

Maddie sighed. "None taken."

"Mia," Tara said, and heard the emotion in her own voice. "I'm sorry. It was a knee-jerk reaction, and I'm sorry."

Some of the tension drained from Mia's shoulders, but not all, as she nodded.

"So you're not having sex?" Chloe asked her.

"No!" Mia said, hugging herself. "Jeez!"

"Good," Chloe said. "Because I really didn't want to be the only one not getting any." She turned to Maddie. "And you. You really thought you might be pregnant?"

Maddie nodded, backed to a chair, and dropped into it. She confiscated Chloe's coffee and sipped. Making a face, she added three heaping spoonfuls of sugar and then sipped again and nodded.

"So since you're not preggers, you're what, going for diabetes?" Chloe asked.

Tara gave Chloe a dark look that had Chloe miming zipping up her lips and throwing away the key. Tara still wanted to strangle her, but even more than that, she wanted to go find Ford and make sure they were okay. Or as okay as they could be when they were . . .

Hell. She had no idea what it was they were doing exactly, except spending a lot of time making each other moan the other's name. In any case, she needed to see him, needed to make sure he knew it really wasn't her. Unfortunately, Maddie appeared to be half an inch from meltdown so Tara pulled a chair up in front of her.

"Jax wants to get married," Maddie whispered without prompting, then let out a shuddering breath, as if a huge weight had been lifted off her shoulders.

"And?" Chloe asked.

"And I think that's just the pregnancy scare talking." Maddie lifted huge eyes to her sisters. "I don't want to get married just because of that."

"It's more," Tara said. "He loves you."

"And I love him. But I don't need the piece of paper."

"How about the diamond?" Chloe asked. "Don't you need the diamond?"

"No. Well, maybe." Maddie let out a watery laugh. "But we haven't been together all that long, really."

"Six months," Tara said.

"Yes, and we're committed," Maddie agreed. "And that's enough for me. Shouldn't that be enough?"

"Are you trying to convince you, or us?" Chloe asked. "Because I'm still on the diamond thing. It'd be pretty hard to turn down a big, fat diamond. And then you get a big party, a cool trip, and use of his credit card." At Tara's slight shake of her head, Chloe rolled her eyes. "And fine. More importantly, you're wild about him. I know you are. He makes you smile. And he thinks your OCD is cute." She smirked at Tara, like *see*? *I can so be supportive.*

"I'm not OCD," Maddie said. "Exactly. And I *am* crazy wild about him. Maybe if I *had* been pregnant..."

"You're just lucky the pregnancy scare happened now," Tara said, extremely aware of Mia soaking up this sisterly exchange. "At a good age with a guy who loves you as much as Jax does." She met Chloe's sharp gaze. "What?"

"You say that like you don't have one of the greatest guys we know wanting *you*."

"Want is not love," Tara said.

Chloe rolled her eyes again.

"If you don't stop doing that," Tara said. "I'm going to pop them in a jar and roll them for you."

"And here I always thought that you were the brightest crayon in the box."

Tara felt her eyes narrow. "And what does that mean?"

"Hey," Chloe said, lifting her hands. "If you don't get it, I'm not going to explain it to you. But his name starts with an F and ends with an O-R-D, and *hello*, he's as head over heels for you as Jax is for Maddie."

Tara stared uncomfortably at Mia, who was nodding. "Okay," Tara said. "It's true, we might have married all those years ago, but seventeen-year-olds shouldn't marry."

"Maybe not," Chloe said. "But Ford's all grown up now, and a pretty damn fine man if you ask me. He's financially stable, hot as hell—sorry, Mia—and would probably die before he hurt you. So what's the hold-up?"

"I've asked the same thing," Mia said. "Minus the hot part, because *ew*."

Tara sagged. "Me. Okay? The hold-up is me. The last time I was with him…" She glanced at Mia. "I didn't handle things well."

"You were a kid," Maddie said and smiled at Mia. "No offense."

"None taken," Mia said politely.

"What a cynic you turned out to be," Chloe chided Tara. "Not believing in the power of love."

"Says the woman who can't even *say* I love you," Tara shot back.

Chloe clammed up, face closed now. "This isn't about me."

Mia looked outside as Carlos pulled in, her entire demeanor perking right up. "I gotta go," she said, and vanished out the door.

Tara sighed, then turned to Maddie. "Back to you."

"I'd rather not get back to me."

"Tough," Tara said. "Because I've had enough of me. Are we happy or sad the test was negative?"

"Aw," Maddie murmured, her eyes going suspiciously damp. "You said *we*."

"Hey, *you* said we were a *we*," Tara reminded her. "About six months ago, when you pretty much demanded we all stick together and act like sisters, remember?"

"Yeah," Chloe said, adding her two cents. "That's true, Mad. You were all about the *we*. Hardcore *we*, actually."

"Since when do either of you listen to me?" Maddie asked.

"Since you made us all hug and kiss and take the blood oath," Tara said, then found herself being squeezed nearly to death by Maddie, who'd pulled her and Chloe in close.

"I love you guys," Maddie whispered.

Tara sighed. "I love you too."

Chloe merely endured the hug and the sentiment.

Maddie pulled back and, still holding their hands, sniffed. "I'm sorry about this. When I didn't get my period on time, I panicked. It's silly. I love Jax so much. And we've talked about getting married, about doing the whole wedding and dress and cake—"

"And dancing," Chloe added. "If you're going to make a production out of it, let's have dancing."

Maddie laughed. "Yeah. And dancing."

"So...panic over?" Tara asked her.

"Yeah." Maddie rubbed her chest. "I mean none of us exactly had the typical childhood. And Jax didn't either. I couldn't picture—I just couldn't imagine being a parent, I don't know how. *We* don't know how."

"You're the warmest, sweetest, kindest person I know," Tara said. "And Jax is smart and sharp as hell. What you don't know, you'll figure out. You'll make great parents."

"Oh," Maddie said, "that's so sweet." And she sniffed again. "But I really just want to be alone with him for a while first. Is that selfish?"

"Hell, no," Chloe said. "If I was going out with Jax, I'd want to be alone with him all the time. Day and night. Naked—"

Tara slid an arm around Chloe and covered her mouth. Chloe freed herself with a laugh. "So if you're done panicking now," she said to Maddie, "maybe you can explain how it is you might have gotten pregnant. Thought you were on the pill."

Maddie winced. "Yes, but apparently they're not effective when you're on antibiotics. Remember last month when I got bronchitis?"

"You were having sex with bronchitis?" Chloe asked. "You weren't supposed to tax yourself."

Maddie bit her lower lip and blushed. "I didn't tax myself. Jax did all the work."

Chloe sighed in jealousy. "Bitch."

"So," Tara said, squeezing Maddie's hand. "Let's recap. Panic is over, and we've established you're madly in love." Which would mean she could go talk to Ford now...

"I'll be better when I get my period," Maddie said. "I've been so distracted. I mean, I ordered full sheets instead of queen-sized for the guests' rooms. I tried to put diesel in my car instead of regular gas. And let's not forget *not* checking the bilge pump on the houseboat and nearly killing Logan."

"Eh," Chloe said with a playful shrug. "He's an ex. Not such a loss."

"*Chloe!*" Tara exclaimed.

Maddie laughed, then clapped a hand over her mouth. "Sorry. But admit it; that was a little funny. And we need to get breakfast going."

"Yes," Tara agreed. "But first I have to go face a man about a pregnancy scare, thank you very much." She sent Chloe a long look.

"My fault," Chloe said, raising her hand. "*I'll* make breakfast."

"*No*," Maddie and Tara said at the same time.

"Hey, I can totally do this. I *want* to do this."

Tara stared at her, then nodded. "Okay, but I'll be back if you need me." With that, she went searching for Ford, but though his car was out front, he wasn't anywhere in the inn.

Or the marina building.

And then she discovered that his Finn was gone. He'd headed out on the water. She boarded his Beneteau and sat on the hull, stretching her long legs out in front of her to catch the rays of the early sun, hoping it would warm her while she waited. Dropping her head back, she closed her eyes and tried to relax. Between the near sinking of the houseboat, the emotional talk with Mia the night before, getting even more emotional—and naked—with

Ford, then Maddie's pregnancy scare, she was plumb done in, all before eight in the morning.

She must have drifted off because the next thing she knew, the boat was shifting as someone stepped on board. She didn't look. She didn't need to. She recognized the buzz along her nerves.

Ford didn't speak, and neither did she. Not when he motored them out of the marina, and not when he took them out of the bay as well, to a secluded area offshore. He dropped anchor and sat beside her, mirroring her pose so that he was sprawled out, face tipped up, the sun gilding his features.

Because she needed to see him for this, she sat up, reached over and pulled off his sunglasses.

He lifted his head and looked at her.

"The pregnancy test really wasn't mine," she said. "I'd have come to you."

His eyes met hers. "Or Logan."

"You really think I'd sleep with both of you?"

He hesitated. "If it were any other guy, I'd say hell no. But there's this little voice inside my head that keeps reminding me that you have strong ties to him. And you were married. I really hate that little fucking voice."

"Logan and I have been apart nearly two years now."

"And we've been apart seventeen."

"I'm thinking the amount of time isn't what matters," she said.

Ford was quiet a moment. "You know, back inside, for just a minute when I saw that stick, a bunch of things hit me."

"Yes. Abject terror."

"And confusion," he said. "And maybe . . . excitement."

His eyes met hers. "I never regretted Mia. Not for a minute. I only regretted what happened to us."

Her chest squeezed. "I hate that I hurt you."

Again he was quiet. "I feel something for you, Tara," he finally said. "You feel it, too. I see it in your eyes when you look at me. I feel it in your touch when you let me in close."

She let out a breath and watched the water. "Yes."

He tugged her onto his lap and stroked a thumb along her jaw, waiting until she opened her eyes.

"I feel it," she said, giving him the words. "And I feel it for only you. Whatever 'it' is. But—"

"No buts," he said. "That sentence was perfect without any buts." He slid his hands beneath her skirt and cupped the cheeks of her bottom in his big hands, yanking her in even closer, letting her feel what this position was doing for him. Kissing his way along her jaw to her ear, he made her shiver in anticipation.

"Here," he said. "Now. With me."

The words weren't spoken with a question mark at the end, but he *was* asking.

"Here," she agreed, cupping his face. "Now. With you. Only you…"

With an agreeing growl rumbling in his throat, he pushed up her sweater and down the cups of her bra, baring her breasts to him. "You drive me crazy," he said against her skin. "*Crazy*."

"Ditto," she gasped, then again when he slid his hand between her thighs. She fisted her hands in his hair and cried out, rubbing against him, needing the friction, needing him inside her with a wild abandon and desperation she couldn't control.

"I think about you day and night." His voice was raw. "And Jesus, the image of you in my T-shirt and those heels, that's going to be fueling my fantasies for a good long time."

"How about doing it on your boat while anchored just off shore in the light of day?" she asked breathlessly. "Is that fantasy worthy?"

His eyes darkened. "Oh Christ, yeah." He pulled off her sweater and yanked her body flush to his, raining open-mouthed kisses down her throat to her breasts. He flicked a nipple with his tongue, causing them both to groan when it pebbled in his mouth. He was pushing up her skirt when she freed him from his jeans. "Please tell me you have a condom," she murmured when he slipped beneath her panties and unerringly touched her so that she writhed for more.

He pulled out a little packet that nearly made her weep for joy. "Now," she said. "You promised now."

Good as his word, he guided her down onto him, inch by glorious inch. "God, Tara. When I'm inside you, I feel like I'm home."

Before she could recover from the beautiful but shocking words, he roughly covered her mouth with his, and gripping her hips hard, gave a slow grind that had her gasping for more. Then he rolled them, reversing their positions. With the warm sun overhead and the pull and thrust of the ocean tide rocking them, Ford moved inside her, taking her to a place no one else ever had. It was the most erotic thing she'd ever experienced, and afterward, they lay side by side, hands entwined, staring up at the clear blue sky as they struggled to catch their breath.

Eventually, Tara rose to dress, and Ford did the same.

In comfortable silence, they sailed back to the marina. After Ford had tied up at the dock, he turned to her.

She looked at him, his last few words still in her head. *I feel like I'm home*. "Ford?"

"Yeah?"

"Me too."

Chapter 17

♥

*"A person who's willing to meet you
halfway is usually, conveniently,
a poor judge of distance."*
Tara Daniel

Tara walked into the kitchen and found Chloe sitting on
the countertop, mixing up something that smelled delicious.

"A new exfoliating face scrub," she explained. "Melon-
flavored. The bonus is that it tastes delicious."

Tara tried not to panic. "I thought you were making
breakfast."

"We are." Mia came into the kitchen from the dining room carrying a huge casserole dish. "I made Good
Morning Sunshine Casserole," she said, looking adorable
in fresh—and tiny—denim shorts and a stretchy tee. "Not
strawberry pie, though I was tempted. It's a casserole
with some leftover ham, Tater Tots, and cheese, all mixed
together." She looked very proud of herself. "It's already
been served and cleaned up."

Tara stared at this creature who was her own flesh and
blood and felt her own pride bubble over. "Wow."

"I know. Cute *and* talented," Mia said.

Carlos came into the room from the back door. Mia turned a smile on him. The poor guy took one look at her mile-long legs in her short shorts, and walked smack into the island.

Chloe shot Tara a smirk.

Tara ignored her in favor of taking a good look at the teens, and didn't like what she saw, because she was seeing a whole hell of a lot of heat. "Busy day," she said to Carlos as he attempted to recover. "We need to hose down the front porch, water the flowers, and fix the flickering lights on the dock in case guests want to walk along there at night."

"On it," he said, and vanished back outside.

"I'll help," Mia said and followed him out.

Tara waited until the door shut behind them. "Those two are—"

"Having sex," Chloe said helpfully.

"She said they weren't."

"Okay, but probably I should add some condoms to the baskets I just put out in the bathrooms."

Tara choked, and Chloe patted her shoulder. "They're seventeen, babe. That's like ninety-nine percent hormones, as I'm sure you remember."

Tara felt her gut clench. "I'm going to have to fire him."

"Are you going to fire every boy that looks at her?"

"That or kill them," Tara said, only half joking.

That night Ford ended up behind the bar at The Love Shack. Earlier he and Sawyer had gone out for a long sail, something that had never once in his life failed to soothe him. They'd had clear blue skies filtered only by a few scattered clouds. Winds had come out of the northwest with knots at twelve to fourteen, which actually was "holy shit" weather on a sailboat. Just the way he usually liked it. It'd taken every ounce of concentration just to stay on the water and not ten feet under. Sawyer had bitched about it the whole time.

The sail should have cleared Ford's mind. It hadn't. He just kept thinking. About his life, and what he was doing with it. About Mia. About Tara... And Christ, he was tired of thinking. Tired of his life being in flux.

And when had *that* happened? He'd thought he had things set up. He had money in the bank, and a job running the bar when he felt like working. He wanted for nothing.

Okay, that wasn't quite true.

He wanted something new, something he'd never really wanted before—a relationship. In the past, any attempt at one had been rough to maintain while sailing eight months out of twelve. Hell, just seeing his own sisters and grandmother had been challenging, although now that he was no longer racing so much, his sisters managed to invade his life on a fairly regular basis.

Which meant that these days, a relationship could actually work.

Slightly terrifying.

Sawyer strolled into the bar after his shift. "Since you saved Logan's ass, you're now ahead in the polls by eighty percent."

Lucky Harbor's gossip train was the little engine that could. Nothing slowed it down—not real news, not decency, and certainly not the truth.

The door to the bar opened again, and in came Logan, not looking any happier than Ford. "Fucking perfect," Ford muttered to Sawyer.

Logan headed straight for the bar. "You cheated," he said to Ford. "I'll take a beer and keep 'em coming."

Ford served him. "What do you mean, I cheated?"

"A kid? You came up with a kid?"

Ford was surprised at this. "You didn't know about Mia?"

"I knew that you'd had a baby. I didn't know that baby had grown up and then shown up."

Ford had been wondering how much Logan and Tara talked, if at all. Not much if it'd taken him this many days to learn about Mia. This fact made him feel marginally better.

"I can't compete with that," Logan said and took a long pull of his beer before turning to Sawyer. "How the hell do I compete with that?"

Sawyer shrugged. "You were married to her."

Ford slid Sawyer a look, and Sawyer shrugged again. "He asked."

"Yeah," Logan said, finding solace in Sawyer's words. "You're right. We were *married*. She used to call me her superhero." He looked at Ford to make sure he was listening. "I was her Superman, her Green Hornet, her Flash Gordon, all rolled into one."

On Logan's other side, a group of women with a pitcher of something pink and frothy were blatantly eavesdropping. One of them was Sandy, town clerk and city manager. Sandy was pretty in a no-nonsense way and never lacked for male companionship, though she'd been ignoring men in general since last year when she'd gotten two-timed by some asshole in Seattle. She was eyeing Logan like maybe she'd finally gotten over it.

"Looks like you're in trouble, Ford," Sandy said. "He's got you with the superhero thing."

"Do you even have to be in good shape to drive a race car?" someone asked.

It was Paige, from the post office. Ford could have kissed her.

"Hey, it takes more core body strength to control a car than a boat," Logan said in his defense. "And I'm completely fit. Look." He raised his shirt to show his abs.

The women all hooted and hollered. "Nice eight pack!" Amy said. She was a waitress at the diner, and tonight she was also Sandy's fearless wingman. In her late twenties, she was tall and leggy and blonde, and in possession of a smile that said she was not only tough as hell, but up for dealing with whatever came her way. "Your turn, Ford," she said with a grin.

This produced even *more* ear-splitting woo-hoos. Ford looked at Sawyer, who raised his beer in a go-for-it toast.

Oh hell, no. "We've had this conversation," Ford told whoever was listening, which was exactly *no one*. "I'm not going to show you my stomach."

This only made them all yell louder.

Logan grinned. "You're afraid of the competition. It's okay; no worries."

Goddammit. Ford wasn't afraid of shit. So he lifted his shirt.

The crowd went crazy.

Sawyer shook his head.

Ford sighed.

"Nice," Amy said. "I declare a tie."

Sandy was on the fence. "I don't know. I think we need more examples."

At this, Amy grinned wider and turned to Ford and Logan. "You heard her, boys—whip 'em out. Sandy, you gotta tape measure?"

Ford, who'd just taken a drink from his Coke, choked. Sawyer smacked him on the back, hard.

"Worth a shot," Amy said with a shrug.

Sandy smiled and nudged her shoulder to Logan's. "Never mind the poll, Logan. Besides, Tara's not the only woman in town. You know that, right?"

He sent her a slow smile. "She's not?"

"Nope." Sandy scooted a little closer to him. "And you can be my superhero any time."

At two a.m., Tara was still lying in bed, gazing at the clock. In a few hours, she needed to be wide awake and making breakfast for their guests' last day, but she couldn't relax enough to sleep.

And this time, it had nothing to do with Chloe's snoring, because Chloe wasn't even home yet. She'd gone out with Lance and friends, and they were God knew where, doing God knew what.

Maddie was at Jax's, safe and sound. One worry off Tara's plate, but she had plenty more. She'd caught Mia and Carlos in the marina building earlier. She wasn't sure exactly what she'd interrupted since they'd leapt away from each other faster than she could blink, but the guilt on their faces had been disturbing.

Short of firing one of them or locking Mia in a chastity belt, what could she do without looking like a first-class hypocrite of the highest order?

And then there was Ford. A small part of her wanted to be cuddled up with him right now. Okay, a big part. She fluffed her pillow and once again tried to fall asleep. It didn't happen. She started wondering if the bills had gotten sent out, and if she had gas in her car, and whether or not she had fresh peaches for tomorrow's pie. And where was Chloe, dammit? Rolling out of bed, she picked up her cell phone. "You'd better be okay," she said to Chloe's voice mail, then hung up and padded into the bathroom, where she took a hot bath. Thirty minutes later, warm and toasty, she climbed back into bed to try again.

Her heart tripped when she saw her cell phone, blinking multiple missed calls on the nightstand. The last time that had happened in the middle of the night, Chloe had been arrested with Lance for staging a sit-in at one of the Washington logging companies up on Rascal Pass. "Be okay," she whispered to Chloe as she accessed her messages, her pulse pounding. "Please be okay so I can kill you myself."

The first message was indeed from her sister. "I'm fine," came Chloe's voice. "I'm alive and playing paintball at an all-night venue—don't wait up. And Jesus, stop worrying, I'm a big girl."

"Oh sure," Tara muttered to no one. "I'll just stop worrying. Cuz it's that easy."

The next message surprised Tara into dropping her irritation.

"Tara," came Ford's voice, not quite sounding like his usual laid-back self. "Yeah, so I thought you should know that I don't think I'm a bad idea. I mean I *can* be bad, but I can be good, too. I can do good things…lots of very good *bad* things…" His voice was all low and husky, and combined with the words, had heat slashing through Tara's stomach. "But," he went on with deliberate slowness. "I don't think I can be your superhero."

At that, she pulled the phone away from her ear to stare at it. Superhero? Where had *that* come from? In the background, she could hear loud music and lots of laughter. Probably The Love Shack.

"I'm maybe, possibly a little drunk," he said, and shock reverberated through Tara. Ford wasn't a drinker. His biological father had been, and one of his stepfathers, and it'd turned him off of alcohol. Plus, for as easygoing as he was, he liked his control.

A lot.

"So this superhero thing," he went on. "All the skills I have, you've already seen. I'm guessing I do okay in the body department, because you seem to like it well enough. After all, just a few nights ago you were licking my—"

At this point, there seemed to be a scuttle with the phone, and Tara could hear Sawyer in the background saying, "Just hang up, man, or I'll do it for you and consider it a public service."

"Back off," came Ford's voice, and then there was another tussle. "Some people have no fuckin' manners," he said, slurring slightly. "I want you to know that if I *could* be your superhero, I totally would. But there's no way my ass is gonna wear a pair of tights, not even for you." He paused thoughtfully. "I could do sex slave, though. That seems like a fair trade, right?"

Tara laughed and covered her mouth in utter surprise. The man was clearly drunk and uncharacteristically out of control, and yet he could still make her laugh. And if the truth was known, in the bedroom Ford had *never* failed to command anything less than her full attention. Which meant he had it backward. *She* was a slave to *him*. To his hands, his mouth...

"What I'm trying to say is that I'll always be there for you, Tara. You need someone to help you, I'm your guy. You need a couple or three orgasms? I'm your personal toy. You need to let off some steam, someone to yell at, I'll be your doormat. Wait. Skip that. I'm not a good doormat— Hey," he said to someone else. "Back the fuck off—"

Click.

Tara was looking at her phone when the last message came on. "Goddammit. Logan's still here, and he stole my phone. *Fucker.* He had his shot with you and blew it." His voice lowered again. "He doesn't see you like I do, Tara. All in charge and bossy and sexy as hell with it. He wants you barefoot and pregnant. Nothing wrong with that, but you're more. So much more..."

Tara felt her throat tighten as the message ended. He did see her. The real her. She took a minute to gather her thoughts, then decided she couldn't possibly *not* call him.

He picked up just before it would have gone to voice mail. "Hey," he said, sounding rougher than he had in his messages. "It's late. You okay?"

"I was going to ask you the same thing, Sailor."

"I'm good," he said. "But I could be better."

"Need a ride?" she asked.

There was a beat of surprise. "You'd do that?"

"Yes," she said without hesitating.

"Would you do it for Logan?"

She closed her eyes and decided to give him the truth. "Not without killing him first."

"But you wouldn't kill me?"

"Maybe just maim or dismember."

"Bloodthirsty," Ford said, sounding cheered by the thought.

"Yeah." She hesitated. "Ford, about Logan."

"Is this the part where you tell me you and I have been nothing but a mistake?"

"No. It's the part where I tell you that Logan's not a factor between us."

Another beat of surprise. "Okay, keep talking."

She let out a huff of laughter. "He never was, you know."

"But you still care about him."

"Very much," she agreed. "But I'm not in the same place I was when I was with him. So what's with the superhero thing? Because you should know, no one's ever been my superhero, Ford. I've never wanted one."

"Okay, *now* would be a really great time for a but. Like, 'I've never wanted anyone to be my hero, Ford, but now that I'm back in Lucky Harbor *you* can be my hero, anytime.'"

Tara laughed and lay back in her bed, wondering at the need to have him here with her right now, chasing away the shadows. "I scare most guys, you know."

"Not me." Ford's voice softened. "I like how tough you are. Tough on the outside, and soft and creamy on the inside."

Again she laughed. "That sounds vaguely obscene."

"Really? Cuz I was going for *overtly* obscene."

"Do you need a ride or not?"

"Nah. Sawyer's got me."

"Oh, God. He arrested you?"

"Hey, I'm not *that* drunk."

"Yes, he is," came Sawyer's voice.

She smiled. "This is unlike you."

"I know. Logan drank me under the table. Fucker."

"Logan's with you too?"

"Was."

There was something in his voice now, something he was holding back. Probably Logan had found female companionship in the bar and Ford was trying to protect Tara's feelings, which wasn't necessary.

She knew Logan. She knew that although he *thought* he loved her, at least the woman she'd once been, above all else Logan loved his career and the lifestyle that went with it. Pretty women were drawn to him. She'd be shocked if he'd managed to sit in the bar tonight *without* garnering female attention. He hadn't cheated during their marriage, but it'd definitely been rough on her ego knowing how easy it would have been for him to cheat if he'd wanted to. She'd traveled with him for a while because of it, but the grueling schedule, plus being in the way and feeling so damn alone even while surrounded by his entourage had nearly done her in. Plus, what did it say about her marriage that she'd felt as if she needed to babysit him?

"So," Ford said. "About that sex slave thing—"

She rolled her eyes. "Say good-night, Ford."

"'Night, Ford."

She closed her phone, not knowing whether to laugh again or simply be touched.

Both, she decided, and shook her head, a smile breaking through. He made her laugh, always. Just as he made her *feel*.

Always.

Her heart knew that, but her brain resisted. Her brain was capable of accessing memories and calculating odds and wasn't ready to believe that this could work. But this time at least she fell right to sleep and slept the rest of the night.

Chapter 18

♥

*"Don't take life too seriously or you
won't get out alive."*
TARA DANIELS

Tara woke up at the crack of dawn, disconcerted to find
Chloe still wasn't back. She got up and showered then
came face-to-face with her baby sister tiptoeing into the
cottage, covered in red, blue, and yellow paint. "Are you
okay?"

"Yes. Barely."

Tara looked Chloe over, marveling at the mess. "You
look like a cross between a rainbow and a combat survi-
vor. What—"

"Don't ask." Chloe dropped her clothes on the spot
and padded naked to the shower. "There's a delivery for
you on the porch."

Tara opened the front door. Sitting on the top step was
a vase of beautiful wildflowers, obviously picked, not
purchased, with a piece of paper that simply read *Tara*.

They were beautiful. The question was, who were they

from? Neither Logan nor Ford were exactly the go-out-and-pick-wildflowers type. Tara carried the flowers across the yard to the inn's kitchen, set them on the counter, and mixed up a batch of muffins. She was back to staring at the flowers when Maddie came in the back door with an armload of fresh flowers of her own and stared at Tara's.

"Hey," she complained, pointing to Tara's surprise gift. "I thought I told you I'd get the flowers."

"I didn't buy these."

Maddie eyed the pretty wildflowers. "Logan? Ford?"

Tara shrugged.

"We should all have two men after us," Maddie said on a dreamy sigh.

"I'm not with two men."

"I would be," Chloe said, coming into the kitchen. She was back to her own color. Mostly. "Except probably after having both men naked and at my mercy, the ensuing asthma attack would kill me."

There was a momentary silence as the three of them contemplated both Ford and Logan naked at the same time.

"Is it hot in here?" Maddie asked after a minute, fanning her face. "It feels hot in here."

Chloe pulled out her inhaler and took a hit. "So who are they from? Logan?"

Tara touched the flowers. "Logan would've sent red roses from some fancy floral shop."

"Maybe they're from Ford," Mia said as she arrived for the day. She tucked her keys and purse into the broom closet. She was in capris and a spaghetti-strapped tank top, looking cool and collected. Tara gazed at her and felt a stab of envy. *She* used to be cool and collected.

Until she'd come here. "Flowers aren't really Ford's style," she said.

"Yes, but you said you two weren't together," Mia said.

"That's true."

"So then how do you know what his style is?" Mia asked.

Chloe smiled. "I like you, niece. I like you a lot."

Mia grinned at her, and Tara sighed. "Don't encourage her," she told Chloe, arranging a pile of muffins into a basket. On second thought, she grabbed a thermos and poured it full of milk as well.

"Where are you going?" Maddie asked.

"To find my Secret Santa." Tara grabbed the basket and flowers. "Hold down the fort; I'll be back in a minute to make breakfast."

"If you're back in a minute, then you're not doing it right," Chloe called after her.

Tara heard Chloe yelp, probably from Maddie smacking her upside the head.

Ford hadn't gotten to bed until three a.m. Sawyer had dumped him at the marina instead of driving him all the way up the hill to his house, then pocketed Ford's keys to both the boat and his car.

"Don't do anything stupid," Sawyer had said, then paused, clearly considering confiscating Ford's cell phone as well.

Luckily Ford had seen that coming and wisely shoved it down the front of his jeans.

With a sound of disgust, Sawyer had left.

Don't do anything stupid. Ford had repeated that carefully to himself several times. Did that include walking up to the cottage and sneaking into Tara's bedroom to make her pant and moan his name as he buried himself deep inside her?

Cuz he'd totally do it.

If he wasn't half certain he'd drown himself getting off the boat. It took all of five seconds to drift off to sleep, only to wake some time later with his head pounding like a jackhammer. Dawn was streaking across the sky, and he was sprawled across the mattress.

With someone sitting at the foot of his bed.

Ford kept very still, eyes closed. "Make it count," he warned whoever it was.

"I can do that."

Craning his neck in surprise, he risked eyeballs popping out of his head to open his eyes.

His daughter was sitting there holding a steaming mug of coffee, which she offered to him.

"Bless you," he whispered in gratitude. With a groan, he rolled over, then managed to sit up to take it.

Mia waited until he sipped. "Alcohol is bad for you, you know," she said. "Kills brain cells. And sperm cells."

He sucked in a very hot gulp of coffee and promptly choked, burning his tongue.

"Sorry." Mia met his gaze, her own bright and intense. "It's just that I don't want to rule out the possibility of a brother or sister someday. You know, when you and Tara get it together and figure yourselves out."

Just looking at her made his heart hurt, this precious kid who—by some lucky twist of fate—he'd fathered. "Honey," he said carefully. "You do realize that things don't always happen all clean and pretty and neat like that in real life, right? Because Tara and I—"

"It could happen." She rose to her feet, eyes and mouth stubborn. He recognized the expression and knew he couldn't blame this one all on Tara.

"Oh, and FYI," she said, heading to the door. "Tara liked the flowers you delivered."

He blinked. "She...I—*What?*"

But Mia was gone.

Ford flopped back on the bed and closed his eyes. When he opened them again, the sun was a little higher in the sky, and there was a different woman sitting on his bed.

Tara let herself onto Ford's boat and made her way below deck. The boat was clean and fairly neat, if one discounted the empty pizza box on the counter and the pile of clothes on the floor by the bed.

Clearly Ford had stripped before climbing into it, which gave her a little shiver as she studied his big, very still body. He was sprawled facedown and spread-eagle across the mattress, wearing only a pair of black knit boxers and all that testosterone—which never failed to make her weak in the knees. His arms spanned the entire bed, as did his legs. And then there was the smooth, sinewy expanse of back and bitable ass...

Controlling herself, she sat at his side, watching as he began to stir. With a groan, he rolled to his back, his hands going to his head as if he needed to hold it onto his shoulders.

"Oh, Christ," he said, his voice all morning raspy. He cracked open one bleary eye, looking like a hot, adorable mess. "Shoot me in the head. I'm begging you."

"I've got something better." She lifted the basket of banana and honey nut muffins.

He closed his eyes and inhaled. "You smell like heaven."

"It's the food."

He didn't move a muscle. "Aren't you busy working?"

"Mia and Maddie are handling the inn for a few minutes. I thought maybe you might need me."

He was quiet for a long moment. "I've never been all that good at needing someone."

She nodded. She understood.

"But for you," he said. "I could try."

Her heart squeezed.

"But maybe later," he said, wincing and rubbing his head. "Because right now I'm busy dying. Do you think you could put down the anchor? The world's spinning."

Tara laughed softly and shifted closer, giving in to the urge to run her fingers over his forehead, smoothing back his hair, making him sigh in pleasure. "Why did you drink so much?" she murmured. "It's not like you."

He muttered something about trying to prove he could be Superman if he wanted to and how no one should dance on a bar while drunk because it was a long fall down.

She laughed again and went to pull away but he caught her hand and held it to his cheek. "You feel so nice and cool." He sighed, eyes still closed. "No idea how I got so lucky to get you both here this morning, but I'm grateful." Very carefully, he sat up and reached for the basket, but Tara held it back.

"Both?" she asked.

"Our daughter showed up with coffee." His arms were longer than hers so he managed to snatch a muffin. "As well as the news that I brought you flowers."

That was so unexpected—a part of her had secretly

hoped it'd been him—that she couldn't control her surprised reaction.

Ford's smile faded. "And," he said slowly, "you thought they were from me."

"No." She shook her head, then nodded. "Okay, maybe a little."

"Fuck." He grimaced and reached for her hand. "I'm sorry, Tara. But honestly, I was far too impaired for a gesture like that."

Tara shrugged. "It's okay. I mean they're not really your style anyway. I knew that. Now if it'd been pizza and beer on the porch..."

He arched a brow. "Are you saying I'm not romantic?"

"It's not your strong suit, no."

He bit into the muffin. "What is my strong suit?"

She thought about how he could make her purr with a single touch, have her writhing in three minutes flat if he put his mind to it, and blushed.

He smiled. "Come here."

"I don't think so."

"Don't trust me?"

"Don't trust *me*."

That made him chuckle, and he finished his muffin. "What are these again? They're amazing."

"They're honey banana, to calm the stomach. The honey also builds up sugar levels, and the bananas are rich in the important stuff: electrolytes, magnesium, and potassium, which you severely depleted with your alcohol intake." She opened the thermos and handed it to him. "And milk. To rehydrate."

"You always name your masterpieces. What are these muffins called?"

She squirmed a little. He knew her well, too well. She'd indeed named the muffins, but she didn't want to tell him. It was too embarrassing. Not to mention revealing.

"Come on," he coaxed.

She sucked in a breath and said it fast. "You'reMy HoneyBunMuffins."

A sole brow shot up. "One more time."

"You're My Honey Bun Muffins." She pointed at him. "And if you laugh, that's the end of our friendship. Or whatever this thing between us is."

Ford grinned. "Aw. I'm your honey bun."

"Stop it." She shoved a napkin at him. "And you're getting crumbs in the bed."

"Don't you mean, 'you're getting crumbs in the bed, *honey bun*'?"

"Okay, that's it. Give me back the muffins." Tara reached for them but Ford laughed and held them out of her reach, leaning back so that she fell on top of him.

Smooth, she thought, scrambling off his hard, warm, perfect body. He was pretty damn smooth as he proceeded to inhale three more muffins and down the milk while she watched. And so...male. Logan had always been a gym rat, his body toned from a rigorous routine of weights and cardio. Ford didn't do the whole gym thing. No, his body was honed to a mouthwatering tightness by running and sailing, and it worked for him.

It worked for her, too. "Are we going to talk about the phone messages?" she asked when he finally stopped eating, looking much better for it.

He winced. "I was really hoping that part of last night was a dream."

She laughed and shook her head. "Nope."

"Can we pretend it was?"

"So you don't want to be my sex slave?"

Ford's expression went hopeful as his gaze flew to hers, then turned crestfallen when she gave him an *are-you-kidding-me* look. "That's just mean, teasing a man when he's down."

"You're not down," Tara said. "You're never down."

"And here I thought you were so observant." He rolled off the bed.

"Where are you going?"

He dropped his boxers to the floor.

"You're naked!"

"Yes, that's usually how I like to shower," he said and walked the finest ass she'd ever seen right out of the bedroom.

Chapter 19

♥

*"If it's going to be two against one, make
sure you aren't the one."*
TARA DANIELS

Back at the inn, Tara cooked up a big breakfast. Then she made bread and put together a slow-cooking soup for later. After that, she cleaned the kitchen, opening the back door to sweep out the crumbs.

When she turned around, Logan was standing there, watching her, eyes bloodshot and red-rimmed with exhaustion.

"Wow," she said. "You look like crap."

His smile was grim. "You make a bedside visit to Ford with hangover muffins, and you tell me I look like crap. Where's the justice in that? And before you ask how I know, it's on Facebook. Lucille reported seeing you board his boat with the muffins. She tweeted it, too, and loaded a pic."

Tara stared at him. "She did not."

"Did."

Tara shook her head to clear it but that didn't help. Neither did the sneaking suspicion coming to her. "So what, you came here to hopefully get caught on camera as well?"

Guilt flashed across his pretty-boy face, but he accompanied it with a charming smile. "Didn't think it could hurt."

She glared at him, then realized that beneath that do-me smile was undeniable misery, and she felt her heart constrict. "Oh, Logan," she said softly, coming around the island to push him gently into a chair.

"Ah, shit," he said, staying where she'd put him. "The *nice* Tara. I'm getting dumped, right?"

"I already dumped you." She made him some green mint tea, his favorite. "And this isn't me being nice," she said, handing him a mug. "It's mercy. It'll help your headache, but what would help even more is not trying to drink other people under the table."

"I didn't try. I *succeeded*. And it wasn't just any other people. It was your boyfriend."

"Ford's not my boyfriend."

"Uh huh."

"Okay," Tara said. "I want you to try something new—*listening* to me for once." She sat in front of him and took his hand in hers. "I'm not looking for a husband. That's over."

"But I'm not done fighting for you."

"I'm not a prize, Logan."

His smile softened. "Yes, you are."

Aw. Dammit, he really had his moments. "I don't want to hurt you," she said, "but you need to know that everything I've told you before still stands. I'm not coming back to you, Logan. We're not going to make this work, you and me."

He looked at her for a long moment. "I'm not ready to concede yet, Tara."

"Logan—"

"Look, I'm enjoying this town. I've been making friends with people who don't bow down to me or want anything from me."

"What you're enjoying is the chase," she said. "And being talked about every day."

"Okay," he admitted. "That too."

Shaking her head, Tara rose. "Go home, Logan. Go back to your life."

"I've never quit anything, you know that." He rose too and snagged her hand, pulling her back around to face him. "And I'm not going to quit this. Not even for you."

He was looking at her just as she'd always dreamed he might, warm and soft and open, and all she could think was *too little, too late*. "Logan—"

"No." He set his finger over her lips. "God, not the pity. Smack me around, tell me I'm an ass, anything but the pity eyes." He paused. "I will, however, take a pity f—*oomph*," he said when she elbowed him in the gut. "Damn, woman."

"Go," she said. Relieved to feel suddenly guilt-free, she shoved him out of her kitchen.

The inn's first real guests arrived as scheduled. A middle-aged couple on a West Coast road trip from San Diego to Vancouver, stopping at a different B&B every night.

Maddie and Tara checked them in together, and Chloe gave them a gift basket full of her natural products. The wife fingered through the items, cooing at the bath salts, the herbal teas, the...

"Massage oil?" the woman asked, lifting the bottle. She had to slip her glasses on to read the label. "Edible strawberry massage oil," she said out loud. "Perfect for that special someone. Put it on your—Oh my."

Mia gaped.

Maddie covered Mia's eyes.

Tara looked at Chloe in horror.

Chloe laughed and reached for the oil. "Whoops, I was wondering where that went. Here, try this instead." And she quickly replaced the oil with body lotion.

"Oh," the woman said, sounding greatly disappointed. "Could I maybe have both?"

"Well, sure." Chloe handed back over the oil. "Enjoy."

The woman glanced at her husband and grinned. "We will."

When the couple was safely upstairs in their room, Maddie and Tara rounded on Chloe, who held up her hands in surrender. "Okay, that was my bad," she admitted.

"You think?" Tara asked.

Mia giggled. A real, honest-to-god genuine giggle, and then Maddie snorted. She slapped her hands over her mouth, but it was too late, and the sound of it sent Mia into a new fit of laughter. Chloe promptly lost the battle as well.

"It isn't funny," Tara protested. "They're going to be up there doing...things." But her daughter was still cracking up, and Tara felt the helpless smile tug at the corners of her own mouth at the sound of it, and the next thing she knew, they'd all slid down the wall to the floor, laughing like loons.

Together.

That night, with everyone tucked into bed all safe and sound, Tara sneaked out to sit on the marina docks. She was staring up at the night sky when she felt a tingle race down her spine. "Ford," she said quietly.

His long legs appeared at her side. Then he crouched down on the balls of his feet to meet her gaze. "The guests?"

"In and settled." She felt herself smile. "They like us, I think."

"There's not much not to like." He had two beers dangling from the fingers of one hand and a pizza box in the other. "It's not flowers," he said, handing her one of the beers.

Throat tight, she accepted it, their fingers brushing together. "I don't need flowers."

"Do you need pizza?"

No. The calories would warrant a damn run in the morning, and she hated to run. But there was this gorgeous man hunkered before her, looking like everything she could ever want. "Actually," she said. "I need pizza more than I need my next breath."

Ford sat next to her, and they ate in comfortable silence. When they were done, he picked up the bottles and the empty box and disposed of them inside the marina building. He came back and again sat close enough that their arms and thighs touched. Around them, the insects hummed. The water slapped up against the dock.

Comfort sounds. "It's a beautiful night," Tara said softly.

"Yes," he said, and she could feel him looking at her. He ran a finger over the strap of her lightweight, gauzy sundress, following the line over her collarbone.

Her nipples hardened. "You're not looking at the night," she pointed out.

"No." Ford kept his fingers on her, stroking lightly back and forth until her thighs pressed together. In her high-heeled sandals, her toes curled a little bit. His gaze toured her body, ending at said toes, and a small smile curved his mouth. He knew exactly what he did to her. "Heard about the massage oil incident," he said.

"Oh my god. Facebook?"

"Yeah. Look at it this way: people will be lining up to book a room now."

She groaned, and he laughed. "It's not that bad," he said. "And it's got to be better than having everyone think you're constipated."

"I was never constipated! And can you never bring that up again, please? *Ever?*"

He grinned, and something warm slid through all her good spots. She pointed at him. "Don't you look at me like that, like you want…" Like he wanted to eat her up. *Whole*.

His soft laugh scraped at her erogenous zones. "Want me to tell you?"

"No!"

From somewhere far off, maybe the pier, maybe Lucille's place down the road, came music. Something slow, melodic, achingly beautiful and just a little bit haunting.

Ford rose with the fluid grace that only the totally physically fit with good knees could accomplish and tugged Tara to her feet as well.

"What?" she asked, sucking in a breath when he pulled her in against him, gently rocking them to the music.

"Are we slow dancing?" she murmured as they moved together.

"Yeah. We're slow dancing."

And she'd accused him of not being romantic. He was warm up against her and strong. He had one big hand low on her back, nearly on her butt, leaving her with the urge to wriggle until his fingers slid lower.

"Keep squirming," he murmured in her ear, still moving them to the beat of the music, "and I'll tell you what I want."

"What do you want?" she asked, unable to stop herself.

He put his mouth to her ear and told her. In graphic detail.

And she promptly, and purposely, squirmed some more.

Ford laughed, then kissed her just beneath her ear. And then touched his tongue to the same spot. When she shivered, he did it again as his hand stroked up and down her back. It was soothing, and also arousing, as it was when he slid a hand down and cupped her. She moaned, and he let out a rough sound of his own at the feel of her. "I can't stop touching you. I think about it all damn day and all damn night, touching you, having you touch me back."

She felt herself completely melt in his arms. The music came to an end, and they stopped swaying. It seemed the most natural thing in the world to tilt her head up and meet him halfway for a kiss.

"Dammit," she said when he lifted his head.

"That's a new reaction to a kiss," he said.

"I mean this is…romantic." She gave him an annoyed look. "And you have some serious moves, too. Good ones."

"Yeah?" His eyes were dark. Intense. "Well then, here's some more." And he covered her mouth with his.

All thinking ceased. It was as if someone switched her brain to OFF, then opened the floodgates for desire. It hummed through her body, making her nerve endings twitch and tingle. A sound escaped her throat, horrifying in its neediness, but she didn't care. She simply pressed herself closer to him, desperately, hungrily seeking more.

More, more, more…

He pulled her in and turned her, pressing her back against a wood pylon, freeing up his hands for other things. Tara wrapped her arms around him, beneath his shirt and up the bare, sleek skin of his back, and then down to his butt.

Which she squeezed.

She couldn't help it. It was a very squeezable butt.

Ford ran his thumb across her nipple while his mouth did something decadent to her neck. She could feel him hard and ready, and she rubbed shamelessly against him, soaking up the feel of him, his scent. She opened her mouth to speak but he nibbled her bottom lip and then kissed her again, making her moan.

"Tell me this is leading back to one of our beds," he said a little hoarsely when they broke apart for air. "I don't care whose."

Everything inside her wanted to say *oh yes, please*. "And then what?" she asked, holding her breath.

"And then I'm going to get you naked, and make you a very, very happy woman. All night long."

That sounded good, but she knew herself well enough to know that by morning, she'd be left fighting the emotions that being with him like this brought. She'd be all that much closer to the point of no return, at least for her heart. Ford was an amazing guy, a good guy. Maybe even The Guy for her—but not just for a night. Or were they past that now? She'd lost their place, she wasn't sure, and more than that, she was afraid. Still so very afraid that this was out of her reach. "And then...?"

"And then all day long," he murmured against her skin, running his hands over her body. "And then all night long again."

Yes. Yes, she knew he could do just that. And she also knew he was missing what she was getting at. That maybe he was missing it on purpose. "Ford, wait."

He didn't. He was, in fact, very busy trailing wet, open-mouthed kisses along her throat, silencing any protest she might have made.

And for a minute, she let him. She couldn't help it. He kissed like heaven on earth, and before she knew it *she* was kissing him. When they were breathless, he cupped her face in his hands, letting his lips brush her temple, her jaw. Then he dipped his tongue into the hollow at the base of her throat, and she felt a shiver wrack her entire body. Her fingers were in his hair now, and she couldn't let go. "Ford? And then what?"

He lifted his head. There was no mistaking the hunger and desire on his beautiful face, or the confusion as he gave one short shake of his head. "What is it?" he asked. "What do you want to hear? Tell me."

No. She didn't want to have to do that. "Never mind. Just quick, kiss me and shut me up."

He did without question, and this time she had to lock her knees. Because it was too late to protect herself, far too late to worry about if she deserved to fall for him because she already had.

Again.

Oh, God. Just the thought left her wobbly. This was going to require a lot of obsessing, and maybe some more chips. Certainly a bottle of wine, and in all likelihood her sisters as well. Not for their wisdom, but to smack her upside the head for even secretly yearning for this.

For him.

For keeps.

"I'm sorry. I have to go," she whispered, still plastered to him like a second skin.

"What?"

She grimaced at herself for being a coward. "Early morning."

Something in her voice must have alerted him to the impending meltdown because he let her pull away, not stopping her when she straightened her dress, or when she left him on the dock.

He let her go without a word; without asking anything of her.

And wasn't that the entire problem in a nutshell? *He let her go.*

He always let her go.

Chapter 20

♥

"Remember, you're unique. And so is everyone else."
TARA DANIELS

The next morning, their guests left before dawn. The woman assured Tara that everything had been great, and then asked for a sample of the oil to go.

Tara put Mia to work sweeping the wood floors, which seemed to gather dust faster than a fat dog could gather fleas. "Careful not to stir it all up into the air," Tara told her. "It irritates Chloe's throat, and she'll need to use her inhaler."

"It's sweet that you worry about her," Mia said.

Tara laughed. She, Chloe, and Maddie were just about anything *but* sweet. No, scratch that, because Maddie was sweet. Tara and Chloe? Not so much.

Mia disappeared upstairs to sweep the hallway, and Tara met with Maddie in the marina office to go over paperwork. Chloe was allergic to paperwork more than dust, so she was outside in the sun, on a yoga mat in the downward-facing-dog position. By the time Tara returned to the inn Mia was nowhere to be seen, although her broom was leaning against a wall in the upstairs hallway.

"Shh!" This came from behind the bathroom door. "She'll hear."

Mia's voice, followed by Carlos's soft laugh, and a second more emphatic "*Shh*" from Mia.

Dammit. Dammit, Tara thought. They were in there messing around. Now see, *this* was why animals ate their young. Ready to rumble, she whipped open the door and blinked.

Her daughter and Carlos sat on the countertop, separated by the sink. Mia had a laptop on her thighs, the screen facing Carlos, who was cracking up. At the sight of her, he sobered and got to his feet. "Ms. Daniels."

Weak with relief that they weren't having sex, Tara leaned back against the door, then realized they were staring at her. "You're not working," she said.

"Well, not *exactly*," Mia said. "But it is about the inn." She turned the laptop in Tara's direction.

"Mia—" Carlos tried to block the view. "Not a good idea—"

"She's going to find out sooner or later, and it might as well be from us." Mia revealed the screen. Facebook, of course, the bane of Tara's existence. She'd been forewarned by Logan, but it was another thing entirely to see it herself.

The picture was grainy and blurry, probably from a cell phone, but it was clear enough. Tara, climbing onto Ford's boat with her basket of muffins, followed by the line:

A secret rendezvous between a certain sexy sailing champion and a very beautiful innkeeper. Guess a certain poll is null and void.

There was another pic of Ford and Tara standing on the marina dock. The shot was incredibly revealing and intimate, Ford trapping Tara against a pylon, his mouth devouring hers. Tara's hands were fisted in his shirt, and he had one hand tangled in her hair, the other tightly wrapped around her back.

Guess this leaves superstar NASCAR driver Logan Perrish out in the cold. No worries, Logan, we're running a new poll starting today. Log in and give us choices for The Bachelor, Lucky Harbor Style. Single ladies, sign up to date sexy Logan now!

Tara stared at the screen in horror. "Did you—"

"No," Mia said quickly. "I didn't take either pic. Neither of us did. You have a spy. I was about to post a comment that people need to mind their own stinking business and leave you to yours."

Tara smiled grimly. "You don't know the locals here very well yet. Minding their own business isn't a strong suit."

Carlos turned to the door. "I should go. I got something to do…"

When he'd vanished, Tara raised a brow at Mia, who shrugged. "He's the tough guy at his school. But you scare him."

"I've never scared him."

"You do. He's worried you're going to kill him."

Tara paused. "Has he given me a reason to kill him?"

"It's more that he thinks you can read minds, and that you'll kill him for what's on his. Boys are kind of obvious that way, you know?"

Yes, Tara knew. She just didn't like that Mia knew.

"You won't kill him, right?" Mia asked.

Tara sighed. "Do you like him that much?"

"Yes. I love him," her daughter said without hesitation.

"Love? Mia, it's only been—"

"I know what I feel," her daughter said with the conviction of a seventeen-year-old. She shut the laptop and leaned back against the counter. "Remember when you said you'd answer any question I might have? Does that still stand?"

Oh boy. "Ask," Tara said bravely.

"I've been wondering why you lost contact with Ford after you had me. You two loved each other, and yet by all accounts, you just walked away."

Tara drew in a long breath. "I went back home. To Texas. It's pretty far from Lucky Harbor."

"Yes, but there are phones. Computers. The U.S. mail service. And your mom lived here."

"Phoebe didn't live here, not yet. She was only visiting that summer, and . . . and well, Ford and I had only met that summer, and we each had our lives." Lame excuses. And Mia deserved better. "Part of it was that I wasn't nearly as mature as you."

"You didn't want to keep in contact?" Mia asked. "You didn't like him anymore?"

"Mia, it wasn't that simple, and we were just kids."

"You could have come back here instead of going to Texas."

"No, because Phoebe didn't stick here, either. But even if she had, I wasn't used to living in a small town. It was different."

"Good different?"

No. Tara had felt claustrophobic and smothered, but she didn't want to say that. "I was used to more. And I wanted to go to school in Texas, to Texas A&M."

"A big college," Mia murmured.

"Yes, and..." Tara trailed off, at a loss on how to make it sound logical when the truth was it hadn't been logical at all. Her reactions had been of sheer emotion. "Honestly, I was just trying to keep it together, and not doing all that great a job." Tara took Mia's hand. "But I'd like to think I've done a lot of growing up since then. If I could go back now, I'd—"

What?

What would she do differently? She wasn't sure.

"You can't go back," Mia said quietly. "Even I know that much. You can't ever go back."

Wasn't that the truth.

With a sigh, Mia turned to the door. Tara followed, just happening to glance down at the trash can.

At the empty condom wrapper right on top.

She stared at it, then slowly looked up at Mia. Who was also looking at the empty condom wrapper, chewing on her lower lip and looking guilty as hell.

"Maddie's," Tara said hopefully.

Mia gnawed on her lip some more and slowly shook her head. "No. Not Maddie's."

"But you said you weren't having sex," Tara said with what she felt was remarkable calm.

"No, I said I wasn't having *unprotected* sex."

"God." Tara pressed her fingers to her eyes. "Mia..."

"Do you want me to go?"

"No! I want..." She dropped her hands from her face and met Mia's shuttered gaze. "I want you to be able to tell me the truth."

"Really? You wanted me to tell you I *was* having sex with Carlos?" Mia asked with disbelief, winding up to a defensive stance.

"Yes!"

Mia shook her head. "Did you tell your parents when you were having sex with Ford?"

Tara staggered back and leaned against the counter. No. No, she hadn't told anyone what she'd shared with Ford. It'd been for them alone. "I'm failing you," she whispered. "This is all my fault, somehow."

Mia sighed. "No, it's not. It has nothing to do with you. And you're acting like I'm too young or something."

"You *are* too young."

"Because you weren't doing the exact same thing when you were my age?"

Tara opened her mouth, then shut it, at a complete loss. "Mia, having sex is a huge emotional commitment, and I don't think *any* seventeen-year-old can possibly be ready for it."

"Yes, well, I need to make my own mistakes," Mia said. "Not yours. Mine. And for this to work, you're going to have to let me."

"Mia—"

But she was gone.

Tara needed a sister bad. Chloe was off God knew where doing God knew what, but Tara found Maddie at

Jax's house on the bluff. They sat outside on his deck, and while he barbecued, Tara filled Maddie in on how she'd screwed up with Mia. "*Epic* failure," she said as Maddie poured them both wine. "And the worst part of all is that I practically hand-delivered Carlos right into her lap. I de-virginized my own daughter!"

"You don't know that Carlos was her first."

Tara went still as she absorbed that, then groaned and covered her eyes. "Okay, not helping."

"Look," Maddie said finally. "Seventeen is nothing but one big pleasure button, from head to toe. You know that. And Mia and Carlos care deeply for each other. You know that too. At least she's with someone who thinks the sun rises and sets on her. He'll make it good for her, Tara."

Tara groaned again.

"What, you'd rather she be with someone who doesn't care about her needs?"

"I'd rather she be with no one at all!" Tara said. "At least not until she's thirty-five, or I'm dead. Whichever comes last. And can we not talk about her having sex?" She winced. "Let's concentrate on getting her to like me."

"She does." Maddie sipped from her glass, her gaze slipping to Jax where he stood at the grill about twenty feet away, turning over the chicken. "Remember how you felt when I wanted you and Chloe to stay with me here in Lucky Harbor, and all you wanted to do was run like hell?"

"Yes." It'd been a tough time for all of them, facing the rush of fresh memories from simply setting foot inside Lucky Harbor. But Maddie had been searching for a place to belong, and at the inn, she'd found it. With Jax, she'd found it. Tara had been thrilled for her sister.

And resigned to sticking around longer than she'd wanted in order to protect their investment—the inn— and to make sure her sisters were okay. Tara had stuck until it hadn't been an obligation. Until it'd somehow become natural to live here.

"Chloe and I won you over with our charm, and that charm is hereditary," Maddie said on a smile. "You'll charm Mia too, you'll see."

"I gave her up at birth," Tara said. "I let someone else raise her. I don't think charm can help me with her."

"You had valid reasons," Maddie reminded her gently. "And Mia knows that. Honey, she came looking for you. Give her some time to put it all together and understand. It's time to stop grieving over what you lost out on and live for the now."

Jax came up behind Maddie and set down a plate of grilled veggies that looked mouthwatering. He squeezed Maddie's shoulder, then leaned in for a quick nuzzle and kiss. "Okay?" he asked.

Just looking at the two of them together had Tara's heart sighing. They were so meant for each other. That they were together was because Maddie had done what she'd just told Tara—she'd taken her *now*.

"We're good," Maddie told Jax. He smiled at her, stole a long swallow of her wine, sneaked another kiss, and ambled back to man his station at the barbecue. Maddie watched him go with a dreamy sigh on her lips. "I love his ass," she said.

Tara laughed out loud, causing Jax to turn and eye them curiously. Maddie waved at him, and Tara murmured, "You'd better snag him up, Mad. Because a good ass is *muy importante*."

Maddie grinned broadly as she blew Jax a kiss. "There's other reasons I want to marry him too, you know."

Tara lifted a brow. "Listen to you, saying the *M* word so freely now."

"He's the one," Maddie said simply. "The only one."

Tara nodded and sipped her wine, and envied the conviction that was all over Maddie's face.

The next morning Ford took Mia out for a long sail. He'd discovered that his daughter liked early mornings, as he did, so they left just before the crack of dawn and caught the sunrise. He taught her how to motor away from the marina and then point the bow into the wind, how to work the mainsail with the halyard and crank it around the winch when she needed to, in order to get it hoisted. He had her unfurl and furl the jib and pull it out with the sheets, and now she stood in the cockpit, hands on the wheel, the sail billowing in front of her, the wind whipping her hair from her face, looking happy and carefree.

Just watching her reminded Ford of a young Tara and warmed a place inside him that he hadn't even realized was cold.

She caught his eye. "What?"

Smiling, he shook his head. "I'm just sitting here thinking how glad I am that you came looking for answers."

"I don't have them all yet," she said.

He loved her bluntness and hoped growing up didn't beat that out of her. "All you have to do is ask."

Mia steered into the wind like a pro, her face thoughtful. Then she suddenly ducked as they hit a swell. The spray hit Ford right in the face, making her laugh out loud, a beautiful sound.

"You're a quick learner," he said, swiping his face with his shirt. "Jax still can't pull that off."

She grinned with pride. "Tara said you were the best of the best."

"She did?"

"Yeah." She nudged him with her shoulder. "She likes you."

Ford laughed, but Mia didn't. She just looked at him earnestly. "I have a couple of questions now," she said.

"Okay. Shoot."

"The first one might seem intrusive."

"Ask."

"Do I have any genetic diseases to look forward to?"

"No. Well, unless you count orneriness," he said. "My grandma's ninety and ornery as hell." He smiled thinking about her. He'd have to fly her up before the summer was over so she could meet Mia. "She'll love you, though. What else?"

"Are you afraid of anything?"

"No."

She rolled her eyes. "That's a typical boy answer. Everyone's afraid of *something*. Spiders? Snakes? Heights?"

"Actually," he said, "frogs."

She stared at him. "Shut up."

"No, it's true, and it's all Sawyer's fault. We were ten. We'd told his dad we were staying at my place, and my grandma that we were staying at his, and then we went camping."

"By yourselves?"

"Yeah. That night he loaded my sleeping bag with frogs. When I got in, they crawled all over me. Slimy suckers." He shuddered. "To this day I can't stand them."

She was smiling, but then her smile faded, and she studied him in that careful way that she'd inherited from Tara. "Are you really not afraid of *anything* else?"

He felt his own amusement drain as well. She was being serious, and she deserved for him to be as well. "Actually, there is one thing."

Her gaze searched his. "What?"

"I was afraid I'd never get to meet you."

Her eyes shone brilliantly, those beautiful, heart-breaking eyes. "Lucky for you I found you then," she whispered.

"Lucky for me," he repeated softly.

Since Mia was scheduled to work at noon, eventually they headed back to the marina. Ford had her reverse their original process with the mainsail and jib, then motor back into the marina and dock. He stood over her as she tied up, but she had no problems, and pride burst from his chest. She was a natural.

Tara came out of the marina office, a few files in her hands. When she saw the two of them standing on the dock, she stopped short.

She looked tired and stressed, and Ford knew she had good reason. She'd been working at the inn and the diner, and working two jobs was stressful for anybody. And here he stood with Mia, the two of them clearly back from a sail, looking carefree, like they didn't have a responsibility in the world.

For years, Ford had purposely cultivated that perception. After the way he'd grown up, he liked living low-key and easygoing. No stresses, no worries. He enjoyed not caring too much about anything. You could care about whatever you wanted: your family, your next meal, whatever, and it didn't amount to squat if you didn't have the means to obtain it.

He realized that having a daughter in his life should have been a threat to that lifestyle, or at the very least disturbed him. But it didn't. And he also didn't feel the same terror that he knew Tara felt about getting involved in Mia's life. In fact, he relished it, because here was a kid who needed them. In return, he needed her, too.

They belonged to each other by blood. No one could take that away.

"Nice day for a sail," Tara said.

Mia grinned as she hopped off the boat. "Yep. You two should go out."

"Oh," Tara said, backing up a step. "I can't. We're really busy, and—"

"Chloe and Maddie are at the inn, right?" Mia asked, giving Ford a sly look.

Oh shit, Ford thought, Look at her go.

"And I'm betting you already have dinner on," Mia said to Tara. "Yeah?"

"Berry Sweet Turkey and Cranberry Quiche," Tara admitted.

"See?" Mia nudged Tara toward the boat, giving Ford go-for-it eyes over Tara's shoulder.

His daughter, the smart, beautiful master schemer.

"Everything's handled," she was saying to Tara, "so go, and I don't want to see you back here for at *least* an hour, young lady. You hear me?"

Ford had to bite back his smile. Oh, yeah. They

were being horribly manipulated by a girl half their age. "Come on," he said to Tara, taking her hand. "Let's do this. Let's go for a quick sail."

"But you just went."

"I could go all day long. And besides, like Mia said, it's perfect out there. An hour, Tara. Let's take an hour."

"I have things to do."

"You always do." He slowly but firmly reeled her in. "Chicken?" he asked softly, pressing his mouth to her ear.

"Of course not."

"One hour," he repeated, then propelled her on board with an arm around her waist.

Mia was beaming. "Gotta run," she said and ran like hell up to the inn.

Tara craned her neck to watch her go. "That girl's going to make a great lawyer."

"No doubt."

Tara turned back and met Ford's gaze, hers troubled. "I'm worried that we're leading her on, setting her up for disappointment."

"You need to stop worrying about things you can't control. In fact, stop thinking altogether. For the next hour, your only job is to live in the moment. In the moment of a gorgeous day and..." He smiled. "Not such bad company."

She hesitated, and he gently tugged on a strand of her hair. "What's the matter? Still don't trust yourself with me?"

When she winced, telling him that was exactly what it was, he laughed. "An hour, Tara. That's all. How much trouble can we get into in one hour?"

She gave him a look of blatant disbelief. "Are you kidding me?"

Ford smiled the most innocent smile in his repertoire. She didn't buy it, but she nodded. "Okay," she said, poking him in the chest. "But no monkey business."

"Define monkey business."

"No nakedness."

"Well, damn," he said. "There goes the striptease I had planned." He gestured for her to step ahead of him into the cockpit, but she hesitated and gave him a speculative once-over.

"Are you good at it?" she asked.

"Sailing?"

"No." She laughed. A glorious sound. "*Stripping*."

He felt his grin split his face. "Actually, I'm a master."

She waggled a brow, and he laughed. "Tara Daniels, are you flirting with me?"

"No!" She turned and busied herself with the halyard. "Ignore me."

"Now there's one thing I've never mastered."

Chapter 21

♥

*"You've grown up if you have learned
to laugh—at yourself."*
TARA DANIELS

Ten minutes later, Ford had them flying across the swells. The sun was at their backs, the wind in their faces, and Tara couldn't have held back her grin if she tried.

"Mmm," Ford said. "Love that look on you." He pulled her in between the steering wheel and his big body, easily holding her steady.

She cuddled up to him. "Okay, but remember, *no* monkey business," she said. "Just sailing."

"Just sailing." His hands urged hers to the wheel, freeing his up to go to her hips as he rubbed his jaw to hers, then kissed her neck. "It's good to see you smiling. And I'm seeing it more and more. I'm thinking Lucky Harbor agrees with you."

Tara was afraid that was true.

"Admit it," he said, running his hands up and down her body, just barely grazing the sides of her breasts.

She ached for more. "Admit what?" she asked faintly.

"That you're right where you want to be." He slowed them down and turned her to face him. "Here in Lucky Harbor."

"I stayed because my sisters needed me," she said. "The inn needed me."

"Maybe, but we both know that neither of those things would have held you here in the past."

Meaning, of course, that in the past, she'd considered only her own needs. Tara absorbed the truth of that for a moment and let out a breath. She could leave it or she could be honest. "I wanted to stay," she admitted.

Ford pulled off her sunglasses. His eyes were intense, and she imagined hers were the same. "Why?" he asked.

Again she could leave it, or give him the truth. "Because my life had fallen apart, and I really had nothing to go back to."

"And?"

"And..." Dammit. "Because I like being a part of a unit. I *like* being with my sisters, even when we fight."

A very small smile played at the corners of his mouth. "And?"

She stared at him, feeling a little...exposed. "Isn't this getting a little deep for you?"

"Deep?"

"Yes. Drawing me out, asking all of life's burning questions. Not your usual M.O. when we're alone like this."

Ford looked into her face for what felt like a very long time, not saying anything. "I need you to do something for me," he finally said.

She shook her head. "Oh, no. I already told you, no monkey business."

She expected a smile at that, but instead there was a spark of very rare temper in his eyes. "Don't paint all men with the same brush as your ex-husband or your father," he said.

"They're both good men," she reminded him.

"Yes, but also by the very nature of their lives, selfish, even neglectful."

"It was their jobs," she said, defending them. "They both traveled and were gone all the time because of their jobs."

"It's about choices. I'm different, Tara. And you need to remember that. Maybe even take a chance on it sometime. A real chance."

Her heart was suddenly in her throat. "We've tried that."

"We should try again."

Oh, God. She wanted to. "You wouldn't know what hit you," she whispered.

The corners of his mouth curved slightly. "I never do when it comes to you."

"I need to be getting back."

"It's been fifteen minutes. You owe me forty-five more. I'd think after working as hard as you have, you'd enjoy this."

She watched as he adjusted their direction slightly so they glided easily through the swells. "I'm used to hard work."

"And not so used to fun," he said.

"No." Tara eyed the horizon, clear and wide open. Gorgeous. "But you're right, I am enjoying this. It'll fill my fun quota for the whole week."

Ford slid an arm around her and pulled her in close,

brushing his mouth to her temple. "I bet we could come up with something even better for you."

"Like old times?"

"If you like."

She tipped up her head and met his gaze, seeing both the heat and the teasing there, and felt her stomach quiver. "I'm not that same girl," she warned him. "The one who used to live her days just to be with you and have fun every night."

"I know. You grew up. Became a smart, amazing woman. But you're still just going through the motions, not allowing for enough fun."

"*No* monkey business," she reminded him, her voice far too unsteady to convince herself, much less him, dammit.

Ford just smiled. "What if you're the one to start it?"

"I won't be," she said with far more confidence than she felt.

He was still looking amused, and she couldn't blame him. She had a history of being very weak where he was concerned. Very weak. And then there was watching him handle the boat, looking quite in charge and at ease as he did so. He stood legs apart, braced for the wind whipping at him. The sun gilded his tanned skin, reflected off his sunglasses. He wore a USA T-shirt and navy blue board shorts just past his knees, which clung to his every line and muscle as he moved with such innate grace that it was hard to believe that he was so big.

"Sheet it in?" he asked.

She was proud to be able to lean over and pull the sail in tight. She was halfway there when a swell hit and leveled her with a wall of water, leaving her dripping from hair to toes and gasping for breath.

Ford grinned. "You're supposed to duck."

Tara narrowed her eyes. "Do you have any idea how long it took me this morning to have a good hair day?" She squeezed the water from it, but it was too late. The frizzies were upon her, she could tell. "I mean *you* get to wash, shake, and go, and come out perfect while you're at it. But look at me."

They both looked at her. Her blouse was thin and wet, and working like a second skin now. Ford had been smiling during her little tirade, complete with hand waving. The corners of his mouth had twitched into the promise of an amused smile, but that was replaced by something darker and hungrier now as he set the controls and stalked toward her.

"Oh, no you don't." She backed up a step and pointed at him. "You stay right there. Or—"

Ford kept coming. "Or what?"

"Things'll happen," she said, slapping a hand to his chest. "Naked things. Really great naked things, but *no*." She shook her head. *Be strong.* "I've gotten it out of my system, Ford. I mean it."

He reached for her. She tried to step back but she had nowhere to go. "Okay, well, maybe not *all* the way out of my system," she admitted, "But we have this little chemistry problem—it's not anyone's fault. We just have to stay strong. *Ford!*" she gasped when he caught her up against his warm, hard body.

His rich laugh washed over her and felt like a touch, a kiss. "Stop," she said weakly. "You're getting me all worked up."

He dipped his head and rubbed his jaw to hers. "I love it when you get all worked up. Your eyes flash, and you say what you're really thinking."

"You're all wet now. You realize that?"

"Mmm, I think that's you." He rocked his body to hers. "Tell me just how wet you are. Slowly. In great detail."

"You're impossible."

"Incorrigible, too," he said. "And like you said, wet. Maybe I should strip."

Oh, yes. "*No!*" But she slid her arms around his neck. "What is it with you and stripping?" She snuggled into him. Lord, she was so damn weak. "How much time is left?"

He tossed his head back and laughed. "Thirty minutes."

She blew out a breath. "Probably I only need ten to fifteen."

He was still grinning. "Is this you starting it?"

She looked into his eyes. God, she missed this. The fun. The teasing. The laughing. Talking...

Him. "If I say yes, are you going to hold it against me?"

"Yes," Ford assured her. "I'm going to hold *it* against you for every single one of those minutes we have left." He dropped anchor and pulled her below deck, nudging her along toward his bed.

As if Tara needed nudging. She was practically running. She hit the mattress and rolled to her back, watching as Ford slowly peeled his wet shirt over his head. He untied his board shorts and let them slide off his hips to join the shirt on the floor.

She heard herself moan as she took him in, one glorious inch at a time, and there were a *lot* of glorious inches.

"I love your uptight, prissy clothes." That said, he stripped her right out of them until she was in just her peach lace bikini panties. He dropped to his knees beside the mattress and shot her a bad-boy smile. He gripped her ankles in each hand and leaned in to kiss her calf before slowly working his way up.

She was writhing by the time he got to her inner thighs.

He hooked his thumbs in the lace at her hips and slid it down her legs, stroking a thumb over what he'd revealed. "Pretty," he said silkily, then lowered his head and worked his usual magic. And, as it turned out, she didn't need fifteen minutes. She only needed five.

"In me," Tara demanded when she could breathe again. She sat up, trying to pull him over her.

But he wouldn't be budged.

Or rushed.

"Shh," he said, not sinking into her. Dammit. Instead, he put a hand to her chest and pushed her back down on the bed. Before she could work up her temper over that, his tongue had stroked her wet flesh again. "Ohmigod," she whispered. Her hands were fisted in his hair, and she didn't care. She thought about tugging him up to be face-to-face with her but he was doing something so amazing with that talented mouth that she held him to her, dying. "I need. God, Ford, I need..."

"Anything," he promised her, but he didn't mean it, the evil, *evil* man, because he was holding her right on the very edge, giving her everything then pulling back, teasing her until she was a panting, begging, squirming wreck, all but screaming his name.

"Ford, dammit!"

That didn't work.

"I don't get mad. I get even," she warned, and whether it was the implied threat or a decision to have mercy on her, Ford gave in. She came again long and hard and was barely back to planet Earth when he grabbed a condom from a drawer by the bed. In a blink, he was covered and sliding home, filling her completely.

"Jesus," he said, his voice low and raw, head bowed close to hers. "Every time. You slay me every fucking time." He pushed inside her again, and then again, making her clutch at him and cry out.

He went still. "Too much?"

"Just right." She dug her fingers into his butt. "And if you don't start moving, I'm going to hurt you, I swear it."

Laughing softly under his strained breath, he kissed her. He slipped an arm beneath her back to better angle her, but she was done letting him be in charge. Done letting him drag out all these raw, earthy, terrifying emotions. It was *her* turn to run the show, and silently thanking Chloe for all the yoga classes that had strengthened her core, she rolled over to claim the top.

He groaned as she straddled his hips, keeping him sheathed inside. And then groaned again when she started a grind that had her eyes drifting shut from the sheer pleasure of the friction.

"Tara, God. God, that's good."

So damn good.

She laced her fingers through his and pulled his arms above his head. Time for some of his own medicine. Leaning over him, she traced his bottom lip with her tongue.

"Mmm," he said, and took immediate control of the kiss, mating his tongue with hers, torturing her with every stroke.

She retaliated by rotating her hips, taking him deeper, and was rewarded when he breathed her name raggedly.

She met each of his movements with a thrust of her own, until it became a struggle to remain in control. She could feel the flutter low in her gut, feel the heat starting at her toes and working its way north.

Definitely losing it...

As if he knew her body better than she did, Ford slipped his hands out of hers and grabbed her hips, forcing a rhythm that made both of them quiver. Startled at the rawness, the utter rightness, she lifted her head and stared at him.

He met her gaze. In fact, he never looked away as they rode each other to climax. She burst first, falling forward onto his chest, panting for air as he followed her over.

"Good Christ," he muttered sometime later. His eyes were closed as he caught his breath, his entire body relaxed except for the hand he had clamped possessively on her ass. "We're going to kill each other."

A distinct possibility.

She buried her face against his neck. "Okay, now I really have to go," she said, but didn't move. Couldn't.

He pressed his mouth to her temple. "We do have a few minutes left..." His fingers dipped between her thighs.

Her entire body quivered, but she shook her head.

With a sigh, he sat up, lightly smacking her butt as he rolled off the bed and strolled casually to the tiny bathroom.

She found herself just sitting there watching him. Finally she shook herself and stood up, wrapping the sheet around her. Her clothes were scattered across the place.

"What's with the modesty now?"

She turned in time to watch him walk—bare ass

nekked—across the room toward her. "I'm...cold," she said and made him laugh softly.

"Tara, I've seen every inch of you. Hell, I've kissed every inch of you. You don't need to hide it."

"Yes, but it's *really* light out."

He grinned and tugged the sheet from her. "I like it that way."

She fought to stay covered. "Well of course you do; you're perfect."

His eyes softened as he won the battle and tossed the sheet behind him. "So are you."

Chapter 22

♥

*"Death is hereditary. Make sure you enjoy
each day before it catches you."*
Tara Daniels

Tara was walking up from the marina just as Chloe
pulled in on her Vespa. "Look at you," Chloe said, pulling
off her helmet. "Glowing again."

Tara ignored that as she opened the door to the cottage, then promptly froze.

Maddie was sitting on their small couch in the living
room, staring open-mouthed at Jax, tears running down
her cheeks.

Jax was on his knees at her side, holding her hand.

"Oh, God," Tara said, hand to her chest. "What's happened, what's wrong?"

Chloe came up beside Tara, took in the sight, and
immediately slid her hand into Tara's. Tara squeezed
it reassuringly, even as her heart landed in her stomach. Not a single one of them was up for another
crisis.

Jax dropped his forehead to Maddie's knee. His shoulders were shaking, and Tara stopped breathing.

"Tell us," Chloe whispered, gripping Tara's fingers hard enough to crack them. "Maybe we can help—"

Jax made a sound. Not of sorrow, Tara noted, and narrowed her eyes.

He was laughing.

When he lifted his face and met Maddie's gaze, his own softened, and he stroked her cheek, wiping away her tears. "I should have known we'd do this by committee. Should we consult the Magic Eight app or take a vote?"

Maddie laughed through her tears. "Oh, no, it's too late for that—I already said yes." She lifted her hand.

Which was weighted down by a sparkling diamond.

"Oh!" Chloe cried and jumped up and down. "I vote yes too, and that's majority. Majority rules!"

"Like I would have voted no," Tara said as she and Chloe stepped forward to hug Maddie. "Sorry we interrupted."

"Actually," Maddie said. "We were done with the proposal. We were just going to..." She blushed. "Negotiate some terms."

"For?"

Maddie and Jax smiled at each other, and their looks were so heated that Tara felt like her eyebrows went up in smoke.

"Aw." Chloe grinned. "You were totally going to do it, right there on the couch." She grabbed Tara and dragged her back to the front door. "Just pretend we never showed up. Carry on."

"We can't now," Maddie said, laughing. "You'll know."

"Yes," Chloe said. "And also, we're never going to sit on that couch again, but don't let that stop you, Ms. Attack-Her-Boyfriend-in-the-Attic."

"Hey," Maddie said, still beet red. "What about Tara in the pantry with her two men?"

Tara sighed. "*Not* a true story," she said to an avidly listening Jax. "Logan and I haven't been together like that in over two years."

Chloe grinned at Maddie. "Notice she didn't deny having Ford 'like that.' She's totally doing him. I mean look at her. Hello, she's *still* glowing. Sex is so great for the skin. Wish I could come up with a skincare formula that gives that same glow. I'd make bank."

Maddie studied Tara's face and grinned, too. "Oh yeah, she's *definitely* doing Ford."

Jax looked pained. "Okay, you've *got* to stop saying that. Bad visual."

Maddie laughed and hugged him close. "Here, baby, let me give you another one to replace it with." She whispered something in his ear and then gently but firmly kicked her sisters out of the cottage, locking the door behind them.

That afternoon, Ford was behind the bar finishing up his monthly inventory. Jax usually helped, but he didn't show up until after it was finished. "Thanks for the help," Ford grumbled, then took in the wide, goofy-ass grin on Jax's face. "What?"

"You'll see," Jax said cryptically, and vanished into the back to do some paperwork.

The place was filling up when Maddie came in wearing a goofy grin that matched Jax's.

"Only one man I know who can put that smile on your face," Ford said.

Maddie laughed, something that had once upon a time been very rare. "Or potato chips."

Ford grinned at her. "What'll it be, Beautiful?"

"Oh, I don't know..." She set her hand down on the bar and nearly blinded him with a diamond.

"Jesus, you need sunglasses to look at that thing." And although he'd already seen the ring—Jax had shown him yesterday—Ford hugged her tight, then lifted her hand and smiled. "Hard to say no to a ring like that."

"Maybe it's just plain hard to say no to me." Jax came in from the back carrying a tray of clean glasses. He took one look at Maddie flashing the ring and smiled from ear to ear. He set down the glasses and hopped over the bar to yank her into his arms. "Hey, wife."

"Not yet, I'm not," she said, laughing as she shifted into him. "You have to get me down the aisle first."

"It's going to happen." Jax lowered his lips to her ear, whispered something that made her blush, then kissed her.

And kissed her.

"Get a room," Ford said and nudged them out of his way, their mouths still fused.

They vanished a few minutes later, and Ford figured that he'd be lucky if Jax surfaced sometime tomorrow. It wasn't a problem; neither he nor Jax was scheduled to actually tend bar tonight. But since Sawyer had a date too, Ford was left on his own with no plans ahead of him. In the old days, he'd have found himself some trouble.

Or a woman.

Neither appealed. So he got in his car and drove, and

found himself at the inn. Carlos was in the yard, hosing out a big pot burned black.

"What happened?" Ford asked.

"Tara burnt the stew."

This was so odd that it took a moment to process. "She did?"

"Earlier. She said she was distracted. And now she's added pissed to the list." Carlos looked around to make sure they were alone. "If you don't have to go in there, maybe you shouldn't. No offense, but you tend to make things worse."

Ford had a feeling he'd already made it worse, that maybe she'd burned the stew when they'd been out on the water. "Does she need dinner for the guests? I can go pick something up."

"No, she's whipping up some fancy burgers right now. She's putting some really stinky cheese and seasonings in with the meat and calling them gourmet. She told me if I wrinkled my nose one more time she was going to rearrange it for me." Carlos let out a rare smile because, as they both knew, Tara could barely reach his nose. "Mia's helping her."

When the kid said Mia's name, a special quality came into his voice that Ford recognized all too well. Carlos was completely and helplessly wrapped around his daughter's pinkie.

They walked into the kitchen together, smelling the burned stew before they crossed the threshold. There was a fan going, and two candles, but they weren't helping yet. The room itself looked like an explosion in *Hell's Kitchen*. The counters were cluttered with cooking utensils and ingredients, and a temperamental Tara stood at the stove, spatula in hand. When she caught sight of Ford, her eyes narrowed and her grip on the spatula tightened as if she was fighting the urge to smack him with it. "You," she said.

"Me," he agreed lightly. A few hours ago, she'd been naked and panting his name. Now she was back to the Steel Magnolia.

"Sugar," Tara said in a voice that was pure Pissed-Off South. "You need to go far, far away."

A few weeks ago, he'd have taken that to mean she didn't want to see his face within a six-hundred-mile radius. Now he knew the truth. He distracted her. He could live with that. "Came to see if I can help."

"I think I know how to make burgers," she said smoothly. "But bless your heart."

In other words, fuck off and die.

Carlos gave him a look like "told you so." He turned to Mia and the two of them exchanged a glance that wasn't all that hard to interpret for anyone who'd ever once been a horny teenager.

"So...I have to run into town to get the mail and fill up the propane tank," Carlos said casually.

"Oh! I'll help," Mia said quickly.

Amateurs. "No," Ford said at the same time as Tara.

Carlos let out a breath and left through the back door. Mia shot Tara a look of perfected teenage annoyance and grabbed the two vases of flowers she's just arranged, leaving through the double doors to display them in the front rooms.

When she was gone, Tara shook her head. "Why don't they tell you that raising a teenager is like trying to nail Jell-O to a freaking tree?"

Ford laughed softly. "Probably because the entire race would die out."

"He looks at her," she fretted. "A lot. He looks at her like…"

Risking his neck, Ford came up behind her and slid his arms around her. "Like I look at you?" he asked against her ear, enjoying the way she shivered before she shoved him away.

"Stop that," she said.

"That's not what you were saying earlier. You were saying 'Oh, Ford. Harder, Ford—'" His sentence ended in an *oomph* when she elbowed him in the gut.

"I have far more important things to do than relive our little…" Apparently she couldn't come up with a satisfactory word for what they'd done because she closed her mouth and inhaled sharply through her nose. "We have a bigger problem."

"I wouldn't classify anything that happened between us today as a problem," Ford said and kissed her jaw.

She pushed at him again, her mood clearly changed by the talk of the teenagers. "We have a mission, Ford. It's called *Keep the Daughter Fully Dressed.*"

He grimaced.

"No, I mean it. That boy takes his job around here very seriously, and I greatly appreciate that. But there's something else he takes very seriously and that's our daughter. Do you hear me?"

"Honey, right now *everyone* can hear you."

Tara shook her head. "It's not happening, Ford. Not on my watch." She pointed at him again. "Or yours."

He arched a brow. "You don't see the irony in all this?"

"Of course I see the irony! I don't give a hoot about the irony!"

Ford very carefully relieved her of her weapon—the spatula—and once again wrapped his arms around her so she couldn't get violent. Holding her tight against him, he pressed his face into her hair. He couldn't help himself. "Even if someone had given a shit about keeping us separated, it wouldn't have helped. We'd have found a way."

"Maybe not."

"We'd have found a way," he repeated. "I was very determined."

Tara sighed. "Smartass."

"You like my ass."

"Yes," she agreed. "That's true, though it's not even your best part—Oh *crap*!" She sniffed, then sniffed again and whipped around to the stovetop. "Christ on a stick, *I did it again*! I burned another meal!" Shoving free, she flipped off the burners and stared in horror at the blackened burgers.

They could hear running footsteps, and then the door flew open. "Fire! Fire, *fire*!" Chloe shrieked, inhaler in one hand, fire extinguisher in the other. When she saw the burned burgers, she stopped and sagged in relief. "Jesus! Jesus Christ, I thought we were burning the place down again!"

Tara sank to a chair in utter disbelief. "I never burn things. And yet I've burned the last three meals I tried to make." She lifted a shocked gaze to both of them. "What's wrong with me?"

Neither Ford nor Chloe was stupid enough to answer that question. Ford poured Tara a fairly large glass of wine and turned to the refrigerator. In less than three minutes, he had the flame going again and was slathering butter on Tara's freshly made bread and slicing cheddar cheese for grilled cheese sandwiches.

"I can't serve plain old grilled cheese," Tara protested, downing her wine.

"It's not plain old grilled cheese," he said. "It's Jax's Chillax Grilled Cheese. It's the only thing the doofus could make until he was twenty-four. Damn good recipe, though."

"You're fixin' this for me," she said.

"Trying."

"You have a habit of doing that, helping me." There was something new in her eyes, something Ford couldn't quite put his finger on but hoped like hell meant that she was finally beginning to see him.

All of him.

Chapter 23

♥

*"Love is when someone puts you on a pedestal
and yet when you fall, they're there
to catch you anyway."*
TARA DANIELS

The summer shifted into high gear, complete with tourist surge and the long, hot, lazy days that were followed by long, hot, lazy nights.

Every Wednesday night, the town hosted Music on the Pier, and Ford always ran a booth for The Love Shack. He'd hired Carlos for help with the setup, and as Ford arrived, he expected that the kid would be working hard.

Instead, Ford found him working hard on swallowing Mia's tongue.

When neither of them noticed Ford's approach—they were pretty busy after all—he cleared his throat.

Nothing. He did it again, putting some major irritation into the sound, and the two teenagers finally jumped apart.

"Hey," Mia said, breathless, swiping a hand over her wet mouth. "We were just…"

Ford raised a brow, curious as to how she was going to finish that sentence. Instead, she fell silent. "Checking each other's tonsils?" he asked her.

Mia grimaced, and Carlos slid his hand into hers. A show of comfort and solidarity, and though his shoulders were a little hunched, he stood his ground right next to her. Ford stared at him, and though Carlos definitely squirmed, he held the eye contact.

"It's my fault," Mia said quickly. "Not his."

"No," Carlos said. "It's mine. Sir."

Ford scrubbed a hand over his face. Sir. Christ, if that didn't make him feel old.

Mia stepped in front of Carlos. Or tried to, but the kid wouldn't let her. "I can kiss who I want," she said with soft steel reminiscent of Tara.

Ford looked into her earnest, sweet face. Seventeen had never looked so young. "Mia—"

"I mean, I know you're my father, but I already have a dad."

Intimidation went out the window. So did the wind in his sails. "Yes, I know."

Mia stared up at him with those bigger-than-life eyes, the ones that haunted him with what-ifs. "And Carlos is a good guy," she said, glancing up at the kid still holding her hand, smiling at him.

Carlos didn't return the expression, but his eyes never left her face.

Ford let out a breath. "I know that, too."

"And so am I," she said. "I'm a good kid."

"My own personal miracle," Ford said with feeling.

Mia hesitated, as if she hadn't been prepared for him to be so agreeable. "So you can trust me to live my life.

You know that too, right? As well as letting me make my own mistakes?"

"Yes, but that doesn't make it any easier for me. Mia..." Ford searched for the right words. "Do you have any idea how many times I hoped I'd get to meet you? Get to know you?"

"No."

"Every day. Every single day."

Her eyes softened. "Yeah?"

"Yeah."

Her eyes filled, and she finally let go of Carlos's hand. She stepped into Ford, wrapped her arms around his waist, and hugged him. "So it's okay with you if after I get back from Spain, I still show up every once in a while?"

Ford tugged on a loose strand of her beautiful hair. "If you didn't, I'd come to you."

Mia's soggy smile warmed the far corners of his heart. "I still want to kiss your employee," she said.

Carlos winced. Mia smiled brilliantly at the teen, and his mouth quirked as if he couldn't help but love her.

Ford knew the feeling.

"I have to go," Mia said. "I promised Tara I'd find her at five." She went up on tiptoe to kiss Ford's cheek, looking him straight in the eyes. "Promise you're not going to do anything stupidly dad-like, okay?" she whispered. "No scaring off my boyfriend?"

Carlos winced again, probably thinking of his tough-guy rep and how easily she crushed it. Still, the kid said nothing as the two of them watched Mia dance off. Only when she was out of sight did Carlos turn his head and look at Ford warily.

"You got anything to say?" Ford asked.

"Would it help?"

"No. Get set up. We're expecting a crowd tonight."

Carlos hesitated, still braced for a father's wrath. "That's it?"

Ford wasn't exactly prepared for this, although he should have been. He'd gone from having no kid to having a hormonal teenager, and he felt a little off kilter. "For now, I need you to work, but stand by later to possibly have your ass kicked."

Carlos hopped to work so fast that Ford's head swam.

The businesses on the pier were making a brisk living today. Tara was out there somewhere with her sisters promoting the inn.

Ford could imagine her in her heels, all elegant and sophisticated and put together, the opposite of how she was when she was writhing beneath him. He thought about that for a few minutes and realized he was no better than Carlos.

The late afternoon was sizzling. The ocean was clear and azure blue, dotted with whitecaps from the light breeze as the sun slowly worked its way down the horizon. Behind him, Carlos was still rushing to set up, sliding the occasional wary glance Ford's way. "*What?*" Ford finally asked.

"Are you going to fire me? Cuz I'd really rather have that ass kicking. Sir."

"Call me 'sir' again and I will."

"So we're okay?"

"Hell, no. You had your hands on my daughter. I want to tell you that if you so much as think about touching her again, I'm going to make sure they never find your body."

Carlos paled a little, and Ford let out another breath. "But I can't do that, either."

The kid nodded. Yeah, he could really get behind Ford not doing that. "Why?"

"Because Mia'd be pissed at me, and I just got her in my life. And because I was seventeen once and incredibly stupid and selfish. Far more than you, actually." Ford paused. "Look, I realize you're just having a summer fling here but Mia—"

"No."

Ford arched a brow at the seriousness and vehemence of that single syllable. "No?"

"No, I'm not just having a summer fling."

"So where do you see this thing going? Because you know she's leaving for Spain when the summer's over. For a whole year. That's a lifetime for a guy your age. I don't want her hurt."

"I'm not going to hurt her. I love her."

Ford looked into Carlos's dark eyes. Whatever a seventeen-year-old could possibly know about love, Carlos meant it. Shit. "Okay, new game plan. If you touch her—"

"They'll never find my body?"

"Just don't. Don't touch her at all. Ever." Ford sighed. "Someday you're going to have a daughter and then you'll understand."

"Actually, I understand now. And what about Ms. Daniels?"

"What about her?"

"Maybe I'm not forty-four or whatever," Carlos said. "But she's a real nice lady. What about *her* getting hurt?"

Ford was so surprised that words nearly failed him. "*Thirty*-four. And I don't intend to hurt Tara. Ever."

"So…"

"I'm in this," Ford said, "to the end."

Carlos looked shocked.

But not as shocked as Ford himself was. He scratched his jaw. "Huh. I didn't see that one coming."

Carlos shook his head. "Does anyone?"

Tara was once again peddling muffins. Mia had started off doing it, but she'd wanted to wander around, so here Tara was. "Double the Pleasure Blueberry Muffins," she said, handing them out, not slowing down enough to engage in conversation until someone came up behind her and grabbed her with two strong arms, snagging a muffin in each hand.

Logan.

He bit into a muffin. "Mmm, damn you're good. Hey, I have some photographers coming in tomorrow from *People*. I made the Hottest 100 List. Your bartender ever do that?"

She shot him a look, and he laughed. "You know, I even miss your Don't-Make-Me-Kick-Your-Ass expression. Anyway, *People*'s bringing a few models in bikinis to drape themselves over a prop car to pose with me. Thought maybe you'd want to take their place."

"Oh, I would," Tara said drolly. "Except hell hasn't frozen over."

He grinned. "Okay, I guess I'll have to make do with the models then."

"Yeah, I bet that's going to be real tough."

Logan tugged on her hair. "I'm still holding out hope for me, Tara. For us."

But the "me" had come before the "us," and it always

would. Logan was a good guy, just not the right good guy for her. She knew that. On some level, she'd always known that. "Logan—"

"Hold that thought, darlin'. My fan club's calling."

She watched as he stepped away to be engulfed by a group of women that included Sandy and Cindy.

With a helpless laugh, Tara turned and found Chloe standing there.

"Want a reprieve?" Chloe asked, reaching for the basket of muffins.

"Yes," Tara said. "But what's wrong with this picture, you offering to help?"

Chloe ignored that and handed out a few muffins with a welcoming smile that Tara couldn't have pulled off to save her life.

Sawyer came walking through the crowd. He was in uniform, talking on his cell when Chloe purposely stepped into his path. "Muffin, officer?"

He stopped and looked down at her, and Tara held her breath. These two hadn't exactly seen eye to eye on… anything. Sawyer was six-foot-three and more than a little intimidating, but the petite Chloe just smiled sweetly up at him as if she hadn't been a thorn in his side since she'd first come to town. "They're Double the Pleasure Blueberry Muffins. Take two and quadruple your pleasure. *Officer*."

He never looked away from Chloe's face. "You make them?"

She laughed. "Why? You afraid?"

"Depends. Answer the question."

"Ah," Chloe said. "You think I poisoned them."

"Maybe just the ones you saved for me."

Chloe slowly eyed him from head to toe and back again. "It'd be a sacrilege."

Tara almost choked.

Sawyer didn't react, other than to slowly remove his sunglasses. "What are you up to?"

She reached over and plucked an invisible piece of lint from his pec. "If I have to tell you," she murmured, "I've gotten rusty."

Sawyer's gaze locked on hers. From five feet away, Tara felt the blast of heat between them, and it nearly knocked her back a step. She had no idea why Chloe was playing with him, why she was jerking his chain, and she had even less of an idea why Sawyer put up with it. But there was a shocking amount of tension there that she hadn't noticed before.

Sexual tension.

Sawyer's radio squawked. Eyes still on Chloe, he didn't move.

"You have to go," Chloe said lightly, as if nothing had happened. She handed him a few muffins. "Stay safe now, you hear?"

Sawyer looked at her for a long beat, clearly perplexed and suspicious of her unexpected niceness, poor guy. "You," he finally said, putting his sunglasses back on, "are a menace."

Chloe smiled and nodded. "Yes. Yes, I am. Don't you forget it now. Buh-bye." She slid her arm in Tara's and steered her away.

"What was *that*?" Tara whispered.

"Me giving away a few muffins."

"I meant the messing with the poor guy's head."

Chloe lifted a shoulder. "It's a give-and-take situation."

Tara slid her a glance. "Meaning?"

"Meaning maybe his head isn't the only one being messed with." Not explaining that cryptic statement, she continued to hand out muffins.

"Chloe—"

"I don't want to talk about it."

"Then can we talk about why you're helping me?" Tara asked.

"What, a sister can't help another sister?"

"Yes, if she wants something."

"Well, I don't," Chloe said, sounding hurt.

Crap. "Okay, that was rude," Tara admitted. "I'm sorry."

Chloe grinned. "Wow, Maddie's right. You *are* a lot more mellow now that you're boinking Ford. I hadn't really noticed. I do want something. I want tonight off to go rock climbing, if you'll wake me in the morning. I'm giving a big spa day tomorrow at the Seattle Four Seasons." She smiled at the guy coming up to her side and handed him a muffin. It was Tucker, Lance's twin.

"We're leaving in half an hour," he said.

"Are we going to get arrested again?" Chloe asked hopefully.

Tucker laughed. "No. This time we really do have permission to be on the Butte. I'm going to go get the gear ready, while Lance works the booth. Jamie and Todd are coming too."

Tara held back her negative comment. She adored Lance and Tucker, but not Jamie's cousin Todd. When he was around, bad things tended to happen.

"Well, then," Chloe said, unconcerned, "I should help." She looked at Tara, who nodded, then handed back the basket and headed off.

"Be careful," Tara said and knew that, of course, she wouldn't be. She looked down at the basket, feeling alone. Both of her sisters had other people in their lives. Tara had neglected to achieve that for herself. An oversight on her part. She'd been so busy trying to make the inn a success, and making sure not to lose herself this time, that she hadn't managed to cultivate many friends here.

Okay, that wasn't quite true. She'd made plenty of time for one person in particular—too much time.

Ford, of course. It always came back to Ford.

She realized that while thinking of him, she'd walked up to his booth. She shouldn't have been surprised, since with him and only him, she seemed to know exactly who she was.

And who she wasn't.

Jax was behind the bar though, not Ford, and she told herself it was silly to be disappointed.

"What'll it be?" Jax asked with a friendly smile.

"Oh, I . . ." She hadn't come for a drink. She'd come for a peek at the man she couldn't stop thinking about. She looked casually around.

Jax raised a brow. "Want a hint?"

Tara felt a tingle at the back of her neck and closed her eyes. "He's right behind me, isn't he?"

"Yep."

With a sigh, she turned around to face Ford. He was looking comfortable and relaxed in a Mariners' baseball cap, cargos, and a T-shirt that said SAIL FAST, LIVE SLOW.

He shot her a slow smile that spread warmth to parts of her that didn't need warming. "Hey," she said casually.

Wow, look at her all composed. Tranquil. "Well"—she backed away—"I hope you get a good crowd tonight."

Not fooled, he stepped in her path. "Going somewhere?"

"I'm working."

"Really? Because it seemed like maybe you were looking for me."

Dammit. "Why would I do that?"

He gave that soft laugh, the one that always made her quiver. "Because you want me bad."

God. She looked around to make sure Jax couldn't hear them, but he'd turned his back and was setting up. "I already had you," she whispered.

"Yes," Ford said. "Hence the bad part. Walk with me." Without waiting for her to refuse him, he took the basket out of her hands and set it behind the bar. With a hand low on her back, he directed her through the throng of people, with the sounds of the music and laughter all around them. The Ferris wheel was slowly revolving, going round and round.

Like her life.

"You know that Carlos thinks he loves Mia."

"Yes. But they're too young for love."

Ford's mouth curved slightly. "That thought would have pissed you off at seventeen."

True. Tara rubbed her temples. "Okay, I'm going to take heart in the fact that they seem to be smarter than we were. Her adoptive parents did a good job of raising her."

"Yeah."

They were both silent as they passed the Ferris wheel, and Tara knew that they were each thinking, thank God that Mia's parents *had* done such an obviously amazing job. Tara was grateful to them, so damn grateful. "And did you know that Sawyer and Chloe are circling each other like two caged tigers?"

"That's actually just Sawyer who's the caged tiger. Chloe's in the center of the ring with the whip, toying with him."

"I'm sorry."

Ford shook his head. "Sawyer's a big boy."

They slowed in front of the ice cream parlor, which was having a tasting party. Lance stood behind the counter offering samples of everything they had. "What'll it be?" he asked them.

Tara pointed to the double fudge chocolate, which melted in her mouth.

"If you liked that, try this one." Lance handed over another tiny spoon. "It's Belgian dark chocolate."

"Oh Lord." She moaned as she swallowed the heavenly taste. "How about that one, what's that?" she asked, pointing to another chocolatey-looking concoction.

"Chocolate E. For ecstasy. Careful with it," Lance warned with a wink at Ford. "They call it pure sin."

Tara tested it and moaned again. She'd never had anything so delicious in her life.

"Want a cone with that?" Lance asked.

Indecision. They were all so amazing that she had no idea how she was going to pick. "Wait, I didn't taste the chocolate butter toffee," she murmured, and Lance patiently offered her another tiny spoon.

She was in mid-heavenly sigh when she felt Ford shift close behind her, his mouth brushing her ear. "Moan through one more sample," he warned in a thick husky whisper, "and I'm dragging you to the closest dark corner on the pier. And Tara?" His breath was warm against her skin, making her shiver. "By the time I'm done with you, you won't remember your own name."

She couldn't remember her own name now. "That's a pretty outrageous threat," she managed.

"Yes, and if you're very lucky, I'll wait until we're alone to carry through on it."

She turned to face him just as he reached past her to accept his own tiny spoon sample from Lance. Eyes on hers, Ford licked at it slowly.

Tara's thighs quivered.

"Order your ice cream," he told her, and took another lick.

Later she couldn't remember what she ordered. All she remembered was Ford holding her hand on the walk back through the crowd, with need and hunger and desire pounding through her veins instead of blood.

By silent agreement, they headed directly to his car. He drove them to the marina and to his boat. Still silent, they boarded.

The moon was nothing but a narrow sliver on the water, lapping quietly at the boat as they turned to each other.

Chapter 24

♥

*"For every action, there is an equal and
opposite criticism. Ignore it."*
Tara Daniels

There was only the faintest glow of a quarter moon on
the water. The night had a hushed quiet to it—with the
exception of Tara's heavy breathing and low moans.

Ford's favorite sounds of all time.

They lay on his bed. As Tara thrashed beneath his
hands, he slowly drew her to the very edge of sanity,
watching, enthralled, as she began to come undone.

She wasn't alone in that.

Always when with her, he was completely undone,
stripped down to raw, bare soul. From her first day back
in Lucky Harbor, it'd been exactly as he remembered, and
something he'd never forgotten in all these years.

His gaze wandered down her gorgeous body, long
and curvy, and spread out across his bed for his viewing
pleasure, and he actually ached.

She opened her eyes. "You're looking at me like..."

"Like you looked at the ice cream earlier?" he asked with a smile. "Yeah, I am. I'm hungry for you, Tara."

Stretching out, she lifted her arms above her head, giving him silent permission to taste whatever he wanted. Something he'd been wanting to do for days—eat her up from head to toe and then back again, until she came for him. Again and again. He started at her throat, tasting every single inch of her, nibbling certain interesting spots, stopping to tease whenever she gasped or wriggled. "So sweet," he murmured against her skin. "You're so damn sweet." By the time he got to her belly button, she was fisting the sheets at her side and murmuring his name in a chant, a prayer, a warning to hurry the hell up.

It made him laugh. "Just lay there and take it, Tara." *Take me...* "Give me the control. I'll get you where you want to go, I promise."

"I—Ohmigod," she managed when he drew her into his mouth and gently sucked, his hands sliding beneath her sexy ass to hold her still. "Don't stop," she demanded.

Still trying to be in the driver's seat. "Please," he corrected. "Don't stop, *please...*"

She slid her fingers into his hair, tightening them to an almost painful grip, holding him to her, making him laugh again. "Say it," he demanded.

"Don't stop, *please*," she ground out, doing her best to make him bald.

"See?" he murmured. "Sweet as hell." And he didn't stop. Not until she begged him to.

Nicely.

Afterward, Tara fell asleep curled into Ford's side, one hand tucked beneath her chin, the other across his chest.

He lay there, relaxed and boneless, listening to her breathe, not wanting to move. Not wanting her to stir and remember that she was trying to hold back from him. Because then she'd get up, get dressed, and walk away.

She was good at that.

And he was good at letting her.

He had no one but himself to blame for that. Bad genes, bad childhood—all excuses and he knew it. And they no longer cut it.

Tara's coming back to Lucky Harbor had been circumstance. Her staying in town even more so. No one would argue that their connection wasn't still there, possibly even deeper than before, but she was holding back, and he couldn't blame her.

She'd been burned.

He knew that. He got it. Hell, he'd even been one of the ones to burn her. Up until now, he'd been willing to give her all the time she needed, because the truth was that he'd needed time, too. Time to deal with some of his own past mistakes. Time to understand that he was in this for the long haul.

Because she made him. She made him laugh. She made him feel. She made him think. She made him happy.

She made him…everything.

And with that everything, she also made him vulnerable. Bone-deep, scary-as-shit vulnerable. Just as gun-shy as she was.

Christ, he really hated that about himself.

With a sleepy sigh, Tara stirred and untangled herself.

"Don't," he said.

She lifted her head in surprise. "Don't what?"

He drew a deep breath. "Don't go. Stay the night."

She smiled softly, and he knew by the light in her eyes that his words meant something to her, said something important. A step in the right direction, that light said, and he smiled back.

But she still climbed out of the bed. "I can't stay tonight. I have to go check on the inn." She slipped back into her dress and bent over the bed to kiss him. "'Night, Ford." Then she was gone, her heels clicking on the deck as she walked away in tune to the only other sound Ford could hear—the roaring of his own racing heart.

Okay, so she'd left a little abruptly, but she'd kissed him first. A step in the right direction, he told himself again, and there, alone in the dark, smiled.

The next morning Tara rose and showered, determined to make their guests the most outstanding breakfast they'd ever had. She would burn nothing. First, though, she went to wake Chloe as Chloe had requested—but her bed was empty. Tara hadn't heard her come in after rock climbing, but most likely she was already in the inn kitchen making a mess.

Resigned, Tara walked to the inn, let herself into the kitchen, and prepared to be annoyed.

But the kitchen was empty. Huh. Tara called Chloe's cell, but it went right to voice mail. She tried Maddie next.

"'Lo?" came Maddie's sleepy voice. "Who's dead?"

"Is Chloe with you at Jax's?" Tara asked.

"It'd be a bit crowded here in his bed if she was. Why?"

"I don't think she came home last night."

"From rock climbing? *Crap*." Sounding more awake

now, Maddie asked the question already on Tara's mind. "You suppose she's in jail again?"

"Anyone's guess."

"I'll be there in fifteen."

"No," Tara said. "You took the late shift here last night. I'll handle this."

"Honey, I was coming in anyway to help you serve breakfast. Give me fifteen."

"Okay," Tara said, grateful to have someone to worry with. "Thanks. You want to call Sawyer or should I?"

"Call Sawyer what?" Sawyer asked, coming in the back door, filling the kitchen with his big build. He was in his uniform and looking very fine as he went straight to the coffeepot.

Tara handed him one of the to-go mugs.

"Thanks." The very corners of his mouth tipped in a barely-there, bad-boy smile as he leaned back against the counter, the mug in hand. "Tell me what?" he repeated.

Tara thought about not going there with him. After all, typically when Chloe got herself in some sort of trouble, poor Sawyer was the one forced to deal with it.

But if Tara didn't tell him and something had happened to her sister... She sighed. "Chloe didn't make it home last night."

He didn't so much as blink, and yet there was a new stillness about him that told her he wasn't happy to hear this. "And she was supposed to?"

"Yes."

"Was she with the group of rock climbers out on the Butte?"

"Possibly," Tara said warily. "Why?"

"Because I arrested one of them this morning."

Oh, God. "Who was it, and for what?"

"Todd Fitzgerald. Public intoxication."

Todd. Of course. Tara sighed, and Sawyer pushed away from the counter. "I'll make some calls."

She knew he meant he'd call the station, the hospital...the morgue. But before he got to the door, Chloe came in—hair wild, face flushed, wearing yesterday's clothes and carrying her shoes.

Sawyer looked at her impassively.

"Don't start," she said and brushed past him. Limping.

He eyed her body carefully. "You okay?"

She turned to face him. "I'm always okay."

There was a long, awkward beat between the two of them. There always was. Tara had no idea what to make of it or how to help.

"Don't you have sheriff-type stuff to do?" Chloe asked him.

Sawyer gave a short shake of his head, one that clearly said *fuck it* before he moved toward the door. Tara gave Chloe a recriminating *you-are-so-rude* look, and Chloe rolled her eyes. "Sawyer," she said with reluctant apology.

He pulled open the door. "Glad you're home safe."

"We were at the Butte," Chloe said to his broad, tense back. "We ran out of gas and had to wait until daylight to catch a ride."

He looked at her. "It's illegal to party out there."

"We ran out of gas," she repeated.

"Did you lose your cell phone too?"

Chloe sighed dramatically. "I forgot mine at home, okay? And Lance doesn't carry one."

Sawyer locked eyes with hers. "Were you with Todd?"

"For a while."

"He had a phone."

"How do you know?" she asked.

"Because it's now residing in his personal possessions baggie for when he bails himself out after he sobers up."

"You arrested him? Seriously?"

Sawyer was unapologetic and unmoved. "He staggered into the convenience store at five this morning, knocked over three displays, and urinated on the magazine stand." He shook his head. "And you and Lance have a serious death wish, you know that? What if he'd had a medical problem out there?"

"He needed to do this, Sawyer. It isn't my place to babysit him and tell him what he can and can't do."

"Jesus, Chloe, his cystic fibrosis isn't a fucking summer cold!"

"And you think he doesn't know that?"

"And what about you?" he asked. "Does the inhaler always do the job? I don't think so. You can't tell me you've never had to make a trip to the ER because of an asthma attack while climbing."

"*Nothing happened*," Chloe said. "So I don't get it. Why are you so pissed?"

"I'm not pissed." His face was impassive. The cop face. "That would imply that there were feelings between us."

Chloe stared at him for a long beat. "My mistake then," she finally said.

Sawyer stared at her right back, then swore beneath his breath and left without another word. When the door shut behind him with quiet fury, Chloe let out a breath.

"Gee," Tara said in the silence. "No tension there."

"Don't you start too." Chloe headed directly for the refrigerator and some leftover Not Yo Mama's Apple Pie.

"Was it just you, Tucker, Lance, and Todd up there?" Tara asked.

"No. Lance brought a bunch of friends, and one thing led to another."

So Sawyer was right. It *had* been a party. "I thought you can't have sex without landing yourself in the hospital."

"No one had sex. Or at least I didn't." Chloe sighed. "Bunch of stupid boys in this town."

"Sawyer isn't stupid."

"And he's not a boy, either."

Tara watched as Chloe shoveled away the pie like she hadn't eaten in a week. "What is he, then?"

"Hell, Tara, do I need to give you the birds and the bees talk? Why can't you get the deets off the Internet like all the other kids these days?"

When Tara laughed, Chloe relaxed slightly. "I really don't want to talk about it," she said.

"A common theme amongst us sisters," Tara said.

"What's this?" Chloe asked. "Regret? From the most private sister of them all?" Without waiting for an answer, she took her plate to the sink and headed to the door. "I'm out."

When Tara was alone, she sighed. "Yeah. I'd definitely call it regret." Shaking it off, she began pulling out all the ingredients she needed for the Good Morning Sunshine Casserole, which she'd adapted from Mia's recipe. She was grating cheese when the back door and the door leading to the hallway opened at the same time.

Logan came in one, and Ford the other.

Immediately, the testosterone level shot up and hit maximum velocity in two point zero seconds as both men stared at each other over Tara's head.

"Well, if it isn't the drinking buddies," Tara said dryly. "Should I break out the mimosas, boys?"

"I just came by to help," Logan said. "Since you keep burning meals and all."

"How are you going to help?" Ford asked. "You actually cook?"

"Well, no, but I give real good help," Logan said with a charming smile in Tara's direction.

"*I* cook," Ford said.

Logan's eyes narrowed, and Tara felt yet another competition coming on. She'd heard about the abs of steel contest at The Love Shack. Part of her still couldn't believe it, and the other part of her wished she'd seen it herself.

"Okay, you know what?" She dropped an empty bag into Logan's hands and gave his leanly muscled, warm body a push out the back door. "I need some apples. Go pick me some, would you?"

Ford, looking big and bad and very cocky, leaned back against the counter with a smile.

"Oh, no." Tara shoved him out after Logan. "You too. And play nice." She shut the door on them both, threw the casserole into the oven, and turned and met Mia's amused glance.

"I showed up to make sure you didn't have any trouble," the teen said.

"Well, the trouble part is taken care of. Other than that, everything's the same old status quo. My life is pretty boring."

"Yeah." Mia laughed. "Okay, let's work on *not* burning breakfast today."

"I swear I'm a good cook," Tara said, needing to be

good at *something* in her daughter's eyes. She walked Mia through the steps to make dough for fresh bread. "This won't take long to bake and then we can—" Tara broke off as she got a good look out the window. "Oh, for the love of God."

Logan and Ford had each shimmied up a tree—Logan with the help of a stepladder—and were making piles of apples. Big piles.

More than she needed for the next month.

Not that they were doing it for *her*. Nope, they were competing again.

Mia joined her at the window and raised a single brow—yet another talent she'd inherited from her father. Together they watched the guys pick apples.

"And you think your life is boring," Mia murmured.

"You're sleeping with her." Logan repeated this grimly to Ford from somewhere inside his apple tree. With his arm injury, he'd been slower to climb up.

Ford, having the free use of both arms, hadn't needed a ladder to climb the adjacent tree. "This is not news," he told Logan. "You read Facebook."

"Christ. I should just kill you. Or me. It'd be less painful to be dead."

"You're not in any real pain," Ford said in disgust. "It's just your fucking ego. You hate to lose."

"Said the pot to the kettle," Logan muttered.

Okay, that might be true, but this was more than about winning for Ford. It was about Tara, a woman he couldn't live without. He pulled himself up to the next branch and dropped another three perfect apples. He glanced down. Yep, his pile was bigger than Logan's. Even as he thought so with deep satisfaction, an apple whizzed by his ear, so close it disturbed his hair. "Hey—"

Logan flashed a grim smile and chucked another one. Ford saw this one coming and ducked again, and slipped. "Shit—"

That's all he got out before he lost his grip, his temper, and his balance all at once.

And fell out of the tree.

Chapter 25

♥

*"Families are like fudge—mostly sweet
with a few nuts."*
TARA DANIELS

When Ford opened his eyes, he was flat on his back staring up at the sky.

"Jesus H. Christ," came a horrified, disembodied voice from the next tree over. "What, you can't hold on to a branch?"

"You beaned me in the forehead," Ford said. "With an apple."

"And you call yourself an athlete." Logan was hauling ass out of his tree as fast as he could with one arm in a brace, swearing colorfully as he went.

Ford prayed he'd fall, too, but it didn't happen. Fucking karma.

"I didn't even hit you that hard," Logan was muttering. "You weren't supposed to fall like a fucking pussy!"

"Nice," Ford said, very carefully *not* moving. "Calling me names when I'm down."

"Hey, you're the one who's always going on and on about me not being an athlete."

That was true. He had no excuse.

Okay, he did.

Jealousy. "All I'm saying is that a race car driver isn't necessarily as fit as say, a sailor—"

"Jesus, would you give it up already? And why are you just lying there? Tell me you're not hurt. You're going to fucking milk this, aren't you? You're going to get laid out of this deal, I just know it. How bad are you hurt?"

Ford let out a breath. "I'm putting all my energy into *not* figuring that out."

Logan swore again and hit the ground.

"I'm surprised to see you move so fast," Ford said. "For someone who sits on his ass for a living."

"I don't—Goddammit, *shut up.*" Logan dropped to Ford's side to look him over, his eyes widening on Ford's legs. "Fuck."

"No. Don't tell me." He already knew. He could feel the fire from his toes to his groin. And not a little baby-ass fire either, but a to-the-bone burning that made him want to scream. But because he *wasn't* a pussy, as Logan had accused, he refused to make a sound. Sweating, however, was allowed. He was doing a lot of sweating. And possibly going to throw up, too.

Then came a buzzing that told him this was it. His life was fading before his very eyes—

"*Bees!*" Logan jumped up and started leaping around, running in circles, flapping his arms.

"It's just the gunk from the bruised apples," Ford told him. "Ignore them and, gee, I don't know, *help the guy you knocked out of the tree.*"

But Logan kept doing the bee dance, and it was actually kind of fun to watch. "Man, if you'd just stand still—"

"I'm allergic!" Logan yelled.

"You're kidding me, right?"

"Fuck! Ow!" Logan slapped at his collarbone. "I'm hit, I'm hit!"

Ford wanted to ask Logan who was the pussy now, but that seemed kind of asshole-ish. And then there was the fact that Ford was suddenly feeling weird, sort of woozy . . .

There were running footsteps, feet pounding the ground toward him. Ford closed his eyes as the pain began to burn a path to his brain. Yeah, he was definitely going to throw up.

"Ford," Tara breathed. "Oh my God. Your leg."

He felt her drop to her knees and had the vague thought that he wished she was going into that position for a different reason altogether.

"Is he dead?"

This from Chloe, and Ford huffed out a laugh. "Not yet," he assured her.

Tara whipped out her cell phone, punched in 9-1-1, and glared at Chloe.

"What?" Chloe asked innocently. "Look, some sisters help you move, but a *real* sister helps you move bodies." She patted Ford's shoulder. "Glad it's not necessary, Big Guy."

"Me too," he muttered.

"Help," came a whisper.

Everyone looked over at Logan. He was sitting on the ground, hands clasped around his throat. His face was sweaty and beet red.

"Logan, not now," Tara said. "Ford's hurt."

"I was...stung by a bee," he rasped out and fell over.

Tara gasped and abandoned Ford, crawling over to Logan. "He's allergic!"

Great, Ford thought. Fucking great. Even while passed out, Logan could upstage him.

The ambulance came. Tara burned breakfast again. And within thirty minutes someone had already updated Facebook with:

Tara nearly kills both of her men!

Mia saved the day, coming up with pancakes that she'd learned to make in Home Ec class. She served the guests with Maddie's help while Tara rode in the ambulance with both Ford and Logan.

An hour and a half later, Tara was sitting in the hospital waiting room with Mia on one side, Chloe on the other. Maddie had taken over inn detail.

They hadn't had any news on either Logan or Ford, and Tara felt herself losing it. "What's taking so long?" she asked for the tenth time.

Chloe sat calmly reading *Cosmo*. She turned the page, eyed the very good-looking, half-naked guy there, and hummed her approval. "Maybe they're surgically removing their *In Love with Tara* gene."

Tara narrowed her eyes. "What does that mean?"

"It means I *still* don't get it. How is it that you have those two guys falling for you? You're grumpy and bossy and demanding and anal—not to mention slightly obsessive compulsive." She paused. "No offense."

Tara looked over at a quiet Mia. "Still glad you found your parents?"

A smile curved her lips. "I have my moments."

Chloe laughed. "I really, really like you."

Tara elbowed her, then turned to Mia again. "Thanks for your help in the kitchen during the fiasco."

"No problem. I've been wondering something."

Oh God. Another question, Tara thought.

"Amy, the waitress at the diner, told me you never burned anything over there. Ever."

"That's true," Tara said over Chloe's snort.

"Why is that?" Mia asked.

"I have no idea."

Finally, a doctor came out to talk to them. Logan had been treated for his severe allergic reaction to the bee sting and was going to be fine. Ford had a broken leg and had been drugged up to have it set. He was loopy, but would also be fine—in six to eight weeks.

Mia went in to see Ford first. While she did, Tara called the B&B and checked in. According to Maddie, their guests were fine and out for the day. Two more people had checked in but all was well.

Taking a deep breath, Tara walked down the hall, stopping to buy two balloons. Both the men in her life had acted like children today; so she figured what the hell.

Logan's room came first. He was sitting up in his bed, flirting with a pretty nurse who was hovering over him taking his pulse. "I've always wanted to meet a real-life NASCAR driver," she was saying.

Tara rolled her eyes and knocked on the jamb. "Am I interrupting?"

The look on the nurse's face said yes, she was absolutely interrupting, but she was professional enough to shake her head. "I just have to get the doctor to sign his forms and then he can be released." With one last little longing glance in Logan's direction, the woman was gone.

Logan smiled at the balloons. "For me?"

"One of them." Tara handed it over and kissed his cheek. "You're an idiot."

"Gee, thanks."

"But I love you anyway."

"Yeah." His smiled faded. "But you're not *in* love with me."

Tara sat at his hip and looked him in the eyes. "And you are, Logan? In love with me? *Truth*," she said when he opened his mouth. "Are you in love with me, the me I am right now?"

"Well not *right* now," he said, brooding. "Right now you're kinda mean."

"How about the me who has a life now separate from yours? The me who's now involved in her sisters' lives, the me who can no longer drop everything and travel the world to be your greatest cheerleader without a care to her own life? *That* me, Logan. Are you in love with *that* me?"

Logan looked at her for a long beat, then expelled a breath. "I don't know that you."

"No, you don't." Tara reached for his hand. "Which means you can't love me."

He was quiet a minute. "I didn't expect us to turn out this way," he finally said. He brought their joined hands up to his mouth and brushed his lips across her knuckles.

"I do see what you love about Lucky Harbor, though. It's a cool place."

It wasn't the place. Tara knew that now. It was the people in it, and the relationships she'd made here. It was...home.

"So if you're not coming back to me," he said after a while, "what are your plans?"

"I'm moving on."

"Moving on while staying in Lucky Harbor?"

"Yes," she said, admitting her newfound realization. "I'm staying."

"With Ford?"

"I don't know," Tara said honestly.

Logan laughed, and in it was a wistfulness and vulnerability she hadn't expected. "*I* know," he said softly.

Chapter 26

♥

*"Never do anything that you don't want
to have to explain to 9-1-1 personnel."*
TARA DANIELS

Tara left Logan's hospital room and went looking for
her next most pressing problem. When she heard Mia's
voice, she slowed her pace. Peeking in the door, she
found Mia sitting in a chair by Ford's bed.

All she could see of Ford was a set of long legs, one casted.
Still standing out of sight behind the curtain, Tara smiled in
spite of herself. They were playing cards. Blackjack.

"Hit me," Ford said.

Mia dealt him a card.

"Hit me," he said.

Mia obliged again.

"Hit me."

"Um," Mia said hesitantly. "You have thirty-six."

Ford blinked blearily at his cards. "You sure?"

"Wow." Mia giggled. "They must have given you
some good stuff, huh, Dad?"

Ford went still and stared her. "Did you just—"

"Yeah," Mia said softly. "Weird?"

"Yes." He smiled at her dopily. "The absolutely *best* kind of weird. You should probably ask me all my secrets now. I'm mush *and* high. I'll sing like a canary."

Mia grinned. "What kind of secrets do you have?"

"Deep, dark ones."

"Like?"

"Like how I watch *Hell's Kitchen.* Shh," he said, bringing a finger to his lips and nearly taking out an eye. "And I change the locks at the bar just to mess with Jax's head. Oh, and I push Tara's buttons cuz I like it when she gets all pissy."

Mia laughed. "You really *are* high. Make me understand why you two aren't a thing again?"

"Me and Jax? He's engaged to someone else now, so..."

"You know I mean Tara," she said, still laughing.

Ford looked at his cards as if they might hold the answer.

"Come on, it's not that tough a question."

"Yes, it is. And didn't I tell you all this already?"

"No, actually," Mia said. "You never have. Tara did. Well, kind of. But not you."

Standing in the doorway, still half-hidden behind the privacy curtain, Tara covered her mouth with her fingers to avoid interrupting them.

"It's complicated," Ford finally said. "But that's also a bullshit answer, and I've always promised myself if I ever got the chance to know you, I wouldn't bullshit you."

He'd thought about this, Tara realized. About getting

to know Mia, being with her. He'd thought about it, and he'd wanted it.

It was to her own shame that she'd tried *not* to do the same, otherwise the guilt would have killed her a long time ago.

"I'm glad, cuz I have a highly sensitive bullshit meter," Mia said.

A half-smile curved Ford's mouth as he reached for the teen's hand. "You get that from Tara, you know. You get a lot from her. Your inner strength, your determination, your brains. All your best parts actually, they come from her, not me."

Tara pressed her free hand over her aching heart.

"So would you finally just tell me?" Mia asked softly. "Will you tell me about you two, how it was back then? You know, since you're high and all."

Ford let out a long breath. "I was bad news for her, Mia."

Tara's breath caught. Out of all the things she expected him to say, that hadn't been on the list.

"Did *she* tell you that?" Mia asked. "That you were bad for her?"

He hadn't been, Tara thought with a lump in her throat. He'd been wonderful. Exactly what she'd needed. She'd been inexperienced, but he hadn't taken advantage of her. And the truth was, she'd wanted him as badly as he'd wanted her. When she'd gotten pregnant, he'd felt guilty as hell.

It hadn't been his fault. Not all of it, anyway. There'd been *two* of them in his bed, and once he'd taught her how good their bodies could feel together, it'd been all she'd wanted to do with him.

"No," Ford said. "She never said that."

"Probably because she didn't see it that way," Mia said.

Ford shrugged, and hands still over her mouth and heart, Tara shook her head. She hadn't seen him as bad for her. Ever. She'd seen past his roughness, the tough exterior, to the caring, warm boy beneath.

"It wasn't going to happen," Ford said. "Us. I couldn't have taken care of her any more than I could have taken care of you, no matter how much I wanted to. Truth is, she was made for better things than being stuck with me in this small town that she hated."

"What about love?" Mia asked. "If you loved each other—"

"We were seventeen," Ford said gently. "We didn't know real love."

Mia made a sound that said she disagreed. Vehemently. But still out of view, Tara nodded in understanding. Maybe she would have said they'd been at least a *little* in love, but she wouldn't judge him. She was the last person to judge.

"Okay," Mia said. "So Tara left, and you ... what? You just let her go?"

She sounded so disappointed, and Ford laughed softly without mirth. "God, you really did get so much from her." He paused. "Yeah, I let her go. She wasn't happy with me over that. It took nearly six months of her being back in Lucky Harbor before she'd even talk to me."

"She was mad at you for letting her walk away?"

"Oh, yeah. And I deserved that."

"But you did it out of love!" the romantic Mia said dramatically. "You thought she deserved better."

"It wasn't all altruistic," he admitted. "I've tended to

go the easy route. And Tara doesn't know the meaning of the word easy."

He sounded...proud, Tara thought. Proud of her.

"And what about now?" Mia wanted to know. "Now that you're both older and together in the same place, it might end differently. Right?"

The ache deepened, spreading through Tara's entire chest as a nurse brushed past her and in the room. "Okay, Mr. Walker," she called out. "You've been cleared and released. You're free to go if you have someone to help you home."

Tara stepped into the room as well, and raised her hand. "That would be me."

Ford's eyes locked with hers. "Sawyer could—"

"It was my tree," she said, oddly loath to let anyone else help him. "It's the least I can do."

Ford took up the entire backseat of Tara's car with his stretched-out leg, leaving the front seat for Logan, which he gleefully took.

Sawyer picked up Mia and Chloe. He offered to take Ford as well, but Tara was still unwilling to part with him and used the excuse that he was already loaded in her car. She got behind the wheel, and nervous with both Ford and Logan watching her, took the first turn a little rough, nearly dumping Ford to the floor.

Logan smirked and eyed Ford in the rearview mirror. "Got to lean into the turns, Mariner Man. Learn to use your body."

Ford gritted his teeth. "I know how to use my body just fine."

"So do I. Tell him, Tara."

Tara glared at Logan. "Don't you make me stop this car. Because I totally will."

Unrepentant, Logan shrugged. Tara went out of her way to drop him off first. When she pulled up to his rented beach cottage, he slumped in the seat. "Hey. Why do *I* have to go home first?"

"Because you're the one most likely to be strangled," she said. "By me."

At that, Ford stopped scowling in the backseat and sat up a little straighter.

"Fine," Logan said. "But I need you to walk me in."

"Why?"

"Maybe I'm dizzy from the meds."

"Cortisone makes you dizzy?"

He lifted his chin. "Yes, for your information, it does. I feel a little sick, too. I almost died, you know."

Tara sighed, threw the car into park, and looked into the rearview mirror at Ford. "Wait here."

"Right," he muttered. "Because I might leap out of the car and make a run for it."

Logan smiled evilly.

Ford flipped him off.

"Let's go," Tara said tightly to her ex. "Behave," she said to Ford.

His expression told her that she shouldn't count on it. She walked Logan up the porch. Sandy was there waiting for him, looking cute and perky.

"Oh, you poor baby!" she said, rising to her feet and moving to Logan's side. "I heard all about it. Are you okay?"

Of course, Logan played it up. "Well, it was touch and go there for a while." He shuddered. "But I'm going to make it."

Sandy fussed all over him. "Let me help you inside."

"Good idea," Logan said, setting his head on her shoulder. "Nearly dying from anaphylactic shock is exhausting."

Tara rolled her eyes so hard that they nearly popped right out of her head.

Paying Tara no attention, Sandy slipped her arm around Logan. "Are you really okay now? What can I do for you? Anything, just name it."

"Oh, darlin', that's so sweet, but really, don't worry about little ol' me."

"Don't be silly," Sandy exclaimed. "You need some serious TLC."

"Maybe you're right," Logan murmured, leaning into her some more, sighing in pleasure.

Tara shook her head. "I assume you're in good hands," she said dryly.

"Yes." This from Sandy. "I'll take care of him from here."

Tara got back in her car and glanced at Ford. "To your house or boat?"

"House," he said morosely, jaw dark with the day's growth, eyes hooded. "I can't maneuver enough to get around on the boat."

Fifteen minutes later, Tara got patient number two settled on his couch, his leg elevated on the coffee table. His crutches, water, snacks, and the remote were all within reach. She'd also given him two pain pills.

He looked miserable, and she melted. "How bad are you hurting?"

He didn't answer. Shifting behind him, she began to rub the knots out of his shoulders. "Better?"

He gave a little grunt of affirmation so she kept at it until the knots loosened and he finally relaxed. "Thanks," he said gruffly.

She didn't want to take her hands off all his gorgeous muscles but she had limits, and jumping his bones when he was on drugs and hurting was one of them.

Probably.

"You'll get used to the crutches," she said, hoping that it was true. "But until you do, we'll all take shifts here to make sure you have what you need."

"I have what I need." He grabbed her hand when she tried to move away. "My own private nurse."

She laughed. "I was a nurse once for Halloween, but you should know, I'm not all that good at it in real life."

"I bet you made a really hot nurse." His eyes went a little glossy as he thought about it. "You and a short short, little white uniform, with white lacy thigh-highs and a devastatingly tiny thong. Or no thong. Yeah, no thong at all."

"You've given this some thought," she said, amused. And also a little turned on to be the center of his fantasies.

"I have a very active imagination." He looked at her, no humor in his face when he said, "Something became clear to me today when I thought I was going to die."

"Ford, you fell out of a tree and broke your leg. You were never going to die."

"Could have," he insisted.

"Did I give you too many of the happy pills?" she asked, checking the bottle. "Maybe the hospital meant for me to wait until morning to dose you again." Shaking her head, she took a long pull from his soda.

He smiled. "I love you, you know. Probably, you should just marry me."

Tara inhaled soda up her nose and choked for air as she wheezed and gaped at him.

"You okay?"

"I will be," she managed through a raw throat. "When the shooting pains down my left arm go away." She drew in a ragged breath. "What did you just say to me?"

"I want to do it right this time with you," he said. "I want to get married. No more stupid Facebook, no more Logan, no more what-are-we-doing-with-each-other shit, and no more bad endings. Just you and me, and a piece of paper to make it official."

She stared at him some more, then picked up the pills again. "Okay, seriously. *What did I give you?*"

With a deceptive laziness, Ford snagged her hand and tugged her on top of him.

"Careful," she gasped. "Your leg—"

"Is fine. Since you aren't in the mood to discuss getting married, there's something else you can do."

"What?"

"Kiss it and make it better."

He was crazy. *She* was crazy. "Ford—"

"*Please*, Nurse Daniels?"

She let out a breath, then cupped his face. It was lined with exhaustion and drawn with pain. He was beautiful. She leaned in and kissed him softly on first one rough cheek, and then went for the other; but he turned his head and caught her mouth with his, kissing her hard and deep.

"Better?" she asked breathlessly, a long moment later.

"No," he said very solemnly. "More."

"Ford, about..." The marriage proposal. Had he

meant to say it? Did he even remember saying it? She looked into his eyes and had no idea how to bring it back up. "When you—"

From within her purse, her cell phone rang with insistence.

"Maybe Logan's gotten stung again," Ford said hopefully as Tara dug the phone out.

"Hey," Chloe said when Tara answered. "Our guests want to know if they could pay you to make them a dinner basket to go. They want to watch the sun set somewhere with a picnic."

Tara was standing between the couch and the coffee table, her legs bumping into Ford's uncasted one. "Uh..." She nearly jumped out of her skin when a big, warm hand slid up the back of her calf. "Sure. But—"

Ford's warm, determined fingers headed north and her brain stuttered.

"They want wine, too," Chloe said. "Do we have what you need for them?"

Ford palmed Tara's ass. Squeezed.

"Um..." she said, closing her eyes when Ford groaned softly at the feel of her.

"I know it's a bad time," Chloe told her sympathetically. "And that you have your hands full."

Actually, it was *Ford* who had his hands full. He slipped beneath her panties now, and she trembled as she smacked at his wayward hand.

The wayward hand was not deterred.

"Hang up," Ford said.

"*Shh.*"

"Hey." Chloe sounded insulted. "I'm just passing the information on here."

"No, not you." Tara bit her lip to hold back her gasp when Ford slid his uncasted leg between hers, forcing her feet into a wider stance. "Oh, God."

"What the hell are you doing?" Chloe asked suspiciously. "You sound like you're running a marathon."

"I'll make the dinner," Tara managed. "Anything else?"

"Yes, lots else," Ford whispered. "Hang up first."

"Well," Clueless Chloe said in her ear, "I get the feeling that this is going to be one of those meaningful Hallmark moments for our guests, so I thought we could also do up a really nice basket with some of my—"

Ford nipped the back of Tara's thigh to get her attention.

He had it.

She gave him a push to the chest to slow him down, but he was a man on a mission. A quick tug, and her panties hit the floor.

He was nothing if not resourceful.

"Your leg," she hissed, then bit back her moan when he lightly stroked right over ground zero.

"Not going to use my leg," he said.

Good grief.

"...*Hellllooooo?*" Chloe said. "When will you be back?" There was something new in her voice now. Definitely still suspicion, but with a big dose of humor now, too. "After you've taken care of Ford?"

"Yes. *No.* I have to go," Tara said, desperate to get off the phone before she got off in Ford's hands. He already had her halfway there. "I'll be there to get the dinner together."

"Okay, but fair warning—Maddie's going to be

coming by there with some stuff for Ford so he can manage better on his own. Jax is with her."

"'Kay, gotta go." Tara dropped the phone and tried to remember why this was a bad idea.

She couldn't come up with one reason. "Maddie's going to come."

"No, I called Jax when you were in the kitchen and told him I was fine." His voice was thick with arousal. "But you. You're going to come, Tara. You're going to come hard."

"Ford. We can't... *you* can't..." She shook her head, hoping he'd see reason.

But he was most unhelpful in that regard. He'd produced a condom from God knew where and tugged her down to straddle him. He was wearing basketball shorts that Sawyer had brought for him at the hospital, which meant easy access. With a single thrust of his hips, he drove into her, pushing her to sweet ecstasy. He murmured something in her ear, something soft and sexy, but she couldn't hear it over the roaring of her own blood as he hurled her toward climax.

"Careful of your leg," she gasped.

"It's not my leg you should be worried about."

Oh boy. He was right. As she flew over the edge, her heart and soul shattering in tandem, she heard herself cry out his name. And the very last thing on her mind was his leg.

Chapter 27

♥

*"It's frustrating when you know all the answers,
but nobody bothers to ask you the questions."*
Tara Daniels

Touching Tara kept the leg pain from hitting the circuits in Ford's brain. There was only room for one sensation at a time, and his hunger for her won out.

That worked for him. *She* worked for him. He couldn't get enough. He had no idea how it was that he was lucky enough to have her with him here, but since he'd made a lifelong habit of not questioning things, he just accepted it. Accepted that she'd once again worked her way into his heart and made herself right at home.

For good this time. He knew that much.

They were still both breathing unsteadily, sweaty and tangled. He stroked a hand down her back, and she practically purred. He could hear his phone vibrating from the pocket of his shorts, but with his hands full of warm, sated woman, he couldn't give a shit.

"Are you okay?" Tara murmured.

"I just came so hard my eyes rolled back in my head. I'm so okay I can't believe it."

"I meant your leg." She slipped out of his arms. "But good to know where you're at."

"And where's that?"

"Mellow from the great sex," she said, looking around for her clothes. "Or maybe it's the drugs."

"No, pretty sure it's you," he said mildly. "And I hate to disagree with a very gorgeous, very naked lady, but that was more than sex."

Someone knocked at the door. Tara clutched her dress to her chest and peeked stealthily out the window. "*Sawyer*," she hissed, bending over for her underwear, giving Ford a world-class view.

"So," he said, getting hard again. "I guess the question is—how much more than sex was that?"

She stopped in the act of buttoning her dress. "What?"

"If you ask me, I'd say it was *way* more than just sex. But 'way' probably isn't an apt descriptive adjective."

Tara stared at him. "And maybe our definitions of 'way' are different."

"Dilemma," he agreed. "Maybe you should just tell me in your own words."

"Now? With Sawyer at the door?"

"That'd be great," he said with relief, pulling up the basketball shorts and adjusting himself since round two was apparently not in the cards. Fucking Sawyer.

"I'm going to need more time than we have available," Tara said.

"Really? You couldn't just say, 'It's a fucking boatload more than just sex, Ford, thanks for asking'?"

She shoved her feet into her heels. "Did you hit your head when you fell?"

He caught her with his crutch and reeled her down to the couch next to him, ignoring Sawyer's next knock. "Stop waiting for me to let you walk away."

She eyed him speculatively. "What should I do instead?"

Fair question, he supposed. "How about we give each other everything we can, and not blame each other for what we can't?"

"That didn't work out for us before."

"Because you left without looking back," he pointed out.

"I had a problem, if you'll remember. I was pregnant."

"*We* had a problem," he said.

Sawyer knocked again, less politely this time. "Ignore him," Ford said.

"I don't run anymore," Tara said quietly. "I stay and fight."

"Well, good. Because—"

The front door opened, and Sawyer stood there looking pissed off. "Okay. When you're alive," he told Ford, "you pick up your damn phone and answer your damn door." He took in the two of them squared off on the couch, nose to nose, with Ford half dressed and Tara looking uncharacteristically mussed up. "Need a moment?"

"No," Tara said.

"Yes," Ford said, holding firm to Tara so she couldn't bail, because if he had to chase her he was going to lose and that would be embarrassing.

Without a word, Sawyer vanished into the kitchen,

and they heard him foraging around in the cupboards, no doubt planning on eating Ford out of house and home.

Ford looked at Tara. "Stay and fight then," he said. "For us."

She looked at him with a mixture of anxiety and hope. "While giving everything I can and not blaming you for what I can't?" she asked softly.

"That's right." He liked the look on her face, the one that said she was tempted.

"I like to analyze things," she warned him. "Obsess. Think too much."

"No," he said straight-faced. "Not you."

"I'm serious."

He smiled. "Yes, I know. Look, I'm sure I'll give you *plenty* to analyze and obsess over. Let's start now. I have certain parts that need analyzing and obsessing."

"Sawyer's in the kitchen!" she hissed.

"He won't listen." Ford yawned, fighting against the sudden weight of his eyelids. "Or he'll pretend not to, at least."

"Your meds are making you sleepy." She sounded concerned.

"No they're not." Yes, they were. But he didn't care. He wanted her again. And then again. Maybe she'd do all the work this time, just this once. He'd owe her. He was good for it.

"Ford, I listened to what you told Mia at the hospital."

"I know. I saw your heels beneath the curtain. So you know that I like to change the locks on Jax."

"And that you think you were bad news for me. Or that I was made for better things than being stuck with you in a town I hated." Her voice shook. "I never felt that way, Ford. Ever." She shook her head. "You were very important to me. You were my best friend. I just didn't know how to be *your* best friend. I didn't know how to give myself. I didn't learn that for a long time. When I got married to Logan, I *still* didn't know, and I went the other way and gave too much. I'm only now learning the happy medium."

Tenderness filled him. "I know," he said gently. "And you've seemed happier lately than I've ever seen you."

"Yes. That's because of you."

"Me?"

Tara smiled. "You." She kissed him, then hopped up, pulling her hair into some complicated twist. "I have to go. Our guests at the inn need me to get a picnic dinner together." Turning back to him, she was all put together again—cool and calm and gorgeous.

His.

He hoped.

"Ford?"

"Hmm?" he said, or he thought he did. He felt her come closer and smiled. "You smell good."

"I love you," she whispered.

Emotion burst through him, and he closed his eyes for a second to absorb it. He could hear her moving around as if she was at home. He liked that. A lot. Liked watching her. But then he realized he wasn't watching her; he was looking at the backs of his eyelids.

Huh. By the time he forced his eyes open, he was alone. "Tara?"

"Not exactly. But I can put on a Southern accent and get all pissy and bossy if you want."

Sawyer.

Ford looked around. He was still on the couch. Sawyer was leaning back in a chair eating chips and watching TV, his boots on the arm of the couch near Ford's face.

Ford shoved them. "What happened?"

"You needed a time-out," Sawyer said.

"Tara?"

"Gone." Sawyer cocked his head. "You're not firing on all cylinders."

No shit. Tara was gone, and Ford wasn't sure if he'd really heard what he wanted to hear—what he'd wanted to hear for a very long time—or if he'd just dreamed it. "Did she say…?"

"Say what?"

I love you… "Nothing. Forget it."

"She totally fondled you when she kissed you goodbye. You don't remember?"

"No."

Sawyer shrugged and lifted the bag to pour the last of the crumbs straight into his mouth. "Your loss. A woman like that fondles me, I remember."

Tara headed back to the inn. Although it felt as if she'd been gone all day, it had only been four hours from start to finish since she'd looked out the kitchen window in time to see Ford fall from the tree.

She never wanted to feel her heart hit her toes like that again. The run out to him had seemed to take forever, and then seeing his leg, his pain, had nearly killed her.

She thought of how she'd just left him, sated and relaxed and feeling no pain, and felt a little better. Inside the inn, she found Chloe in the sunroom, giving their guests facials. For a minute, Tara stood in the doorway watching her baby sister work, appearing both surprisingly professional and yet so sweet. Chloe had everyone laughing and smiling and completely at ease in a way that Tara could never have managed. She was still marveling over that when Chloe looked up and caught sight of her.

"Just lay back and relax now," Chloe said to their guests, and light on her feet, moved toward Tara, pushing her out into the hallway.

"Hey," Tara said. "Smells good in there."

"It's the oatmeal and honey mix in the facial. It smells delicious when it's warmed. Don't panic; I realize the inn doesn't have a license for a spa, but I'm not charging; it's a freebie. I'll make sure to have Maddie start applying for the right licenses before I ever think about charging anyone."

"I wasn't going to say that."

"Okay, what were you going to say? Let me have it. Or should I save you some time? Yes, I stole your heavy cream, but I replaced it this morning. It helps make the facial smooth."

"I don't mind," Tara said.

But Chloe was on a roll. "And yeah, okay, I ate the last of your Not Yo Mama's Apple Pie. But..." She flashed her poker-faced smile. "You're getting sex, *great* sex by the look of you, so in all fairness, you don't need the pie, right? And I made brownies to replace it anyway. You can add them to your picnic dinner."

Tara felt a little dizzy with the quick subject changes, not to mention that this Chloe—a non-lazy, responsible Chloe—was a welcome surprise. "You did?"

"Okay, no. Mia made them. That girl most *definitely* inherited Ford's talent in the kitchen." Chloe waited a sly beat, just long enough for Tara to frown before laughing softly. "And yours, of course. Anyway, the husband's allergic to a lot of veggies, did you know that? So instead of veggie oil, Mia used applesauce, of all things. And the brownies came out *fantastic*. If I hadn't seen her do it with my own eyes, I'd have sworn you made them."

Tara shook her head. Definitely dizzy. "Chloe…"

"Yeah, yeah, yell at me for all of it later, okay? I've got to get back in there."

"No, Sugar. You don't understand." She reached for Chloe's hand. "I'm not mad at all. Are you kidding? You used your own spare time to do my job, you covered my ass, and you're making the inn a day spa on top of it? You're a lifesaver."

Chloe narrowed her eyes. "You take some of Ford's pain meds?"

"What? No!"

"You sure?"

"Yes! Chloe, I'm trying to say that I'm impressed. And that maybe I was too harsh when I said you never grew up. I shouldn't have said that."

Chloe arched a brow. "Well butter my butt and call me a biscuit. Did you almost—*almost*, mind you, but not quite—admit you were wrong about me?"

"Listen, I know I've been hard on you—"

"You were wrong," Chloe said flatly. "Say it."

Tara sighed. "Okay, fine. You're right. I was *wrong*."

"Wow. And you didn't even choke on it." Chloe grinned. "Now if only you'd get that stick extracted from your ass and admit that you're also over your head in the love department, we'd all be able to enjoy ourselves."

"My relationship with Mia is a work in progress."

"I meant Ford." Chloe leaned in and sniffed at her neck. "You smell like him, you know."

Tara felt the heat on her face. "You should probably get back to the guests."

With a soft, knowing laugh, Chloe headed into the sunroom. Tara blew out a breath and moved into the kitchen to get the picnic dinner together. She was planning on ham pinwheel sandwiches with brie, herbs, and nuts. She was going to call them Pigs-in-a-Wheel Delectables.

Mia came in and silently began chopping the herbs and nuts. Tara felt a little burst of pride and affection fill her. They really did work well as a team. She smiled, then felt her smile congeal when she caught a good look at Mia's face. "You've been crying."

"No." Even as Mia said it, her eyes filled. She sniffed and swiped angrily at her eyes. "I'm not crying." And then she burst into tears.

Crap. Shit. Damn. Tara very gently took the knife out of Mia's fingers as the teen babbled something in a long watery string. The only words that Tara caught were "stupid ass," "thinks he knows what's best," and "going to hunt him down."

Tara nudged the knife farther out of their way and risked both her heart and the silk of her dress by hugging Mia in close.

Mia slumped against her. "H-he said that when the s-summer's over and I go to S-Spain, we won't see each other anymore. *Ever.*"

Ah. Carlos. "Well, Spain's pretty far away and expensive to get to, but I'm sure when you're back in Seattle, you'll—"

"No, it's not the distance. He says that he'll hold

me back. That I need to go and have the whole college experience. He thinks it's unrealistic to expect…he says it's easier to break clean now. Like ripping off a Band-Aid."

"And you said…"

"I said that's the *stupidest* thing I've ever heard! That he's just a big chickenshit! That if he loved me, it wouldn't matter how far away I was; we'd make it work."

Oh God, the irony, Tara thought. "Maybe he's trying to protect you. Maybe he wants to make sure you get everything you deserve out of life. And the only way he thinks he can make sure you do that is to push you away."

"Well, that's just stupid," Mia cried. "I'll get what I want out of life on my own. It's not up to him to get it for me, or to make my decisions."

Tara hugged her as the girl sobbed with the abandon of a despairing teenager. God knew Tara herself had cried buckets when she'd been this age, but then again, she'd been in a different situation.

Sort of.

She thought about Carlos trying to protect Mia and felt her heart squeeze for him. For the selflessness…

And then closed her eyes as her heart nearly stopped beating. Back in Ford's hospital room, when she'd been eavesdropping on him and Mia, all the reasons he'd given their daughter for the two of them not being together— they'd all been for Tara.

To protect *her*.

His answer was like a knife to Tara's gut. His unselfish answer. She'd accused him of letting her go because he hadn't cared enough, but that hadn't been it at all. He'd let her go, thinking she deserved better.

What was it that she'd told Mia way back when? That she'd never spent any time in a small town, that she was used to more... God. All her reasons for leaving Lucky Harbor had been about herself.

She was made for better things than being stuck with me, Ford had said.

Carlos was doing the same thing, cutting off what he wanted and yearned for in order to give Mia the life he thought she deserved. Because in his eyes, she deserved more, not realizing that he deserved it, too.

She thought of Ford and physically ached. Because what about now? They were no longer seventeen, and she could decide for herself what she wanted, what she deserved.

What they both deserved.

How about we give each other everything we can and not blame each other for what we can't, he'd said. She'd assumed he'd been talking about himself, that he didn't want her to blame him for what he couldn't give.

But he'd meant her, she realized. He wouldn't blame *her* for what she couldn't give.

Tara waited until Mia was reduced to hiccups before offering her a kitchen towel to mop her face.

"Mascara check," Mia said, lifting her raccoon eyes to Tara's. "Am I a wreck?"

Tara took back the kitchen towel and swiped beneath Mia's eyes herself. "You're beautiful."

There was a knock at the back door. Carlos stood there wearing his baggy jeans and tight T-shirt, piercings glinting, eyes hooded, holding a case of cranberry juice. "Jax sent me over with this from the bar. They got a double shipment. He thought you might get use out of them." He glanced at Mia, and his mouth went grim. "You've been crying."

"Yes," Mia said. "It's what happens when a stupid guy dumps me."

Still holding the case of juice, he grimaced in misery.

Tara pulled Carlos the rest of the way into the kitchen. "Could you load that into the pantry?" She turned to Mia. "He'll need your help."

Mia looked surprised. "But the other day you said I couldn't be alone with him in the pantry except over your dead body."

"You have three minutes," Tara told her. "And if you don't emerge exactly as you are, there *will* be a dead body—just not mine. Take it or leave it."

Mia was staring at Carlos. "Take it," she said softly.

Tara watched Carlos wait for Mia to go ahead of him before he looked back at Tara.

"There's always a way to make things work," she told him quietly. "If you want it bad enough."

He nodded and followed Mia into the pantry.

Tara looked around at the empty but chaotic kitchen and for once realized she didn't feel an ounce of the usual panic and anxiety over the mess. Instead, she felt...

Utterly at home.

She stepped out the back door and drew a deep breath of the salty air. She bent and picked a pesky weed out of the flower bed. Then she looked at her watch. Their three minutes were up. Back inside, she moved to the pantry and knocked.

No answer. Dammit. Give teenagers an inch, and they'd take a mile. She should know; she'd taken hundreds of miles when she'd been a teen. *Thousands.* "Hey," she said, knocking harder, "I wasn't kidding about the dead body."

"It's okay, Mom."

Tara whirled around, her throat locked at the word "Mom." Mia and Carlos stood there, holding hands. "Oh," she breathed, scarcely able to talk. "You called me Mom."

"Yes. Is that okay?"

"*So* okay," Tara managed. "Did you two work it out?"

"No," Mia said softly, looking at Carlos.

He looked at her right back, not smiling, but with a world of warmth in his eyes.

"We've decided to enjoy the rest of the summer," Mia said, never taking her eyes off of him. "Take it as it comes. When I leave and then come back . . ." She lifted a shoulder. "We'll see."

"Sounds very grown-up," Tara managed, nearly losing it at the look on Carlos's face as he watched Mia. He was doing his best to be cool. Calm. Collected. She recognized the technique.

But he was hurting, and her heart ached for him. He'd wanted to rip the Band-Aid off as much for him as he had for Mia. But he'd agreed to wait, knowing the painful sting was coming eventually. Very likely, he didn't believe in good outcomes for himself. That was okay. She had a feeling that Mia believed enough for all of them. "How about helping me out in here?" she asked them.

They chopped. Sautéed. Stirred. Tasted. By the time the food was finished, Tara was red-faced and sweaty, which she knew because Mia forced her to view her own reflection in a spoon.

Mia was grinning. "You look . . ."

Tara stared at herself. "Like a mess. A complete mess."

"I think you're beautiful," Mia said.

That afternoon, Tara had her first real success right there in the kitchen, both with the meal *and* her time with her daughter, and she realized it was because of love.

If she cooked with love, things came out right.

So maybe if she lived with love...same thing? With love maybe she could be a real chef, a mom, a sister, a lover.

She could be anything she wanted.

She could have anything she wanted.

God, she really could. She looked at Mia. "I have to go for a few minutes. Can you man the phone?"

"Of course. Maddie and Chloe are here, too."

Tara grabbed her keys and ran outside. She had to go to Ford, had to tell him all she'd realized, but there he was in the yard, struggling out of the passenger seat of Sawyer's truck.

Chapter 28

♥

"You haven't lived until you've loved."
TARA DANIELS

As Ford stepped clumsily out of the truck, concern and worry choked Tara, and she ran forward.

He stopped her with a single, violent shake of his head.

"Yeah, don't bother," Sawyer said over the hood. "He gets all PMS-y if you try to help."

Tara took a good look at Ford. He was pale and sweaty, and unstable on his feet. Dammit. "You need to be inside. Off your leg."

"In a minute," he said.

"Ford, please," she said. "Just wait, let me—"

"Actually," he said. "I'm done waiting. Done doing things the easy way and letting things happen as they will."

Her heart caught. "What does that mean?"

"It means this is too important to let slip away again.

You're too important." He leaned back against the truck with a low grunt of effort, eyes dark, jaw clenched. "I love you too, Tara."

She stopped breathing, and he went still. "You did say that you love me, right? Oh, Christ, don't tell me that was the drugs."

She choked out a half-laugh, half-sob and shook her head.

He stared at her. "Okay, for the poor drugged man—is that no it wasn't the drugs, or no you didn't say it?"

She swallowed hard past the lump of emotion and gave him the words that she'd previously only managed to whisper when she'd thought he'd been sleeping. "I said it."

"Good. Because I love you, too. I think I always have. I always will." One of the crutches clattered to the ground. He started to bend for it and stopped short, going from pale to green.

"*Ford.*" Tara was at his side in two seconds, slipping an arm around him as Sawyer came around the other side.

"No," Ford said, resisting them both. "Just give me a damn minute. I think...Fuck. I think I'm going to pass out now."

"Okay, that's it," Tara said and nodded at Sawyer. "Inside. Now."

"Love it when you're bossy," Ford murmured. "Especially in bed. Can we do that again soon?"

"You don't listen to me when I boss you," she said, holding on to him.

"If you get naked, I'll try. I swear."

Sawyer looked deeply pained. "Hello, I'm right here."

When he tried to steer Ford toward the inn, Ford dug in his heels.

Or heel.

"Don't," Ford grated out. "Not yet. Sawyer—"

"Let me guess. You need a minute."

"Yeah."

"Ford, you're hurting," Tara said, and just sighed when Sawyer gave in and backed away, heading to the porch.

"My pain meds wore off," Ford announced.

"I know, which is why—"

"I need to do this, Tara. I came here to do this."

"You're trying to tell me something," she said.

"Yes. Actually, I'm trying to *ask* you something. The last time I asked, you didn't take me seriously because I was high as a kite. I'm not high as a kite this time, Tara." His eyes held pain, but also warmth and affection and love.

"I know this because I've been watching the clock," he said. "Waiting."

Before she could say a word to that, her sisters and Mia, along with Carlos, came out of the inn. So did their two guests with their picnic basket. Everyone crowded onto the porch with Sawyer.

Ford looked at them and let out one low oath.

"Oh, no," Tara said, ignoring their audience as she gripped his shirt. "No more waiting. You said so. Now ask me, dammit."

He seemed surprised that she'd managed to follow his rambling logic. "Now?"

"*Now.*"

"I ask you to marry me when we're alone, and you assume I'm out of my mind and don't respond. And now you want me to ask you while we're being stared at by..." He paused to look at all the people on the porch.

Everyone waved.

Shaking his head, Ford waved back. "I don't even know some of those people but the ones I do know are probably going to mock me for the rest of my life. And Jesus, is Chloe videotaping this?"

Chloe had her phone aimed at them. "For Facebook," she called out.

Tara turned her back on them. "Just do it!"

He stared at her. "You really are the most stubborn woman on the planet."

"Yeah, yeah, I'm working on that. *Ask me!*"

"You sure do like to tell people what to do. You know that?"

"Yes, but to be fair, I'm good at it. Ford—"

"*And* impatient," he mused. "Interrupting me when I'm trying to outline the reasons I love you."

She blinked. "You're...you mean you love my stubborn, bossy, interrupting self?"

"Well, I'd say you were more perversely inflexible and mule-headed, but yeah. I also love the way you drop your *g*s like a Southern belle, and the way you talk to yourself when you're cooking. And how you think you're so badass cool, calm, and collected, when really, if you know what to look for, you show everything in your eyes, and usually you're not cool, calm, or collected at all."

Her breath caught.

"Yeah," he said softly. "I know all the secrets. I love them, too." He pressed his mouth to her temple. "I love you, Tara. Love me back. Marry me."

She pressed her forehead to his and felt all the little

pieces of her heart knit together. "Yes," she said, and the crowd on the porch erupted into cheers.

"I did that," Mia told Maddie and Chloe proudly, pointing to Ford and Tara embracing. "I totally brought them together."

Ford grinned at her, then looked down at Tara. "I even have a ring," he said. "I've had it since right after you poured me a glass of iced tea while you were serving the Garden Biddies." He lifted a shoulder. "It was wishful thinking. It's on my boat," he said and waggled a brow.

She laughed. "Are you trying to lure me back to your place?"

"Yes. Is it working?"

She thought about it for a beat. "It'll be hard."

He lowered his voice for her ears only. "I can promise you that."

"I mean I'm no picnic, Ford."

"No," he agreed, closing his eyes when she slid her arms around his waist, brushing his lips along her jaw. "But you sure taste good."

With a sigh, Tara turned her face, pressing it against his chest. He wrapped her in his arms and held on, although to be fair, she was doing most of the supporting. "How long do you figure until you fall down?" she asked.

"Maybe ten seconds."

"Sawyer!" she yelled, without taking her eyes off of her new fiancé, who cupped her face, and looked deep into his eyes.

"*Forever* this time," he said as Sawyer strode toward them.

Tara sighed blissfully. "You know what this means, right?"

"I'm done guessing," he said. "Tell me."

"It means you're mine," she said. "And I'm yours. No more walking away. We are going to get it right this time."

His smile was slow and easy, and just for her. "Well, finally."

Good Morning Sunshine Casserole

Ingredients:

1 layer of tater tots

1 layer of ham or sausage cubes
(or crumbled bacon, whatever makes
your skirt blow up)

1 layer of grated cheddar cheese
(there's no such thing as too much cheese
for breakfast)

Mix the following together and pour on top:

6 beaten eggs

1/2 tsp. salt (or more, if no one's looking)

1/2 tsp. pepper

1 tsp. dry mustard

1/2 cup of chopped onion

3 cups of milk

2 tsp. Worcestershire sauce

Add 1/2 cup melted butter over all that. Shh, don't tell…

Cook 1 hour at 350 degrees uncovered.

Kissing
Santa Claus

Chapter 1

"Merry Christmas," Sandy Jansen murmured to herself, staring in her office mirror. She closed her eyes, trying to avoid the sadness in her own reflection. She loved Christmas, loved the decorations, loved the festivities, loved the joy of the entire season, but this year that joy was sorely lacking.

It had been for five months, ever since the day she'd watched Logan Perrish's very fine ass walk out of her life.

It was silly because she'd known he was just a fling. Hell, it'd even been her idea. But she hadn't known that she'd miss the NASCAR star as much as she had.

Or that all these months later, she'd still remember his smile, his warm, dark eyes, how she'd melted at the sight of him. And when he'd touched her . . . well. She'd gone up in flames for him, all of her, including her damn heart.

Sandy opened her eyes but didn't meet her own gaze

again. Instead she looked at the rest of her. As the town clerk of Lucky Harbor, she'd come to the annual employee Christmas cocktail party in a cute little red dress, her "holiday" dress, which never failed to cheer her up. Being all of five foot two was a bit of a problem, but her four-inch Manolo knockoffs helped.

What *hadn't* helped her was the costume she now had on over her sexy little red dress, complete with a stuffed belly and butt, white beard and wig, red fur-lined hat, and the final touch, thick wire-rimmed glasses.

Santa Claus.

From outside her office and down the hall, there was only silence. The party had emptied out, leaving her alone in the building. Tomorrow night, Christmas Eve, everyone in town would be here for the annual Christmas parade, which Santa would head up in the same 1972 Buick convertible, aka rust bucket, that they'd been using for years. The evening would culminate at the end of the pier, with all the kids lining up to sit on Santa's lap so they could whisper their holiday wish.

Sandy's wish, if anyone had asked, would be that Anderson hadn't caught the flu so *he* could play Santa as planned. She'd tried to get a last-minute replacement, oh how she'd tried. But Jax Cullen, Lucky Harbor's mayor, was master of ceremonies of the parade. Ford Walker and resident hottie had taken his new fiancée to Palm Springs for a holiday getaway. Sandy's third and final choice, Sheriff Sawyer Thompson, was going to be on duty at the parade, handling crowd control.

There was no one else to ask, which panicked Sandy. No one but her... She took her role of town clerk very seriously, but this... this was going over and above the call of duty. Yet all she could think of was the kids of Lucky Harbor, and how disappointed they'd be without Santa. Dammit. She sighed and took one last look at herself. She did actually look a little bit like Santa, albeit a very short one.

"You, Sandy Jansen," she told her reflection. "Are a sucker."

The biggest. And she had a broken heart to prove it. With a sigh, she reached around behind her to unzip the Santa costume, but the zipper wouldn't budge. She tried again. And then again. "*Really?*" she said to the room in general, most specifically to her karma. "Are you kidding me?"

Karma wasn't listening. The zipper was stuck.

"Dammit," she said, and tried again to no avail. "Well, isn't this just perfect." With an eye roll, she snatched up her purse and her keys and headed out into the night, hoping a neighbor was still up. But if anyone so much as smiled at this *I Love Lucy* predicament, Sandy was going to smack them. "Christmas," she muttered, but it wasn't annoyance she felt so much as bone-deep sadness. Her family was back East. She didn't have a date, and she felt... alone. It was a feeling that someone who'd grown up as the nerd, the bookworm in a family of charismatic, outgoing people, should be familiar with by now. Shaking her head at herself, she hurried out to her car, her heels clicking on the asphalt, and she realized how she must look in the Santa costume—with her heels.

Santa in drag...

Good thing she was all alone. Except she wasn't.

The lot was empty but for her rundown Toyota and another car, a convertible BMW.

And leaning against her car as if he belonged there was the cool, sophisticated, gorgeous Logan Perrish, as if she'd conjured him out of her nightly fantasies. Except in her nightly fantasies, he returned her rambling but heartfelt e-mails...

Clearly she was hallucinating. Because no way would karma be so cruel as to stick her in the Santa costume and then produce the man who'd crushed her.

"Sandy?"

At the low, almost unbearably familiar voice that she'd expected to never hear again, she dropped her keys. To give herself a desperately needed moment, she bent over, and her hat and wig fell off. What were the chances he'd believe she really was Santa?

"Sandy."

Dammit! Oh, how she wished she could turn back time. Because then, when she'd gotten that sexy "hey, babe" voice mail message a few days after he'd left, she wouldn't have then poured her heart out to him via e-mail.

To which he'd never responded...

She scooped up both the hat and the keys and hugged them to her padded belly as she straightened and shook her head wildly. Nope, not Sandy. No Sandy here—

"It is. It's you," he murmured, and then laughed.

Which settled it. He'd hurt her *and* laughed at her. She tended toward a mild-mannered and easygoing temperament, but this was too much for her. She was going to have to kill him.

Chapter 2

Logan pushed off of Sandy's car and shook his head. He couldn't believe it when, through the mist of the frosty night, came a very short, round Santa, wobbling through the lot toward Sandy's car.

In four-inch FMPs.

It hadn't been until Santa dropped the hat and wig that he realized he recognized that wavy mass of dark hair. Choking out a laugh, he took a step toward her. His smiled faded when she just stared at him. Her baby blues, usually so soft and warm, were putting out a chill to rival the December night air.

Not exactly the welcome he'd envisioned. And he *had* envisioned. His fantasies had involved her throwing herself at him, and shortly thereafter divesting them both of all clothing.

"Hey," he said. "You okay?"

"Why wouldn't I be?"

Hmm. That didn't sound like she was gearing up to throw herself at him at all, much less anything indecent after that. Logan looked at her thoughtfully, rubbing his jaw. In his world, decisions were made in split seconds. Sandy had always made him want to slow down and enjoy. Take his time... It was to his shame that he hadn't realized how much she meant to him until he left Lucky Harbor.

He was going to have to leave again, but not until he'd made her his. Which apparently wasn't going to be as easy as he'd thought. He took another step toward her, but her hand came up, eyes flashing, and she pointed at him. "No. Do *not* touch me."

They'd spent a week together, during which she'd spent a fair amount of time begging him to touch her. He'd loved touching her. In fact, he'd spent seven long nights doing just that... every inch.

Logan wasn't unsure of much. Of anything, really, not that he could think of. Things tended to go his way. Sure, there'd been a failure or two along the way, and disappointments, even heartbreak.

But mostly things fell right into his lap. His mom had always told him it was because he was the last of seven kids, born early. He'd been in a rush to get ahead of the pack from the get-go, and that had never changed. Which is what made the sweet, warm Sandy Jansen so confusing. He'd wanted her, he'd had her, and that should have been the end of the story.

Except that after their one-week, holy-shit-hot affair, he'd left Lucky Harbor, gone back to the racing world, and then proceeded to do nothing but think of her. He'd called her. What had he said? Hell, he couldn't remember.

Probably just "hey," but she hadn't returned the call. He'd had his manager send a round-trip ticket to his next race, but she hadn't shown up.

He could admit, he'd been surprised. Disconcerted.

And utterly bewildered.

People called him back. Women called him back. He'd busied himself with his season, telling himself it didn't matter. There were other women, lots of them.

But not a single one had attracted him. It'd been five months since he'd seen or heard from Sandy, and he should have been over it, but he wasn't. So he'd come to see why…

Sexy Claus was tugging at something behind her, and swearing the air blue. "Goddamn, stupid, shitty, crappy, piece-of-shit zipper…"

"Do you kiss Mrs. Claus with that mouth?" he teased.

She stopped wriggling and narrowed her eyes at him.

Okay, so she wasn't amused. He'd figured they'd be naked by now, sweaty and working their way toward round two.

And three…

"Need help?" he asked.

"Not from you."

There was no one else in the parking lot. Across the street was the diner and the pier, and that lot was full. There was a group of Christmas carolers standing outside the diner, doing a rowdy rendition of "Jingle Bells."

Sandy yanked off the wire-rimmed glasses and began to look more like herself. Well, except for that red suit, which was making her look wider than she was tall.

"And what are you even doing here?" she asked, but then, without waiting for an answer, she reached past him and unlocked her door, tossing in her purse, the Santa hat, and the wig. She tried to slide in behind the wheel, but she wouldn't fit with her padded belly. "Cheese and rice!" she burst out, and with a deep sigh, dropped her head to the roof of her car and thunked it a few times.

"You're going to rattle something loose," Logan said.

She turned only her head and gave him an eat-shit-and-die look. "It's been five months, Logan."

Right to the heart. That was Sandy. She knew no other way. Out of all the women he'd known—and there'd been quite a few—she was the most open, the most direct. The most hardheaded. It was a huge part of the attraction for him, how she kept her own mind and didn't take any shit from him. He dropped the smile and got serious. "I told you I'd be back."

"Someday. You said you'd be back someday. You tell all the women that!"

Well, he'd meant it when he'd said it. Okay, so maybe he hadn't. Maybe it had been a line, but he'd changed. From the moment he'd left her, he'd changed. Not that she wanted to hear that from him right now. "It was a busy season, and I couldn't get away. If you'd have come to see me, this would have been a lot easier."

"I didn't want to be that girl."

"What girl?"

She sighed. "The one who e-mails you her entire heart and then chases you around the whole frigging world."

"I usually stay within the continental United States."

This earned him another sigh.

Across the street, the carolers switched to "Oh Holy Night."

"And what e-mail?" Logan asked.

"You know what e-mail," she said, and she turned slightly, presenting him with her back. "Undo me."

"Is this a sexual invitation?"

She craned her neck and eyed him long and hard.

Okay, *not* a sexual invitation. Got it. He gently stroked her hair from her nape and reached for the zipper of the Santa costume, brushing her creamy skin with his fingertips.

She shivered, and he went still. Coincidence? To test, he ran the pad of his thumb over the same spot, and she shivered again. Ah, he thought with a surge of fierce relief. She wasn't completely over him, at least not yet.

"I didn't get any e-mails, Sandy."

"Fine, so I went to spam. Whatever. I didn't get any e-mails from you at all."

This was true. He was more of an in-person sort of guy. "Know what I wished for from Santa?" he asked quietly.

She remained silent, but he knew by the stillness of her body that she was listening. She'd always listened to him, like no other. She'd listened, and she'd cared. He'd underestimated how much that meant to him. *His* fault. He'd clearly hurt her. Also his fault. But he was good at turning shit around.

"I wished for you," he said, and slowly unzipped her. His heart caught as the costume opened, revealing more creamy skin.

And nothing else.

Her breathing quickened, and so did his.

"Logan," she whispered.

"Yeah, babe?" Anything. *God, anything you want. My car, my wallet, my life…*

At the base of her spine, he ran into red silk. Before he

could get any farther, she stepped clear and shrugged, and the Santa suit fell away, revealing the petite but lushly curved Sandy wearing a slinky red dress that made his mouth water. "There you are," he managed.

"Thanks." Bending, she scooped up the costume and shoved it into her car. "Appreciate it."

"What are you doing now?" he asked.

"Now?"

"Yes, right now. Let's go talk."

"I have a very busy schedule," she said. She glanced around her and narrowed her gaze on a group of carolers standing outside the diner across the street. "I'm supposed to be caroling. I have a date to be caroling."

She was making that up right on the spot. He knew it. She knew it. "You have a date. Caroling."

"That's right. He's probably over there right now, wondering why I'm standing here talking to you instead of holding his hand and singing with him." She gave him a narrow-eyed look. "You don't believe I could get a date? Because I have lots of dates."

She was warm, soft, sexy, and adorable. He believed she could date anyone she set her mind to. But no, he didn't believe she had a date tonight, caroling. "You'd best hurry over there then. Looks like they're getting ready to move on. I wouldn't want you to stand anyone up."

She lifted her chin to nose-bleed heights and crossed the street.

Logan remained where he was, watching. When Sandy walked up to the group of carolers, she glanced back.

He waved.

It was dark so he couldn't be sure, but he thought maybe she bared her teeth at him before sidling up to one of the men. Then she glanced back again and shot Logan a "see?" look.

Logan gestured that she should do her thing. Sandy hesitated, then slipped her arm in the man's.

This earned her a startled stare; then the guy disentangled himself and shifted closer to the man on the other side of him. That man then curled a possessive arm around Sandy's "date," and they both shifted away from her.

Logan grinned.

The carolers finished their song and moved on.

Sandy came back across the street, and without a word to him, slid behind the wheel of her car, clearly intending to leave. She was a speedy thing.

But he was speedier. He blocked her move by stepping close, one hand on the roof, the other on the door, as he crouched down to look into her face.

Her eyes met his and softened, but then she shook her head and closed them. "Okay, so I didn't have a date tonight. Dammit."

"Sandy."

With a sigh, she opened them again, and leveled him with those killer baby blues, which were filled with a shocking, staggering sadness. "Hey," he said gently, and unable to help himself, leaned in and kissed her lightly. "Missed you."

"Oh, Logan," she whispered, as if maybe she'd missed him too, but there was something in her voice that disturbed him.

She didn't believe him. "I should have told you sooner," he said. "I've been thinking about you. Wanting you."

"So this is what, a booty call?"

"I wanted to see you," he said, smart enough not to touch that question with a ten-foot pole.

"Your season's over now, right? Everyone's off for Christmas, and you got bored. You were probably on the West Coast visiting your San Francisco relatives, so you thought why the hell not look up that cute little brunette you hooked up with from Lucky Harbor because she was easy enough?"

He stared at her, stunned that she'd think that. "You're wrong."

"Am I?"

"Yeah." And he pulled her into his arms and kissed her to prove it.

Chapter 3

♥

One moment, Sandy was sitting there behind the wheel of her car in her righteous resentment, and the next, Logan's lips had covered hers. His hand cupped her jaw, and he sucked hungrily on her bottom lip, like a starving man in search of a meal.

Confused, dizzy, and extremely turned on, she threw her arms around his neck and pressed even closer. Logan answered with a low, rough groan and stood up, pulling her out of the car with him. He threaded his fingers into her hair while his other arm slid around her hips, hauling her up onto her tiptoes for a better lineup of their parts.

And, oh Lord, how their parts lined up.

She heard herself moan with the sheer pleasure of his hard body. He broke the kiss to stare down at her with a triumphant gleam.

"What was that?" she demanded.

"A reminder of what we had."

"What we had was a fling," Sandy said. "A very hot, wonderful fling, but then you left."

"I had contractual obligations," he reminded her. "And you're not remembering all of it." He brushed his lips across hers. "We said we'd keep in touch because we had something."

"Chemistry."

"Yeah. Let me remind you just how much."

This kiss was deeper, hotter, and *far* more intimate as he opened his mouth over hers. She told herself to shove him away, to regain some badly needed dignity, but her brain sent the wrong message to her fingertips, and she hauled him closer instead, pushing herself against him. He was hard. *Everywhere.* She was on the edge, and he'd barely touched her. This did not say much about her will to resist him.

And truth be told, she had just about forgotten why she wanted to.

Because he made you fall for him—hard—and then he walked his sweet ass right out of your life. It hit her like a bucket of cold water. She unfisted her hands from his shirt and gave him a push.

Logan stepped back and looked at her from beneath his sexy, hooded eyes.

"Don't do that," she said, annoyed at her own breathlessness.

"Don't kiss you?"

"Don't kiss me. Don't touch me."

He smiled. "Because you can't resist me?"

His smile weakened her knees. She gave him another

push and then slid into her car again. "And don't do that either."

"Talk?"

"Smile." She turned the key and started her car. "In fact, don't anything in my presence. Go back to your bigger-than-life world, where women drape their panties on your hotel room doorknob and scream your name and want to be with you."

"I don't want to be with any of them. It's Christmas, and I want to be with you."

But could she really believe that? "You should go home, Logan."

He was quiet, *too* quiet, and she made the mistake of looking at him. He was standing there all leanly muscled and gorgeous by moonlight. "That's the thing, Sandy," he said, his voice low and husky. "*I am* home."

Until the season starts up again, she told herself, and revved her engine. "Stand back. I don't want to run over your foot."

Not a stupid man by any means, he took a step back, but his eyes never left hers. "I'm going to prove myself to you, Sandy."

Afraid of him doing just that, she hit the gas and drove off into the night. *Don't look back...*

She totally looked back. Logan was standing in the middle of the lot watching her go.

Sandy spent the evening staring at her bedroom ceiling, her body bereft and achy, like she'd betrayed it by not taking Logan home with her.

Sleep, she ordered herself. *Concentrate.*

But the truth was, she hadn't been able to concentrate in months. Sleeping through the night had become a forgotten luxury. Instead, she'd toss and turn, remembering the feel of Logan's hands and mouth on her body, and how he'd made her burn for him...

You could be burning right now, instead of lying here staring at the ceiling.

Ignoring herself, she gave up trying to sleep and showered, then drove to work. She pulled into the lot and blinked in surprise. The old '72 Buick was gone, replaced by a...BMW.

She stared at it, then strode into the building. "Where's the Buick?" she asked Kali, the front-desk clerk.

Kali was twenty-four, an avid snowboarder who supported her habit with this minimum-wage position, along with her minimum experience. She was quivering with excitement. "I can't tell you."

"Excuse me?"

Kali flipped her cute blond ponytail to the left and then the right, and when she'd satisfied herself that no one was looking or listening, she leaned close and whispered, "He paid me not to tell you."

Sandy already knew damn well who "he" was, but she asked anyway. "*Who* paid you not to tell me *what*?"

"Well, not *me* exactly..." Kali swiveled her chair and pointed to the side counter, which was set up with three large money jars, each for a different charity, the Humane Society, the senior center, and disabled athletes.

Each was full. Shocked, Sandy moved closer. "Oh my God." Each jar had been crammed with money.

"And those aren't just one-dollar bills, either," Kali said in an awed whisper. "Those are *twenties*. He said he'd have done it in hundreds, but the bank wasn't prepared to give him that many hundreds on such short notice."

Sandy's eyes narrowed as a bad feeling came over her. "*He*."

Kali smiled. "The cutest guy in the history of all cute guys." From her desk, she pulled out last week's *People* magazine and opened it to the Star Tracks page. There was Logan in full color in his racing gear, hot, sweaty, gorgeous...holding up a trophy and giving the grin that never failed to melt her panties.

Oh, no. No, no, no, no...this was bad. "*Logan*," she hissed through her teeth.

"Yes!" Kali beamed at her. "Got it in one."

He was just trying to impress her with the charity jars, she told herself. That was all. And he had more money than God himself, so it wasn't like he'd done that much.

Except stay up all night and get the old Buick piece-of-shit towed away.

Replace it with his BMW.

Go to the bank and clean them out of twenties.

And stuff the charity money jars full. "Kali, you have one thing to do today."

"What's that?"

"Find me a Santa."

Sandy was head deep in a mountain of paperwork at noon when sushi was delivered.

From a little place in Seattle, her favorite.

She eyed the small card that had come with it. She blew out a breath and opened it.

Sandy,

Enjoy.

Love, Logan

Love? He wouldn't know love if it bit him on his very fine ass. But then again, she admitted with a soft sigh, she wasn't sure she would know love either. Mostly she preferred books or work over men, not that they were beating down her door.

All she knew was that Logan was back in town—for how long she had no idea. She couldn't imagine it would be more than a few days—and she couldn't eat, couldn't sleep, couldn't do anything but think of him.

She eyed the sushi, and her mouth watered. Okay, maybe she *could* eat, just a little...

Jax Cullen, town mayor and longtime friend, walked by her office and stopped, brows up. "You went out for sushi and didn't ask me?"

Jax was leanly muscled and broad shouldered and... well, gorgeous. They'd almost had a thing once, a very long time ago, but they'd settled for a friendship, a comfortable one. "I didn't go out," she said. "This was delivered."

"You have a secret admirer?"

"Not so secret. Logan's back in town."

Jax leaned against the doorway, settling in. "You going to admit to him that you've been pouting since he left?"

"Hell, no," Sandy said.

"You going to admit to him that you've always wanted to stop being a small-town homebody and travel the world?"

"Hell, no."

Jax shook his head. "Are you going to admit anything?"

"Would you?"

Jax smiled at that. "You suggesting I out-stubborn you?"

"I'm not suggesting," she said. "I'm flat out saying it."

"Yeah." Jax nodded with a laugh. "Maybe. But I've

changed my ways, and now I've got the woman I want in my bed every night. Change your ways, Sandy. He might surprise you."

She wasn't ready to go there. "Don't let the door hit you on your very fine ass," she said.

He laughed again and left, and Sandy spent the afternoon at her desk, with one ear glued for Kali's footsteps to come down the hall and tell her that she'd located a Santa replacement.

"Nothing," Kali said at the end of the day.

Sandy put her pen down. "Are you telling me that there's not one man in this entire county willing to be Santa for the kids of Lucky Harbor?"

Kali rolled her lips together. "Um. Yes. No. I mean, not exactly."

Sandy narrowed her eyes. "Then, what exactly?"

Kali covered her face. "Okay, so there was something else he paid me to do." She said "he" like he was the second coming. "He paid me not to find you a Santa."

This took a full moment to compute. "So . . . you didn't make the calls."

Kali bit her lip. "He said—"

"He who?" she asked, knowing damn well who.

"Logan. The one in my *People* magazine."

"I know who he is, thank you."

"Right." Kali giggled.

Sandy worked on not completely losing her ever-loving mind. "So what was it?"

"What was what?"

"Why weren't you supposed to find me a Santa?" Sandy asked with what she felt was remarkable calm, even though she wasn't calm. Not even *close* to calm.

"It's a secret," Kali said; then with a softly uttered apology, she whirled and ran off. "See you at the parade in an hour!" she yelled back.

Sandy turned and stared at the costume in the corner chair. She was wearing her favorite emerald-green wraparound dress, but that was about to change. "Great. I'm going to be merry and fat for Christmas."

"I think we can do better than that."

With a startled gasp, Sandy whirled to find Logan lounging in her doorway, looking like he didn't have a care in the world. "*Logan.*"

His eyes heated. "You look like a Christmas treat. Good enough to eat."

She pointed at him. "No. No charming me, remember?"

"You said no talking, touching, kissing." He pushed off the doorjamb and stalked her across the office. "You didn't say anything about charming."

Well, shit. She was in *big* trouble.

Chapter 4

Logan didn't have to get any closer to Sandy to see that she was stressed, anxious, and exhausted. Poor baby needed some TLC, and he was just the man to give it to her.

"This isn't going to work," Sandy told him, backing away as he advanced. When she nearly tripped over her own office chair, he put his hands on her hips to hold her steady. Surprised to find her quivering beneath his touch, he softened his hold. "Sandy," he murmured softly while brushing a stray strand of hair from her cheek.

"You can't charm me." She shook her head from side to side. "You can't." She fisted her hands in his shirt and glared up at him, her eyes huge and wide. "I don't have time to be charmed, Logan!"

"I know." He ran his hands up and down her arms. "I know."

"I don't know what kind of game you're playing, but

having Kali not get me a Santa... There are kids out there. *Kids*, Logan, and they came to see Santa. So no matter what the hell you think you're doing here playing with me, I can't have it, not now. You're not what I need right now."

"I'm exactly what you need."

She stared up at him, then dropped her head to his chest with a little moan. Because he couldn't help himself, he stroked a hand down her slim back and brushed his cheek along her hair, loving the scent of her, the feel of her against him. "I'll prove it," he said.

"What?" She lifted her head and leveled him with her pretty eyes.

He slid his fingers into her hair and stroked her cheekbone with his thumb. God, he'd missed the feel of her skin. The way she looked at him. How she challenged him at every turn, treating him like...

A regular guy. "I'll prove it," he said again. "That I'm exactly what you need." He gestured to the Santa suit lying lifeless in her spare chair.

She stared at it, then at him. "You? But you're a national celebrity, and you're... *gorgeous*, and you have a lot of really good qualities, but sweet isn't one of them, and—"

He yanked his shirt over his head and tossed it to her desk.

She abruptly stopped talking and stared at him.

Nice to know that he had that power. He kicked off his shoes, unbuckled his belt and slid it out, tossing it down on his shirt.

Sandy's mouth was open, as if maybe she needed it that way to breathe. "Um..."

He unbuttoned and unzipped his pants and shoved

them down, kicking them off. She took in his only item
of clothing left—black knit boxers—and drew in a shaky
breath. She seemed to like what she saw. Ditto. Maybe he
did have a few good qualities as she'd pointed out, but if
that was true, *she* was his best quality.

The very best.

And he couldn't lose her.

"Logan?" she whispered, her eyes glued to his body
in a way that was working for him. So was her new
breathlessness.

"Toss me the Santa suit, babe."

She didn't move.

"Sandy?"

She nibbled on her lower lip, worrying it between her
teeth, making it all plump, her eyes locked on his abs—
which wasn't even his best part. "Hmm?"

"The Santa suit."

She blinked, then jerked her eyes to his. "You're actually going to wear the Santa suit. For me."

She sounded bowled over at this, so utterly shocked
that he felt a tightening in his chest. Hadn't anyone ever
offered to do something nice for her? "Yeah. I'm going
to wear the Santa suit."

"It's going to be cold on the pier. Don't you think you
should leave your clothes on?"

Yeah, he probably should have. "I was trying to make
a statement."

She shook her head, still looking bowled over. Because
she wasn't moving, he walked by her and grabbed the
suit, pulling it on.

It was thick and itchy. And Christ, what was up with
the fat belly? "Santa needs a gym," he said, looking down

at himself. "And a whole hell lot less carbs and fat in his diet."

Sandy snorted, then covered her mouth, still staring at him.

"Are you laughing at me?"

Hand still clamped over her mouth, she shook her head. Then she nodded. Yes. Yes, she was laughing at him. Her eyes were sparkling. She was smiling. She was beautiful. Leaning in, he kissed her on the end of her adorable nose. "You can trust me to have your back."

She hesitated, then nodded, but he could tell she didn't believe him, not wholly. That was okay. He was well used to proving himself, over and over again. It was one thing he could do and do well.

Or so he hoped. Because this wasn't a race, and it wasn't a game. Getting Sandy to believe in him, in *them*, was going to be the most important thing he'd ever done.

Sandy stood at the end of the parade, watching as the crowd celebrated and the kids rushed Santa.

Logan.

He was in the hat, glasses, wig, and beard, and he'd even let her redden his nose. The costume was too short for him, but they'd stuffed the hem of the red pants into the black boots to be less noticeable. The belly was over-the-top—hell, the whole thing was over-the-top—but Logan was completely immersed into the role.

It shocked her.

He shocked her. She had the world-famous NASCAR driver wearing a Santa costume for a small town he'd never even heard of until five months ago.

He isn't for me. She'd finally convinced herself that

he was too into his career and the glitz and glam world that went with it, that he'd never be interested in making anything work with a small-town girl like herself.

But then he'd shown up.

For how long?

He glanced up and looked at her with that soft, tender, heated expression, the one that told her that she was the only woman on his mind.

Her.

When he could have had anyone. He sat on the throne at the end of the pier that had been set up for Santa, complete with a faux winter wonderland and lights and all the decorations the evening called for. As Sandy mingled and made sure the line stayed in control and that everyone was enjoying themselves, she kept one eye on Logan. Kid after kid jumped into his lap and whispered their greatest wishes for Christmas morning.

He had a smile for each of them, and she had to admit, she couldn't tear her eyes off of him. He was doing this, coming through for her like no one else ever had, and he was doing it with good grace and utter sweetness.

Realizing that the line had died down, she slowly walked toward him. The only part recognizable was his eyes. Eyes that tracked her approach.

He let out a slow smile. "Got a wish, little girl?"

Yes, for you to stay. "I'm a little old for wishes."

His smile went from playful to serious. "You're never too old for wishes."

Chapter 5

♥

Logan watched Sandy absorb his words and realized that she wanted to have faith in him; she wanted that badly.

But she wasn't sure she could.

His own fault. He'd had things pretty fucking easy most of his life, and he knew it. He was spoiled, and he knew that, too. But now was the time to change, time to learn from his mistakes.

Time to work his ass off for what he wanted, for what really mattered.

And that was Sandy. She mattered. She was his.

She just didn't know it yet.

She hadn't had anything easy, ever. She gave so freely of herself to others, and she cared. Deeply. She wasn't used to people noticing, but he noticed. He wanted to kiss away her worries and keep them away forever.

The crowd was gone. He gave her a "come here"

crook of his finger, and she surprised him by sitting on his lap. "I can't tell you my wish," she said softly, hooking her arms around his neck. "Or it won't come true."

He would have liked to make her tell him. He could have done it too, sliding his hands under her dress until she lost herself. But he'd prefer somewhere far more private. Rising, he set her on her feet, stretching, going still when she laughed.

"You look like an old man," she said.

"An old, *fat* man," he corrected, and narrowed his eyes when she laughed again. Enjoying her amusement, he grabbed her hand. "In fact, I'm so old, you'd better take me home." He led her up the pier to the BMW, which she stared at with open fascination. He knew for a fact that she had several speeding tickets and a few fender benders, so it was a real testament to his feelings for her when he handed her his keys.

She stared down at them in her hand, then lifted her face to his. "I can take it for a spin?"

"Yeah," he said, sliding into the passenger seat. "Though I should have installed a three-point seat belt system."

"You don't have to let me do this."

He knew she didn't want to be in any more debt to him. But he was in debt to her, for opening his heart. "Just watch fifth gear," he said. "It's an instant ticket maker."

"'Kay." But she chirped out of the lot on two wheels, and he grabbed the "oh shit" bar. In a Santa costume *and* he'd lost his balls. She flashed him a wide grin that made putting his life in her hands worth every second.

Half an hour later, after tearing up the mountainous roads with wicked glee, Sandy pulled back into the pier lot and regretfully turned off the car. "Thanks for that, Logan. Thanks for everything. Tonight was—"

He leaned in and kissed her. Kissed her until she let out a soft little moan that went straight through him as she slid her arms around his neck. Cupping her face, he stared into her eyes and saw his own hunger reflected back at him, so he dove back into the kiss, plundering her mouth until they were both panting for air.

Invite me to your place, he wished on a Christmas spirit he wasn't even sure he believed in. *Invite me into your heart*.

"Good night," she whispered instead, starting to get out of the car.

He grabbed her wrist, meeting her gaze, unable to let her go.

"I'm running a soup kitchen at Vets' Hall until midnight," she said softly. "I'm the only one of my staff without family in town. I always do it. I've got to go."

Slowly he released her and nodded. She got out of the car, walked to hers, and drove off into the night.

Logan drove to the Lucky Harbor B&B. He knew one of the owners well.

His ex-wife, Tara Daniels.

They'd burned hard and bright in their early twenties, back in his wild days. He'd been an ass then, and hadn't any idea how to nurture a relationship, much less a woman.

Tara was Southern, a real Steel Magnolia. Tough as hell, with a soft, warm heart.

She'd forgiven him, and they'd even become friends, of all things. He sat with her in the B&B's big, homey kitchen that she ran like a drill sergeant.

"Word around town is that you're whipped," she drawled.

"*Whipped* is such a strong word."

She laughed at him. "Sugar, you're here in Lucky Harbor, when you could be on a warm, deserted island with an assortment of babes. Give it up. You've finally fallen. Hard."

He looked into her amused eyes and admitted defeat. Not easy for him. "I was a lousy bet in my twenties," he said in way of apology to her, though she already knew this. "I screwed up, made mistakes. I'm better now. And I know what I want."

"Don't you even think about screwing this up," Tara said. "Sandy's a friend, a good one. She's too sweet and kind for the likes of you."

"I know."

"You go after her this time, you have to keep her."

"I know that, too," he said, and pulled the small ring box from his pocket. He'd been carrying it around for a month now, ever since he'd realized he couldn't live without her. "I wanted to wrap it in something she couldn't resist. I was thinking something sweet. Can't you make me a fruitcake or something?"

"Bless your heart," Tara said. "But no one likes fruitcake. I'll fix you up with just the thing. You'd best be sure, Logan Perrish. If you screw this up..."

"I won't." And God, how he hoped that was true.

It was twelve thirty a.m. before Sandy let herself into her house. Her place was high above the town on the bluffs. It was a tiny little thing, but she loved it because it was all hers.

Inside, she turned on the lights to her Christmas tree

but nothing else. For a long moment, she just looked at the cute little tree, flickering for all it was worth. She very carefully avoided peeking beneath it, where there were no presents. Her family was all back East, but she couldn't afford to go this year. Her parents had sent her a check, but she hadn't bought herself anything yet. Now she wished she had. When her phone rang, she jumped, startled. It was Logan.

"Merry Christmas," he said.

She melted at the sound of his voice, even as her heart panged hard. She imagined he was already back in San Francisco, maybe celebrating with friends and family. "Same to you. How's your Christmas so far?"

"To be determined. There's a present at your door."

"No," she said. "I just came in..." Biting her lip, she whirled to the door and pulled it open.

Logan stood there with a smile brighter than her Christmas tree, one hand braced above him, the other holding his cell to his ear. "Hey."

"Hey," she said breathlessly. Because she was a chronic idiot, she just stared at him. He shoved his cell phone into his pocket, and she walked into his arms. He wrapped them around her and kicked the door closed behind them as he eyed her tree. "It's missing something."

"It is not," she said, insulted.

He set her loose and pulled a brightly wrapped present from his pocket and set it beneath the tree.

Her heart stopped. How had he known? She stared at the present, then dropped to her knees in front of it. "I bought myself a new hair straightener the other day. I almost wrapped it and stuck it beneath the tree just to have a present to unwrap on Christmas. This is much better."

"Babe." His voice was low, husky, and full of far too much understanding.

Her heart took a direct hit, and she busied herself with fixing an already perfectly placed decoration.

"Sandy, look at me."

No. If she did, her mouth might run away with her good sense and ask how long he was sticking this time. Another week?

Less?

If she asked, he might feel the need to be honest, to remind her that come next season, he still had an entire world counting on him, a world that was far from here. It was also a world that she secretly yearned to see and experience—but how could she ask that of him? She knew she could have gone and seen him these past few months. She should have, but the truth was she wanted to go as his one woman, not as *one* of his women. And worse, if she looked at him, he'd see all of that along with her entire heart. That would be the biggest mistake of all.

Logan crouched before the woman he knew he'd never get enough of. She had her head bowed away from him, and she was breaking his heart. He reached for the box and handed it to her.

She pulled on the ribbon and gently tore away the paper, then sucked in a breath at the robin's-egg-blue Tiffany box. "*Logan*," she breathed.

"Open it."

She pulled off the lid and gasped, then lifted the diamond pendant necklace from the box. "It's beautiful," she whispered, and her eyes filled.

"Hey," he said softly. "Hey, it's supposed to make you happy."

She flashed a brilliant smile, if not a little soggy. "I am," she assured him. "It's just the most wonderful gift anyone's ever given me." She saw the card on the bottom of the box and reached for it.

For Sandy,

The only woman I want to be with for Christmas.

Love, Logan

He took the necklace from her and placed it around her neck. She fisted her hand around the pendant and held it to her heart. "I love it, Logan. Thank you."

"Looks good on you." He looked at her for a moment, hoping she was starting to understand how serious he was. Cupping her face, he stared into her eyes, slowly leaned in, and caressed her mouth with his in a gentle kiss. "I have another present for you. I've had this one for a while."

"No," she said. "You've given me too much. It's my turn to give you your present," she whispered against his lips. "It's wrapped and everything." She took his hand in hers and brought it to the bow at her hip, the one that appeared to hold her wraparound dress together.

"Mmm," he said, pulse leaping. "My favorite kind of present." The bow came loose, and her dress fell away, revealing a black silk bra and thong, and the soft, curvy body he'd been dreaming about every night for six months. "Exactly what I wanted," he whispered, and pulled her down to the rug.

Sprawled out over her, he felt his heart roll over, and his smile slowly faded. "Sandy, about the other present. I—"

"Later," she murmured. "Much later." And she pulled his head down to hers.

Chapter 6

♥

Logan's mouth ravaging hers again after all this time sent a thrill through Sandy. She'd accepted that she loved him, that this was what he had to give her, and for tonight, it was enough. It would have to be. So she dug her fingers into his shoulders and arched up into him.

She was rewarded when his mouth continued its quest to own hers, his tongue stroking in tune to his hands on her body, which felt like a tightly strung instrument, playing just for him.

Only for him.

"Tell me what you want, Sandy."

She was pretty sure he didn't want the answer to that, because the answer was everything. She wanted everything from him. "Well... you're overdressed," she managed to say, and tugged at his shirt.

He reared up and stripped out of his clothes, leaving

nothing but muscle and sinew and testosterone wrapped up in sleek, smooth skin. She couldn't take her eyes off him.

He didn't come back over her. Instead, he kneeled between her thighs and slowly slid her bra straps off her shoulders. "Tell me, Sandy…"

"I want you to keep going."

He smiled, then reached beneath her with one hand and unhooked the clasp of her bra. "I *am* going to keep going." He tossed the scrap of lace over his shoulder and then set his attention to her panties.

He removed those with his teeth.

She was panting by the time he crawled back up her body, touching every inch, following each of those touches by nips and kisses and licks of his tongue. She was panting, begging, and beyond desperate as he finally settled his weight over her.

With a moan, she arched her back, lifting herself to him. He smiled as if she'd given him the best Christmas present of his life, then went back to stoking her inner fire, caressing her until the flames consumed her, making her breath catch with each new touch. She wanted more, she wanted him, all of him, but hell if she'd beg.

For anything.

Then he stopped.

"What?" she gasped. There'd better be a fire…

"Just wanted to look at you."

Oh, she thought, melting. Oh, damn. It had taken her five months to get over him, she still wasn't over him, and now she wasn't sure she wanted to be.

He leaned over her, his eyes telling her he could read her thoughts. "Trust me," he said, his lips so close that they brushed hers as he spoke. "Trust me with you."

She opened her mouth to tell him that she did, in spite of herself, she really did trust him, but he'd produced a condom and slid home and what came out was an erotic, sensual cry.

His attention was on her body, his gaze heating every inch of her skin as he trailed his fingers in a line from her breasts to her legs, which he wrapped around his hips. He slid in deep, and with a rough groan, dropped to his elbows so that he covered her completely. She wrapped her arms around his neck, and then his lips were on hers as he began to move.

She lost herself in the delicious, overwhelming sensations, unable to think or even remember the reasons she'd hesitated to let him love her again like this. His arms slid beneath her, pulling her even closer to him, plunging deep, then deeper still, until she burst. He went over the edge with her, pulsing inside her until they collapsed together, spent.

Afterward, he carried her to her bed and started over...

Much later, she snuggled in against him and everything was forgotten as she fell asleep. She awoke to the sun poking her in the eyes and panicked. It was eight o'clock on Christmas morning! She was supposed to be at the diner for the breakfast buffet. Everyone in town was coming and she was in charge. She tried to jump out of bed but found she couldn't.

Because a very warm, tousled, leanly muscled man had her wrapped up tight in his arms. "Got to go!" she said, and kissed him on the jaw before shimmying loose.

He rolled over to catch her, but she was too fast, making quick work of pulling on jeans and a sweater. "I'm late!"

"It's Christmas," he said in a rough morning voice, and sexy as hell.

"Exactly!" She shoved her feet into boots, grabbed her purse, and headed for the door, but something bright nearly blinded her.

Her necklace.

She looked down at it, then at the naked man sprawled in her bed. "Thanks for last night."

"And this morning?" he asked in that husky male morning voice that made her tremble.

They'd dozed and woken each other up somewhere around three a.m. to tear up her sheets again. Her thighs rubbed together, and she felt the slight sting of the whisker burn there. Her face heated. "That too."

"I wanted to talk to you last night," he said, rolling off the bed and coming toward her, completely unconcerned about his nudity.

And if she were him and looked that good, she'd be unconcerned too. "It's okay," she said, and patted his chest. "I understand now. We're...explosive. I couldn't resist you, and vice versa. No regrets, Logan." And with a soft kiss, she left him alone.

And if maybe she shed a tear or two in the car on the way to the diner, well, no one had to know but her.

She arrived just in time. She jumped behind the counter to help the owner, Jan, and her waitress, Amy, serve the crowd. And it was a big crowd. Everyone was inhaling stacks of pancakes and eggs, and bacon and sausage, when suddenly the low level of mayhem ceased altogether as the diner door opened.

Sandy looked up just as Logan strode in.

The squeals of delight were genuine and real. The

residents of Lucky Harbor had fallen in love with Logan on his first visit, all those months ago. Logan smiled but moved through the crowd, heading straight for Sandy. "Hope you don't mind if I steal Sandy away for a second," he said.

Sandy told herself to be brave, but she wasn't feeling brave. She stood there in a bright red apron, a serving spoon in one hand and a coffee carafe in the other, and shook her head. "I can't," she said. "I'm busy."

Logan looked at her for a long beat. He took the spoon from her hand and set it down, then did the same with the coffee. He cupped her face. "I've been trying to tell you something. But I'll do it right here if I have to."

Oh, God. He was going to end things now. She wasn't ready. Maybe tomorrow she'd be ready. "No, that's not necessary—"

"I know you thought this was just a fling. Hell, *I* thought this was just a fling. I wanted it to be. I wasn't looking for this, and I sure as hell never wanted you to get hurt."

Someone in the crowd "ahhed" at that.

Logan ignored it. "But there's something about you, Sandy. Something that I just can't get enough of. That was proven when I left here and thought of nothing but you."

"You raced every weekend," she murmured, trying not to think about their audience. "You were too busy to think of me."

"Believe me, I had room to think of you no matter what I was doing. Just don't tell my team. That sort of thing is frowned upon since it tends to get people killed." He flashed a grin. "I would fly you out every weekend to ensure my safety, if you'd let me."

Her heart felt instantly lightened, and now butterflies were bouncing off the walls of her stomach. The good kind of butterflies. "Oh my God."

"Tell him you love him back!" someone yelled.

"Hurry, before he changes his mind!" someone else called out.

"How about hurry, my eggs are getting cold?" a third party griped.

Logan never took his eyes off Sandy. "I don't want anyone's eggs to get cold. Let's speed this up." He handed her the basket. "They're peach muffins. Because apparently no one likes fruitcake."

"What?"

He sighed and pulled out the muffins. Beneath, nestled in the bottom of the basket, was another Tiffany box, this one smaller than the first.

A ring box.

Her mouth fell open, and she slowly reached into the basket. Her fingers were shaking so badly that Logan took over and opened the box, revealing the diamond ring he'd picked out for her.

"There is no other woman for me," he said. "You're it, Sandy Jansen. You're warm and sweet and kind and funny, and you make me feel like I'm more than just a good driver. You make me feel...everything." He removed the ring from the box and slipped it on her finger. "I love you," he told her. "I love you more than I've ever loved anyone or anything. I want you to marry me, even though you drive like a crazy person."

There was a collective "ohmigod" around them, but Sandy paid them no mind. She stared at the ring, then up into his face, clearly stunned. "You do? Really?"

He was going to work on that, on making sure she never doubted or wondered how he felt. Ever. "I do." He loved the dreamy look in her eyes, but she hadn't said anything, and he was starting to feel a little bit like he was out in public without a stitch of clothing. He slid a look at their avid audience, then leaned in closer. "This is the part where maybe you could say you want me, too. I've kinda got my ass hanging out here. Say yes, and I'll throw in the BMW. You know you love that thing as much as you love me."

"Hey." A little kid tapped Logan on the arm. "You look a lot like Santa."

Sandy choked out a laugh and covered her mouth.

Logan looked down at the kid. "Santa already came this year. Did you get what you wanted?"

"Yeah," the kid said, waving a handheld game. "Did you?"

"I don't know." Logan looked at Sandy. "Did I?"

"Yes," she breathed, and threw herself at him. "You got everything you ever wanted. Forever."

"Does this mean you love me, too?"

"It means I love you. With or without the BMW." She waited a beat, grinning up at him mischievously. "But with is better."

Under
the Mistletoe

Chapter 1

♥

Holding on to her hat, Mia ran along the streets on her killer four-inch red heels, her matching red skirt ruffling in the breeze. Late. She was late.

It was the story of her life.

"Hey, Mrs. Claus!" a construction worker yelled. "I need some holiday spirit! Come on, mama, bring it over here!"

This was accompanied by the hoots and hollers of the guy's coworkers.

Mia flipped them off and kept running in tune to their raucous laughter. She might not be New York born or bred, but she'd learned to fit in just fine.

"Wow, are you real?" a little kid asked in marvel a block later, taking in her costume. "Is Santa real?"

"Yes!" she told him, and kept running.

Except if there'd really been a Santa Claus, she'd have

happily crawled onto his lap and whispered her greatest wish—to be picked. For her softball team, for her internship, for a relationship, it didn't matter. Getting picked meant everything to her, but somehow, she always ended up doing the picking.

Finally, she skidded into the restaurant and stopped to catch her breath, smoothing down her Mrs. Claus outfit. She had a change of clothes in her bag; she just needed to get to the ladies' room. Whirling to do just that, she plowed right into a warm, hard body.

Nick.

Her first reaction was embarrassment at her costume. Granted, she'd just made two hundred bucks serving drinks at a corporate Christmas party, but she'd hoped to get into her cute little black dress before Nick caught sight of her.

And then there was her second reaction, which was *wow*, because he looked heart-stoppingly great tonight.

"You're thinking so hard your hair's smoking," he said, his voice low and sexy. Teasing.

Mia reached out to touch her hair, but Nick caught her hand in his and smiled. "Like the look," he said. "Is it for me?"

"No!" But she smiled back at him because it was impossible not to react to Nick. "I have my date night LBD in my bag. *That's* for you."

He took her hands and spread them out at her sides, studying the skimpy Mrs. Claus costume. "Mmm, I'm happy to settle for this." His sun-kissed hair was the same color as the aged whiskey in the bottle on the bar behind him, and matched his eyes as well. He'd come right from work. His tie was loosened, his shirt sleeves shoved up past his deliciously corded forearms. His yummy build came from daily runs and long summers working as a manual laborer for tuition money.

But it wasn't his looks that stopped Mia's heart.

"Love that smile," he murmured.

That. It was that way he had of making her feel like the prettiest woman in the world. She had it bad for him, and knew it.

The hostess seated them before she could change. Each table held a flickering candle and a sprig of mistletoe. Nick picked the mistletoe up, held it over Mia's head, and then leaned in for a kiss. He squeezed her hand, his callused thumb slowly gliding over her palm. She'd never considered her palm a particularly sensual spot before, but his touch altered her breathing and made her shiver.

Or maybe that was just him.

His eyes darkened as he pulled back. "Hmm," he said, his voice like sex on a stick. "I definitely want to know what you're thinking now."

"It's you," she blurted out. "You have the most amazing eyes."

He brought her hand up to his mouth and nipped the pad of her thumb. "And just think, my eyes aren't even my best part."

She laughed. "And as I've seen all your parts, I'm in a position of authority to verify this as fact."

"Maybe you should re-verify later. Just to make sure," he said, flashing her a panty-melting grin.

Mia knew she could get lost in him. *Had* gotten lost in him. But she didn't want to get distracted by his sexiness, not tonight. She'd come here with a plan. She was giving him his Christmas present early, which was a flight to her aunt Chloe's Christmas Eve wedding. It would mean flying across the country on a whim and meeting the people who meant the most to her.

Nick was good with whims, and she was excited at the prospect of spending the holiday with him. But she held back, waiting, because this was a beautiful, expensive restaurant that they'd talked about but had never been to. It was intimate, and exquisitely decorated for the holidays, and she hoped that maybe Nick had a surprise of his own up his sleeve.

They'd been dating for six months, through her graduating NYU with a BA in psychology and Nick working his very fine butt off studying for and passing the bar exam. Mia had gotten into graduate school and was currently halfway through her first year, and Nick was working around the clock to make a name for himself and reduce his monumental college debt—which was currently rivaling the size of the national deficit. So his restaurant choice had to mean something.

Was tonight the night he'd finally use the L-word?

Her heart picked up at the thought because *that* would be a most *excellent* Christmas present. But whatever his plans, Nick seemed in no hurry. He ordered appetizers, teased her about what she might have on beneath the Mrs. Claus outfit, and coaxed the details of her day out of her.

They ordered wine, and he touched his glass to hers, his eyes warm. "To a night like last night...," he said silkily.

Last night had involved the secluded, deserted—and thankfully enclosed—rooftop patio of his five-story walk-up, where he'd loosened her inhibitions with slow, steady hands and an incredibly talented mouth, until she'd begged him to take her.

He'd acquiesced, twice. Just the memory made her go damp. "It's supposed to rain tonight," she said, her voice all Marilyn Monroe whispery, giving her away.

His smile was as slow and steady as his hands, and bad-boy wicked. He didn't care about the rain.

"You're wearing your new clothes," she pointed out. "You'll ruin them."

He shrugged. After a lifetime of not having money, he never seemed to put much importance into possessions. In fact, he'd applied to work at a nonprofit law office providing restorative justice across the country. He wanted to try to save the kids who'd made some bad choices and needed help. If he got the job, he'd be traveling far and wide, and she'd lose him. She'd known this.

She'd fallen for him anyway.

Helplessly.

The question was still the same—had *he fallen as well*? They'd both been given up at birth, but Mia had been adopted by a wonderful couple who'd become mom and dad to her. Nick hadn't been as lucky, and didn't feel the same need for ties that she did. He was a lone wolf.

She, on the other hand, had been born to be part of a pack.

Nick leaned in close and kissed her just beneath her ear. "Have you ever had sex in the rain, Mia?"

Her breath caught, and there was a lot more tingling in places that had no business tingling in a restaurant. "Is sex all you think about?"

"No. But I think about it a lot. With you." He flicked her earlobe with his tongue, and somehow all the bones in her body liquefied.

"Are guys really that much of a slave to their libido?" she managed.

"It's the testosterone. A guy'd follow his girl all the way to Siberia if he thought it might get him laid. Barefoot. Uphill in the snow, both ways."

She laughed, and he smiled. "Love the sound of your laugh," he said. "You don't do it enough."

She'd been a serious kid, and not just because she was adopted. She loved her family, both her adoptive parents *and* her birth parents. She was lucky enough to have them all in her life. But there was no denying that in spite of her luck and the wealth of love she'd been showered with, she was...well, serious.

And still looking for her place to belong.

She thought—hoped—that her place to belong was with Nick, and it filled her with a giddiness that was hard to contain. *He* filled her with giddiness.

Dinner came and was delicious, and still Nick didn't seem inclined to get to the point of the expensive restaurant. When the check arrived, he scooped it before she could. He always did that, even though he was drowning in college debt and, thanks to her four parents, she was not.

Outside, there were no cabs to be had. There was only a light mist in the air so they started walking. The construction crew was gone. Not that it mattered. No one would have bothered her with Nick at her side. He held himself in a way that spoke of a tough, easy confidence. He never went looking for trouble, but there was an edge to him that said if he happened to come across some, he wasn't opposed to kicking its ass.

And growing up as he had, she had no doubt he could do so with little to no effort.

They made it to her tiny place, enjoying the crazy, over-the-top lights and Christmas decorations of the city. At her door, Nick playfully pushed her up against it. "You're all wet, Mia…"

She took a moment to enjoy the feel of his hard body holding her pinned, then tipped her head to his. The flight confirmation was burning a hole in her purse. "Nick? Before we go in…"

He bent and kissed her cheek, her jaw, her throat, his hands slipping inside her coat. "I'm as adventurous as the next guy," he murmured hotly against her skin, making her shiver because she knew exactly what his hands and mouth could do. "But out here in the hall?"

She went still and then smacked him on the chest. "That's *not* what I was going to say."

He laughed and straightened, leaving his hands on her hips. "No?" His eyes were gleaming with mischief and a sexual promise that made her rethink turning him down for anything.

"*No*," she repeated, her heart speeding up a little. "Nick—"

He kissed her again, full of intent and purpose, and only when her bones had melted did he pull slowly back. "Sorry," he said. "You're just so damn sweet."

"You can gobble me up inside," she promised. "But I sort of have a Christmas present for you."

He dropped his hands from her. "You said no Christmas presents, that we'd go away together for a weekend next month when we both have off, and that would be our gift to each other."

"Okay, so it's not a Christmas present," she said. "Call it a *present* present. Do you remember months ago when I told you I was going home for Christmas for my aunt

Chloe's wedding?" She hesitated. "Well...I bought two plane tickets, not just one." She pulled his confirmation from her purse and handed it to him.

Mia's aunt Chloe and her fiancé, Sawyer Thompson, had been together for five years now. Being committed but not tethered had suited both of their wild souls, but recently Chloe had caught baby fever from her sister Maddie, who'd just had her second child.

Nick stared down at the paper Mia had handed him. "The wedding in Lucky Harbor?" he asked. "In Washington State?"

"Yes," Mia said. She'd spent her first summer there five years ago at age seventeen, where she'd found and met her birth parents. She'd discovered her first crush there, too, her first love.

She and Carlos had done their best, but they'd been so young. Too young. Their teenage romance hadn't survived, but she'd still gone to Lucky Harbor as often as she could over the past five years. "I realize it's all the way across the country," she said. "And also that it's short notice, but I've been wanting to ask you for a while now. I just didn't want you to feel obligated."

He wasn't looking like he felt obligated. He was looking like she'd clobbered him over the head with her purse, and some of her happiness faded.

"You want me to meet your birth parents?" he asked slowly.

"No," she said slowly. "Well, yes. But mostly I just want to spend the holiday with you." She knew the holidays had never been kind to him, and she wanted to show him how magical it could be. "This'll be our first Christmas. It'll be fun." She smiled.

He didn't. "Mia, I can't."

She took in his blank expression and got suddenly cold. "Can't?" she murmured, not understanding.

"Okay, won't," he corrected, voice soft but his meaning brutally clear.

Shocked, she stepped back, coming up against her front door.

Nick reached for her, but she lifted a hand, holding him off. "You know it's just a trip, right?" she asked as lightly as she could. "It's not a request for a diamond or anything like that." She'd never make *that* request of him. Maybe she'd secretly hoped that someday *he'd* make that request, but *she* certainly wouldn't.

"I can't," he repeated.

No warm smile, no explanation to soften the blow, nothing. She actually looked down at herself. Was she bleeding? It felt like she was bleeding. But she wasn't. She was in perfect working order as Mrs. Claus. Feeling stupid, she lifted her chin. "Okay," she said quietly, even as her heart seized. "Never mind." A little numb, which was a good thing at the moment since she didn't want to fall apart, *yet*, she unlocked her door and stepped inside. *Don't look back, don't look back—*

She totally looked back.

Tension radiated from Nick, but he wasn't giving anything away. A moment ago, he'd been touching her as if he needed her more than air, and now he was a complete stranger.

She quietly shut and locked the door, then leaned back against it.

He hadn't picked her.

Chapter 2

♥

Nick spent the next hour studying the ticket confirmation Mia had given him as if it held the answers to the universe. Not that he was actually seeing the piece of paper. Nope, he kept flashing back to Mia sitting across from him at the table earlier, her long brown hair falling like silk to her shoulders, her mossy green eyes full of affection and heat.

For him.

He loved the way she looked at him, though he'd managed to ruin that pretty well tonight. Disgusted with himself, he set the paper aside, turned off the lights, and got into bed, where he proceeded to stare up at the ceiling, counting the ways in which he'd screwed up.

There were too many to count.

He could argue that his life was in crazy flux, but that was an excuse, and he hated excuses. His reaction to Mia's invitation had been knee-jerk, and he'd hurt her.

He felt like shit about that, but he knew in the end, it was for the best. He had no business going to meet her family. One, he had no family experience. None. Two, he had even less relationship experience. Three, he'd applied for a job that was going to take him places, the first of which was around the entire country for the next two years.

It was what he'd wanted, to defend the kids who were falling through the cracks of the system—as he had. Mia, more than anyone else, understood this need. She'd been given up at birth, too.

But she'd been adopted. Nick had been shuffled from home to home his entire childhood, never quite belonging anywhere. Mia knew all this about him. It was what drew them together.

But what she didn't know was that he'd gotten the job.

He'd been planning on telling her at dinner, and then they'd have celebrated. Except that being with her, as always, took him out of time and place. She made him forget everything but her and how he felt when he was with her.

And then there'd been the real problem.

Sitting with her at that candlelit table, watching her smile at him, *for* him . . . suddenly he hadn't wanted to go anywhere.

He'd been wrestling with that when she'd dropped her wedding invite like a bombshell. She wanted him to go spend Christmas—a holiday he'd never believed in—with her family. Her *family*, something else he didn't quite believe in.

When he finally fell into an exhausted, restless sleep, he dreamed about the first time they'd met, in a Human

Behavior class that he'd needed in order to counsel teens on a volunteer basis.

She turned her head and gave him a long look when he slid into the class ten minutes late on the first day, thanks to a monster hangover. She was in glasses, her eyes nondescript, her brown hair piled up on top of her head. She had a laptop perched carefully on her lap and the required reading opened in one hand.

A nerd, he'd immediately decided, and knew he'd sat by the right girl. He always tried to sit by the smart ones because they were great study partners. He smiled at her.

She frowned and went back to concentrating on the lecture.

He realized he must have missed something important, as she had a full screen of notes. He leaned in to try to read over her shoulder at the same moment she turned back to him.

Their lips nearly brushed.

Her eyes widened and her lips opened in a little oh! of surprise. His reaction wasn't all that different. Had he thought her nondescript? She was the furthest thing from nondescript, starting with her eyes. They were deep green and brimming with intelligence. She stared at him for a long beat, and then turned her laptop his way to share her notes.

"Oh, whoops," she said, quickly closing a screen. "That was my research project for a different class." She bit her lower lip. "You're probably wondering about it now."

Actually, he wasn't. He wasn't even looking at her screen. He was wondering how it was that she smelled so amazing, how her eyes could be so... green. He was wondering if she was wearing a bra beneath that thin sweater, or if she was just chilly...

"I'm writing about human sexuality," she said.

Okay, now she had his attention. "You're researching sex?" he asked. "As in how to have it?"

"Hey, I know how to have it," she said, and then blushed gorgeously when she caught the teasing in his gaze.

Later he found out she'd been adopted, too. Drawn by this thing they had in common, he bought her a burger that night, and they ended up in Central Park beneath the stars watching an unexpected meteor shower. Mia made wishes on every falling star, big wishes, little wishes, wishes for everyone in her life... and he found himself entranced big-time.

Normally he never talked about himself, but she pulled him out of his shell, and they talked until dawn. Talked. Never in his life had he just sat and talked with a girl he hadn't yet even gotten to second base. But she was different, and he shared things with her that he'd not shared with anyone.

The next night, she brought him homemade brownies. And unlike the brownies his roommates always made, hers weren't illegal.

They'd been together ever since. Nick flopped over in his bed. They'd had fun exploring the city together. Exploring each other. Getting closer than he'd ever let someone get before.

And that's about when her ex had shown up.
With a ring.
Yeah, that had been fun.

Carlos knocked on Mia's door late one night. Mia was shocked at the visit. Nick was shocked when she asked him to go home so she could talk to Carlos alone.

Nick went downstairs and stood on the sidewalk, wondering if he was about to lose the best thing that had ever happened to him.

The longest hour of his life later, Carlos came out of the building, hood up and hands in his pockets as he headed down the sidewalk, never looking back.

Nick took the stairs at a jog, his gut in knots.

Mia's shower was running, and he waited until she came out of the bathroom. In just a towel, steam surrounding her, she stared at him, and slowly shook her head.

And then her eyes filled with tears.

His heart squeezed as he strode to her and pulled her in close.

"He wanted me to marry him," she said against his chest.

Nick went still. "And you said...?"

"I loved him when I was seventeen," she said soggily, "with everything I had. I wanted to make it work, but he didn't. He told me to move on. So that's what I did. He broke my heart, and I just broke his."

Nick let out the breath he hadn't realized he'd been holding and pressed his jaw to the top of her head.

"I think you should go," she whispered.

Nick had made it a lifelong policy to never stay a moment longer than he was wanted. Ever. So he headed out of the building much the way Carlos had only a little while before and walked home. The last thing he remembered before falling asleep that night was the feel of Mia's tears on his neck.

Rolling over again, he punched his pillow. He'd made a choice back then, and he'd been wrong. He shouldn't have left her.

And he'd made the same mistake tonight.

At the crack of dawn, he gave up trying to sleep. He dressed and went to Mia's apartment. He needed to see her, talk to her. Touch her. He had a key, but it didn't feel right to just let himself in this time. But she didn't answer, which is what happened when one acted like a complete ass. A complete, stupid ass. "Mia," he said, "let me in."

At the deafening silence, he blew out a sigh and pulled out his phone. But either she'd turned hers off or she'd hit Ignore because his call went right to voice mail. "Come to the door, Mia."

Three doors down, an older lady peeked out and frowned at him. "So you're *all* stupid then," she said.

"Excuse me?"

" 'Let me in.' 'Come to the door.' You always demand like that? No wonder she isn't answering. Try *asking* sometime. Not all women will stand for that *Fifty Shades* crap, you know." She gave a disgusted headshake and slammed her door shut.

Nick had no idea what "*Fifty Shades* crap" was, but

he looked at Mia's door. Had he been demanding? He knocked again. "Mia? Can we talk?"

When the door still didn't open, he gave up and tried a text: *I'm at your place, come to the door.* He paused, and then added *please*.

Hoping that covered all the bases, he waited a minute. Mia always responded to his texts right away, even when she was busy at school or work. She wanted to be a high school counselor when she finished grad school, and was working on getting an internship. But swamped as she was, she always made time for him no matter what—which never failed to make him feel special. Wanted.

Needed.

She was the first person to ever make him feel those things, and it meant a lot to him. *She* meant a lot to him.

But his phone remained ominously silent and her door remained shut, neither of which boded well.

He knew his own issues—he'd always been reluctant to let anyone get too close. But if he knew his own, he knew hers even better. She was the opposite. She *needed* to let people close, to be surrounded by those who cared.

And he also knew something else, something she'd never verbalized to him: for as well adjusted as she was, she needed her people to make a stand for her.

Nick had failed her in that, big-time, and both his heart and gut were churning over it. She'd never asked for a thing from him, but he'd known that need of hers was there and he hadn't fulfilled it.

He could fix that. He *would* fix that, and then she'd never doubt him again.

The door behind him opened, and he turned to face Mia's other neighbor. Cindy was twenty-something, rumpled but pretty, with an infant in her arms and a toddler in a Santa hat wrapped around one leg.

"Hey, Nick," she said in surprise. "Mia left already."

"Left?"

"Yeah, she caught a cab a few hours ago."

Chapter 3

Mia landed in Seattle and took a shuttle to Lucky Harbor. It was a long drive, and she hadn't wanted to inconvenience anyone to come get her.

Okay, that was a lie. Her heart hurt and felt too big for her rib cage, and her emotions were all over the place. She needed time to get herself together.

Tara and Ford Walker—her birth parents—might not have formally met her until she sought them out at age seventeen, but there was no doubt that having them in her life had completed her. She belonged to them. She loved them. But...

But *she'd* found *them*. *She'd* picked *them*. She'd picked Nick, too, though, and look how that had turned out.

Shoving away the unproductive thought, she inhaled deeply, taking in the thick, lush forestland of the Olympic Mountains as the van cut through them. On the other side, as they came down to the coast and into the little bowl where Lucky Harbor was nestled, she found herself relaxing a little. The ocean churned wildly beneath a gunmetal-gray sky, and the air was scented with sea salt and pine—unique to Lucky Harbor. The town smelled perennially of Christmas, which never failed to make her smile.

Being back here made it hard to hold on to a bad mood, but she intended to give it a try. Except it wasn't a bad mood. It was a broken heart.

Nick never promised you anything.

That thought came with another—maybe he'd only liked her because she understood being abandoned. Maybe she'd been nothing more than a mental crutch for him. This thought tumbled in her brain for a few minutes, giving her a headache. But she couldn't blame him for this. He'd never given her false hopes. He'd never said that they were going anywhere with this relationship.

Hell, he'd never even said they *had* a relationship.

She'd just assumed, and everyone knew what assuming anything got you. Good and hurt.

Realizing she'd never turned her phone back on after her flight, she pushed the power button and watched as a few texts loaded from Nick.

I'm at your place, come to the door.

And then the shocking *please*.

She called him, but it went straight to voice mail. Since she had no idea what to say, she hung up.

He'd gone to her place. There was a terrible beat of hope, but realistically she knew it'd been to make sure she was okay. He'd made it clear how he felt; that wasn't going to change. It didn't mean he was a bad guy.

He wasn't. He was one of the good guys. One of the best...

And wasn't that just the problem.

The van entered Lucky Harbor and made its way along the quaint Victorian main street, past the pier and the Ferris wheel, and finally down the narrow road to the Lucky Harbor B&B. The B&B was run by her mom, Tara, and her two sisters, Maddie and Chloe. They'd turned away all reservations for the next two weeks to concentrate on the wedding. But Mia knew the place would be abuzz with craziness, and in spite of her heartache, her spirits lifted slightly at what lay ahead.

A wedding.

The B&B had been decorated for the holidays, with a fresh garland lining the wraparound porch. At night, the two-story Victorian would be lit up with strings of white twinkling lights. In the light of day, the flower beds were filled with festive red poinsettias.

Mia tipped her driver and got out. The sun peeked through the clouds, piercing the sky with long, shimmery beams that shifted into a rainbow over the water. It was all so amazing and gorgeous, it could have been a painting, and a very small part of her happiness returned.

A gardener was hard at work on the yard, his back to her. He was digging holes for planting, the shovel moving steadily in and out of the dirt, the muscles of his shoulders, arms, and back flexing and bunching effortlessly, and Mia went still as stone, as recognition hit hard.

Carlos.

The past five years fell away, and just like that memories of a far simpler time washed over her, back to when a teenage crush had been the most important thing in her life.

It'd been four months since he'd come to New York to ask her to give him another shot, and she hadn't seen or heard from him since. Before Mia could say a word, a young woman came around the corner of the house and threw herself into his arms. •

Carlos easily caught her up and with a megawatt smile, lowered his head and kissed her.

And kissed her.

Feeling intrusive, Mia took an involuntary step back, unable to put a finger on what she felt exactly. Envious that she'd broken up with the love of her life while Carlos was clearly so happy? As unflattering as that was, yes. She must have made a sound because Carlos broke from the kiss and turned to face her. He was wearing dark, reflective sunglasses, which he slowly shoved to the top of his head. And then he smiled.

The woman in his arms disentangled herself and turned with curiosity in Mia's direction. Carlos murmured something soft to her, squeezed her hand, and then left her, heading toward Mia.

"Hey," he said, genuine affection in his voice as he reached for her. Mia was so relieved that it wasn't awkward that she walked right into his arms.

It wasn't the same kind of embrace he'd just shared with the woman still watching them, not even close. Nor was it the same kind of embrace that Carlos himself would have given Mia once upon a time. It was warm and friendly. Not sexual.

Mia waited for the hit of disappointment over that, but though being held by Carlos was bittersweet, she ached for someone else.

For Nick.

She missed his solid warmth, the way he always tightened his grip on her in a way that made her feel like she was his everything.

His pick.

For a moment, she closed her eyes against the sorrow that was threatening to bring her to her knees and held on to the oh-so-painfully-familiar Carlos. Then she stepped back and gave him as big a smile as she could manage.

"It's good to see you," he said sincerely. "You look beautiful. You must be fighting the guys off left and right."

No, just scaring them off...

"Yes," she said lightly, "and it's quite the chore."

Carlos smiled, and then turned to the other woman and held out his hand for her. When she came close, he said, "Theresa, this is Mia."

Theresa's smile was as reserved as Mia's. "Ah," she said, "the one who got away. I've heard a lot about you. You're the one who taught him how to treat a woman right, which makes me eternally grateful to you." She moved into Carlos a little bit, marking her territory. "Hope you enjoy your stay."

Mia found everyone in the large B&B kitchen—her parents, Maddie and Jax, Chloe and Sawyer. They were all in an assembly line, wrapping what appeared to be an entire Toys "R" Us warehouse of stuff.

After welcome hugs and kisses, Mia was put to work wrapping presents for Maddie and Jax's two kids.

"We might have gone overboard," Maddie said, passing Mia a pair of scissors.

"Might?" Sawyer asked drily, attempting to fold a neat corner and failing.

Chloe took over for him. "Tell us, Mia."

"Tell you what?"

She smiled gently. "Why you're looking like you just found out there's no Santa."

"I'm fine," she said. And then she burst into tears.

Chapter 4

♥

Mia told everyone about Nick over eggnog and more wrapping, which temporarily halted when a baby's cry came through the monitor. Jax left the room and came back holding his sleepy three-month-old son, Ryder, in one arm like a football. "Sierra's still sleeping," he said.

A relieved Maddie went back to the discussion at hand. "I think the text means he's sorry," she said to Mia. "It's actually kinda sweet."

Nick was a lot of things. He was strong of mind and body, he was both street and book smart, and he possessed a wicked sense of humor. He treated Mia like she meant something to him.

But she wouldn't classify him as sweet.

"I like the 'please,'" Chloe said. "The 'please' is always good." She gave Sawyer a secret smile.

"If he's long term," Maddie said, wielding a spool of

ribbon like an expert, "he needs to be the kind of guy who thinks you're beautiful when you're not. So, for example, he wouldn't care if you live in yoga pants even though you hate yoga."

"You hate yoga?" Chloe asked. She was Maddie's yoga instructor. And a tyrant. "You said you liked it."

Jax choked on his beer, making Ryder mewl in his sleep.

Maddie shot her husband a look as she soothed the baby. "He needs to let you know how much he cares," she said to Mia. "He needs to see you and think you're it for him."

Jax tugged on Maddie's hand until she moved in close. "You're it for me, Mad. For always. And I love your yoga pants."

Maddie smiled and kissed him over Ryder's head.

Mia's heart sighed.

"Oh good Lord, get a room," Tara said before looking at Mia. "Look, Nick let you go. Not okay. As I see it, he's got to earn your heart back."

"Harsh," Ford said.

Sawyer snorted. "Says the idiot who once had to do the same thing."

Ford leveled a long look at Sawyer. "You want to tell tales?"

Sawyer just smiled. "In two days, I'm going on a honeymoon to a South Pacific beach. We're packing sunglasses and sunscreen, and that's it. Nothing you say can bug the shit out of me."

Mia woke the next morning to a knot in her gut that came from missing Nick like she'd miss a limb. She'd clearly misread things. She'd mistaken affection for a deeper emotion. She'd mistaken passion for love.

Could she go back to New York and resume right where they'd left off and accept less than she'd hoped for?

If she was being honest with herself, the answer was no. She couldn't do it. It would kill her slowly.

She opened her eyes. She was on Ford's boat, docked at the marina at the B&B. He and Tara had a house on the hill above town, but Mia had wanted to sleep on the water. They'd stayed with her, taking the tiny cabin. She had the narrow couch in the galley area. Sitting up, she saw that they were cooking breakfast.

Tara was the chef in the family, but Ford could totally out-cook her when he wanted. Proving it, he jostled a pan and expertly flipped the eggs.

Tara rolled her eyes at him. "Show-off."

He grinned and gave her a smacking kiss on the lips.

"Morning," Mia said, and they both turned to her. They were still smiling, but she could see worry in their gazes.

"I'm fine," she said.

"Of course you are, sugar." Tara's southern drawl came out as she made up three plates with quick efficiency. "You're a Daniels *and* a Walker." She shot Ford a wry smile. "That means you're ninety-nine percent *fine* stubbornness, tenacity, and resilience combined."

"And the other one percent?" Mia asked as they sat at the tiny galley table and ate elbow to elbow.

Ford wrapped an arm around her neck and pulled her in close. *"Perfection."*

Turning her face into his chest, Mia closed her eyes and ignored the burn in her throat as he stroked her hair.

It was going to be okay, she told herself. Somehow, it

would. So she'd made a mistake and had fallen for a guy who hadn't fallen back. *Welcome to Womanhood.*

"There's something you should know, Mia," Ford said quietly.

She lifted her head. "What?"

"Actually, it's more a confession than a what," Tara said.

Oh, God. "Is one of you sick?"

"No." Tara took Mia's hand. "Nothing like that. It's just that your phone was buzzing off the hook while you were sleeping, and I didn't want it to wake you up, so..." She grimaced.

"So you turned it off?" Mia asked.

Ford chuckled softly, and Tara reached over Mia to smack him.

Ford simply caught Tara's hand. "Your mom doesn't quite have that much control," he said to Mia. "What she's trying to tell you is that she not only answered your phone, she meddled."

"Hey, it's in my blood," Tara said, sounding like a Steel Magnolia. "And I'm not sorry for it. Okay, maybe I'm a little sorry for it, but not as much as *he* will be if he screws this up."

Mia's heart stopped. "If who screws what up?"

"Maybe you should just go see him," Ford said. "He's at the B&B waiting for you. He's been there since dawn."

Mia blinked, unable to fully process this.

Ford handed her a coffee, which she gratefully sipped. The caffeine hit her system in thirty seconds. "Okay," she said, "that's better. Because I could have sworn you just said there was a guy waiting at the B&B for me."

Tara just looked at her, and Mia's heart kicked. "You aren't kidding."

"Sugar, I never kid about men."

Ford lifted his wife's hand to his mouth, smiling at her over their entwined fingers.

Normally, Mia would take a moment to think about how sweet it was that they loved each other so much, but...*Nick had come?* With wobbly knees and a rush of blood through her head, she set down the coffee and started to scramble above deck, but Ford gently pulled her to him by the back of the sweatshirt she'd slept in. He looked down into her face, his own unusually serious.

"I remember that look," she said. "It's the look you once gave Carlos right before you threatened to kick his ass."

"I can still kick ass," he said with absolute steel. "I just wanted you to know that."

Mia went up on tiptoes and kissed his cheek. "No worries. I inherited the ability from you."

Once again, she started to go, but quickly backtracked to brush her teeth, making Tara and Ford laugh. Then she hit the deck. The tide was in and choppy, knocking the boat around some. She jumped to the dock and crossed the wide yard to the Victorian B&B with...well, she didn't know what exactly was humming through her veins. Hope? No. Even if he'd come, he couldn't take back what had been in his eyes the other night.

But none of that mattered because the man staring down at the flower beds wasn't Nick.

It was Carlos.

He turned and took in her baggy sweats and undoubtedly rumpled bedhead, and the corner of his mouth quirked. "Like the look," he said.

She tried for a smile and failed, and then his faded, too. "What's wrong?" he asked.

"Nothing." *Everything*... "I thought..." She shook her head, not trusting her voice. She wasn't going to cry again. Hell no. She'd save it for really important events, like watching *The Notebook* after a round of brutal finals, or the Humane Society commercials.

"Ah, hell," Carlos said. "He fucked it up, didn't he? Did he hurt you, Mia?"

Throat burning, she shook her head.

With a sigh, he pulled her into him.

"I'm a mess," she whispered.

"A cute mess."

She found a smile after all. "I did miss you, you know."

"I missed you, too."

They paused, then at the same time both said, "but..."

Carlos pulled back and gestured for her to go first.

"But..." She drew in a deep breath. "I don't love you anymore. Not the way I used to."

He nodded. "I know. It's okay, chica. We're both okay."

She wanted desperately for that to be true, but was afraid it wasn't. "Do you love her? Theresa?"

Carlos hesitated. "Mia."

"It's okay. Really," she said softly.

He looked at her for a long moment. "I didn't think I'd ever get over you. But I was wrong," he said. "She's the one for me, Mia."

She nodded, wondering what Nick would say if someone asked him if he loved her. Would he hesitate? Say no? She thought about how he'd pretty much done exactly that, and felt her face heat with embarrassment and hurt.

She'd been so sure that they'd been in a very different place...

"Mia," said a low, unbearably familiar voice behind her.

Mia went still, then whirled around, coming face-to-face with Nick, silhouetted against the morning sun slanting across the water.

Chapter 5

♥

Nick watched Mia's emotions chase each other across her face. Hope, hurt. Temper. He was going to hold on to the first one, in spite of the fact that Carlos was standing at her back.

"Nick." The genuine surprise in Mia's voice was a direct hit. Clearly, she hadn't expected to see him, hadn't expected that he'd come for her. He took a step toward her, but before he could say a word, the door of the B&B opened. In the doorway stood Mia's uncles, both of whom he'd met when he'd arrived last night. Clearly interested in his and Mia's reunion, their imposing, impenetrable vibe was broken only by the little girl and huge brown Labrador at their feet.

Mia's aunts were in the window. They'd been incredibly kind but incredibly vague about Mia's exact location. Not up to par on family protocol, Nick figured he had some serious ass-kissing to do. He was prepared to do that. What he wasn't prepared for was the glacial wall of protectiveness from Maddie's husband, Jax, and Chloe's husband-to-be, Sheriff Sawyer Thompson.

The dog and little girl weren't imposing. The little girl was offering a soggy cookie to the dog.

"Baby, don't feed Izzy," Jax said, and hoisted her up into his arms.

The dog shot Jax a look of reproach and sighed.

Everyone else looked at Nick.

This was possibly the most important moment of his entire life, and he had an audience. Well, what the hell. He was good at tuning out the bad shit. He'd been able to tune out unfavorable foster parents, nosy teachers, menacing bullies…everything. It was a unique gift. So he used it now, and looked only at Mia.

But she'd craned her neck and was watching Tara and Ford walk across the yard toward them. Perfect. Now everyone was here to witness this.

Mia was wearing sweats—his, he was relieved to note—and her hair was piled precariously on top of her head. She had a sleepy-eyed look to her, one that he knew well. Normally, the heavy-lidded look was accompanied by a sweet yet sexy-as-hell smile as she woke up, stretched, and then climbed all over him.

She'd clearly just very recently woken up—hopefully *not* with the tall, dark, and attitude-ridden Carlos, who was *still* standing too close at her back.

Nick wanted to be alone with her to talk, but apparently she didn't have ESP because she looked at him for a long beat, then gestured to the couple who'd just crossed the yard. "I'm assuming you met my parents, Ford and Tara."

They shook hands. Nick noted that they were watching him with guarded sympathy.

"And you've met the rest of my family?" Mia asked him as she swept a hand toward the B&B.

Nick nodded.

"And Carlos?"

Carlos sent Nick a narrow-eyed glance that said, *You screwed up*.

There was no doubt.

Nick's life had been only what he had made of it. He was used to being responsible for his own emotions, just as he was well used to controlling them tightly. But he hadn't slept for two days now, and his control was slipping big-time. Plus, Mia wasn't showing much. Since she'd always shown him her feelings before—no holding back—this was a bad sign.

"We need to talk," he said.

She arched a brow. "You came across the country to talk?"

"I came for you. Look," he said, all too aware of their company, "I know I suck at this, but can we talk? Please?"

It may have been wishful thinking, but her eyes seemed to warm. "Okay."

Nick let out a breath and eyed their avid audience pointedly, but not a single one expressed any embarrassment at shamelessly eavesdropping. Finally, one of the aunts took mercy and stepped in. "All right, show's over," Maddie said, soft-spoken though her voice was laced with steel as she turned and gave the entire gang a shooing motion.

To Nick's relief, everyone actually listened to her and began to move off.

Except Carlos. He grabbed the shovel from against the porch railing and leaned on it, staying right at Mia's back.

"You've had a long trip," Mia said to Nick. "Though why you made it when you so clearly didn't want to, I can't imagine."

"I was hoping we could discuss that. Privately." This last word he directed at Carlos.

Carlos didn't move.

"Nick," Mia said quietly.

Christ, he thought, she was going to turn him down.

"It's a really busy day here," she said. "There's last-minute fittings, and the rehearsal dinner, and I have to help."

"I'm not leaving," Nick said.

"You're leaving if she wants you to leave," Carlos said, and set aside the shovel.

Nick stared at him. "This is none of your business."

"Did I say that to you when you waited like a vulture in New York to swoop in and pick at the bones?" Carlos asked.

"Oh, for God's sake," Mia said. "This is ridiculous. Both of you need to—"

"She was *mine* then," Nick said, stepping closer. He could feel Mia's surprised reaction at this, and couldn't blame her. It was the first time he'd laid public claim to his feelings for her. He was surprised as hell, too. But oddly enough, it felt natural.

And right. "She's mine now," he said.

"Hey," Mia said with a frown, "I'm—"

Carlos stepped up to Nick so that they were toe to toe. "You need to go. I'm going to stand here and watch you. Then *I'm* going to pick at the bones this time. How's that?"

"You have a real problem," Nick said.

"Yeah," Carlos said. "It's you." And he punched him.

Perfect, Nick thought, swinging back. A fight was *just* what he needed, and the next thing he knew, he and Carlos were in a tangle, rolling around on the ground, fists flying.

Carlos landed a few good hits, but so did Nick. In fact, he was getting the best of the fight when they were suddenly blasted with icy water.

He and Carlos rolled away from each other, flat on their backs, gasping for breath. Nick swiped dirt and water from his face and blinked as an old lady came into view. She was in a pink velour sweat suit with white sneakers, and she was holding a hose.

"That'll do it every time," she said to Mia.

Mia's mouth was pinched tight. "Thanks, Lucille," she said. Then, with one long, hard glare at both Nick and Carlos, Mia stormed inside the B&B and slammed the door.

The sound of the lock clicking into place was unmistakable.

Lucille tossed the hose aside and brushed off her hands. "Hello," she said to Nick. "Nice to meet you. I run the art gallery down the street." She looked at Carlos. "You two are good now? No more silly boy stuff?"

"Yeah," Carlos said and sat up, rubbing his jaw. "We're good."

Nick sat up, too, rubbing his aching ribs as he nodded.

"Great," Lucille said. She pulled a cell phone from her pocket and snapped a picture of them. "Behave now." And then she was gone.

Nick glanced at Carlos. "She for real?"

"Unfortunately."

"You going to tell me what the hell that was about?" Nick asked.

"Does it matter?"

Nick thought about it. "No." Taking a careful breath, he rolled to his feet. "We are done, right?"

Carlos gave him a long, considering look. "Depends on how stupid you are."

Nick shrugged. He tried hard not to be stupid, but apparently where Mia was concerned all bets were off. Wet, dirty, and off center, he walked around the B&B until he came to the back. As he suspected, there were steps leading up to the wraparound porch and a sliding glass door, which was thankfully unlocked.

Inside, Mia sat on the couch with her smartphone, working on a word puzzle. "I have a problem," she said when Nick walked in. "I need a three-letter word for ass-hole, and I don't know if it's M-E-N or Y-O-U."

"Either, no doubt." He walked over and crouched in front of her, his hands on her thighs as he looked into her face. "Am I too late, Mia?"

Chapter 6

♥

Mia was startled by Nick's question. "That's an odd thing to ask," she said carefully, "for a guy who was too afraid to come to a wedding with the girl he's been with for six months."

"I wasn't afraid."

She just looked at him and he grimaced. "Okay, maybe a little."

Carlos appeared at the slider, as dirty and wet as Nick, and Mia narrowed her eyes at him as well.

"Hey," Carlos said, raising his hands in surrender. "I'm just working here." But he didn't go anywhere.

Mia stood between the only two men she'd ever been with. The only two men she'd ever loved. "We need a moment," she said to Carlos.

"You going to dump him?" Carlos asked. "Because if you are, I should get to watch. It'd be nice to be on the other side of the fence on that score."

"*You* dumped *me*," she reminded him.

"Yes," he said. "So that you could go live your life." He looked at Nick. "Not to get hurt."

"Carlos," she said, and knew he heard the warning in her voice because he sighed.

"Yeah, I know," he said. Ignoring Nick completely, he leaned in and kissed her on the cheek, taking his sweet-ass time about it, too. "Give him hell," he whispered against her ear. "Neither of us deserves you."

And then he was gone.

She drew in a deep, steady breath and looked at Nick. "So. You want to talk?"

"Not here," Nick said, and pulled Mia to her feet. He knew damn well her uncles hadn't gone far. Maybe Carlos didn't intimidate him, but Jax and Sawyer sure as hell did. He wasn't scared of much, but this—Mia's family—terrified him. They'd loved her a hell of a lot longer than he had, and he was pretty sure he hadn't made a great first impression.

Or a second...

Mia led him through the inn. There was mistletoe hanging in various spots, and he longed to shove her beneath it and kiss her until she melted against him and remembered that she liked him.

But since steam was still coming out her ears, he resisted.

She took him to the kitchen, where Sawyer stood against the counter drinking a coffee. He didn't express surprise at the sight of Nick all dirty and rumpled from the fight. "Nice right hook," was all he said.

Mia let out a sound that managed to perfectly convey

her annoyance, probably with the entire male race, then went to the freezer. She grabbed a small bag of frozen peas and brought it up to Nick's right eye with exactly zero gentleness.

"Hold it there," she said tightly when he winced. "You're swelling."

Nick took some heart in the fact that she hadn't offered Carlos a bag of peas.

"We're making a getaway for a few," she said to Sawyer. "You going to have our backs?"

"Sure." Sawyer looked down at her, his eyes softening. "You know where to find me if you need anything."

"Come on," Mia said to Nick, and tugged him outside. They walked across the yard to the marina and into a small building, where she snatched a set of keys off a desk. From inside a closet, she grabbed two life vests and carried them with her.

Because she didn't look like she was ready to talk, he followed her to the docks to a rickety old houseboat that had definitely seen better days.

"It came with the marina," Mia said. "My dad taught me how to operate it several summers ago."

Nick eyed the shabby houseboat and then the dark, choppy water. "It's December."

She glanced over at him, her eyes showing the slightest amusement and also the hint of challenge. "So?"

"The water looks cold."

"Yeah. Don't fall in," she said.

He rubbed his jaw and studied the death trap. "Is this thing seaworthy?"

"Mostly."

What the hell. He boarded behind her, watching as

she tossed the life vests down but within reach, and then turned on the engine compartment blower and checked the outdrive and propeller.

"Untie the mooring lines," she said, "and FYI? You're my rear lookout."

"My pleasure," he responded, and checked out *her* rear.

She rolled her eyes but let out a low laugh that was music to his ears. "The *boat*," she said. "Make sure we're clear." She went inside the houseboat to the controls, leaving the door open so she could hear him as she started the engine. "I've got to run this for two minutes at 1500 rpm," she called to him. "Time me."

Two minutes later, he told her "time," and then was amused when she began barking directions at him like a drill sergeant.

"This bossiness is a new side of you," he murmured, entertained. "I like it."

"Just keep your eyes on the water. Pulling this bad boy is tricky, and I don't want to clip the dock. Jax hates it when I do that, because he's the one that fixes everything around here. Oh shit, am I close? Stop checking out my ass and go look! Hurry!"

"I'm not much for hurrying," he said, doing as she asked and moving to where he could see their hind end. "I'm more a fan of the slow and thorough." He slid her a look through the door. "I'm going to remind you of that you when it's my turn to be in charge."

She stopped moving, nibbling on her lower lip as her eyes went a little glossy.

"Mia?"

"Yeah?"

"The boat."

"Oh!" She jerked back to attention.

When they cleared the marina safe and sound, he joined her inside. She wiped her brow and turned to him. "Slow and thorough?"

"Have you forgotten?"

She blushed. "No. I remember."

"Do you?" He liked the look of her standing at the bridge. He came up behind her, a hand on either side, caging her in. "I was starting to wonder..."

She closed her eyes when he leaned over her and brushed his mouth along her jaw. Taking that as a good sign, he concentrated on the sweet spot beneath her ear. She let out a shuddering sigh, but gave him a nudge back.

"I need space," she said. "I can't think when you're so close. I'm not going to run this thing into the ground because you're distracting me."

The sensation of needing more room had figured prominently in Nick's life. He'd always needed far more room than he'd been given. Then he'd turned eighteen, been free of the system, and made sure to never be cornered again. That she needed room from *him* sucked. "I never meant to hurt you, Mia."

"Is that what you came all the way across the country to tell me?"

"Yes," he said. "Partly."

"You could have said that much on the phone."

"You didn't answer your phone," he pointed out.

"I was on a plane. And I called you back, and *you* didn't answer *your* phone."

"Because *I* was on a plane," he said.

She sighed. "You shouldn't have come."

There was something terrifying in her voice. A distance, he thought, and felt the licks of a newfound and very unwelcome emotion blocking his throat. Panic.

She apparently didn't have the same problem. "We've said all that needed to be said," she told him.

"Not by a long shot." Turning her to face him, he pulled her in close, which took some doing because she was stiff as a board. "I didn't come out here just to apologize, Mia," he said, cupping her face. "I wanted to be with you. I've wanted to be with you since day one, when you saved my ass."

"You'd have figured it out. That class wasn't hard."

"I don't mean the stupid class," he said. "I mean life. You saved my ass in life. And you've been saving it ever since. Keeping me on track when no one else ever gave a shit, encouraging me to go after what I want. And what I want, Mia, is you. I want you in my life, in a relationship with me."

She searched his gaze for a long beat. "When I asked you to this wedding," she finally said, "I really just wanted your company. I wasn't asking for—"

"I know. I was an idiot, Mia."

She rolled her eyes again but definitely warmed toward him. "Look at us," she said. "Two ridiculously scared peas in a pod."

He shook his head. "Scarred, maybe. Not scared. I'm not scared of this."

"Well, that makes one of us." She let out a breath. "I thought I knew what and who we were. But I was wrong."

"I screwed up."

"No," she said, shaking her head. "No one can blame you for not being ready for a relationship. I thought I was ready, but the truth is, I'm not even sure what a real relationship is." She paused, and a frightening solemnity came into her eyes. "We were both given away once. I've made peace with that. I grew up loved, so I know what it feels like. Now I have my birth parents in my life, too, and have had nothing but acceptance. I even had a teenage love that I have nothing but fond memories of. But the fact is that *I* picked these relationships. *I* found my birth parents. *I* forced my way into their lives. Hell, I forced myself on Carlos, for that matter. He had no choice; he never knew what hit him. I've always done the picking, Nick, and—"

"—And for once you want to be picked," he said softly. "I know. I'm picking you, Mia."

"No, listen to me…that very first day when you strolled into class? There were two girls sitting in the seats on one side of me and my backpack on the other. I saw you come in and my heart stopped." She put a hand to her chest as if it ached. "I told the girls that James Franco was in the back row, and when they scampered off to check, I quickly kicked my backpack beneath the seat in front of me, making it look like I had nearly a whole row to myself so you'd take one of the seats. And then…" She sucked in a breath. "Then I broke the cardinal girl rule."

Nick was confused. "Girl rule?"

"I didn't wait three days to see if you'd contact me. I made sure to run into you the next day with brownies. I threw myself at you, Nick. Don't you see? You had no choice."

He stared at her for another beat and then laughed.

She smacked him. "I'm serious!"

"So am I." He let his smile fade, let his own intent ring clear in his voice. "So now *you* listen. Mia, I think of you from the moment I open my eyes to when I close them at night. You make me smile, you make me ache. You make me think, you make me strong. You make me frustrated as shit, and I honestly can't see myself without you. I know you don't quite believe that right now, and that's okay. I can wait for you to catch up."

She shook her head. "I'm so confused. I really thought that this whole thing was your fault, but now I'm confused because you've changed your mind about commitment. I'm going to be a counselor, Nick. How can I be a counselor when I'm so confused? God, I was such a smug idiot."

"No, you're the smartest woman I know. And if anyone's the idiot, it's me. A slow idiot."

She didn't disagree with him, which might have made him smile if this hadn't been so serious. "I didn't change my mind, Mia. I always knew."

She stared at him, and he touched her, running a finger along her temple. He couldn't help himself. "I just didn't know how to make this work," he said.

"And you know now?"

"No, but I want to figure it out. Together. Mia, I heard back about the job."

Her breath hitched, and she stared into his eyes. "You got it."

He nodded, taking in her expression. She was happy for him. He could see that clear as day. Past any sadness for her own heart, her relief for him was tangible. Tugging her close, he buried his face in her hair. Carlos was right. Neither of them deserved her, himself especially. But hell if he'd walk away. "I was going to tell you about it at dinner the other night, but then I couldn't."

She pulled back and stared into his eyes. "Because you thought I would hold you back?"

"No." He tightened his grip on her. "I knew you wouldn't. But you were talking about us going skiing next month, and then on a Valentine's Day trip. I want to do those things, but I probably won't be able to. And I didn't know how to tell you."

"So you told me nothing?"

"Not my finest moment," he admitted. "Look, this is going to be a challenge for us, but it can work. Tell me you know that, that you still feel something for me."

"I feel lots of things for you, Nick. Probably too much. But that doesn't change anything." She turned away from him to the controls and adjusted their course. "It's just too complicated," she whispered. "You shouldn't have come."

"I'll always come for you."

Chapter 7

♥

Mia kept her eyes on the horizon, but she didn't have to turn around to know that Nick was there, right at her back, so close that a sheet of paper wouldn't have fit between them.

"Anchor us," he said.

Her heart sped up, in reaction to both his low, sexy voice and his proximity. Her body always reacted to his like this. Zero to sixty. This condition wasn't improved when he brushed a kiss to her jaw, and lingered. "Nick—"

His mouth slid over her throat, his warm palm settling on the nape of her neck to hold her steady. "It's my turn to be the boss, Mia."

She had no idea what it said about her that this made her quiver in anticipation, but she hurriedly steered them into a quiet, deserted bay and dropped anchor.

Turning her to face him, Nick took her hands in his

and directed them to his chest. Unable to help herself, she let them wander. She loved his body. Lifting her head, she found his eyes on hers.

"Do you want this?" he asked quietly. "Do you still want me?"

"Yes," her mouth said without her brain's permission.

With a groan, he pressed her against the controls, pinning her there with his deliciously warm body. His mouth skimmed over her jaw to her lips as his big, warm hand palmed her breast. With a sound that said it wasn't enough for him, he slid his hands beneath her sweatshirt and thin tee. Another sound escaped him at finding her braless, this one of rough, male appreciation while his thumb strummed over her nipple. "God. God, I missed this," he said, his lips hovering over the pulse beating frantically at the base of her neck. "I missed you."

She didn't want words. She wanted him to banish the hurt, just for a little while. Rocking into him, she reached for the zipper on his jeans. "We have to be quick."

Catching her hands, he pinned them on either side of her.

"Nick—"

"*My* turn," he said firmly, and dropped to his knees in front of her.

Pushing up her sweatshirt, he cupped her breasts, leaning in to take a nibble of her quivering abs. "Mine," he said, untying the sweats.

She had no idea if he meant the sweats, or herself. Had no idea how she felt about that either.

Okay, so that was a total fib. She knew exactly how she felt about it. She'd just gotten a rush that was a millimeter short of an orgasm.

When he tugged the sweats down, she gasped.

"Commando," he said huskily. "My favorite."

"I was sleeping, and I don't like wearing underwear when I sleep." A little panicked, she searched their immediate surroundings. How had she gone from so hurt to so nearly naked? "Uh..."

"No one's around," he assured her. "Not for miles. Relax, Mia. This is for you."

Relax? She had no idea how she was supposed to do that with her emotions seesawing, not to mention the fact that her pants were at her thighs and Nick's hands were cupping her ass, pulling her to his mouth, and—"Ohmigod." She slid her hands into his hair, holding him to her because his mouth—good Lord, his *mouth.* It took her an embarrassingly short amount of time to come, which she decided to attribute to adrenaline and not to his considerable skills or the fact that she was still helplessly in love with him.

When her knees buckled, he caught her. Feeling incredibly emotional, and far too vulnerable, she tried to push him away. He simply and devastatingly pressed a sweet kiss to her hipbone. Then just beside her belly button.

She stared down at him, nearly choking on her heart. "Nick."

He tugged off her sneakers and then her clothes, and surged to his feet. "I need you, Mia."

He did. She could feel his erection pressing against her through his jeans. She let her hand glide down his chest, his abs, and then she palmed him.

He groaned but took her hand. "Not there." He slid their entwined fingers back up to his chest against his heart. "Here."

Undone, and unable to resist, she went up on tiptoes

and kissed him, long and deep. They'd do this, and she'd hold the memories warm and safe inside her forever.

Nick pulled a condom from his wallet and Mia freed his essentials—and oh how she loved his essentials—and then he lifted her up. "Wrap your legs around me," he said, and when she did, he slid home.

And in that moment at least, her world was complete.

He was going too fast with her, Nick knew it. But the pent-up lust and longing had drawn them into this explosion of deep, wet kisses and slick, needy bodies, and he couldn't slow himself down. When she came, shuddering in pleasure, his name on her lips, she took him right over the edge with her.

They ended up on the floor of the houseboat flat on their backs, staring up at the sky through the skylight, panting for breath, trying to recover. He wasn't even sure he could move, but somehow he managed to pull her into him, holding her to his side, gliding a hand up and down her satiny, still-damp skin. She shivered at his touch and arched into him as if needing more, and he discovered he *could* move plenty. Catching her hands in his, he rolled, tucking her beneath him.

She stared up at him, her eyes two fathomless pools, and he felt his heart give a hard kick to his ribs.

She was it for him.

"Mia," he said quietly, brushing her hair from her face, breathing deeply of her scent—part shampoo, part satisfied woman. "I love you." He kissed her before she could respond because he wanted her to absorb the words and believe. He kissed her as if he could breathe the truth into her lungs.

But she eventually pulled back. "I don't need promises, Nick. I never did. I just wanted you here with me. For now."

For now. A guy's dream, those two words. But he'd come to realize that he wanted more, so much more. He wanted her heart.

Chapter 8

♥

By the time they got back to the B&B, Mia had received no less than ten calls from her mom and aunts, and Nick could feel her pulling away.

On the porch of the B&B, she turned to him, face solemn. "Today was wonderful, Nick."

There was an unsettling finality to her words, like she was saying good-bye. Did she think he would just go home now that he'd gotten laid?

"I'll never forget it," she said.

Yeah, she did. She expected him to go. "I want to stay, Mia." He ran his hands up her arms and felt her tremble at his touch. She closed her eyes and he cupped her face, running the pads of his thumbs over her cheekbones. "I know you don't quite believe in us right now," he said, "but I believe enough for the both of us."

"Nick—"

Maddie burst out of the B&B. "Thank God," she said at the sight of Mia. "Someone I can boss around."

"What do you need?" Mia asked.

"Everything. A builder, a gopher, an errand runner... No offense, honey, but your mama's gone off the deep end. Her elevator isn't hitting the top floor, she's a few fries short of a Big Mac Meal, she—"

"*I can hear you!*" Tara yelled from the open window.

Maddie winced, then leaned in and lowered her voice. "Help me. Chloe's *this* close to killing her, and if she goes to prison, I'll be the only one left to deal with her."

"Sure," Mia said. "Whatever you need."

"Me too," Nick said.

Both women stared at him in surprise.

"But you're leaving," Mia said.

Nick shook his head.

"Either way, you're a guest," Maddie told him. "And guests don't help."

He'd spent much of his life telling himself he didn't need a family, but right then, for the first time ever, he'd have loved to have been included as a family member and not a guest. "I want to help."

Maddie stared at him for a long beat, but apparently she decided to take him at his word because she put him to work. Hours later, he and Jax had assembled a big white tent and outside heaters to keep the guests warm, set up all the tables, including hanging mistletoe at each one, assisted Tara in the kitchen, and run around town picking up more Christmas trees and decorations by demand of Chloe herself. He even set up the trees with Carlos. They didn't speak much, but they didn't brawl either, so that was a bonus. Halfway through, Carlos's girlfriend, Theresa, showed up with a basket of cookies, which Carlos reluctantly offered to share with Nick.

Not a martyr, Nick dug in. "If you have a girlfriend," he asked, mouth full of delicious chocolate chip cookie, "what the hell was earlier about?"

Carlos shrugged. "Still care about her."

"You have a girlfriend," Nick repeated.

"Yeah, but you never really get over your first love."

Nick chewed on that statement along with the cookie. His first love was Mia, too. And since he couldn't imagine moving on or forgetting her, he finally nodded his understanding.

The rehearsal dinner was a blur, and afterward Mia vanished with her mom and aunts doing...whatever girls did the night before a wedding. Nick was politely shown to his room at the B&B.

He got up early the next morning, made himself useful some more, and knew he'd won over at least half the clan when Tara made him a big breakfast and Maddie hugged him for all he'd done to help out.

By the time the guests showed up and the ceremony began, he was hungry for a peek at Mia.

And then she was walking down the aisle in a beautiful forest-green dress, flowers in her hands, hair flowing behind her in the slight breeze, a warm smile on her face. Just looking at her, Nick ached. She was a part of him. The very best part.

Halfway down the aisle, their gazes caught and held. He wasn't sure he recognized the look on her face, but he couldn't tear his eyes off of her.

Tara was next, and then Maddie, holding her son. Her three-year-old daughter was walking at her side, carefully and precisely dumping a fistful of flowers out of her basket with each step. When she ran out of flowers, she stopped short, refusing to go another step. "I need more flowers!"

Maddie shot her husband a desperate look where he stood with Ford and Sawyer. Jax jogged down the aisle and gave Maddie a quick kiss, and then picked up his daughter.

"Daddy, I need more flowers!"

"I know, baby." Jax adjusted her in one arm and slid the other around Maddie, and they walked the rest of the aisle together.

Then the crowd hushed and it was Chloe's turn to walk toward Sawyer. Nick was struck by her expression as she smiled at her soon-to-be husband from brilliantly shiny eyes. And then it hit him like a one-two punch—it was the same expression Mia had worn only a moment before when she'd locked gazes with Nick.

Love.

Stunned, Nick sat there and missed nearly every word of the ceremony, which apparently had been incredibly touching because there wasn't a dry eye in sight when it was over.

Then the music started and the bride and groom had their first dance. Nick caught sight of Mia dancing with Ford, and then Sawyer. And then Carlos.

Nick stood. Pocketing the swig of mistletoe from the table, he made his way toward the dance floor. He knew this wasn't going to be on the top ten list of the smartest things he'd ever done, but he didn't care. "Can I cut in?"

Carlos looked at Mia, who nodded. Nick took her hand and brought it up around his neck, pulling her in close, drinking in her familiar scent and the warm, soft feel of her curves. He molded his body to hers and felt her react by melting into him.

It was almost as good as being inside her. Unable to help himself, he ran his hands down the length of her back, closing his eyes to savor the feel of her.

"Nick?"

He opened his eyes and met hers, surprised to see a glimmer of uncertainty.

"What are we doing?" she asked.

"Dancing."

"It feels like a lot more."

"Good." He held the mistletoe over her head.

She let out a low laugh. "You want a kiss?"

"To start," he said, and leaned in and touched his lips to hers. "You are so beautiful, Mia."

"You really do have some pretty fancy words lately."

"Yeah." He put the mistletoe in his pocket and pulled her in closer. "And here's three more...I love you."

"I've waited a long time to hear you say that." She stared up at him. "I love you, too, Nick. So much. But—"

"No. No buts," he said, dropping his forehead to hers. "Not tonight."

She relaxed slightly in his arms, and as the beat of the music flowed over them, he wished the song wouldn't end. As if she felt the same, her hands tightened around his neck. Again she pressed her face into the curve of his throat, but this time his heart dropped in his chest when he felt the wetness of her tears against his skin.

"Mia," he said, devastated. "Don't cry. I'm sorry." He wasn't exactly sure what he was sorry for, but he'd be sorry for breathing if that was the problem.

"No, they're happy tears," she said, and sniffed. "It's

Christmas Eve, it's Chloe's wedding, and it's all been wonderful." She lifted her head and met his gaze, her own drenched. "And you're still here."

"I'm not going anywhere."

Her mom and aunts cut in then, and the women all danced together for a while, laughing and sharing a few happy tears. Afterward, Mia went looking for Nick, and had a moment's panic when she couldn't find him. She didn't think he and Carlos would fight again. Earlier she'd actually seen them hauling in cases of beer and wine together. They'd even been laughing at Jax's brown Lab, Izzy, who was napping in the center of the aisle all sprawled out, forcing everyone to literally take a flying leap to get past her.

Watching Nick interact here with her family, with the people who mattered so deeply to her, had been a jump start to her aching heart.

"I know that smile," Chloe said, coming up beside Mia, slinging an arm around her shoulder and nearly drowning Mia in white silk. "It's the smile of a woman in love."

"How do you tell the difference between lust and love?" Mia asked.

"If you can wear your laundry panties on a date with him, you know it's true love."

Mia put her hands to her butt and tried to remember what panties she was wearing.

Chloe laughed softly and hugged her. "Baby, you're so lovable you don't have to worry about it. Your heart will talk to you."

Her heart was talking to her plenty. "How do I know

it's not just heartburn?" she asked. "Is there a magic handshake?"

Chloe smiled. "Yes. You don't marry the first guy you can see yourself living with."

"I don't?"

"No. You marry the first guy you can't live without."

Mia smiled. "Says the woman who strung along the town sheriff for five years before caving and marrying him."

"Hey, some things take time," Chloe said unapologetically. "The *best* things take time."

And one thing Mia did have was time. "Have you seen Nick?"

Her aunt turned and pointed across the dance floor to the bar—where she could see her dad and her uncles talking to a tall, handsome Nick.

He looked relaxed enough, even perfectly at ease. "He's handling it," she said, relieved.

"Handling what?" Chloe asked. "Looking fine? You got that right."

Mia smiled. He did look especially fine. If fine was hot as hell. "He doesn't have family, you know. He doesn't come from roots and ties. He never had anyone teach him loyalty and unconditional love."

"Some things you don't have to be taught," Chloe said.

"He was uncertain about my big family, and how he might feel out of place, but he came anyway."

Chloe squeezed her gently. "We're a bunch of misfits ourselves, aren't we? All of us. But we fit together. Including Nick."

Mia's throat tightened, and she turned into Chloe. They hugged for a long moment, then Mia pulled back. "I have to go."

"You're going to go eavesdrop on them," Chloe said.

"Hell, yeah."

Chloe grinned. "Me too."

They skirted around the dance floor and made their surreptitious way toward the bar, hiding behind a white lattice that Chloe totally blended into with her wedding dress. Not so much Mia, in her forest green. In fact, with the lights flashing on the other side of the lattice, she probably looked like a Christmas tree.

But the guys were paying them no attention at all.

"You know she's only twenty-two," Ford was saying to Nick.

Mia opened her mouth at this because she was twenty-*three*, dammit. Or at least she would be next month. But Chloe squeezed her hand to keep her quiet.

"Yes," Nick said. "She's twenty-two. A grown-up. Listen, I get that you're her family and you're all very protective of her, but she kicks ass at life. You can trust her to make her own decisions."

"She hasn't decided on you yet," Sawyer pointed out smoothly. Calmly. Eyes steady. He wasn't wearing a gun on his hip today, not with his tux, but Mia would bet he had one hidden on him somewhere.

Chloe rolled her eyes at her new husband and muttered something about him being the sexiest stubborn ass she'd ever met.

"I realize she hasn't chosen me," Nick said. "But I'm still going to be here for her."

"Even if she dumps you?" Jax asked.

"Yeah."

"That's quite a promise."

"It's a fact," Nick said.

Chloe sighed dreamily.

Mia did the same. And her heart melted into a puddle of love that swelled against her rib cage.

"We weren't always here for her," Ford said quietly. "So we're a little overprotective. I won't apologize for that. But she's everything to me, and I'm not a complete idiot. I can see that you're everything to her. All I want is for *her* to be someone's everything."

"Done," Nick said without hesitation. "And maybe you weren't always a part of her life, but you gave her life. A *great* life. And she's made the most of it. She's really amazing."

Chloe sighed again.

Mia didn't have breath left in her lungs to sigh. Pulling free of Chloe, she walked around the lattice, eyes only on Nick.

Some things take time, Chloe had said. And that was true. It'd taken her seventeen years to get to meet her birth parents and find this great big family waiting to embrace her.

And six months to give her heart to Nick.

He'd come here for her. He'd picked her.

She walked right up to him and into his arms, which closed hard around her. "Mia," he breathed into her hair, burying his face in her neck, inhaling deeply. Taking comfort, she realized. It wasn't something he'd ever done before, actively sought comfort from her. She whispered his name and hugged him to her, aware that everyone had moved off to give them some privacy.

He pulled back enough to shove his hand into his pocket and come out with a small black box.

Her heart stopped. She pulled it open and stared down

at the delicate white gold promise ring that was two rib-
bons woven together leading to a knot lined with tiny
sapphires.

Her birthstone.

"It's after midnight," he said softly. "Merry Christmas."

"We weren't going to give each other a present," she
said just as softly, mirroring his words back to her from a
few days ago as she ran a reverent finger over the beautiful ring.

"Then it's just a present present," he said, a smile in
his voice. "A promise for the future. Our future."

"Oh Nick," she breathed, slipping the ring on, so
happy she could scarcely contain herself. "I wasn't sure
you wanted a future."

"I do, very much. I think about my life before you
came into it, Mia. It sucked." He met her gaze. "I need
you. I want you to know that. I should have told you
sooner, but I thought that made me weak. I was wrong
about that. You're the only thing I care about. You're the
only thing that matters to me. I turned down the job—"

"Nick," she gasped. "No. You—"

"I took a different one, with the same company. Still
restorative justice, but I'll be staying within the state of
New York."

"But you wanted to travel."

"Wanted. Past tense. I want to be with you, Mia.
You're it for me. You're everything." He paused and let
his gaze touch her every feature. "You're the best choice
I ever made. You're my only choice."

She pressed her forehead to his, her words brushing
against his lips. "I was just thinking the same thing about
you."

Leah is a brilliant pastry chef—
who's somehow botched all her
opportunities for success.

Jack is an ex-hotshot wildfire
fighter who's back to taming the
fires of a small town.

When these old friends reunite
in Lucky Harbor, can they
handle the heat?

♥

Please turn this page for a preview of

Always on My Mind.

Chapter 1

♥

Saying that she went to the annual Firefighter's Charity Breakfast for pancakes was like saying she watched baseball for the game—when everyone knew that you watched baseball for the guys in the tight uniform pants.

But this time Leah Sullivan really did want pancakes. She also wanted her grandma to live forever, world peace, and hey, while she was making wishes, she wouldn't object to being sweet-talked out of her clothes sometime this year.

But those were all issues for another day. Mid-August was hinting at an Indian summer for the Pacific Northwest. The morning was warm and heading toward hot as she walked to the already crowded pier. The people of Lucky Harbor loved a get-together, and if there was food involved—and cute firefighters to boot—well, that was just a bonus.

Leah accepted a short stack of pancakes from Tim Denison, a firefighter from Station #24. He was a rookie, fresh from the academy and at least five years younger than her, which didn't stop him from sending her a wink. She took in his beachy, I-belong-in-a-Gap-ad-campaign appearance and waited for her good parts to flutter.

They didn't.

For reasons unknown, her good parts were on vacation and had been for months.

Okay, so not for reasons unknown. But not wanting to go there, not today, she blew out a breath and continued down the length of the pier.

Picnic tables had been set up, most of them full of other Lucky Harbor locals supporting the firefighters' annual breakfast. Leah's friend Ali Winters was halfway through a huge stack of pancakes, eyeing the food line as if considering getting more.

Leah plopped down beside her. "You eating for two already?"

"Bite your tongue." Ali aimed her fork at her along with a pointed *don't mess with me* look. "I've only been with Luke for two months. Pregnancy isn't anywhere on the to-do list yet. I'm just doing my part to support the community."

"By eating two hundred pancakes?"

"Hey, the money goes to the senior center."

There was a salty breeze making a mess of Leah's and Ali's hair, but it didn't dare disturb the woman sitting on the other side of Ali. Nothing much disturbed the cool-as-a-cucumber Aubrey.

"I bet sex is on your to-do list," Aubrey said, joining their conversation.

Ali gave a secret smile.

Aubrey narrowed her eyes. "I could really hate you for that smile."

"You *should* hate me for this smile."

"Luke's that good, huh?"

Ali sighed dreamily. "He's *magic*."

"Magic's just an illusion." Aubrey licked the syrup off her fork while managing to somehow look both beautifully sophisticated and graceful.

Back in their school days, Aubrey had been untouchable, tough as nails, and Leah hadn't been anywhere in the vicinity of her league. Nothing much had changed there. She looked down at herself and sucked in her stomach.

"There's no illusion when it comes to Luke," Ali told Aubrey. "He's one-hundred-percent real. And all mine."

"Well, now you're just being mean," Aubrey said. "And that's my area. Leah, what's with the expensive shoes and cheap haircut?"

Leah put a hand to her choppy auburn layers, and Aubrey smiled at Ali, like *see?* That's *how you do mean…*

Most of Leah's money went toward her school loans and helping to keep her grandma afloat, but she did have one vice. Okay, two, but being addicted to Pinterest wasn't technically a vice. Her love of shoes most definitely was. She'd gotten today's strappy leather wedges from Paris, and they'd been totally worth having to eat apples and peanut butter for a week. "They were on sale," she said, clicking them together like she was Dorothy in Oz. "They're knock-offs," she admitted.

Aubrey sighed. "You're not supposed to say that last part. It's not as fun to be mean when you're nice."

"But I am nice," Leah said.

"I know," Aubrey said. "And I'm trying to like you anyway."

The three of them were an extremely unlikely trio, connected by a cute, quirky Victorian building in downtown Lucky Harbor. The building was older than God, currently owned by Aubrey's great-uncle, and divided into three shops. There was Ali's floral shop, Leah's grandma's bakery, and a neglected bookstore that Aubrey had been making noises about taking over since her job at Town Hall had gone south a few weeks back.

Neither Ali nor Leah was sure yet if having Aubrey in the building every day would be fun or a nightmare. But regardless, Aubrey knew her path. So did Ali.

Leah admired the hell out of that. Especially since she'd never known her path. She'd known one thing, the need to get out of Lucky Harbor—and she had. At age seventeen, she'd gone and had rarely looked back.

But she was back now, putting her pastry chef skills to good use helping her grandma while she recovered from knee surgery. The problem was, Leah had gotten out of the habit of settling in one place.

Not quite true, said a little voice inside her. If not for a string of spectacularly bad decisions, she'd have finished French culinary school. And not embarrassed herself on the reality TV show *Sweet Wars*. And…

Don't go there.

Instead, she scooped up a big bite of fluffy pancakes and concentrated on their delicious goodness rather than her own screw-ups. Obsessing over her bad decisions was something she saved for the deep, dark of night.

"Jack's at the griddle," Ali noted.

Leah twisted around to look at the cooking setup.

Lieutenant Jack Harper was indeed manning the griddle. He was tall and broad shouldered and looked like a guy who could take on anything that came his way. This was a good thing since he ran station #24.

Fire station #24 was one of four that serviced the county, and thanks to the Olympic Mountain range at their back with its million acres of forest, all four stations were perpetually busy.

Jack thrived on busy. He could be as intimidating as hell when he chose to be, which wasn't right now since he was head-bopping to some beat only he could hear in his headphones. Knowing him, it was some good, old-fashioned, ear-splitting hard rock.

Not too far from him, leashed to a bench off to the side sat Kevin, a huge Great Dane. He was white with black markings that made him look like a Dalmatian wannabe. Kevin had been given to a neighboring fire station where he'd remained until he'd eaten one-too-many expensive hoses, torn up one-too-many beds, and chewed dead one too many pairs of boots. The rambunctious one-year-old had then been put up for adoption.

The only problem was that no one had wanted what was by then a hundred-and-fifty-pound nuisance. Kevin had been headed for the Humane Society when Jack, always the protector, always the savior, had stepped in a few weeks back and saved the day.

Just like he'd done for Leah more times than she could count.

It'd become a great source of entertainment for the entire town that Jack Harper II, once the town terror himself—at least to mothers of teenage daughters everywhere—was now in charge of the *latest* town terror.

Another firefighter stepped up to the griddle to relieve Jack, who loaded a plate for himself and stepped over to Kevin. He flipped the dog a sausage, which Kevin caught in midair with one snap of his huge jaws. The sausage instantly vanished, and Kevin licked his lips, staring intently at Jack's plate as if he could make more sausage fly into his mouth by wish alone.

Jack laughed and crouched down to talk to the dog, a movement that had his shirt riding up, revealing low-riding BDUs—his uniform pants—a strip of taut, tantalizing male skin, and just the hint of a perfect ass.

On either side of Leah, both Ali and Aubrey gave lusty sighs. Leah completely understood. She could feel her own lusty sigh catching in her throat but she squelched it. They were in the F-zone, she and Jack. *Friends*. Friends didn't do lust, or if they did, they also did the smart, logical thing and ignored it. Still, she felt a smile escape her at the contagious sound of Jack's laughter. Truth was, he'd been making her smile since the sixth grade, when she'd first moved to Lucky Harbor.

As if sensing her appraisal, Jack lifted his head. His dark mirrored sunglasses hid his eyes, but she knew he was looking right at her because he arched a dark brow.

And on either side of her, Ali and Aubrey sighed again.

"Really?" Leah asked them.

"Well look at him," Aubrey said unapologetically. "He's hot, he's got rhythm, and not just the fake white-boy kind either. He's also funny as hell. And for a bonus, he's gainfully employed. It's just too bad I'm off men forever."

"Forever's a long time," Ali said, and Leah's gut cramped at the thought of the beautiful, blonde Aubrey going after Jack.

But Jack was still looking at Leah. Those glasses were still in the way but she knew his dark eyes were framed by thick, black lashes and the straight, dark lines of his eyebrows. And the right brow was sliced through by a thin scar, which he'd gotten at age fourteen when he and his cousin Ben had stolen his mom's car and driven it into a fence.

"Forever," Aubrey repeated emphatically. "I'm off men *forever*," and Leah felt herself relax a little.

Which was silly. Jack could date whomever he wanted, and did. Often.

"And anyway," Aubrey went on, "that's what batteries are for."

Ali laughed along with Aubrey as they all continued to watch Jack, who'd gone back to the griddle. He was moving to his music again while flipping pancakes, much to the utter delight of the crowd.

"Woo hoo!" Aubrey yelled at him, both her and Ali toasting him with their plastic cups filled with orange juice.

Jack grinned and took a bow.

"Hey," Ali said, nudging Leah. "Go tip him."

"Is that what the kids are calling it nowadays?" Aubrey asked.

Leah rolled her eyes and stood up. "You're both ridiculous. He's dating some EMT flight nurse."

Or at least he had been as of last week. She couldn't keep up with Jack's dating life. Okay, so she *chose* not to keep up. "We're just…buddies." They always had been, she and Jack, through thick and thin, and there'd been a lot of thin. "When you go to middle school with someone, you learn too much about them," she went on, knowing damn well that she needed to just stop talking, something she couldn't seem to do. "I mean, I couldn't go out with the guy who stole all the condoms on Sex Education Day and then used them as water balloons to blast the track girls as we ran the 400."

"I could," Aubrey said.

Leah rolled her eyes, mostly to hide the fact that she'd left off the real reason she couldn't date Jack.

"Where you going?" Ali asked when Leah stood up. "We haven't gotten to talk about the latest episode of *Sweet Wars*. Now that you're halfway through the season and down to the single eliminations, the whole town's talking about it nonstop. Did you know that there's a big crowd at the Love Shack on episode night?"

Yes, she'd known. At first, she'd been pressured to go, but she couldn't do it. She couldn't watch herself if anyone else was in the room.

"You were awesome," Ali said.

Maybe, but that had been the adrenaline high from being filmed. Leah had pulled it off by pretending she was Julia Child. Easy enough, since she'd been pretending that since she'd been a kid. After the first terrifying episode, she'd learned something about herself. Even as a kid who'd grown up with little to no self-esteem, there was something about being in front of a camera. It was pretend, so she'd been able to break out of her shell.

The shocking truth was, she'd loved it.

"And also, you looked great on TV," Aubrey said. "Bitch. I know you were judged on originality, presentation, and taste but you really should get brownie points for not looking fat. Do you look as good for the last three episodes?"

This subject was no better than the last one. "Gotta

go," Leah said, grabbing her plate and pointing to the cooking area. "There's sausage now."

"Ah." Aubrey nodded sagely. "So you *do* want Jack's sausage."

Ali burst out laughing, and Aubrey high-fived her.

Ignoring them both, Leah headed toward the grill.

Bad girl Aubrey Wellington has a
plan to make all of her past
wrongs right.

Ben McDaniel doesn't know it
yet…but he's on the top of her list!
♥

Please turn this page for a preview of

Once in a Lifetime.

Chapter 1

It was early when Ben walked out of Lucky Harbor's deliciously warm bakery and into the icy morning. His breath crystallized in front of his face as he took a bite from his fresh bear claw.

As close to heaven as he was going to get.

He glanced back inside the big picture window to wave his thanks, but pastry chef Leah currently had her arms and lips entangled with her fiancé, who happened to be Ben's cousin Jack.

Jack looked to be pretty busy himself, with his tongue down Leah's throat. Turning his back to the window, Ben watched the morning instead as he ate his bear claw. Tendrils of fog had glided in off the water, lingering in long, silvery fingers.

After a few minutes, the bakery door opened behind him, and then Jack was standing at his side. He was in uniform for work, which meant that every woman driving down the street slowed down to get a look at him in his firefighter gear.

"Why are you dressed?" Ben asked.

"Because when I'm naked, I actually cause riots," Jack said, sliding on his sunglasses.

"You know what I mean." Not too long ago, Jack had made the change from firefighting to fire marshal, and no longer suited up to respond to calls.

Jack shrugged. "I'm working a shift today for Ian, who's down with the flu." He pulled his own breakfast choice out of a bakery bag.

Ben took one look at the cheese croissant and shook his head. "Pussy breakfast."

Unperturbed by this, Jack stuffed it into his mouth. "You're just still grumpy because a pretty lady tossed her drink in your face last night."

Ben didn't react to this because Jack was watching him carefully, and Jack, unlike anyone else, could read Ben like a book. But yeah, Aubrey had nailed him—and not in a good way.

Not that he wanted the sexy-as-hell blonde to nail him. Well, okay, maybe she'd occasionally done just that in a few of his late night fantasies, but that was it. Fantasy. Because the reality was that he and Aubrey wouldn't mix well. He liked quiet, serene, calm.

Aubrey didn't know the meaning of any of those things. "It was an accident," he finally said.

"Oh, I know that," Jack said. "Just checking to see if you know it too."

Ben looked at his watch. "Luke's late."

The three of them had been tight since age twelve,

when Ben's mom, unable to take care of him any longer, had dropped him on her sister's doorstep—Jack's mom, Dee Harper. Luke had lived next door. The three boys had spent their teen years terrorizing the neighborhood and giving Ben's aunt Dee lots of gray hair.

"Luke's not late," Jack said. "He's here. He's in the flower shop trying to get into Ali's back pocket. Guess that's what you do when you're engaged."

Ben didn't say anything to this, and Jack blew out a breath. "Sorry."

Ben shook his head. "Been a long time."

"Yeah," Jack said. "But some things never stop hurting."

Maybe not. But it really had been forever ago that Ben had been engaged, and then married. He and Hannah had had a solid marriage.

Until she'd died five years ago.

Ben went after his second bear claw while Jack looked down at his vibrating phone. "Shit. I've gotta go. Tell Luke he's an asshole."

"Will do." When he was alone again, Ben washed down his breakfast with icy cold, chocolate milk. *You drink too much caffeine*, Leah had told him all bossy and sweet at the same time, handing him the milk instead of a mug of coffee.

He planned to stop at the convenience store next for that coffee, and she'd never know. It was early, not close to seven yet, but Ben liked early. Fewer people. Quiet air. Or maybe that was just Lucky Harbor. Either way, he found he was nearly content—coffee would probably tip the scales into *all the way* content. The feeling felt...odd, like he was wearing an ill-fitting coat, so as he did with all uncomfortable emotions, he shoved it aside.

A few snowflakes floated lazily out of the low, dense clouds. One block over, the Pacific Ocean carved into the harbor, which was lined by three-story-high, rugged bluffs teeming with untouched forestland. The Olympic Mountains. Around him, the oak-lined streets were strung with white lights, shining brightly through the morning gloom. Peaceful. Still.

A month ago, he'd been in South America, elbows-deep in a project rebuilding a water system for the war-torn land. Before that, he'd been in Haiti. And before that, Africa. And before that... Indonesia? Hell, it might have been another planet for all he remembered. It was all rolling together.

He went to places after disaster hit, whether man or nature made, and he saw people at their very worst moments. Sometimes he changed lives, sometimes he improved them, but at some point over the past five years, he'd become numb to it. So much so that when he'd gone to check out a new job site at the wrong place, only to have the right place blown to bits by a suicide bomber just before he got there, he'd realized something.

He didn't always have to be the guy on the front line. He could design and plan water systems for devastated countries from anywhere. Hell, he could become a consultant instead. Five years of wading knee-deep in crap, both figuratively and literally, was enough for anyone. He didn't want to be in the *right* hellhole next time.

So he'd come home, with no idea what was next.

Polishing off his second bear claw, Ben sucked the sugar off his thumb. Turning to head toward his truck, he stopped short at the realization someone stood watching him.

Aubrey, and when he caught her eye, she said, "It *is* you" and dropped the things in her hands.

Her tone of voice had suggested she'd just stepped in dog shit with her fancy high-heeled boot. This didn't surprise Ben. She'd been a few years behind him in school. In those years, he'd either been on the basketball court, trouble-seeking with Jack, or with Hannah.

Aubrey had been the Hot Girl. He didn't know why, but there'd always been an instinctive mistrust between them, as if they both recognized two like souls—*troubled* souls. He remembered when she'd first entered high school, she'd had more than a few run-ins with the mean girls. Then she became the mean girl. Crouching down, he reached to help her with the stuff she'd dropped.

"I've got it," she snapped, squatting next to him, pushing his hands away. "I'm fine."

She certainly looked the part of fine. Her long, blond hair was loose and shiny, held back from her face by a pale blue knit cap. A matching scarf was wrapped around her neck and tucked into a white wool coat covering her from chin to a few inches above her knees. Leather boots met those knees, leaving some bare skin below the hem of her coat. She looked sophisticated, and hot as hell. Certainly perfectly put together. In fact, she was always purposely put together.

It made him want to ruffle her up. A crazy thought.

Even crazier, she smelled so good he wanted to just sniff her for about five days. Also, he wanted to know what she was wearing beneath that coat. "Where did you come from?" he asked, as no car had pulled up.

"The building."

There were three storefronts in this building, one of the oldest buildings in town, the floral shop, the bakery, and the bookstore. She hadn't come out of the floral shop or the bakery, he knew that much. He glanced at the bookstore. "It's not open yet."

The windows were no longer boarded up, he realized, and through the glass panes, he could see that the old bookstore was now a new bookstore, as shiny and clean and pretty as the woman before him.

She scooped up a pen and a lipstick, and he grabbed a fallen notebook.

"That's mine," she said.

"I wasn't going to take it, Aubrey," he said, and then, with no idea of what came over him—maybe her flashing eyes—he held the notebook just out of her reach as he looked at it. It was small, and like Aubrey herself, neat and tidy. Just a regular pad of paper, spiral bound, opened to a page she'd written on.

"Give it to me, Ben."

The notebook was nothing special, but clearly his holding on to it was making her uncomfortable. If it had been any other woman on the planet, he'd have handed it right over. But he didn't.

She narrowed sharp, hazel eyes on him as she waggled impatient fingers. "It's just my grocery list."

Grocery list, his ass. It was a list of names, and there was a Ben on it. "Is this me?"

"Wow," she said. "Egocentric much?"

"It says Ben."

"No it doesn't." She tried to snatch at it again, but one thing that living in Third World countries did for you, it gave you quick instincts.

"Look here," he said, pointing to item number four. *"Ben."*

"It's Ben and Jerry. *Ice cream*," she informed him. "Shorthand. Give me the damn notepad."

Hmm. He might've been inclined to believe her except there was that slight panic in her gaze, the one she hadn't been able to hide quick enough. Straightening, he skimmed the names and realized he recognized a few. "Cathy Wheaton," he said, frowning. "Why do I remember that name?"

"You don't." Straightening as well, Aubrey tried to crawl up his body to reach the pad.

Ben wasn't too ashamed to admit he liked that. A lot.

Frustrated, she fisted a hand in his shirt, right over his heart. "Dammit, Ben—"

"Wait…I remember," he said, wincing since she now had a few chest hairs in a tight grip. "Cathy…She was the grade in between us, right? A little skinny? Okay, a *lot* skinny. Nice girl."

Keeping her hold on him, Aubrey went still as stone, and Ben watched her carefully. Yeah, he was right about Cathy, and he went back to the list. "Mrs. Cappernackle." He looked at her again. "The librarian?"

With her free hand, Aubrey pulled her phone from a pocket and looked pointedly at the time.

He ignored this because once his curiosity was tweaked, he was like a dog with a bone, and his curiosity was definitely tweaked. "Sue Henderson." He paused, thinking. Remembering. "Wasn't she your neighbor when you were growing up? That bitchy DA who had you arrested when you put food coloring in her pool and turned it green?"

Aubrey's eyes were fascinating. Hazel fire. "Give. Me. My. List."

Oh hell no, this was just getting good—"Ouch!"

She'd twisted the grip she had on his shirt, yanking out the few hairs she'd fisted. She also got a better grip on the pad so that now they were tug-o-warring over it. "You could just tell me what this is about," he said.

"It's none of your business," she said, fighting him. "That's what it is."

"But it *is* my business when you're carrying around a list with my name on it."

"You know what? Google the name *Ben* and see how many there are. Now let go!" she demanded, just as the door to the floral shop opened and a uniformed officer walked out.

Luke, with his impeccable timing as always. Eyeing the tussle before him, he raised a brow. "What's up, kids?"

"Officer," Aubrey said, voice cool, eyes cooler as she jerked the pad from Ben's fingers. She shoved it into her purse, zipped it, and tugged it higher up on her shoulder. "This man"—she broke off to stab a finger in Ben's direction, like there was any question of which man she meant—"is bothering me."

"Lucky Harbor's beloved troublemaker Ben McDaniel is bothering you?" Luke grinned. "I could arrest him for you."

"Maybe you could just shoot him?" she asked hopefully.

Luke's grin widened as he gave Ben a speculative glance. "Sure, but there'd be a bunch of paperwork, and I hate paperwork. How about I just beat him up a little bit?"

Aubrey seemed like this idea worked for her.

Ben gave her a long, steely look, and she rolled her

eyes. "Oh, never mind." Still hugging her purse to herself, she turned, unlocked the bookstore, and vanished back inside it, slamming the door behind her.

"I thought the store was closed," Ben said, absently rubbing his chest where he was missing those few hairs.

"It was," Luke said. "Mr. Lyons is her uncle, and she rented the place from him and reopened the store. She's gone with a soft opening for now because she needs the income from the store, but she's wants to have a grand opening when the renovations are finished."

"How do you know so much?" Ben asked.

"Because I know all. And because Mr. Lyons called. He needs a carpenter so I gave him your number."

"Mine?" Ben asked.

Luke shrugged. "Everyone in town knows you're good with a hammer."

"Yeah." Ben's phone rang, and he looked at the unfamiliar local number.

Luke looked too. "That's him," he said. "Mr. Lyons."

Ben resisted the urge to do his usual and hit ignore. "McDaniel," he answered.

"Don't say no yet," Mr. Lyons immediately said. "I need a carpenter."

Ben slid Luke a look. "So I've heard. I'm not a carpenter. I'm an engineer."

"You know damn well before you got all dark and mysterious and broody that you were also handy with a set of tools," Mr. Lyons said.

Luke, who could hear Mr. Lyons's booming voice, grinned like the Cheshire cat and nodded, pointing at Ben.

Ben flipped him off. An older woman driving down the street rolled down her window and "tsked" at him.